PRAISE FOR

Moriah Jovan is synonymous with grand passions and political intrigues, epic allegories of good versus evil—but at heart, Moriah's effortless writing is shockingly, unflinchingly, beautifully human.

—Louisa Edwards,
New York Times bestselling author

Regardless of your preferences as to genre and content, it is impossible to miss the quality of Jovan's writing. She is clever, coherent, furiously fast-paced and exciting. She uses just the right amount of detail, writes characters that are somehow both incredibly improbable and extremely relatable, and overall hooks a reader and keeps her driven through to the very end.

—Sarah Dunster
book reviewer and critic

Kenard Chronicles

Book 1: *Black as Knight*

Book 2: *A Babe in Winter*
(forthcoming)

The Tales of Dunham

Book 1: *The Proviso*
Book 2: *Stay*
Book 3: *Magdalene*

The Past: *Dunham*
The Legend: *1520 Main*

LaMontagne 1: *Paso Doble*
LaMontagne 2: *We Were Gods*

Friends & Family: *Black Jack*
Friends & Family: *Lion's Share*
Friends & Family: *Twenty-Dollar Rag*

Black as Knight

Kenard Chronicles
Book 1

Moriah Jovan

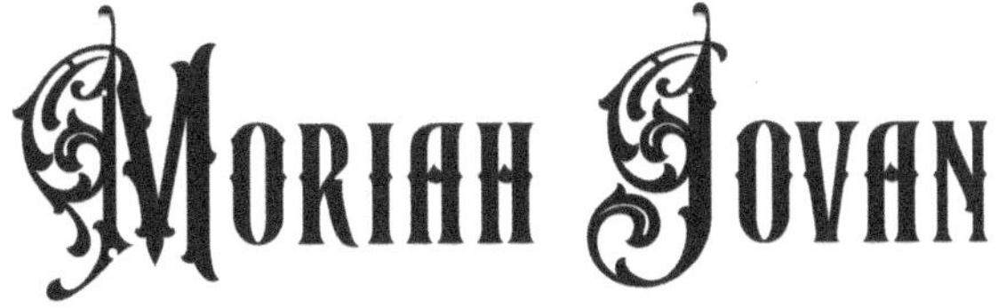

B10 Mediaworx
Kansas City Missouri

PUBLISHED BY:

B10 MEDIAWORX

PO Box 1233
Liberty, MO 64069-1233
b10mediaworx.com

Black as Knight
Book 1 in the Kenard Chronicles

ISBN: 978-1-7320302-8-2 (paperback)
ISBN: 978-1-7320302-7-5 (ebook, all formats)

Cover, print design, ebook formatting: Elizabeth Beeton of B10 Mediaworx

To my brother Nick.

1

EAST LOTHIAN, SCOTLAND
APRIL 1420

" ... DAY OF BINDING, if any man do allege and declare any impediment—"

BOOM!

The cathedral shook from the force of the narthex's massive doors blowing open such that they bounced off the stone walls.

Lady Brìghde Fàileach and her groom whipped around whilst an hundred people leapt to their feet, the men's swords drawn from sheer habit.

A giant mail-clad intruder stood in the doorway, one big gauntleted hand resting on the pommel of his broadsword.

"I object." He said it calmly, in English, almost as if he were bored, but his voice was deep and it resonated in the nave all the way up to the apse where Brìghde and her groom stood gaping.

"What ho!" bellowed Brìghde's father as he scrambled around the end of the pew, his sword already drawn as he strode down the choir toward the nave and the stranger. "Who are ye an' by what authority do ye object?"

"My own." His accent was Sassenach with a hint of French. "I need that bride."

Brìghde's father gasped. "Ye canna burst into weddings and appropriate brides as if this were a merchant's faire tent!"

"Watch me," the giant said wryly and lifted a finger, whereupon three more well-armed mail-clad soldiers erupted from behind him and ran down the nave to the apse. The intruder engaged in swords with Brìghde's father, and quite handily defeated him, for Walter Fàileach, once a famed swordsman, was forced to fight with his left hand. His left shoulder was not much better than his right.

The second soldier engaged the groom's father, who had never been much of a swordsman at all.

The third soldier engaged the best man, which was somewhat of a struggle.

The last soldier picked Brìghde up, threw her over his shoulder, and sprinted right back out of the cathedral, trampling her fallen wimple and bouncing her all the way, her long black hair falling out of its coif and nearly dragging along the ground.

It was a most unpleasant experience, and even had she a mind to scream or fight, she was too out of breath to scream, it would be painful and futile to pound on the soldier's well-armored back, and she couldn't kick because her legs were clasped so tightly against the soldier's chest.

Thus, she did not protest as the men ran for their horses. She did not protest when she was thrown over the mounted giant's lap. She did not protest until they were well away from the kirk and she gathered her remaining bits of breath to yell over the wind and thundering hooves, "*May I please sit up?!*"

"*Nay, my lady!*" the giant yelled back, and pushed his horse to go faster. "'Twill have to wait until we are clear."

Brìghde sighed and braced herself. She would have many bruises upon her belly and ribs tomorrow, as she was wedged in the tiny space between the pommel and knit metal.

No one could follow: It was five miles from her home to the kirk. The whole family had traversed it by carriage without a mounted guard. Brìghde's menfolk would have to return to her home to fetch horses that could catch the knights. Even if they managed to do that in a timely fashion, they would not know where she had gone once she and her captors rounded the turn in the road and plunged sharply into the woods.

It was darker here and it would be darker still in an hour or two as the sun set and the fog rolled in. She did not know how they would go in the dark or even if they would. Stopping and lighting a fire might not give them away through the dense forest and fog, but she was quite sure these men would take no chance of being found.

Thus, with nothing to do but bear the offenses against her body and wait for an opportunity to answer nature's call, Brìghde determined that she was going to chastise her mother mightily for not thinking to supply her a horse.

Soon the woods grew black and the soldiers slowed their horses to a walk. After some time passed, they stopped. Three men dismounted and one wrangled Brìghde from the giant's lap, clearly expecting her to fight, but even if she wanted to, she was too tired and sore and stiff. He put her on her feet. Her head spun, her legs buckled, and she fell over. The giant dismounted and gently assisted her to rise and held her whilst she regained her balance.

"Well!" she croaked, still holding on to his gauntleted arm. "That was an adventure."

"Mea culpa, my lady," he said, "but we are in a rush."

"Hoooo," she breathed and plopped on her arse. Then she flopped on her back and clasped her fingers over her belly.

"My lady," the man said solicitously. "We need to go."

"I'll not go anywhere until my head stops spinning. Didn't my family tell you to get me my own horse?"

Silence. "What … are you talking about, my lady?"

"When my family hired you to abduct me, didn't they tell you to get me my own horse? I'm quite sure you would have been paid enough."

More silence. "Uh … " he finally drawled, surprise in his voice. "No one hired us to abduct you."

Brìghde lay there on the forest floor and opened her eyes to see four silhouettes looming over her. She thought for a moment. "You just … happened … to be out abducting brides today?"

"Aye."

Now she was furious. "Of course! Because that level of planning is just beyond their ken!"

The four men exchanged glances, then one said, "Why would you think your family had anything to do with it?"

"I don't want to discuss it. I'm too angry. Not at you."

"Are you saying," one of the men began carefully, "that you *wanted* to be abducted?"

"If you saw my groom, you'd want to be abducted too!" she snapped.

There was a minute pause and then they all started to laugh.

"Good Lord," one of them wheezed.

"Who are you, then?" Brìghde demanded. "And where are you taking me?"

"I am Earl Grim Kenard," the giant said. "I'm taking you home with me."

"I have never heard of you," she said flatly, "and I know who all our neighbors are on both sides of the border."

"Aye, well, you missed one. My earldom is small and only five years old, with a bare fifteen miles of Scottish border, 'twixt Sheffield to the west and south, Tavendish to the east, and Dunham to the north. The king granted it to me for my service at Agincourt."

"Hrmph. And you are taking me there?"

"Aye."

"Why?"

"May we discuss this when we are farther along our journey?"

"Very well. All I ask is that you not ravish me."

"We have no intention of it, my lady."

"Well then!" She held her hands up so that the gentlemen could pull her to her feet. "Let's be upon our way. Do we plan to walk through the night, good sir?"

"'My lord.'"

"Oh, no," she said. "Nobles who lower themselves to do their own abducting don't get obeisance."

He snorted. "I'm a warrior and, since I am not in France with Henry, I was itching for a battle. Sadly, your people disappointed."

"They disappoint me every day."

"Apparently. We will walk. You may ride, although we do not have a sidesaddle."

"No need," she replied. "I am able to ride astride, prefer it in fact, so long as no one need see my bare legs."

"'Tis pitch black, my lady," he answered dryly. "As well, we have business to tend."

"Speaking of business to tend, I have need of a bit of privacy."

The earl took her hand and began to pick his way carefully to a nearby tree, then released her. "Stay close, my lady," he warned.

"Where would I go?" she asked with irritation. "'Tis dark, 'tis in a fog-bound forest, I have my wedding slippers on, I have no provisions, and I think I'd go with you even if you *did* want to ravish me."

"That bad, eh?" a different man asked.

"You could not imagine."

"I have no imagination," said the earl.

"Aye, it was that bad." Once she was finished and back at the horse's side, he began to wrap a cloth 'round her face. "'Tis really not necessary. I did not cry out all this time."

"Because you thought your family hired us," he returned dryly.

With a series of jostles and grunts, Brìghde was soon astride a very tall, very broad horse. The four conferred among themselves whilst she arranged herself, tucking her skirts around her legs to protect them from the chafing of the leather.

"Show your hands, my lady," the earl said, after which a rope was wound 'round her wrists tightly enough so that she could not escape and loosely enough that she could hold onto the pommel.

They set out again, though now very slowly and impossibly quietly for four mailed men and their horses. The earl led the way for what must have been the better portion of two hours. Brìghde's eyes had gradually accustomed themselves to the dark enough to see shadows, trees and such, downed logs they must traverse, a stream at which they stopped for a long drink and to replenish their flasks. Brìghde's gag was removed and she was given to drink, of which she did, for a long while and requested more.

"Need you answer nature's call again?" the earl asked, and again she wondered at his consideration, within the rules (she presumed there were rules) of abduction.

"No, but I might as well, whilst we're here."

He took the ropes off her wrists, then lifted her down from the horse. Once again, she stumbled, even more sore than before and starting to feel all her bruises. She grimaced and groaned with every footstep around a big tree. Once she had finished, she emerged to find all four with their heads together and murmuring. She was only a few feet away from them and still could barely hear their voices at all.

She tilted her ear back the way they had come and heard nothing but faint rustles she assumed were night rodents.

"We camp tonight, my lady," whispered the earl in her ear.

She jumped, startled out of her wits, as she had not heard him approach even though she was listening to her surroundings.

"'Twill go very badly for you should you run."

"I *just* told you I needed to be rescued," she said snidely.

"And it could be you are cooperating and telling tales so as to effect your escape from us, in which case, I commend your quick thinking."

"Fair," she said approvingly, "and thank you for the compliment. However, I am drained and I hurt. I am also hungry. As you have promised not to ravish me, I shall seek the better part of valor."

"We do not ravish you, you do not run or cry out? Is that our bargain then?"

"Also feed and water me, don't bind or gag me, and don't make me walk."

"Done."

With that, he lifted her back onto the horse without replacing her gag and bonds, and led it across the swift-running stream. The horse's hoof slipped on the moss on the bank and it was all Brìghde could do to hold her seat whilst the four men and their beasts navigated into the stream.

Brìghde knew where they were. She had played here endlessly with her brothers during her childhood and was fairly certain of the terrain. Ever being one to turn a situation to her own advantage, she did not doubt her ability to do so now. The questions were: Could she think of it quickly enough and how long could she go without food?

"If I told you where we are and how to get to the nearest town away from the kirk, would you believe me?"

"No," all four men said at once.

"Fair," she said again. "But for my own comfort, I am compelled to suggest we ford this stream for a generous mile. There is a good area to make camp on this side of the stream, and 'twill not leave tracks, although I do not think anyone saw us go into the woods, nor would they think to look there, nor do they know who you are. Besides, they would all have had to spend time running to Fàileach to fetch their horses and armor, which is a good five miles away from the kirk. The *other* direction."

No one moved or spoke for a good two or three minutes. When the silence lengthened, she said, "I know you don't want to trust me, but I would really like to go to sleep."

"As it happens," the earl said slowly, "that was our exact plan."

"Oh!" she chirped. "Now you have proof I am willing to fall in with you."

"Do not make me regret trusting you, my lady," he warned.

When she escaped, it wouldn't be back to Walter Fàileach, for a certainty. She needed to plot.

They set off down the stream. Once they arrived at their campsite, Brìghde said softly, "There is a ledge some two hundred feet away from here under which you may light a fire."

"How do you know these things, my lady?" one of the knights asked as the earl lifted her off his horse.

"My brothers and I played in these woods for years."

No one said anything else, but presently she heard a flint and saw a spark in the darkness. She waited patiently whilst the earl and his men divested themselves of their mail, leaving them clad in their leather gambesons. By the meager light, they draped their mail over tree limbs, then loosened the girths on their horses' saddles. They led the beasts to the stream from which they drank greedily. 'Twas a cool night and Brìghde's wedding dress was heavy, but her slippers weren't, and the moisture from the moss seeped through. She sighed. Cold, wet feet were the bane of her existence.

"My lady," the earl said quietly as he led Brìghde to the fire and gallantly seated her on a coarse blanket, "you may sleep next to me and trust I will not ravish you, or you can sleep on your feet, tied to a tree."

"With you," Brìghde said immediately.

"I cannot believe your groom was that undesirable."

"The entire circumstance was untenable."

The men chuckled low in their chests, then sat around the fire with their packs, digging in. She took her slippers off and set them by the fire to dry, then she stretched out to warm her feet. The earl threw a canvas sack in her lap before sitting beside her with his own.

"You came well prepared," she muttered as she explored her sack to find a goodly amount of bread and cheese, as well as several pears. There was also a full bladder. She uncorked it, but the earl snatched it from her.

"Careful, my lady. 'Tis a fine vintage of wine I enjoy, but do not suck it down as if 'tis a cheap ale or fresh spring water."

"Oh. Thank you," she said as he gave it back to her. She sipped and savored it. "Good Lord, that is excellent."

"I told you."

Then Brìghde fell silent as she ate—the first meal she'd had since breakfast, after which the day had been taken up with wedding business. The bread was hearty. The cheese was of a quality to match the wine. The pears were crisp and sweet and perfectly complemented the cheese. "'Tis likely the most delicious meal I've ever had," she muttered to herself around her bite. She might be a lady, but she had been brought up with boys and these men were warriors. They should have no reason to take offense at her lack of propriety.

"Hunger is the best sauce."

"Indeed. May I fetch more water?"

"Nay," he said as one of his men arose and went to the stream to fill a bladder. Whilst he was there, he settled the horses for the night. When he returned he handed the water to Brìghde without a word.

"Thank you."

Brìghde had no idea what time it was, but now that she was a little rested, fed, watered, and her feet warm and dry, she was beginning to grow sleepy. It had been a very long day, and she was far more pleased with this ending than the one she was fated to endure. Fortunately, she had spent so many a night sleeping in this tiny, sheltered glade with this brother or that brother scattered about that it almost felt like home. She had a favored sleeping spot, but she wasn't sure she would be … able to … make …

2

THE SOUND OF horse tack and men's low murmurings awoke her at dawn. The fog was still thick and she sat up to look for the earl. There, next to the stream, through the fog, she saw a dark blob squatting, filling his flask whilst his men destroyed the evidence of their passing. A good tracker would be able to tell in the moss that someone had made camp here, but not even the best hunting dogs could follow a scent in the water.

"Good morn, my lady," the earl said from above her suddenly.

She smiled and said, "Good morn to you, too, my lord."

He held his hand out for her to take. She did, and, forgetting about her sore and bruised body, attempted to spring right to her feet, but instead was met with aches and pains all over. She arose with great difficulty, not bothering to hide her grunts and groans. Finally she was on her feet, but she wished for nothing more at the moment than to lie down and go back to sleep. Finally she gathered her courage and stretched against the pain. She groaned some more.

"You're beautiful," he said matter-of-factly, "which surprises me, really, but you need not fear me. You are not to my taste."

She came down from her stretch. "What do you intend to do with me, then?"

"Wed you."

Brìghde threw up her hands. "If 'tis not one forced marriage, 'tis another. What do I care? At least you have some manliness about you."

He blinked, then began laughing after his men started to snicker. "You do not seem overly distressed, my lady."

"Hrmph. I am property," she said bitterly, "so does it matter what I think of my owner?"

"Not really," he said blithely, then swung up onto his enormous dark red destrier with a luxurious black mane, tail, and feathers. "Let us be upon our way before the fog burns off. We will eat in the saddle."

Brìghde bent and pulled the back of her skirt forward to tuck it into her girdle, making of her beautiful red and azure wedding kirtle a peasant woman's working garb. She groaned whilst she did so—

"Are you going to mimic an old woman our entire journey?"

"Aye," Brìghde groaned and struggled to stand upright, clutching her back. "I've never been thrown over a shoulder or the back of a horse before, nor have I struggled to stay in the saddle of a warhorse whilst bound and gagged."

"I could not have anticipated such a willing captive," the earl said. "In the village, we will see if there are any horses for purchase. But for now, 'tis time for your creaky bones to move."

With that, he signaled for one of his men-at-arms to pluck Brìghde off her feet and plop her onto the earl's horse's rump. The man handed her the earl's pack, which she spread over her lap. The earl twisted to look at her whilst she arranged herself.

"My lady," he said politely, "do not think to escape."

She hooted. "I *am* escaping."

"So you say."

"To prove it yet *again*, I shall tell you. Continue in the stream. It feeds the village of Laight. There will be provisions there, an inn, stables for the horses. 'Tis a full day's hard ride by road. How far it is or how long it will take by woods and in a stream, no less, I cannot guess."

"Two days," all four men said in unison.

"Ah, well then. You know we will need to camp again."

"We did not set out upon this errand without knowing our way, my lady," the earl said with irritation. "Stupid men don't survive on the battlefield as long as we have."

"Forgive me for my air of superiority, my lord," she said haughtily. "I am only trying to help and to prove my trustworthiness. Please keep in mind that I do not know what you know."

He harrumphed. "Very well."

In the fog, she could only see that his hair was a dull gold and his eyes were dark. His skin was ruddy, his nose long and straight, his jaw strong, his teeth good, and his face overall, not loathsome.

She nodded. "You'll do."

His eyebrow rose and he chuckled. "I will, will I?"

"Of course, but compared to my groom, anyone would."

His men laughed, and with that, the earl turned and tapped his horse into motion. The four horses were wading in the stream in no time, headed the direction Brìghde wanted to go.

"How far is your home?" she grunted as she adjusted her seat.

"Ninety miles."

"What did you say your name was, again?"

"Grim Kenard."

"You don't seem very grim." He growled, which made her snicker. "I am not terribly original, my lord."

"Indeed," he grumbled. "I may ravish you after all, for that. Listen carefully. 'Tis between 'grim' and 'gram.' Grem."

"Oh, aye," she said and attempted to pronounce it correctly.

"Well enough. So. Marriage?"

She sighed. "Do I have a choice?"

"No. You may be as amenable as you have been and be treated with respect, or you may fight us and be gagged and bound, but 'twould seem to me that simply being wed would free you from your circumstance. Was your betrothed a noble of consequence?"

"The *second* son of a clan chief."

He grunted. "Couldn't your father have made a better match for you?"

"He doesn't care about me," she scoffed. "It was sufficient for his purposes. It would make him *furious* were I to become an English countess." And once she had the earl's name, *then* she would escape. "But why me?"

"You were the most convenient noblewoman of marriageable age and circumstance I could find in the time I had."

"Ah … you're a Sassenach and I am Scots. We are enemies."

"I am beyond caring."

"Hm. Interesting. If you *need* a noble bride, would that not imply you also need an heir from her? If not also a spare?"

"Under normal circumstances, it would; however, I will not rape a woman, much less force her to bear my babe, so I had planned to gently woo and seduce you—"

At that, his men began to quietly snicker and snort.

"You made your task more difficult than it had to be, abducting her," Brìghde observed. "Could you not have done that *before* offering marriage?"

"Time was of the essence, and aye, I am well aware that abducting a woman is not the most effective way to woo; however, I would think treating her with kindness and respect would go far toward establishing some trust. Even if time were *not* of the essence, would your father have allowed me to court you?"

"Ah, nay. My marriage was arranged when we were children, and I would not even have my groom as a playmate, though our borders march. He is ugly and stupid and we hate each other. I didn't want bairns from *that* ass, as I would be obliged to slay them in mercy."

"And there it is. I *do* need an heir, that is true, but bedding you is not the most pleasant of thoughts for me and, I'm sure, even less so for you. Mayhap careful *wooing*," he said snidely at his men, who now did not bother to hide their amusement, "will make a difference for both of us. But until I can force myself to bed you, I shall continue as I have always done."

Brìghde found this very odd and a mite hurtful, should she be honest. She was bonny. She knew it because she had been told so her entire life. There were few men who saw her out and about, or visited her estate who did not watch her endlessly and, betimes, attempt to seduce or even force themselves upon her.

She is contracted, Walter would growl. *Keep your eyes in your head.*

Even the earl himself had remarked upon it. Why *wouldn't* he want to swive her? Unless ...

"You swive men, then?"

He laughed. He had a wonderful laugh. "No."

That ... hurt.

"My keep is full of women who are happy to see to my needs. I simply have a deep and abiding aversion to brunettes." Then it was not specific to *her*. That made it a mite less hurtful. "Knowing that, then, will you accept my suit with the goal of bearing an heir?"

Having bairns was not her biggest goal in life, but it *was* what she was expected to do, had thought she would be doing anyway, and she'd rather do it with almost anybody but Roger.

"If you continue to treat me as kindly as you have thus far," she mused, "I see no reason not to."

"You do ken what I mean by bedding you, do you not?"

"Aye. You will swive me until I am with child."

"And you know what swiving is?"

"I have brothers," she drawled, which made him chuckle.

"What was so awful about your circumstance that you are willing to loan your womb to any man who abducts you?"

"Many reasons, which I may or may not tell you later, but my immediate concern was avoiding that jackanape's spindle."

All four of them laughed.

"This adventure has been far more preferable to swiving *him*, and at least I can bear to look at you without vomiting. Indeed, I should thank you. But since you *did* abduct me, I shall keep my gratitude to myself until you prove your claims of kindness, gentle wooing, and steadfastness."

With great amusement, the earl said, "That, I can do."

"So ... why did you need a noblewoman to wed so urgently that you would risk abducting one, much less a Scot? If my people find out who you are, your small earldom will be as good as destroyed. Are Sassenach noblewomen that thin on the ground that you would risk it?"

He took a deep breath. "I need a noble wife before I am killed, and, hopefully, a legitimate heir."

"Killed?" she asked, now alarmed.

"'Tis a very long story and I would rather not think about it, much less tell it at the moment, and I would beg your leave to enjoy your very amusing cooperation as a respite from my problems. I will tell you anon."

Brìghde could appreciate the need for a respite from one's problems and she could also hear the weariness in his voice, so she would wait.

"If you would be so kind as to feed me ... " he said.

"Of course," Brìghde said and dug in his pack. He held his hand over his shoulder, palm up. She slapped a good portion of bread into it. For herself, she looked for the cheese. The five of them ate in silence whilst the horses made relatively good time for picking through a stream.

"Pear."

Without a word, Brìghde handed him one and continued to feed and water him thusly for the next half hour whilst she fed herself, almost giddy she had not greeted the day despoiled by that buffoon Roger.

"But since you are so cooperative and forthcoming," Kenard said suddenly, breaking the companionable silence, "I would ask: Are you learned in the art of housekeeping? I would have simply assumed so, but you ride astride, so ... "

"I ride astride, as I am the only lass amongst a litter of lads, with barely a year between each of us. But aye, I was also trained in a noblewoman's duties. My mother is a virago about it—that is what my father calls her, and not approvingly—and she trained me."

"If you must be away from your groom so much that you will bargain your womb for the protection of my name, you and I may be able to fill each other's needs. My earldom is in shambles."

"Oh?"

"My castellan is—was—an excellent steward in his day. In fact, he built my earldom to what it is now. But he is old and feeble and deserves his rest. To be blunt, it has grown at such a rapid pace that he cannot keep up and my household has slipped into such chaos that I have noticed and it has begun to affect me, which I will not tolerate. He has found and attempted to train others, but they have not been able to do the job to his satisfaction. His standards are a bit above mine but that is an extra source of distress to him that now he cannot keep to his own expectations. I can offer you a title, a roof, food, wine, more coin than you can spend in a lifetime, and all the freedom you want once I know I can trust you. Ideally, I would like for you to bear me one or two sons and then rule the earldom in my stead so I can go back onto the battlefield where I belong."

Kind, handsome, titled, wealthy, intelligent, and offering her the freedom to rule an earldom the way she wanted to in exchange for ... a son. Mayhap. If he could bear to bed her. She might not want to escape at all.

"I am amenable to the bargain. I only need endure your amorous attentions—"

"*Not* amorous."

"—until I produce at least one son—God grant me easy fertility—"

"Aye," he agreed fervently. "But if you are *not*, I may be forced to use a surrogate, which I do not want to do, either."

"—and in the meantime and forever after, I may rule your earldom. I am a power-hungry lass, I will have you know, and I *covet* the chance of having a fair bit. Aye, I can settle for being a countess with an iron fist, especially if you are gone most of the time and won't be getting in my way."

They all laughed.

"I need your assurance you will be absent."

"With any luck, aye."

"Also, that wine."

"I did not expect the wine to be such a point in my favor. To the production of an heir, as you seem amenable to that, I need to have your word in turn that when the time comes, you will not gainsay me. I will leave you be otherwise and after a second son, you may take a lover as you please. I care not, but I will not rear another man's get."

"Considering whom I would have been obliged to bed last night, you are far more preferable, my lord. You have my word."

"Very well, then."

It was late afternoon when she heard the dogs, but from which direction, she did not know. "Stop, my lord."

But his party had already halted. Brìghde twisted to look around, as did the earl and his men, but they did not stray from the stream.

"That's my father's voice," she whispered. "My deerhound may be amongst that pack, and considering he has slept in my bed since he was a pup, he will know me instantly."

With a sharp gesture from the earl, one of his men took off to the north, and one to the south. With a click of his tongue, he, Brìghde, and his last soldier continued onward. For Brìghde to leave the safety of the stream now when there were hunting dogs about would be the height of folly, and she only prayed that she would not be obliged to walk in it to throw off her scent. The foliage was dense here, too, and it was relatively dark, the forest an old one and little disturbed except by, perhaps, wee laddies exploring. Brìghde was not even sure her brothers had ever come this far.

Brìghde could feel the earl's big body, tense now, whereas all day he had been relaxed. She did not know how much time had passed before one of his men returned from the north, but the sun was about to set.

"'Tis indeed her people, my lord. Perhaps thirty. Ten dogs, none deer-hounds. I followed them into the village. They have settled at the inn for the night. They intend to return home early on the morrow to search elsewhere."

"Very well," the earl muttered. "We will make camp now, then, whilst we can see without aid of a fire."

3

BRÌGHDE WAS TOO tired to do anything but eat and drink. The earl admonished her once again to sleep with him or sleep tied to a tree, but as she had the night before, she fell asleep before she could feel his arms around her.

It was pitch and the forest was absolutely still when she awoke to tend her needs. The earl was spooned against her back, his arm heavy in the curve of her waist. She moved slightly and his arm tightened just a bit. She did not know if he was awake or if it was a reflex. Carefully she inched out of his grasp, but as she stood, he grabbed her skirt and made her trip.

"Ooof," she grunted.

"I told you not to run," he growled.

She sighed. "Nature calls, I am thirsty, and I have every reason to stay with you. I did not want to wake you, particularly since your man is standing guard somewhere out there in the darkness."

He released her slowly. "Do not bolt." She attempted to hurry, but her body was sore and she groaned at every twitch of muscle. Still, he growled at her when she returned. "You took too long."

"Shall I give you a detailed report?" she asked testily as she lay again on the blanket he had smoothed out for both of them, his strong chest against her back. Since he had no lust for her, she did not mind. It was no different from how her deerhound took over her bed of a night, and really, what was the earl but a human deerhound?

He made no answer but shifted to allow herself to settle so he could again drape his arm over her to make sure she did not run away.

The next time she awoke, the sun was high in the sky, the fog completely burned off. Hearing nothing, she quickly scanned the area. There was the earl's red-and-black destrier calmly drinking from the stream. She closed her eyes.

"I know you're awake, my lady," the earl said dryly from behind her. "Do not go back to sleep."

She groaned. "Where are your men?"

"Scouting. We are out of provisions and must go into the village today, whether your people are there or not."

"Oh."

"Come, 'tis time to be off."

Brìghde got to her feet with less groaning than the day before, but still a bit. She picked up the blanket, shook it out, then folded it. "I'm hungry."

"Sadly, the only thing I've to offer you is more wine."

Her stomach rumbled. "I'll take it!"

He laughed. "Here," he said as he handed her the bladder. "Don't drink too much, lest you fall off the back of the horse."

She looked up with a smile, which she fought to keep on her face because now, in the sunlight and with her first opportunity to truly study him, she realized he was not only not loathsome, but possibly the most breathtaking man she had ever met—and she had met many a breathtaking man in her travels.

Until I can force myself to bed you …

… deep and abiding aversion to brunettes …

Brìghde drank deeply with her eyes closed to disguise her thoughts. He was much taller than anyone of her acquaintance, brawnier. His hair was a blonder red in the sunlight, his growing beard bright copper. His face was sharp and lean, his nose and jaw strong. His smile was … devastating.

After everything she had heard and seen, she had dreaded mating because she knew the only man she would ever swive was Roger. Thus, it had made her absolutely ill. But with *this* handsome giant in front of her and Roger suddenly removed from her future, she knew exactly what she was feeling.

She would not hesitate to swive her new betrothed.

However, if she were not careful with her expressions, he would know what she thought of him and, as she had never been able to bear mockery of any sort and she could not laugh at herself, she did not want to have to bear any manner of teasing should he catch her out.

Soon enough they were on the horse and into the stream, riding silently. Brìghde had nothing to say and she doubted the earl wanted her to make any noise anyway. The sun had traversed into the west enough to become blinding when one of the earl's scouts appeared.

"My lady's people are gone, my lord, back to their lands. I have secured lodgings and food for us and the horses, and found a priest."

"Another horse?"

"I felt it best to leave that to your judgment, my lord. There are few for sale, and they are of questionable quality. Yet there is an impoverished knight seeking to sell his destrier and tack. I would have purchased it, but I did not know if my lady would be amenable to riding so much farther on a warhorse."

"What say you, my lady?" the earl asked over his shoulder.

"'Tis preferable to riding on a rump or squeezed between your mailed belly and your pommel with your knees poking my ribs."

He chuckled. "Aye, then. I shall see to it on the morrow."

It was close to sunset when they made the road at the outskirts of the village. They gathered no attention at all in such a large town. Once at a stable, a young groom met them and helped Brìghde dismount.

The earl dismounted and turned to Brìghde, who now could see that he was haggard and clearly exhausted. "I know you are hungry, as am I, so first we will—

"My lord, the priest awaits," his man murmured.

"—go see the priest," the earl sighed heavily.

She nodded.

They walked down the lane to the kirk and entered its cool dimness, where the rest of the earl's contingent was also awaiting them.

The five of them waited patiently in the pews whilst the priest finished speaking to an old woman, then sent her on her way with a smile.

"You are the two needin' to be wed?"

As one, Brìghde and the earl said, "Aye."

The priest's brow rose and he looked at Brìghde. "Where's your father?"

"We don't need him," the earl rumbled. "We are of age, not related, and consenting."

"Ye don't need me fer that, then."

"We need your register."

"Aye, then. Your name, please?" he asked Brìghde once they reached the book.

"Lady Brìghde Fàileach, daughter of Walter Fàileach, clan chief of Fàileach. That's B—"

"*What?!*"

Brìghde, startled, jumped at the earl's bellow. "What what, my lord?"

"You are not Lady Margaret Dunham?"

"If I were," she said testily, "I would have said Lady Margaret Dunham."

"I heard the banns myself!" Kenard insisted.

"Aye, you did! Lady Margaret wed my brother in the ceremony just before the one you interrupted. 'Twas a double wedding. I was to wed Roger MacFhionnlaigh, thereby uniting our lands between MacFhionnlaigh and Dunham."

His men groaned, and the earl clapped his hands to his face. He dropped his head back and began to pace.

"You snatched the wrong woman?" Brìghde asked incredulously.

"I snatched the wrong woman," he croaked.

The priest heaved an irritated sigh. "If ye've no need of me services, I've other things to do."

No one spoke. Brìghde was suddenly on the verge of tears, afraid that, having made such a grievous error, the earl would simply take her back. If he did, she would request he take her to her brother at Dunham. The earl had been generous thus far, and 'twas not *her* fault!

"How can I turn this to my advantage?" Kenard whispered at the ceiling as he paced, his hands clasped behind his neck.

"Did you need to wed Lady Margaret specifically?"

"Aye."

"You cannot wed she who was already wed when you arrived, and she is now my sister-in-law ... "

Kenard grasped her upper arm—hard—and dragged her out of the kirk and into the lane. His men followed.

"You said you know all your neighbors to the north and south of you, save me. Do you know the Duke of Sheffield?"

"Of him, though I have never met him. Walter—my father—thinks he is not of fit wit to be a duke."

"He's right, but that is neither here nor there. As I said, the dukedom of Sheffield is my neighbor to the south and west. Sheffield was unofficially promised my speck of land before the king granted them to me."

She grimaced.

"'Tis worse than that. Sheffield is my liege, and he has ever been envious of my friendship with King Henry. If I die without a wife or issue, there is a very good chance he can get my land. As long as I was on the battlefield, he was content to wait until I was killed, but I am a very hard man to kill. A year and a half ago, Henry sent me home to solidify my earldom so that I could return to the battlefield with a strong estate that could support and defend itself against a border war. It has been able to support itself for three years, but it could not defend itself nor could it withstand a siege for long. It has taken me that long to build another army after Henry took most of my force with him to France. Now, it can both defend itself and withstand a siege, so I thought I would be free to go back to France. But a month ago, I was warned that Sheffield has grown impatient with my refusal to die, and is plotting to do it himself."

"*Ohhhhhh*," Brìghde breathed. "You need a wife to assure your estate's longevity in the case of your death."

"Aye, that, but here is the nut of it: Sheffield is a man who, it is rumored, killed his cousin and his cousin's legitimate heir—a babe—to gain the dukedom. The duchess also mysteriously disappeared. Since this happened thirty years and two kings ago, few people remember or care. Henry knows of these rumors, but can do nothing, even if he had time. He doesn't like Sheffield, doesn't trust him, but Sheffield is a title that goes back centuries and thus far, Sheffield has proven his loyalty to Henry.

"If I die under suspicious circumstances, Henry will *never* let him have my lands. Sheffield knows this; thus, his plot to kill me without raising Henry's suspicion will take time to implement. If I am wed to a noblewoman and I die suspiciously or not, Henry will not let him have those lands, as he will back my wife and her right to it, so killing her would be suspicious and futile. If I *also* have a legitimate heir, there is no point to killing me at all, as he will have to go through three people and that is nothing but suspicious when he already has a cloud hanging over him.

"Know this: I do not fear death. I fear for the future of my family, as he will not kill me first. He is evil and cruel and will delight in killing everyone for the sport of it *in front of me* before killing me."

Brìghde closed her eyes, took a deep breath and released it slowly through puffed cheeks, suddenly not so sure about this bargain after all. Yet she had her own weapon and the wherewithal to use it. "I ken you need a noble bride and quickly. But why do you need Lady Margaret specifically?"

"Firstly, *if* Dunham found out who snatched his daughter, he would descend upon me, but most of Dunham's force is in France fighting *my* force, so holding off that siege indefinitely would be no feat. It would give me time to *woo* and *seduce* Lady Margaret to my side. I could also hold off Fàileach—" She didn't bother to correct his atrocious attempt at Gaelic. "—if he could be arsed to care enough to join in, and I gambled that he wouldn't, as I am told Dunham and Fàileach don't much care for each other."

Brìghde nodded. "That's true. My brothers have all but disavowed Fàileach so he would not lift a finger to avenge an insult to Dunham, allied by marriage or not."

"Secondly, I did not know you existed."

She harrumphed. "That is because I have been held prisoner for the last three years and I doubt you had any reason to scout MacFhionnlaigh."

"Indeed. But now Fàileach has a reason to lay siege to me, and I will have to fend off him *and* MacFhionnlaigh *and* Dunham, for you are his son-in-law's sister. I cannot hold off a siege of that magnitude. Sheffield won't have to do anything, Tavendish—my neighbor to the east—won't assist as I have committed a vile act of war, and Henry—"

"You won't have to outlast any siege at all!" she chirped, interrupting him as excitement pooled in her breast.

That brought the earl up short. "Why?" he asked suspiciously.

"Firstly, Dunham will *also* not lift a finger on my behalf."

"Why not?"

"You may never have heard of me, but *I* am infamous throughout the Lowlands for outwitting Walter—we don't refer to him as our father—time and time again. *Everyone*, including Walter, will assume that I had arranged for my own abduction."

Kenard and all his men gaped at her.

"Aye, he's enraged right now, but my mother, brothers, and Dunham are laughing themselves silly that I did it again, in *spite* of being held at swordpoint, and then it will spread to the other clans and Walter will be humiliated he canna keep his daughter under control or outwit her. I will be blunt: I need the protection of your name so that I will be forever free of MacFhionnlaigh and Fàileach, which is why I am willing to stand as assurance against your death and provide an heir in trade for it.

"I will write my brother and tell him 'twas indeed a plot 'twixt you and me, which was in the making for some time. Walter will want to make war on me for outwitting and defying him, but he has to cross Dunham lands to do it, and Dunham won't allow that. MacFhionnlaigh will do nothing alone as he is wet as moss and as easily trampled. Furthermore, Dunham and your Sassenach neighbor to the east, Tavendish, are good friends, no matter that the Scottish border separates them. Through me, you would be allied with Dunham *and* Tavendish, who might assist you with Sheffield if you laid out your plight to them. You didn't commit a vile act of war by abducting an enemy bride, my lord. You conspired with that cunning Fàileach lass for your own purposes and hers, which are well known, and came out politically stronger with two strong nobles at your back. Your king canna be but even more impressed with you than he is now."

The earl immediately offered his hand for her to shake. "Done."

4

GRIMME REMAINED silent the entire next day, sunrise having made his panicked plan to abduct a bride look utterly foolish. He knew better than to panic and normally, panic was not something he felt. But this was not war; it was politics, about which Grimme knew little. He was a knight, a soldier, and a commander. He need not worry himself with anything but that his men functioned well together, and if they didn't, to find out why and repair the situation.

The night before, all five of them had taken their meal in the taproom, Lady Brìghde happily eating and drinking all of them to shame. Of the inn's proprietor, she had requested parchment, quill, ink, and sealing wax.

"Bra— Bri— Bre— By the bye, how in God's name do you pronounce your name?"

"Bree-juh."

"*In English.*"

"Oh. Bridget. Fallack."

"Thank you. Do not expect me to pronounce it in Gaelic, *Bridget.*"

"Very well," she said smartly, then drawled, "*Grim.*"

He grunted. "Point taken."

The writing implements arrived. Brìghde looked at Grimme. "Do you have anything you want to say?"

"I'll leave that to you, as he's your brother."

Brìghde sat up and began to write. "'Dearest Baldy—'"

"What?"

"His name is Archibald, but I always called him 'Baldy' because I am his bratty younger sister and that is my purpose in life. This way, he will know 'tis from me, in case my penmanship does not convince him. 'I have wed Earl—' How do you spell your name?" She wrote carefully as he spelled. "'—Grimme Kyneward. Inform Walter that the abduction 'twas a plot of my and my husband's own devising because I will not be bent to his will. Be sure to press the point that I will not be bent to his will, and demand he admit it was an ingenious plot. In writing.'"

Grimme laughed.

"'Further, my husband the earl wishes to assure him that any attack on Kyneward will be met with fatal force.'"

Grimme and his knights snorted. "Seven hundred men is not a fatal force."

"'If he cannot be dissuaded, please discourage his march across Dunham lands. Your sister, Countess Budgie Kyneward.'"

That had made Grimme grin. "*Budgie?*"

She held up a finger. "Don't you dare. 'P.S. Please have Mum send my possessions to—'" She looked at him expectantly.

"Kyneward Keep. South to Catlowdy then twenty miles west to Hogarth and 'tis twenty miles south beyond that."

She wrote. "'—and if she cannot do that, please at least send me Mercury.'"

"What's Mercury?"

"My dog. Sign this." He did. Quite satisfied, she folded the parchment, wrote the direction on it, dripped wax on it and slid it over to Grimme for his ring's seal, then gave it to one of his knights.

Grimme sighed, handed the man some coin, pointed at another knight, and muttered, "You two leave at first light for Dunham."

"Aye, my lord."

"Thank you!" she said brightly. "Did you purchase something for me to wear that is better than my wedding dress?"

"Aye, my lady," said one of his men and gave her a package with breeches, a shirt, and boots. "You're about the size of my page."

"Oh, well done, good sir! I don't have to wear a dress all the way."

Grimme's men bid their good eves and went to sleep in the stable. Grimme had been eyeing a tavern wench who matched his tastes precisely and was about to escort Brìghde to the room he'd taken for her so he could fuck the wench. However, it occurred to him that just because *he* did not find his little wife to be at all to his taste—the exact opposite of it, in fact—did not mean that no *other* man felt the same way.

She was attracting a lot of attention. She wasn't *trying* to attract attention. She was a beautiful noblewoman in a tavern full of men who weren't used to seeing noblewomen, beautiful or otherwise. He looked at her more closely.

Aye, she was comely. She was short, reaching only to Grimme's shoulder, if that. She had long, thick midnight-black hair that shimmered blue in the sunlight. She had the biggest green eyes he had ever seen punctuated by thick black lashes in a bit of a heart-shaped face, with a straight but delicate nose. Her skin was pale, with a plethora of very faint freckles. From what he could tell of her body from having slept next to it for two nights, she was curvaceous with generous breasts and hips.

He liked curvaceous, all breasts and hips and arse, but there was that *blonde* over there awaiting him. "Time for bed, Brìghde, and you cannot stay down here without me. Long day ahead."

Grimme did not awaken terribly rested, as he had indeed spent his wedding night fucking the blonde, and breakfast was again a competition who could eat and drink the most, with a bright and well-rested Brìghde, dressed in boy's clothes and looking in no way like a boy, winning handily.

The second she saw the war stallion he had purchased—named Troy—she practically ordered Grimme to give her coin to buy pears, which she promptly shoveled into the beast's mouth.

Once on the road south, both beast and saddle far too big for a tiny woman like Brìghde, she was as silent as Grimme and his remaining man-at-arms, but she was an excellent horsewoman, keeping up with the punishing pace he set, and did not complain except for her incessant groaning whenever she moved a muscle. Whenever they slowed from a canter to a walk to rest their mounts, she happily busied herself looking at the scenery as if she had never seen a tree or a meadow or a brook.

When they halted for the night some ways off the road in a small copse, though she could not lift the saddle off the horse, she requested of his man a currycomb and set herself to grooming the animal and speaking to him as if he would answer her questions. Grimme watched her work in the boy's clothes, stroke and scratch the beast, saying,

"Who's a good laddie? *You're* a good laddie, aye, you are."

"That is a temporary mount, my lady," Grimme said wearily.

"Not anymore," she said crisply. "Oh, what a *good* lad." Troy craned his neck around so he could get his cheeks scratched too, and pulled on her sleeve with his lips then snuffled all the way up her arm until he was snuffling at her cheek and pulling her braid. "What's this? Why, 'tis more pears! For you! He's a good lad. Who's a good lad? *You're* a good lad. I will grant you dessert before your supper."

"I thought you gave him all the pears."

"I bought two bags."

"You're going to make a pet out of a destrier?"

"I make a pet out of *every* animal who catches my fancy. Aye, I do, don't I? And he is absolutely breathtaking, aye, you are. But 'tis because of his name, mostly. Troy. You're a *Trojan horse*!" She chortled at her own jest, making Grimme roll his eyes. "Somebody had a sense of humor, aye, they did, didn't they, laddie?"

"Or he really is that much of a knight," his man muttered.

"He won't be by the time we get home," Grimme retorted.

By the time she had given him *two* rations of oats and they had all bedded down, Grimme still sleeping with his arm in the curve of Brìghde's waist, the beast was in love with her.

Grimme had dodged matrimony for years but now he'd married a strange girl who had more motive to wed *anybody* but her intended. Grimme was an earl, true, but that was mostly parchment. Other than his reputation as a knight, no one knew who he was. He had very little power, very little land, and a small keep. But what he *did* have was men and money. Aye, most of his army was in France, but Grimme had spent the last year and a half gathering more men to rebuild it. He could do that because his father was clever and had nurtured Grimme's earnings from the lists and spoils of war and profits from his various enterprises, and turned it into a moderate fortune with wise investments and strict control of the purse-strings. Several seasons of good weather had helped. Grimme chafed under his father's thriftiness, but knew it to be for the better.

Though Grimme was relatively wealthy in coin, he was land poor—yet Duke Sheffield wanted Grimme's measly holdings anyway. Grimme could not, in all honesty, blame Sheffield for being angry about it when he had had good reason to expect it. What he *could* blame Sheffield for was his sudden need to possess everything that Grimme loved. King Henry had decreed the lands to be Grimme's and Sheffield could not go against the king without incurring his wrath. Grimme had sworn fealty to Duke Sheffield, which left a bitter taste in his mouth, but he had no choice if he wanted to be an earl.

And he did.

'Twas not every day the bastard son of a merchant was elevated to nobility.

Now, on their second day homeward, he was in a bit better mood, or at least enough to start getting to know this girl he'd married.

"How old are you?" Grimme asked. Not that it would matter.

"Two and twenty. You?"

Not a mere girl, then. "Six and twenty."

She was clearly surprised. "That is a bit young to be a newly made earl, is it not?"

"I grew into my frame quickly, and was able to finish my apprenticeship as page and squire well before usual, attained knighthood, then rode out onto the battlefield."

"And you are also more clever than usual, apparently."

He shrugged listlessly. "Not clever enough, if the last three days is anything to consider."

"You are having second thoughts?"

He took a deep breath and decided to confess. "I am now dismayed that I felt I had to abduct a bride at all. I was advised to take my time and find a noblewoman to wed the usual way of nobility, but I cannot think of one noble in England who would wed their girl to me, I felt pressed for time, and I panicked. At the moment, I am contemplating how very wrong it *could* have gone if I'd snatched the woman I meant to."

"Ah," she said softly.

"I am a soldier. I am accustomed to taking what I want, vanquishing people without thought to their wants, because that is the nature of war. I find myself in a war of politics that I cannot simply hack my way through. I do not know how to wage this war. I assure you, I am not usually this dimwitted."

"Does it not ease your mind a bit that I needed to be rescued and thus, it benefited both of us?"

He shook his head. "That I did *not* snatch the woman I meant to means I failed my quest. I do not consider near misses, when the cause is mistakes I made, to be victories. I do not like to credit luck, as luck is outside my control and I cannot tolerate that which is outside my control. I may have won this battle, but I won in spite of my mistakes, not because of my intellect, skill, and experience."

"Not luck," she returned. "Never luck. 'Tis God's hand."

He pursed his lips and thought about that. If 'twere God's hand, then God had also planted the panic in his breast that sent him on this quest.

"I must ponder that a bit more. It sits little better than luck, for I have ever been aware of what God wants me to do. Why would He keep such a task from me?"

"Mayhap He did not want you to ponder it so much that you decided He would never ask you to do such a thing, and 'twas your fear driving you to it, and therefore would decide against it."

He looked at her sharply. "You speak as if you know God's will."

She shook her head. "Nay. I assume my success is God's will."

"And your failures?"

She looked at him and soberly said, "I never fail. Success may take time, and what you consider failure, to me is only God protecting me from an unfortunate end. The only question of success is *when* and what circumstances I must endure and plot against to ensure the success He is guiding me toward."

He understood exactly what she was saying and in general, she was right, but he could not see past the fact that he had snatched the wrong woman.

"You failed at outwitting your father," he persisted.

"I had to endure the wedding and marriage to get away from Walter to plot against people who are easily led," she corrected. "God removed from me that burden. I *was*, in fact, plotting my own abduction, but I could not go anywhere without Walter's hand-chosen guard. I wasn't allowed to ride any but the slowest horses in the stables. Thus, I could not slip the fortress, nor could I outwit or outrun my guard, and they are immune to my charms."

"Oh?"

"Not *that*," she huffed. "They are Walter's closest and most trusted men. They also hate me because he does, so they were eager to have me under their thumb."

"That's not why they hate you and that's not what they wanted you under," his man said matter-of-factly.

The earl barked a laugh, but Brìghde said, "Very astute of you and also true, but I was not going to crow about my irresistibility in front of a man who finds me resistible." Grimme and his man exchanged grins. "If he ever even suspected one of them had taken advantage of their opportunities to throw my skirt up, he'd have them killed in the most painful and long-lasting way possible."

"I must ponder this," Grimme repeated slowly, chirruping his horse into a canter and leading in silence until the horses needed to rest.

"Tell me of your household," she said. "I would be at least a little prepared for what I might find. You said it is in shambles?"

"Aye," he sighed, wiping his hand down his face. It did not bother him until it affected him directly, but that was happening more and more often. If Brìghde could do what she said she could do, then mayhap he should simply accept that it was God's grace and pray to feel gratitude he did not yet. He crossed himself.

"My castellan is also my father," he began. "My legitimate brothers—I have three—have no use for him. His wife and mistresses, including my mother, are all dead, and he was tired of the demands of being a merchant, so I asked him to come live with me and he took it upon himself to build my earldom for the same reasons you are eager to take his place."

"Why did you take him in?" Brìghde asked sharply. "Not one of Fàileach's children would take him in were he destitute, so your brothers must have their reasons. Why do you not have such a reason?"

Grimme shrugged. "I love him. I enjoy his company. I am grateful to him for my profession and my wealth. You see, my legitimate brothers got as much attention from him as they would allow, but *their* mother was bitter, and she poisoned their minds against him. Also, I am twenty years younger than my next oldest legitimate brother, and they resent that my father set me up as well and gave me his surname. So they twisted it in their minds that I am his favorite, when I am not. And then there's my next oldest brother, who is also a bastard. His mother died when he was an infant, so my mother reared us together until I was sent for a page and he disappeared for a while. He's a thief by trade and never made any effort to hide it, so our legitimate brothers despise him for his own acts. I'm quite sure my father has other bastards elsewhere and I have no doubt he either supported them or doesn't know they exist."

He slid a glance at Lady Brìghde to see that her mouth was pursed in surprise. "You must admit, it *is* odd. Most men don't acknowledge their bastards."

"Aye, and that is what my legitimate brothers would prefer."

"You have spoken with them?"

"Nay, 'tis what my father confessed to me once in a drunken stupor. They are successful merchants, as my father was, but they resent that though I am a bastard, I have done as well as they."

"And then you earned an earldom."

"I don't know if they know about that. You questioned my youth; 'tis because my father had the funds to outfit me as a page and squire and was friends with a very old knight who was desperate for apprentices and would sponsor me as if I were nobility, for I could fight in his stead. My father could see no brighter future for me than as a knight, as I was ill-suited to commerce and too restless to be a smith or scholar, and did not take pleasure in scratching out a living stealing, as my brother did. Does."

"I cannot imagine a father who loves his legitimate sons, much less his bastards."

"You will see. My hope is that you and he rub along well with each other."

"I, too. You have women in your keep to see to your needs, you said? You plow the maidservants?"

"I do, but my four mistresses take precedence." He grinned at her stunned expression.

"Is your lust so vast that you must keep a stable of paramours?"

"That is an odd thing for a lady virgin to ask, particularly when she is your wife and 'tis not proper to share such intimate details."

"I have six brothers," she said flatly. "They talk frankly and vulgarly. I have heard and seen many things I should not have and would rather not have. My sensibilities will not be offended by anything you say, and I feel it is something I must know to do my duty."

"It is not. Your curiosity is aroused."

"Are they or are they not part of the household?"

"Aye."

"Am I or am I not now the ruler of said household?"

"Hrmph. Very well, then. Remember you asked. Aye, my lust is that vast. 'Tis a Kyneward trait. I can break any one woman with my lust, and I have, every last one."

She gaped at him, then she started to chuckle. Then she started to laugh. "*Break her?!*" she squealed, laughing until she was snorting and squeezing tears out of her eyes. She mimicked nearly falling out of the saddle.

He glared at her. "I am glad that amused you, *Budgie*—" He gave her a smug smile when she stopped laughing and glared back.

Then she snickered until she snorted again. "'Break her.'"

"—but I say that in all seriousness."

She looked to Grimme's man-at-arms for confirmation, which irritated him.

"'Tis true, my lady."

"Oh. Huh."

"You think I boast, but rather, 'tis a complaint. 'Tis frustrating to enjoy a woman for some time and then hear her say, 'I cannot accommodate you further. My body hurts.' Or 'I will not do this thing you ask of me.' Or 'I am with your child.' Then, I must find another. 'Tis why I keep them all near. Each enjoys something the others will not do and I rotate amongst them to give their bodies time to recover. Not one of them alone could satisfy all my tastes or the frequency I demand. 'Tis also why I need a maidservant."

"Or three," his man muttered.

Grimme laughed. "Aye, that too. And I take my opportunities when I am at war or traveling."

"Oh," Brìghde said, seeming a little dazed. "Well. Then." She gathered herself enough to ask, "Do you have children?"

"Aye, four sons."

"I would hope you do not show any favoritism toward them than any child I might bear you."

"Nay. My boys believe each other to be my favorite, but I have none. They are *different*. They have different needs. They are different ages. Their needs change as they grow, wax and wane. Further, it depends on how much their mothers want or expect or allow me to do. So whether I show favoritism or not, *they* believe that I do. I cannot make them understand."

"Ah. We do not have that problem. Walter hates all his sons equally, and I far more than them."

"I cannot imagine that."

"So! Your household functions around your women?"

"It does indeed. They demand much, and they refuse to obey my father."

"Why do you not rein them in a bit? Surely you can order them to obey your father."

"Oh, no. I do not involve myself in household affairs. 'Twould be a disaster for me should I get between four women."

"Five, now," Lady Brìghde said dryly.

Grimme and his knight laughed. "They get along well—"

Brìghde hooted. At that, his man did, in fact, snicker.

Grimme scowled at both of them. "—and they know what my quest was, so they are prepared to welcome another woman into the household."

"*Welcome,*" she snorted. "Why did you not simply wed one of them and declare one of her sons your heir?"

He hesitated. "I needed to wed a noblewoman."

She looked at him for quite a while, her eyes narrowed. It was possible this girl could see through his vague answer to the truth, but it didn't matter. If she was as quick-witted as she seemed, she had probably already deduced and if not now, she would soon enough.

But the only thing she said was, "Your stamina is commendable." Again Grimme laughed. "Well? Tell me of them."

"There is Emelisse, with whom I have been for eleven years."

She gasped. "Why, that would have made you fifteen when you bedded her!"

"Aye. She is five years older than I and the mother of my two oldest. Ardith has no children. Dillena is the mother of my next oldest. Maebh is the mother of my youngest."

"French, English, Welsh, and Irish, respectively."

Grimme cast her a quick glance. "Aye."

"And a Scots wife. Your children?"

"I have no daughters. My sons are Gaston, who is ten—"

"Sweet Mary and Joseph! You were a father at sixteen!"

"Aye. 'Twas why I went on the battlefield and lists early. I had a family to feed."

"I find that quite commendable also, that you did not abandon them."

"My father didn't abandon his bastards or their mothers, thus, it didn't occur to me to abandon mine. Max is nine, Terrwyn is seven, and Pierce is five, so I had had four children by the time I was twenty-one."

"And you haven't had another in five years?"

He slid a look at her. "Ardith is learned in remaining without child. I assume she has taught the others. I prefer it that way. I do not want any more children with them."

She pursed her lips. "I see." What *did* she see? "You have a bit of a French accent. Where is your birthplace?"

"London. I spent most of my adolescence in France. I was there so long I not only acquired the language, but also an accent. The wine you enjoyed is from Bordeaux."

"You said your earldom is only five years old?"

He nodded. "It was granted to me at Agincourt, on my twenty-first birthday. It was in need of repair, so in between my knightly duties of battle, I competed on the lists and bred my stallion to build my coin chest, whilst my father turned Kyneward into a proper keep, villeins, crops, sheep, suchlike."

"How many servants? How many serfs or villeins?"

"My father will know. What do you know of husbandry?"

"Enough to get myself in trouble," she quipped.

Brìghde was sounding better and better. "You read then? Write? Do sums?"

"Why, of course! Who ever heard of a castellain who could not keep the books?"

"Are noblewomen not usually sent away to a convent or such to learn … something *other* than reading and writing?"

"I was sent to a convent when I was twelve, aye, and we learned to read and write and sum. But since I already knew how to do those things, it was terribly boring. I didn't have any friends to help ease the time. I can play the lyre very well, but I don't like it enough to practice on my own. I can embroider, too, but 'tis difficult for me to sit still and do such fine work. I loved my history and philosophy classes, but not enough to stay. I was supposed to be there six years; however, because it *was* boring, I ran away. It took me three years to get home, and I did not know until I returned that Walter had never meant to send for me until it was time to marry Roger. He was furious."

"Ahhh, *that* is why you were so competent in the woods."

"One reason."

"What if he had sent you back?"

"I would have left and found another way in the world. I shouldn't have gone home at all, but I was tired of scraping by and I missed my comforts—and then I was promptly imprisoned, so that was an embarrassing lapse in judgment."

"You seem to have led an unusual childhood."

"I am the fifth child, only daughter, of seven children. Walter was angry with my mother for producing me for he had a vanity that he could have seven sons, as he was a seventh son."

"A seventh son is the head of a clan?"

Lady Brìghde shrugged her shoulders. "They all died in the plague. Or so I am told."

"You do not believe that?"

"I would not be surprised should I find he had murdered one or two of them, mayhap three, when the plague did not oblige him. When you took me, he had a sword in my back."

"That is often the case with willful daughters, and clearly you are one."

She cast him a grin. "Indeed, but I was not speaking figuratively. He had the point of it *in* my back. If I moved a muscle, I was dead."

"I believe I begin to see why abduction was preferable."

"Aye, it has been most agreeable. Should we continue thusly, I think I shall be very happy."

Suddenly troubled, he said, "Loyalty does not seem to be one of your virtues."

Lady Brìghde scoffed bitterly. "Loyalty is a weapon used by those who demand it. You are supposed to be loyal to your liege, but he is evil and wants to kill you."

"Aye, but my liege's interests are the king's interests, and the king is my friend. He and I share a mutual respect, and I am loyal to him because he is worthy of it. It is unfortunate that I must follow the chain of command to do so. As I am one who demands loyalty, I pray you not force me to regret trusting you."

"Keep your word and enforce my position as castellain, and I will have no reason to want to betray you. My loyalty can be earned, my lord, but it cannot be compelled."

5

THE JOURNEY FROM Fàileach to Hogarth, the biggest town closest to Kyneward, took another day, and Brìghde and Lord Kyneward chatted happily for the whole of it. He was witty and learned, even for a young man who had spent most of his life on a battlefield, as both his father and the ancient knight for whom he had served as page and squire valued education. Further, Brìghde engaged his man-at-arms in conversation as well, drawing him out, learning of him. It was easier to rule a household when one knew who was in it.

Every night, the earl slept with her for reasons she did not know, but did not mind.

"I'm not going to run away," she had said testily, although, she thought as he draped his bare arm over her waist, he did make a fine substitute for her dog.

He did not explain himself.

The closer they got to Kyneward, the more Brìghde looked forward to taking over as castellain until she was quivering in anticipation. She would miss her mother, of course, but it meant she would be in total control, without having to do everything the way her mother did it, having to avoid Walter, having nothing at all to do in the MacFhionnlaigh household where she would *not* be a countess and enduring Roger's mother to boot, or having to tip-toe around the four women—seven including maidservants—her husband was bedding. She felt it best to keep that to herself. If he didn't know how that many women could share a man's bed and *not* have strife, he would never know what Brìghde might have to do to them to rule the household.

They might not obey the earl's father, but they *would* obey Brìghde with or without the earl's sanction. Indeed, her mother had broken more than a few contentious women over her knee, as had her mother before her, and Brìghde was her mother's daughter.

"Brìghde," asked the earl as they drew closer to Kyneward land, "do you think it is possible we will both benefit disproportionately from this arrangement?"

"If there is to be an arrangement, it should always be disproportionately advantageous."

He laughed. "You are delightful company, my lady. Do you perchance play chess?"

"Aye, I do!"

"Excellent. Ahead is the village of Hogarth. 'Tis twenty more miles to Kyneward, but there is a smaller hamlet between the two."

Hogarth was in fact quite a big town, with fine clothiers and merchants of other refined goods that were not to be had in tiny hamlets and villages. There were several inns and liveries, and many, many taverns.

"When you are settled," Kyneward said as they stopped at a livery and took an inn for the night, "we will come outfit you as befits a countess. We would do that tomorrow, but it will take many days and I am eager to get home to my family."

"My lord—"

"Grimme."

"Thank you. Grimme. I have nothing to wear but my wedding dress and these clothes for a lad. Surely we could find something already made that I can wear until we can shop properly? And as to that, I have nothing *else* either. Brush, hairpins, dagger."

He grimaced. "Of course. I apologize."

"I must also go to the kirk."

"I, too," said the earl, surprising her.

"You do not seem the devout sort," she said as they walked in the direction the innkeeper had pointed.

"As much as I can be, whilst keeping a harem," he grinned at her.

She was still laughing when they entered, and he poked his elbow in her ribs to make her stop laughing, but she could barely bite back her giggles.

"Shhh," he teased, then whispered, "What are you praying for?"

"I want to give thanks for my disproportionate advantage. And you?"

"Same thing."

THE EARL AGAIN slept with her.

"We're not in the forest anymore, my lord."

"It occurred to me that I should not have left you alone in the room in Laight. This inn is far nicer than the one there, but I do not want to house a woman who is in my care in a room alone. If you were not my wife, I would sleep on the floor or have my man stand watch, but he also must rest if he is to be of any use to me."

She shrugged. Why not. Nothing untoward would happen and even if something *did* occur, she *was* his wife and she had promised him sons (or at least to attempt them), so it would not, in fact, be untoward at all. She had bargained with full knowledge of having to bed him and, thanks to her brothers' big mouths and a few—many—moments of witnessing the act, knowing exactly what bedding entailed.

The earl might have an amorous aversion to her, but *she* certainly did not have an aversion to *him*, and after several delightful days of conversation and laughter, and his admission of his appetites, she wouldn't mind if he *did* have amorous intentions.

That could be, she reasoned, simply by comparison to Roger MacFhionnlaigh, from whom the earl had saved her by a breath.

Aye, that was it. She had never had a true suitor because everyone knew her final destination was Roger's bed.

She felt his body relax and his breathing shallow out, and was oddly disappointed.

THE THREE OF them spent the next morning gathering basic necessities: two plain kirtles of uninspiring colors—

"I ... would rather you not wear black," the earl said when she fingered a fine linen. He was staring between her and the cloth as if he feared she would suddenly betray him. She could not decipher his expression, nor fathom what about the black disturbed him.

Confused and a little wary, she said, "Is it *important* to you that I not wear black?"

"Ah ... well, aye, it rather is."

"Why?"

"Please," he said courteously, his voice strained.

—girdle, hairpins, ribbons, brush, comb, a glass—

"My lord—"

"Grimme."

"Grimme. That is expensive."

"Do you have one at home?"

"Aye. We are wealthy and my mother gives me anything I want."

"Then you should have one here. You do not have to worry about the state of my coin chest."

"Until I do," she quipped, but he did not laugh.

"Aye," he mumbled distantly, as he had been since he asked her not to buy black.

—parchment, quills, ink, a lovely dagger she saw in a window and sighed over, stockings, two pairs of sturdy daily slippers and one pair of leather boots, and a lovely pouch to carry it all in.

"Will that do?" he asked, concerned when she said she was ready to get back on the road.

"For the next week or two, aye."

They had stayed in the most expensive part of Hogarth, so they traveled south around the less savory part of town, and headed out.

In another fifteen miles was the hamlet of Waters. It boasted only the basic necessities to support a keep and goods that knights and peasants needed and could afford. But it also had an overabundance of taverns for a hamlet.

"My forces eat here. I supply rations, but I also pay them enough to find their own food."

"Ah."

The earl was greeted with bows and curtsies and smiles and well wishes, and then they were through it in a blink. The road from Waters to Kyneward was a well-trod five miles of rolling hills that presently forked, giving way to a route around the keep that continued south, a road that continued west, and the third a long lane leading to the keep, which was, indeed, small. To either side of the lane were tiny thatched cottages with kitchen gardens just beginning to sprout, and beyond, more green rolling hills as far as the eye could see, covered in sheep, and, beyond the keep, fields of grain just showing their green heads.

The lane itself was lined with tall, deep, neatly trimmed boxwood hedges.

"That's lovely," she said.

"That is not their purpose."

"Oh?"

"My arbalists will hide there in case of an invasion. What think you, Lady Brìghde?" Kyneward asked earnestly.

"Your keep might be small, but your lands are prosperous," she said approvingly.

"My father's work."

"You, ah … your west curtain wall … " She said hesitantly, not wanting to be like her mother, finding fault with everything first. "'Tis crumbling."

"There are architects and stonemasons at the back of the keep rebuilding the walls and building a third bailey to protect the villeins within the fortress. You can hear them if you listen to them closely enough."

"Oh, aye," she chirped. "You have no moat."

"No need. The whole fortress is dug down to solid rock."

"Excellent!"

This was getting better and better.

Then they were noticed.

"My lord! My lord! Lord Kyneward is home!"

And, as had happened in the village and in the hamlet, Kyneward was suddenly swimming in goodwill from the villeins, serfs, and cottagers, which he returned wholeheartedly, with laughs and waves and jests and good-natured taunts.

Indeed, Lord Kyneward's homecoming was like nothing Brìghde could imagine. The villeins in the fields stopped and waved enthusiastically. Servants emptied the keep and ran down the slope to meet their company, gathering around their horses like the foam of the sea around a rock. "Come now, come!" he called, laughing. "Let us through. We may celebrate when we have rested."

They all ignored his command, men, women, children, dogs, all too excited to see their lord to allow him to get out of their reach.

Brìghde's father would never have gotten a reception like that, and her good fortune was looking more and more disproportionate. She could not be more pleased.

"Papa! Papa's home!"

Brìghde saw four boys racing out of the keep and the biggest threw himself at Kyneward, who laughed and hoisted him up onto his lap.

"Papa! Papa!" One of the big ones pulled the smallest away so hard, the little boy fell on his arse. "I want a turn!"

Kyneward flashed Brìghde a grin and dismounted so he could gather all four boys in his arms. He arose and tossed the two oldest on the back of his horse, threw the next youngest on his own back, and plucked the littlest one off the ground to hold him in his arms.

Something within Brìghde suddenly began to ache. Walter Fàileach would never have greeted her thusly, and in fact, no one had ever been that happy to see her. Her mother had barely noticed when she'd arrived home from the convent except to note that she was happy to have her second-in-command back and Brìghde immediately needed to see to this task and that errand.

"Lord Grimme! Lord Grimme! You're *home!*"

Brìghde looked up the hill to see the most beautiful woman she had ever seen in her life running down the lane, followed closely by three other equally bonny women. They were all tall, blonde, fair of skin, and light of eye. In fact, they were so alike, she would have thought them sisters if Grimme had not told her about them. Brìghde, who had never had a reason to doubt her own beauty, felt embarrassingly out of place, with her black hair and deep emerald eyes (though equally fair skin) and being so appallingly underdressed in her boys' breeches, shirt, and boots. It was far from the first time she'd felt so very out of place, but it was here she would be expected to stay for the rest of her life.

The woman in the lead threw herself at Kyneward and gave him a lusty kiss, which he returned wholeheartedly, her arse filling his big hand. Brìghde simply watched, curious how the other three reacted to that kiss, but … nothing. Then it was their turn and they each gave and received an equally lusty kiss.

They acted like a family, which shocked her. After the way he had so lightly spoken of them, she had assumed his "household" was a collection of wenches who had had his children, but that he did not pay attention to until he wanted to satisfy his lust.

Treating all his women as if they were dear to his heart was not normal. The mistress—*one*—who may or may not have the lord's heart, had her own residence and the wife pretended to be ignorant of the mistress's existence.

The fact that all these women and children and its lord lived together as a *family* was an unfortunate development, for it would be a much more delicate balance than women who were, in fact, dear wives.

"Where is she?" she heard one of the women demand.

Kyneward gestured toward Brìghde, who gave a little wave and smile.

All four of the women's jaws dropped.

"Please don't mind my garments," Brìghde called helpfully. "I was getting married to someone else, but then I was compelled to ride for an hundred twenty miles. I know I am a fright."

"She doesn't act abducted," a different mistress said, still looking at Brìghde with some suspicion.

"I really didn't mind," Brìghde assured them, which was likely the wrong thing to say, since all four of them then glared at Grimme, who held his hands up in surrender.

"Were you hoping I would bring home an *un*happy wife? Emelisse, Ardith, Dillena, Maebh, this is Lady Brìghde Fallack."

"Have you not married her yet?" the first woman demanded. In French. "*Must* you torture me with a wedding, too?"

"I have wed her," he returned in the same language. "It so happens that we are preferable to her own family."

"Does she know who we are?"

"Oui."

Again all four sets of eyes, light blue, looked at her as if she were a ghost.

"You're going to bed *her?*" the French one practically screeched.

"Not until I absolutely must," Grimme said as he turned away and strolled up the hill toward the portcullis, his arms draped over two of the women's shoulders, the children dancing around them, the other two women walking backward in front of him to chatter at him excitedly.

"If you could dismount, my lady," said a boy from below Brìghde, "I would take your horse to the stable."

Brìghde watched Grimme and his family. She had never felt so empty, watching what she had never seen, much less hoped for for herself.

"My lady?"

She shook herself. "Yes. Um, of course," she murmured and dismounted with the boy's help.

"'Tis too much horse for you, pardon my sayin' so."

"Mayhap," she muttered vaguely. The boy stood with the horse's reins whilst Brìghde gathered her meager things and clutched them to her breast.

Now what?

She was the wife, the countess, the lady of the manor, the castellain, the Lady portion of Lord and Lady Kyneward, yet here she stood in a dusty road dressed like a bedraggled boy, with serfs, servants, and knights flowing around and past her as if she were not there, whilst the Lord portion of Lord and Lady Kyneward capered with his family and forgot she existed.

Almost a sennight of his most delightful company and ... he'd forgotten all about her.

She looked over her shoulder, back toward the forest-lined road from which they'd come. She could walk away right now and no one would ever notice.

"Brìghde!"

She looked around to see Kyneward far away, surrounded by people who loved him, whom he loved, smiling at her, waving and shouting at her to join them.

His women were not smiling.

"Come!"

She cast him her brightest smile, pulled her shoulders back, and marched herself up the hill to the castle entrance as if she were the lady of the manor.

"Well!" she exclaimed brightly. "Isn't this lovely!"

The lands were, but the keep wasn't. It was much bigger than he had led her to envision, but it was not nearly as big as Fàileach. The ditches outside the walls were littered with rotting wood and other building materials. She was glad there was no moat, for moats stunk. The outer bailey was almost all stables, well built and pristinely kempt. The inner bailey, however, was a disaster. The sheds and outbuildings in the inner bailey close to the keep were in dire need of demolition and rebuilding in more efficient spots.

The women and children continued to talk at the earl, who answered as he could get a word in. He was happy here, she saw, and she wanted to be happy here, too, but she was not sure that would be completely possible, with four women who were not mere whores, as Brìghde had thought, and thus, set against her already by virtue of her station.

His head mistress should be his wife and she was understandably bitter about it. He didn't *need* to marry a noblewoman. He *wanted* to marry a noblewoman, likely to establish to himself that he was a noble. He'd only been an earl for five years and before that had had no expectation of becoming one. If he hadn't wed the woman in eleven years, there had to be more reasons than that she was not a noblewoman.

Brìghde's best course of action would be to make sure none of the women had reason to fear Brìghde would take over the earl's spindle. Aye, he was extraordinarily pleasing to the eye, but he wasn't worth going to war over. If he really wanted a legitimate heir, she'd get his spindle eventually anyway, and she'd have his naked beauty right next to hers until she caught.

Her former betrothed could not lay claim to any beauty more than as a particularly ugly imp. Unfortunately, she had once informed him of this, and though they had been a mere six and eight years old, he had never forgiven her. Of course, if he had not been mean to her, perhaps she would not have been forced to make such an observation. She had not been able to look into his face since, and God help her if she had not been abducted to escape a wedding night with him.

She and Roger *hated* each other, and she was quite sure Roger was as happy about her abduction as she was.

"You're welcome, Roger," she muttered.

Brìghde followed them up the stairs and into the keep. In the great hall, a priest stood next to an old man leaning on a cane. He would have been the earl's height as a younger man. His expression alit when he saw the earl. "My son," he croaked as he held out his arms.

"Papa," the earl said warmly and embraced him. "I have brought you a gift," he said as he released him.

"Oh?"

The earl gestured to Brìghde. "Come."

Brìghde squeezed through the paramours, who deliberately blocked her way until she elbowed one in the ribs, and stood in front of the earl's father. Even hunched over he was far taller than Brìghde.

"My bride, Lady Brìghde Fàileach Kyneward." The priest and old man both gaped at the earl, who shrugged sheepishly. "I unwittingly snatched the wrong woman, but 'twas a fortunate turn of events for both of us. Lady Brìghde, this is Sir John Kyneward, my father and castellan of Kyneward."

"Lady Brìghde," he said tremulously and attempted to bow.

"No, no!" she breathed, concerned, and held onto his arms so he would not fall, then grasped his hand. "None of that."

"She assures me she will be a good candidate for the position of castellain. I will leave it for you to decide."

The man's face softened even further and his smile was one of joy and relief. "Oh, I pray so, my lady."

Brìghde gave him a saucy wink. "You shall see."

"*Castellain?*" the French woman cried.

"Oui," Grimme said with some measure of excitement. "And was that not fortunate!"

"I am not going to allow her to tell me what I can or cannot do."

He either had not heard that or he was ignoring it. "And this is Father Hercule."

"Father."

He bowed. "Welcome, my lady."

"Come, come, my dear," said the old man, weakly tugging her hand. "You've had a week to get acquainted with my son and now I would see what you know."

He led her slowly through the great hall, past the chapel, and into a large study. "This is my domain," he murmured as he bid her enter and closed the door behind her. "The witches can't come in here, even if they wanted to. Sit, sit."

"All pardons, but I have been sitting for the last week," she said dryly.

"Of course, of course." He shuffled toward a chair and fell back into it with a sigh. His head tipped back and his eyes closed as he caught his breath. "I do not know you, know of you, know any of your qualifications, but I know that my son seems to be happy with your presence, and he is an excellent judge of character."

Brìghde coughed into her hand.

"Mostly," he amended with a fleeting smile, his eyes still closed. "He is also dazzled by tall, willowy, blue-eyed blondes, but the Kyneward men have always been a lusty lot and my son is no different."

Brìghde decided to walk around the study, which was lined with books. There was even a clock and a globe. "I heard all about his insatiable lust and his ability to break women," she teased.

He barked a laugh. "You are forgiving."

"Forgiving, no. Uncaring, aye. The women may want to claw my eyes out, but I do not care enough about them or Lord Kyneward to want to claw theirs out. He has no amorous intentions toward me, so I am perfectly happy to ply my trade far away from home and free from a marriage contract I abhorred."

"And what of a legitimate heir?"

"When he feels he can bear to bed a brunette, I will be happy to comply, which was one reason I made the bargain."

He laughed. "Does he know that?"

"I would rather he not," she mused as she walked around looking at the lovely things Sir John had. "He is only attractive to me by comparison to my other groom and I have never been allowed other options, so he is a novelty simply because an option was presented to me. It will fade, but he would tease me about it forevermore, and I canna laugh at myself."

"Then rest assured, I will not tell him."

"Thank you."

"Now tell me about your trade."

Thus, Brìghde began to list her qualifications for the position of castellain, what her mother did, how she did it, how Brìghde would have liked to do it but for her mother's insistence that her way was better. When he nodded, she was encouraged to forge on. She told him how she would stock the larders and storage rooms, what supplies she would lay in, how, when, and in what season, and how the outbuildings should be arranged.

"Good, good," he murmured.

Even more emboldened, she revealed her ability to do many of the jobs in the castle: candle-making, baking, weaving, spinning, sewing, brewing, dying, laundering—

"How did you come by such extensive knowledge?"

The half-lie rolled easily off her tongue. "My mother made sure of it, you see, to give me reference for what was a reasonable time spent in each occupation."

She did not notice, but dusk had fallen whilst she spoke—

"Light some candles, will you, my dear?"

"Goodness! I have chattered your ear off."

"'Tis a lovely way to lose an ear, if I must. I am impressed."

So very, very pleased with his approbation, she was nearly in tears. Now, if he only *stayed* happy with her. She found the flints and lit the candles she saw, then returned to her chair when she had gathered herself and said nothing more. The noise in the great hall rose and the soft swish of the door opening to admit a servant interrupted the peace in the study.

She dropped a curtsy. "My lady, Sir John, my lord requests you join him for supper."

"Please inform my lord that I am in council with Lady Brìghde and would request the leisure of dining here. Then bring us our supper and wine."

The servant curtsied again and scurried away.

"Will my lord not find that a slight?" Brìghde asked.

He waved a hand. "Grimme gives me whatever I want. He'll not insist. You read, write, and work sums?"

"Aye." She hesitated. "Ah, but … I cannot manage the estate outside the inner bailey walls. I do not know how."

They sat in silence for a few moments, awaiting their suppers, which came promptly, and ate in companionable silence. As she ate, she began to wonder if the earl's father did not deem her fit for duty after all, if perhaps his words were simple courtesy.

Then he spoke. "The outer bailey is all stables and training pen. The stable master keeps a tight rein on it."

She snickered at his jest, and he winked at her.

"We will hire a steward together. 'Tis too much for one person. I should know."

"Ah … mayhap a housekeeper also? Once I've the house running the way I want, I mean," she added hastily. "We also need carpenters to rebuild almost the whole of the inner bailey."

"Whatever you need, my dear. If you can do all you have said, I will die a happy man, knowing my son is in good hands."

At that, tears *did* begin to swell. "Do you intend to do so as soon as you have stepped back?"

"Oh, no. I have other plans. Should you find yourself in need of help, I would be willing to keep the books, but I would rather not."

"The earl said your other candidates were inept."

He sighed heavily and sipped at his wine. "They were quite adept, in fact. I was too exacting and gave them no time to learn. I was not ready to cede my position, and took any opportunity to find fault."

Brìghde's eyebrows rose to hear a man confess his mistakes so easily.

"And now we come to the end of my life when I cannot do half so much they did."

"Surely you have your own servants."

He puffed an unamused laugh. "Every time I get a servant trained, one of the witches sends him on an errand and never lets him go. Female servants disappear even more quickly."

"Do they do this purposefully?"

"I do not believe so; they simply think only of themselves and appropriate the first servant they see and then keep them milling about waiting for commands."

"And you have not asked my lord to assign any to you permanently?"

He huffed impatiently. "Grimme does not interfere in the workings of the household at all. He thinks I should be able to assert my authority, but he has never given me any over the women, much less my grandsons. If I cannot control the women, I cannot control anything else. He might as well put me out on a wintery hilltop to die. I do not fault him for keeping his women, but I am angry that he ties my hands so, and I do not care for those particular women.

"All my mistresses were intelligent with interests, or at least a willingness to learn new things. They were also kind and the ones who had my babes were good mothers. I could not keep a mistress unless she was my friend. Grimme's mother was an illiterate wet nurse when I met her, but we became lovers when I noticed that I was spending more and more time with her simply talking. She had educated herself when I wasn't paying attention. They were all quite different in appearance, as that was never my first reason for taking a mistress. Thus, I do not understand my son's habits. I tell you this in all good faith. However, should you carry tales, 'twill make no difference as the witches already know what I think and Grimme does not care.

"Emelisse is deceitful and vicious. Ardith is as sharp as a wheel of cheese and without any interest whatsoever. Dillena is the quiet one. She keeps to herself, so in truth, I have no complaint there. Maebh is almost as insatiable as Grimme and she acts childishly sometimes, so she is merely irritating."

"Do *none* of them have any redeeming values? The quiet one excepted."

His shaggy eyebrow rose. "Other than their ability to please my son?"

Brìghde couldn't help her snicker and the old man winked at her with a hint of a smile. "He said he did not like brunettes, but I find it extraordinary that he has such specific taste."

Sir John shrugged with confusion. "I cannot explain. I appreciated variety. I will credit them: They *do* love their children, and they *try* to be good mothers, but 'tis as if they are too dimwitted to learn how."

"Oh?"

"Emelisse is the mother of Gaston and Max. She keeps them by her side or in their chambers, though they chafe. She is afraid they will get hurt outside, does not want them to be knights, but does not allow them to spend time with Father Hercule at studies, as then they are not within earshot. She treats them like dolls. Beloved ones, but dolls nonetheless. When they can sneak out of their chambers, they run about endlessly, break things, get in the servants' way. They are everywhere, no one can control them, and no one can find them, which sends her into the trusses, screeching with fear that they are dead, blaming anyone and everyone for their escape, which makes her cling to them that much tighter.

"Dillena is learned and writes stories for her son, teaches him how to read and write, sees to his needs, but other than that, seems utterly baffled by what a boy needs.

"Maebh practically ignores hers, allowing him to do what he pleases, but when she does pay attention, she hugs and kisses him, tells him what a good boy he is, then forgets he exists. None of them make any attempt to discipline them. The youngest, Pierce, Maebh's, enjoys his studies, but he is the only one. The next youngest, Terrwyn, Dillena's, doesn't like his studies, even with his mother, so he will coax the older boys into mischief, over which Emelisse will then panic and scream at Dillena about her 'monster.' The older boys resent the younger ones' freedom and the younger boys resent the attention Emelisse showers upon the older two. And Terrwyn feels completely forgotten by everyone until Emelisse screams at him."

Brìghde was confused. "Do they not have a nursemaid?"

Sir John shook his head. "We have had several. Emelisse would never give her babes over, and she drove the ones for Dillena and Maebh away."

"Why?"

"Because she 'didn't like them,'" Sir John mocked in a high-pitched voice.

Brìghde laughed.

"No, in fact, Emelisse believed them to be contemptuous of the women's place in the household and she could not bear it."

"Were they? Contemptuous?"

"Not particularly, but Emelisse will allow no one else to be happy if she is not happy, and she has not been happy since Grimme brought Ardith home ten years ago." Brìghde could understand that completely. He looked at her pointedly. "The boys need a strong hand."

"Oh, noooo," Brìghde breathed. "I'll not get between a woman and her bairn, and as I am the wee laddies' stepmother now, 'twould be putting fire to a hayloft. The lord's first priority should be to see to the proper instruction of his sons. If I remember correctly, are not three of them of age to be apprenticed as pages?"

The old man nodded wearily. "Aye. I have spoken with Grimme, but because it involves the witches' objections, he sees that as household business. He loves the boys and does not want to send them away, thus he claims he has simply not gotten around to arranging for it. The truth is, he does not want them to leave home and he dotes. He is far too indulgent, in my opinion."

"Where are their chambers?"

"The women and the boys live on the third floor. Emelisse is in the chambers over Grimme's. Dillena is across the hall from her. Ardith and Maebh are next door to Dillena. The boys have the two chambers at the end of the hall near the back stairs, across from each other."

"Two of the women share a chamber?" Brìghde asked, surprised.

"They share more than that," he drawled.

Brìghde pondered that for a second or two, then— "*Ohhhhhh,*" she breathed, eyes wide in comprehension. Then she laughed. "Well. Isn't that special."

Sir John barked a laugh. "Aye, 'tis. How do you know about such? You're a maiden, no?"

"Aye," she said airily, "but I have six brothers, we are all a year apart, we played together, and even now, most of the time they do not remember I'm a lass, so they speak freely enough."

The old man chuckled softly.

She saw no need to mention that which she'd seen, so there was a companionable silence in the room and Brìghde sipped at the lovely wine she had had on the journey here.

She was about to open her mouth to ask something else when she realized that Sir John had fallen asleep, his chin to his chest. He was snoring. She finished her supper and her wine, then went to the door and peered out. The great hall was still loud, but the platters were being cleared away. There was Lord Kyneward lounging in his chair in the middle of the head table, looking out over all his people.

"Psst! My lord!"

Lord Kyneward craned his head around his chair and Brìghde beckoned to him. He shot his chair back and crossed the room in four long strides. "Is something wrong?" he demanded.

"No. He is asleep. I ... don't know whom to fetch. I don't know where his chambers are or I would take him myself. I haven't even bathed yet."

Lord Kyneward smiled and caught a passing servant and instructed him to put Sir John into bed, his chambers through the door at the back of the study. He caught yet another servant and told her to prepare Lady Brìghde's chambers and bring her a bath.

"Pardon me, my lord. Which chambers are hers?"

"Across the hall from mine."

Lord Kyneward was turning away so he did not see the minute expression of disbelief the servant flashed him before scurrying away.

"Across the hall from you?" Brìghde asked.

"Aye," he said with a grin. "'Tis so I can bid you play chess with me and I will not have to fetch a servant to drag you down a flight of stairs."

Brìghde grimaced. "Ah … did you displace someone else to put me there?"

"No," he said, puzzled. "Those chambers have been empty since we moved in."

"Ah."

"Emelisse wanted them," he continued blithely, "but I want all my women on the same floor."

Brìghde barely kept from dropping her face in her palm.

"If she begs you for them, do not give in."

"Oh, I won't," she murmured, seeing a very long war in her future.

6

GRIMME WAS IN a terribly good mood. No, Brìghde had not supped with him and so his welcome-home supper was a bit dampened by her absence, but he was so happy his father had taken to her so quickly and easily that he was jubilant anyway.

He made his way up to the third floor and walked into Emelisse's chambers to find her in the bath, her maidservant washing her hair.

"Leave me," she snapped at him in French.

"I have been gone three weeks," Grimme said testily, immediately irritated. "Could you not be a little more welcoming?"

"After you brought home a wife?" she snapped. "When you should have married *me?*"

Grimme's good humor began to fade, but he shouldn't be surprised at her anger. Aye, his trip to Scotland had been met with a slight problem, but he'd expected resistance and had gone prepared. That he had not had to use any had pleased him. Abduct bride. Marry her himself. Be upon his way. Very simple, all according to plan. No, he had not snatched Lady Margaret, but God had saved Grimme from his own stupidity and directed him to snatch the right woman after all. He was pleased with his new bride and though he was glad to be home, he had enjoyed their journey immensely.

Only God could have planned something so perfect.

"You knew this day would come, yet here I am here with you. Nothing has changed."

"Nothing has changed?!" she screeched. "Nothing has changed but that there is another woman in the house—"

"Whom I will not be bedding until I must."

"—for whom you put me out of my rightful place at your side! And then she did not even bother to appear for supper to sit there!"

"'Twas never your rightful place and you knew I was going to bring home a wife. What did you expect?"

"I *expected* her to be bound and gagged and locked in a chamber at the top of a tower."

He shrugged his concession. "So did I, but isn't it fortunate for all of us that she needs us as much as we need her?"

"*We*," she growled, "*don't* need her."

"You do understand that if Sheffield killed me before I wed, he would have killed you first, do you not? Or you would have had nowhere to go and no coin to get there, so you would have died out in the wilderness."

"You should have wed *me!*" she screamed.

There were many reasons he would never have wed Emelisse, none of which he felt like enumerating. "I needed a noblewoman."

"You didn't *need* one," she retorted. "You *wanted* one."

"I'm an earl," he said flatly. "Henry would expect me to wed according to my station. What if she looked like you?"

That made her pause. "She doesn't."

"Mayhap you should be grateful, as if she did, I would have fucked her before the ink was dry and I would have taken her straight to bed as soon as we arrived home and I wouldn't be here talking to you."

She snarled at him. "I also did not expect that you would make her castellain. I hope you do not expect me to obey her every command."

Grimme scowled in confusion. "What commands could she possibly need to give you?"

"Any command Sir John feels free to give me now."

"Which you do not obey, so … ?"

That calmed her a bit. "What chambers did you put her in?" she mumbled.

"The ones across from me."

She gasped in horror. "You *didn't!*"

"I did," he returned blithely.

Grimme and Emelisse had had their fallings out before, when she expected him to obey as if she were his mother. It was a hazard of bedding a woman five years older than he when he was barely fifteen and growing into his manhood on the battlefield and the lists. He couldn't tolerate her overbearing nature, but in the end, he always came back to Emelisse.

Tears sparkled in her eyes. "Did you do that on purpose?" she croaked. "To hurt me?"

"The things I do might hurt you," he returned, "but I have never done them for the purpose of hurting you."

"When you know what hurts me and you keep doing those things, then you are doing them to hurt me."

"Emelisse," he said firmly, "we have been together for eleven years. You know my habits and you know I am not going to change. I am home now. There is a wife somewhere in this keep, but I know not where because I am with you, my lover. Do you want me to come to you tonight or not?"

She sniffled, then muttered, "Oui."

7

BRÌGHDE OPENED HER chamber door very late that night after having sat with the earl at table and watched the after-supper amusements. His second-in-command was on his right and they were trading jests, trying to out-do each other, getting more and more vulgar as the night went on.

She didn't mind. Which jests she understood, in both English and French, were funny. The ones she didn't ken used Sassenach words that had other meanings she did not know.

No one else spoke to her; indeed, no one else noticed her. The mistresses had been nowhere in sight when she left Sir John, so she had slipped into the chair to the left of the earl, where the lady of the manor should normally sit.

When she could no longer keep her eyes open, she had requested excusal and the earl had bid her a quick but hearty good eve over his shoulder so he could go back to his conversation.

Thus, here she stood, still dressed in a peasant boy's clothes, alone in a close, dark, cold keep in an inadequately lit hall with her meager possessions in her hand, looking into a vast nothingness. She trudged down to the farthest end of the hall and counted six doors not including hers and the earl's. She snatched the last torch and returned to her chambers.

The chamber was large, but not as large as hers at Fàileach. There was a massive four-poster bed along one wall, but it looked like it would collapse any second. At least it had linens on it.

There was a man-sized hearth in the corner of the room, but there was no fire, no wood laid, no wood in the chambers at all, and no chairs in front of it. In fact, she saw now, the bed was the only furniture in the room. There was no place to put candles, so there were none of those, either.

There were two large diamond-mullioned windows that had no drapes. There were no tapestries on the walls. There were no rugs covering the stone floor. There were no hangings on the bed.

She took the torch into the antechamber. There was no bed for a chambermaid, no chests, no bathtub, no water pitcher and basin. She went to the garderobe. At least it did not stink, but only because it hadn't been used in years.

She sighed and dropped her face in her hand.

No one had curtsied or bowed to her when she came in as the new countess. The villeins and servants had ignored her. The groom felt free to chastise her for riding a horse too big for her. The servants had not been gathered and introduced to her. Chambers should have already been prepared for any bride's arrival, but not only had that not been done, the earl's explicit order to do so had been completely ignored.

No one had taken her things from her to place them in the chambers if they *had* been prepared. Not even Sir John noticed she had her possessions with her.

Aye, this household was a complete and utter disaster.

Dispirited, she decided to go to sleep and start fresh in daylight. She threw back the linens to find there were no sheets, no blankets, and no pillows. Just one thin coverlet.

"It's not Roger MacFhionnlaigh," she whispered to herself, near tears. "It's not Roger MacFhionnlaigh."

She was just tired. The situation would not seem so awful after a good night's rest and a hearty breakfast.

She closed the door, dropped her things by the bed, doubled up the coverlet, donned her heavy wedding dress over her boy clothes, and gingerly climbed into the bed hoping it wouldn't break with all the creaks and groans it made, covered herself, and tried to go to sleep.

WHEN SHE AWOKE, it was still dark outside. She was freezing, her feet most of all. Now she was too cold to go back to sleep, too tired to find a servant, even if she knew where to look, or get wood and make a fire herself, if she knew where that was, either. It was dark, and she was cold and tired.

She walked across the hall and knocked on the earl's door.

The chamberlain answered the door. "Aye?" he drawled contemptuously.

"Is Lord Kyneward here?"

"He is not," he sniffed, and slammed the door.

Of course not. He would be with one of his mistresses after so long away.

Wrapped in her coverlet, she made her way downstairs where many knights were barracked, obliging her to pick her way through them to get to the hearth. The fire was banked. She threw more wood on it because she was too tired to take it upstairs and start afresh, poked it to blazing, pulled up an upholstered chair and ottoman, plopped in it, curled up, and went to sleep.

"What the devil are you doing?"

Brìghde was fairly certain that the question was directed at her, but her eyes would not open.

"Brìghde!"

"Mmrmph."

"Why are you not in your chambers?"

"Cold," she mumbled. "No blankets. No fire."

"What?!"

She turned over on her hip away from the earl and mumbled, "Will see to it tomorrow."

"Aye, you will, but for now—"

She gasped when she was jolted from her warm cocoon and swept into the earl's arms, but he moved so fast, she had no time to ask him what he was doing before he took the stairs, bumped his door open, and dropped her on his bed. She sighed and relaxed whilst he tucked her in. She vaguely heard the earl poking his own fire to life whilst the chamberlain apologized profusely, and then felt the earl climbing into bed beside her before she finally fell asleep.

8

BREAKFAST WAS long over by the time Brìghde dragged herself out of the earl's warm bed, the chamberlain nowhere in sight, went across the hall, divested herself of her coverlet and wedding dress, leaving her in her peasant boy's clothes, pulled on a pair of her new sturdy slippers, then went down to the great hall, which was empty. She continued on down the stairs to the cellar kitchen for food. It was a relaxed chamber of household servants, cooks, and bakers eating and chatting. She cleared her throat, and was cast glances of contempt and suspicion.

"Who are ye an' where'd ye come from an' why're ye dressed like a boy?"

Brìghde slipped into a familiar role. "New 'ere. Was told to come to the kitchen for a meal 'fore gettin'a work."

"Who told you that?"

"Some ol' man."

"Aye, right, then."

A cook arose and put together a very fine platter of food for her, far too rich for a servant, much less one they'd never met. "What's yer name, girl?"

"Bridget."

"Whatcher duties?"

"The ol' man said he'd assign me soon's I ate. Who is he?"

"That's Sir John, the keep's steward."

"Don'tche worry he'll catch ye lazin'?"

Someone snorted. "Sir John canna get down the stairs. He's'na been down here for a year and a half."

"More."

"Aye. Ol' codger don't know nuffin 'bout what goes on 'round 'ere."

"No housekeeper?"

"Never had one. Earl don't know how to be an earl—" Brìghde already deduced as much. "—an' the old man's a merchant by trade, so he don't know either."

Brìghde made sure to talk with food in her mouth. "Fine eatin' for servants."

"With Sir John not bein' able to keep count, we eat what we want when we want 'ow much we want. An' then we take more 'ome. Only thing's sure is don't let the earl suspect nothin's goin' on. Feed 'im an' 'is men good, an' you can 'ide everythin' else from Sir John, so long's it's not on the main floor."

"What about pay?" Brìghde asked.

"Didn't 'e tell ye? Pay once a week, 'stead o' every day. Old man takes some time to get 'is body creakin' to the coin chest. Don't wanna do it ever'day"

That also made sense.

"So it's like this. Ye do as little as ye can get away with—and pray to God ye don't get one o' the hags, 'cuz they run ye ragged if they notice ya doin' a good job—take food 'ome at night, sit on yer arse 'ere or catch up on yer work at 'ome, collect yer wages."

"Hags?"

"Earl's got four 'arlots who fancy 'emselfs ladies of the manor, mostly that Frenchie one, what's been widdim for years."

"Four, eh?"

"Aye, an' any blonde maidservant 'e can get 'is 'ands on."

"We only got three," someone else said around his food.

"Seven women's enough, don't ye fink?"

"Not fer 'im."

Brìghde snickered. "Ol' man said ye got a countess yesterday."

"Ain't seen her," someone said flatly. "Still abed, like as not."

"'Ja see the look on the Frenchie's face when the earl put her out o' her chair?"

The room exploded in cackles and Brìghde didn't bother to hide her grin.

"Can't wait to see what the new lady'll do widdem."

One of the bakers sobered. "Don't wish too hard. She may be the death of all of us, worse than all the hags put together. So we'll have them *and* her."

That was, indeed, a sobering thought.

"I'd best be on up to the ol' man," Brìghde said as she wiped her mouth on the back of her sleeve, "see what he wants me ta do."

"Good luck. Come back for supper, after the betters've eaten. I'll send a bundle home wit' ye."

"Aye, and thank ye."

"Oh, ye might wanna watch out for the earl's bastards. Four o' them, too. They get inta all sortsa things and last thing's we need's the hags down here. They ain't bad boys, but they're … "

"Lads," Brìghde finished.

"Aye, cooped-up ones, which are the worst kind."

She nodded and waved, then climbed the—

"Not *those* stairs, girl! The *back* stairs. Where's yer brain? Ye wanna get caught?"

Back stairs. Aye. She'd forgotten. Brìghde managed to look just confused enough.

"That way."

With another thanks, Brìghde climbed the back stairs and emerged in a covered walkway in the bailey. She stood there and thought. The servants were stealing the food and getting paid to do as little as possible, but instead of being angry, Brìghde was sad. Sad that Sir John had built the earldom to prosperousness, tried to control the spending, but did not know what was going on in his stewardship anymore simply because he couldn't climb stairs, which meant he *also* could not go outside to supervise the villeins.

The earl did not want to be bothered with household business. The keep had never had a lady, so it was no better than a barracks that happened to have four women and four children ensconced at the top of the tower demanding things. None of the mistresses seemed to have any authority to do anything at all, even if they knew what to do or wanted to try. Sir John had been a merchant, so the earldom might be prosperous, but he had no idea how to run a household and *did not know* that he did not know. A skilled and strict housekeeper would have gone a long way, but neither the earl nor his father nor the commoner mistresses knew how a noble house functioned.

"Sweet Mary and Joseph," she whispered.

She didn't blame the servants; that was what a rational person would do when left unsupervised with the most minimal of duties having to be performed to keep from detection. She didn't *like* it, but it *was* logical and once upon a time, she would have gloried in serving in a household such as this one.

Brìghde wouldn't put them out. The food, whether it was being stolen or not, was excellent. She snorted. It was excellent because they were cooking for themselves. All she had to do to keep them in line was visit the kitchen every so often without warning, take quill, ink, and parchment, and make notes. That, to a servant, was terrifying.

She turned to go up the back stairs to the second floor and hoped she could find her chambers. She needed a gown and to rearrange her hair.

She did, indeed, find her chambers, doffed her boy's clothes and donned one of her new kirtles, a deep rich green that the earl had suggested. It didn't fit as well as she'd like, being too snug over her breasts, the waist too low, and the hem too long, but it was the best she could do in a color other than black. She still found his reaction to a mere length of cloth a tad disconcerting.

She dug in her pouch for her glass and groaned when she saw what a mess she was. The kitchen servants would *never* suspect the peasant girl they'd fed was the countess. Unfortunately, they would also not suspect this woman was a countess because she was not richly dressed and coifed enough. She looked for a water pitcher, which had not magically appeared in the night.

She dug her brush out—she was ever so happy she had requested the stay in Hogarth—fixed her hair quickly, then licked her fingertips and scrubbed her face. She checked her glass. It would do.

Well rested, well fed, with daylight streaming through her beautiful (if undraped) windows, she felt more able to tackle the day. The trick was to keep herself from getting overwhelmed with all that must be done, and to discern the proper first steps.

She opened the door next to hers. Empty. The door next to the earl's. Empty. All four of the remaining chambers were also empty.

She went up the back stairs to the third floor where maidservants were milling about looking bored, some sitting on the floor, one lying down. They did not notice her. Brìghde counted. Fifteen.

"What are you doing?" she asked, startling most of them. Two others were sound asleep.

"We're waitin' on the ladies' pleasure," one said a bit snidely. "Ain't you here for the same thing?"

"Nooooot quite. I'm Countess Kyneward, and I am not happy."

Their eyes narrowed as they swept her up and down. "Ye think we're stupid, do ye? Ain't no countess dresses like *that*."

This was unfortunate, but entirely foreseeable.

"Which door is Lord Kyneward most likely to be behind?"

They all pointed to the same one.

Brìghde took a deep breath, marched herself through the gaggle of maids who were so surprised they did not try to stop her (that would have been a mistake), went to the door and started pounding on it.

"GRIMME, GET YOUR ARSE OUT OF BED!"

The maids gasped and stepped back.

There was much cursing and scrambling behind the door before it was snatched open to reveal an enraged woman—until she realized the intruder was Brìghde. Before she thought to take advantage of the situation and deny that Brìghde was the new countess, which would have caused Brìghde no end of problems, she dropped a bare curtsy and said, "My lady," through gritted teeth.

Two other doors opened and three other tall, willowy, blue-eyed blondes stepped out, who also curtsied and murmured, "My lady."

Thus began the scramble of the maidservants to wake up, hop to their feet, curtsy, and deliver many apologies.

"What's your name again?" Brìghde demanded.

"Emelisse."

"Let me make one thing perfectly clear to all four of you. I do not care about you, I do not care about your dealings with Lord Kyneward, I do not care that you are here, I do not care *why* you are here. I *care* that you—" She twisted and swept her finger at them, then turned back to the favorite. "—have a stable of fifteen maidservants doing *nothing* whilst awaiting your pleasure, I have none, I spent the night freezing in a bed that was not made before I slept in the barracks with the knights before the earl found me and dropped me in his bed."

"You *slept* in his bed?" the French one shrieked.

"I did, because *I HAD NOWHERE ELSE TO SLEEP!*"

This was not an auspicious beginning.

"Brìghde?"

Oh, and there was Brìghde's husband, naked, hair rumpled and swinging around his shoulders, jaw stubbled, coming up behind his mistress. He was more beautiful naked than clothed and she did not bother to look away from his spindle.

"What's the matter?"

Brìghde repeated it, only louder this time, because now she was beyond furious.

He spread his hands. "What do you want me to do? This is household business. You told me you would relish taking over. Here you are. It's yours."

"The problem is—"

He held a hand up. "No. I do not want to get involved. That was the bargain."

"Your chamberlain goes first."

He paused. "I'm listening."

"Your order to prepare a room for me last night was ignored," she growled. "The bargain was that you enforce my position here. How can you enforce *my* position if your servants ignore *you* and they do not know who I am? Such as, say, your *chamberlain*, who slammed the door in my face last night, forcing *a countess* to sleep *with soldiers* for some warmth."

His face flushed and he immediately disappeared.

With a smug look, the mistress slammed her door in Brìghde's face. But conveniently, she had slammed it so hard it bounced, so the latch did not catch such that the door stood minutely ajar.

Brìghde cracked her neck this way and that, looked at the maids who were trying not to giggle, said, "Watch this," stood back, raised her skirts, and kicked the door open.

The mistress, shocked, looking half terrified, skittered out of Brìghde's way as she stalked through the chambers until she found the one with the bed by which her husband was dressing.

"Grimme Kyneward!"

"Aye, aye," he grunted from inside his tunic as he pulled it over his head. "I take your point. No need to kick doors in." Then his head popped out and he grinned at her. "That, my lady, was very impressive. I shall have to get you a velvet glove for your iron fist." Brìghde gaped at him, but he pointed at her and chortled. "The look on your face."

She huffed and slumped over, her rage leaving her in a whoosh. "Stop trying to make me laugh. This is serious."

"Are you laughing? You're laughing. Try not to laugh. *Grimme, get your arse out of bed!*" he mocked in a high-pitched voice then roared with laughter.

She broke down and snickered.

"Aye, I know it's serious," he grinned, "which is why I am going out of my way to involve myself in household business. You're welcome."

"I have nothing to thank you for," she said as he brushed by her.

"Roger MacFhionnlaigh!" he called on his way out the door.

Brìghde huffed and stalked back through the chambers and out into the hallway where four identical blondes and fifteen maidservants stood frozen. She jabbed her finger at the stairs. They all bolted.

9

GRINNING, GRIMME clipped down the stairs and into the great hall and waited for all the women to gather. That, he thought, was the most rousing entertainment he'd had in a while. *Grimme, get your arse out of bed!* He laughed until he was bent over and started to cough. She'd *kicked the door in!* He straightened, met Brìghde's somewhat sheepish expression and started to laugh again. She flushed, huffed, and crossed her arms over her chest, but would not look at him because she was trying not to laugh.

That girl was trouble, and he could not *wait* to see what she did next.

He inhaled, his chest expanding, then bellowed,

"IF I PAY YOUR WAGES, REPORT TO THE GREAT HALL IMMEDIATELY!"

It took some time and he gestured for Brìghde to come stand beside him. He started to laugh again and draped his arm over her shoulders, squeezing her to his side, planting a kiss on the top of her head.

"Och!" She dropped her arms and leaned against him.

He was going to lose his chamberlain today, which would *hurt,* but she wanted him to enforce her position as he'd bargained, so that was what he was going to do.

Father Hercule appeared at the door of the chapel, the boys popping up from behind him and squeezing past.

Sir John's door opened and he shuffled out. Grimme waved him over to his side also.

"What is the meaning of this?"

"My countess is not impressed with her reception last night."

"Oh, I know I—"

"Not you."

They waited. And waited. And waited. Until no more servants trickled out. He remained silent until all of them looked appropriately terrified. His women were off to his left, on the side, also looking terrified. His sons were watching with anticipatory glee.

"Papa," Grimme asked, "does this look like the correct number of servants?"

He sighed heavily. "I don't know."

Grimme began. "This is Lady Kyneward, my countess. Other than I, she is the supreme authority here. And with that, I am off."

"Oh, no," Brìghde said, grabbing the tail of his tunic before he could flee.

He huffed and dropped his head back. "Very well."

All eyes were on her as she studied them for a few long moments, then she looked at Grimme's chamberlain. "You," she said sweetly, "are dismissed. No reference. Present yourself to Sir John's study with your belongings and you may collect your wages after I have ascertained that you have not stolen anything."

The chamberlain, his color gone and his eyes wide, looked to Grimme. "My lord … "

Grimme shook his head. "Did it not seem odd that a *brunette* in an expensive gown whom you did not know was knocking on my door in the middle of the night? *After* I had just returned with a countess? Did you think that *perhaps* you should have fetched me? Or even inquired as to who she was? Begone. Now, my lady," he said, sketching a deep, mocking bow and sweeping his hand out toward the gathered servants, "they are yours to do with what you will." He straightened. "Do not involve me in household business again."

And with that, he sauntered out of the great hall, howling with laughter all the way.

10

BRÌGHDE LOOKED at Sir John and began to laugh. She laughed so hard she was squeezing tears out of her eyes and the befuddled look Sir John gave her made her laugh harder. "Oh," she breathed, fanning herself as she wound down, wiping her eyes, "what a *splendid* morning!"

Thus she was happy and smiling as she looked around. The chamberlain had dragged himself up the stairs to pack his belongings. She could paw through his things all she wanted and wouldn't know what he had or had not stolen, but he didn't know that.

First, she looked at the mistresses. "The maidservants referred to you as 'ladies.' You shall not be referred to as ladies, because you are not. You shall be addressed as 'Mistress,' as is proper for commoners." She waited a few seconds for effect, then looked around at the fifty or so servants. There should have been three times that many for a keep this size.

"Today, we start anew. We will consider that today is your first day, and that you have no history here. I do not plan to dismiss anyone else. *Yet.*" She looked directly at the cooks and bakers who had fed her that morning until every one of them recognized her and their eyes grew wide. "Carry on as you have been for now. That is your reward for excellent food and being kind to a stray. We shall go over menus later."

They bobbed curtsies and bowed and whispered, "Thank you, my lady."

"I intend to make this a noble house. How many of you know what this means?" About half the servants raised their hands. "Excellent! If you have suggestions, bring them to me. I will listen. You won't believe me. I ken. Hopefully you will come to trust me as I find problems and repair them. When I have everything the way I want it, I will hire a housekeeper. *Tomorrow morning,* after lauds, you will line up at Sir John's study, where I will take your names and positions. Now!" she said breathily, clapping her hands together and looking at the mistresses. "Which one of you is the favorite one again? I can't tell you apart."

Sir John bent to whisper, "Emelisse."

Ah, yes, the French one whose face was contorted with rage. "Who is your chambermaid?" Her jaw grinding, she slowly pointed. The girl stepped forward. "Are you happy with her?" Now she looked suspicious, then nodded. "Excellent." She looked at the chambermaid and said, "Shoo." The girl ran up the stairs. "Now you may choose another maidservant."

She looked very, very shocked, then she surveyed the gathered servants and pointed. "Her."

That girl looked as if she had just been told to eat pig shit. "All right, then," Brìghde said. "Go. Go, go." She looked at the mistress. "You're excused."

"Gaston," the mistress said sharply at the boys in the doorway of the chapel. "Max. Come."

Brìghde looked between them and their mother. They did not want to go. "Go!" she barked. The boys, startled, also ran up the stairs. Their mother gave her a dagger stare and Brìghde called, "You're welcome! Who's next?"

Sir John advised, "The next one is Ardith, the one with no children."

Brìghde repeated the process with her and the last two mistresses. The sons of those women were left behind. "Who takes care of the young masters' chambers?"

Four hands went up. "Go on." They too, flew up the stairs. She looked at the two remaining boys and said, "Go to the kitchen for some sweetmeats or … whatever suits you, then go out and play."

Shocked, they stayed frozen for some seconds, then raced each other across the hall and down the stairs.

"Who would like to be my chambermaid?" Not one hand. She snickered. "Who is the most experienced one here?" Everyone turned to look at one girl, who shrank into herself. "My bedchamber *only* has a bed that is about to collapse. It has no linens. I want you to oversee my chambers' transformation as best you can with what little furniture may be in this keep, and I suspect there is not much. I want to see how you do without direction. If you please me, you shall be well rewarded. You have my permission to command anyone to do anything so long as it is for my benefit." The lass's eyes were wide. "Who here is the *least* experienced?" Everyone turned to look at another girl, who nearly whimpered. "You shall be my other maidservant, and take direction from my chambermaid. I will ask you your names later. I will never remember all of you at the moment. My chambers are across the hall from Lord Kyneward's. Go. Make of it the absolute best with what is available, as you are outfitting for a countess. You have until midnight."

They didn't move, but exchanged glances.

"Aye?" Brìghde asked kindly. "Speak."

The experienced one curtsied. "My lady. We will need manservants to move furniture."

"Oh, aye. Of course you will. Stay there." Brìghde studied all the men. "Who would like the chance to earn the position of chamberlain for Lord Kyneward?" Multiple hands went up. "All of you stand over there."

She tugged on Sir John's sleeve and when he bent, she whispered, "What did Grimme's chamberlain do?"

"Grimme *hates* shaving himself," he whispered back, "and he's meticulous about it. A decent barber could be his chamberlain and he'd never know, and he's been able to dress himself since he was three."

She chuckled, then looked at the pile of men. "Who wants to try shaving the earl's face without a nick or bump?"

Not one hand. She traded glances with Sir John, who looked down in an effort to hide his impending laughter.

"Very well." She looked to her new maids and said, "Take whom you please." Some silent communication passed between the two girls and all of the men, and four men disappeared up the stairs with the girls.

"Kitchen staff, you are excused." That left a fraction of servants left. "I do not know what you do, and right now I do not care. Go about your normal duties if you have any."

Father Hercule disappeared into the chapel and she and Sir John were alone. A grin slowly started to widen his face. "Oh, my lady. I don't think Grimme realizes what he has unleashed."

She smiled and clapped, looking up at him and quivering with delight. "I know."

11

"'GRIMME, GET your arse out of bed!'" he mocked at Brìghde once he seated her at table for supper. His knights roared, and she grinned. "We have been laughing about that all afternoon."

"So happy I amuse you, my lord."

"You have amused me since I abducted you. So much so, I missed you at supper last night and breakfast this morn."

"You abducted me eight days ago. How can you miss me?"

"And spent most of every day and night together, and sleeping together. I grew accustomed to laughing and chatting with you."

"Oh." Her mood dimmed a little.

"Brìghde?" His smile faded. "What did I say?"

"Oh, 'tis not you," she hastened to assure him. "I do not make friends very easily. Well, I *do*, but I canna keep them very long. I very much enjoy your company too, but I would rather not spend so much time with you that you grow tired of me."

"Why do they grow tired of you?"

"That, my lord Grimme—"

"Just Grimme. My mistresses call me Lord Grimme."

"Ah. Very well. Ply me with food and drink, and I will tell you."

"You'll do anything for good food and drink, won't you?" he asked wryly as he poured wine into her goblet.

She laughed and raised the cup to him. He clinked his goblet to hers. "And plenty of it." She looked around whilst she sipped.

The tables were arranged in an E shape. The head table was perpendicular to the other three, on a dais. People sat on both sides of the three parallel tables. Grimme's place was in the middle of the head table, Brìghde to his left, Sir John to his right.

The mistresses sat at the middle table at the end closest to Brìghde and Grimme, two on each side. The laddies—the only children in the hall who were not servants—were to sit next to their respective mothers. Emelisse was flanked by her two. Ardith the barren sat next to Grimme's oldest. On the other side of the table, Dillena sat closest to the head table, her son next, then Maebh, then the littlest boy. Emelisse's children were hungry, angry, and restless. The other two were sleepy and slouching from all the sweetmeats they'd eaten all afternoon and tired from being outside, but they were happy.

In the hall, there were almost three dozen knights called vingteniers, who each commanded a group of twenty men called a vingtaine. There were another seven knights, called centeniers, who each commanded a section of five vingtaines to make an hundred men, called a centaine. Three knights, each of whom commanded a force of one thousand, were gone with almost three thousand of Grimme's men to France. Their seats sat empty to honor their absence.

Grimme's deputy, Sir Drew, who commanded the entire force of seven hundred that remained at Kyneward, sat to Sir John's right, leaving four empty seats to his right. Father Hercule sat to Brìghde's left, leaving another four seats to his left.

"The mistresses and children all used to sit up here, my lady," Father Hercule whispered to Brìghde when she asked him why there were so many empty chairs.

"He displaced *all* of them?"

"I advised him thusly," he replied softly, "so as to honor your place as Lady Kyneward. 'Twould not be seemly for Lord Kyneward's mistresses to sit in a place of honor with his wife, and 'twould be even more an insult if the favorite mistress and the wife were to sit together."

"Thank you. I appreciate that."

"You're welcome," he murmured with a comforting smile.

Grimme knocked his knife against his goblet and stood, tugging Brìghde up to stand with him. Everyone else stood then. "This," he said, splaying his hand on Brìghde's back, "is my new wife and countess, Lady Brìghde Kyneward. Please make her welcome."

The knights applauded and cheered loudly, and the one who had assisted in her abduction and returned with her and Grimme led the cheers. She grinned and waved at him.

The mistresses, however, remained silent and stone-faced.

Grimme seated Brìghde, then his father, then himself. Everyone else sat, and the food and wine was put out in abundance. In this, the kitchen servants and bakers did not laze about, and 'twas no wonder no one noticed anything else falling apart. Or rather, that it had never been put together in the first place.

"You were telling me why you have no friends," Grimme murmured after everyone settled in to eat.

"Oh. Aye. You see, I *want* to have friends, but once I make one, after a while, she will get tired of me and either lose patience or drift away. In some cases, when she is too polite to do either, I can still tell, so I drift away to relieve her of my presence. Mostly I have just learned to keep to myself. 'Tis not rare for me to make an immediate friend, such as you or Sir John, but none have ever *stayed* my friend after a few weeks or, if I am lucky, months. My brothers are my only real friends, and that is because we have a common enemy and we can fight amongst ourselves until we're all too weary and bruised to be angry."

"Neither I nor Sir John is going to get tired of you."

She looked at him from under her brow. "You have known me a sennight and Sir John barely one day. Overmuch familiarity engenders disparagement. By the time a friend wishes to part company with me, there is much anger and resentment built up, and friendships do not survive that sort of anger."

"Mayhap if you argued as you went along and came to agreement, or agreed to disagree, 'twould not build up until you cannot reconcile."

"In my experience, that is an extraordinary accomplishment."

"I had a friend once. My very best friend. We had known each other from the cradle, 'twould seem. My mother, brother, and I, and he and his mother, lived across the hall from each other above my father's shop. My friend had even less of a future than I. My father outfitted us both as pages and sent us to a noble. We learned together. Studied together. We competed at everything. I would win one. He would win the other. We were equally matched. We grew and attained knighthood very early, as both of us were large for our size, and smart. We have even been taken for brothers. We fought together on the battlefield. We had saved each other's lives again and again." Grimme hesitated, then continued slowly, "Once, I carried him off the battlefield when he was injured so that he would not be slain in mercy."

She laid his hand on his arm, and he blinked at her, surprised. "You don't have to tell me," she said softly. "I can see that it is an unpleasant tale for you to tell."

He laid his other hand over hers and gave her a pained smile. "Perhaps it needs to be told, and I would like to tell it to you, if you will grant me the honor."

She smiled, pleased that he wanted to confide in her. "As you wish."

He took another deep breath. "Aye, well. We were at the Battle of Agincourt, where I earned my earldom and he didn't, though he had an equal hand in what happened and deserved one as much as I."

"Aw," Brìghde sighed.

"But that was not the worst of it. He had already begun drifting away from me before that, as he could not bear the burden of his gratitude for carrying him off the battlefield. He would have feigned his happiness for me and finished fading away. It was that I seduced his lady love."

She grimaced.

"I swear to you, Brìghde, I did not know she was his lady love. He spoke of a woman he was wooing. I thought nothing of it, as I do not woo."

"You *don't?*" she asked breathlessly.

He grinned. "She claimed that she allowed him to woo her because she wanted *me*."

"Mmm hm," she hummed and pulled her hand away to take a bite off her platter.

"He accused me of taking everything away from him, his dignity, his honor, his chance at nobility, and then his lady love, which, he told me, was why he had never introduced me to her. He refused to believe that I did not know and would not concede that it takes two. She rebuffed him."

He stopped talking and began to eat in earnest, as did she, but after a few bites, she said, "Well, I am sorry." She was.

"I am not finished."

Her eyebrows rose and she looked at him out of the corner of her eye as she ate.

"You do not even let a good tale get between you and your food, do you?" he laughed.

She grinned and popped a bite in her mouth to punctuate the jest. "Go on."

"We had had a philosophical disagreement of many years' duration, which was what finally turned us from friends to bitter enemies."

"And that was ... ?"

"I," he said slowly, now looking at his platter and toying with his food, "am not an honorable knight."

"How so?"

He raised his eyes to hers. "I want to win. By any means necessary. I identify my enemy, I do what I must to conquer him. I will ambush. I will sneak through the night and slit the throats of hundreds of men silently, like a snake, then lick the blood off the blade. I will lay traps, spy, poison, and run a sword through the backs of retreating soldiers so they do not return to bedevil me another day."

Brìghde was confused. "What about ransom?"

"Only when I'm not outnumbered, and those battles have been few and far between. If I do not have the force to take knights for ransom, I take their armor and horses when I'm finished laying a field to waste."

"That is the nature of warfare."

He blinked at her as if he had expected her to judge him harshly. His expression softened. "Not when one has been reared to adhere to the chivalric code. The only place I have always fought honorably is on the lists, and that is because I could not win otherwise. My friend found my philosophy dishonorable, but he tolerated it as we fought our way through France, victorious always. He could not see that he needed my warcraft to make it possible for him to ply his.

"And I did not come to my philosophy lightly," he hastened to assure her, as if he'd argued this point for years. "It was difficult to change my thoughts, but I was simply tired of losing. I do not lose well or graciously and finally determined I would not tolerate losing at all. So, he saw my having had his lady love as the final manifestation of my dishonorable and cowardly way of waging war."

She studied him for a long time, her mouth pursing, her nose scrunching, her lips twitching back and forth. "He believes your earldom to be illegitimate."

"Aye, and the fact that he fought honorably, by his code, and deserved one as much as I, and 'twas only that Henry saw my fleeting valor, but did not observe his steadfast valor that made the difference."

"Oh," Brìghde said sadly. "How long were you friends?"

"Twenty years and then a few more. We have been enemies since Agincourt."

"What was his name?"

"Aldwyn Marchand. He is Sheffield's deputy, prime commander of all Sheffield's forces."

Brìghde gasped. "Leading the charge for your death?"

"I'm told no, and I would believe that, for that is not Aldwyn's way. On the other hand, he remains in the service of Sheffield, so he may have changed; I know not. You will likely meet him soon as I expect the duke will insist on visiting to *celebrate* our marriage. If he is still the Aldwyn I know, I have great sympathy for him, as it chafes for any intelligent knight to be subject to a dull-witted noble. Divine right of kings," he scoffed. "So many men too *simple* to wage an effective war, and too many men too prideful to wage war to *conquer*, chivalry be damned."

Brìghde sighed sadly and dropped her head, shaking it.

"Do you judge me now, my lady?" he asked coolly.

She raised an eyebrow at him. "Trojan horse."

He looked confused.

"Someday—not today—I will tell you why and how I was to be the Trojan horse to destroy Clan MacFhionnlaigh."

Comprehension slowly overcame his features. "My God," he whispered, aghast.

"I told you you rescued me from more than marriage to an imp."

"The horse," he whispered.

Brìghde smiled wistfully and picked at her food. "Aye. But!" she said, sipping at her wine. "Do you care, I am *sad* for both of you, as I understand both your philosophies. My father believes as you do, but his bloodlust is never sated. He continuously looks for battles to pick just to go to war. *That* is dishonorable. I didn't *like* the MacFhionnlaighs and I certainly did not want to breed with that pack of disgusting dimwits, but they did not deserve to be slaughtered simply because my father is carrying a grudge over a slight."

He blinked. "Would you have done it?"

Brìghde's mouth tightened and she looked away. "I … like to think I would not have once I was no longer under his control." She shook her head. "We are discussing the nature of friendship, not my moral failings. Your point is that you are not angry with your friend, but he is angry with you. And you saved his life, which he cannot bear at all because it means you are no longer equal in all things. He is in your debt. In his mind, he is inferior, not only because he does not have an earldom whilst you do and he is more deserving, but because he sees himself as having been the weak one and you the strong one, and having lost his lady love to you was the final insult to his manhood."

"Aye," Grimme muttered with a sigh, looking down at his platter, only half eaten, whereas Brìghde was busy licking hers clean. "But that does, in fact, prove my point. For twenty years, Aldwyn and I argued incessantly. Fought. Grew angry with each other. Yet those small contentions did not damage our friendship. One large philosophical contention alone did not break us. It took many contentions and much of fate to do so."

"I would argue that that is the privilege of history. My brothers and I are loyal to each other because we are so close in age and we have experienced the same things. 'Tis not something that can be claimed with just anyone."

He pursed his lips and thought, then nodded. "Aye, I see your point."

Brìghde looked up to see that the hall was quiet. Everyone was finished eating and were bored awaiting Grimme's order for the entertainments to begin. She quickly glanced at the mistresses, two of whom were trying to coax their sons to eat more, but they had come to the table stuffed. One mistress was staring at her empty platter morosely, and the last sat back with her arms crossed, glaring at Brìghde.

"Dismissed," Grimme rumbled, and slid his half-eaten platter over to Brìghde.

"Oh, thank you!"

As the hall emptied of those who did not wish to stay and the mummers appeared to begin the evening's amusement, he snapped his fingers and bid more wine be poured for both him and Brìghde. The mistresses scattered and took their sons with them.

"Good eve, Papa! Good eve, Grandpapa!"

"Good eve, boys!" Grimme and Sir John called back to them as one.

"Excellent wine," she breathed under the cacophony as she sipped, her eyes closed. "Thank you, Husband."

He smiled. "I believe we have indeed been disproportionately advantaged."

"I agree."

"And so I ask again, what makes you so unlikeable?"

She put down her goblet and dropped her knife. She leaned back, crossed one leg over the other, stared at the opposite wall. She crossed her arms over her chest. Her jaw slid back and forth, then she turned her face toward him but looked at the floor. "I'm right." She raised her eyes to his. "I'm *always* right. Even when I'm wrong, I'm right."

Grimme started to grin. "That is the most winsome thing I have ever heard a woman say."

She laughed, but a little sadly. "I want a friend like yours so badly," she said softly, "that I will beg like a dog to have his ears scratched. Sometimes, I make immediate friends, as I said. *Sometimes,* someone will pursue me to be my friend—*those* I am suspicious of, but will still take because I am so desperate."

"Is that why you acquiesced so easily to this marriage?"

She shrugged. "One reason. You seemed friendly and did not ravish me."

"Your expectations are too low."

"You see, I do not *want* to have small arguments along the way because for me, any argument at all always ends the friendship. I try to be kind. I try to listen and be a good friend, give good counsel. It is not returned, but still I ignore slights and hurtful words, I ignore annoyances and pranks. I ignore the gossip about me, I ignore things I overhear. I ignore my resentment of the hints for coin or this and that and give her what she wants, until I don't, at which point she stops speaking to me. As for philosophical differences ... " She sighed. "I've never had a friendship last long enough to *have* a philosophical difference. I try. I try, Grimme, but at some point, she is wrong and I am right, and I can no longer bear the weight of my righteousness silently."

Grimme held his hand out, palm up. She looked at it, confused, then raised her eyes to his. He gave her a crooked grin and flexed his fingers. She hesitantly put her hand in his. "If you will let me, I will teach you that friendships don't end with an argument or two. You don't have to beg for ear scratches from me."

12

GRIMME SAT IN his chair just after midnight and Brìghde had requested excusal. It was quiet but for the scraping of tables being pushed to the side and the erection of cots for his men. He had not realized that all through the meal, his father had been listening and there the two of them sat, father and son, silently contemplating.

"Trojan horse," Sir John murmured.

Grimme nodded slowly. "It worries me, her lack of a sense of loyalty."

"Son, she has no reason at all to be loyal to you. You abducted her, and the fact that it suited her purposes does not make it worth any loyalty, for you would have brought her here against her will anyway."

"Aye." He paused. "After our wedding, she wrote a letter to her brother absolving me of an act of war."

"Oh? That's … "

"Loyalty to herself."

"But she *told* you about her father's plan, which, considered the proper way, is a gesture of good faith."

He did not answer for a long time. "She has been very free with information. What if … she is not disloyal or acting in bad faith, but so desperate for a friend she will tell anyone who is kind to her anything and everything in the hopes that they will like her?"

"That occurred to me whilst she was speaking."

Grimme shrugged. "No matter. I don't befriend those I fuck and I don't fuck my friends."

"If you don't intend to bed her, why did you wed her and bring her home?"

"I *do* intend to bed her," he said testily. "Just not … today."

"I don't understand you. How are you able to turn down even the most beautiful of brunettes?"

"Papa, *you* fucked a dwarf."

"She was comely and the price was right."

Grimme rolled his eyes.

"I'd bed Brìghde myself if I thought she'd accommodate my infirmities."

"I knew you would before I brought her home. I regret to inform you she's married."

"Never stopped me before," Sir John said blithely.

Grimme laughed and clapped his father on the back, rubbing his shoulder. "That's my papa."

"And with that, I shall find my bed."

"Sleep well."

"And you, my son," he said with a pat on Grimme's arm.

Grimme sat slouched, his foot on the table, his chin on his fist, still contemplating what it meant to have in his household a woman capable of slaying an allied clan at her father's behest for … a slight. How *large* a slight it was, well … Grimme had avenged himself for a slight before, but not to that extent. The thing that bothered him the most was that she *did not know* if she would have gone through with it once she became Lady MacFhionnlaigh and took up residence.

"Grimme."

"*Lord* Grimme," he growled without turning.

"Lord Grimme," Emelisse pleaded, pulling out her—no, Brìghde's—chair and sitting in it. She clutched Grimme's hand and held it to her breast as she leaned forward, tears in her eyes. "Don't let her come between us," she whispered in French.

Grimme rolled his head on the back of his chair until he was looking at her. "Did we not discuss this last night? How many times must I tell you that I am not at all interested in bedding her—"

"But you must! For legitimate heirs. What if you acquire a taste for her?"

Grimme laughed suddenly.

"I am not laughing! She is beautiful."

"That does not signify. She is not beautiful in a way that appeals to me."

Her nostrils flared. "You sat at supper whispering with her the *entire* time. I tried to get your attention. Your harlots tried to get your attention. Your *sons* tried to get your attention. A few of your men tried to get your attention. You have *never* sat at supper and whispered with me all the way through."

That was because he and Emelisse had nothing to talk about. He preferred it that way, but even if he didn't, Emelisse had nothing of interest to say.

"Nothing could take your attention away from her. She pounded on my door and you laughed. She ordered you to get out of bed and you laughed." Grimme started to snicker again. "You see? You would have put me away for *days* had I done such a thing to you. Never mind *kicking in my door!*"

"Make sure it's latched next time."

She gnashed her teeth. "Gr—*Lord Grimme!*"

"She amuses me. Think of her as … Aldwyn."

"That is not what I see. You left my bed when your knight summoned you and you did not return until late morning. Then I learn she slept in your bed last night. You slept with her, did you not?"

"Aye. I slept with her almost all the way home from Scotland, too."

She whimpered. "But—"

He huffed, no longer amused. "You misunderstand my marriage to her. I did not wed a woman. I bought a measure of safety from Sheffield's plans for my death, and also had God's blessing to get a castellain and a willing womb. She just happens to amuse me. Now, I weary of this conversation. If the boys are distressed by my having snubbed them, send them to my chambers." That was the *last* thing he wanted to do, as they would want to wrestle and he was too tired to wrestle little boys.

"She is different," she said flatly. "There is something about her that draws you to her."

"I am not drawn to her *that way*."

"*Non*, there is something else. I am going to lose you."

"If you continue with this, oui, you might," he burst out, exasperated.

"I mean, I am going to lose you *to her*."

He looked at her with something akin to astonishment. "You see things that are not there. I bed *you*, not her."

"You bed three or more others, too," she said bitterly, "and do not tell me you did not get your cod satisfied on your journey to get her."

"This *again*?" he asked with a raised eyebrow. "You know why. Do not expect me to curb my lust simply because you cannot pace me."

She flushed.

"I do not disrespect you by demanding you do what you don't want to do, so do not badger me with your unhappiness that I go elsewhere for those things. As to Brigitte, if you are cordial to her, she will be cordial to you."

"After this morning's display?"

"She told you immediately that she does not care about you or why you are here. She was angry *at me* because she was tired because my orders were not carried out because the servants are not under control and you four hoard them all and my chamberlain dismissed her and no one knew who she was so could not command anyone. That was all *my* fault. She has *no* interest in you as anything but a member of the household for which she, as castellain, is responsible."

"I will not be commanded, much less by her."

"I cannot think what she could possibly want you to do."

Her eyebrows rose. "Oh, you cannot think. *This morning* she felt free to kick in my door—"

He somehow controlled his snicker.

"—and storm into it as if it belonged to her. Then she lined me up with your other harlots as if I were a servant and ordered me to choose two maidservants, then ordered me upstairs. *Then* she ordered Gaston and Max upstairs with me."

Grimme found nothing truly untoward about that, but kept his thoughts to himself. "She is just getting the household settled. She will not need to command you to do anything once everything is put to rights."

"Tell her she is not allowed to command me for any reason at all!" she demanded.

He sighed. "Go to bed. I will be there anon."

It wasn't long after she left that he heard, "Papa!"

He smiled to see his youngest son, of Maebh's womb, running to him with a big smile.

"'Tis very late, Pierce," he said and pulled the boy onto his lap. "Why are you not in bed?"

He blinked. "No one put me there."

Of course not. "Would you like me to do so?"

"Aye, Papa, and will you tell me a story?"

"Mmm, let me see. I will tell you the story of how I plucked Lady Brìghde straight out of her wedding."

Exaggerated for best effect, of course. He had not gotten through their first night in the woods before the boy drifted off and his body grew heavier against Grimme's chest until he released tiny snores.

He looked up to find that most of his men were in their cups around the hearth or sleeping. Grimme sighed and stood, the boy cradled in his arms and took him to his chambers, sliding him gently in bed beside his snoring brother. Once tucked in, Grimme looked down at his sons and smiled a little. Sometimes he did not feel as if they were his blood, just any four of many, many children in the keep and the bailey. How did a man *feel* his sons to be *part* of him? The boys' mothers certainly felt them to be part of them, but Grimme could not capture that feeling. Any sons Brìghde bore him would be his legitimate sons, but he could not imagine caring for them any more or less than he cared for the ones he already had.

He should start preparing them for their future, the way his father had prepared Grimme, Grimme's brothers, and Aldwyn. They could be warriors or respected scholars or doctors of medicine or merchants or clerics or craftsmen, sure of themselves. He wanted them to enjoy their occupations as much as Grimme enjoyed his, and he didn't much care what they were, so long as they weren't thieves like Grimme's older brother.

He simply … did not want them to leave him.

Troubled by his neglect of his sons' educations, he clipped down the stairs to his own hallway and slowed as he reached the span between his door and Brìghde's. Hers was wide open, candles and torches blazing, hearth also ablaze. She had servants running in and out, fetching buckets of hot water and leaving with empty ones.

He leaned against her door frame, his arm up over his head to watch. The girls curtsied to him as they went in and out of the chambers. One, a tall, willowy, blue-eyed blonde, didn't curtsy. She gave him a long look up his body, met his amused gaze, looked back down his body, then settled her attention on his cod. He smirked. She raised an eyebrow at him.

He shook his head with a wry grin, and she rolled her eyes and shrugged, then went about her business, cupping and squeezing his half hard cod as she went past. He looked over his shoulder and watched her disappear down the stairs. He puffed out a long breath.

"Oh! Grimme! Good eve."

"Are you going to keep the maidservants up all night?" he asked, because if she didn't, he would.

"Sweet Virgin Mary, I hope not," she breathed, then flopped in an overstuffed chair and wiped her forehead with the back of her arm. "I'm *drained.*"

"Food?"

"Nay, but wine would not come amiss."

He ordered one of the girls to fetch wine for both of them. She curtsied and scrambled, and he watched after her too.

"What is that scowl for, Lord Husband?"

He grunted. "I have never seen the servants work this hard or this fast."

"There is a reason for that," she said lazily, then yawned.

"Which is?"

"They haven't been working much at all, but this wanders into things you do not want to know about."

"Indeed." He looked around at her chambers. "I would you acquire things of your own taste, not pieces scavenged from forgotten corners. If these chambers are not to your liking, you are free to choose different ones."

"Aye, I will, bu—" A huge yawn caught her. "—but there are too many things to be done first, particularly if your duke is going to be visiting anon. Do you know! There are one hundred thirty-four guest chambers in this keep that do not have furniture!"

"Twenty-four total."

"Well, it *seemed* like one hundred thirty-four. We shall need carpenters. And wood."

"We will go to Hogarth and fetch some as soon as I can get away."

"Thank you. Did you need me for something?"

"I *was* going to ask you to play chess with me, but I see you have a bath awaiting you."

She nodded wearily, and said nothing whilst the remaining maid left. His brow wrinkled and he tilted his head to see if— "Brìghde, are you crying?"

She dashed her fingertips against her cheeks. "I miss my dog," she whispered. "I have never slept a night that he did not sleep with me since he was a pup and now … "

"You slept without him on our journey."

"I slept with *you* and you are almost as big as he is, and almost as intrusive into my sleeping space. Last night, for example."

Grimme laughed. "Would you have been allowed to take him to MacFhionnlaigh?"

"He was awaiting me there," she muttered.

"What's his name?"

"Mercury."

"Roman? Commerce?" he asked, confused.

"Speed. Mercury has winged sandals and helmet."

He smiled wistfully and sighed, his smile fading. "Aye."

"What's wrong?"

"I had a horse once," he said, for some reason compelled to tell her things he had either never told anyone else or had forgotten. "Ares."

"Greek god of war," she murmured.

"He was born small and weak. He'd be dead in a couple of days, but my patron knight told me I could have him if I could save him. I was thirteen. I think. I sat with him and his dam night and day, slept with him, kept him warm, poured goat milk down his throat until he could nurse. His dam wanted him to live too; without her, he wouldn't have survived. I spent every penny I had to keep him alive.

"So then, my knight took us to the best trainer in France, and loaned me the coin. I did the bulk of the training, with the trainer's help, and he trained me how to train a horse to war. Ares carried me through every battle I ever fought as a knight, every tournament I ever entered, across France, up and down England." Grimme wiped his hand down his face, wishing he'd never said anything, but now could not stop speaking. "I've never owned or ridden another horse that could match him. Intelligent. Fierce. A warrior." She was watching him carefully, which made him angry because she saw too much. "I was approached about breeding him. I was very careful to breed him to mares who could match him and I made a lot of money. I have two of his sons and I only ride one or the other."

"What happened to him?" she asked softly.

Why had he thought he could end the story there?

Because the story didn't end there. It hadn't ended at all.

"Sheffield has him. Marchand—my friend—rides him."

Brìghde gasped, her eyes wide and her hands over her mouth. Indeed, her eyes were glistening again, and now he was happy because she could cry for him, that he had someone who *would* cry for him.

"Sheffield demanded him as tribute," he muttered, looking down and scuffing his boot on the stone. "I had no choice. You will likely get to see him, too, when the duke visits."

"Oh, Grimme," she whispered.

He pushed himself away from her door jamb. "Good eve, and sleep well." He halted, then said over his shoulder, "When the duke comes, he will tour the stables. Whatever you do, do not let him know how much you love Troy. He'll demand him and I'll have to give him to him because he's my liege and God knows, Sheffield wants to possess everything I love."

13

"MY LADY. LAUDS."

Brìghde sighed at the hand on her shoulder, but did not open her eyes. She was so very comfortable in the old but sturdy bed with a new mattress. "Thank you, Avis. Bring me the green kirtle."

She arose, allowed her chambermaid to help her dress, then sat on a stool whilst the girl brushed her hair, braided it, and dressed it. She looked in the glass. "That is very lovely. Thank you." She could see the girl blush and smile in the glass. Brìghde turned and said, "You did very well with my chambers, and by the time I set. I am pleased. If you continue to serve me this well, I shall double your wage."

"Thank you, my lady," she whispered.

She looked around. "Does *nothing* match? Where is everything? Certainly the last occupant of this keep left *something*?"

Avis shook her head apologetically. "Not very much, my lady. We searched every corner of the keep for even this much and—" She shrugged helplessly.

"That's a new mattress. Where did you find it?"

She pulled her lips between her teeth.

"Tell me," she teased.

"You said all maids were to obey our orders, aye? We ordered one of the hags'—*mistresses'* maids to bring us one of their mattresses that had not been swived upon. They have several, stacked upon each other."

Brìghde beamed, and the girl ducked her head to hide her smile. "Excellent work. Very good thinking." She leaned closer. "Which hags and how did they react?"

The maid giggled before she caught it in her hand. "Maebh and Ardith, mum. They only grumbled because they had to get out of the bed before we could get to it."

"You and I should get along very well."

"Aye, mum," she whispered shyly. "You must hurry, however. The servants are lining up for roll."

"Ah, aye. Thank you."

If Brìghde wanted to get all the servants accounted for before breakfast, she would have to skip morning prayers and go straight to Sir John's study, where he was awaiting her with his ledger. She went to the study door and said, "Kitchen staff first."

They went quickly, Sir John checking them off, verifying their positions and wages. The serving staff next, who had to hurry to get the tables readied for breakfast. Next, the chambermaids and on down to the last servant in the keep.

There were many not accounted for and many important positions not filled. Sir John shook his head wearily. "I cannot keep up," he murmured. "If they were dismissed, if they disappeared ... " His eyes were shiny with tears of frustration, and Brìghde would have comforted him, but it was time for breakfast.

"Come, come. A good meal will make everything look brighter. Can you go outside?" she asked as she accompanied him to the table.

"Only with help. Getting down the stairs outside the keep is dangerous business."

"Ah."

She and Sir John stood by their chairs and awaited Grimme, who appeared in simple breeches, tunic, and boots, which was standard clothing for a soldier to wear under his gambeson, mail, and armor.

"Good morn, Papa. Brìghde," he said cheerfully.

"Good morn, Grimme."

He seated her, then his father, then he sat. Everyone else then sat and breakfast was served. Brìghde looked at the mistresses' spots. "Where's your family?"

"Emelisse is sleeping. The boys are likely also asleep. The others, I don't know. When are you going to get me a new chamberlain?" he muttered, scratching at the copper-gold stubble on his jaw.

"I asked who would like to shave the earl's face without a nick or a cut and no one was interested."

Grimme and Sir John chuckled.

"Is there anything *else* you need from a chamberlain?"

"See to my clothing," he mumbled as he ate. "See to my comfort when I'm there."

"Did you like him?"

"He's been with me for eight years, so ... aye."

Brìghde pursed her lips and thought mayhap she had been a little too quick to take offense.

He slid a glance at her. "But I want someone I don't have to train. I train enough pages and squires and men-at-arms. And horses. I don't want to have to do it at home, too."

Brìghde nodded. "Fair. Who occupied this keep before you? There is *no* furniture in this house."

"So you said," Grimme said around a bite. He was wolfing down his food and must want to get out to the training field. "It was empty when we got here. Papa saw to furnishing it for our needs, but that was five years ago, so … Kyneward has a dower house that may have something in it, but I doubt it. It's boarded up. I haven't been there, nor has anyone else, I don't think. Papa?"

"Nay."

"Where is it?"

"In the southwest corner, just inside the border between Kyneward and Sheffield."

"How far is that?"

"Seven miles."

"Where are the keys?" she asked breathlessly.

"I have them," Sir John said.

Grimme slid her another glance. "Not this week. I will send knights with you, but we are conducting important training practice. Sheffield guards the border heavily to make sure we know they are there, and I don't want them to mistake you for a wench who's lost her way, and they would be *very* happy to see a beautiful woman alone and vulnerable. *Wedding* you would not be at the forefront of their thoughts."

It irritated her, but she could see his point. "Very well. I have things to do."

"Aye, and one thing you must do is adjudicate the villeins' and merchants' complaints against one another and against us."

She looked at him, aghast. "You do not have a manorial court?"

"A what?"

Brìghde thought she would never overcome the shock at what this earldom lacked. "Uh … do *you* not adjudicate them?"

Grimme shook his head with finality. "No. My method of adjudicating conflict is to let the soldiers fight it out until one of them surrenders or dies."

"Then … who does do it?"

"Father Hercule, when he can. Otherwise, no one."

"So they've been arguing amongst themselves all this time?!"

"Aye."

She leaned over her platter to look at Sir John. "Do you not have a lawyer here?"

Sir John and Grimme both looked at her strangely. "We should have a lawyer?"

"Oh, sweet Virgin Mary and Joseph," she moaned, planting an elbow on the table and rubbing the bridge of her nose.

"Brìghde," Grimme said stiffly, "I am the bastard son of a wealthy merchant, *not* a noble. I should not even have been made a knight, much less an earl and I have very rarely been in a noble's home, and that only to sup occasionally. I have been an earl a mere five years, more than half of which I have spent in France. Neither of us knows how a noble household runs, which is something that has become painfully obvious to both of us over the last two days. We have done as well as we can with what little knowledge we have. There is no such thing as lessons in how to be an earl."

"And I," Sir John said darkly, "have been busy building a fortune, at which I excel, in case you haven't noticed."

Brìghde swallowed at the chastisement and wondered if she would lose both her new friends in all of three days.

Grimme went on, "I don't even know how to get my sons legitimized, and my incessant missives to London have gone unanswered. We understand that you are learned in these matters, and we are grateful that you are, and that you have consented to see to putting us to rights. However, if you could refrain from pointing out how dimwitted we are, we would appreciate it."

She flushed. "I'm sorry," she muttered. "I— My mother is— I try not to be like her but … "

"Forgiven. *Do* you know how I can legitimize my sons?"

"I only know Scots law," she mumbled, flushing, utterly ashamed of herself because she had suddenly turned into her mother and she had sworn never to do so. She looked at Father Hercule next to her. "Please tell me you studied law before you took your vows."

He smiled. "I did."

"How can Lord Kyneward legitimize his sons?"

"He doesn't have to legitimize them; he only has to declare an heir."

"That is not what I want," Grimme said. "I want to legitimize them, not name one of them my heir. Making a wise decision as to an heir amongst my sons is not only difficult at their ages, it would cause much strife amongst their mothers. I want my heir to be legitimate because none of my women have any expectations as to their sons being the heir. I don't want the conflict."

"You cannot legitimize them, my lord," Father Hercule returned.

"Out of curiosity," Brìghde asked Grimme, "which one would you name?"

"I – don't – know!"

She turned back to Father Hercule. "You know the laddies. What do you think?"

"Pierce," he said immediately. "He is shrewd, learns quickly, and he also has a bit of a ruthless streak, which, if it can be nourished in the correct way, will be what he needs to be earl."

"He's five," Grimme drawled impatiently. "How ruthless can he be?"

"That is whom I would choose and that is part of my reasoning," Father Hercule said firmly.

"You're hired," Brìghde told Father Hercule. "Send for a new priest."

WHEN SHE RETURNED to her chambers just after midday meal, after having sequestered herself with Father Hercule to build a list of complaints to be heard and to set a regular weekly court day, her chambermaid was stacking wood by the hearth.

"Oh! Good afternoon, my lady," she said, curtsying.

Brìghde smiled. "Come. Let us talk." She offered her one of the mismatched chairs in front of the hearth and Brìghde took the other. The girl looked scared.

"Do you know Lord Kyneward's chamberlain?"

She flushed. "He's … me uncle, mum."

"Oh, is that so!"

"Aye, mum."

"Take me to him." Her eyes popped out of her head. "I am not going to accuse him of thievery. Lord Kyneward values him, and I would offer him his position back."

Her face lit up. "Oh, mum, *thank you!*"

Brìghde hopped up and gestured at the lass to hurry. She clipped down to the kitchen, surprising the kitchen staff, and asked where she could find carrots. They scurried to get them for her and she sweetly said, "Thank you," then ran back up the stairs. It was pleasant to walk outside, as she had not been outside in a full day. "Come, we must visit my pet first." She led the girl to the stables and Troy snuffled at her as soon as he saw her. "Good day, my sweet wee laddie," she said and puckered up to smooch his snout. He lipped her nose. "Today I have carrots for you." He gobbled them as fast as she could pull them out of the sack. "Sweet Mary! Do they give you *nothing* to eat?"

"Pardon, my lady, but he's spoilt."

She turned to see whom she assumed to be the marshal. He bowed, but was trying to keep his smile in check.

"Are you accusing me of spoiling this magnificent charger?"

"Aye, my lady, I am."

She turned to Troy and nuzzled his snout again. "I can spoil you all I want, can I not, my beast?" She looked over her shoulder and said, "He's a *Trojan* horse."

"Aye, mum," he chuckled. "Do you need him saddled?"

"Oh, no. I am going to walk. I just stopped by to pet my pet. Aye, he is. Who's a good laddie? *You're* a good laddie."

"Ah, mum, I was wondering— We do need him to train and—"

"Any day, any time after breakfast. If I need him, I will try to request him in advance. Tomorrow, in fact."

He bowed again. "Thank you, my lady."

"Are you going to breed him?"

"Already done, by Lord Kyneward's orders, mum."

"Let me see her."

The marshal led her across the outer bailey to a different stable. "This is where we keep the breeding mares."

"Oh! 'Tis why you have so many horses!"

"Aye, mum. Lord Kyneward breeds and trains horses for sale. As he had Ares and now his sons, his horses are much in demand and nobles from all around come to purchase."

He took her to a stall where a lovely bay mare who was almost as big as Troy stood munching oats. "Oh, good day," Brìghde sighed, holding her hand out for the lass to sniff. "What's her name?"

"Helen." Brìghde gaped at him. "All our mares are named Mary until Lord Kyneward decides upon a name. We have mares who've been with us two or more years who still haven't been named. Since this one and Troy took a liking to each other almost immediately and she was already in heat, 'twasn't difficult to get him on her. So my lord named her Helen. He has a gift for knowing which stallions to breed to which mares and he spends quite a bit of time with their lineages."

"Oh, what a lovely lass you are," Brìghde cooed, but Helen did not seem to appreciate her attentions, so she stepped back. "I suppose I'll not be riding *her*."

"No, you will not. Nobody has been able to ride her but my lord and then only barely. She's thrown him dozens of times."

"Ah, 'tis not just me, then."

"No. She is five, but her previous owner practically gave her away for she could not be trained. If anyone can train her, 'twould be my lord."

"Does Ares have a consort?"

"Aye, he does. Come."

The mare was mostly white with big black splotches, and mixed black-and-white mane, tail, and feathers. She too was almost as big as Troy. "Why, good day to you, Mistress Aphrodite."

"Oh, no, mum. Her name is Enyo."

Brìghde searched her mind for an Enyo, and could think of nothing. "Why?"

"I don't know. You'd have to ask Lord Kyneward."

"Do you breed her?"

"We do, but Lord Kyneward would rather not, as we don't have Ares and Lord Sheffield will not allow him to mate her. At the moment, she's not in heat, but we cannot afford to leave her fallow, as her foals are too fine."

"Why did Sheffield not take her too?"

"He doesn't care about mares."

"Idiot."

The marshal chuckled.

Unlike Helen, Enyo seemed to like her quite well, even going so far as to wrap her neck around Brìghde's shoulders to hug her, and Brìghde fell in love. "Oh, you bonny lass," she cooed, with her arms around the mare's neck, scratching her. "I am pleased to make your acquaintance and shall return to see you soon, aye, I will. What a bonny wee lassie you are! Thank you, Marshal. We'll be off!"

The day was overcast, but warm for April. Brìghde paid careful attention to the villeins' cottages, all of which needed a few repairs. Kyneward would need a land steward before those few minor repairs turned into many major repairs.

"This way, mum," Avis said softly, and led her off the main lane through a pathway cut between cottages three rows back from the lane. She stopped at a cottage and knocked.

"Go'way."

"Hamond, 'tis me, Avis."

"Girl!" came the gasp and the door was ripped open. "Ye shouldna be away from the keep! Go back afore ye get—"

Avis tilted her head to the left. He looked at Brìghde and though he was surprised, he kept his expression carefully back.

"I made a mistake," Brìghde said crisply.

Both Avis and her uncle gaped at Brìghde. A noble admitting error was unheard of and possibly scandalous, but doing so made one seem trustworthy.

"Lord Kyneward values you highly and he allowed me to dismiss you to honor a bargain he and I made, but he did not like it. Thus, since he has said nothing about it, much less complained, and he will not ask me to request your return, I would like to honor his gesture to me. If you would care to return, I will double your wages."

Avis gasped and Hamond's jaw dropped open. "My lady," he breathed, stepping out into the small pathway.

"Before you accept or refuse," she said, "we must have a bargain amongst the three of us. I don't know you. You don't know me. Hamond, Lord Kyneward values you. Avis, you showed me your worth when you put my chambers together within your power and in the time I gave you. This is all I have to guide me; however, I *must* trust *someone*. You two must be my eyes and ears. I mean to set the keep to rights the way a noble household should be run. I need to know what goes on belowstairs or I will be crawling all over the keep at all hours of the day and night and nobody will see or hear me and I do not like to hear bad things about myself because then I will get angry. I want to know all the household goings-on. Who's swiving whom. Who has a grudge against whom for what reason. Who is stealing what from whom, where, and how. Who's a layabout. Who causes trouble. And I need to have your word you will not let your personal grievances against a good servant inform me whom to dismiss."

Hamond was nodding along and Avis seemed to be soaking up the instructions as if she had accepted the terms.

"I do *not* want to know anything about where Lord Kyneward puts his spindle."

They both choked.

"Do we have a bargain?"

"Aye, my lady."

"Avis?"

"Oh, aye, my lady."

"Excellent. If we hurry, we can have you in livery by supper."

And the livery was awful. Brìghde grimaced when she saw Hamond dressed in his finest. The three of them stood in Grimme's chambers and Brìghde tilted her head. "When was the last time you had new livery?"

"I couldn't say, mum."

Brìghde groaned and dropped her head in her hand. "So much." She mimicked sobbing for a moment and then drew up a deep breath. She turned to Avis. "How long have you had that?"

She shrugged. "Don't know, mum."

Then Brìghde glanced at the unmade bed, which a maidservant should have made, which Hamond would have made sure she did. She pointed to the bedsheets. "Those are very worn. In fact, so are mine. That's not something an earl and countess should be sleeping on."

"That's the best we have, mum."

Brìghde sighed and closed her eyes. "Very well."

Suddenly the chamber door opened and there stood Grimme, in his mail, who stopped short. "Oh. Good afternoon, Hamond."

"Good afternoon, my lord," he said, bowing.

Avis curtsied.

Brìghde opened her mouth, but Grimme held his hand up. "Household business." With that, he dropped to his knees, looked under his bed, pulled out a sword, and left.

"Hamond," she said suddenly, "do you know why Lord Kyneward does not like black?"

He looked surprised. "His tournament armor is black and his horse, Ares, is black."

"Hrmph. Suffice it to say, your new livery will *not* be black. Suggestions?"

14

GRIMME AND HIS knights were deeply engaged in whatever drills they were practicing, so much so that the next morning, he and they all bolted down their breakfasts with barely a word.

"Wait," she said as she caught him when he arose to head out to the practice field. Grimme looked at her, irritated, distracted. She snapped her fingers in his face. "Pay attention."

"What!"

"What's your favorite color?"

His mouth dropped open and then his expression hardened and his nostrils flared. "Brìghde."

"I am absolutely serious. I am going to order new livery. I know you hate black, and I want to know what would please you."

"Black," he snapped and scraped his chair back so fast it fell over, then stalked out of the hall, all his knights following him.

She and Sir John exchanged looks. "Did you say you are going to order new livery?"

"Aye, and bedsheets. Why?"

Sir John's brow wrinkled and he slowly arose and shuffled toward his office, gesturing for her to come with him. He sat heavily at his desk and sorted through his very tidy stack of papers that were arranged in some way she did not understand. He pulled out a bill and handed it to her. "That is from the seamstress in Waters. Livery. Bedsheets."

Brìghde studied the bill. "Firstly, I would not order good livery from Waters. Secondly," she said slowly, "there is no new livery in the larders and nothing but worn bedsheets upstairs. I had my maid ask the paramours' maids about the state of their bedsheets, and 'tis the same. A countess, an earl, and his mistresses should not be sleeping on bare threads. Thirdly, if you didn't order it, who did?"

"I'm sure it's just an error," Sir John said wearily.

He didn't believe that.

"I will rectify it," Brìghde murmured.

He flopped back in his chair and said, "How long will it take you to get the keep into the order it should be?"

"Uh … I don't know. Grimme is convinced the duke will be coming soon, but I don't know what that means. We must be ready, and I am hurrying. Why?"

"I am tired and I want—" He snapped his mouth shut.

Brìghde's mouth twisted and she looked away.

"Go," he muttered. "Just … go."

"I … will need coin," she said uncertainly in a small voice.

"Coin?" he barked. "To go do … whatever you do?"

"No," she said, confused. "I'm going to Waters. To find out about this bill."

He blinked. "Oh. Aye. I suppose you will." He made shooing gestures as he arose and she left his study, closed the door, and waited for him to open it and put a pouch in her hand. She counted it.

"That should be enough." She smiled at him. "Thank you."

He did not smile back. He nodded wearily and closed his door.

She hurried up to her chambers to tell Avis where she was going, then across the hall to ask Hamond if he felt Lord Kyneward needed anything. Razors. She clipped down the stairs, out the front door, and ran across the inner bailey to the outer bailey, to the stables. "Good day!" she called.

Grooms popped out of the stalls and fell all over themselves to bow and serve her. No, here, they would not be able to laze about as the indoors servants had done before Brìghde had come to set them aright. This was the marshal's domain and he would know if the slightest, most insignificant straw were out of place.

"I would like my horse, please."

"All pardons, my lady," one ventured. "Which one is yours?"

"The golden destrier with the white mane and tail."

Their mouths dropped open, which Brìghde found extraordinarily satisfactory, and she preened.

"But … my lady … that's … a *really* big horse."

"Now, please."

Once Troy was led out, she admired his deep golden hide and nearly white mane and tail, and the thick white feathers about his hooves.

"My lady, all pardons, but the only side-saddles we have belong to the mistresses, and they are not big enough for your horse. Are you *sure* you would rather not ride one of the palfreys? Or at least a gelding?"

"No," she said airily, "I would not. Saddle him with what he came with." She put her nose against her horse's and scratched his cheeks. He huffed and nibbled her nose with his velvety lips. "I grew rather attached to this lad on our journey, did I not? Aye, I did," she told the horse. "You are a pretty lad, aren't you? Aye, you are." She hugged his neck and spoke to him, then fed him carrots whilst the grooms saddled him. "Have you seen your consort today? She doesn't like me." When her bag of carrots was empty, they assisted her in mounting.

Once again, she arranged her skirts so that they would protect her against the leather yet allow her knees movement. She started when a saddled sway-backed nag was drawn up next to her and a groom mounted, then looked at her expectantly.

"What."

He gestured to the portcullis. "Whenever you're ready, my lady."

She laughed. "Oh, no. You are not coming with me."

"But if I don't, my lord will—"

"And if you do, I will. You stay here."

"My lady," he begged. "*Please.*"

"*Nooooo.*" With a laugh, she kicked her stallion into a flat run and thundered out the portcullis and down the lane, leaping carts, children, sheep, and gates.

For the good livery the upper servants would wear, the clothier had to visit Kyneward for an extended stay, but she had no furniture. It would have to wait until they had some. But the candle was burning down quickly until there would be an unannounced visit by the duke. She would go to Hogarth soon to start outfitting the keep in earnest.

She let the horse have his head for as long as he wanted. After years of being pent up in either her chambers or her father's study, allowed out with the heaviest of guards on the worst horses in the stable, it was absolute heaven being alone outside on a powerful horse, free to go where she would as fast as she wanted to.

When Troy finally slowed, she pulled him back to a walk for a while, then cantered the rest of the way into the village.

She garnered many a shocked look as she clip-clopped merrily into the hamlet. She waved. "Good morn!" she called to that farmer. "Good morn!" she called to this baker. "Good morn!" she called to the seamstress, which shop was the first place she was headed. She stopped her horse and dismounted (not without some difficulty). "I am Lady Brìghde Kyneward," she said to the still-dumb woman.

"I know," she whispered. "Ye came through here three days ago with the earl."

Brìghde smiled. "Excellent! Then you likely know I need clothes."

"Aye, but my lady, I do not carry such finery, nor do I know the latest fashions. I provide linens and rough livery for scullery maids and the like."

Her eyebrows rose. "But I do not *need* the latest fashions today. I need *you* today. Would you rather I take my business elsewhere?"

She gasped. "No, no! Welcome. Welcome, my lady. Come in, come in." With that, she yelled a boy's name into the shop and presently, one popped up. "Take my lady's horse to the livery."

Brìghde nodded approvingly and followed the woman into the shop. She looked around. It was unimpressive at first and stayed that way throughout her inspection. The fabric was rough and in uninteresting colors, half of it black. She sighed.

Black was her favorite color.

"Now, I must tell you," Brìghde said finally, "that I am a working lady, and will soon take over Sir John's duties."

"Oh?" she asked carefully.

"Aye. Serve me well today and you shall have all the business you could dream of."

She bobbed a curtsy, but looked more afraid than delighted. She might not know how to manage more business. Oh, well. She would learn.

"I am in need of more rough gowns such as I am wearing and servants' clothing for myself. 'Tis why you are perfect for my needs."

The woman's jaw dropped. "But my lady—!"

"No, no. I am serious. Please take my measurements and get me three daily gowns, ten white shifts, and four sets of pages' clothing. Can you do that in a week?"

She gulped. "Yes, my lady."

"And … oh. Sir John was teaching me the ledgers, and I saw some of your bills and I thought that mayhap a delivery of bedsheets and livery was not accounted for properly? I could not find the merchandise."

The woman struggled to keep her smile in place, but her skin paled. "I must have mixed up the bills, my lady. The bedsheets are awaiting delivery when the livery is finished."

"Excellent! Also, I was wondering if we have any credit against future purchases? Or perhaps we have not settled our accounts properly? I have not been able to go over all the bills, you see. I would not have you go unpaid."

She gulped. "I don't think so, but I will go over my records and calculate it. If so, 'twould have been an honest mistake."

Brìghde waved a hand. "Everyone makes errors," she said reassuringly. "I'm sure everyone in Waters has made errors at some point or another, no?"

"I—I wouldn't know, my lady."

"Mayhap," Brìghde said softly, "some other merchants might like to be made aware of any errors in calculations for goods to the keep. Oh, and in future, please direct the deliveries to me. Now!" she resumed brightly. "About my new clothing … "

SHE SPENT THE day going through the hamlet ordering what she could from the few resources available and making sure every single merchant knew they would be undergoing scrutiny by the new countess. Kyneward had merchant credit all over Waters so she needed few coins. Now, how to keep that from Sir John so as to spare his feelings, she did not know.

She bought a good pair of scissors and several razors from the blacksmith in coin, as the blacksmith would admit to no credit there. She went to the cobbler and ordered another pair of boots, but could not order slippers or fine shoes, as he did not trade in finery, either. She purchased an entire set of sewing implements. The only other thing she purchased outright was a wheel of a particularly good cheese (which made the cheesemaker preen) and a loaf of bread, then a bag of pears for Troy.

She sighed sadly. His name was particularly poignant to her, considering the task Walter had assigned her in anticipation of her becoming Lady MacFhionnlaigh. Aye, it was indeed worth promising children to a strange man who intended to force her to marry him if it meant she would be forever free of Roger and her father. That the earl was kind, funny, and handsome was even more fortuitous. When the time came, lying under him would be no hardship.

Her brow wrinkled. Unless … he was *so* averse to brunettes he could not rise for her at all, ever, and if his collection of tall, willowy, blue-eyed blondes (including three maidservants) was anything to go by, it would be quite the hardship for *him* to lie with *her*.

She could admit that did bruise her vanity, as she was not accustomed to being rebuffed for her appearance. Why would it be a pleasurable experience for *her* if she knew all along that he was disgusted by her? She couldn't bed him if he had to force himself, for she would have to beg and why should *she* beg to carry *his* babe? It wasn't *her* earldom under attack.

She was not so desperate to keep him as a friend as to be able to swallow that insult without stating her opinion.

His aversion to brunettes was one thing, but his insistence that she not wear or buy black made her wonder if one had anything to do with the other.

'Twas almost sunset when she and Troy trotted into Kyneward's stable, where the grooms barely spoke to her, would not look at her, and stayed as far away from her as possible. She huffed and stomped her foot. "What has happened that you barely acknowledge my existence?"

"They have been roundly berated for allowing you to go out alone," came the earl's deep voice, filled with anger, from the entrance to the stable. She turned to see him standing by his destrier, reins in hand, glaring at her. "And they may be even more severely disciplined, once I decide upon it."

She clucked. "Oh, *really*," she huffed. "They tried, and I ordered them not to. Then I outran them. They had no chance even had they disobeyed my order, especially with that nag they had saddled. And then *I* would have berated and disciplined them. Recant your beration."

"Wife," he growled.

"*Hus*band," she mocked with wide eyes and fluttered her eyelashes at him.

She knew she had him when his mouth started to twitch. He opened his mouth, pointed at her, took a breath, and said— Nothing. He simply started to laugh. "'Beration' is not a word."

"It is now. Give your reins over, tell them you won't discipline them any further, and inform them that I will go out whenever I please with or without whomever I please on *that* horse—" She turned and looked at a groom. "His name is Troy. He is *mine*. No one else rides him when he is not occupied in training or warfare. Have my purchases taken to my chambers, the ones across from his lordship's."

"Aye, my lady," he whispered.

She turned back to the earl. "—and to pamper him *shamelessly* with pears and carrots and whatever else he asks for."

Grimme sighed and threw up a hand. "You heard her." He handed over the reins to his horse and offered her his arm, which she took, and strolled with him out of the stable, through the outer bailey, inner bailey, and up the stairs to the great hall.

"I never thanked you for offering me your bed the first night."

"You're welcome," he smiled warmly.

"How did you know where to find me?"

"You disturbed one of my knights, who fetched me, as he was horrified that a countess had to sleep in a chair amongst men of war. And," he said slowly, "I… apologize for snapping at you this morning. I have much to think about."

"'Tis well."

"Thank you also for returning Hamond to me."

"I was very angry," she said simply, "but after some thought, I realized that because you immediately honored the bargain at great sacrifice to yourself without complaint, I wanted to show you my appreciation."

He slid her a glance. "You didn't want to find a new chamberlain."

She snickered.

"Green."

"What?"

"My favorite color is green."

15

BRÌGHDE WAS IN the chapel early the next morning to pray as she had always done at home but had not yet had a chance to do here. Her customs were all awry, but they would have been anyway, as the last time she had had any custom was the morning before her wedding, after which she would have had to establish new customs at MacFhionnlaigh, which would have involved avoiding Roger's mother. And father. And Roger.

Whilst she plotted to disappear forever.

If she lived that long.

Kyneward was not MacFhionnlaigh, and she was here to stay, so she was free to create customs she would not have to abandon. The only person who commanded her was her husband, who did not seem to care much about commanding her at all. Here at Kyneward, there were no plots, no angry fathers, no overbearing mothers, no husband she could not abide, much less his family, no swiving a disgusting imp (although now *she* was the disgusting imp) and she had a *friend*. Finally. *Two* friends!

Until she was right and could no longer suffer being right silently.

She finished her prayers, crossed herself, and stood, turning to see Grimme kneeling with his rosary. She sat quietly so that she would not disturb him as she passed by to leave.

"Amen," he whispered.

She arose to leave, but he caught her with a smile. "Good morn."

"Good morn," she said, taking a seat beside him when he moved over. "How was your night?"

"Busy," he said.

Her brow wrinkled. "What could you— *Ohhhh*."

He chuckled.

"Do you go to confession for that?" she asked cheekily.

"Why bother?" he drawled. "Do you suppose God has blessed us? You and me."

Brìghde looked at him, once again noting how fine of face he was. "I do," she answered simply.

"Tell me about the Trojan horse."

Surprised, though she should not have been, she began. "'Tis not much more than you could deduce from what I said. The finer point was that once established as Roger's bride, I was to host a feast of all the MacFhionnlaighs from far and wide, choose a propitious moment, and poison the lot of them. And then Walter would ride in with his army and lay waste to MacFhionnlaigh's troops, who would, hopefully, be dead drunk."

"You speak of it as if 'twere just another Sunday for you. It … bothers me, as your propensity for loyalty—or lack thereof—bothers me."

She supposed she deserved that, and he wasn't wrong.

"You said your loyalty could be earned, but not compelled. You profess no loyalty to your father, yet you were poised to do as he commanded you. Please help me understand."

She took a deep breath. "No one knew of the plot except Walter and I. I was supposed to wed Roger two years ago, but MacFhionnlaigh offended him somehow—don't ask, I don't know what happened—and he wanted revenge. If he had said, 'They are weak and I want their lands and I will go to war to obtain them,' I would have thought nothing of it, for they are weak and I don't like weak men. But for a slight … It didn't have to be anything big."

Grimme was nodding. "If my neighbor's weakness bore a consequence to my land, say, allowing invaders to cross because of a lack of defense, then aye, I would take it. If not, no. But certainly 'I want your land' is a better reason than 'You hurt my feelings.'"

She laughed. "It is. Thus, he kept me at his side for two years, plotting and planning. I learned potions and poisons. I learned how to wield my dagger and sword more effectively. Not once did he say a derogatory word to me the entire two years. He didn't praise much, either, but I didn't expect any. It was … Grimme, it was *wonderful*. In those moments when I was at his side, I would have done whatever he asked to keep his approbation. But then I would go to my chambers and wonder what spell he had me under."

Grimme tensed just slightly. "But at the wedding, he had a sword in your back, and you said he walled off all your options for rebellion."

She heaved a sigh. "Aye. After all that and he didn't trust me not to rebel."

"You said no one would be surprised if you had been plotting to do so."

"Aye. But since I could not outwit him *before* the wedding, I would have to do so *after*. I intended to run away, as I did from the convent, but how long would it take me to prepare so that I never had to return? Could I hold Roger off long to escape his spindle and Walter's plan? Could I keep from doing it at all if he caught me before I did what he wanted?"

Grimme looked a little befuddled. "Once you were with MacFhionnlaigh, wouldn't you have his protection?"

"Not … necessarily. Walter would have visited often, ever threatening to kill me if I did not do as he said. He would have gotten impatient enough eventually to do so. But if I *did* do as he wanted and succeeded, the other clans would have executed me. He would have disavowed all knowledge."

"*What?*" he breathed.

"I do not *know*, but I *believe* that his intent was to be able to take MacFhionnlaigh, aye, but stage it as if I had acted alone and his seizure of it would have been to protect MacFhionnlaigh from me and he arrived too late. Then he could turn me over to the clans for execution. I was terrified to do it, and terrified not to do it. Either way, I would have died, by the clans' hand or his."

"Brìghde," he whispered, looking quite horrified.

"If I am right—and some days I could not believe he would go to such lengths to avenge himself for my rebellions—"

"Why could he not simply kill you?"

"My mother. She has some hold on him that none of us has ever been able to ken. He gives her whatever she wants. He had to have a way to get me killed without doing it himself. At this point, I could easily be convinced he will do anything to kill me without making my mother suspicious that he had done so."

They sat in silence for a moment or two before Brìghde realized she needed to wipe a tear from her cheek.

"Why didn't you poison your father?" he finally asked.

"Och!" She waved a hand. "He's had tasters for as long as I've been alive, and that's simply because he has not hardened himself to *every* poison in the world."

That seemed to intrigue him. "Are *you* hardened to poison?"

"Only the one I was to use. He wouldn't dare poison me."

"Because your mother would know."

"Aye."

Grimme nudged her. "Should I fear you will wreak havoc upon my household and supplant my rule with yours?"

She snickered at his teasing. "Were your brains suddenly to turn to mush, I would of course assume power," she teased in return, "but I've no fear of that."

"You might," he said wryly, "should my helm be battered on the battlefield and I return with the wits of a vegetable."

"Then you shall go into battle knowing your estate is safe in my hands."

"But I do *not* know. I've yet to see you with complete control."

"You've seen my iron fist already."

He started to chuckle again. "I've yet to get you that velvet glove." He paused. "I shall think on what you have said, but know this: I will not let him harm you."

She smiled softly at his sincere tone. He believed what he said, and he would do what he could to protect her, but in the end she would offend him and he would no longer be her friend and then he wouldn't care.

"Ah … " he began delicately. "On to something entirely different."

"Am I in trouble?" she asked warily.

"No, no! My youngest son, Pierce. Maebh's. The five-year-old."

Brìghde nodded encouragingly.

"He lurks and skulks about the keep. He has seen you pass through, and is distressed that you have not said good day to him though I tell him time and time again that people who cannot see or hear him cannot say good day. He doesn't understand. He finds you fascinating."

Brìghde blinked. "Why?"

"He hates Emelisse," he said flatly. "You showed him Emelisse is not as powerful as she thinks she is. He wants your protection from her—"

Brìghde had many thoughts on *that*. "Oh."

"And perhaps a little attention. May I introduce you? And … will you be kind?"

"Of course," she said in a small voice, hurt.

"Brìghde," he said softly, picking up her hand and running his thumbs over the veins, "I don't know you. Please do not hold my requests against me. I don't want them to fear their stepmother."

She took in a deep breath and nodded. "I— Hm. Um … "

"Say it."

"Very well. Sir John asked me to intervene, as I have brothers and might understand your sons. I said no, because I do not want to get between a mother and her child. Yet … what little I have seen—and it has been *very* little—and have heard, they need to be allowed to be wee laddies. More, they need your guidance."

He nodded wearily. "I know. I hesitate to take them away from their mothers, as they are so attached— Rather, Emelisse is attached." His mouth tightened. "I know that Gaston and Max need to be apprenticed out to a knight as pages, and Terrwyn is that age now. Pierce enjoys his studies with Father Hercule, so I suspect he may thrive as a scholar. I was surprised at Father Hercule's assertion that Pierce has a bit of a ruthless streak, as he is only five."

"He gets it from his father," Brìghde said wryly, which made him laugh.

"Aye, I suppose. But quite frankly," he said, his voice a little hollow, "I don't know them as well as my father knew me, my brother, and Aldwyn at those ages, so I cannot tell which of them are suited to the battlefield or possibly commerce, as my father and brothers are."

"You do not send them away so that you can observe and do for them what your father did for you."

"Aye."

"Have you been?"

"Have I been what?"

"Observing them."

He slid her a glance that made his irritation clear. "No."

She refrained from saying *I didn't think so.*

"But you knew that."

She shrugged. "How can you observe them when they spend their days in their chambers or running around the inside of the keep and you are out on the practice field?"

"Come," he said, assisting Brìghde out of the pew, walking together out of the chapel to see the boys already running about. "Boys!"

"Papa!"

Then they were surrounding him, jumping on him like excited puppies. He picked up the littlest, who watched Brìghde with great curiosity. "Good morn, Master Pierce," she said with a smile, and held her hand out.

"Take her hand like this," Grimme murmured and demonstrated, "and then kiss her knuckles."

He tried it and pressed his mouth so hard against her knuckles he would wake up with a fat lip. Brìghde kept her laugh to herself. "Thank you."

"Boys, this is Lady Brìghde. She is my wife."

"We know," Gaston muttered with a hateful glare.

Brìghde looked at him with a wry expression and said, "I am not going to try to be your mother, but if you allow me to, we might be able to be friends."

He rolled his eyes and turned away.

Brìghde looked at the other two and said, "Max? And Terrwyn? Aye? Very nice to meet you also."

The three older lads looked to start playing tag in the great hall whilst the servants were readying breakfast. "Grimme," she said softly, "will you allow them to run in the bailey?"

"Aye, I think so," he said, putting Pierce on his feet. "Come, boys. I will play with you."

They turned into the four happiest lads in the world, and she waved at Pierce, who was craning his neck around to look at her as he was shuffled out the door. He returned her wave hesitantly.

"You stay away from my sons."

Brìghde turned to see the French mistress snarling at her. Brìghde rolled her eyes and took a few steps away from her, but was jerked back by a long bony hand wrapped around Brìghde's entire upper arm. It hurt. But she merely looked at the hand, then up at Emelisse and murmured, "Get your hand off me before I cut it off."

The woman was so shocked she did, in fact, drop her hand.

"We can be friends," Brìghde said flatly, "or we can ignore each other, but I would rather not be enemies because I dispose of my enemies, which requires more work than I care to perform. Do not make me work harder than I absolutely must."

"You have Grimme. You do not get my sons, too."

"I do not *have* Grimme. I do not *want* Grimme."

Emelisse was surprised, if not shocked.

"Nor do I want your sons. But," Brìghde said low, stepping forward and looking up at the utterly beautiful woman Brìghde could not hope to compete with even if she wanted to, "I will treat them—and you—any way I feel moved to. Stay out of my way and we will have no trouble."

With that, Brìghde stepped around her and continued upon her way.

"May your womb one day find too many choices to make."

Brìghde did not stop walking, but shivers ran down her spine. It was said in a whisper, in sing-song French. It *sounded* like a curse, but instead of panicking, she simply raised her hand with the middle finger up prominently.

Brìghde smirked at the witch's gasp of outrage.

There were advantages to having grown up with six brothers.

16

"SIR JOHN," BRÌGHDE murmured after breakfast as the two of them sat on the same side of his desk whilst Brìghde wrote out her purchases of the day before and their exact amounts. "You referred to the paramours as witches. Did you *mean* that?"

He cast her a sober glance. "Why?"

"Emelisse *cursed* me."

"She has cursed me also."

She dropped her quill and wrung her hands. "Has it come true?"

Sir John heaved a sigh. "Brìghde. The thing you must know about curses is that they only work if you believe them, and even then almost never."

Brìghde was confused. "But that's … *witchcraft*. 'Tis of Satan!"

"Consider: If you were Satan—"

She gasped, her eyes wide at his blasphemy.

"No, no. Listen to me for a moment and ponder. I want an answer. If you were Satan, and you wanted to exploit all the evil in the world, would you waste your time on trifles such as curses and potions and possession of animals?"

She worried that in her mind.

"With all the evil that humans are capable of—say, your father. Sheffield. When those two are wandering the earth wreaking havoc on anything and everything for sport, when men have warred with each other from the dawn of time— The man my son idolizes, Henry of Monmouth— He is not a good man. Grimme was with him when they took Rouen. They starved the town out, so it released twelve thousand of its poor, thinking Henry would let them through his forces to find sustenance." He shook his head. "No. He let them starve and *my son* was there at his side and saw nothing wrong with it."

Brìghde looked at him without understanding.

"Well?" he barked. "Is that or is that not evil?"

Confused, Brìghde said, "That's … war."

Sir John's forehead thunked on his desk. "There's two of you," he groaned. He raised his head and rubbed the bridge of his nose. "Do you pray to God?"

"Of course!" she said, horrified that anyone would question her devotion.

"Mm hmm, and does God give you what you want when you do what He says?"

"Aye," she said firmly.

"Oh, *really*," he drawled with a bit of disdain. "What was the last thing you prayed for that you got?"

"A miracle to keep me from marrying Roger MacFhionnlaigh," she said flatly.

Sir John, shocked, blinked at her but looked at Brìghde's list. "Ah. And so where is God on the battlefield?"

"With the victor," she replied helplessly, unable to understand his point.

"One innocent person is slain, it is murder. Slay twelve thousand, but that is just … war?"

"Aye."

"And what about your father's plan for MacFhionnlaigh?"

Brìghde's mouth tightened. "You say Satan does not waste his time on trifles such as potions and curses, but exploits the larger evils that men do."

"Aye."

"Walter wanted to lay waste to MacFhionnlaigh because they offended him in some way that they probably don't know they did. Instead of saying, 'Och! Ye hurt me feelin's!' so MacFhionnlaigh could say, 'Och! I'm verra sorry!' he plotted for two years to slay the entire clan. His vanity is a trifle that Satan exploits. Do not say Satan will not use every trifle, even the fancies of a jealous French mistress; he has the time, energy, and demonic army to do it."

Sir John heaved an exasperated sigh. "Never mind."

"Does Grimme know? About Emelisse, I mean?"

"He can't. He prays every morning. He is superstitious and has a very deep fear of witches, demons and such, which I don't know how he acquired, so if he thought she were a witch, he would've put her away immediately. As for her witchcraft, I don't find it any worse or better than anything the church teaches, and St. Augustine was clear on its irrelevancy to the gospel or anything else, but let's not debate theology any longer, as I am a bitter old man."

It bothered Brìghde that her friend Sir John had such a blasphemous opinion of the church, and she wanted to talk about it, but trying to show him where he was wrong would distress him and she did not want to lose her friend, so she tried not to think about it.

"My son believes in witchcraft, but I do not. Emelisse is *not* one. I have seen no evidence that she has been any more detrimental to a household than any other man's mistress, which is to say if she *is* a witch, she is a very inept one. There is no reason to plant those seeds in his mind, which would throw the household into more chaos than it already is, and my very strong advice to you—since I cannot command you—is to keep your belief to yourself. He doesn't need to know, I don't want to discuss it, and it would immediately make him suspicious of you and your motives."

"Aye," she murmured, properly chastised.

He then went back to her list. She could tell when he began paying attention and shrank in on herself in dread.

"Brìghde," he said slowly, "what … Do I read this correctly? You spent almost no coin yesterday, but you returned with merchandise."

She pulled out the coin purse and dropped it on the list. "There is the balance," she sighed. "Sir John … I don't know how to say this, but … "

By the time she was finished, he was nearly in tears, and she despaired that she had had to hurt him so. She did not like hurting her friends, as those hurts built, and then the friendship ended.

But she was training to be castellain of Kyneward and she was right, and she also could not bear the burden of being right without a way to repair the situation. To repair it, he had to know and she was the only one who could tell him. Hesitantly, she reached out and put her hand on his back, but he waved her away, so she decided not to tell him about the kitchen staff, as she had already managed the situation. She arose quietly and left the study, pulling the door closed and standing there, sad and helpless. She had made her friend cry.

The midday meal was called then and she stood behind her chair to await Grimme, as did his paramours and their children. He entered the hall with three of his men, laughing. One of his men said something, which made the rest of them roar. Grimme's face was red and shiny with sweat. His blond-roux hair was wet and dark. Though he had taken off his mail and gambeson, clad in only breeches and a belted tunic over it, he was still a very large man, at least twice her size, as he could sleep curled around her almost doubled over.

"Brìghde!" he called, grinning at her. He turned to his man and said, "Tell my lady."

His face flushed. "Ah, 'tis not fit for a lady, my lord."

The others jeered him, so Grimme turned and, as he walked toward her, as his men stopped at their own chairs, he told the jest. It was bawdy, she knew, but this jest also used Sassenach words whose double meaning she did not ken. She laughed anyway when the rest of the knights began to roar yet again.

She took quick glances at the paramours, three of whom seemed to understand the jest no better than Brìghde and one who rolled her eyes. Brìghde supposed that was the English one.

"Boys!" Grimme called.

The lads, standing behind their own chairs restlessly, waved at him. "Papa!"

He stopped and, squeezing between two of his men, he stepped up on the table, his leg perfectly defined in his hose, flexing with his effort, then he dropped onto the floor behind his smallest son with a thud. The wee laddie fair jumped into his arms, whilst Grimme clasped the next youngest to his side and ruffled his hair. Then he looked across the table with a wide grin to inquire of his two oldest, flanking their mother, as to how their morning studies had gone.

"They were not present this morning, my lord," Father Hercule said matter-of-factly from beside Brìghde. She had not even noticed he'd joined the table.

Grimme's smile disappeared and he looked stonily at their mother. She met his look defiantly, her chin high. His mouth tightened and his nostrils flared as he took a deep breath. He set his second youngest aside and put the youngest down. He leaned across the table and pressed the woman's ear to his mouth and spoke for quite a while. She flushed, her jaw tightening angrily, then she whirled and ran down the aisle, around the end of another table to the stairs, then disappeared up them.

Without a look in Brìghde's direction, he stepped on that table, then stepped on the head table, his foot right between her place and his, then dropped with a thud next to Brìghde. He scraped his chair away from the table and plopped his arse in it. The rest of the household then were free to take their seats and the meal was served.

"Are you and Troy going out this afternoon, Brìghde?" he asked pleasantly as he stuffed a piece of meat in his mouth.

"He's in the field today. Tomorrow, we are going to Hogarth. I must discuss livery with the clothier, drapes, hangings, and such. I must order nice gowns and slippers. Then we must hire carpenters for new furniture, as I must fetch the clothier here, but I have nowhere to put him or his retinue. I need to hire a clerk, a land steward, and a housekeeper. As well, I need everything else, as my bridegroom did not allow me to bring any of my possessions with me."

"All apologies," he said, not at all apologetic. "If your father refuses you your possessions, I will send for your things."

She gasped a little, her hand to her breast. "You would do that for me?"

He cast her a glance as he ate. "Aye. I'd not have you go without your pet."

"Thank you!" she breathed.

"Would you like company tomorrow?"

She gestured to his knights.

"They've trained without me before."

She looked at him with mock suspicion. "'Tis to keep me from going alone, aye?"

He flashed her a grin.

She huffed. "Then a 'no' would be ignored."

"Very much so."

She laughed. "I would enjoy it. After breakfast. How was your morning?" she asked to be courteous, but apparently he heard it in her voice.

"I will not bore you with my occupation any more than I will allow you to bore me with yours."

"Thank you," she breathed, which made him laugh.

As a servant passed behind Brìghde's chair, she caught her and murmured, "I want several barrels full of water heated to boiling by the time this meal has been completely cleaned up. Find all the soap in this keep, brooms, brushes, cloths, scrapers, and such, and gather every unoccupied servant in and out of the keep, and I know there are many of those."

The girl, looking half terrified, curtsied, said, "Aye, my lady," and scurried off.

Brìghde turned back to her platter to see Grimme looking at her. "Time to clean the floor," she said archly. He grimaced, but she refrained from pointing out how filthy it was; that was something her mother would do. "Oh! I was perusing your stables with your marshal yesterday."

"I heard. How did you find them?"

"*Very* impressive," she said sincerely.

He gave her a warm smile. "Thank you."

"He said this is a breeding estate."

"Aye. 'Twas something I started by accident once my trainer and I had Ares battle-ready."

"Who is Enyo?"

"One of Ares's consorts. Goddess of war, Ares's counterpart."

"Ah, *that* is why you did not name her Aphrodite, as I assumed."

He nodded. "Enyo has been considered Ares's wife, sister, mother, or companion-at-arms, 'tis not clear, but I think of her as his wife and dearest companion, who rides at his side into battle, along with his sons Phobos and Deimos."

Brìghde looked at him in confusion. "You don't have a mare named Aphrodite?"

Grimme shook his head.

"But Enyo is also Ares's lover?"

"Only to produce warriors like them. Enyo is more valuable to Ares than Aphrodite."

"Ah. Who are the sons you said?"

"Phobos and Deimos, gods of fear and dread. Deimos is the red I rode to Fàileach. Phobos is silver with the same black mane and tail as Deimos."

"Who's their mother?"

"The beasts or the gods?"

"The gods."

He hesitated. "They're Aphrodite's sons. As for the beasts, they've got different dams. I've bred Ares to a dozen select mares across France and another two dozen in England. The royal stables are filled with his get. God only knows what Sheffield's done with him or even if it's occurred to him at all, and I'll never know if Ares has sired any others whilst he's in Sheffield's possession, which will disturb my recordkeeping."

"I would like you to take me on a tour of your stables, if you please."

"I will soon, but not this week. I was told Helen was not pleased to meet you."

She sniffed. "Enyo loved me. What is wrong with Helen?"

"She's difficult and she doesn't like anybody."

"Then why would you buy or breed her?"

"Firstly, I would pay any price to have her dam and sire, but they will never be for sale. Secondly, she was cheap. Whether she can be trained or not, I could spare the coin to at least try. Thirdly, she is—was—a maiden. I hadn't found a stallion yet that could mount her, but she fell in love with Troy the minute I walked him past her stall and is completely tractable in his company. I decided to see what comes of it. Thus far I'm the only one who's been able to ride her, and only for a few seconds before I land on my arse in the dirt." His brow wrinkled. "Would you be so kind as to ride the mares when Troy is out on the field? The stable is growing, my marshal can't hire enough grooms fast enough to exercise them, and they need to be ridden. My women go riding almost every day, but they have their own mounts and are not willing to ride any others and they won't ride astride."

Flattered, she said, "Of course! Thank you."

"The grooms will tell you which ones need to be ridden. In fact, mayhap you and I should go out together and see if Helen is as tractable with Troy whilst riding."

"That sounds like fun! Speaking of Ares and the duke, you said he will call upon us? To *celebrate* our marriage?"

"Aye," he said around a bite.

"How soon can we expect him?"

"A month at the latest."

"Whether he does that or not, 'tis not proper. He and the duchess should be expecting an invitation to Kyneward Keep. *We* shall prepare a celebration of our marriage and invite all the local nobles. But we must decide on a date soon so as to forestall a surprise visit."

He paused. "Summon the enemy on our terms and our territory," he mused, then looked at her. "I hadn't thought of it. We have never hosted any such thing, I have no wife, and I'm always gone."

"*Had* no wife."

"But if you think an invitation three or more months hence for a fête will forestall a surprise visit, think again."

She grimaced. "That is what I fear. However, our cooks are excellent and I shall have them prepare a feast for the ages."

"That look in your eyes is terrifying."

She grinned at him.

Grimme leaned against her and whispered in her ear, "Please do not poison my liege."

"You *want* me to," she whispered back.

"What I want is of no matter. Just *don't*."

She started to laugh, then realized he was not jesting. She decided not to protest. "Aye," she grumbled.

"Promise."

"I promise I will not poison your liege." Grimme sat back in his chair and continued to eat. "This time."

He looked at her out of the corner and she granted him a sunny smile. He pursed his lips as he studied her, then said abruptly, "When I give the order."

That surprised her. "*When?*"

"He covets what I love, aye, and he is bitter about having been promised this land, but he has not been here in years. Once he sees Kyneward as it is now, once you have it repaired and dressed in finery, he will be ravenous for it on its own, not because it was denied him after being told to expect it. I am generally of a mind to strike first, but I need evidence he is about to plot my death to be able to justify it to the king."

Brìghde's bottom lip slowly dropped open and her eyes had widened. "You fear him," she whispered.

"No," he corrected as quietly. "I am wary. He will enjoin Aldwyn to lay the plans, and he is who worries me. Aldwyn is clever and we have not fought together since Agincourt. He will have learned much since then and I do not underestimate my enemies."

"But you are wily. He can't know what you have learned since then, either, and wily defeats frontal attacks."

"And what he does not know," Grimme again said in her ear, "is that my wife is a Trojan horse and I will wield her to her fullest capacities."

He drew away from her and studied her soberly. She was no less sober. "You trust me?"

"No," he rumbled. "But I need you and I can only pray you will not betray me."

17

THAT NIGHT BRÌGHDE dropped into her bathtub with a hiss and a sigh, leaning back and thinking about how sore she was going to be on her ride to Hogarth with Grimme in the morning, to which she was looking forward a little less now. Riding forty miles round trip after a day of hard labor was no mean feat.

It had taken a mere fifteen minutes for some forty servants to scrub all the tables and chairs in the great hall with hot water and lye soap to her satisfaction and take them out to the bailey to dry.

However, it had taken hours for the forty of them—and Brìghde—to dig up several inches' worth of compacted filth, discarded rotting food, and dog shit upon the stone floor with scrapers. It had taken Brìghde a half hour to teach them what she expected and *how to do it* and *on her hands and knees*, by the Virgin Mary, and she had spent the rest of the afternoon tending them to get the floor completely clean and a thick carpet of rushes and herbs laid by suppertime.

Three of the paramours had drifted down the stairs just in time to see Brìghde, dressed in her boy clothes, on her hands and knees digging and scrubbing. They had begun to snicker and whisper. She had looked up and said, "Unless you want to join us, I suggest you go find something else to do."

They simply curled their lips at her. She got to her feet and approached them. In disgust of her filthy clothes and hands, they backed up with contemptuous grimaces—all the way up two flights of a spiral staircase as Brìghde stalked them with a vicious glare, threatening to touch their persons with hers.

Unfortunately, the lads, who had been ordered to stay indoors although the day was a perfect day for four wee laddies to be outside playing, thought all the water on the floor was for splashing.

Finally, Brìghde could take no more.

"Lads!" she said with forced gaiety. "Let's go out to the stable."

They stopped splashing immediately. Pierce dashed outside. Terrwyn followed. That left Gaston and Max, the two oldest. "We don't take orders from you," Gaston snapped, crossing his arms over his chest.

Brìghde shrugged. "'Tis not an order. You may stay here if you want." She gestured to Max. "Shall we?" When he hesitated, she said, "Your father approves."

That got him out the door. She left Gaston behind without a glance. Once she'd gotten the other three to the stable, she asked the grooms to take them in hand and have them brushing the warhorses. "'Tis a great responsibility," she said gravely down at them, "grooming knights' steeds. They must be *beautiful*."

"My lady," the head groom whispered to her, "they're all out in the field. May I suggest the ponies? They do need to be groomed."

"I don't care. Just put them to work."

"Aye, my lady."

When she walked back into the hall, there was Emelisse standing at the bottom of the stairs, unwilling to walk in the water, Gaston beside her looking triumphant.

"What have you done with Max?" she demanded.

"He's working in the stable," Brìghde grunted as she walked around to correct this servant or that servant, and to point out missed spots.

"Gaston, go get him and bring him back."

"Sweet Virgin Mary!" she burst out. "*Nothing* is going to happen to him in the stable with a legion's worth of grooms. Quit being such a bloody coward and let him go play with his brothers."

Emelisse snarled at her and snatched Gaston up the stairs after her, but Brìghde didn't miss the quiver of his bottom lip and his longing look at the keep door.

Sir John did not appear at supper, and she dared not seek him out to see to his welfare though she did send a lass with a tray and wine. Grimme did not ask her about it.

Now she lay in the bath, her eyes closed, almost asleep, when the door opened suddenly, and she started and whirled, crossing her arms over her breasts.

"Emelisse said you sent my sons out to the stable today," Grimme growled.

"Get—out."

"This is *my* house."

"I am in the bath *with no clothes on* and you are holding my door open for any passerby to see."

He slammed the door.

"Again. I have *no clothes on*. Go away until I am bathed and dressed, and we can argue like civilized people."

"You're my wife," he said flatly. "I have the right to see you naked and I will argue with you whenever and wherever I bloody well please."

She curled her lip at him, turned and laid back down in the water, hoping it was dark enough he couldn't see. "What is wrong with having sent them out to the stable?"

"'Tis not that you *did*. 'Tis how you did it."

"Oh, sweet Mother Mary and Joseph," Brìghde grumbled, her brogue thickening with her irritation.

"Do *not* speak to my sons that way again."

"Like this? 'Lads! Let's go out to the stable.' Like that?"

"That is not how you said it."

"You weren't there."

"I didn't have to be. Emelisse told me all about it."

"She has absolutely *no* reason in the world to lie to you about me, none at *all*, nooooooo."

He was silent.

"Did you ask your sons?"

"They're asleep."

"Wake them up."

He sighed heavily, went to the hearth and dropped into a chair, his back to her, and dropped his head back on its top. "I do not," he muttered, "want to be drawn into a war."

"What, exactly, do you think happens in a household of four women sharing the same man's spindle? And what did you think would happen when you brought a wife home?"

Silence.

"I did not draw you into any war. Your mistress did. The laddies were splashing in the water all over the floor—as if that is the most interesting thing in the world, which is pathetic. I wanted them out of the house for the duration, so I bade them do something productive. Wee laddies make trouble in a house when they are bored, and they are intolerably bored."

"Intolerable for you or for them?" he muttered.

"For all of us in equal measure. *You* aren't paying attention to their needs. *I* need them out from underfoot. *They* need firm guidance *away* from their mothers, who need to keep their hostilities to themselves. I care not what your women think of the way I treat your sons. Someone has to take them in hand, and since this is my domain, it is my responsibility."

"What of my opinion?"

"You have had no opinion for ten years, so it is of little use now. As far as I can see, the laddies' only value to you is their devotion to an indulgent father. Papa! Papa! Papa! Papa!"

"That is not true. And although I might be willing to concede all the rest of your points, I demand you leave my women be. They are the mothers of my sons and they have done nothing to earn your hatred. Did you call Emelisse a coward?"

"Firstly, I do not hate them. I don't care enough to hate them. Secondly, aye, I did call her a coward because it's true. And there poor Gaston goes, up the stairs, when his brother is out in the stables having a semblance of fun, and he wants to be allowed to go too. He thought she'd go fetch Max and the boys could be miserable together, but that is not what happened."

"Brìghde," he sighed wearily.

"Grimme," she said crisply, rolling her R contemptuously, "the bargain was that I would bring order to your house and you would enforce my rule so that I could do that. You have forced your father to work around them for years, and look what has happened. I will not work around them because my primary goal is to get this earldom working like an earldom *in spite of itself.* That was the bargain."

"What has happened," he said tightly, "is that my father and I don't know how an earl's household works."

"But I do and you are now asking me not to do it. You cannot have it both ways. *No one* wants things to change, and your bringing home a wife is a most drastic change indeed, much less one who intends to turn the house upside down and shake it out, which they and everyone attached to Kyneward fears, including the merchants in Waters. And with good reason. If you do not want to be drawn into these battles, keep your women away from me and your sons occupied in the things they *should* be doing. The two older boys *should* have been sent out two years ago to apprentice as pages."

"What have the merchants in Waters to do with anything?" he asked slowly.

"Household business," she sing-songed.

"Indulge me."

"They and the servants are cheating you. Sir John is overwhelmed and too frail to keep up. I had to tell him and by the time I left, he was sobbing over his desk, and I didn't tell him about the servants because I have managed that already. 'Twas why he was not at supper. This is what happens when you willfully ignore household business. This is *your* earldom, *your* ultimate responsibility, but you have not paid attention to the burden your father carries, which is vastly heavier because you gave him no authority over your women and children. If you expect me to pull you out of this mess, I need you to keep your women away from me and your sons occupied."

There was a long silence.

"Grimme, the water is cold and I want to get out."

She saw the silhouette of his hand waving in the firelight. "Get out," he sighed. "Even if I were looking at you, I am not going to suddenly find ardor that wasn't there an hour ago."

Brìghde was starting to shiver, so she took the chance. He didn't turn when she snatched her towel and scurried to Avis's antechamber to dry off, then she peeked around the threshold and saw him still facing the hearth. She bound to her bed and dove in, pulling the covers up to her head.

He chuckled, but it was a sad, weary one.

"I ken you don't want to send your sons away to apprentice," Brìghde said quietly as she arranged herself under her covers as well as she could without throwing them off to start again. "So why not assign them to men in your forces?"

"Their mothers would harry me and I do not want to get involved in their squabbles."

Brìghde said nothing to that. Her mother harried her father over many things, but sending her sons off to become pages to other knights was not one of them. 'Twas the way of nobility.

"You're the earl," Brìghde said softly. "You have the ultimate authority here and you are allowing women to lead you around by your spindle." He growled at her. Well, she'd already lost Sir John. What did it matter if she lost Grimme too? She was here permanently, she had a task to perform, he didn't want to bed her anyway, and she was *right*. "They are your sons. They aren't three years old anymore and wee laddies grow into men. What kind of men do you want them to be? And are you going to allow their mothers to rear them as useless, simpering ones lazing on their father's successes simply because you don't want to tell your women to shut up and sit down? Because if you don't, I will."

18

GRIMME STORMED out of Brìghde's room and slammed the door behind him, then stalked up the stairs and down the hallway to the second door on the right and opened it to find Maebh and Ardith asleep. He slammed the door closed, which jolted both of them awake.

"Lord Grimme," Maebh yawned, rubbing her eyes.

"My lord," came the breathless voice of the blonde maidservant who'd offered herself whilst putting Brìghde's chambers to rights. He looked at her standing naked in the threshold of the antechamber. He pointed to the bed.

She skittered across the floor and snatched a pillow, gave him a sultry look, and strolled toward him, her hips swaying temptingly. She dropped the pillow on the floor in front of Grimme, knelt, eased his hose down to his knees and took him in her mouth.

Grimme shoved his fingers in her hair and dropped his head back to feel her mouth working his cod. He grunted with his release, shooting his seed straight down her throat.

He opened his eyes and slowly tilted his head forward to see her on her knees in front of him, looking up at him with those beautiful blue eyes. He loved blue eyes.

With a slight gesture, the maid arose and undressed him slowly, caressing him lightly all over the way he liked, the way that made him wish he could purr like a cat because the delightful shivers were absolutely luxurious. Soon he stood in the middle of the chambers with not a stitch on and his cod was still hard and ready for more.

She leaned toward him for a kiss, but he put his hand in her face and pushed her away. Not after she'd swallowed his seed. She pouted and he raised an eyebrow that commanded her to back away.

"Come, then," she whispered, taking his hand and leading him to his women's bed. He lay upon his back and allowed Maebh and Ardith to caress him, to play with his hair, to nigh put him to sleep, but soon Maebh's hand was 'round his cod, stroking him, rousing him from his near-slumber. He linked his hands behind his head and watched her climb on, slowly easing his cod up into her. She burdened his hips with her entire weight and she sighed, rolling her hips around, her head back. His cod was hard as a rock.

Ardith leaned down to kiss him and he did so for a long time, reaching up to fondle her breasts whilst Maebh slowly pleasured herself upon his cod. Ardith broke the kiss and climbed over Grimme's chest only enough for him to suck her nipples. She whimpered when Grimme slid his hand up under her and entered her with his fingers. Maebh set the rhythm on his cod and he followed it to fuck Ardith with his hand. Then he withdrew, leaving her wanting, but she was not close to release just yet.

She twisted and arose and straddled Grimme with her arse facing him so she and Maebh could embrace and kiss with a passion Grimme could never muster for any of his women, not even Emelisse.

Ardith and Maebh were lovers, their feelings for each other far more than any feeling either of them had for him. He would not fulfill all their needs, nor did he have to. They were here for him, not he for them.

Maebh broke free of Ardith's embrace and arched her back, riding Grimme's cod with fury, gasping, clenching, crying out. Ardith sucked her nipples as she gained her release—loudly.

Yet Grimme was not satisfied. "Move," he commanded. She wasn't quite finished yet, but he didn't care. She climbed off and Ardith immediately took her place, Maebh's juices providing the slickness she had not yet attained. She began to rock slowly, and Maebh turned to suckle Ardith's nipple, which made her gasp, and slid her hand down to fondle Ardith's nymph.

It would take forever for Ardith to get her release, which was her own concern after Grimme had gotten his. He could fuck them both all night and did, frequently.

"Off."

Ardith dismounted immediately and Grimme rolled off the bed to allow the women to arrange themselves, Maebh on her back, her legs splayed, Ardith between her knees, her back arched and her arse in the air. Ardith dove into Maebh's muff whilst Grimme climbed back onto the bed on his knees and impaled Ardith. He did not find Ardith's cunte particularly satisfying, so he impaled her where he would get the most satisfaction.

She cried out, but Maebh was getting her release and shoved Ardith's mouth back to her nymph.

Grimme pumped viciously, gritting his teeth, throwing his head back, now reaching for his release. It finally came and he rammed himself into Ardith, who cried out again. Or was it Maebh? He didn't remember. He didn't care.

He withdrew and went to the dish of water to clean his cod thoroughly whilst his women continued to fuck. Presently he dropped into a chair and slouched there to watch, his leg draped over the arm. He looked across the room to the maidservant who was looking at him with hunger, and came eagerly when he pointed to the floor in front of him, dropping to her knees and immediately putting his flaccid cod in her mouth.

It would be a while before it would rise again, but he liked the feel of a mouth on him and he wasn't too particular about which woman's mouth it was. She worked and worked and worked, and he simply relaxed, looking off into the darkness, thinking about his household.

Brìghde thought he was naïve for believing the four women he was bedding could live under the same roof without strife. To be truthful, he'd never really given it a lot of thought. He would fuck whomever he pleased and the women he supported were free to leave at any time. He didn't know what they would do, but he was not keeping them hostage.

Did they get along?

Mayhap. Mayhap not. But they managed. Throughout the years, Emelisse had made her displeasure at having to share him known, but she didn't have a choice if she wanted his attentions, and she had from the first time she'd seen him, surreptitiously watching him in a rare bath his patron knight had ordered for him.

She had taken him that night and they had been nigh inseparable from then on.

Except Grimme was a randy cur and when Emelisse grew heavy with babe, he sought somewhere to bury his cod. Enter Ardith.

Emelisse had thrown a fit when she caught him midstroke, but, undaunted, he told her if she wanted his cod ever again, she'd sit down, shut up, and watch. That was when she realized that if she'd hoped for a biddable boy who could be commanded by his cod and a beautiful twenty-year-old woman, she'd bedded the wrong fifteen-year-old.

Presently he noticed that the maidservant had managed to make his cod rise again. He looked over at Maebh and Ardith who were cuddled up in bed, fondling each other, kissing, and watching.

He didn't force the maidservants to pleasure him if they did not make it clear they wanted to. This one was particularly talented with her mouth and she was Maebh's maidservant for this purpose. Grimme was not the only one in these chambers she pleasured. Maebh was a lusty wench and would fuck all day long if she could.

He had one rule for all his women: They were not to fuck other men. He didn't care if they *fucked*. He would not to raise some other man's spawn. The moment one of his women fucked another man, they would be out on their arse. Preferably in the winter.

The maid was beginning to whimper. "Ardith," he commanded. She rolled out of Maebh's embrace and grabbed her brush. Dropping to her knees behind the maid, she eased the brush handle up into the girl, who gasped around Grimme's cod. Grimme could see her arse pumping against the brush that Ardith was working and feel her mouth at the same time.

No, Grimme simply did not care enough about his women's squabbles to get in the middle of them, and he was certain Brìghde could go to war with all four of them at once and win. He did not have to worry about her reception so long as he didn't have to listen to it.

The maidservant (whose name Grimme did not know, or care about) got her release and her gasps against his cod were pleasant.

"Don't stop," he warned coolly when she gave in to the throes of her ecstasy and completely abandoned him.

"Aye, my lord," she gasped and went back to her job.

Ardith went back to bed, the brush abandoned on the floor, her hips swaying, to be welcomed back into Maebh's awaiting arms. They wrapped themselves up together to watch Grimme's pleasure. They were a beautiful sight, sitting there in the middle of the bed, acting the veriest of lovers, kissing softly, watching, fondling each other's breasts and nethers.

Grimme was not going to get his release with this maid's mouth and he pushed her away, then snapped his fingers at the bed. "Maebh."

She scrambled off the bed and scurried toward him. He twirled his finger to make her turn around before impaling herself on Grimme's cod. He grasped her hips to keep her from moving and she sunk her entire weight onto his hips. He gently nudged her until she was doubled over her knees and released immediately.

He sat still. When Maebh would have taken herself away, he barked, "Stay until I tell you you may go."

They sat that way for a long time, so long that Ardith got bored and bade her maid to pleasure her with the brush. Grimme watched whilst Maebh hung limp from Grimme's cod as if she were a fish, hooked.

He stirred again, as he had known he would, and slowly grew until he filled Maebh yet again.

He put household matters out of his mind and spent the rest of the night getting his cod stroked and sucked by his women. He ordered the maid to fetch Dillena, who did not like such activities. He didn't care. She joined in more or less enthusiastically, and at some point, he lost track of which woman did what, nor did he care.

It simply didn't matter.

19

IN THE MORNING, Brìghde went to prayers, but Grimme was not there. She went out to ask the grooms to prepare Troy and Grimme's horse for a day's outing. She spent some time petting Troy and giving him treats, talking to him, and wishing she had Mercury with her. He and Troy would get along magnificently.

She went to Sir John's study to request more coin for her and Grimme's trip into Hogarth, but stopped at the door, hesitating. She rapped her knuckles lightly.

"Come."

She entered slowly to see Sir John sitting in a chair in front of his hearth, staring into it, a goblet in his hand. He said nothing. Brìghde closed the door quietly behind her and remained quiet, her hands folded in front of her.

"Do what you want," he said so abruptly it startled her. "Neither Grimme nor I trust you, but I have come to the conclusion that I don't care."

Tears began to sting Brìghde's eyes.

"You don't seem to need my training or even guidance, even if I were adept enough to give you any."

"Sir John," she whispered, her voice trembling. "I didn't mean to—"

He held his hand up and she clicked her mouth shut. "I keep the daily coin chest in my chambers. Under the bed. The most obvious place. Of course. I will show you where the rest of it is presently. The keys to the keep and the dower house are hanging on the inside of the wall by the door. They're yours now."

"I'm sorry," she croaked.

He waved toward his bedchamber door. "I know you are going to Hogarth today and you will need coin. I think." He barked a bitter laugh. "Who knows how much merchant credit we have there, too."

With a lump in her throat, Brìghde tiptoed toward his chambers, opened it slowly, entered, and reached under the bed for the chest. It was massive and she struggled with it for some time whilst it scraped against the stone, unforgiving of its purchase. It was locked. She fetched the keys and after many tries, found the correct one.

There was more coin in that chest than she had ever seen in her life, and this was the *daily* chest.

She left his chambers with a large pouch full of coins and the keys to the keep, tiptoeing behind … "Sir John?"

He sighed. "Brìghde, leave me to my cups. Please."

WHEN SHE ARRIVED at the breakfast table, Emelisse was the only paramour at table. She was already sitting in her chair instead of standing behind it, her boys flanking her and eating, the other two boys across from them, which was odd. Emelisse would not look at Brìghde. She was angry, Brìghde understood that, but Brìghde had no interest in stirring the embers, so she simply strode to her chair and waited for Grimme to appear so she could sit.

Sir John would not be coming to breakfast, so she caught a servant and ordered a tray delivered to him. Father Hercule entered, looked at Emelisse and took his seat, too. Grimme's deputy entered, looked at Emelisse, then sat in his chair next to Sir John's. Then the knights came roaming in for breakfast, also took note of Emelisse, and took their seats.

"Where is my lord this morn, Sir Drew?"

"Likely asleep. Do not await him; he will not appear until noon."

Brìghde's brow wrinkled as she took her seat. "Is he ill?"

"Nay."

"Uh … he was supposed to go to Hogarth with me today."

"My *lady*," Emelisse snarled. Surprised, Brìghde looked at her, but Emelisse was not looking at Brìghde. "Do you notice Ardith, Dillena, and Maebh are also absent?"

"Aye," Brìghde answered slowly, confused. "But what does that have to do— Ohhhhh," she breathed. Sir Drew and some of the closer knights started to snicker, and Brìghde flashed them a broad grin.

"*Ohhhh*, she says," Emelisse sniped.

Brìghde's brow wrinkled. "All *three?*"

That made the knights start laughing, but the curling of Emelisse's lip was all the answer Brìghde needed, and she realized that Emelisse's anger was not directed solely at Brìghde. If 'twere, she would not have informed Brìghde of the missing facts.

Brìghde gestured to Terrwyn and Pierce and carefully asked, "Do you have charge of them when Grimme has … ah … "

"Who else is going to make sure they eat their breakfast?" she snapped.

The knights subsided and Brìghde pulled her lips between her teeth. How Grimme thought his women got along, she could not fathom, nor did she understand why all *three* were necessary. So far as she understood the act, 'twas only done with two people.

It was all so … *difficult*. Unnecessarily so. Why could a man not confine himself to one wife he rarely visited and only to gather heirs, and one mistress to see to his pleasure all the other nights? Granted, the mistress might change every year or two, but Brìghde truly did not understand her husband's vast lust.

Breakfast had just been served and Brìghde had just begun to eat when Grimme's chair was scraped backward and he dropped himself into it with a sparkling smile at Brìghde. "Good morn, Brìghde."

Brìghde blinked, surprised. "Uh, good morn, Grimme."

His smile dimmed a little. "You act as if you do not want me here," he said as his platter was put in front of him. "I promised to go to Hogarth with you today, remember?"

"I remember."

"Rather, nobody expected you to be arisen this early," Emelisse drawled in French, spearing a piece of meat and shoving it into her mouth. "But of *course* you rousted yourself out of bed for *her*. How was your rest, *Grimme?*"

Grimme's expression gradually turned thunderous, looking first at Emelisse then Brìghde, who simply looked at him, completely mystified why he could not accept that his behavior angered those who felt they had the most claim on him.

"So. The household is angry this morning," he drawled in English, sitting back in his chair to lounge. "I wonder *why*," he sneered.

"I'm not," Brìghde informed him.

His eyes narrowed. "Why not."

"Do you *want* me to be, my lord? I could give a good imitation of it, given some time to practice."

His mouth pursed and his jaw slid leftward as he studied her, but he did not answer her.

"Good morn, Papa!"

"Good morn, my sons. Gaston, Max, mind your mother today. Terrwyn, Pierce, be on your best behavior for Emelisse."

Brìghde stared at him, aghast. "My lord," she whispered, "mayhap it would ease some of the tension if you did not ask Emelisse to look after your sons from other women after you've spent the night swiving them all."

Grimme snarled at her. "I didn't ask for your opinion. I got enough of that last night."

Brìghde simply turned to her meal and tried to remind herself that he believed friends could have arguments and be angry with each other and remain friends, but she didn't believe that. Yet in case he was right, she kept her mouth shut even though she wanted to make Grimme understand how very *wrong* he was to expect his favorite mistress to act as nursemaid for his sons by other women. She simply hoped she could keep her mouth shut all the way to Hogarth.

"Well!" Brìghde said brightly when she finished her platter and arose. "I'll be about my day. Grimme?"

He nodded curtly and continued to eat.

Brìghde strode out to the stables and requested Troy and Grimme's horse be brought out. She attached her provisions of wine, water, and oats to her pack, was thrown into the saddle, and waited.

And waited.

And waited.

She twisted to see the opening to the inner bailey and ... empty. She looked at the sky. Hogarth was twenty miles. If she wanted to get there, shop, and get home before sundown ... Maybe he *was* angry enough with her that he had decided not to be friends anymore. She sighed. His promise had been made when he was in good humor.

"I'm not waiting any longer," she said and tapped Troy to trot out to the lane and to warm up, then cantered, then kicked him into a gallop.

She and the horse flew down the road, dust flying behind them— She didn't see the fawn until she and Troy were sailing over her, and, though she barely kept her seat, she whooped with joy.

Aye, this life was new to her and, after having spent the last two years with Walter preparing endlessly for the MacFhionnlaighs' destruction, she had genuinely relished yesterday's mindlessly hard labor of scraping decades' worth of filth off the stones, and this morning she had felt particularly proud of how it gleamed between the rushes. It smelled good with the herbs in the rushes being crunched under foot to release their fragrance. Nobody cared but her, but that was all she needed.

She would simply put Grimme and his lack of desire for her away, as it was not important. She would enjoy her good fortune, since she had had so little of it in her life. She could not have *everything* she wanted, and had she wed Roger, she would have *nothing* she wanted.

She and Troy trotted into Waters in no time at all, and she went straight to the seamstress.

"Good morn!" she called as she entered.

"Oh, good morn, my lady," she answered with a bit of hesitance. "I've two dresses ready fer ye, three shifts, a set of boy's clothes, all the bedsheets, and half the livery."

Brìghde clapped her hands and said, "Excellent! I will send a cart soon to pick them up."

"Aye, my lady."

Brìghde, feeling very pleased with herself, walked Troy down the lane to the livery and applied to a groom there to help her mount, which he did with alacrity and received a coin for his efforts. "Thank you, my lady!"

It was a beautiful day and the road between Waters and Hogarth became increasingly congested as she grew closer. She drew many looks, which she returned, waving and calling "Good morn!" to everyone as she trotted by, passing heavily laden carts driven by villeins and pulled by mules, palfreys ridden sidesaddle by noblewomen, their noblemen on fine horses (none as fine as Troy, but no horse was), fine carriages that carried more nobles, dozens of various peasant women carrying packs into or out of Hogarth, stalls selling fruits and vegetables and eggs and all manner of foodstuffs.

She stood in the saddle to ease the tension off her arse, which was when she saw mounted, mailed men-at-arms who were not from Kyneward. They spotted her immediately and she suddenly realized this had not been a good idea. Her wedding gown was clean and mended now, but still a bit bedraggled, so if she looked like a noblewoman, she looked like a poor one. This wasn't Fàileach, so no one knew that she was important and to treat her with the utmost respect. She was small and riding a valuable horse far too big for her, in a large and expensive saddle—*not* a side-saddle, as a noblewoman *should* be riding—which made her look even smaller and unlike a noblewoman. She wasn't sure *what* she looked like, but vulnerable was definitely one of them.

She would either have to ride through them or turn around and run. She made to do that, but ... she couldn't. The road was too congested.

Brìghde raised her chin and looked at them as haughtily as she could muster as she continued on through the column—as far as she could make it until they closed in on her.

"Well, my *lady,*" one of them said, reaching out to caress her collarbone. He looked into her eyes and purred, "What a pretty mare."

Brìghde tried to keep her thundering heart from beating out of her chest, her breathing normal, and her hauteur pointed. "Excuse you," she said. "I am Countess Kyneward."

"So nice to make your acquaintance, *Lady Kyneward,*" he sneered.

"Woman who can ride *that* stallion can ride *my* stallion," said another one, and the rest of them laughed. He ran his hand over her breast and sighed, "Oh, aye, you'll be a treat."

Shocked, she slapped him only as an afterthought, and the other one grabbed her arm.

Their horses squeezed in on her, and Troy was throwing his head back, trying to back up, but the other end of the column closed in on her until she was encircled by five men who were not—

"BRÌGHDE!"

Brìghde closed her eyes and heaved a deep sigh of relief. When she heard the ring of metal on metal, her eyes popped open and she twisted to see Grimme in mail, leading a force of ten similarly clad men with swords drawn.

"That's my husband," Brìghde felt the need to point out.

The knights around her were moving, their swords drawn, ready to battle if indeed, this knight was coming their direction.

"Get away from her," Grimme rumbled as he and his men came to a stop some distance away from them, as there were many people and horses between Grimme and Brìghde, where she was encircled by men-at-arms.

"An' who are you?"

"Earl Grimme Kyneward."

They didn't believe him, but they stepped their horses away from Brìghde and fanned out as much as they could. Brìghde, still with her back to Grimme because she and Troy didn't have enough room to turn around, surreptitiously slipped her dagger out of her girdle, gripped it in her fist, raised her arm, and stabbed one of the horses in the rump.

He screamed and reared, tossing the man off his back.

She struggled to control Troy, but managed to switch the knife to her other hand and stabbed the rump of the horse on her left.

That horse also screamed, reared, tossed his rider, and the column opened in front of her. Troy bolted immediately, darting out from between the two screaming, rearing horses, and three men-at-arms who seemed to have no idea what was going on. He dodged this obstacle and that obstacle and leapt over some other obstacle. They stopped some hundred feet away and turned to watch what was going on behind them.

It was a complete uproar, with the knights in the midst of people and other horses with carts, all packed in so tightly they couldn't move, the two injured horses screaming, rearing, and trampling all over their riders, food, villeins, merchandise stalls, and anything else in their way.

And all the while, Grimme and his men simply sat on their horses watching. He looked at her with a steely expression.

"I thought you forgot!" she yelled, her hand cupped around her mouth.

His mouth tightened and his jaw slid one way. "I didn't forget!" he yelled back angrily. "I decided I didn't want to go!"

Her teeth ground and her nostrils flared. "And you did not give me the courtesy of telling me?"

The uproar had grown so loud, Grimme had to stand up in his stirrups and bellow to be heard. "I didn't think you'd be so dimwitted as to go alone when I didn't appear at the stable!"

Brìghde's jaw dropped and her eyes popped out of her head. "Oh … *you* … " She snarled at him, whirled Troy around, and took off, leaving the mess of people, horses, carts, and now food and other merchandise between her and Grimme.

"*BRÌGHDE!*"

Brìghde had no idea where she was going, but her husband could stuff himself down the garderobe. Spend the night swiving three women, toss his bastards onto his favorite mistress to take care of whilst the others slept off their night, turn up at breakfast in a sour mood, ruin Brìghde's day, and then chastise her for it in public, would he?

No, he would not.

Not without retribution.

She and Troy were on the outskirts of town when she finally slowed him and walked him to a fountain from which he could drink. She leaned over him and scratched his neck. "I'm sorry, laddie. Who's a good laddie? You're a good laddie, aye you are. Such a good lad."

She was still drawing looks, but there were no knights around. There were nobles and commoners of means and merchants. Many, many, many merchants.

And she had come to shop.

20

GRIMME WAS ENRAGED, finding out Brìghde had gone to Hogarth without him. Aye, he should have told her when she confronted him about charging Emelisse with the care of all his sons that he had abruptly changed his mind about spending the day with her. After his wife's pointed lecture punctuating his deficiencies as a father and her chastisement this morning, the *last* place he wanted to be was on a forty-mile round trip to shop with her.

But then Pierce had slipped Emelisse's charge, run out to the stable after Brìghde, and was despondent that she wasn't there. A groom had led him back to the keep and he had run to Grimme and cast himself in his arms and wailed, "She didn't even say fare thee well!"

"Who?" Grimme demanded, completely confused by both Pierce's behavior and whoever *she* was.

"Lady Kyneward," the groom told him. "She left a bit ago for Hogarth. She thought you were comin', waited a while, but when ye didn't, she left. We put Phobos back. Do ye need him anyway?"

Grimme thought his heart dropped through his boots. "She went to Hogarth alone?"

"Aye, my lord."

"Good God," he whispered. He put Pierce down, then pushed his chair back so fast, it toppled and clattered to the floor. He ran out to the stables, then put his fingers to his lips and let out a long, sharp, high-pitched whistle. The grooms scattered.

"Papa?"

"Lady Brìghde went to purchase things she needs, that she had to leave behind when I snatched her," he told Pierce, who had chased after Grimme. "She thought you were with Emelisse—"

"I don't wanna be with Emelisse!" he screamed, his little fists clenched at his side, his little face with an expression of such anger, it took Grimme aback. *"I hate Emelisse!"* Then he launched himself at Grimme and started to hit him with those little fists. This shocked Grimme so much he didn't quite know what to do.

"Pierce," Grimme gritted and tried to capture his slippery little boy, but missed. Pierce kicked him in the shin. Finally Grimme was able to snatch the child by his waist, haul him up and into his chest where the child broke down sobbing. Grimme, panicking, could do nothing with Pierce in his arms and he was terrified of what could happen to Brìghde in Hogarth, which looked much different as a lone woman than it did with an armored, mounted guard.

"Come, Pierce," Father Hercule said calmly, coaxing the boy from Grimme's arms into his. "Your father needs to fetch Lady Brìghde before something bad happens to her. She will come see you when she gets home. Mayhap she will bring you something."

The boy was hiccuping so hard he couldn't speak. Grimme stroked his forehead and said, "I promise you Lady Brìghde will bring you a gift, and if you're good, when she returns, she might let you visit her in her chambers."

"Do—do—you, you, you—think—so, so, Papa?"

He had no idea. "I must find her first."

Before she gets herself dragged off Troy and separated from him and her innocence forever.

But in the time it took Grimme to get Pierce inside with Father Hercule, his gambeson and mail on, his horse saddled, ten men were awaiting him to set out after her, riding hard.

She had stopped in Waters, the seamstress said, not an hour before.

They could make Hogarth in three quarters of an hour.

His heart had again stopped to see her penned by unliveried men-at-arms, fondling her, fondling the horse, squeezing her in.

Then she'd stabbed the horses and Troy had taken off, rapidly picking his way through the mêlée like a seasoned battle horse.

Grimme simply sat and watched her bound away and around the corner after she finished roaring at him.

"Chase her down, my lord?"

He shook his head and pointed to his right. "She'll be at the fountain to water Troy, and then she'll want to stay to shop." He chucked his chin toward the five men-at-arms who were still struggling. "Gather the mail and horses. Go back to Kyneward and make sure Marshal knows about the dagger wounds. We may spend a night or two, possibly three, so do not send out scouts until the fourth day."

"Aye, my lord."

Grimme took his time heading to the edge of town and going around it. Soon enough he was upon the very large square with the fountain in the middle of it. And there was Brìghde, in the doorway of the apothecary, with Troy's reins in her hand, whilst she happily called her farewells and turned to stuff her purchase in the pack. She stopped cold when she saw Grimme blocking the road out of town and glared at him.

"Need help getting on your horse, Wife?" he called blithely.

"Not from you!" she snapped.

The north end of Hogarth, its most expensive part, was a very large, tidy square, with shops surrounding it, save for the entrance to the lane that led to the rest of the town. There were dead-end lanes off the square with many more shops. Unlike the middle part and south end of town, this end was clean, with lords and ladies all milling about, going from one shop to the other, stopping at the windows to admire the clever displays.

Brìghde glared at him as she led Troy across the wide square until she reached the pasty shop. Grimme casually clip-clopped along until they met just past the fountain.

"Shall I take your noble steed to the livery, my lady?" he mocked.

"Aye," she snapped, threw the reins at him, and stalked the rest of the way into the shop.

He was still furious, but somehow she had managed to make him laugh. He left to run his errand, and returned to find her sitting on the wall of the fountain devouring a hand pie. He sat beside her and held his hand out. She glared at him, but slapped one in it, the same way she had fed him from the back of his horse on the road from Fàileach.

They ate in silence. She took a long pull from the bladder she had produced, then handed it to him.

"Do not ever," he said mildly, then took a bite of his pie, "come here alone again."

"Do not ever," she returned just as mildly, "invite yourself along on an outing with me and then simply not bother to inform me of your change of heart or fail to arrive at the appointed place and time."

"Hrmph."

She glared at him expectantly.

"I'm sorry," he muttered. "I was— Breakfast was—"

"Awkward?" she suggested with disdain. "The *only* person in that hall who *should* care how you spent your night *doesn't*. You acted as if you *wanted* me to be angry with you and were disappointed I did not glare and stomp at you. Oh, but wait. You were angry with me last night when you left my chambers. I deduce that you went straight to—" She waved a hand.

"Maebh and Ardith," he supplied helpfully.

"I can't remember their names and they all look alike."

He started to laugh.

"And you left angry because I am *right*."

He gestured around. "But when you're wrong, you are *extraordinarily* wrong."

"I don't do things in half measures." She started in on another pasty. "Have you talked to your father?" she said through her mouthful.

"No," he said snidely. "I was too busy rescuing my wife from unsavory knights."

"I would have stuck those rumps anyway. You just happened to arrive in time to witness my cleverness at getting myself out of scrapes. At least they didn't abduct me from my wedding and then get angry because they abducted the wrong woman."

He snorted.

"Sir John is very angry with me," she muttered, turning away from him.

Then he heard the sniffle, and he leaned over to look in her face. His amusement faded.

She looked at him. Her face was splotchy. "He might as well have thrown the keys to the keep at me and told me the coin chest was mine and … *now* what am I supposed to do?"

"Be the castellain," he murmured and rubbed her back. She sighed. "He is not angry at you. He is angry at himself."

"I've been here barely a week," she muttered, "and already the household is on its head. I thought it would take me at least a fortnight to tear everything apart."

"Is that a good thing or a bad thing?"

"Well, bad, in fact. My mother would demand to know why it had taken me so long."

He laughed and wrapped his hand around her arm and hugged her to his side. She laid her head on his shoulder and handed him another pasty. He ate in silence while his wife sulked. He finally finished, took the bladder she offered, washed it all down, then said, "We'd best see to your list if we want to get home by sundown. Otherwise, we will have to take an inn."

"Why not," she said flatly. "I will have to be measured and fitted and need a place to put all my purchases and—"

"If you like, we can inquire about carpenters.

"Oh!" she gasped. "And stewards and housekeepers and clerks?"

He nodded. "Whatever you want."

"Wonderful!" she chirped, suddenly happy again. "Let's get on with it, then, shall we?"

21

ONCE IN THEIR chambers, she had to assist him in removing his mail and gambeson. Underneath all that, he was in his soldier's garb of breeches and plain tunic. It was linen and nothing a noble would wear whilst shopping in the most expensive part of Hogarth. Certainly, she was wearing nothing that said "wealthy countess."

He accompanied her to the very few shops she needed before going to the clothier's and carried her purchases for her without once complaining. They received many contemptuous glances from exquisitely attired people who were nobles and commoners of means.

They were greeted at the clothier's with subtle disdain. She turned to Grimme and said loudly, "Do you think the keep is too far away to send for a clothier, Lord Kyneward?"

His eyebrow rose and he looked straight at the proprietor and, flashing his signet ring, said, "Nay, Lady Kyneward. I can send for one from London, if you like."

The man's expression didn't change. "Do you mean the estate that does not or cannot pay its bills?" He looked Grimme over and sneered. "Cannot."

Brìghde and Grimme stilled and looked at each other. "We pay our bills," Grimme said slowly.

"No, you don't. You've bills outstanding for months." He disappeared and Brìghde began to get a sick feeling in her stomach. Grimme was red in the face and clearly wanted to dash away. "You go," she said softly. "Household business. I will take care of the matter."

He bolted.

When the proprietor emerged, he had a stack of parchments. "Where'd his lordship get off to?"

"I am the new countess and castellain."

He thrust the parchments at her. "Here then."

She looked down at them and perused them. She checked the dates, which were, indeed, months ago, checked the names on the bills, summed quickly, and opened her coin pouch, paying for it all in full without a word.

His eyes popped open.

"On behalf of Kyneward, I apologize. Neither the earl nor his castellan would have left the bills to rot so. In future, do not sell anything to anyone claiming to be from Kyneward if they cannot pay in coin. These bills did not reach the castellan, as he would have paid them." Not happily, but he couldn't do anything but lecture the offenders.

He bowed deeply. "Thank you, my lady."

"Just a moment and I will fetch my husband."

Indeed, Grimme was outside pacing, his head dropped back and his hands wiping down his face.

"'Tis well. Come."

The earl was too embarrassed, but eventually, she barked, "Grimme! I need clothes."

He wouldn't look at the clothier all afternoon.

Unfortunately, after taking measurements and choosing styles, fabrics, and colors, it was too late for them to visit any other shops. They went back to their inn, sat in the taproom and ate in silence.

Then he muttered, "I will assume 'tis the same all over town."

Brìghde hummed noncommittally. "I was expecting merchant credit," she said, "as in Waters." Then she changed the subject. "Sweet Virgin Mary, this wine is good," she breathed, then sucked it down and ordered more.

"Careful, Brìghde," he said, apparently deciding to relax, propping his foot on a chair, dropping his arm over her shoulder, and reaching for the bowl of nuts on the table.

"I can hold my wine like a well-trained knight, I will have you know."

"They can't hold their wine, so that is no compliment to you."

Grimme caught a serving wench going by. "We are Earl and Countess Kyneward. We would like to see the proprietor of this fine establishment, if you please."

She dropped a curtsy. "Aye, m'lord."

Soon enough, the proprietor scurried to them and bowed. He was twisting his hands. "Is something wrong, my lord?"

"We are looking for some learned men and skilled women to hire, and I thought that you might know of such or hear things in passing."

He stopped wringing his hands. "Oh. What kind of help do you need?"

Grimme gestured to Brìghde, who said, "A land steward, a housekeeper for a small keep, and a clerk. Can you find them?"

"It might take me a while, but I can do it."

"When you do, send them to Kyneward Keep. Send as many as might be interested. We will also need carpenters to build furniture for most of the keep. Please tell us where we can find those."

"Aye, my lady. My lord."

"Also, more wine."

Grimme laughed, and dropped a stack of coins in the man's hand.

"Thank you, my lord."

After some time sitting quietly, drinking, and listening to the music, she yawned. "I am ready for bed."

"'Tis all the horses you stabbed today," Grimme said vaguely.

Brìghde turned her head to find her husband looking off into a corner of the taproom, his head tilted. A tall, willowy, blue-eyed blonde looked right back at him with a sultry gaze and a slight smile.

"I suppose I'll have the bed all to myself tonight?" she asked dryly.

"You most certainly will."

BRÌGHDE DIDN'T KNOW when Grimme came to bed, but she did know that she did not appreciate being jostled out of her slumber.

He grunted as he pulled her this way and that. "Brìghde."

"Mmrrphm."

He huffed, stripped her covers, picked her up, placed her on the other side of the bed, climbed in beside her, then covered them both up again.

"Harlot?" she mumbled into the pillow.

"I'm finished. I don't *sleep* with them, you know."

She turned over and went back to sleep. Tried to, anyway.

"Do you know what we did today, Budgie?"

"Shut—up."

"We argued."

Brìghde's eyes opened to the darkness. Grimme grunted as he struggled to make himself comfortable, bouncing the mattress in the process. Soon enough he was at her back with his arm in the curve of her waist.

"We were angry with each other and we argued," he whispered, "and we're still friends."

22

THE NEXT DAY found them purchasing what seemed like the entire town, and, indeed, there were merchants whose bills had gone unpaid, all at the finest shops. The word had gotten out that the new countess was in town and she was settling Kyneward's debts, and the merchants began to come to her.

Grimme was mortified, but Brìghde courteously explained that the castellan had not received the bills or he would have paid them.

Once she had paid them all, however, and they knew she would be paying for her own things in coin, they were only too happy to serve her. Shoes, wimples, girdles, another two daggers she could not help but sigh over. They went to the swordsmith to order something tailored to her, and both the smith and Grimme were surprised at her strength. As a jest, Grimme took her to the armorer and ordered her a full set of mail and a leather gambeson like his. Then Grimme determined he, too, needed some more clothing suited to an earl, and they decided to stay another day.

That evening followed last night's sequence of events: supper, Grimme to his pleasures, Brìghde to bed, Grimme disturbing her sleep some time in the middle of the night.

The third morning, Grimme dragged Brìghde to the tailor's whilst she gave her opinion on his choices of styles and colors, then rolled her eyes when he chose exactly what she told him *not* to choose. They went to the seamstress to discuss good livery for the higher-ranked servants. Naturally, she had no outstanding bills there because the mistresses would not think to order livery, and Sir John could not get here nor would he have had time to do it even if he had thought of it.

He was too busy making the coin to spend it correctly.

Since the seamstress and her retinue would have to come to Kyneward Keep to outfit the household, Brìghde paid for her time and promised that as soon as she had somewhere to put everyone, she would send for them.

"One more thing," Grimme said when they were about to stop shopping for the day. He led her to the jeweler's, and asked the proprietor for rings—*after* they had settled their debt.

Brìghde was running out of coin. Quickly.

"I have more," Grimme murmured when she told him this in a panicked whisper. "Emeralds, please."

"Aw," Brìghde sighed happily when she saw the selection.

He flashed her a grin. "Why not."

"Will that become our philosophy, my lord? 'Why not.'?"

He slid the ring she chose on her finger, and she held it up to admire it, then gifted him a wide smile. "Why not."

They ventured to the other side of town where there were other amusements to be had: jesters and mummers, puppet shows, musicians, and dwarves and giants in colorful clothes turning cartwheels and somersaults. Brìghde and Grimme threw a few coins into the hats of anyone who caused them to stop and watch.

A notice caught Grimme's attention. He sighed.

"What's wrong?"

He planted his finger in the middle of the bill. "Faire in six weeks, with a joust."

"Let us attend then. We can bring the laddies. Will you compete?"

His smile faded and he looked away. His shrug was listless.

"Why not?"

He looked down at her soberly. "I have never competed without Ares."

She sighed. "Grimme. You have his sons. Are they as well trained as their sire?"

"Aye."

"Then why not."

"They aren't him."

"Well ... how about Troy?"

"Troy isn't Ares," he repeated testily. He pressed her away from the notice, but he was unhappy for the rest of the day. He said almost nothing at supper, which he picked at, and he did not notice that the wench he had swived the last two nights was trying to catch his attention. He sat slumped, staring at his signet ring, twisting it round and round his finger. Brìghde gave the wench a helpless, apologetic shrug.

"My lord?" They both looked up to see the proprietor with a well-dressed young man next to him. "This young man says he'd like to speak to you about the clerk position."

Grimme chucked his chin at the chair and the young man bowed before taking the seat offered. "My lord, thank you."

Grimme nodded toward Brìghde. "Talk to her. She's the one you'll be working for if she hires you." He looked shocked. "She is not only my countess, but my castellain. If you have reservations about being in the employ of a woman, you may leave."

"No, no!" He looked at Brìghde. "My lady, my name is William Hughes and I have recently returned from Italy … "

He had a parchment that listed his studies and his accomplishments, and began to read it.

She gestured for it. "I can read." He slid it across the table to her. His handwriting was precise. His qualifications—if true—were impressive. She was particularly interested in— "What is Medici Bank?"

"A money holding and lending institution in Italy, my lady. 'Tis not quite a quarter century in existence, but very powerful nonetheless."

"Why did you leave your position there?"

His eager demeanor faded a little. "I was homesick and my lady love was awaiting me. And then I found that my lady love had *not* waited for me, and that I had nothing *else* here, either. I have been trying to get back to Italy, but I spent all my funds to come home."

Her eyebrow arched. "Should you come to Kyneward, do you stay only as long as it takes to gather your funds?"

He sighed wearily. "My lady," he said flatly. "I would be most happy to settle and create a life for myself *somewhere*. I love Italy, but England is my home."

Brìghde pursed her lips. "What is your direction?"

He flushed. "Um … I … " Didn't have a roof over his head.

"Do you ride?"

He grimaced. "Not … well, my lady."

"You may stay and sup with us tonight. Gather your possessions and present yourself here at nine of the clock tomorrow for breakfast." His look of cautious hope made her smile. "'Tis twenty miles to Kyneward. Rest well, as you will have to ride at least as fast as we do or get there on your own. We wait for no one."

"'WE WAIT FOR no one,'" Grimme mocked in a high-pitched voice as he lay in bed on his side, his head propped on his hand, watching Brìghde brush out and braid her hair.

She snickered until she snorted.

"Budgie."

Her smile faded and she closed her eyes, taking in a deep breath.

"What."

This was the moment she would either insist he not address her thusly and risk his friendship or allow it so that she would not risk his friendship. "Please do not call me Budgie," she said quietly.

"Uh … ah. Very well." He turned onto his back and stared up at the ceiling, his hands clasped over his chest. He seemed to take that rather well, or else he was lying there stewing about it.

"What troubles you?"

"Other than the debts?" he muttered. "The tournament."

Brìghde was relieved it was not her request, so she said nothing, blew out the candles, knelt on the edge of the bed, and crawled over him to get to the other side, against the wall. He grunted then yelped when her knee dug into his spindle and bollocks.

"Bloody hell, Brìghde! Watch where you're going!"

"I did not *mean* to!" she protested as she arranged herself and her shift under the bedclothes, he groaning the entire time. "Grimme," she said, rolling the R long and crisply, "neither of us can afford for your jewels to be damaged. I would do no such thing purposely."

"Hrmph. Intent and carelessness yield the same result."

Finally she was settled on her side facing away from Grimme and almost asleep when he muttered, "I miss it."

"Miss what?" she mumbled.

"Battle. War. I want to be in France, but I am stuck here, seeing to business. If the war still rages once you have borne me a son or two, I will return. Should you prove yourself steadfast in all things, I would feel entirely secure in leaving Kyneward in your hands to rule in my stead. In point of fact, I deeply *hope* that I can do that."

That made her *very* happy with their disproportionately advantageous arrangement. "Compete in the tournament. Surely you can do that on a horse other than Ares."

"I haven't practiced in years."

"You have six weeks and two dozen well-trained chargers to choose from."

He said nothing else and she did not awaken until sunlight crept up the window pane and warmed her as it illuminated the foot of the bed. Grimme was sound asleep, his strong, muscular legs bare of the linens almost to his bollocks. The sun caught the hair on his legs and painted it an almost sparkling copper. She poked her foot out of the linens and held it up to his. It was almost twice hers in length and width and darker. She turned her head and saw that his head was turned away from her, his long golden-red hair spread across the pillow. His jaw was covered in a two-day stubble of copper. His chest barely moved under his muscular bare arm, also covered in that shiny copper hair, his other arm hanging over the floor.

She looked up at the ceiling and wondered what he would look like in full armor, astride a fully dressed and armored horse, a lance in his hand. She had never seen him in full armor, and here, now, he was bare and still looked rather frightening.

She sighed and nudged him. "'Tis Sunday morning. We missed mass, and I told William to meet us at nine."

He growled.

"I do want to get home to Sir John. I worry." She was worried about what he'd say when she presented him all the parchment she had collected.

"My deputy has full control," he croaked and wiped his hand down his face, and even with that bit of exertion, his forearm flexed. "All is well."

Presently, Brìghde found herself assisting Grimme to put on his gambeson and mail. He belted his sword and looked at her. "You'd make a fine squire, Wife."

She rolled her eyes. "I've done this for my brothers once or twice."

They met William at breakfast in the taproom, fed him, then Brìghde organized the transfer of their possessions and what purchases they could carry to the livery and supervised its packing. Grimme purchased another horse and saddle for William, and tossed him on the beast's back. He possessed almost nothing for himself except two expensive sets of clothing, quills, parchment, ink, and other such tools of a clerk. He seemed to be able to ride better than he had hinted the night before, but his skill needed refinement. Grimme was carefully and patiently instructing him when a groom made to assist Brìghde onto Troy. Grimme said, "One moment," and moved the groom out of the way. He grasped Brìghde around the waist and plopped her in the saddle, then turned back to William.

Soon enough they were on the road headed south. They walked along and chatted merrily with Brìghde's new clerk, who rode between them. He was an utterly delightful young man with whom, Brìghde was quite sure, she would get along and hoped Sir John would find him adequate. At some point, they broke into a trot and assisted William with his seat. When he seemed to capture that quite well, they moved to a canter, which seemed to be easier for him. By the time they reached Waters, however, Brìghde and Grimme were exchanging impatient glances over the lad's head.

"William," Brìghde said politely. "We are five miles from Kyneward, on this road. You can't miss it."

"Aye, my lady?"

"We will see you there." With that, she rose in her stirrups and kicked her mount into a full gallop, her husband a bare nose behind her, his laugh rich and deep.

"Catch me if you can, Wife!"

With that, he eased past her, but she was lighter and urged Troy harder. She laughed almost all the way to Kyneward, which only took a blink. They rounded the turn leading to the lane.

"What's that, Husband?!"

She squealed with delight as everyone scattered, terrified looks on their faces, both mounts thundering through and flying over everything. She was still laughing when they halted in the outer bailey and the grooms rushed to take their reins. Their mounts were heaving and their coats were foaming.

"That," Grimme panted, "was fun."

"You have had fun with me since you abducted me," Brìghde replied breathlessly as he swept her off her horse.

"That I have," he agreed agreeably, and draped his arm over her shoulders whilst she plucked something out of her pack. It had only been a week and a half ago they had ridden in to Kyneward. He had draped his arms over his women this way, left her behind in this new place he had brought her, and now they were together, breathless, laughing as they emerged from the stable.

Aye, this was home and it had only taken a few days.

23

"PAPA!"

"Papa!"

"Papa!"

"Papa's home!"

The lads came running, as did his women, whose welcoming smiles faded as soon as they noticed Grimme's arm around her. She acted as if she hadn't seen their expressions, and soon enough Grimme dropped his arm to stoop and gather his sons to him. The clamor was happy and Brìghde stood patiently, her hands folded behind her. She noticed little Pierce casting shy glances at her from the circle of Grimme's arms and she smiled at him.

She crouched then and gestured for him to come to her. He cautiously wiggled out of Grimme's arms and approached her warily. "Good afternoon, Master Pierce."

"Good afternoon, Lady Brìghde."

"I have something for you."

His eyes lit up. "You *do?*"

"Aye," she said softly and pulled her hands from behind her back to show him the toy she'd purchased for him after Grimme had explained his dilemma in riding out after her. "I'm sorry I did not tell you fare thee well." But he did not seem to hear her. He was looking at the toy in her hand.

"Look," she murmured, holding a short wooden stick that looked like a spoon with its bowl cut out. Attached to it was a ball with a string. "You must get the ball through the hole, do you see?" But Brìghde failed at it as she had since she'd purchased it, making Grimme laugh because he could do it easily. "Here," she said, offering it to him.

She was watching Pierce handle it carefully and look at it with pleased awe when it came to her attention that the other laddies wanted toys.

"Aye, aye, we brought something for you," Grimme was saying, then handing each lad a toy chosen specifically for him.

Brìghde watched, smiling, then happened to glance up to see the paramours all standing quite a way from them watching with varying expressions on their faces, but none she could identify. She stood and looked down at Pierce, who looked up at her with a bright smile and twinkling eyes. "If you promise to make yourself known to me, I will promise not to ignore you. I canna say good morn or fare thee well to a laddie I canna see."

He nodded, then turned away, still looking down at his toy as he walked up the lane, past the mistresses, and disappeared.

Brìghde looked at Grimme and he looked back at her with a grin. "That went well."

"It did," she agreed with a smile.

"Lord Grimme!"

He looked up and his grin grew. "I'm home." With that, he threw his arms wide open.

And they ran down the lane like wee lassies to jump all over him. Again, he gave each of them lusty kisses and groped their arses.

Brìghde called, "I'm going to find Sir John. When William arrives, please direct him to us."

He nodded, and she trudged up the hill, through the portcullis, across the bailey, up the stairs, into the great hall, and across it to Sir John's study. She raised her hand, hesitated, but knocked softly.

"Come."

She opened the door and peeked into the room, then around the door to see the old man sitting in a chair reading a book. "We're home," she said softly.

He smiled at her and she released a long breath. "Come in, come in." She did, closing the door behind her.

"You look much happier than you did when we last spoke," she said as she took the chair beside him.

"Aye, well, as soon as you left with the keys, 'twas as if a great weight had lifted from my shoulders." He leaned forward and took her hands. Looking into her eyes, he said, "I know that I have left you a dreadful mess, but I have every confidence that you can set things aright."

She blushed. "Thank you," she said softly. "I spoke with Grimme about it. I informed him that it was his ultimate responsibility to see that you had help and the authority to do what he wouldn't. 'Twas because he refused to be involved in the household at all yet refused you authority that he had put that burden upon you."

He blinked and pulled back a bit. "And what did he say to that?"

She shrugged. "Nothing. He simply stormed out of my chambers."

"When was that?"

"The night before we left for Hogarth."

He released her hands and sat back with a contemplative expression.

"What is the matter?"

"He *listens* to you," Sir John whispered more to himself than to her. Then he shook himself and flashed her a wide smile. "Oh, Brìghde. I am so glad you came here."

"If you keep saying that, my head will grow so big I canna get through the portcullis. How did things manage whilst we were gone?"

He waved a hand and said airily, "I don't know. I napped, read, ate, drank all the wine I could hold, and thoroughly enjoyed myself. I was even able to go outside with help from a manservant."

Brìghde grinned. "That makes me happy. I was afraid I had made you so angry with me you would no longer be my friend."

He tsk'd. "Oh, my dear. I will never *not* be your friend and advocate."

"Why?" she asked softly. "I have not been here yet a fortnight, and I was gone four days of that, and you don't trust me."

He shrugged mischievously as if he knew but would not tell her, then waved a hand. "As for trust, I have decided simply to do so. Whether or not you are disloyal, 'twould be what we deserved for snatching you."

"But I *wanted* to be snatched."

"Any other maiden would have had to be bound and gagged, forced to sign her name to the register, and kept in her chambers under lock and key, possibly without food, until she could be trusted not to run away, at which point, Grimme would have had to force her to bear his children, which he would have never done, so the exercise would have been entirely pointless. Your cooperation *could* be an elaborate act to lull us into complacency, but if so, you have extraordinary endurance for such a ruse, you have already benefited Kyneward, you have all the opportunity and resources you need to escape but you haven't, and you are enjoying yourself whilst you lure us to our destruction."

That should have been obvious to them from the first, but she held her tongue so as not to offend him.

He sat forward. "Tell me. Did you enjoy yourself in Hogarth?"

"I did, but let me give you the bad news first."

She barely made it through a recitation of her experience at the clothier's, his expression a study in humiliation, when he said, "Stop. I can guess the rest of the story. You settled the bills?"

"Aye, all of them so far as I know. I told the merchants not to sell to anyone claiming to be from Kyneward if they have not coin, but since I won't allow the paramours to go anytime soon, that will not be at issue."

"Well, then!" he said with forced cheer, "tell me the good news."

Then she regaled him with the tale of how Grimme thought he rescued her, but did not truly, as she was going to stab the horses anyway. She had him genuinely laughing by the time she finished with every detail and then—"Oh! Look!" She held out her hand and waggled her ring finger.

His expression melted in wonder and he took her hand gently to turn it this way and that. "It matches your eyes," he murmured.

"Grimme cheated. He bid the jeweler show me only emeralds." Suddenly there was a tear at the corner of the old man's eye and her smile dropped. "Is something wrong?"

He puffed a laugh and let go of her hand, wiping his eye. "*Nothing* is wrong, my dear," he beamed. "Not. One. Thing."

WILLIAM HAD arrived no worse for wear and a little earlier than Brìghde had expected him to be able to, but he seemed happy enough to have a roof over his head and three good meals a day. She bade a servant to prepare a chamber in the servants' quarters, where he would stay until Brìghde could get furniture to move him somewhere more suited to his station, or unless he determined he would like his own cottage outside the keep.

Sir John was ecstatic to make his acquaintance and offered to teach William how he kept the books in return for stories of Medici Bank and the Italian way of doing business, of which he had heard much. Brìghde blinked. Italians did business differently from anyone else? William was just as happy to meet Sir John, and they were fast friends.

Brìghde, Grimme, and William had attended evening mass with the villeins, some of the knights and men-at-arms, and other people from the keep, and now they sat at supper, William to Father Hercule's left. Brìghde bade the servant to keep William's platter full.

In the middle of the meal, Grimme's two men-at-arms who had been tasked with taking Brìghde's message to her brother dragged into the hall. One approached the table, bowed, and handed a return message to Grimme, who handed it to her.

She inspected it. Her name was in her brother's penmanship, but the seal was Dunham's. She opened it and read it, her heart sinking.

"No Mercury?" Grimme murmured.

She shook her head. "No Mercury." Then she handed the parchment to Grimme, who looked at it and handed it back.

"It's written in Gaelic."

"Oh, so it is. 'Dearest Budgie: We, Walter excepted, are happy to learn of your circumstance, as we were worried when we could not find you. He refused to admit that it was an ingenious plan (it was, and I would expect no less from you), but when has he ever admitted any such thing of a foe? And he does consider you a foe now, for you have dealt him a great slight, and the consequences for this slight he intends to be greater. My father-in-law did, in fact, tell him he would not be allowed to cross Dunham lands to wage war upon you—'" She looked at Grimme. "He means *me*, specifically, as I defied him. You are incidental, a hapless victim of my machinations, who, unfortunately, must bear his wrath caused by my rebelliousness. He will think I plied my wiles and used my beauty to seduce you into it."

Grimme started to laugh, then laughed until he was coughing.

Brìghde nodded. "Just so. '—for he cannot afford a conflict and Earl Tavendish, who was visiting Dunham when we received your missive, said he will back your husband.' That is news we can use."

"Just as you foresaw. I wonder if I could apply to Tavendish to back us against Sheffield."

"Asking won't hurt. 'But Dunham has the whole of the border and he cannot protect all of it. Tavendish also reminded Fàileach that Sheffield surrounds Kyneward on the west and south, and Sheffield will not tolerate incursion. Thus, you can expect a force to descend upon you, but whether tomorrow or ten years from now, no one can say.'"

"Stop. He was threatened with the force of four nobles that span and straddle the border who all have standing armies, was told he would not be allowed to cross it, and he still will plan an attack?"

"He loves making war."

"I love war, too, but only ones I can win."

"'Alas, he will not allow your possessions to be forwarded to you, much less Mercury. 'Twas all Mum could do to keep him from burning the lot and killing the dog, and that only because it is still at MacFhionnlaigh. She went to MacFhionnlaigh, packed it all up and bade Lady MacFhionnlaigh to store it there without destroying it in retaliation—'"

"Why would she acquiesce to that? You cheated her of a daughter-in-law."

"Och, Lady MacFhionnlaigh is an absolute rug. She will do whatever she is told, and my mother—"

"Is a virago. I tremble in my boots."

She snickered. "'Roger is ecstatic and bid me thank you, but did make a point to say he still hates you. He may help me snatch the dog, but I promise nothing. Your brother, Sir Baldy Fàileach. P.S. Mum is utterly delighted and says that if you have not taken total control of Kyneward immediately, she will invade you herself to thrash you.'"

Grimme chuckled. "Does she mean take control of me or the estate?"

"Both."

24

AT BREAKFAST THE next morn, she leaned toward Grimme and whispered, "Did you talk about the bills with your paramours?"

He looked at her, confused. "No. Why would I? The merchants are paid and you told them not to serve them if they had no coin and you said you wouldn't allow them to go shopping in the foreseeable future anyway. That is household business and your domain."

Brìghde sighed and left the subject.

After breakfast, Grimme took Brìghde to the mares' stable and introduced her to all of them. Half of them were named Mary. The other half all had names of Greek goddesses that he said fit their temperaments, but none named Aphrodite. His explanation held so much more information than the words, but she was not yet able to imagine what that could be.

Then they came to a halt at Helen's stall.

"If you could fetch Troy … " he asked politely.

"Of course!"

Once she returned, she found Grimme with Helen out in the middle of the aisle, trying to control her. As soon as Troy entered, he snuffed and she calmed immediately, craning her neck around to look at him. Brìghde drew him abreast of her and she could clearly see that Helen was a woman in love. Brìghde smiled, delighted.

Grimme saddled her himself whilst Brìghde held her. Helen didn't care. She and Troy were nuzzling.

"Very well," Grimme muttered when he finished and then helped Brìghde mount Troy. He untied Helen, then walked the mare out to a training pen at the back of the keep that Brìghde had not seen. "Bring Troy up a little and let's see what happens." He took a deep breath and swung into the saddle. He had firm hold on the reins, but Helen didn't buck or bolt. She wasn't paying attention to Grimme at all.

"Walk him."

Brìghde followed Grimme's directions and Helen followed Troy like a puppy.

"Leave the pen. I don't want her to get too attached."

As soon as Troy was turned away, Helen tried to follow, but Grimme had firm control. She protested. Troy followed Brìghde's directions, but he didn't like it. A groom opened the gate. She and Troy went outside the pen but stayed at the rail to watch.

Helen was trying to get to Troy but Grimme wouldn't let her. He turned her this way and that—but soon enough she started to misbehave, rearing slightly, bucking, then rearing sharply, protesting. But Grimme held his seat.

Brìghde had many times watched Fàileach grooms ride recalcitrant horses, but none this misbehaved.

"Open the gate," he called.

The groom did as he was told. Grimme struggled to get her pointed in that direction, but then she saw Troy and calmed instantly. She trotted over and they touched noses.

"Run," Grimme said tightly. "Don't look back."

Brìghde wheeled Troy and she let him have his head. They thundered out of the bailey and down the lane. She heard hooves running after them, and she turned Troy off to a field occupied only by sheep. It took a while for Helen to catch Troy's flank, but she could not pass him and even fell back a bit.

"Canter!"

Brìghde slowed him and a perfectly behaved Helen caught up to them. Brìghde and Grimme cantered along side by side for two or three miles, and Brìghde finally realized that Grimme wanted to wear her out whilst accustoming her to commands. She slowed Troy to a walk and Helen followed suit.

Grimme grinned at her and she returned it. "Come. There's a stream ahead." It was a clear-running stream, gurgling, and there were sheep drinking from it. The horses did too.

"Why don't you want her to get attached?"

"Troy's trained for war. I don't want her to pick up habits that, for a mare, would be undesirable."

Brìghde's mouth pursed.

"What?"

She shrugged. "Simply reminds me that my mother didn't succeed in training out male qualities that make me undesirable as a woman."

She caught his slight wince, but he only said, "Hold her for a bit."

Brìghde held Helen's halter as Grimme dismounted, but as long as the mare was near Troy, she didn't mind being held. Grimme untied a bag of oats and, once he had Helen's attention, began feeding her out of his hand. "Bloody hell," he muttered when she bit him, but not purposely, happily gobbling up every last grain of it. "Hand me the carrots, please. I'll feed Troy in a bit."

Thus he gave Helen some carrots and he petted her. As Grimme fed Troy, Brìghde gathered Helen's reins and dropped her halter to allow her to drink again, patting her withers and telling her what a good wee lassie she was.

When the horses were sated, Grimme mounted, took a deep breath, and said, "Let's see what happens *now*. Stay here for a bit."

She did and watched whilst Grimme turned Helen away and tried to chirrup her into a trot, but she balked and pawed the ground. "Dammit," he muttered to himself. "Run out a little way so I can run her in circles around Troy." Brìghde turned Troy and they cantered easily, Helen following and obeying Grimme's commands. "Stop." Brìghde did. Grimme asked Helen to trot, which she did, so long as she could do so around Troy. Then a canter, in ever-widening circles. Then a gallop, but Grimme broke the circle and galloped away from Troy back toward the keep.

Helen stopped cold and Grimme went flying over her head, landing on his back some distance away. Brìghde didn't laugh; that hurt.

She chirruped Troy into a walk. It took a while to get to them, but finally she drew up alongside Helen and took her bridle. She tried to snap, but Troy snuffled. She stood still and allowed Brìghde to gather her reins and lead her to Grimme, who was groaning.

"Is your back broken?"

"I do not believe so, no." He struggled to his feet, stretched and twisted this way and that. "My head is pounding," he muttered as he swayed on his feet. Brìghde and both horses stood quietly whilst Grimme retrieved his equilibrium and could mount Helen again. When he did, he sat and blinked, shaking his head as if to clear it.

"Why would it be bad for her to acquire Troy's training? She is almost as big as he is."

"Mares do not belong on the battlefield."

"Why?"

"Firstly, because a mare's value is in breeding. I will not send a mare into battle with the possibility of her being killed, no matter how well trained, if she can give me an excellent foal every year. Secondly, stallions are aggressive and can be trained to fight in a mêlée. Helen *might* have been an excellent warhorse if she had been trained from a foal, but it's too late for her now. She must be able to act with a human's direction, without depending on a stallion she's mated to direct her, never mind being taught to think and act independently. One trains a warhorse from birth." He pointed to Troy. "Now, him. I would give my left arm to find out who sired and foaled and trained him, as I suspect he's a match for Ares."

That pleased her more than was warranted, but she didn't want to mention the tournament again.

Helen was clearly tired, but Troy wasn't, so Brìghde sent him on another gallop. Grimme gave Helen her head and she followed until she simply could not. Her sides were heaving, she was lathered, and her head hung. It was at that point, Grimme dismounted and walked her slowly toward the keep, leaving Troy behind. She was too tired to fight anymore. Brìghde watched until they were almost out of sight and then turned Troy.

"Good laddie. Who's a good laddie? *You're* a good laddie."

She cantered Troy around to cool him off, then trotted toward home.

When she crested a rise, there was Grimme standing with an exhausted Helen, but talking to Emelisse, who was riding side-saddle. As he spoke, he plucked handsful of tall grass and rubbed Helen down. Emelisse's palfrey was small, little bigger than a pony, and she cast Brìghde a hateful glance as Brìghde rode up on Helen's other side. She turned Troy so the beasts could touch noses. Emelisse was still speaking to Grimme. In French. Very, very *polite* French thrumming with obvious rage if one could speak French.

"Why do you not ride with *me* in the morning?"

"I don't ride with you when I'm training."

"You *never* ride with me at all." He sighed. "You're training and you're riding with *her*."

"Emelisse, I do not owe you an explanation for anything I do. I do not want to have a discussion with you right now, as I am sore and tired and I have a headache and I must still take care of my horse, who is also tired and lathered. I need to get her back to the stable to groom her properly. You may help me take care of her if you wish."

Disgust ran across Emelisse's face.

"That's what I thought," Grimme said.

"Why do you allow *her* to ride your warhorses anyway?"

"Because she *can*," he said darkly. "If you could be bothered to ride astride on something more powerful than that nag, I would, in fact, appreciate it. My mares need to be ridden and I'm running out of grooms with time to do so."

She sniffed haughtily.

"It would help me a great deal," he said firmly, "if you and the other three would learn to ride astride and ride my mares every day."

"*Non*."

"Then don't question me when I go out with my wife."

"She has a name," she sneered. "You don't have to keep reminding me you married her instead of me."

"Oui, she has a name, but since we are being rude and speaking in a language she does not know, I don't want to say her name so that she does not know we're discussing her."

"Why has Lady *Brigitte*," she returned, Brìghde's name said crisply and undeniably, but with the French pronunciation, "earned such high regard from you?"

Grimme sighed heavily and simply refused to answer. He continued to rub Helen down, and Brìghde had to stay because Helen needed Troy near to encourage and comfort her back to the stable.

"Grimme!"

"*Lord* Grimme," he growled.

"You were a fifteen-year-old squire when I met you!" she snapped. "*I* was your first. *I* taught you how to be a man. You were sixteen when *I* had your first child. You were seventeen when *I* had your second child. You were eighteen when you were made a knight. You were twenty-one when you were made an earl. I refuse to call you *Lord* Grimme one more time, especially since *she* may call you Grimme. All you want is for someone to remind you constantly that you are a noble, because you are *not* one, you know it, you know *nothing* about being an earl, and now that you are one, you are ashamed of your beginnings, and you *know* this was a stroke of luck and that you did *nothing* to earn it."

Brìghde had already deduced that, and it was an astute observation, but she was shocked Emelisse was intelligent enough to make it, and she was curious as to how he could respond.

"That is one reason she's here, to teach me how to be an earl."

"She is here because you couldn't *bear* to wed a commoner!"

That, too, was true.

"What has you in such a toss?" he asked testily as he moved to Helen's right side and plucked more grass. "You've been angry for months, long before she came."

"I am tired of sharing you. With *anyone*. I have put up with it for ten years."

"Then leave."

Silence, but Brìghde wouldn't look at her. She busied herself admiring the grass and the … grass. That was all there was to admire, really.

"You would send me away?" she croaked.

"*Non*. But I would not grieve if you left."

"Grimme!" she cried. "*Eleven years!*"

"Oui, and you've been angry for most of them. You alone cannot satisfy me. You won't let me have your arse—"

Brìghde almost choked, and he was so matter-of-fact about it!

"—you won't suck my cod, you won't let me take you from behind, you won't join in with the others—"

Brìghde was glad she was already looking away.

"—you don't like being punished—"

Brìghde didn't ken that. Who *liked* being punished?

"—and you hate being tied up."

What?!

"You *also* can't go more than twice in a night."

"Twice in a night?!" she hooted. "Your *once* is *three times* for me! Six times in a night, more like."

Brìghde didn't understand that, either.

"What else am I supposed to do?"

"Learn to control yourself," she hissed.

That was the first and probably last time Brìghde would ever agree with Emelisse.

"Control myself? I give you your release first and you immediately start complaining though I am not finished. So I go find somebody else to finish me off. It is not unreasonable for *any* man to expect that if his woman gets her release, she will be courteous enough to allow him one. *One*, Emelisse, not six. You won't even give me that much, and then you have the gall to complain that I go elsewhere."

Brìghde could see his point. That was very selfish of her.

"I won't control myself. I don't have to. *You* alone of the seven women I'm fucking are the only one trying to put a leash on me. It hasn't worked in the last eleven years. Why do you think it'll work now?"

"*Brigitte* has you on a leash!"

"Mother of God, do you *want* me to slap you?"

She gasped. "You wouldn't!"

"*Yesterday* I would have said *non*. Today ... "

He finally left off rubbing Helen down and began walking, Helen plodding along behind him.

"You've changed since you brought her home."

"I have not changed. I have a different circumstance I must learn how to manage. You and I have been through many changes in our life. Why can you not simply see this is another one?"

"*Non*. This *is* different because you are trying to earn her favor."

He shook his head wearily. "If *you* wanted to earn *my* favor, exercise my mares. *Not* side-saddle."

"I shouldn't have to earn your favor," she muttered. Very well, Brìghde agreed with her *twice*. "I can simply let myself catch."

"You won't," he said with some amusement. "Because as soon as you're showing, I won't fuck you and then you'll believe I've forgotten you. Finish your ride and do whatever it is you do in a day. If you won't help me, then I've nothing more to say."

"*I* am your wife! Your *true* wife!"

"I see your reasoning." Brìghde gulped. "But I must have a legitimate heir from a noblewoman, and you are not it."

"You *want* a legitimate heir from a noblewoman because you cannot bear for one of your bastards from a commoner to inherit."

He said nothing.

"Why do you not allow La—*her* to take a lover and pass his babe off as yours?"

"That is an excellent idea—"

Brìghde's insides roiled like a cauldron. That would make her nothing more than a brood mare, mated off to the best candidate. She had bargained for *Grimme*, not some nameless, faceless stallion!

"—but I do not want to rear another man's child if I can help it."

"Or get a babe from a maidservant and pass it off as hers. You will never have to fuck her, much less look at her."

"I don't want a babe from a maidservant, either. No, I don't want to fuck her—"

Brìghde barely kept from wincing.

"—but she is intelligent, courageous, and strong, and I want that for my heir. *She* can give me a warrior. You haven't."

"You don't want them to be!"

Grimme halted abruptly, so Brìghde did too.

"You will not let me have them," he snarled. "You want to keep them to your breast, coddle and control them. If you could, you would still have them suckling. They should have been out in the field two years ago and you would not allow it, so do not now speak to me about their lack of strength. *How* am I supposed to make warriors of them when you barely allow me to speak with them? You don't even allow them to attend their studies with Father Hercule, and I will not have illiterate children! I have respected your wishes all these years, but I am at the end of my patience. They are *infants*. Ten-year-old and nine-year-old *infants* who can barely read, and not allowing Gaston to go to the stables with Max is a perfect example. Do not now tell me it is my fault for not training them."

"You have *never* said a word to me about how I rear our sons until *she* came."

He was silent for a moment, then started walking again. "That is true. She has made me consider things I should have been considering all along, but I allowed you to do what you will because you love them so much. If you didn't, it would be a different thing."

"You're going to take them away from me, aren't you?" she accused. "Leave me with *nothing*. Nothing of you, nothing of them. Because of *her*. Mayhap I *will* allow myself to catch."

"I do not want another child with you!" he barked. "I don't want any more children with any of you!"

"And so what would you do if I *did*?" she taunted.

"I would give it to my wife."

Not that Brìghde would want the babe, but that would indeed keep Emelisse from catching again just to keep Grimme tied to her.

"I am finished with this conversation," Grimme said abruptly. "Unless you want to assist me with Helen—"

"Helen?" she asked, apparently startled out of her rage. "Who's Helen?"

"This horse," he answered with overdone patience. "She is named after Helen of Troy, who was the most beautiful woman in the world."

"So?"

"The horse my wife is riding—his name is Troy."

"So?"

Grimme dropped his head until his chin bumped his chest. "Never mind. I wish—" He clapped his mouth shut.

"You wish what?"

"I wish you would find something to do other than keep our sons in their chambers and lie around waiting for me to fuck you."

Brìghde *almost* couldn't control her snicker, but she caught it in time.

"I embroider," Emelisse said, her voice filled with hurt and confusion. "I ride."

"My God, Emelisse!" he burst out. "Can't you do *anything* else?"

"What should I do?"

"*One* thing you could do is teach the boys to ride!"

"They'll fall off."

"Oui, they will. How did *you* learn to ride?" Silence. "Ask Father Hercule to teach *you* to read and write."

"Why would I need to read and write?"

They were now walking into the outer bailey. "Go finish your ride," he said wearily. "I have work to do." When she didn't, he snapped, "*With my wife*."

She turned in a huff and cantered off.

"I apologize," he muttered in French, then repeated himself in English. "I apologize. That was very rude of us. She cannot express herself as well in English."

Brìghde was quite sure she could express herself as well as she needed to and that was a conversation that should have been had in private, but having an extended conversation in a language they thought Brìghde didn't understand was a show of dominance by Emelisse.

Yet Brìghde only said, "Apology accepted."

"Join me?"

"Aye, in a moment." Whilst Grimme rode to the mares' stable, Brìghde handed Troy off to a groom— "Pears, two rations of oats." —and found Grimme, who was just beginning to wipe down Helen properly.

She joined him and together they spent an hour grooming her, pampering her with pears and carrots, which she seemed reluctant to take, and talking.

"She has been mistreated," Brìghde observed.

Grimme nodded and he was moving with difficulty. He would be very sore in the morning. "Sheffield was her first owner."

Brìghde's eyes widened. "Ares!"

Grimme shook his head. "Aldwyn won't allow his chargers to be abused. The duchess has many ladies in waiting, so their mares are for the women to ride side-saddle, no more, no less and in that case, they don't care about quality. They don't breed. They buy, but Sheffield won't buy my mares. They're too expensive and are for breeding, not for ladies' pleasures. I don't know why Sheffield bought this one, as she is valuable and she must have cost him a great deal, but someone ruined her. I bought her from her second owner soon after he had bought her."

"If Sheffield wants what you love so much, why has he not taken more of your horses? They are fine animals."

"Henry would have something to say about it, and he would not be kind. However, I'm not going to run to the king over one horse, no matter how much it hurts."

"The king is your friend, then, not just a grateful liege?"

"Aye. When you battle together, titles melt away and you become companions-at-arms. He knows me. Trusts me. He simply happened to be the companion-at-arms whose life I saved. I didn't even know it was the king. But with that, we forged a friendship that has lasted. I am loyal to him, he is loyal to me, and that is not something I take for granted."

"What is the duke to him?"

He pursed his lips as if trying to decide what to say. "I told you," he began slowly, "that Sheffield murdered his cousin and the cousin's babe to take the title, and that the duchess disappeared."

"Aye."

"After the old duke was killed, Sheffield challenged the babe's legitimacy, as the old duke did not care for women, and it was rumored he was not the babe's father. That challenge did not hold, as the babe was born in wedlock and the old duke declared him his, then the old duke was murdered. Soon after that, the babe disappeared. Was he murdered? Did someone spirit him away to save his life? A babe's dead body was eventually found, possibly … six months later. I am not quite sure on that. But it was too fresh; it was not the body of a babe long dead."

"So there *could be* a legitimate duke somewhere."

"'Tis very possible, and most who remember or care believe that the legitimate duke is still alive."

She narrowed her eyes. "*You're* that duke."

He barked a laugh. "I'm twenty-six. Do your sums, my lady."

Now wasn't *she* embarrassed! "Oops," she snickered.

"My main concern is if, in light of the fact that he's killed a duke, a duchess, and possibly a babe to gain the dukedom, will he do it again? Is a measly twenty thousand acres worth killing another three people if it gains the attention of a king who would believe it and keep it from him anyway? Kill me, aye, that's worth it. Kill me *and* a countess? I'm not sure. Kill me *and* a countess *and* a legitimate heir? Who knows? He is evil enough to do it, but is he smart enough to make it look like an accident or alternatively, not to do it at all? That is what gives me pause."

"We simply must not travel together, then."

"That will not always be feasible."

She could concede. "Is the king your *only* protection?"

"At the moment, aye. I haven't made any other alliances."

"Did you tell Henry about Ares?"

"No. I cannot go running to him every time Sheffield looks at me with vicious envy in his eyes. If I could kill Sheffield without raising suspicion from the other nobles, I would. I'm not sure Henry would do more than smack my hand."

"What an unholy mess," Brìghde muttered. "Walter is as Sheffield, only worse, because he is intelligent."

Grimme's eyebrow rose. "To my ears, your father is truly evil."

"He is," she said flatly. "There have been times I wonder if he's sold his soul to Satan." Then she caught his expression and his very pale face. "'Twas a jest, Lord Husband," she said quickly. "My humor is not always so obvious."

He cleared his throat. "'Tis well."

"And now I have ruined any trust I might have built," she sighed.

His brow wrinkled then. "I'm not sure what to think of you. You needed rescue, aye, I can see that. You told me the entire plot almost immediately when you knew that doing so, and what the plot was, would damage you in my sight."

"I wanted you to be my friend," she muttered, embarrassed again, but not so humorously this time. "I practically told you that, too."

"And so all this ... is your way of trying to earn a friendship? That you will abandon as soon as everything we say or do that hurts you has built and become unbearable to you?"

She was about to cry with embarrassment. "If I abandon you, 'twill not be for Fàileach, so you need not fear that. I found my way home hundreds of miles from a convent by myself. I told you that."

He was silent for a time. "How old were you?"

"Fifteen. It took me three years. I worked my way home, seeking employment in noble houses. I have been a scullery maid. I have been a laundress. I have been a serving wench. I have been a chambermaid. I have been a nursemaid. I have been a housekeeper. 'Tis why I treat my servants differently from other housekeepers and noblewomen."

"That is why you are not spoiled."

"I *was*," she said lightly, then admitted reluctantly, "I was a scullery maid far longer than I had to be because of my behavior. I was dismissed from three noble houses before I realized I was my own worst enemy. In my last noble house, I determined to be silent and work my way up, as I could not bear being at the bottom. I hated the way the household was run, so cruelly, but worse, so inefficiently. I determined to be the housekeeper and eventually I was. I was going to gain control of that household one way or another."

He chuckled. "Of course you were. Did you kill the housekeeper?"

"In point of fact, I did, but not intentionally. Quite by chance, I startled her as we both came around the same corner in opposite directions and she dropped dead right there. I was startled enough I *thought* I was going to die, but alas."

His laughter was infectious, and she began to laugh with him. "Aye, it was funny, but I dared not laugh. Anyway, I went to the lady and gave her my qualifications in writing as William did, and she promoted me. No one else could read or write, you see, and a housekeeper must be able to. I made a good wage. I could have stayed there, but for the fact that the old lord, who would not lower himself to swive a servant, died and the new one liked to swive the servants whether they wanted to or not. The first time he tried it with me, I swung a pitcher at his head, and I gathered my things and left before he regained consciousness."

His laughter had turned into roars, and he was coughing and wheezing. She grinned whilst she waited for his laughter to subside. "Do you know," he said as he wiped his eyes, "I think I would trust you on the strength of that alone. I truly admire that."

Warmed to the seed of her soul, she flushed and smiled shyly. "Thank you, Grimme."

"How did you keep your innocence all the way through it?"

"Virginity, aye, I kept that. Innocence, no. I have seen many things I would rather not, which is why I could, with all assurance, tell you I know what swiving entails. Once I had enough coin that I did not have to work anymore, I cut my hair. I dressed like a boy. I was very careful about when and where I traveled and with whom I spoke."

"And your need for friends?"

"I didn't need them so badly I would risk my life or possessions." She paused. "I had been gone from the convent for a fortnight when I met a dog. She was a very large, very vicious beast who seemed to have come out of nowhere and attached herself to me. I didn't know why. She killed for me. More than once. She would herd me from places she didn't want me to go, and snap at me if I didn't obey. One time, I stopped at a pasty stall but she wanted me to keep going. I was hungry. She kept pushing me. I wouldn't go. Then she bit me in the arse. Hard. I was angry with her, but I obeyed. We got down the road a bit. I heard a scream and I turned around. There was a boy being dragged kicking and screaming behind the seller's cart. She barked at me as if to say, 'Do what I tell you to do next time.'"

"What happened to her?"

"She was killed rescuing me from a place she had not wanted me to go." Her eyes stung and she wished she hadn't said anything, for it renewed her grief and guilt.

"What did you name her?"

She decided that a warrior of twenty-six who could command and pay a force of almost four thousand should not need his fear of witchcraft indulged. "Hades."

"For a bitch?"

Brìghde shrugged. "She was vicious enough to have come from hell, so why not?"

He cleared his throat. "And … your households where you worked? What did you do with her then?"

She shrugged. "How many dogs do we have in the keep who scrounge for food at table?"

"Oh, aye."

"She was one of many. She slept with me. I was always surprised no one said anything. 'Twas as if God Himself had blessed me with safety in my travels, and now He has once again blessed me, sending me you."

His smile was warm. "Rather, God has blessed *me* with you." She flushed with pleasure. "Now it seems we have groomed Helen to sleep."

"Who's a good lassie?" Brìghde crooned. "*You're* a good lassie, aye you are."

"She will be," Grimme grunted as he gathered the currycombs. "Would you do this with me every morning for a while, if you can spare time from your duties?"

"Of course!" Brìghde said, more than willing to let the keep go to rot whilst spending time with Grimme training a skittish horse how to be loved—and needling one very jealous mistress.

25

BRÌGHDE SPENT the next week with Grimme in the mornings riding Helen and Troy, accustoming the animal to being cared for gently, which seemed to be her biggest problem. Helen still threw Grimme if he wanted her to run without Troy, but the distances she covered before doing so were getting longer and longer.

After the first day, Brìghde requested that they not take Helen out or allow her to see Troy immediately, but that they take time to comb her and feed her a small treat and speak to her gently before she was saddled. It took several days before Helen would believe that where Brìghde and Grimme went, treats went also.

The third day, they met a groom teaching one of the mistresses how to ride astride; not long after that, they saw two others doing the same. They seemed to be acquiring the skill rather well.

"Did they object?"

"No," Grimme said shortly.

Thursday was manorial court, or something approximating it, which she and Sir John attended. Father Hercule seemed to be a reasonable judge, only looking to her or Sir John in case he wasn't quite sure what to believe or, if a monetary value was involved, what proper compensation should be.

Brìghde spent the rest of the afternoons with William surveying the servants with positions in the inner and outer bailey, and assessed their needs or opinions for improvements. They met with the architect who was directing the work on the curtain wall to discuss new outbuildings and expanded storage. Sir John suggested they start surveying the villeins also, their abilities, their leaseholds, their crops, their services, and their families in anticipation of hiring a land steward. She surveyed them as to their contracted days of service to Kyneward as foot soldiers. They ended their task with Grimme's two youngest sons in tow.

She had caught the two playing hide-and-seek in the keep and getting in the servants' way.

After midday meal, she commanded them to accompany her to protect her honor.

Surely you have swords.

Aye, my lady.

Go get them. Go on. We have much to accomplish before supper.

They were only too happy to fetch their light wooden toy swords and set off, yet they were no less restless whilst she and William conducted business, so she set them to herding goats who had gotten loose from their goatherd.

When they returned to the keep for supper, she was greeted by one furious mother, who snatched Terrwyn to her side.

"You have no right to my son! I have been looking *everywhere* for him!"

"I had requested his services as a knight-in-training."

That seemed to confuse her. "He is not a knight."

"He will be one day."

She gave Brìghde a long look, clearly not knowing what to say to that.

"What is your name again?"

"Dillena."

"Dillena, I apologize. I should have instructed him to ask permission or at least tell you where he was going." She stared at Brìghde as if she were a ghost. "Would you give your permission to allow me to see to his care when you are unable to?"

"I … suppose?" She paused, then blurted, "God knows, Emelisse has ruined our chance of having any nursemaids."

"'Tis unfortunate," Brìghde agreed.

Her eyes narrowed. "Why are you being nice to me? You know exactly why I would be unable to care for my son, yet you offer to assist in my— Um. With Lord Grimme. You are his wife. Should you not be angry? I would."

"I am here for the position of castellain," she said wryly. "Sadly, matrimony to a noble includes the bearing of children, but if my lord's lust for me continues unabated, I will die a virgin."

She smiled hesitantly, and she cleared her throat. "Um … well then. 'Tis pleasant to make your acquaintance."

"Please do not be offended if I cannot remember your name for a while."

She shrugged. "We all look like Emelisse. There is a reason for that."

Brìghde watched her go, taking Terrwyn. To Brìghde's eye, the women and children were Grimme's family and they had greeted each other that way when he returned. Yet when she searched her mind, she could not recall that he had spoken to any of the lesser three mistresses, even at mealtimes, much less carried on an entire conversation.

The only conversation he had had with any of them in Brìghde's presence was the one with Emelisse, which involved rancor, with no expressions or overtones of love at all. Grimme had even dared Emelisse to leave, telling her he would not grieve her absence, yet he did not put her out and he continued to swive her. What did they talk about deep in the night after the swiving was done? Brìghde assumed that the only two words involved in the act of mating were "Oh" and "God."

Thus, Brìghde began to wonder exactly what Grimme's women were. Dillena believed that her only value was her cunte, and that she was chosen only because she looked like one of the other women Grimme was swiving. Was that … true? And if so, was that any better or worse than being repulsive?

"Come, Pierce. 'Tis time for supper."

Once at table, Brìghde saw that Grimme's two oldest looked as if they were ready to drop and Emelisse was furious.

"What happened to them?" Brìghde whispered to Grimme.

"I sent them out to the stables to muck stalls all afternoon," he replied shortly. The other two were happy and telling their mothers all about their adventures with Lady Brìghde and William.

The next morning at breakfast, Grimme and Terrwyn's mother—Dillena, she reminded herself—were the only parents present, and the only children present were Terrwyn and Pierce.

Brìghde didn't dare ask after the other mistresses, but she did ask after Gaston and Max.

"In bed," he said tightly.

He didn't say much on their morning ride, except what he wanted Brìghde and Troy to do, and he left off grooming Helen in the middle, storming out of the stall in a rage.

Suddenly, Helen was much less calm, snapping at Brìghde and trying to bite. She would not take the treats Brìghde offered and she started to buck and kick the stall walls.

"Oh," Brìghde whispered as she tried to calm her. "'Twas a woman who mistreated you, aye? Oh, me wee lassie," she soothed as she backed out of the stall slowly and closed the door. Once Brìghde was out of the stall, Helen calmed and hesitantly took the offered treats over the door.

Presently, she heard Grimme's angry voice far off, and then she heard children crying. As he got closer, she could see he had his two oldest sons with him, lecturing them in French, and telling them he was not going to allow them to sleep through breakfast. Every day but the Sabbath, they would be up, they would eat, and then they were to report to the head groom and do whatever he needed done. On the Sabbath, they would go to mass with him and Lady Brìghde, then they may rest.

The head groom met them. Grimme repeated his orders in English, and they were led off to the pony stable to muck stalls. They were not happy, nor was Grimme. He stalked into the mares' stable and down the aisle, and Brìghde put her hand up when he was two stalls away.

"Stop. Release your anger first." His nostrils flared, but she said, "Helen." He blinked and his expression cleared, then she explained that Helen would not tolerate Brìghde alone in the stall with her.

Thus together they finished their pampering of Helen.

After midday meal, from which both Gaston and Max were absent, though a fuming Emelisse was not, Terrwyn's mother would not allow the boy to once again accompany Brìghde and William—until Grimme barked at her that Terrwyn would be going and that he should take his sword.

She was utterly cowed, whilst Pierce's mother cast a sly little glance at Pierce, which the boy did not notice.

"I did not want to get *that* battle started," Brìghde grumped at William as they trod down the lane, boys in tow, "but it seems I did."

William grimaced in sympathy.

At supper, Gaston and Max were nearly asleep in their chairs, whilst Terrwyn and Pierce were still ready for more adventures and could barely stay in their seats.

"I will not be able to go for our morning ride tomorrow," Grimme muttered, but did not elaborate. He was in a foul mood that clearly concerned his sons, so Brìghde said only,

"Very well."

It was around midnight before she plopped her arse on her stool and bid Avis to brush her hair.

The door opened and Grimme stuck his head in. "You're sleeping with me tonight. We have things to discuss." The door slammed shut.

"Oh, I am, am I?" she drawled, as amused as she could be whilst she was so tired. Once her hair was braided for the night, she dismissed Avis, and went across the hall to find Grimme half asleep, with his hands linked behind his head. "We do, do we?"

"Aye. Tell me *exactly* what happened yesterday with Terrwyn."

She dropped into bed, locked her fingers behind her head, too, and merely said that Dillena was concerned when she couldn't find her son, which was understandable, as he did not tell her where he was going, and that Brìghde had apologized for not thinking before taking him along.

"Grimme, I *really* do not want to get between your women and their children, as I would not want another woman to come between me and *my* children. But you *must* set some sort of daily custom before they force me to. They will blame the wicked stepmother instead of the castellain bringing order to the keep. Sweet Mary and Joseph, my brothers would have destroyed the keep by now, locked up that way, and *that*, I will not tolerate."

"Hrmph."

"And *why* must we have these councils in bed?"

"Because," he said snidely, "*you* are my castellain and I can wake *you* up in the middle of the night to speak my thoughts when they are new, which I will not do to my father, and even if I would, I would have to get out of bed, dress, and go down the stairs. *Or* I would have to remember something until daylight when I can speak with him. Which I never do until the most inconvenient moment."

"That is why you have a chamberlain."

"You are also my wife. You will sleep with me whether you want to or not." With that, he heaved himself to his side facing away from her and went to sleep.

Brìghde rolled her eyes, then rolled away from him and went to sleep.

The next morning after breakfast, William went about doing the surveying alone as he had every morning she had ridden with Grimme, and she was not terribly surprised to find Terrwyn and Pierce waiting for him at the front door, their toy swords in hand. She grimaced. "William's gone already and I am going into Waters. I don't know whether I can take you with me. Do you ride?"

They deflated and looked at the floor in shame, shaking their heads.

"You do now," came Grimme's deep voice from the threshold of the chapel.

Their heads snapped up and they gaped at their father. Brìghde almost caught herself gaping as well.

"You are coming with us, my lord?" she asked carefully.

"Nay. I am going to spend the day teaching my sons to ride."

The boys jumped and whooped for joy, then bounded out of the keep. Brìghde looked at him, happy but confused. "Last night, you … "

His jaw tightened again and he looked away. "You've made your point and I don't want to continue to hear it."

Brìghde pulled her lips between her teeth to keep herself from saying anything more. He followed the boys, brushing past her and saying only, "I will see you at midday. Or supper. Don't go to Hogarth alone."

"I am taking the cart," she called after him. He stopped and merely tilted an ear toward her, and she skittered after him. "I must pick up my things from the seamstress, so 'twill be slow enough for them."

He looked at her then, confused. "Why do they not deliver them here?"

"I want to count them myself as they are loaded."

He shrugged. "Aye, then. Can you wait for me to instruct them a little? Or will you bound off when I am not quick enough for you?"

"Oh, *stop* it," she huffed. "You were wrong. Admit it."

"I already did," he said dryly as they walked into the stables where Troy and Phobos and four ponies were saddled. "I won't do it twice. And I will *never* admit I was wrong in writing."

She chortled.

He bellowed for his two oldest to come, and when they found out they would be released from their brand-new duties for the day and why, they were ecstatic.

The lads did know how to get into the saddle, but that was all. Whilst Grimme gave them a swift lesson, Brìghde ordered a cart hitched, a groom, and two manservants. Then she went to Troy, who had been begging her for attention, stretching his neck out and craning to look at her. She grasped the horse's face between her fingers and touched her nose to his. He snuffed and nibbled at her cheek with his lips. She planted a kiss on his nose and fed him oats and carrots whilst her cart was hitched and Grimme got the laddies ready to ride.

He helped her mount, and then, in deference to the boys, walked Phobos. They were barely halfway down the lane that led to the main road when Emelisse came running out of the keep, screaming at Grimme to stop. He did and turned with an annoyed scowl.

"Where are you taking them?" she demanded in French.

"Riding," he snapped, "which should be obvious."

"But—"

Grimme threw Phobos's reins at Brìghde, stalked toward Emelisse, took her by the arm, and half dragged her up the lane toward the keep. He swung her around to face him and started speaking and gesturing. All four lads and Brìghde twisted in their saddles to watch this, straining to hear. When he was finished, he pointed to the keep. She turned angrily and stormed the rest of the way until she disappeared. Grimme started to stalk back toward them.

"Where was *your* mother, Pierce? Terrwyn?" Gaston, the oldest, taunted.

"Aye," Max echoed just as contemptuously. "Don't *they* care whether you'll get hurt or not?"

"*Our* mother is Papa's *favorite*," Gaston added for good measure.

"*My* mother doesn't treat me like a baby!" Pierce retorted. "*I* get to do what I want and *you* never get to go outside!"

"Like a *baby*—wah wah wah," Terrwyn finished up.

Brìghde's heart ached, but she did not step in because she didn't know if she should. She would simply have to discuss it with Grimme, although thus far, her opinions of his sons had not been welcome.

They had, however, been effective.

"And Papa made *you* go work in the stables whilst *we* got to play with Lady Brìghde."

She grimaced. That was the *last* thing she needed.

Brìghde tossed Phobos's reins back to Grimme, and they continued on. About a mile down the road, Grimme decided the boys could ride the rest of the way without his intervention, so he mounted Phobos. Both Phobos and Troy wanted to race, and Brìghde traded glances with a very impatient Grimme.

She reached out and patted his arm. "Be as patient and consistent as you are with Helen. 'Twill get better."

"How do you know?" he snapped, and all four laddies whipped their heads around in anticipation of a spat.

"I have brothers," she said with a simple smile. "I've watched pups trained to hunt, horses trained to saddle. I have not yet known of a trained cat, but they know their jobs from the litter, so there is no point."

Grimme lost some of his tension and relaxed, then patted her hand. "Thank you, Wife."

"You're welcome, Husband."

Brìghde was looking at the boys out of the corner of her eye or she would have missed it. Gaston and Max were angry. Terrwyn was confused. Pierce was hopeful.

"Very well, boys. Shall we trot?"

They trotted toward Waters, all the lads finding it difficult. Gaston fell off not once, but twice, then Max was thrown when he confused his reins and his knees. Each time, Pierce and Terrwyn, neither of whom fell off, giggled themselves into fits of coughing.

Grimme either didn't notice or care.

Siblings fought; she knew this so very well. However, Brìghde and her brothers had a common enemy, so when they fought, it was always with the knowledge that when they got home, they would be allies. This felt different because Gaston and Max had obviously been poisoned and were punishing the littlest two on Emelisse's behalf.

Soon enough they were in Waters, having ridden in to bows and curtsies and "my lord"s and "my lady"s. Brìghde instructed the groom to drive the cart to the seamstress's shop, and she would meet him there shortly.

Grimme helped her dismount in the stable. "I'll stay here with them for a while to teach them grooming and such."

"Aye. Shall—" She hesitated to mention it. "Shall we have our midday meal here? Mayhap allow the lads to roam alone with some coin?"

He shrugged. "Aye. 'Twill do no harm." She hesitated, and he sighed wearily. "Say it."

"Firstly, they are at each other's throats. I would advise you to allow them to fight it out. My brothers and I always battled until we were black and blue and bloody and broken, and tensions were gone. You said yourself that you adjudicate by allowing soldiers to battle to surrender or death. Secondly, have they ever been here? Or Hogarth? Your women must go to Hogarth quite often, but the laddies are far too happy to have an outing."

His brow wrinkled and he turned. "Gaston. Have you ever been here? Any of you? Or Hogarth?"

"No, Papa."

"Have you ever been outside the outer bailey wall *at all?*"

"Just when you come home, Papa," Max said.

"I have," Terrwyn offered hesitantly.

"*My* mother lets me go where I want," Pierce taunted.

The two oldest snarled and advanced on him, but he stood his ground, then Grimme growled. The lads stopped cold and all of them looked a little frightened.

"'Tis not you," Brìghde hastened to assure them. "Grimme! You're scaring them."

"Papa, I've been here," Pierce said with great satisfaction, preening at his two oldest brothers whose resentment flared.

Grimme was silent for a second or two, then said with strained patience, "How have you been here when none of your brothers has been?"

"I walked," he said matter-of-factly.

Brìghde gasped, her eyes wide.

"By … *yourself?*" Grimme asked carefully.

Pierce nodded as if it were the most reasonable thing in the world. Grimme slowly turned to gape at Brìghde as if he'd been felled by a caber, which was not much different from how Brìghde felt.

She looked back at Pierce and said crisply, "Do not do that again without permission, please. You will not like the consequences."

He slumped. "Very well," he pouted.

Grimme shook his head, then turned Brìghde away and off to the side. "I can see why no one likes you."

She looked up at him, hurt.

"'Tis because you are *right.*"

Her hurt gave way to smugness. "I know," she trilled. "Say the words, Grimme."

"You were right," he growled.

She cackled. "In writing."

He gave her a wryly amused glance and said, "Never. Go on, now."

26

GRIMME HAD TO do something. Gaston was ten. He should have been gone to apprentice as a page three years ago. Max was nine. He should have been gone two. Terrwyn was seven, and he should be preparing to go right this moment.

They could barely get into the saddle, much less ride. His head groom had told him the boys were so defiant about grooming, they were affecting the horses, so Grimme had ordered them to muck stalls and had had to stand over them to get them to work. He didn't *want* to thrash them, but he was willing to, and since he had never expressed anger toward them before, this was dire.

First it was Brìghde's tale of being willing to work to get what she wanted in spite of being a spoiled adolescent noblewoman, working her way up England and Scotland hundreds of miles to get home. Then it was the unpaid bills. Then it was Emelisse's flat refusal to exercise the mares when he asked; the fact that she had never, in his recollection, done *anything* of value to him, and the list of what she wouldn't do in bed made him only too aware she wasn't of much value *there*, either. Then Maebh, Ardith, and Dillena had happily acquiesced to exercising the mares, apparently eager for something new to do and know that they were helping. They had shocked Grimme into a confused, "Uh … thank you" and his sudden recollection of their temperate and helpful natures had befuddled him a little. *Now* Emelisse's sons' refusal to work had him in a thunderous rage.

It was *not* the boys' fault, but he continued to have to remind himself of it.

Then! He learned that only the two youngest had ever gone outside the keep's walls at all, and five-year-old Pierce had walked to Waters and back alone at *least* once! It was infuriating, and he didn't know with whom he was more angry—their mothers or himself, and suddenly Father Hercule's opinion of Pierce's aptitude for ruthlessness started to make more sense.

"When I was your age, Gaston," Grimme began gently, whilst showing each of them how to unsaddle their ponies, "I was doing everything for my knight's horse."

"We can't help it, Papa," Max said. "We aren't allowed out of the keep."

"But now that Lady Brìghde's here—" Terrwyn put in.

"I *hate* Lady Brìghde!" Gaston yelled.

"Me *too*!" Max echoed.

"Well, *I* don't!" Terrwyn screamed.

"I *like* her!" Pierce declared.

Grimme closed his eyes and rubbed his fingers in his eyes. "I do not care," he said wearily, but the argument was getting louder and soon they would be pushing and shoving, "whether you like her or not—" They weren't listening. War was about to break out, just as Brìghde had said. "—she is here to stay."

It was when Gaston and Max started shoving their younger brothers that he stepped in and picked up Gaston and Max by the backs of their necks. He looked at each of them in turn. They were squirming, but Grimme's hands were huge compared to little boys' necks, so he held on easily. "I am going to let you go. You will not touch your brothers." Yet. "Understand?"

"Aye, Papa," they squeaked, but when he dropped them they rubbed their necks and glared at the younger two, who were snickering. Max pointed at them and accused, "Do you see, Papa, what they do? They poke at us until we want to thrash them, then they run outside like cowards. '*You* can't go outside,'" he mocked. "'*Your* mother makes you stay inside like a *baby*.' 'Where's *your* toy sword? Did your mother take it away from you?'"

Grimme scowled at him. "Well? Did she?"

"Aye," he grumbled.

Suddenly, Grimme wished Brìghde hadn't left. He sighed and propelled them all toward the door.

"Where are we going?"

Behind the stable and beyond the pen, where there was soft grass and few people milling about.

"Sons," he said, "you may continue your fight."

They looked at each other, confused. To Grimme's not-altogether shock, Pierce took the first swing, such as it was.

Grimme simply stood and watched whilst his sons brawled, his arms across his chest and his legs wide. The fight went to ground almost immediately, which was normal.

Men gathered around. After the appropriate bows and respectful "my lord"s, the conversation with Grimme gradually turned as if he were one of them, commenting on each boy's strengths and weaknesses, and eventually, wagering on which boy would conquer.

Grimme and all his villeins flinched and winced and grimaced every once in a while and poor Pierce was on the receiving end of a lot of it, but he battled as fiercely as a five-year-old could against two boys twice his size, save when Terrwyn rescued him from one or the other and then it was again one to one.

The fight shifted as they tired and their strengths and weaknesses really started to show. The younger boys had an advantage the older two did not: they had more endurance, likely because they went out to play and the older two weren't allowed. They would outlast the two older boys easily.

While Grimme was happy it was a somewhat fair fight, he was *not* happy about the reason, and he *certainly* was not happy to have to tell Brìghde she was right. *Again.*

By the time Terrwyn and Pierce had beaten their two older brothers into submission, they were all worn out, lying on the ground panting, crying (every one of them—Grimme shook his head wearily); they were also bloody, cut, swollen, and bruised. Nothing seemed to be broken.

Grimme and his villeins continued to calmly discuss the fight and its particulars.

Finally, Grimme said, "Is everyone happy now?"

"*No!*" cried Pierce, who hopped up, his tears immediately dry. He went over to Gaston and kicked him in the bollocks.

The entire huddle of men groaned, flinched, and clamped their knees together whilst Gaston screamed in pain.

Gaston rolled over in sobs and curled up to protect himself from a five-year-old's kicks, wailing, "Papa! Papa!"

Pierce was ready to go again, and Terrwyn not soon after, who went after Max.

After a while, Pierce slowed down, then stopped when he started limping around panting. Gaston and Max were still curled up sobbing and crying, "Papa!"

Terrwyn also finally stopped raining clumsy punches down on Max's head, then kicked Gaston for good measure and flopped to the ground on his back, splayed out to pant and rest. Pierce joined him.

The villeins cackled and collected their bets, bid Grimme a respectful "my lord," and faded away.

"Gaston," Grimme finally rumbled once the two older boys' weeping had subsided to hiccups. "Max. Get up."

They slowly, painfully, lumbered to their feet and then trod to him for comfort, but Grimme stepped away and they stumbled. They looked up at him shock and confusion.

"Mayhap that will teach you not to start battles you can't win. Terrwyn, Pierce. Up. Back to the stable. We have a lot of work to do."

27

BRÌGHDE SUPERVISED the loading of her linens and livery, which was a true count according to the bill Sir John had received. Furthermore, she had all the clothing she had ordered. She beamed at the seamstress, for the clothes were well sewn and softer than they looked.

"'Tis too plain for you, my lady," the seamstress said. "You should be in green or black velvet."

"Oh, I will be!" she assured her. "I ordered many new gowns in Hogarth. Only one black, but don't tell Lord Kyneward. He hates black. But the clothier *tried* to sell me *yellow*, do you believe." The seamstress studied Brìghde's complexion then grimaced, and Brìghde nodded in agreement. "Just so. 'Twas the most expensive cloth in the shop, which is no surprise. My wedding dress was a red split kirtle over an azure skirt."

"Oh, that sounds lovely."

She sent the cart back to Kyneward with all her purchases, then she pulled the seamstress aside and whispered sweetly, "If you *ever* attempt to cheat me again, I will burn down everything you hold dear. Make sure every merchant in one hundred miles in every direction knows I will destroy anyone who attempts it."

The seamstress dropped to her knees, sobbing and begging, pulling at her skirts, pleading and apologizing.

"And now we will act and converse and conduct much business together as if this never happened, aye?" Brìghde said brightly, practically dragging the woman to her feet.

"Aye, my lady," she sobbed. "Aye. Thank you, my lady."

Brìghde next attended the cobbler, who afforded her *four* new pairs of boots where she had only ordered one out of merchant credit. Brìghde exclaimed over the workmanship and gave him a sweet smile. "We understand each other now, do we not?"

"Aye, my lady," he said nervously.

"You may be assured of Kyneward's continued patronage."

"Thank you, my lady."

The only tradesperson in Waters who had *not* puffed up his bills to Kyneward was the blacksmith, from whom she bought daggers for the boys, and requested small swords of metal be fashioned.

"Oh, my lady, I already have some," he said, surprised. "The pages at Kyneward need them. I thought the boys would already have their own."

"They don't," Brìghde said flatly. "There are many changes afoot at Kyneward now that I am in charge."

The corner of the big man's mouth curled up and he winked. "Are there now?"

She grinned and leaned in. "Oh, aye, there are."

He lost his humor, looked away, tapped his fingers on his anvil, and twisted his mouth.

"Speak freely."

He looked at her warily.

She sighed with irritation. "I cannot repair it if I do not know."

He sucked in a breath. "You have made it clear you know about the bills the merchants here send to Kyneward."

Brìghde was surprised he would approach it so bluntly, but was careful to keep her expression calmly interested and she nodded.

"There is a reason for that, my lady. The mistresses. They come here to shop. They do not pay in coin, and they do not seem to give Sir John their bills. If they did, he would pay them. The other bills are higher to account for what the mistresses take but have not paid for."

Brìghde's jaw dropped on the floor and her eyes widened. Her hand went to her breast. "On the sweet Virgin Mary," she breathed.

"The merchants asked me to deliver ye this news, as the mistresses have not cheated *me*, and thus I have had no reason to attempt to reclaim the loss."

"Why did you not go to Sir John? Or send a duplicate bill for what they took? You know he would not cheat you."

He shrugged. "The merchants are very angry, my lady. 'Twas easier to manage this way, and, well, aye, the overages *may* have gotten a little out of hand." He paused at Brìghde's flat look. "*Very* out of hand."

"What about Lord Kyneward?"

"He does not ... " The blacksmith considered his words very carefully. "Ah, that is to say—"

"Aye, I know," she snorted. "He doesn't get involved in household business."

"Aye. And there is no estate court. Even if there were, we could not find a lawyer, must less pay for one."

"There is now, but 'twill not come to that, as I will deal with this. Tell every merchant in this village to sum what the mistresses have taken, to subtract the overage Sir John has paid, and to account for whatever merchant credit I have assumed today, and if Kyneward still owes them, I will pay it *personally,* and I will forgive what is owed Kyneward. I want a *true* accounting, though. I will not cheat you if you do not cheat me. Mayhap— Oh, I know! I shall call a meeting to reconcile."

"We would appreciate that, my lady."

"*No one* is to *ever* serve the mistresses again if they have not the coin to pay in full."

He bowed deeply. "Aye, my lady. Thank you. Now, about those swords for the young masters … "

Hugging four boy-sized swords and matching daggers to her breast and feeling very proud of herself, she strode to the livery, where Grimme and his boys were getting along magnificently, Gaston helping Terrwyn and Max assisting Pierce where their heights made the difference in the task. But as she watched, she noticed that they were all moving very slowly and painfully and groaning. Then the swords slipped from her grasp and fell in a crash, startling everyone, even the horses.

"Sorry!" she called and crouched to pick them all up.

"What's this, Wife?" Grimme said as he strode to her.

"The boys need swords of metal, and daggers too."

His eyebrows flew up into his golden-red hair and she smiled. "You thought of my sons whilst you were out?"

"We are here today for them, are we not?" she asked softly.

His expression faded to confused wonderment. "Aye," he said vaguely, looking at them from across the stable. "Aye we are. Boys, come see what Lady Brìghde has brought you."

She gasped at the sight of them. Their lips were fat and bloody. Their faces were covered in bruises. There were tiny crusts of blood around their noses. Their arms were also bruised and they were limping. Slowly. Gaston seemed as if he could barely breathe and he was clutching his side. He was also waddling just the tiniest bit. Brìghde had six brothers. She knew why he was waddling.

As they stood in front of her, weary, bleary-eyed, aching, and listless, she pulled her lips between her teeth. She looked at Grimme, who could barely keep from laughing.

She looked back at the boys because Grimme was going to make her laugh if she looked at him much longer, put her hand over her mouth, and said, "Oh my."

"I!—won!" Pierce barked, glaring at Gaston.

"Me too!" Terrwyn chirped.

"Well! Maybe you four need not have daggers and swords after all. I doubt your mothers would appreciate your killing each other."

"I *hate* their mother!" Pierce screamed.

"We hate yours too!" Max returned.

Gaston glared at Brìghde. "We hate *you* too."

"I don't care."

He looked puzzled.

"Gaston," Grimme growled. "Do not *ever* speak to her that way again."

"Oh, no, he may," Brìghde said matter-of-factly. "That way I know what their mother is telling them."

Grimme looked at her strangely.

"Well, *I* have been perfectly reasonable and have been willing to give them what they want, but their mother is keeping it from them. Their hatred has to come from *somewhere*."

"You made Papa send us to the stables to work."

"No, she did not," Grimme snarled, making Gaston's eyes go wide with fear. "Now. Do you want the swords and daggers *Lady Brìghde* bought for you or not?"

"Aye, Papa," Gaston and Max whispered, cowed.

Terrwyn and Pierce snickered, but that, too, earned a glare from their father. It did *not* keep them from continuing to snicker, much less cow them.

Brìghde thought it was all entirely appropriate, with the appropriate responses, and she was pleased. "Hm. Grimme?"

"Aye, parcel them out. They'll need them tomorrow on the fields."

They all gaped up at Grimme. "All except Pierce." He looked at Gaston and Max and said pointedly, "He's too young."

They looked like they were about to cry.

"I will assign you each to a knight so that you may begin your instruction. I cannot send you out to another knight anywhere in England or France at your ages to be trained from anew. 'Tis shameful, a ten-year-old and a nine-year-old not knowing the most basic of tasks, unable to ride, unable to take a five-year-old and a seven-year-old in a fight, *crying* and *wailing* like babies."

Tears sparkled in their eyes.

"Grimme," Brìghde said firmly. "'Tis not their fault."

"Aye, 'tis mine," he replied, gently placing one hand each on Gaston's and Max's heads and squeezing very lightly, then stroking down their backs to rub them, pressing them to his body.

"But Papa, I hurt," Max whinged.

"You will be hurting for the next several years. Accustom yourselves to it. Enjoy your chambers and your mothers and your meals tonight, because by sundown tomorrow, you will be sleeping in the encampment with your knights. Now, collect your weapons Lady Brìghde has bought for you."

They started digging in the pile before she could catch them.

"No, no, no, no, no, no!" Brìghde cried as she shooed them away. "They each have your initials on them so you do not mix them up." She picked up a sword and looked at the end of the pommel. "Gaston." She checked the daggers and gave him his. "Terrwyn." And so forth until all the boys had their own swords and daggers. She took Grimme's hand when he offered it to assist her to her feet. She looked up at Grimme. "He did not have scabbards," she apologized.

"We will get those in Hogarth," he murmured, looking down at her with an uncertain expression.

Brìghde then wondered if she had offended him. "Are you … angry with me?"

His face cleared. "Nay," he hastened to assure her, bringing her hands to his lips for a kiss. She nearly melted in relief. "I simply— I had not thought— Their mothers—"

Brìghde's mouth flattened and she turned away, clutching Grimme's hands and swinging him around with her. "Your women," she hissed, "have been stealing from the merchants. *That* is why the bills are so puffed up."

His eyes widened.

"I have taken care of the situation with the merchants and hopefully have established some goodwill and trust. I have instructed the merchants to let them take *nothing* they cannot pay for with coin, and I suspect that the only reason Hogarth's merchants were not doing so is because they did not want to spend the coin or time to ride forty miles to deliver duplicate bills. I want access to your women's chambers to take an inventory—"

His mouth dropped open.

"—*before* I allow them any more coin at all."

"Brìghde!" he whispered harshly, his eyes wide, "I won't order that."

"I have the keys to the keep," she growled. "And I will not tolerate such behavior. If you do not rein your women in, *I* will, and *no one* is going to be happy. What are you afraid of? That they will deny you their cuntes? Ha! Hardly. That seems to be their *sole purpose*."

His eyes narrowed throughout her speech. "Brìghde—"

She pointed at him and whispered hotly, "No. For too long you have set aside your responsibility to your father and to your sons because you do not want to face your women, and the proof is that you said *nothing* to them about the bills from Hogarth. They didn't give them to Sir John because they didn't want to be subject to his anger that they didn't ask first because they knew he'd refuse them coin, *and* he would not allow them to go to Hogarth again. Yet all he can do is rage. He has no power to do anything the way it should be done because you will not give it to him. I am here to do what you will not do because I will *take* the power whether you want me to or not. If I have to lock them in the donjon whilst I take inventory of their chambers, by all that is holy, I will do it."

He stared at her, his nostrils flaring, his chest heaving, but she would not look away.

"Our bargain," she said low, "was that you would enforce my position as castellain in return for a legitimate heir and a spare, and you could get sixteen daughters out of me before you get one son, and women *die* in childbirth, you ken! You do not fulfill your part, I do not fulfill my part. All you have to do is *stay out of my way* and pay the bills."

"They will come to me endlessly!" he hissed.

She rocked back on one heel, crossed her arms over her chest, and gave him a dead stare, her jaw grinding.

He closed his eyes and took a deep breath. "Very well. I will order their chambers opened for inventory *only*. Do *not* take anything."

She growled, and he held his hands up in apology. "I can see why you were dismissed," he grumbled.

She grinned. "And if they don't comply or get in my way or otherwise make it more difficult than it has to be?"

He looked over his shoulder at his sons, who were each off on their own admiring their swords and daggers instead of clanging away at each other. He looked back at her and sighed. "Put them in the donjon."

28

THE SCREAMING commenced as soon as the six of them were spotted rounding the turn into the lane that led to the keep just after suppertime. At first it was faint, but got sharper as it grew nearer.

The boys were slumped in their saddles, half asleep, more than ready to let their ponies carry them without direction and simply hold on to pommels and manes.

Grimme and Brìghde were leading the ponies from horseback, and *their* horses hadn't had a good run all day so they were antsy and irritated, dancing and prancing and pawing. Grimme could almost see the ponies rolling their eyes.

Emelisse ran almost all the way down the lane, and if Grimme thought the screaming was intolerable then, when she got a good look at the boys—

"Emelisse!" he barked.

She didn't hear him, sobbing over Gaston, hugging him as they plodded along. "Come, come!" she wailed in French. "Off that beast. We'll get you into a nice hot bath—Max!" Grimme looked over his shoulder at Gaston with a stony expression *daring* him to submit to his mother's coddling when that was *exactly* what he wanted to do. He wanted to cry in Emelisse's lap whilst she rocked him and told him how evil Brìghde was and this was all her fault.

Gaston, cowed, said, "I'm well, Mamá."

"You are *not* well! I *knew* I should never have allowed you to go! Max! My love!"

Grimme turned the same look upon Max, who also reluctantly rebuffed his mother, staring at Grimme the whole time.

That was when Emelisse got a good look at Pierce and Terrwyn. She gasped and ran in front of Grimme and Brìghde to walk backward and scream at Grimme in French. "How could you allow this?! Were you not paying attention? I trusted you! You were off fucking *her*, weren't you? Leaving my babies alone with those two little *monsters*!"

He rolled his eyes as villeins gathered to watch this. Dillena came running down the lane whilst Emelisse threw obscenities at him and Brìghde. It was a good thing Brìghde and the villeins, who were gathering in great numbers now, didn't speak French. As Dillena came closer and saw Terrwyn, she began to grow angry, and would continue to be once Grimme told her Terrwyn would be going out to the field. She wouldn't like it, but at least she was sensible enough to understand that this was the way of noble sons.

"What— What *happened?!*" Dillena breathed as she went to Terrwyn and inspected his injuries.

Emelisse stopped walking, bringing everyone to a halt. "*Your* monster did this to *my* babies!" Emelisse screamed.

"And look what yours did to mine!" Dillena screamed in return, in French.

"He's less bruised than mine are!"

"Which only means that yours are weak! Good boy, Terrwyn!" Grimme almost laughed.

Emelisse released an ear-shattering scream of pure rage. "I *hate* you! You took Grimme away from me!"

"If *you* gave Lord Grimme what he wants, he wouldn't need *me!*" And Dillena was the *quiet* one.

Bloody hell. Grimme didn't know what to do or say. He was in the middle of a war he didn't want to be in, but he was having a very hard time keeping a straight face. Suddenly he remembered Brìghde's hoots when he told her his women got along—and that was *before* she met them.

It was a *very* good thing Brìghde and the villeins couldn't speak French.

The argument between the women escalated into which acts Emelisse would and would not perform for Grimme, Dillena neatly outwitting her on every point.

He wondered if he should allow them to come to blows right here, in front of his people, the way he had allowed the boys to do. He bowed his head and rubbed his temples.

Sadly, it took him quite a while to notice that Maebh was nowhere to be found, but as soon as he did, anger shot through him. He did not care about the battle raging between his first and third mistresses whilst the whole of Kyneward watched with barely disguised glee. He cared that the victor got no welcome home, no loving mother, no one to fuss over his wounds.

He twisted to look back at Pierce, who sat with an expression of utter resentment, looking to the portcullis to see if his mother would come. Brìghde turned to see what Grimme was staring at and he supposed she saw the same thing he did, because she looked back at Grimme and solemnly nodded, as if she knew what he was thinking and would do whatever she felt needed to be done. Mayhap she did.

Emelisse was still screaming, but it was weaker now that she had screamed her throat raw.

Then, apparently realizing that Dillena was not going to be cowed, and not going to lose the argument, Emelisse turned on Grimme and Brìghde, and jabbed a finger at Brìghde. "It's *her!*"

Grimme pursed his lips and nodded slowly.

"Choose, Grimme!" she snarled. "Her or *me.*"

"Her," he said immediately.

Emelisse gaped at him and Dillena chortled.

"Recant your demand and I will forget you ever said it," he said calmly. "Take the boys. Both of you. Give them their hot bath and their meals in their rooms and all the smothering you can give them because tomorrow they go into the field and they will not come home until their knights give them leave."

"What?!" Dillena breathed, aghast. "But—"

"He's seven," Grimme told Dillena gently, "and he won the fight against his older and bigger brothers. It's time."

She gulped, tears in her eyes whilst Emelisse stood heartsick in front of him.

"The only thing I apologize for," he said, "is not taking them in hand sooner. Emelisse, I have allowed you to baby them too long, so much that boys smaller and younger defeated them." Gaston and Max began to weep quietly again, but Grimme was ashamed. Ashamed that a knight of his caliber had set aside his duty to his sons because he didn't want to hear their mothers' complaints and let them do what they wanted. He tilted his head toward the boys and said, "Go on. Take them. Because after breakfast tomorrow, they come with me and you will not see them again for a long time."

Dillena and Emelisse scurried to get their sons. Grimme twisted to see Dillena merely assist Terrwyn off the horse and brace him so he could walk his soreness off. Emelisse dragged Gaston off his pony and held him to her like a baby, his arms and legs wrapped around her, whilst she twisted and rocked and stroked and cried. Gaston was big, but she could do it, which meant she had a lot of practice. But Gaston caught Grimme's look and he squiggled down. She went to Max and did the same thing. He too wormed his way out of her arms. She took their hands and began to march them up the lane, but they resisted.

"We have to take care of our ponies, Mamá," Max muttered, looking at the ground. Terrwyn and Gaston nodded in resignation.

Now *that* surprised Grimme and he smiled. "Well done, my sons," he said immediately. They peeked up at him, then looked away in relief, but Gaston and Max were still discomfited that they had defied their mother and now she was pleading with them to allow her to take care of them.

Then Emelisse turned on Brìghde. "It's *you!*" she raged hoarsely, in English now.

Brìghde nodded matter-of-factly and said, "Aye, 'tis me."

"You have hated me and my sons from the beginning because you're jealous! You want *my* husband!"

"I don't care about you or your sons enough to hate you," she said in a bored tone, but curiously, did not refute Emelisse's assertion that he was Emelisse's husband. It irritated him, but if Brìghde didn't care, why should he? Then she chirruped to Troy, wheeled him around and took off into the fields for a well-deserved gallop.

Grimme watched her go, wishing he could go with her, particularly since Phobos was just as restless and wanted to follow Troy. He looked at Emelisse, who was shocked. "Recant, or I will never visit you again."

She started to sob. "Grimme!"

"Boys, take your ponies to the stables and groom them as I showed you." The three whose mothers had come to save them walked slowly and painfully, leading their ponies.

Pierce chirruped his and trotted on by. He was clumsy about it, but he rode out of sight long before his brothers disappeared. Father Hercule was right: Pierce did indeed seem to have a penchant for ruthlessness.

Grimme waited until they were out of sight, then dismounted and gathered both his women to him, kissing each of them on the temple. The reins in his hands, he walked the weeping women back to the keep.

Ordering the inventory would have to wait.

29

"PIERCE?"

Brìghde knocked on his door, but he didn't answer. She opened it softly, and crept into his chambers to find him fast asleep on his bed, still in his filthy clothes. He had refused to stay for supper, though Grimme commanded that the others do so. Pierce had not eaten from the tray Brìghde had had sent up.

She sighed and turned to creep out quietly again.

"Lady Brìghde?" he said softly.

"Aye," she said, rushing to the bed and sitting upon it, stroking his hair and battered face.

"I won."

"I know. I'm verra proud of you."

He turned his head and looked at her as if she were mad. "You are?"

"I've a hot bath awaiting you in my chambers, and you can tell me *all* about it. Every detail."

His eyes flew open wide. "Do you mean that?"

"I do. I don't know if your father told you, but I have six brothers. We used to get into scraps like this all the time. Once 'tis over, all the anger is gone and you can be friends."

"I'm still angry," he muttered.

"Sometimes it takes two scraps," she conceded. "Mayhap three. Come, come! I will bring your food. And I have a surprise for you, but you *must not* tell your brothers."

He was curious enough that he climbed off the bed, moving like his grandfather, and left, Brìghde following with his tray. She bumped the door of her chambers open with her hip and set the tray down, then pointed to the bath. "I shall turn my back so you can get undressed and hop in." Once the water stopped splashing, she gave him a glass. "Mead." And willow bark.

He grimaced at the bitterness of the willow bark, but drank it anyway. She filled his cup again, drew up a stool and put the pitcher on it. Then she went to her parcels and found his treat.

"Look," she said, placing it on the stool. "A cake."

He gasped softly, a small smile forming, but then fading likely because it hurt.

"Now," she said breathlessly as she lay on her bed, "tell me *everything*."

He started with excitement, but after innumerable *And then I*s, interrupted by eating, he had run down, the water was cold, and he was almost asleep. She ran across the hall and asked Hamond if he would fetch his mother to tend him.

"All pardons, my lady, but I believe Lord Kyneward would rather do that himself."

"Oh!" she said, surprised. "Fetch him, then."

Grimme, rumpled, barely dressed, gave her only the slightest glance when he entered her chambers and shook the boy awake. "Time for the conqueror to go to bed," he said gently, taking him out of the tub, drying him off, and dressing him. The boy was so tired and sore he could barely stand.

"Papa, I won."

"Well done, my son."

"Aye?"

"In any battle, there can be only one conqueror, and today you are it."

With that, Grimme swept his wee conqueror up in his arms and left.

Brìghde heaved a sigh of relief. Laddies.

Soon enough, Avis had her chambers put to rights again and Brìghde was in the middle of changing when Grimme trudged in and softly closed the door.

She was naked, holding her shift in her hand, and gaping at him. "Grimme!"

He looked at her oddly and said, "Stand up straight."

She did, slowly, her heart beginning to race, her breath coming faster, her lower body tingling and swirling, then settling between her legs.

Kiss me.

"Grimme—"

"You're my wife," he said harshly. "Turn around."

She did, slowly, dropping her kirtle to hold her arms out so he could see all of her.

"Come here."

She approached him and he swept his hand down her body a hair's breadth away from her skin without touching her.

Touch me.

He cupped her breast, her nipple hardening with delicious pain, and it was all she could do to hide her sudden and intense longing for him to do more.

He thumbed her rock-hard nipple, seeming to over-concentrate.

Swive me.

His gaze went to her right arm, then stopped. His hand left her breast and lifted a lock of her hair. He rubbed it in his fingers, studied it, clenched his jaw.

He looked very, very unhappy.

His mouth twisted, he dropped her hair, turned around, and walked out.

GRIMME STOPPED as soon as he reached his chambers and thunked his head back on the door.

"My lord?"

"Is there … *something* that can make a man rise when his mind is eager, but his cod refuses to cooperate?"

Hamond hesitated. "There … might be … someone I could ask."

"Find it," he said, frustrated beyond belief. "Find it before I am driven to lunacy."

30

THEY DID NOT take his order to open their chambers well.

After gathering his mistresses in his chambers the next morning, he paced in front of them, his hands behind his back, and barked,

"This is not up for discussion! You cannot *imagine* how embarrassed I was to be told our bills had not been paid, and in front of *my wife!* Why could you not have simply given the bills to Sir John?"

"He would snap at us," Emelisse hissed, "and I do not like being snapped at by that—"

Grimme turned a stony glance on her that quelled her immediately. "You do remember who helped us through our first years together, do you not?" he murmured threateningly.

She gulped.

"If you refuse to do anything useful, at least be grateful to the hand that feeds you." She looked away. "We understand each other, then. So now. Let us discuss our children. You—" He pointed at Emelisse. "—have kept the boys penned up and made them angry at the younger two for their freedoms. You do not allow them to attend their studies, so they are practically illiterate. You—" He pointed to Dillena. "—have made Terrwyn angry that you do not give him as much attention as Emelisse gives Gaston and Max, nor as much freedom as Maebh gives Pierce, and you do not enforce my order to tend to his studies."

"That is not true," she said with angry dignity, "but I refuse to discuss that with you here and now."

"Hrmph. And you—" He pointed to Maebh. "I'm furious with you. Did you know that Pierce *walked* to Waters and back *by himself?*"

All four of them gasped, and Maebh went white.

"Ten miles. On foot. A five-year-old. Alone. He would only admit to having done it once, but I have my doubts. You have completely ignored him. *They*—" he said, swiping his finger from Emelisse and Dillena, "met their sons when we came home and fussed over them. Pierce won the fight, but *his* mother was nowhere to be found. He should have ridden in the victor, but he was completely forgotten."

Maebh had the grace to flush and look away.

"Then! There are their studies! They are *my* sons and no son of *mine*, bastard or not, will I allow to grow up as illiterate wastrels." He looked at Emelisse. "They are not babies and I am tired of them acting that way. *Crying* and *wailing* that their younger, smaller brothers won the fight."

"This is *her* fault!" Emelisse screamed, hopping to her feet and pointing her finger in his face. He slapped it away. He tolerated that from Brìghde because she was his friend, gave good advice, and had thus far not led him astray, but he would *not* tolerate it from his women. "*She* has been here not even a month and has caused utter chaos!"

"No!" he snapped. "She has *revealed* it. I will allow her to repair it and to do that, she must have free rein, which I have given her. You *will* submit to her orders."

"There is something about her," Emelisse hissed, "something you want, something you're drawn to."

"Aye, there is," he sneered. "Her mind, her willingness to work, and her *womb*."

"And her nobility!"

"That too," he agreed.

"You have never met a woman you either did or did not want to bed. You bed the ones you do, and ignore the ones you don't. You do not bed her, but you *certainly* do not ignore her."

"That's true," Ardith said matter-of-factly.

The other two nodded, though they were not upset.

Grimme closed his eyes and rubbed the bridge of his nose. "She is my wife, which is an entirely different circumstance altogether. We are all treading into the unknown together, including her." He opened his eyes and swept his finger across the four of them. "*All* of us. I want her to be happy here because it will make *all* our lives easier. At the moment, I am being a welcoming and gracious host."

"'*Welcoming and gracious host?!*'" Emelisse hooted. "You spend more time with her than you do all of us put together, and you would jump into the trusses if she snapped her fingers!"

"Also true," Ardith once again volunteered, with the other two agreeing.

"She tells you to take our sons away from us. You do. You get up early from a long night of fucking three women—"

"Four," Maebh said helpfully.

Emelisse snarled at Maebh, who pointedly yawned.

"—*four* women to take *her* to Hogarth. She goes alone because you changed your mind for some reason. You drop everything to marshal a force and chase after her. She tells you to let our sons fight to the death." Grimme snorted. "You do. She tells you to throw open our doors for her inspection, and you do that too! You are a *nettle*, clinging to her skirt, unable to be plucked off."

Grimme ignored that. "When she is more settled, I will leave her to her business and she will leave me to mine, which is to go back to France with Henry. Until she gets everything running smoothly, *her* business is *my* business and, since *you* are my business, you are now *her* business too. Cooperate, and she will be courteous. Do not cooperate, and she will get cruel."

"And you will *allow* that?!" Emelisse screeched.

He narrowed his eyes at her. "If this demonstration is anything to go by, I may allow her to *keep* you in the donjon as long as she wants."

"If you do," she snarled, "you will *never* have my cunte again."

He laughed and pointed to the other three. "Aye, I will. And the three maidservants who look like you, as well."

She bent over at the waist and released a blood-curdling scream. "I *hate* you for that!"

"Emelisse," he said archly, "that is the *second* time in as many days that you have threatened me with that. One day you will wake up and realize that I have complied. If you hate me that much, you are welcome to go back to France with everything I have ever given you. I will give you the funds to last you the rest of your life in some comfort, so long as you shepherd it carefully, which I doubt you know how to do."

"I want my sons back!"

"No." He raised an eyebrow. "Stay and obey, or go and be free of me and Brìghde."

"You *said*," she hissed, "that I would not have to obey her."

"I *said* that I could not imagine what order she could give you. Now I can and I know why and I agree. You *will* obey her. Make a decision."

Furious, she crossed her arms over her chest and flopped in her chair.

"Do we understand each other?" Grimme looked at each of them in turn until they acquiesced with varying expressions, none of them good.

"When does she take count?" Dillena asked with quiet dignity. She did everything with quiet dignity—except fuck.

"She will tell you." He looked around at them. "Do not force me to involve myself between you and her again. The boys are gone, assigned to knights far out in the encampment where I have no reason to go, much less you. Emelisse, if I catch you riding out there to see them or take them treats or abduct them home, I will turn you over my knee. Dillena, I understand you will miss Terrwyn, but you know this is the proper thing to do."

"Aye," she muttered.

"Maebh, I dare say you would hand Pierce over to Brìghde with a smile, aye?"

"Not with a smile," she returned, entirely serious.

"What does that mean?"

She shrugged. "You think I don't pay attention, but I do. I give him everything he wants—"

"You give him what you *think* he wants."

"I *try*!" she snapped.

"He *wants* your attention."

"What do you say to a child?" she demanded. "What conversation is there to be had?"

Maebh wasn't a conversationalist.

"He's *five*. All you have to do is fuss over him a little and make sure he won't walk ten miles by himself."

"He wants her," she said doggedly. "She makes him happy and I want to make my baby happy. I don't know how to do that. *She—does*. Clearly she has a gift for rearing boys and I don't. *None* of us do." Emelisse opened her mouth but Maebh pointed at her and snarled. "Shut up. You are cruel to my baby and your brats torment him endlessly and I have told you before to stop and make them stop, but they only get worse. You encourage it and *their father*," she sneered at Grimme, who stayed silent because he deserved it, "doesn't want to hear it. I cannot protect him from you, Lord Grimme *won't*, but *she* can. *She* won't put up with you *or* your little monsters because *she doesn't have to!*"

"*My* monsters?!" she shrieked. "*Yours* terrified and humiliated mine yesterday in front of an entire town!"

"He's five and he beat your ten-year-old!" Maebh sneered. "I'm proud of him."

"It needed to happen," Dillena added serenely.

Grimme's eyebrows rose.

He let this go on for quite a while, as he was now fully immersed in his sons' upbringing and he needed to know what he had never cared about before. He was ashamed of that, ashamed it took a twenty-two-year-old abducted virgin all of two days to see it, know what needed to be done, and risk a new friendship to correct it. But of course she would know how to rear boys. She had six brothers and had worked as a nursemaid, which he respected far more than he respected any of these women, mothers of his children or not.

When they started repeating themselves, he said, "Silence."

There was silence. Except for Maebh. Of course. "If he hates me for drawing away from him, but he's happier with her, I will have no regrets."

Mayhap he had severely misjudged the mother of his youngest son. "I've never known you to demonstrate such selflessness."

She snarled at him, and he decided to think about that later, as that was, indeed, one of the most selfless acts he could imagine.

"Cooperate with Brìghde—and I will order her to be nice—and you will have no problems. Ignore her the rest of the time, and she will ignore you. But remember this: *She* does not want to bed me any more than I want to bed her, so you do not have to fear her. No, Emelisse, I was *not* off fucking her whilst the boys were fighting. I was right there, watching with half the townsmen whilst *she* was off buying them weapons."

She gasped. "*Weapons?!* I don't want them to have weapons!"

"And that is part of my quibble with you. They *should* have weapons, and you took away the toy ones I gave them, which makes me furious."

Her face was flushed. Her jaw was clenched. Her eyes were narrowed.

"To your other point: I fuck *you*."

"*All* of us," Emelisse snarled.

Grimme spread his hands. "I cannot help my appetite. If any *one* of you could sate me, I would not need the rest of you. I will not control it if I don't have to, and I don't have to because I am the earl. I want what I want, and what I want is my house filled with women I can fuck anytime, anywhere, any way I want as many times as I want."

Grimme looked at Emelisse expectantly.

She huffed. "But not *her*."

"Not her," he said flatly. "Until I can force myself to it, and you—" He pointed between Ardith and Maebh. "—will have to sit in a corner where I can watch *you* fuck so I can get my cod in her. Unless my chamberlain finds me some magic potion."

"Can I have a go at her?" Maebh asked brightly.

"Maebh!" Ardith cried, slapping her arm.

"Ow! What? She's pretty and I like her bubs."

Emelisse huffed in utter disgust.

"You may not fuck my wife."

"But her *bubs!*"

"They are very nice," Grimme agreed, "but you have the pick of every wench in this entire keep. You can't have mine."

"But—"

"Why don't you allow her to choose a lover and have his child?" Dillena asked quietly, logically. "No one would ever have to know."

"That's what I said!" Emelisse said with excitement.

"While that is an excellent idea, I am not rearing some other man's by-blow. Unless one of *you* has another child and I can pass it off as *hers*. I could accept that solution."

He looked directly at Emelisse, who flushed and looked away. The others were silent.

"Mmm hm," he hummed smugly. "Don't be careless. If any one of you catches ever again, it's Brìghde's."

"Why can I not have her?" Maebh demanded. "I can't get her with child. Oh, I know! I could swive her whilst you watch and 'twould be enough for you to get it in her. She will lie flat, I will lie atop her. You put your cod in her and pretend it's me!"

"*Maebh!*" Ardith cried again, louder this time.

"*Also* an excellent idea," he said firmly, "but no. Don't ask again. Now. When you pray, if you do, beg for her easy fertility toward boys so I don't have to think about this anymore. Dismissed. Not you, Emelisse."

When they were finally alone, Grimme loomed over her. "If I ever hear of," he whispered threateningly, "or catch you treating Terrwyn and Pierce with anything less than perfect courtesy, I will beat your arse so hard you won't be able to sit down for a week."

Her face went white and her eyes widened. She gulped.

"They are *my* sons and you have no right to them."

She gathered herself and hissed, "Then mayhap you should not drop them on my head after fucking their mothers all night. As they are *your* sons, don't expect me to look after them."

Grimme drew himself up. "You're right," he said quietly.

That surprised her.

"The reason I changed my mind about going to Hogarth with Brìghde was because she chided me for expecting you to take charge of them when I'd kept their mothers up all night long."

She looked stunned.

"She advocated on your behalf. In fact, was quite horrified on your behalf, and I was furious with her, but she was right. I apologize for asking you to do that. I now understand some of your frustration and anger."

"Uh … oh."

"But my warning stands. You are free to ignore the boys, but do not be cruel to them. Do you understand?"

"Oui."

"Dismissed."

31

GRIMME SLID Brìghde a stony look at supper when she raised her eyebrow in question. "Well?"

"'Tis done, but do not make me do that again."

Then she smiled sweetly at him and fluttered her eyelashes.

He dropped his head and started to laugh.

"Have some wine," she said playfully and filled his goblet from the pitcher sitting in front of her. "Ye're more amusin' with a few goblets in ye."

"You have a *pitcher* now?" he asked incredulously, noting that her brogue was quite thick, which made him wonder how much she'd had to drink.

She looked in the pitcher, poured the rest into her cup, and signaled the servant for another, which was promptly placed in front of her. "Walter," she said archly, "once said he could outdrink me three to one an' still work as if he had not drunk at all. He couldn't, an' me moom ridiculed him endlessly fer it. He didn't speak to me fer a month. That was a wonderful month."

Grimme closed his eyes and shook his head. "Why has he not put you in the ground? Or your mother, for that fact?"

"Hrmph." Her emerald eyes darkened and she stuck a piece of meat in her mouth. "I'm nae sure," she muttered after she'd washed it down with an entire goblet full of wine. Then she poured another. Drank that. And a third. "He once accused me o' bein' a spawn o' Satan. Then he sent me flyin' 'cross the room wi'the back of 'is hand."

Spawn of Satan. Grimme's chest tightened a little, but this time he was careful not to show his discomfort. He wasn't sure what his father had said to her, but clearly she knew that any talk of witchcraft or Satanic things unnerved him. "Is that why it was important to you to fall in with his plan to destroy MacFhionnlaigh whether you wanted to or not?"

She nodded hesitantly and wouldn't look at him. Her mouth was turned down in a frown and she was suddenly picking at her food. Another glass, down her throat.

"What did you do that he accused you of such?" Grimme asked carefully.

"I dinna *do* anythin'," she muttered. "Me brothers had all gone off to different knights, so they'd nae been there to serve as a shield fer me. Moom was bedevilin' him over somethin', I walked into the room, he turned 'round, there I was, he accused her o' bearin' some other man's bastard because he couldna possibly ha'e spawned somethin' so ugly as me, she screamed back that she had to bear another man's bastard so I wouldna be as ugly as *him*, an' then he slapped me. I landed in the hearth. He said, 'I am sorry, Brìghde.' I said, 'Very well, Walter.' He said, 'I am sorry there was no fire there.' 'Twasn't the first time, but it *was* the last."

"Brìghde," he said softly, covering her hand. "You are *not* ugly."

"I know that!" she snapped and snatched her hand out from under his. "Do ye know how many men woulda been glad to wed me, who'd treat me well, mayhap even *love* me?" Her lip curled in contempt. "Mayhap touch me and not run away as if I were a leprosy-befouled *witch*. Were ye afraid I'd raise me hellhound from the dead to attack ye?"

His breath caught and he looked away, his jaw tight, only to catch his father's dead stare. He turned back to her and met her contemptuous glare and murmured, "I'm sorry. I … " He did not want to admit this, but he owed her an explanation. "I was embarrassed."

"Aye, and so was I," she drawled hatefully, then continued airily with another goblet down her throat. Oh. Her father wasn't why she was drunk. *Grimme* was.

"How much have you had to drink?"

"Not. Enough," she said stoutly.

He decided to leave that alone.

"Alas, I was already betrothed an' couldna be courted properly by a proper man who'd take me to wife properly." She put her elbow on the table and her cheek on her fist whilst she used her knife to stab at her food as if 'twere an unwelcome suitor. "I woulda liked that," she said wistfully, her eyes sparkling with tears. "Verra much." Then she reached for her pitcher, poured another glass of wine, and gulped that down, too. "Me grandmoom was a bonny lass," she muttered. "We have a portrait. Me moom— She is also. Walter, now," she said, her brogue now so thick he could barely understand her, "*he* is uglier than a deerhound."

Grimme would have laughed if he weren't stinging from both his failure and her contempt.

"Ha'e ye e'er seen one? They're *ugly*. Me Mercury is beyond ugly, but I love 'im." She paused to pour more wine, but the pitcher was, once again, empty. She held it up and waggled it for a servant to pass by and take it, then replace it with a full one. "My God, this wine is bonny," she sighed in ecstasy as she sipped at her next glass.

"And your mother? You said she rules the household. How does she do it when he is in disagreement with her decisions?"

"I tole ye she must ha'e somethin' keepin' him on a leash."

"What did she do when he sent you into the hearth?"

Brìghde began telling a story, her hands gesturing, but he couldn't understand a word.

"Speak English."

"That *was* English," she said with exaggerated enunciation.

He took the almost-empty pitcher and casually handed it to his father. "What did your mother do?" he asked again.

"She threw a poker into 'is shoulder like a spear. Whoosh! Straight through. 'Twas magnificent. His sword arm, too."

Grimme was shocked. "How long ago was that?" he asked low.

"Three years. She'n'I could take MacFhionnlaigh and Fàileach by ourselves. She punished him ever' time he raised a hand to me, but it didn't stop him. Until that last time."

"And he hasn't learned how to fight left-handed yet?"

Brìghde said something—

He snapped his fingers in her face. "English, Brìghde."

"His left shoulder, he injured long ago. It ne'er healed. She completely destroyed the right one. 'Twas why 'e ne'er struck me again. He *couldn't*. I think— Sometimes I think they *enjoy* the constant warfare. I don't. I don't wanna be at war wi' me husband, but I also doona want— Roger, me groom." Her Rs were rolling off her tongue in rich waves, and her accent was musical. Grimme found himself charmed by the rhythm of her voice and her speech, whether she was drunk or not. "He was born a beaten puppy. An *ugly* one. Uglier'n'Mercury. I coulda commanded him to clean the garderobe wi' 'is tongue an' he woulda done it wi' a 'I hate you, Budgie, but o' course I will!'" she chirped. "I dinna want that, either." She looked up at him then, tears now spilling over. "Ye rescued me," she said in a very small voice. She sniffled. Her mouth trembled. "Ye were kind to me an' ye befriended me. I'd give ye as many bairns as ye want just for that."

Grimme sighed heavily.

"I'm goin'a bed."

"Good eve."

He twisted around the chair and watched her go. She was steady on her feet and skipped up the stairs lightly.

He looked at his father, who returned him a stunned expression.

"Well," Sir John finally said. "That explains much."

"Papa," Grimme asked with threatening levity, "why does she seem to know that the only thing I fear is Satan and witchcraft?"

"Don't use that tone with me, Son," he said softly, tightly. "I taught it to you."

"She is going to use that as a weapon every time I hurt her feelings."

"Explain 'leprosy-befouled witch' and 'hellhound,' and I will tell you what I said and why, for she is not the witch in this house."

Father and son looked at each other with locked jaws, neither giving ground.

"I didn't think so," the father murmured with a slight sneer. "See me to my chambers."

32

OVER THE NEXT few days, Brìghde was able to establish somewhat of a custom: Arise just after lauds, go to her morning prayer and confession, ride Troy harum-scarum through all of Kyneward without Grimme and Helen, arrive in time for breakfast, get about her inventory, have supper, then exercise a mare. She and Enyo got along famously, as she did with all the other mares but Helen. Helen would still not allow Brìghde alone in her stall with her, but would take the treats she was offered and suffer being petted and told what a good lassie she was.

Brìghde explained to Sir John and William about the circumstance between the mistresses and the merchants. She explained the arrangements she had made for a fresh calculation. She explained that she was now going to take an inventory of the mistress's chambers. And that once everything was reconciled on the Kyneward books, she would meet with the merchants and reconcile with them.

Sir John gaped at her. "Grimme's going to allow you to take inventory?"

"Aye."

"I have wanted to do that for years, and stopped asking when I could no longer climb the stairs."

Brìghde relayed the whole of the conversation because she relayed the whole of almost all of her conversations with Grimme to Sir John.

He was howling with laughter by the end of her recitation, and though William was amused, he couldn't quite grasp why it was that amusing. "I would give the next five years off my life to have been a fly on the wall at *that* family council," Sir John said, wiping his eyes.

Brìghde nodded crisply as he wound down. "Just so. Thus, William, you and I are going to start with Ardith and Maebh. She's the newest; she cannot have that many things."

Maebh did not protest. She did, however, sit in a dressing gown with her legs spread, watching Brìghde suggestively. Ardith was nowhere to be seen.

"You've got to be off your tot!" Brìghde finally exploded when she could turn in no direction without Maebh there flashing a bit of skin or looking Brìghde up and down as if to devour her. William was utterly mortified and busied himself in the maidservant's antechamber, which had not yet been counted. "I'd no more swive you than I would Grimme if I didn't have to!"

"But you *do* have to," she purred with a lilting Irish brogue, wrapping a lock of Brìghde's hair around her finger, "so when you have, then you're welcome to come to me. You might like what a *woman* can do for you. You don't even have to wait since *I* canna get you with babe and he'd never have to know."

Brìghde huffed, smacked her hand away, then turned, only to have her arse squeezed. She yelped and gaped at a very smug Maebh.

"I am not 'off my tot,'" Maebh said matter-of-factly. "I am completely serious. You are beautiful and I want to see all of you and I wanna suck your bubs and lick your muff."

Brìghde took a deep breath. "While I appreciate that you appreciate my beauty—"

"Maebh!" Grimme barked from the doorway. "I told you you could not fuck my wife. If you can't keep your mouth shut and your hands to yourself whilst she's here, get out."

She huffed and stomped her foot. "You *said* you would have to watch Ardith and me swiving in the corner so you could get it in her."

Brìghde's mouth opened a little bit, feeling sick to her stomach, tears stinging her eyes for more than a few reasons, and she looked at Grimme wide-eyed, who was furious.

"*I* can do better than that with my little bitty nymphie. *You* don't want her but *I* do. Mayhap she would like to be swived by someone who *wants* her. And why do you care so much anyway? You've no reason to be jealous."

"Maebh," he growled. "Out."

She huffed her way out the door.

There was a long silence. Grimme's face was flushed and he would not look at Brìghde. She turned away and said, "Thank you," as clearly and brightly as she could, but it was not very bright.

"Brìghde, I'm sorry," he sighed. "When she starts talking, she ... "

She waved a hand. "This is what I asked you for," she said crisply. "You have made it easier for me and I appreciate it." She faked a laugh. "I canna write when I am being seduced!" With that, she strode to the first chest and tried to see through her tears. There were dresses upon dresses upon dresses upon dresses, all stuffed in many, many chests with no care. She would have to take them all out, spread them across the bedraggled bed, and describe them.

She stiffened when she felt his hands on her shoulders. She gulped down the lump in her throat.

"You are beautiful," he whispered. "But my taste is very specific."

"Why?" she asked as disinterestedly as she could manage.

"Emelisse was my first." Brìghde nodded. "When I first got her with child, she barred me from her bed, and I was in need of release. I found Ardith. I went back to Emelisse, but got her with child *again*. Then I found Dillena. Then Dillena was with child. Then there was Maebh. In short, they all look like Emelisse because I want Emelisse, but I very often cannot have her."

That was oddly logical.

"Do they mind?"

"Emelisse is the only one who cares. The rest simply enjoy themselves. Maebh— She will fuck *anyone* who catches her eye, man or woman, and I have to credit her—she has very discerning taste. You should be flattered. She is not to fuck any other man but me, but she is free to have any woman she wants, except you, so now you are even more attractive to her."

Brìghde nodded. Truthfully, it *was* nice to know that *someone* in this keep found her bonny enough to seduce.

"But they each do something different that I like, that Emelisse will not do—" And didn't Brìghde already know what those were! "—and I will not force myself on a woman who cannot bear my attentions. It is convenient you are as reluctant to bear me as I am to be upon you, but it is also inconvenient to the necessity of the deed. I will feel as if I am forcing myself upon you and that never makes me rise."

That, too, was logical; in fact, utterly courteous.

If it had any basis in truth.

"If that is so, then what would you have done with an unwilling captive?"

Silence. "I … don't know. Now that you are here, I cannot remember my reasoning."

Brìghde didn't know what to think about that. "You said something about a surrogate? One of them may have another child."

"I already asked," he said dryly. "There were no volunteers."

He was the earl. He could command them. "Maidservants?"

"I would rather not have a child by a maidservant."

He was closing down all avenues except Brìghde but he could not swive her without his harlots in a corner. She gulped.

"It is not simply that I am a brunette?" she asked, hating herself for asking.

He sighed. "I cannot rise for brunettes, no. I have tried. I tried the other night. It's humiliating."

"You … did not want me to buy or wear black. Is that … ?"

He hesitated. "That is … difficult to explain and I would rather not."

So they *were* connected. 'Twas not her. 'Twas not brunettes. 'Twas the color black—and he feared witchcraft.

No, a warrior like him would not want to confess that.

She did not know what to think about any of this, and she rubbed her forehead. "Well! You must do what you must do, I suppose."

"I intended for you not to have seen Maebh and Ardith whilst you and I did the deed."

"Can you not simply use your imagination?"

He laughed. "I don't have an imagination." He turned her around and looked down at her. Fortunately she had managed to blink back her tears and none had fallen so her face wasn't wet. "Brìghde, when the time comes, I will take my time. I will teach you how to have pleasure, because if you are frightened or hurt or stiff or … anything but relaxed and willing, I won't be able to do it. There is an additional complication. Because I consider you my friend, I value you for something other than your cunte, mouth, arse, or womb. 'Twill be difficult for me to separate my friend from the act.

"If you will allow me to teach you pleasure, I *may* be able to do it without Maebh in the corner, and I *may* even find it changing my taste a little. Furthermore, when you have had my sons, I would that you find a lover of your own, and engage with him—or her—without fear. You will have to ask my women how not to conceive with any other, however." Oh. It wouldn't matter if he ordered them to have his child to pass off as Brìghde's, then. They simply wouldn't comply. "I'll not rear another man's whelp. Would you allow me to try?"

"That was the bargain, was it not? I did not gainsay you the other night when— Um."

"Aye, I am sorry. I know that was hurtful. I saw a beautiful woman, not a leprosy-befouled witch. But then I saw the glint of your hair in the firelight, which … But here," he said softly, "this is what I want you to know: I have not *slept* with Emelisse since I was a squire. I have not *slept* with any of the others at all. I don't *want* to. I have known you for a month, and I have *slept* with you for a third of that. That is something they covet desperately." He shrugged. "Emelisse. Dillena is so quiet, I'm not sure what she wants most of the time. Maebh and Ardith sleep together. I would likely not be welcome." He chuckled.

"Why are you telling me all this? I do not need to know the details of your relations with them. Would rather not, in fact."

"I am telling you this because we are friends and I want you to know everything, and know that I value our friendship enough to tell you these things. I value that you and I can sleep together. I also wanted to apologize again for the other night."

"You said you do not swive men, but did you sleep with your other friend? Aldwyn?"

He shrugged. "In the same tent. We'd lie awake at night and plan how we were going to conquer the world. He would get one half, and I the other, and then we would change places. We were more brothers than friends, which is—should be, anyway—a deeper bond, and I wish my sons had that. 'Tis why I want you near when I want to talk, the way Aldwyn and I did."

"I am Aldwyn," she said dully.

"Aye!" he said with excitement. "Precisely! Thank you. 'Tis what I told Emelisse to reassure her. If I could not talk to you, if we were not friends, I would not want to sleep with you. And that, my dear wife, is *far* more important to me than where I stick my cod."

He left, happy that, in his eyes, the argument was satisfactorily resolved, whilst Brìghde could barely keep herself from crying. If she said what she thought, he would take umbrage that she dared tell him he was wrong.

She was his former dearest friend's replacement. That was all.

Friends. And this one, she couldn't simply drift away from when she'd had enough.

"He's not Roger MacFhionnlaigh," she whispered, as she got on with her chore, "he's not Roger MacFhionnlaigh."

33

IT TOOK BRÌGHDE and William a full sennight to complete the inventory of the paramours' chambers, and Brìghde threw herself into it wholeheartedly not because she wanted to paw through Grimme's mistresses' things, but because she had to do something other than attempt to drink herself into a stupor to keep from remembering his brutal rejection of her, and then the fact that he had spoken so vulgarly of her behind her back to his mistresses. *All* of them.

Friendship.

Brìghde wasn't Grimme's friend. She was *Aldwyn,* a mere replacement for a dear friend he had lost.

She felt completely and utterly betrayed, and what had she done? Kept it to herself instead of punching him in the face.

It was getting more and more difficult to be content with the fact that he didn't want to swive her because he continued to remind her of how she repulsed him. Seeing her naked, touching her, then walking out angry had been a devastating blow to her vanity. No apology was going to salve that wound.

It wouldn't hurt quite so much if she did not want to swive him.

During the week of inventory, all but Dillena had ridden into Waters with their grooms, likely to test the strength of Brìghde's order, and returned furious, for they could not even purchase bread to eat at midday and they were hungry. Brìghde greeted each one of them with a tiny smirk of victory.

Dillena was the one with the fewest possessions. She was thoughtful about what she purchased and had nothing that was not important to her. She had a writing desk, piles and piles of parchment, many quills, and lovely, expensive inks. She had an entire chest full of parchment she had written on and illuminated beautifully. "Ohhh," Brìghde breathed in awe. She handled them gently and profusely complimented Dillena on her talent, then respectfully put the chest back without digging in it at all. She didn't care what the parchments were hiding; the art was too beautiful to touch. Dillena's jewelry was simple but elegant, and at the conclusion of the inspection of her chambers, Brìghde could not with any certainty say that she had anything that could have come from Waters or Hogarth without having been paid for. Thus, she apologized sincerely, to which Dillena gave her a small, dignified nod.

Maebh and Ardith had the most, but they shared everything, and they flung their jewels throughout, under the mattress, in their shoes, wrapped up in blankets.

"Why don't you keep them in their boxes so they won't get lost?" Brìghde asked, confused.

"Oh, we do," Maebh said. "The ones you found are used for—" Ardith slapped a hand over Maebh's mouth. Brìghde sighed and rolled her eyes. There were many things there that had come from Waters and Hogarth that she marked as possible theft.

Emelisse had ... everything. Her chambers were a wonderland of sparkling jewels, sparkling satins and velvets in light blue that matched her eyes, sparkling trim, sparkling shoes, sparkling trifles and toys for the lads that did not seem to be used. Brìghde was careful to ask Emelisse to present her items so that Brìghde could write them down and not disturb anything. She also was careful to compliment her on her taste. It wasn't hard. Emelisse's taste was exquisite and though it was much, it was not *over*much.

Emelisse did not know how to respond to either the respect Brìghde showed her or her compliments.

"Thank you, Emelisse," she said courteously when she closed her ledger and prepared her quills and inks to return to Sir John's study.

"What did you need that list for?" she asked sharply.

"To discern what you may have stolen from the merchants in Waters and Hogarth," Brìghde said matter-of-factly.

Emelisse's face flushed. "If Sir John does not pay a bill, then that is *his* doing, not mine!"

"He can't pay bills you don't give him. I don't know if Grimme—"

"*Lord* Grimme to you," she snapped.

"Noooooo. *I* am to call him Grimme. Or anything else I feel like calling him."

"May I ... " She gritted her teeth and closed her eyes. Her fists clenched. "May I have coin for Waters?"

"Not one farthing."

Emelisse opened her eyes and her expression was pure poison.

"*You* will not be getting *any* coin for anything anytime soon, nor will I allow you to go to Waters or Hogarth for the foreseeable future."

Emelisse's expression twisted. "You *bitch*."

Brìghde nodded. "Aye." She looked around. "Tell me where you acquired your new hangings so I may compare them to the bills I paid."

She did, through gritted teeth.

"If you are nice to me," Brìghde said airily as she left Emelisse's room, "I could be persuaded to change my mind."

That stopped her cold. "How nice?"

"Not *that,*" Brìghde huffed. "Be cordial to me and I will be cordial to you, and if you can do that long enough, I'll forget how angry I am that you were cheating the merchants in Waters and giving us a bad reputation in Hogarth. I want goodwill amongst those we need, as 'tis easier to get what you want when you're pleasant and fair. Brute strength is so *tiring* because you must needs *always* watch your back."

Thus, after having just surveyed Emelisse's chambers, when Brìghde went back to her own, she looked around and her shoulders slumped. It was awful, a hodge-podge of mismatched furniture found in dark corners at the farthest parts of the keep, left behind from its last occupant, simply thrown in any chamber to land wherever it might. Aye, she had hired carpenters, who were here, but the wood was being cut out in the forests, which would take quite a lot of time, and furnishing all the chambers would take at least a year. Could she get away with postponing a wedding celebration for one year just so she could get the keep in order? Would anyone understand? How terrible a breach of etiquette was it?

It still didn't solve the problem of a surprise visit from the duke. If that happened, the only place she could put him was Grimme's chambers and even then she would have to put the duchess *with him*. It was an appalling display of barbarism.

She had not yet been to the dower house, but as the keep had been stripped of every odd thing to put in Brìghde's chambers, she had no hope of anything in a boarded-up relic.

She needed livery, hangings, drapes, but she couldn't have those until she had furniture to house the clothier and his staff and his goods.

As to her wardrobe, her new gowns should start arriving any day now. The only nice gown she had was her wedding dress, but she was loath to wear it. It reminded her too much of the sword point in her back.

She rubbed that spot.

"Why are you not at supper? I am waiting for you."

Brìghde looked over her shoulder at Grimme, who was leaning against her threshold. "I'm sorry. I ... did not realize it was so late," she muttered.

"What's wrong with your back?"

"Nothing. 'Twas where Walter had the point of his sword and sometimes I can still feel it."

"Would you like me to send up a tray?"

"Aye, please. Thank you. And wine."

He didn't move. "Brìghde?" he said softly, coming into the room, framing her face in his hands, and tilting it up. "What's wrong?"

Other than his opinion of her? She gestured around, her mouth twisting. "I want my things. I appreciate that I will have new furniture, but I wish I had my other things. My own clothes. My own jewelry. My own brushes and ribbons and suchlike. And my dog."

"Your belongings and your dog are all at MacFhionnlaigh, aye?"

Brìghde nodded.

"I will send out a company to fetch them and since we would not have to go through Fàileach lands, we can easily avoid your father. I doubt your father's army would be interested in a procession of villeins moving elsewhere anyway."

She raised her eyes to meet his soft brown ones and sighed. He was so handsome, with his strong jaw and straight nose and long golden-red hair and … he would have to force himself to bed her, and involve his women to do it.

It was humiliating.

She nodded hesitantly. "If … if that is something you are willing to do, then, yes. I would like that."

He pressed his mouth to her forehead. "You are my friend, Brìghde, and I will do most anything for my friends. Sleep with me tonight? I'll rub your back for you."

No. She did not want to sleep with him. "Aye, that would be good, thank you."

He was true to his word: He sent up a tray with twice as much food as she could possibly eat (she ate it all) and two pitchers of wine. Whilst she was eating, one maidservant after another brought up hot water and filled her tub.

"Lord Kyneward said to bring ye a hot bath, m'lady," one girl said.

"That was thoughtful," she said softly, a smile curving her face. "Thank you. Two more pitchers of wine. No, three."

They curtsied and then, once she had finished her meal, Avis helped her wash her hair. When that was finished and she was otherwise bathed, she relaxed there looking at the wall and drinking.

So she didn't have her things or her dog. Her circumstance was disproportionately advantageous. Five weeks ago …

She had been on the verge of a life she would have abhorred, ordered to complete a task she was terrified to carry out and terrified not to, with a plethora of problems to solve quickly if she wanted to live.

Now ...

She was married, so she could not be forced to wed.

She had the permanent protection of a wealthy English earl with a standing army and who was a dear friend to the king of England.

She was an English countess, which outranked a Scottish clan chief.

The earl was kind, generous, thoughtful, enjoyed her company, considered her a dear friend also, and made her laugh.

She was the prime ruler of a keep with power she had coveted since she had served as her mother's apprentice and then as a housekeeper.

The earl's father treated her with kindness and praise, something she craved.

She felt at home here, as if she had lived here forever, as if she had known Grimme and his father forever.

Though Brìghde did not know how to feel gratitude, she hoped her work here demonstrated her good faith in holding up their bargain.

The disadvantages of her circumstance were so minor as to be a mere annoyance and yet ...

Why was it so hurtful that her husband did not want to swive her? Any sensible abducted lass would be glad about that. Was her vanity that vast, that she could not stand for *one* man to find her repulsive? She did not expect him to lust for her the way he did his mistresses and the maidservants, but finding her repulsive, the way she found Roger, was something else again.

It was that, she realized. She did not mind if someone didn't find her attractive; not everyone was attractive to everyone else. It was that he considered her a replacement for his dearest friend, who was a male, and he found men repulsive. That still didn't explain it all, however, because—

But then I saw the glint of your hair in the firelight ...

There was something very, *very* wrong with her husband.

'Twas late when the water grew cold enough to wake her up. The candles had sputtered out. The fire was still well fed, and she saw that Grimme was asleep in her bed. She smiled a little. Would a man who found her *repulsive* want to sleep with her or offer to rub her back for a wound that never existed?

It was all so confusing.

She climbed out of her tub, dried herself, and put on her shift. She stood looking down at her husband, so still and peaceful in sleep.

His big body.

His long, strong legs.

His wide, muscular shoulders.

His broad back that was, at this moment, bare to the waist.

His long golden-red hair.

He was ... *dazzling.*

After the third time she was dismissed from being a scullery maid, she had stopped lying to herself about whose fault it was. It was not, in fact, the housekeeper's fault that she did not see Brìghde's worth. No. It was Brìghde who could not accept that her status in the world was sleeping in cinders and eating porridge. If she wanted to *remain* sleeping in cinders and eating porridge instead of outside in the dead of winter with only a dog for warmth and stolen bits of food to eat, she was going to have to stop acting like the lady of the manor and start acting like a scullery maid.

She had never lied to herself again, for her survival depended on her ability to accept and manage the brutal truth. So she could not now continue to lie to herself that she did not want her husband in her bed for something more than sleep.

What she *could* do was keep her imagination from running amok with what *could have been* if he had the least amount of lust for her. She had many times witnessed people in various stages of the act, but once, unfortunately, she had witnessed it from start to finish. It had been an interesting and somewhat arousing thing to watch—until she realized that she would be expected to do *that* with Roger. Then she vomited. Here, now, looking at her husband asleep in her bed, she wanted that for herself.

She stood looking at him, rather, *through* him, when she realized that swiving him for the heir she promised was one thing. Wanting him to swive her for her pleasure was another. It would make her one of many—and not at all his favorite.

Did she really want that? Could she be content with that?

No, she decided. No, she would not. She was a lady, by the Virgin Mary, not a commoner a squire picked up off the street in whom he planted seed. Brìghde was the wife. *Other* noblewomen might tolerate it by husbands who did not care about them, whom they almost never saw, but Brìghde was not *other* noblewomen and her husband *did* care about her and demanded her company quite a bit of the time—just not ... *that way.*

She refused to be one of many, but she wanted ...

It was maddening.

"Och!" she huffed. She checked the fire, climbed into bed beside her husband, and took care not to touch him. It was a big bed; that was simple enough.

Brìghde clutched her crucifix and brought it to her lips. "At least he's not Roger MacFhionnlaigh."

"What's that?" he muttered.

"You're not Roger MacFhionnlaigh," she repeated.

He looked over his shoulder. "Where did *that* come from?"

"I was thinking of our disproportionately advantageous bargain."

"Ah."

"Um … there is something … " She grimaced.

"Say it," he said flatly, turning over onto his back.

She took a deep breath. "As we await you to sit for meals, 'tis terribly inefficient for us to wait for you at breakfast when you do not appear without notice. Business must be gotten on with, your knights need to be in the field, and it is embarrassing to Emelisse that we know if she is sitting, you will not appear because you have been swiving the night away. Twice this week you have slept until noon. It weakens my credibility for all to look to Emelisse to know whether to be seated or not." It also hurt.

"That's fair," he agreed agreeably.

Brìghde released a sigh of relief.

"Aye, see? Friends. That wasn't even an argument. Now turn over and I'll rub that sword point out of your back."

She sighed with pleasure when his big hand pressed into her back and wished it were more.

"Go to sleep, Brìghde," he murmured. "As long as I live, no one will ever have a sword in your back again."

34

"THANK YOU, Grimme," she said, smiling up at him.

Grimme returned his little wife's smile as they stood in the outer bailey at sunrise whilst a company of knights and men-at-arms disguised themselves as villeins moving from town to town looking for a lord to serve. "You're welcome," he said warmly, happy that at least *one* woman in his household was not furious with him.

A week had passed before he could put together a company to fetch Brìghde's dog and other belongings from MacFhionnlaigh. In that week, he had had to confront each of his women privately.

Ardith was angry that Grimme had introduced someone to the household her lover wanted to fuck. "How was I supposed to know that would happen?" he asked. She gave him a stony glare. He should've known.

Maebh was angry that he would not let her have Brìghde since *he* wasn't fucking her, nor would he acquiesce to allowing her to warm Brìghde up for him to fuck. And—

"You keep that bitch Emelisse and her little monsters from Pierce, and I know very good and well he won that fight because I do give him all the freedom he wants."

"Aye, he did. But the other boys are gone now. I apologize for allowing the situation amongst them to go on and I have already told Emelisse I will punish her severely if she so much as breathes in Pierce's direction."

That had surprised her out of her pique.

Dillena was angry because she did not appreciate being accused of thievery when she had not done any such of a thing (although Brìghde had apologized), for which he did not blame her. She was also angry that he had accused her of neglecting Terrwyn's studies, and denying him attention or freedom.

"*I* teach him to read and write," she informed him with soft rage. "Father Hercule teaches him his sums. I believe the amount of attention Emelisse gives her sons is detrimental. I also believe that the amount of freedom Maebh gives Pierce is dangerous for a five-year-old, walking to Waters and back alone, and no one missed him. *Terrwyn* might believe he is neglected for not getting what they do, but *I* do not and I don't intend to change. Emelisse and Maebh don't, either, but at least I will tell you that and why."

Grimme couldn't fault her logic and he couldn't fault her for being angry.

"I am not angry about the fight amongst the boys, for it has been brewing for some time and Emelisse's sons deserved what they got. I am angry that you do not see what Emelisse and her sons do to mine. I am angry that you chastised me in front of the others instead of simply coming to me and speaking calmly. I am angry that it took another woman with more power than any of us to get you to see."

He shrugged. "My parents didn't mitigate the conflicts my older brother and I had."

She was surprised. "You have an older brother?"

"Four, three legitimate. 'Tis the way of men, to settle their differences in the dirt. The best men won, and Gaston and Max will have to live with the humiliation of having lost to a five- and seven-year-old. It won't be easy, trust me. That is a better punishment than any I could have given them."

"Hrmph. I am sad that you have sent my boy out to apprentice. But he is an earl's son and I want him to have the privileges and responsibilities that entails. I appreciate that you don't treat him like a bastard."

It was likely the longest conversation he had ever had with her, so he was quite impressed and assured her that now that she had explained, he agreed with all points.

And Emelisse was just angry.

She had been angry for years. He never cared because she was free to leave and she chose to stay. Now he cared because he had discovered a friend—a *female* friend who did not seem to be given to such intractable moods. Oh, Brìghde had a temper, but as soon as everything was resolved, which took almost no time at all, she went back to being as happy and amusing as Aldwyn had been before their bitter parting.

He watched the company roll out of the bailey to fetch her belongings. It wasn't an easy task, but he didn't mind doing things for her. She was so grateful for any expression of approval and was so willing to work that it made his mistresses seem like selfish, spoiled, pampered princesses.

But then there was the subject of his sons and that was a sore point for everyone. The entire household was in upset because he had taken Brìghde's words to heart about his sons' needs, and no one was happy.

"Papa? Is Brìghde going somewhere?"

Except Pierce. He was very happy.

Grimme looked down at him in surprise. "Why, no. They are going to her home to fetch her belongings back to her."

"She's going to be here forever?"

He smiled. "That is generally what a wife does, my son."

With that, Pierce merely leaned against his leg and Grimme laid his hand gently upon his head. His other three sons had been gone almost a fortnight now, and he missed them more than he thought possible, missed seeing them every day, missed hearing an excited chorus of *Papa!*s.

Though he had forbidden Emelisse to ride out to the farthest reaches of the encampment to see the boys, *he* had gone—to "inspect." No one was fooled, and he drew many glances askance, particularly from the knights who were training them. He just wanted to see them. It was shockingly difficult for him to let them go, but he must do for them what was right, and what was right was to send them out.

What really had him in contention with himself was that Pierce had attached himself to Brìghde, who did not seem to be ready to be a mother, but Maebh was insistent that she wanted to make Pierce happy and if that meant he would abandon Maebh for Brìghde, then that was what that meant. After some thought, he had approached Maebh with a new proposition.

She had been furious. Maebh would throw tantrums and be angry, but she was *never* enraged.

Nay, I'll not have another child with you to immediately hand over to her! You wanted to wed a noblewoman because you couldn't bear to lower yourself to wed one of us! You got one, but now you can't bear to bed her—God only knows why because she's beautiful—and I even offered to help, but you won't let me *have her, either. And now you come begging me for another babe so you don't have to touch her. What is* wrong *with you?*

He was not in the habit of talking to his women, so it didn't occur to him to explain.

Out! Get out! Don't come back until I tell you!

It gave him a new look into an otherwise flighty girl with whom he shared no more than a betrayal, a bed, and a boy. As for Brìghde, she was happy to indulge Pierce and seemed to understand what he needed, but she acted more like an older sister than a mother.

He didn't dare tell Brìghde that Maebh was willing to give him up to her just to make Pierce happy.

"Lady Brìghde?"

She started and looked around Grimme's body to find Pierce. "Good morn."

"Do you go to confession this morn?"

"Aye, I have already been, my wee laddie. Why?"

"I didn't see you."

"Mayhap," she said conspiratorially, "I have been taking lessons from you, skulking about, hiding, watching, and listening." Then in a flurry of skirts, she whirled around Grimme and captured Pierce, making him squeal with laughter, and picked him up.

He watched her play with Pierce, tickling him gently and blowing in his ear, making him giggle. All his sons were blond. That was what happened when a blond-roux mated with a blonde. He began to wonder what a son of his and Brìghde's would look like. Would he be blond? Would he be roux as his father had been before it had turned white? Would he be brunet?

Gaston and Terrwyn had blue eyes. Max and Pierce had brown. What would a son with Brìghde have? Brown? Green?

He tilted his head. What would she look like, heavy with his child? How would she act? Would she turn into a shrew, as Dillena had been? Would she be so fatigued she could not walk up a flight of stairs without breathing heavily, as Maebh had been? Would she be bedbound for fear of losing the babe, as Emelisse had been? Twice?

"What are you thinking?" she asked, breathless from twirling Pierce around by his arms.

"What our children will look like," he mused.

Her eyebrow rose. "Oh?"

He waved a hand. "Your play with Pierce. It makes me feel as if we are a family. You, me, him."

She blinked. Pierce leaned against her and wrapped his arms around her legs. "But … Pierce is not mine and his mother is … " She waved her hand toward the keep. "And you have three other sons and we are already a family, albeit a rather strange one."

Grimme nodded. Aye, he and his women and his sons and his father were a family. He had never questioned this; it simply was. "I feel as though you and I, and Pierce, are a *different* family, apart from the rest. As one, we slide into it, and as one, we slide out of it."

"Um … "

He said nothing else, because he could not explain that he was now seeing Brìghde as Pierce's mother, and he could not disagree with Maebh that Brìghde would be better for Pierce all the way around.

He sighed. Maybe … maybe he *did* have a favorite son. He hadn't, not before the fight, but Pierce had clearly dominated his older, bigger brothers, and Grimme could do naught but respect that in ways he could not respect his other sons.

The thought did not sit well. It was Emelisse's fault he could not respect his oldest two. It was to Dillena's credit that he could respect Terrwyn for holding his own. But no matter how much he didn't like Maebh's mothering,

Pierce had won the fight *because* she allowed him to do anything and go anywhere he wanted.

How far out in other directions had he explored? How many villeins' children had he scrapped with? What did he know, what had he done and seen?

Grimme once again looked at Brìghde, absently caressing Pierce's back as they watched the procession, and thought about the welcome-home Brìghde had given Pierce—a hot bath, a cake, medicine. Then she had encouraged him to give her a full recounting of the fight wherein she praised him excessively for being ... a boy, doing what boys did, and for conquering.

Dillena's mothering was the middle ground between Emelisse's and Maebh's, but Maebh was exactly right: Brìghde could rear *boys*. She understood them, knew what they needed, where to rein them in, and would bring a bit of a woman's touch to it.

The company was down the lane and then out of sight. With any luck, they would return in a fortnight without having seen battle, and Brìghde could have her things and her dog because he *hated* it when she cried.

It was so ... sad, and with Brìghde ... it *meant* something when she was sad, *especially* when she had been drinking. She was a very sad drunk.

Never, when he set out on this course to snatch Lady Margaret Dunham, had he thought he would end up in such a favorable circumstance.

"*Now* what are you thinking?" she teased, "staring off into the sunrise like a cockerel who didn't crow because he was too captivated."

He grinned. "I'm happy that you're happy."

She blushed and shrugged, turning away so he couldn't see her smile. She was so lovely. "Well!" she said breathlessly, "I am going into breakfast. Are you coming with me?"

"I will in a moment. You go on."

35

TO BRÌGHDE'S surprise, Emelisse was *sitting* in the chair next to the empty lord's chair. Sir John, standing behind his chair next to Grimme's, looked entirely furious. The rest of the hall stood behind their chairs, silent, waiting.

Emelisse gave her a victorious, challenging look. Brìghde took a deep breath and, shaking her head at the prospect of a long war with her husband's favorite mistress, glided to the head table. "Get up," she said quietly, but firmly.

"This is my chair, *Brigitte,*" Emelisse growled low, glaring at Brìghde from under her brows. "I am the mother of his two oldest sons and have been at his side for eleven years."

"And I am the countess," Brìghde said matter-of-factly. "Get up."

"No, you little bitch," she hissed. "Just *try* to get me out of this chair."

Brìghde grabbed her by the chin as hard as she could, jerked her face up, and touched her nose to Emelisse's. Emelisse struggled with small noises as she was unable to speak, her hands clawing at Brìghde's, but Brìghde's grip was too tight. "Do not challenge me in my home again, Emelisse," she murmured pleasantly enough, dragging Emelisse up and out of the chair by her face. Emelisse was taller and heavier than she looked, so Brìghde had to look up. Emelisse was struggling, but she, like her sons, was weak. "You will lose. You can be my friend or you can be invisible or you can be my enemy. Choose wisely because I can snap your skinny little neck right now."

"*BRÌGHDE!*" Grimme roared from the doorway. "*LET – HER – GO!*"

Brìghde turned her head and looked at him whilst tightening her grip. Emelisse was trying to cough but couldn't so she began gurgling, yet still Brìghde held on. "This is household business, my lord," she called pleasantly. "I would not burden you with it."

Grimme bolted into the hall and around the tables to grab Brìghde's wrist and squeeze it painfully enough to force her to set Emelisse free. Emelisse fell back into Brìghde's chair, sprawling, trying to catch her breath. "Is this what you meant?" he hissed, grabbing her other wrist between them and lifting her until their eyes met and her toes did not touch the floor. Brìghde could simply lower her arms a few inches and she would be on her feet, but she was strong and she held her elbows to her side so as not to show weakness. "About your iron fist?"

"Aye," she said calmly.

"The punishment did not fit the crime."

"'Twas no punishment, my lord," she said matter-of-factly, her arms trembling from the effort to keep herself elevated, her wrists aching from his grip. "'Twas a warning. I may hate Walter Fàileach, but I learned enough about politics and warfare from him to be able to muster a force and seize a castle, never mind evict one jealous whore—" Emelisse gasped. "—from my rightful place. Only strength is respected and only the strong lead."

Grimme's brown eyes darkened and his jaw ground. He released her, likely intending that she should stumble, but she landed on her feet quite tidily and refused to rub her wrists, which throbbed.

"Don't touch my women again."

"Get—her—out—of—my—chair."

Grimme said nothing, but his nostrils flared.

"You said you would enforce my position, but every time she challenges me and I assert my authority, you balk until I remind you of the bargain. You enforce my position here, I give you legitimate heirs. That's the bargain. How many more times must we go through this?"

"You laid hands on her," Grimme growled.

"*I*," she snarled, "am demonstrating my authority because *you* will not enforce it."

She had him.

She did not *like* having him, particularly in front of the entire household and all his commanders. It weakened his credibility as lord for the lady to challenge him at all, much less so publicly, and that was the *last* thing the castellain needed.

"Your inability to control your women," she whispered, "is damaging your credibility with your men. She dared me to pull her out of that chair, so I did. Get control of them or stand back and allow me to do it. Either way, your credibility stays intact."

Grimme leaned to his right and said over Brìghde's shoulder, "Emelisse, go to your chambers."

She released an astonished, horrified breath in a sharp whoosh. "Grimme—" she croaked.

"*Now!*"

He looked back at Brìghde and snarled, "I will deal with you later," then stormed out of the hall.

Silence reigned for all of thirty seconds before Brìghde looked over her shoulder at Emelisse. "You were told to go to your chambers. Do so. Now."

Emelisse tried to squeeze between Brìghde and the table, but she had barely enough room. "I'm not done with you," she hissed as she clambered by.

"I look forward to our further conversations, Mistress Emelisse!" Brìghde called brightly at her retreating form. Then she turned to the hall and said with a smile, "Eat! Eat! Don't let me interrupt your meal."

With that, she sat and slid a glance across Grimme's chair to Sir John, who gave her a sly grin.

36

GRIMME PACED IN his chambers, furious, but how much at which woman, he could not say, which was even more maddening. If Grimme knew only one thing about his favorite mistress, it was that she would do anything in her power to destroy Brìghde in Grimme's eyes. Unfortunately for Emelisse, Brìghde didn't care what Grimme thought; she was not interested in a petty scrap. If Emelisse provoked her enough, Brìghde would simply break Emelisse over her knee like a dry twig.

Brìghde had every right to expect her seat to be empty and he was furious with Emelisse for challenging both his and her authority *after* he had told her never to sit there again. Though Grimme had told Emelisse he would never wed her, he hadn't wed anyone else, either, which gave Emelisse hope that he would one day. She was angry and bitter, which he understood, but had no sympathy for. He should have known Emelisse would make things difficult for any woman he married, but had given it no thought whatsoever.

But he was also furious with Brìghde, so much so that he could understand why her father had had to stick a sword in her back to say her vows. She had challenged Grimme's authority in front of the entire hall, his knights, servants, mistresses, and son, and that could not be borne. If she had wanted, she could have killed Emelisse right then and there before he could forestall it, and never mind her skill with poison!

That girl was trouble and he dreaded what she would do next.

But now she was not an amusing oddity and he needed her for far more than a surety against his murder.

Hamond appeared. "My lord, Sir John begs an audience."

Of course he would.

Once he clipped down the stairs and entered his father's chambers, he noted the small, filthy, prone male on the rug in his path. He stepped over it and threw himself in a chair across the desk from Sir John. "What," he sighed, rubbing the bridge of his nose.

"I will be blunt," his father said with a strength in his voice Grimme had not heard in a long time. He opened his eyes to see Sir John fussing with the parchments on his desk, organizing them, tapping them square. "You were wrong to question Brìghde's handling of Emelisse."

"Papa," he sighed wearily, "you take Brìghde's side because you don't like Emelisse."

Sir John looked up, his expression one of fury. "I *despise* Emelisse. She is a poison in this household and she has been since you bedded her. God knows why I supported her all those years."

"I was fifteen."

"How many times did I tell you not to stick your cod in madwomen? How many times did I tell you that no matter how beautiful a woman is, someone, somewhere, is tired of her nonsense? How many times did I warn you away from her? But nooo," he mocked. "You were *in loooove*."

This was a lecture Grimme had suffered through for years. "And I'm not anymore. Why are you so angry? She has no power and Brìghde did what you have wanted to do for years. You should be giddy."

Sir John chortled. "No power? No power but that of negligence. Since you have not allowed *me* to have command over them, and *you* have not taken them in hand, they have the ultimate power. I did not realize it until Brìghde came, but this would have happened whether or not I could climb stairs because you have given them right of refusal to me. And before you deny that, remember the bills in Hogarth and Waters that went unpaid for months. What could I do but grumble and rage at them? And they *still* would not bring them to me. Now that Lady Brìghde, who has rule over *me*, has shown she can and will take power by whatever means necessary, you will be *forced* to see and do what I have been begging you to for years, if only to keep Brìghde from killing Emelisse with her bare hands."

"You are angry," Grimme whispered in some awe, as he had never seen his father so.

"I am," he snapped, "but I did not know *how* angry until this morning when Emelisse usurped Brìghde's place. I warned her it was not seemly but she scoffed at me, as she has done for years also, *then* she dared Brìghde to evict her. And now the entire household knows the lord of this keep is the hapless, helpless fool being led around by his cod by four women, and the new lady of the manor is the only one amongst you with any sense and strength at all. Brìghde is the ruler here and she demonstrated that to every one of your commanders."

"It is not being 'led around by my cod,'" he sneered, "when I have a house full of women who have always gotten along—"

His father hooted.

"—and all I want as a man coming home is to have a happy household and a happy family. Then I bring home this, this, this—*woman* who turns everything upside down."

"Did you or did you not ask her to do so?"

"No! I asked her to take your place!"

"You cannot have both, Son. She can rule everyone, including your mistresses, or she can sit by the hearth and embroider for all the good she can do when you refuse to make them behave as part of a household. Take them in hand yourself or allow Brìghde to be the enemy. She is clearly willing to be seen as such and has no investment in the opinions of anyone here save mine. For her, her word is law and by God everyone *will* bow to her. If you sit at her side being lord of the earldom and leave everything else to Brìghde, you will be seen as a powerful pair who can rule more than a mere twenty thousand acres with one small hamlet on its outskirts. Is that not why Henry sent you home?"

"Aye," Grimme mumbled.

"Ply your women in private and soothe the wounds Brìghde inflicts upon them, berate Brìghde in private, but *never* take their side against her in public again. Your credibility as a lord and leader depends upon it. If you had brought home any lesser of a woman than Brìghde, nothing would have changed."

Silence.

"Are you finished?" Grimme asked.

"Aye."

"I will not tolerate Brìghde assaulting my women at all, much less in public."

"If they defy her, they must pay the price whether in public or private. Brìghde is asserting her power in the most efficient and unmistakable way possible. What would it say that Emelisse challenged her to use force and then she backed down? It would say she was not fit to rule here and that she would be no more effective than I am. You would not hesitate to put a soldier to the lash should he defy you as Emelisse defied Brìghde."

That was true.

"Order cannot be maintained without a strong leader, and I could not be it because you tied my hands."

There came a knock upon the door, which startled all three of them. The prone male hopped up and sped to a corner behind some drapes with remarkable speed. Sir John said, "Come."

It was Brìghde herself. She hesitated when she saw Grimme, but squared her shoulders and skirted around the desk to Sir John's side and presented him with a parchment. "I would like to give William permission to transfer the bulk of our funds into the Medici Bank. Would that be something you would advise for or against?"

Grimme watched his father's face light up. "I have been wanting to do that since William told me about it. 'Twill safeguard any losses from an attack by Sheffield. We may not even have to go to Italy—"

"I approve of *a* bank," Grimme said, "and the reason, but not one in Italy. Transporting that much coin is a risk I will not take. There are banks in England, surely. Mayhap even France."

"No, there are not," Sir John said with overdone patience. "And we can purchase a sea insurance contract."

"This is household business," Brìghde growled.

"This is *my* money," Grimme snarled back, and was satisfied when she looked away. "We have hiding places that are sufficient."

Cowed, she went back to conferring with Sir John. She was humble in Sir John's presence, almost bowing to him, grateful for any sign of approval, and after what she'd said of her father, Grimme could see why. Although she had been here over a month now, she still flushed slightly when Sir John praised her. Her expression was soft and open, unlike how it had been when confronting Emelisse then Grimme. To walk into his home and see her as a "virago" was something else again, and it thoroughly discomfited him.

If you do not rein your women in, I *will.*

Maybe his father was right, Grimme thought. Perhaps the best course of action would be to step out of the fray completely as he had always done and tend the business of acquiring more knights, training them, and fortifying the keep. What did he care about his women versus his wife, so long as his wife could control them, and he continued to bed the four and sit next to the one at supper?

And most certainly, his wife could control them—if he let her.

"Brìghde," he grunted, startling both her and his father.

"My lord?"

"I apologize, on Emelisse's behalf, that she sought to usurp your position at breakfast."

She blinked. "Uh … oh."

"I will not interfere with your disciplinary decisions again, as I simply do not want to be bothered. I would request, however, that you find some other way to control them than touching them, much less hurting them."

"Mayhap you should instruct them not to dare me to, as I have never met a dare I would not take."

"That is fair," he conceded.

Brìghde chewed on her bottom lip. "What," she began carefully, "did you expect when you brought home a wife? You never answered."

And she had not acceded to his request, but he let it go for the moment. "I expected that my wife would be no different from them, and that the household would simply have one more woman in it who would be grateful not to be subjected to my unwanted advances overmuch."

She nodded thoughtfully and mused, "Aye, I suppose 'tis not a large expectation when one plucks just any noblewoman out of her wedding."

"Tall, willowy, blue-eyed blonde noblewomen were in short supply."

Her face flushed. Ah, so she knew it for the insult it was. Good. Grimme *almost* regretted saying it, but Brìghde needed to be punished and that cut was as far as he would allow himself.

"If you had not been so dimwitted as to snatch the wrong bride, *my lord*," she said softly, the fury in her expression clear, "you could have had a tall, willowy, blue-eyed blonde noblewoman who is also capable of being castellain."

Grimme's eyes widened and his bottom lip eased downward, his mind spinning with what *could have been* if he'd listened to the banns more closely and arrived in time.

"I am *so* sorry you got me instead of Meg Dunham. One look at her and your spindle would have been hard as a rock. You wouldn't have had another thought in your head but that you had to have her and you wouldn't have waited until you got to the register, never mind *wooing* and *seducing*."

That was when he noticed her mouth was tight and trembling and she was swallowing quickly, which meant she was about to cry.

He whispered, "I'm sorry, Brìghde."

"I will take your name and some coin and Troy as payment for my work here, and be on my way to my brother at Dunham. I can find my way there without getting into trouble. You will have to look at me no longer. Get a babe on someone else, say I was in confinement, and then that you sent me away because our bargain had been fulfilled and I was no longer needed.

"*I* am the only thing between the duke and the survival of your earldom. *I* was the only one between Fàileach and this pitiful piece of property. Do you know how easy it would have been to escape you? But *nooooo*. You'd rather endure a siege by an enraged father to have the blonde. And I agreed to bear the heir of a man who can't stand to touch me. God, I'm an idiot."

He shook his head. "No. Please, let me—" He stood and reached for her, but she skittered away from him and ran out of the study.

He made to go after her, but his father snarled, "Don't. The look on your face was disgusting. *Bloody hell, I could've had the blonde and got you instead!*"

Grimme lowered himself into his chair slowly and looked at his father, who shook his head.

The small, filthy male came out from behind the drapery snickering. "*That* was worth the journey," he cackled and planted one arse cheek on the corner of Sir John's desk.

"Mouse!" Grimme barked. "Go take a bath. You stink."

"Aye, I will, as that's the only reason I visit. But first! Tell me exactly what your favorite whore did that you had to apologize to your *beautiful* bride on her behalf?"

Sir John gave Mouse such a vividly gleeful account, Mouse grew an evil grin. "Beautiful *and* vicious," he purred. "Where is she? I'll go take a bath right now and give her a babe. You'll never have to worry about it." He looked at Sir John. "You and I have trod this ground before."

Sir John shrugged. "I don't really care whose babe she has, just so that she has one," he said smoothly, glaring at Grimme, "since the only male in this room who doesn't want to fuck her is the only one who needs to."

"May I have her, Grimme? *Please?*" Mouse whinged. "I'm more handsome than you are, and I'm not a grotesque giant."

Both were true. "I'm also not thirteen. *Boy.*"

Mouse snarled and kicked his shin. Grimme chuckled when he winced.

"Tell me what she meant about your dimwittedness," Mouse commanded. "I thought your plan with her was brilliant. Sheffield was furious, which was delightful for me to witness, but not so delightful for the poor wench he slapped across the room for daring to serve him what he asked for."

"He meant to snatch Lady Margaret," Sir John said.

"Aye, I know that. I just assumed he found a better candidate and made a sensible bargain."

Grimme slid down in his chair.

"It was a mistake!" his father snapped. "He snatched the wrong girl by accident, and just completely devastated her by so obviously regretting he didn't get the blonde."

Mouse gaped, then he started to laugh. Then he roared until he was coughing. "And all these years I was jesting about your dimwittedness. This is *perfect!*"

Grimme deserved it, and Mouse was the only person in the world other than his father who could get away with mocking him so. Finally, Mouse managed to calm down, but he was wiping his eyes. "I told you to take some time to go about gaining a wife the usual way of nobility."

"What else should I have done?" Grimme barked. "You *also* told me I was in imminent danger."

"Not that imminent, but you didn't give me a chance to explain before you stopped listening to me. *As usual.*"

"What noble father is going to give his girl over to a bastard whose holdings are tiny, five years old, and on the Scottish border? There is *nothing* to recommend me."

Mouse gaped at him. "Nothing to recommend you?" he gasped, horrified. "You've a title, wealth, a standing army, *and* the king's ear. There is nothing more a noble father could beg for!"

Grimme scowled in confusion and met his father's equally confused look. Grimme looked back at Mouse. "But I have no influence—"

"You have a great deal of influence!" Mouse huffed. "You see your worth solely as it pertains to Sheffield because you have been in France, so you act like a naughty squire serving his cruel knight, desperate not to get his arse beaten. You sneak around to get what you want when *you do not have to*. No noble in England would turn his nose up to have you as an ally."

"But I only have twenty thousand acres."

"And a standing army of almost four thousand, which is *far* more than most nobles have no matter their acreage! *Why* did you not tell me this?" he pled, genuinely upset.

Grimme was oddly warmed by Mouse's distress. "I … hadn't put words to it yet, I suppose," he answered vaguely.

"Grimme! Do you not understand why Henry sent you home?"

Grimme looked at him helplessly. "To put the earldom to rights so I can go back."

"No! To be his political ally *here*. A king needs loyal nobles. You are *far* more valuable to him as a noble than you are as a knight on the battlefield. He sent you home to establish yourself amongst the nobility, to make alliances, which, aye, included marriage and you made a fairly powerful one. You will *never* be on the battlefield again so long as Henry needs your voice amongst his leadership. Did he not tell you any of this?"

"No, and don't lecture me," Grimme snapped, angry at the possibility he would never be able to war at Henry's side again. "You know who you are."

"And you need to know who *you* are, which is *not* insignificant!"

"Well, he thinks he is," his father grumbled. "Both of us, rather. Not knowing how to— Knowing *nothing* about nobility— I can make money and he can make war, but that's all! I didn't think about his chances for an alliance with another noble any more than he did. And then he—" Sir John waved a hand at Grimme in frustration. "Just *happens* to snatch the exact girl he needs, who wanted to be snatched, can teach us both, and set this earldom on its feet, but neither one of us knows quite what to do with her. We don't trust her, we don't even know enough to ask the right questions—her first observation was that we had no lawyer. How were we supposed to know we needed one? Aye, as a *merchant* I needed one, but an earldom? We must allow her to do whatever she wants and hope she doesn't betray us."

Mouse scowled. "*Wanted* to be snatched? Start from the beginning."

Grimme sighed and relayed the entire story, including Brìghde's Trojan horse dilemma and Walter Fàileach's plan for her death.

Mouse didn't laugh, which surprised Grimme, but he was contemplating. "That's the devil's own luck," he mused. "For both of you."

"Not the devil's!" he barked. "God's hand."

Mouse sneered. "You've not done one bloody thing in your life to earn God's favor."

"Mayhap He has things in store," Grimme said archly, "a greater purpose for me."

Mouse rolled his eyes and Sir John snorted.

"Very well. You snatched the wrong girl, you both seem to have outwitted your masters, but sadly, she is a brunette."

Grimme nodded wearily. "Worse. She has become a very good friend—"

"I'd hate to have *you* as a friend. Bad enough working for you."

"—and I do not befriend those I fuck, and I do not fuck my friends."

Mouse blinked. "Oh. Well. Then I see your dilemma."

"Aye, I knew *you* would."

Mouse threw up his hands. "I cannot advise. There's a reason I don't fuck my female friends. If I had any left. I stopped making them because of dilemmas such as this. And you—" he said to Sir John. "You fucked every female friend you ever had. Couldn't keep a male one to save your life."

"Don't make friends with women you don't want to fuck."

"Do I have to listen to this *again*?" Grimme groaned.

"Aye, that lecture is a bit rug-worn," Mouse agreed.

"Neither of you have ever listened to a bloody word I say anyway!" Sir John planted both elbows on his desk and clapped his palms to his face and rubbed it. "Brìghde is the first female friend he's ever had. 'Tis simple enough to avoid fucking one's male friends."

Grimme gnashed his teeth and looked at his father. "Since you are the font of wisdom of all things women, what do I do?"

"Why don't you try *kissing* her?" Mouse asked, exasperated.

Grimme grimaced.

"I hope you have not allowed her to see *that* face! *Now* I am serious," Mouse continued, entirely seriously. "Get me some good clothes and a haircut, and I will look something approaching my age. Trust me, I can seduce her."

"I am not going to rear your get," Grimme said flatly.

"Grimme," his father said gravely, "either do it or let Mouse do it. Bloody hell, summon *Aldwyn,* as we all know how *he* feels about brunettes. She will make his heart stop and *he* knows how to seduce a woman."

Grimme snarled.

"Son, I do not want to spend my last days listening to you make an ass out of yourself with a girl who's been nothing but good fortune for you. If you want sympathy, you'll not find it here. Now, out. You both stink, albeit of different filths."

Thoroughly chastened, Grimme took his leave and trod heavily up the stairs and then up another flight to Emelisse's chambers. He walked in to find her with her maidservant brushing her long flaxen hair. The finger-shaped bruises on her fair skin were already starting to form from her chin to jawbones to cheekbones, and she was holding cool cloths to her face.

"Begone," he said to the maidservant with a wave of his hand. As soon as she left, he growled, "Do not ever gainsay me again. You embarrassed me."

Emelisse sniffed. "You are angry because I showed you your *wife's* weaknesses."

"Don't challenge her to lift you out of her chair with one hand, and mayhap she wouldn't have to show her *weakness,*" he sneered.

"Is that what she told you? That I dared her to?"

"You lie to me all the time, but I never cared before. Now I do. I have no reason to believe her, but I have every reason to disbelieve you. Stay out of her way. You will not like the consequences."

"I *told* you I will not be ruled by that *bitch*."

"You will."

"No!" she screamed. "I will *not!*"

"No arguments!" he snapped, infuriated all over again. "Circumstances are what they are, and Brigitte is my wife. You are first in my bed, as you have been for the last eleven years, and Brigitte is nowhere near my bed, so you must console yourself with that."

"Oui! *After* she announced your bargain to the whole of Kyneward! Her as castellain in exchange for legitimate sons!"

"Marriages *are* bargains!" Grimme roared. "That is its entire purpose! An exchange of wealth and land. Usually it is between the groom and the bride's father. In *this* case, 'tis between the groom and the bride herself because we need each other to further our own goals. Her statement should take *no one* by surprise."

"But what of love?" she whinged.

"Love! Love is a fairy story made up by bards to entertain bored nobles!"

"But *I* love you!"

"You *lust* to possess and control me, which you cannot do, which you should have learned ten years ago. So what did you do? You had my babes so you could control and possess *them*. Know this: I am *Brigitte's* husband. I am glad to be Brigitte's husband. God has blessed me with the privilege of being Brigitte's husband. There are many reasons I did not wed you, so do not *ever* refer to me as your husband again."

37

BRÌGHDE HAD taken supper in her room that evening, for she could not bear to sit beside her husband. Now it was late and she was in a chair in front of her hearth drinking. She *tried* to remind herself that Grimme was not Roger MacFhionnlaigh. That worked for a little while, but then Grimme's expression at losing Meg Dunham would flash across her mind and dispirit her once again.

Of all the indignities she had suffered throughout the years, childhood friends, the lasses and nuns at the convent, the months she had spent as a servant, and, biggest of all, Walter Fàileach, why did Grimme's manner of friendship hurt so much? He might not be the best friend in the world, but he was *trying* to be one. She understood that he was now in a position he had not expected nor wanted to be in, between his wife and his women. She understood that all he wanted was a nice, quiet family to enjoy. Why *shouldn't* he choose women he'd been with for years, women who had had his bairns, over a woman he'd known a little over a month? It was entirely reasonable and she was honest enough that she could admire his loyalty to them.

She was alone here. Being alone whilst surrounded by a legion of people was a familiar circumstance. She was accustomed to being the one not chosen. She was accustomed to a new friend changing into a different person as soon as other people were introduced. She had no claim on him or his friendship.

Yet, for a sliver of time, she had felt like she had a friend, a real friend, because on the road from Fàileach to Kyneward, she had had his undivided attention. It was that sliver of time that had tricked her into thinking it would always be that way between them. After all, how much regard could a man have for mistresses he rarely saw and that only to swive them? But no. He saw them as his family and had expectations of home and hearth with them. Meanwhile, he had left his new friend to her own devices as soon as he was home. She might have thought she lost him as soon as he was with his people again, but the truth was, she had never had him in the first place.

Her chamber door opened and she sighed heavily. "I have had enough of you today."

"And I you," he agreed agreeably, closing the door and taking the other chair in front of the hearth. "And yet, here I am."

"Why," she said flatly, then took another drink of wine.

"I told you I would teach you how to argue and still remain friends. 'Tis time for a lesson."

She started when he reached out, gently wrapped his big hand around her wrist, and caressed her bruises with his thumb. She snatched her arm away from him.

"I do not like that I put those there," he said low, clearly discomfited.

"The *bruises* are not what hurts, *my lord*."

He heaved a resigned sigh. "Aye, I'm an ass for—"

"You are an ass," she said, trying to control her rage, "for interrupting my discipline of Emelisse. You are an ass for throwing that insult at me. And you are an ass for so blatantly wishing you had Lady Margaret instead of me. You didn't even have the grace to hide it. You are an ass for touching me and then walking out angry, without so much as a blush or an explanation. You talk of friendship and not hiding hurt feelings and arguing over every little thing so they don't become big things. But your blows are not little, Lord Spindle. They are magnificent! I must retreat every time just to heal enough and regain enough strength to look at you again. I have *never* had a friend whom I have allowed to hurt me with such regularity and force. Bruises. Pffftt. I would rather you stick a dagger in my belly and let me bleed out. 'Twould be more dignified."

"What would you like me to do?" he asked slowly, but sincerely.

"Nothing! You smack me into the hearth and apologize and when I say, 'Very well, Grimme,' you say, 'I'm sorry there was no fire in it.' Do you not understand? Unless you tie me up, which you won't, *I do not have to stay here.* You need *me* far more than I need *you*. I already have your name so I canna be forced to wed and I will *never* agree to an annulment. I can seek protection with my brother at Dunham. *Or* I can simply disappear and let you explain to my mother and brothers you misplaced me. You say to me, 'Do you tell us everything to make a friendship that you will abandon as soon as we have hurt you enough?' I am long past being hurt enough to abandon you, my lord, yet … here I stay, with a husband who cannot decide what to do with me or remember why I'm here, who resents me for doing exactly what he asked me to do, and I'm stuck with women who hate me. I am almost as dimwitted as you are."

He arose and took her hand, coaxing her out of her chair and to the bed. She sighed, rolled her eyes and sat. He sat beside her. "I am sorry."

That was all.

She waited for more, but more never came.

"Now you say, 'Apology accepted.'"

"But I don't."

"Brìghde! I *apologized!*"

"That does not make the hurt disappear. *Resolution* does not happen until both parties can put away the hurt. I am *angry* with you, and I am not going to *stop* being angry with you until I stop being angry with you. I cannot force that to happen and a mere 'I'm sorry' with no knowledge of or expression of genuine penitence for *what* you did does not hasten it."

He bent over and clasped his hands behind his head.

"This is why I have no friends. They say they are sorry—*if* they say it, that is—I cannot accept the apology until I have gotten rid of the hurt, they do not acknowledge that they are in any way responsible, and they are angry that I do not simply act as if it never happened. It *happened*. They did the thing that hurt me. *My* anger has not concluded. *They* want immediate forgiveness—if they're even that penitent—and *I can't do that*. Oh, I *say* I do to try to keep the friendship, but I don't. Laddies, now—they can do that. They get angry. They have a fight. They are bruised and battered and broken, but all is well and they are friends again. Mayhap 'twill take two or three scraps, as Pierce is still angry, but it would come to some resolution. I wish I could do that."

"We could," he said, looking up at her now.

She looked at him in confusion. "We cannot."

He pointed to the floor. "There is a rug. We may wrestle until you have beaten all your anger out on me."

She hesitated, then scowled. "You're twice my size. You would win and I would be even angrier because I hate to lose."

He nudged her. "You thought about it, though. What if I gave you a dagger? You could stab me in the arse the way you did those horses in Hogarth. *That* would get me out of bed."

"Stop it," she muttered.

"Stop what?"

"Trying to make me laugh."

"Is it working?"

She drew back her fist and punched him in the arm.

"Ow." He snickered. "It's working." He draped his arm over her shoulder and brought him in to his body, caressing her hair. "Brìghde," he said soberly, "I said what I did to punish you for hurting Emelisse."

"I know that. I should not have been punished at all."

"You're right. My father pointed out that it would have been politically foolish, mayhap dangerous, for you to do nothing once she dared you. I killed a man for defying me thusly, so I can appreciate the necessity and fullness of your act. So. I apologize."

"Thank you," Brìghde murmured, completely appeased. "Accepted."

"I am sorry that I could not control my expression enough so that you did not see what fleetingly went through my mind. I am sorry that it even went through my mind; however, those types of thoughts are a habit to me so I could not have stopped it."

That was adequate. "Very well. Also accepted."

"Thank you," he said, and sounded sincere. "As for touching you and walking out—I have already apologized for that. Will you accept my apology or should I expect to be smacked in the face with everything I have done wrong no matter how many times or ways I apologize?"

"I canna tell," she muttered, "when an apology is sincere or if the person just wants the argument to go away, thus I assume 'tis the latter. I bring it up until I get an apology I can accept as sincere, but I will try to be more careful in the future."

"Thank you. I do not want to hurt my friend, but I do and I will because we are still learning each other's sore spots. 'Tis a time we must get through. And you will hurt me and then you will want forgiveness and you will tease me out of my pique, the way you do. Now. I told Emelisse something I feel I need to tell you."

She tensed.

He took a deep breath and puffed out his cheeks. "I feel God has given me the privilege of being your husband."

That wasn't what she had expected.

"I am very glad to be your husband, and I told her never to refer to me as her husband again."

Confused, unnerved, and suspicious, she turned to look him in the eye. "You would say that to soothe my ruffled feathers."

He shook his head solemnly. "If I did not mean it, I would not say it. I should have taken more time to find a wife the proper way, that is true, but I was panicking and thinking only of what would happen to my family should Sheffield kill me."

Her eyes narrowed at him. "Do not tell me that, given the opportunity to court both of us and you found us both equally matched in the ability to rule Kyneward, you would have chosen me."

"That, my lady," he said low, threateningly, "is a question only a fool would attempt to answer, as there is no right answer *and* it is entirely irrelevant. Why can you not simply be grateful for what has happened?"

She bit her lip. "I … give thanks," she murmured reluctantly, "but I do not *feel* gratitude here." She thumped her breastbone.

He was silent for a moment. "I find," he mused, "that when I cannot feel gratitude here—" He mimicked her gesture. "—'tis because I am not satisfied with what I have and want something more, and usually 'tis something very specific."

Brìghde gulped. He was getting too close to the truth.

"What do you still want that you cannot be grateful?"

I want you to desire me.

"I canna think of anything more I could want," she lied. "I canna feel—" Here again she thumped her breast. "—gratitude for the rescue, as I feel that my work here is a fair trade and I will do my best to repay that debt. 'Tis a much better life than I would have had with Roger."

"I don't need your gratitude or payment in kind," he said softly. "I just need your friendship. If I had known you, known of your predicament, I would have rescued you anyway."

She gulped.

"'*Grimme, get your arse out of bed!*'"

Surprised, she snickered in spite of herself and dipped her head when she felt herself flush.

"Risking the wrath of two Scottish clans was worth it just to hear you kick the door in."

Her smile widened even though she didn't want it to. He crooked a finger under her chin and lifted her face to grin at her.

Her smile slowly changed to a grimace. He rolled his eyes and gestured for her to say whatever she needed to.

So she did. "Well. Then." She cleared her throat. "Speaking of Emelisse, I … have a question, but … you said you wanted to tell me everything … "

He sighed heavily. "Is this going to lead to another argument?"

She looked down, wrung her hands, and wondered if her next question would be the one to disrupt their friendship.

"Ask it. I might be angry, but I will still consider us friends, and we will come to some conclusion. If not tonight, tomorrow. If not tomorrow, the next day."

She took a deep breath, for she had to approach this carefully. "Why have you stayed with her all these years if you never had an intention to wed her? She does nothing but harry you and you are clearly as well as done with her."

He shrugged. "She was my first."

"No."

"I'm loyal," he said flatly. "I did love her once, if one can count an adolescent infatuation with his first as love, but that died long ago. Which is only to say, if I can endure her all these years with no love, no intention of wedding her, and no intention of putting her out, can you not trust me to be loyal to you and our friendship enough to weather our contentions, no matter how hurtful?"

That was reasonable and logical and somewhat comforting. "Aye," she said finally. "I understand."

"When the time comes for us to mate, I must have your cooperation, and I want you to trust me."

"'Tis not *my* cooperation you need beg!" she cried, immediately exasperated. "'Tis your spindle's."

He dropped his head.

"Do not imply that *I* am the one responsible for our lack of breeding. And to the point: Why do you find brunettes so distasteful? It has something to do with the color black, doesn't it? Mayhap even ... witchcraft? That is what you do not want to discuss, is it not?"

He released her and stood, walked across the entire width of her chambers and back again. It was not a very long trip, as her chambers were the smallest in the keep. In the firelight she could see him with his head back and his hands rubbing his face. "Are you *trying* to find ways for me to hurt you?"

"I want to understand. If I understand, mayhap 'twill not be so hurtful."

"'Tis a trap," he barked. "You know there's a reason and you aren't going to let go of it unless I tell you, and thus, you will be angry with me no matter which I choose, aye?"

"Aye!" she blurted. "It is hurtful that you find me so repulsive you intended to elicit your mistress's harlotry to enable you to perform the act. It is *also* hurtful that you think of me not as a female Aldwyn, but a *male*. It is *not* a compliment."

He paused. "It's not?" he asked carefully.

"No."

"Oh."

"I want to *ken*, as if I do, mayhap I can find a way to *repair* it—"

"It cannot be repaired!"

He stopped pacing and dropped his head forward until his chin touched his chest. After a moment, he muttered, "Remember that you asked, and know that my answer is your punishment for trapping me thusly."

She couldn't promise that. "Aye."

38

"YOU'RE EVIL," HE said flatly.

Her breath caught. "*What?*"

"All of you," he continued ruthlessly.

"No!" she cried. "No! I'm sorry. I don't—"

"Dark. Ruthless. Demonic. And aye, witches."

"I am not a witch," she choked, desperately wishing she could tell him about the curse Emelisse had laid upon her and that Emelisse had also cursed Sir John.

"I know that." He strode across the room and sat beside her on the bed again. She scooted away. He followed her. "Brìghde, you asked. Now I'm going to tell you. Sit still.

"When I was a very small boy, my brother the thief, who is six years older than I, would tell me about a raven witch. The raven witch was a small, beautiful, black-haired woman in a flowing black kirtle who could break herself apart, and all her parts would become a flock of ravens to swoop down upon any unsuspecting person to bedevil them for sport. Woe betide if you had done something naughty for which you must be punished, as that would get your eyes pecked out. My mother and the priest said witches were ugly so that one would know them for what they are; my brother said Satan disguises evil with beauty. The more beautiful, the more evil. For his own amusement, betimes, he would say he would send the raven witch after me."

"Grimme," she said weakly, "that's what older brothers do. You're not four years old anymore. You're six and twenty, a knight who loves war."

"I'm not finished. When I was a page, mayhap eight or nine, Aldwyn and I were in the woods hunting rabbits for our knights' supper. Ravens attacked us. There were hundreds. Thousands, mayhap. Mayhap only ten. They chased us out. Miles, mayhap. Mayhap only a few feet. I don't remember. We looked back. They were tearing through the rabbits we'd skinned. The first thing I thought was that the raven witch had come to get me."

Brìghde gulped. That did indeed sound frightening.

"When I got older, I realized that they simply wanted what we had and did what they had to do to get them. They taught me a great lesson that day. To do what I needed to do to win. To conquer. It is also why I do not carry fear onto the battlefield. Compared to those ravens, death is *nothing,* and I *still* have nightmares about the raven witch and her demon parts."

She swallowed and tried to keep her mouth from trembling. Demon parts! *Nightmares!* This was, indeed, a great hurt.

"I have never been able to look at a dark-haired woman—*any* dark-haired woman—without remembering the raven witch, especially if she is clothed in black. Thus, I simply ignore brunettes entirely."

She was about to cry. "Is that what you thought when you first saw me in daylight?" she asked in a tiny voice.

"I first saw you in daylight when you were thrown over my lap," he said wryly. "So, no. I might have noted that your hair was black, but I didn't have a lot of time to think about it."

That did make her chuckle a little.

"By the time I could study you in good light, we had laughed, you had made it clear you were all in with us, you were wearing red and blue, so I didn't give it another thought beyond noting that you were a brunette. Then, you turned our disparate situations to our advantage. You enjoyed the adventure, took pleasure in the smallest things. You were delightful, and I never thought about it once—until you wanted the black linen."

Brìghde tried to quip, "Black is my best color."

He did chuckle, so that was successful. "Aye, well. Now you know why I asked you not to, and I am grateful that you respected my request before I had to command you. I have never told anyone about the raven witch. I have never told the story of the ravens in this way. Aldwyn and I told it many times to our men over our cups, painting it as a great adventure, but Aldwyn didn't know how terrified I was and I don't know if he was at all. You aren't the first person to ask me why I don't like brunettes, but you're the only person to whom I've told the truth. I knew you would not like it, but there it is.

"Long, dark, *beautiful* glossy feathers," he said with reverence as he reached around her to grab her braid and caress the end of it. "The more beautiful, the more evil. I *hate* ravens, but ... I cannot forget them, cannot keep from being enchanted by them, cannot look away when I see them. And since they gather in the bailey, I see them every day. So bold. So clever. So shrewd. So terrifying. An *unkindness* of ravens. The stuff of my nightmares. You are beautiful," he continued matter-of-factly. "I have never denied that. But you are dangerous. Shrewd. Bold. Ruthless. I do not look at you, Brìghde Kyneward, and see a witch, but you—brunettes, collectively—are the raven witch."

"And blondes?" she croaked, cut to the core.

"Doves," he answered immediately. "Soft. Kind. Light. Smart, but calm and wise. Angels."

But Emelisse cursed me!

"Do doves enchant you?" she asked in a very tiny voice.

"No," he said flatly. "Enchantment is witchcraft, and I will not tolerate witchcraft. Apparently, my father told you that already."

She nodded hesitantly. "I, too, fear the things of Satan, but not every brunette can be a witch."

"I know that."

"Could not blondes also be witches?"

"How would I know?" he asked helplessly. "What happened that caused such a conversation with my father to happen?"

EMELISSE CURSED ME!

"We were talking about the church and miracles."

He nodded. "Aye, he hates the church, and has tried to argue me free of my fear of all things Satanic."

"But I was praying for a miracle to take me away from my wedding, and you were there. 'Twas God's hand, but Satan has almost equal power to God."

"I agree, but my father scoffs. He does not believe either God or Satan has a hand in men's fortunes or misfortunes, nor anything men do."

Brìghde was holding herself together by a thread. Aye, she had correctly guessed his hesitance, but she could not have guessed the cause of his fear, much less the depth of it. Her voice was trembling when she whispered, "You were right. That was very hurtful. It may ... take some time."

"I know that *you* are not a witch," Grimme said earnestly, reaching up to caress her cheek. She looked into his eyes that she knew were velvety brown and it hurt to know that they would never look at her the way they did a mere tavern wench. "It is figurative, and my mind chastises me for holding onto this foolishness. I *know* you are not evil, nor a demon. You are delightful company and a good friend. I value your opinions and you give wise counsel. But you are most definitely shrewd, dangerous, bold, and ruthless. By your own words, your loyalty is only to yourself. Your purpose in wedding MacFhionnlaigh, as well as your purpose in wedding me, is proof of that."

"You canna *possibly* hold that against me!" she cried, feeling betrayed. Again. "I was contracted to wed him when I was a bairn and then I was further trapped! My end was near the moment I said 'I do.'"

"Aye, you're right. I forgot momentarily. But you also believe yourself to be always right no matter what and you will sacrifice a friendship for your righteousness once you have had enough of swallowing your opinions. You took the chin of a woman much bigger than you and pulled her out of her chair with brute strength, then held yourself off the floor whilst I held you by your wrists.

You ride a warhorse when you should be riding something half Troy's size. You threatened to lay waste to a town because its merchants stole a little money in retaliation for being stolen from. You had a bitch you named Hades who killed for you. More than once. I could go on. *How* am I supposed to think of you any other way but shrewd, dangerous, bold, and ruthless?

"You, my lady, my lady wife, my *beautiful* lady wife, with your hair black as night, shimmering blue in the sun, are the most enchanting raven I have ever seen. Their queen. I seek your company because everything about you enchants me."

She could see no compliment there.

"I do *not* find you repulsive, and I can understand why you would think that and that it would be hurtful. I understand why you are hurt by my reaction to Lady Margaret's description and I will apologize for that as many times as you need me to. But everything about you that makes me seek your company, that makes me wish to sleep with you, that makes me laugh and play with you, to listen to your counsel and follow it, that makes me feel privileged and blessed by God to be your husband, is that for which I cannot rise. You are the very essence of what I find terrifying about ravens. On the other hand, you are *also* the very essence of what I find admirable in men. I would feel privileged to know you were at my back during a battle, and I *do* feel privileged that you are at my back here. Enyo, Ares's wife and dearest companion-at-arms. This is how I think of you."

Could he possibly say anything *worse?* "That's ... a problem."

"Aye! And I do not know how to solve this problem—*or I would.*"

He stopped speaking, wrapped his arm around her shoulders, and pressed his mouth to her temple.

Brìghde sat with her head bowed and her hands in her lap. She stayed that way for a long time, not knowing what to do. He valued her for things that, a year ago, she would have been proud to claim. What was different now? Why was this hurtful at all when he valued her for exactly whom she had always taken pride in being?

They both had problems that, no, could not be repaired.

"Ye're not a wee laddie anymore, Grimme," she said low. "I will not quibble that witches are real and things of Satan are to be feared. Aye, that is true. But ravens canna hurt you."

He threw up his hands. "You say nothing I have not told myself."

Still she remained silent, her insides tumbling like dark thunderclouds. "My older brothers," she said low, "told us the same types of tales. I told them to my younger brothers. I was frightened and sometimes I still am, but I do not see real people in them."

"I can't explain it. Sleep with me?" he asked warily.

"No," she murmured. "I don't ken what I feel. 'Tis not anger. I don't think. 'Tis somewhat of relief, that 'tis not *me*, that you *know* 'tis a defect in you. That you know this about yourself is comforting. 'Tis somewhat flattery that you value me so highly and that I have somehow risen above suspicion. But please understand. I am *not* male, and though I feel privileged that you see me as your dearest companion-at-arms, I am a *female* and my female vanity is bruised."

He nodded. "Fair."

"I may be angry tomorrow or I may never be angry or ... I don't know. Please be patient, as we made a bargain and 'tis a fair one and we must live and work together for the rest of our days. But you rescued me and were kind to me and you befriended me and you saved my life. I will do anything for you to repay that debt."

"Never mind who owes whom what or how much. 'Tis not important. What *is* important is that you have brought something to me that I have grown to cherish, and I do not want to harm that. But I will, and you will, because that is the nature of people. *Promise me* that you will not keep your hurts and thoughts from me, so that we may argue as we go along, for I do not want to lose your friendship."

"I canna promise that," she said low. "'Tis a lifelong habit."

He paused. "Then I can only hope that I can earn your trust. Try?"

"I will try."

39

BRÌGHDE SAT AT breakfast the next morning noting that there was very little tension between her and the mistresses. Of course, part of that could be that she had never had any quarrel with the three lesser mistresses and she was actually quite flattered that Maebh wanted to swive her. Ardith was, indeed, as sharp as a wheel of cheese. Dillena was quiet, but also dignified, elegant, and refined, which was not something Brìghde could lay claim to and thus, admired and some days even longed to be.

It could also be that Emelisse was not at table, but that was likely because her face was too bruised to show it. Brìghde looked down at her wrists that were also ringed with thick, ugly bruises, the right far worse than the left. She caressed one with a finger. She was proud of them. It had taken all her strength to keep herself elevated to face Grimme on his level and her arms and shoulders were still sore.

Brìghde had tossed and turned all night, dozing, stewing about what Grimme had said and how he saw her—

Ravens!

Witches!

Nightmares!

and worst of all

A man!

—but otherwise she had no reservations about sleeping here at Kyneward. It was a realization she had had upon arising. Here, she felt safe. She could allow herself to sleep deeply with the knowledge that she did not have to keep one eye open for predators animal or human, or Walter, who was wont to awaken her at any time of night with the next idea he had for the fate of MacFhionnlaigh. She also did not have to awaken in time to do her servant duties.

The only person who would barge into her room was her husband and that only to sleep with her. He might awaken her upon getting into bed, but she did not fear any nefarious intentions nor did she have to think, which would have left her sleepless for the rest of the night.

She wished he *did* have nefarious intentions. Indeed, it was precisely the fact that he didn't that had her in an upset. It didn't matter, though, because that wasn't going to change, either. She could not repair the defect in his mind, so she had to learn how to manage the situation in hers.

"Good morn, Brìghde!" the earl said cheerfully as he sat next to her.

"Good morn, Grimme."

"You look fetching today." Her eyebrows rose and he slid her a wry grin. "I am allowed to notice when you are fetching, am I not? Men don't normally go about in kirtles and their hair in rolls."

She chuckled. "'Tis true."

"Is our argument behind us or are we still stinging?"

She waggled her bruised wrist. "My vanity is still bruised, but 'twill fade."
He grimaced. "I will try not to reference those things in future arguments."

"Thank you. What do you have planned for today?"

She suddenly couldn't remember, but whatever it was, she'd let it go in a heartbeat. "Why?"

"I know you wanted to go to the dower house. I can put a force together."

She would *love* to go to the dower house. She was desperate to find furniture, and though she was absolutely certain there was none there, she could leave no stone unturned. Yet with all the tension of the last few days, she had forgotten.

He hadn't, and offered his men when they were busy. She cleared her throat and decided to take the olive branch. "I would like that, thank you."

"I will have them meet you in the stable as soon as I can."

That was why she put up with his manner of friendship. He was as thoughtful as he was hurtful.

Thus she was perched upon her trusty steed awaiting her guard when they came in from the encampment with smiles and a cheery, "Good morn, my lady!"

"You are a centenier, are you not?" she asked one of them, surprised that a commander of a force of one hundred had been selected.

"Aye, my lady," he said with a smile and a wink. "Sir Thom. He felt you deserved the best."

"That's because I do!" she said, suddenly much happier. Aye, Grimme was clumsy with her feelings, but he was also carelessly thoughtful and when he was, he was magnificently carelessly thoughtful. "Well? Lead the way."

To entertain both them and herself, she set about regaling them with the tale of how Grimme had snatched her out of her wedding, and had them roaring by the time she got to *Grimme, get your arse out of bed!* She referenced the vulgar jests she did not understand and they hesitantly explained them to her, but only because she commanded them to as Lady Kyneward. Then she offered a few vulgar jests of her own she'd learned from her brothers. She also wanted to race, but they kept allowing her to win, so she huffed in disgust and did not attempt to yet *again* order them to allow her to lose if she deserved to.

"I have a warhorse, by Mother Mary and Joseph. I grew up riding shires bareback against six brothers! I need a challenge!"

But no.

By the time they reached the old crumbling dower house, they were fast friends and breathless from laughing.

There were, indeed, armored knights on horses bearing Sheffield's standard patrolling the border, which seemed to be a mere ten feet from the dower house.

Once they came into view, her knights ceased laughing and spread out to cover the Kyneward side of the border whilst she trotted around the house twice, inspecting the exterior. "Stay back, my lady," Sir Thom said low.

"I'm going inside."

They looked up at the crumbling dower house, looked at the knights who were eyeing her speculatively, and sighed. "Be careful."

She went back around the house to the front stoop, which was on the opposite side of the border, facing Kyneward Keep, sidled Troy up to the stoop, and dismounted easily. "Stay there," she firmly commanded the beast and fed him some more pears. She shook out the key ring and finally found the right one. While the iron bar across the iron door was heavy, she was equal to the task, then she unlocked the front door. It took all her little might, but she finally got the iron door open.

The inside was dim, of course, boarded up as it was, with only slivers of light streaming through and creating sparkles out of dust motes. It wasn't as decrepit on the inside as it was on the outside and she went about pulling drapes open to allow even a smidgen more of light. To her surprise, the ground floor rooms were *filled* with furniture, all covered with cloths that were coated in many inches of dust. She coughed as she ripped them off and gasped. It was an hundred years out of date, but it was *beautiful.*

She ripped another cloth off. More beautiful furniture that matched! She started running from room to room, snatching cloths off and squealing in delight. She ran up the stairs, or tried, since the stairs were rotting, but that did not deter her. There were rooms and rooms full of furniture that had once been well loved, cared for, and left protected. The third floor, too, was thoroughly furnished and it *all matched!*

There were rugs and tapestries, drapes and bed hangings all protected from fading by the boards. In the pantries there were hundreds and hundreds of beautiful platters and knives and spoons, goblets and tankards.

She was in the middle of looking around at all these treasures with utter joy when she heard the faint scrape of a sword leaving its scabbard. She had lived with a warmonger too long not to know it instantly. Startled, she went to a window and peeked out through a slit between planks to see that her knights were squared off against Sheffield knights, and they were outnumbered by one.

That was when she heard the long, low sound of a horn.

The battle started. She ran to the front door. Troy was still standing there by the stoop, grazing. She mounted him, turned him sharply, and kicked him into a flat-out gallop toward the keep, which was not visible. Presently, she heard the faint thrum of galloping hooves behind her and, terrified, she urged Troy faster. Now the keep was at least in sight. She was getting closer to the keep ... closer ... closer ...

A dark spot just outside her vision, behind her, to the left, grew from a tiny shadow to a threat.

schwoop

It was just a whisper that went right by her ear.

Troy darted right, nearly unseating her, and she struggled to get back in control.

schwoop

schwoop

schwoop

schwoop

As if driven by instinct, Troy darted left again, across the fields, flashing past a dozen knights racing the other way, until she and Troy thundered onto the road that ringed the keep, around the turn, up the lane, leaping children, carts, and goats, through the portcullis, and into the outer bailey where there were grooms anxiously awaiting her.

She was panting as Troy, his sides heaving, paced almost angrily around the outer bailey, and did what she could for her pet to cool him off before she had to release him to the grooms. "Thank you," she croaked, her heart racing. "Thank you, laddie. I wanted a challenge," she quipped weakly, because if she did not quip, she would slide right off and start to sob. "I should be careful what I wish for, aye?"

"Brìghde!"

She was panting through her nose and she couldn't catch a deep enough breath and still she trotted Troy around. The portcullis wasn't closed. They weren't under attack. There was Grimme alongside her, gently taking Troy's bridle and slowing them down until they were walking to the stables.

She thought.

Perhaps.

Her eyes were clamped shut and she was going to start sobbing right in front of her husband.

"We'll get them," he said lightly, taking her chin in his hand and gently forcing her to face him. "No one's chasing you anymore. Open your eyes."

She didn't want to, but she did. They stung from the salt in her tears and she blinked rapidly against the glare. She still couldn't breathe.

"Cup your hands and put them over your mouth to breathe." She did. She knew to do that. Why hadn't she thought of it? "Good girl," he said soothingly. "Gooood wife. That's my good countess. No one's chasing you anymore," he repeated. Now he was rubbing her back. She felt his mailed leg scrape against her linen-covered one. Troy and Deimos touched noses and Troy huffed. Grimme scratched Troy's withers. "Good boy. Who's a good boy? *You're* a good boy."

That made her drop her hands and the corner of her mouth turned up a little. "What happened?" she croaked. "I— Our border. They— My guard and—"

"Shhh. Listen."

She heard the faint sound of another set of horses racing away from the keep, men shouting, metal clanging, and then it faded.

"All those knights … I'm just … one … wee lass … " she hiccupped.

"You're my wife," he corrected gently and cupped her cheek, his thumb caressing her cheekbone. "And countess. These men have sworn fealty to you."

"How— Chasing me and then—"

"My watchers saw the skirmish begin and sounded the alarm. The archers had to wait until he was in range."

"Troy, he—almost threw me—" She demonstrated with her hands.

"A warhorse is trained to think and act independently when his knight is otherwise engaged. He did that to get out of your pursuer's reach, then doubled back to get to the keep."

"But why would they do that?" she cried. "It's our land!"

"Brìghde, look at me. See me."

She looked at him. She saw him. That handsome carved face and those velvety brown eyes and the long golden-red hair currently fluttering in the breeze, the man that had abducted her but treated her with respect and tenderness, lain with her to keep her from escaping, and to protect her, then because he simply … liked to. Never, from the moment one of his knights had thrown her over his shoulder, had she felt real fear. She couldn't—she was too afraid of Walter's sword point in her back, being Roger's wife, that she would be forced to poison Roger MacFhionnlaigh to keep his spindle out of her, then poison an entire clan, which would have meant her death, too.

Kiss me, Grimme. Please.

"This is what is going to happen: I will send a missive to Sheffield informing him that I have his knights in my possession. He will pay the ransom for his knights and I will keep the horses and armor. It will be called a simple misunderstanding, but we will all know what happened and why, which is why he will pay the ransom. When the king finds out he *did* pay the ransom, he will demand an answer and I will give it to him. And Aldwyn—"

"Your *former* friend."

"Aye. Aldwyn will see that they get the lash once they are back at Sheffield. He will not tolerate such behavior in his ranks. They will be made an example of."

"But I'm *your* wife. He would—"

"Being my wife has nothing to do with it. You are a woman and, moreover, a noblewoman, and a chivalrous knight does not rape women. He adheres to the chivalric code, and part of that is to protect women at all costs."

The tears were starting to spill over. He took her face in both hands and wiped them away with his thumbs, smiling gently at her. "I just found you, Brìghde. I'm not going to let anything happen to you, now or ever. There are too many servants left for you to terrify."

Take me to your bed. Undress me. Swive me.

She couldn't smile.

He gently pushed away from her and said, "'Tis time to put Troy away. You need to go to bed."

She shook her head. "No. I will feel like a coward."

"Very well. You must do what you must do, but first Troy needs to be taken care of. Give him a bushel of carrots and discuss the event with him." He scratched Troy's ears and cheeks. "Who's a good boy? *You're* a good boy."

40

"EXPECT THE DUKE within the fortnight," Grimme muttered at her at supper that night.

"What?" she whispered, panicking, heart racing. Where would she put all those people? She couldn't get a mansion's worth of furniture moved and arranged in two weeks without enlisting her husband's knights' help. After her ordeal, it was too much to think about.

"Not his retinue. Him, Aldwyn most definitely, possibly a few knights who will set up their own encampment. This is business, not a social visit or a tutor visiting to check on his pupil's progress and make sure he is showing his work," he said bitterly.

Her heart began to slow. "I will put him in your chambers. You will sleep with me."

"'Twill not be a hardship, my lady."

Brìghde poured herself another cup of wine, but her hand was trembling and Grimme noticed. He took the pitcher and poured for her. "Thank you," she croaked. "I left the door of the dower house unlocked and I want to fetch the furniture as soon as possible. May I have some knights?"

"Use villeins. They owe us three days a week. I'll not have my knights moving furniture. However, I *will* send another guard with you."

"Aye, because I would not know that knights are not furniture movers."

He slid her a glance, but said nothing.

"I would like for you to assign Sir Thom to me permanently."

"Aye."

"He may sit up here with us, aye?"

"Sir Thom!" Grimme barked. "My lady would like you to join the head table as the captain of her guard. You will have full command of Kyneward when she is in residence, but I and Sir Drew are not. Do you accept?"

Surprised, he said, "Of course, my lord. I am privileged."

"I'm sure she will get in enough trouble that you won't be bored."

That made the hall laugh, and she did, in fact, chuckle in spite of herself.

As he moved himself, Brìghde happened to see Pierce looking at Brìghde, his mouth trembling. Brìghde smiled. "All is well, Pierce," she said.

"I need to talk to you about him," Grimme whispered. "Would you sleep with me tonight?"

Truth be told, she needed to sleep with him tonight. She was still trembling from her day's misadventure, but she didn't want anybody to see her weakness. She could lie beside Grimme and have his comfort and protection.

When she nodded, Grimme stood calmly and held his hand out to Brìghde, who put her hand in his. Calmly, deliberately, they went to the stairs, glided up them like dignified nobles, then, once they were in his chambers he folded her in his arms and she burst out into sobs.

GRIMME LAY AWAKE with Brìghde cradled to him after she had cried herself to sleep. The aftermath of any battle was difficult, especially at first, with very young, untried soldiers. Grimme had always considered the ravens to be his first battle.

In some ways, he was grateful for that very early experience, for because of it, he had never feared war or death on the battlefield. It was also when he had learned that he must *conquer*. Victory wasn't enough. Where other men saw terror and death, he saw complete subjugation of his enemy. But he remembered his terror all too well, and he knew that Brìghde had held herself together as long as she could before she broke. Everybody did.

The oddest things broke people, and today, it had been the news that she would have to quickly prepare the keep for the duke's visit.

He knew what Brìghde had needed, but he couldn't give it to her. He could only offer his chest for her to soak through.

Hamond, any word of something that will help me?

My ... friend ... thinks something is possible, but has not—ah, that is to say—

Take me to him. I will pay anything.

Ah, my lord, if I do that, it will never happen at all.

Then again, he remembered, she didn't want him any more than he wanted her. She was perfectly willing to comply to fulfill the bargain to get it out of the way, and he was even reasonably certain that once taught, she would be a wonderful lover. She was only upset because she continued to be reminded that he did not want her, and he could see how that would wear a person down. She was passionate and lusty about everything: food, wine, horses, dogs, her position here at Kyneward Keep. Why would she fuck any less passionately or lustily than she did anything else?

As he lay there staring up into his hangings, the knowledge that she didn't want him, which was only convenient to his deficit, undulated into a *realization* that this woman lying in his arms, his wife, Brìghde Kyneward, *did not want* to fuck Grimme.

He scowled. But for God's sake, why didn't she?

How many times had he told her she was beautiful?

He was handsome, but she'd never so much as given him a side glance or hint that she *might like* for him to fuck her.

Women competed for Grimme's attention all the time. They had since he'd grown into his paws at such a young age. The second Emelisse had seduced him as a fifteen-year-old, he had been insatiable, just like his father, just like his grandfather, just like his brothers, with the bastards all over England to attest to it.

There weren't a lot of men in Grimme's circle as handsome as he, except for Aldwyn, who looked quite a bit like Grimme, so that was another area where he and Aldwyn had always competed. But outside of the two of them, there just wasn't that much competition for women.

Mouse *was* right about being more handsome than Grimme, but he was Grimme's exact opposite: normal height, strong but thin and wiry, with dark brown-red hair and blue eyes. His skin was pale in the winter, but darkened easily in the summer if he could be bothered to go outside in the daylight. But he looked barely into puberty, which made it difficult for him to find anyone but young girls who swooned over him. No, Mouse was no competition, for several reasons.

Mayhap that was Brìghde's problem: Mayhap Grimme was simply too big for her taste, and she would rather have someone like Mouse. Some women liked grotesque blond giants. Some women liked tricky brown mice who didn't look their age. He wondered what she would think if she ever saw Mouse clean and in rich clothing, but she would never get the chance, so it didn't matter.

His father's suggestion to summon Aldwyn to get a babe on Brìghde had been a jest, but he was not wrong: Aldwyn loved brunettes and he knew how to seduce women. In a fortnight, Aldwyn would be here to collect his knights, riding Ares. He would take one look at Brìghde and the fire of challenge would be there again. The temptation to have Grimme's wife—before Grimme did—for revenge and simply because she was beautiful might even be too much for chivalrous Aldwyn. Fucking her. Planting *his* seed before Grimme planted his, because Aldwyn would *know* Grimme hadn't fucked his wife the second he saw her, and it would not be in the least bit difficult. Between her need for friends and Aldwyn's skill at wooing, she'd topple immediately.

Grimme closed his eyes, impatient with himself. That would *never* happen. Aldwyn wouldn't seduce another man's wife, no matter how great the temptation, and Brìghde had agreed to having no other lovers until she'd had one or two sons for Grimme.

But … what if it did?

He started thrumming his fingers on the mattress, his jaw grinding. Oh, aye, Brìghde would stop Aldwyn's heart immediately.

Grimme did not want to fuck Brìghde, but he didn't want anyone else to, either, including Maebh.

But why didn't Brìghde, his lusty little bride, want to fuck *Grimme?*

41

GRIMME HAD, FOR two nights following the incident, insisted that Brìghde sleep with him in his chambers. She did not hesitate for she felt safest with him. Today, three mornings later, she had awakened after a fitful night filled with dreams of ravens and witches.

Since ravens were mere birds and Brìghde was fully capable of killing the only witch in this house at her leisure, she did not awaken frightened. She did, however, awaken with a headache, stinging eyes, and a sour mood.

As if that weren't enough, when she appeared for breakfast, there was a messenger awaiting her, outfitted in purple and yellow livery.

"My Lady Kyneward?" he asked politely.

"Aye," she said warily.

"I am from the Dukedom of Sheffield. I come on behalf of His Grace the Duke and request a return message."

She opened the message he gave her, scanned it and turned away from the man before she allowed him to see how frightened she was.

Aye, the duke would arrive within a fortnight of the incident, as Grimme had predicted. His visit was for the sole purpose of paying to ransom his knights, which was a business negotiation. Aye, Grimme was right about that, too. So why was this missive addressed to *her*? *She* didn't have anything to do with the exchange of coin for men.

It was an insult, nigh unto a taunt.

We'll get you, Lady Kyneward, never fear.

She closed her eyes and took a deep breath. She was allowing her imagination to get away with her, or else she was still so frightened by her narrow escape she felt a simple missive to be a weapon.

She ran up the stairs and burst into Grimme's chambers. "Grimme. Wake up. Please tell me I am making too much of this."

He twisted toward her, his arm up to keep the sunlight out of his eyes. "What?"

"Sheffield." She thrust the note upon him.

He read it. "What's wrong with it?"

"It's addressed to me."

He bolted upright and looked at the other side of the parchment. "God damn him," he swore, tearing off his sheet and hunting around for his hose.

She looked away from his naked body because she could not stand to know he saw her as the stuff of nightmares whilst she saw him as a ray of sunlight.

He looked up at her as Hamond was combing his hair. "Why are you upset about this? Why did you bring it to me?"

"It feels like a threat."

"Aye, it is," he said tightly. "You've good instincts, but I shouldn't be surprised."

Then he was out the door. She ran after him and saw him slam into Sir John's study. She followed to see him penning his own missive, writing quickly. As soon as the ink was dry, he folded it and sealed it, then stormed out to the waiting messenger.

"You tell His Grace," Grimme snarled, slapping the missive in the messenger's hand, "that he negotiates with *me*, not my wife."

Unless I'm dead.

Brìghde heard it as loudly as if he had said it.

The messenger bowed. "Thank you, my lord."

Brìghde scurried to the door where Grimme stood watching until the messenger was out of the fortress and down the lane. "What did you write?" she asked quietly.

"I told him to send another message and this time address it to the man with the power."

Brìghde's eyes went wide and she puffed her cheeks out. He turned then and caught her look. "I don't fear death, Brìghde," he said quietly. "But you need to get this keep operating like your mother has Fàileach before he kills me because then you *will* be negotiating with him."

"How?" she whispered. "Your sons are illegitimate, the duke will challenge any heir you name, and you and I don't have any. Without a wee laddie, I would have no power. Grimme," she said helplessly, "we *must* have a bairn."

"Pierce," he said, then bellowed for Father Hercule to meet him in Sir John's study. "Just in case it will hold, I will name Pierce as my heir right now. You're his stepmother. You will be in control."

He directed her into the room behind Father Hercule. Brìghde sat heavily, wondering how many excuses Grimme was going to find to avoid bedding her. If Father Hercule was right, it was probable that a document drawn up by the earl's lawyer would hold, but what if it didn't? Sheffield had already once challenged the legitimacy of a babe simply because the old duke did not care to swive women. He would of course challenge this.

"Brìghde," Grimme said earnestly, as if he were panicked, "what I needed to talk to you about the other night— Maebh would like you to take Pierce as your own."

Brìghde's mouth dropped open.

"I stated that incorrectly. Maebh gives Pierce anything he wants because she wants him to be happy. She fails at that miserably because she doesn't know what will make him happy, and she is torn up about it, but she has noted that *you* make him happy *and* she correctly ascertained that you know how to rear boys better than any of my sons' mothers. She wants the best for him, she thinks *you* are what's best for him and I agree, so she doesn't want to give Pierce to you. She wants to give *you* to Pierce."

Before Brìghde could say anything at all, he was out the door. Presently, he returned with Maebh and bustled her to Brìghde's desk and said, "Are you sure?"

Maebh looked up at Brìghde and, with tears in her eyes, said, "You're better for him than I am. He … " She sniffled. "Loves you more."

"I haven't been here long enough for him to love me," Brìghde croaked.

Maebh shrugged helplessly and prepared a quill then swore out in writing her intention of giving Brìghde to Pierce should anything happen to Maebh or Grimme.

It's not Roger MacFhionnlaigh. It's not Roger MacFhionnlaigh.

No one was paying attention to her. Grimme was striding between what Father Hercule was penning and what Maebh was penning. It didn't involve Brìghde at all. She would not be missed, so she left the study. Breakfast was being served, but she wasn't hungry, so she went out to the stable.

"Troy's training today, m'lady. Would ye mind takin' Enyo out?"

Enyo … Ares's … wife and dearest companion, who rides with him into battle.

She had always taken pride in her privileged place in a room full of men, but now … She was most definitely Enyo, and for the first time in her life, she didn't like it.

"Mary Seven, mayhap?"

"Aye, good choice."

"Brìghde?" came Pierce's small voice.

She looked around. "I canna see you, Pierce." He peeked around the door of the stall and gave her a sweet smile. There were worse sons to have, as, say, Gaston and Max. "Would you like to go riding with me this morn on your wee pony?"

His little face lit up with a smile so wide it made her heart ache. He looked so much like Grimme it was uncanny. His blonde hair was almost white like his mother's and it didn't gleam red in the sun, but he had the same face and same velvety brown eyes. She put her hand on his head and smoothed his hair, looked down at him and felt her tears sting her eyes. "Ye look so much like yer da," she whispered.

"What's wrong?"

"Everythin', me wee laddie. Everythin'."

THE RETURN message came a day later.

It was addressed to Grimme.

The whole of the message was a date.

The duke would arrive in a sennight.

42

IT TOOK A full week for Brìghde, sixty villeins and servants, many carts, teams of oxen and shires, and six carpenters to strip the dower house and get it all back to Kyneward Keep, in place, and finished off with the trappings. Every morning after her prayers, she supervised the servants placing the furniture that had been delivered late the night before. She stopped to eat whilst Avis and Hamond took over directing the placement of it all where they felt best it should go.

Brìghde, Pierce on his wee pony, Sir Thom, and a guard of ten rode out after bolting down their breakfast to see the villeins and manservants already wrestling the next enormous pieces of furniture onto the carts lined up at least a mile. The carpenters carefully dismantled the beds and tables and anything else that could be dismantled for transport. They did not stop for the night until they could no longer see the pathway they had carved from the keep to the dower house.

Under Hamond's and Avis's direction, as the beds were assembled in the rooms they designated, as more furniture arrived from the dower house, they directed others to bring the rugs and bed hangings and linens and tapestries. The servants in the larders barely had enough room to put all the kitchenware. The cooks and bakers were thrilled with the plethora of cooking pots, pans, and utensils. The rugs and tapestries and mattresses were beaten and aired out. The larders full of linens were laundered.

By the morning before the duke's arrival, Kyneward Keep still had eight chambers of twenty-four that were empty, but they would have no shortage of places to put their guests.

Thus, in the midst of panicked preparation from chambers to menus to cleaning, Brìghde had an excuse to avoid Grimme all week, but Sir John noticed. The day before the duke was to arrive, once Brìghde declared all the chambers in acceptable condition to receive guests, Sir John directed her to his study and demanded an explanation of her behavior. Exhausted, frazzled, and still upset, she tearfully laid out almost the whole of it, save the brother's tales and the ravens, but when Sir John waved it away, she was even more hurt.

"My dear, there are more ways to a man's cod than through his eyes or his stomach."

"I don't *want* his spindle!" she lied.

His eyebrow rose. "Well if you don't want it, why is it that hurtful?"

"I just don't want him to see me as a witch, *enchanting* him with black magic, by Mary and Joseph! When *Emelisse* is an *actual* witch! I might as well be a *man!* Just because I have black hair!"

He sighed impatiently and closed his eyes. "Brìghde, take what you can get. He has given you a gift he gives no one but his closest friends. You are getting what Aldwyn got, which is rare and special. More even, as you sleep with him, no?"

"Aye."

"Don't let your vanity mar what he has given you. He is not now nor has he ever been a *chivalrous* knight and he does not *woo*. He does not know how to talk to women and he has never had a female friend before, which means you must bear his practice. As he inherited his lust from me, I know how he thinks and what he needs. You are used to attracting men's eyes, but you have now met the first and only man who has ever deliberately snubbed you for your beauty. Boo hoo." He shooed her away. "Go on now. The duke will be here tomorrow afternoon."

She refused to go away. "Sir John," she insisted, "there is also the question of issue. At what point does the duke ask himself if he really needs that plague of an earl and finds another way to lure him into a trap? What if it is true that naming an heir will not hold no matter what legalities are observed? Sheffield has already tried to challenge the legitimacy of one babe, aye?"

Sir John nodded.

"If it doesn't hold, what happens to the rest of us? What will Sheffield do to me? If Pierce is accepted as the heir, I, as his stepmother am still in danger because it doesn't give *me* as much power as a legitimate heir. Even nobles who swive men manage to get their wives with child, yet Grimme canna do that much. I—am—frightened. Frightened enough to seek protection with my brother and abandon the rest of you. *I do not have to stay.*"

"Take a lover," he said shortly.

"But I promised—"

He looked up at her with narrowed eyes and she clicked her mouth shut. "When you first arrived, you said you took the bargain in part because you found him handsome enough to bed him."

"I remember. I also said it would fade—"

"It hasn't. It won't. You knew that when you said it, and it has only grown." She gulped. "I am seventy years old, my dear, and I have a long history with women as friends *and* lovers, as I never took a mistress unless she was also my friend. So don't try to lie to me about what you do and don't want from him. You couldn't care less about a babe, and if you were that frightened, you would have already left."

She bit her lip and looked away.

"But I am very happy about that, as it makes me feel much better about the entire situation. He will get over this impediment—" He couldn't promise that because she hadn't given him all the information. "—but it will take time. The problem is that we do not have that kind of time."

She sighed.

He rubbed his temple. "Let us get through the negotiations. The duke is not going to kill anybody this week, and then we can discuss the matter with Grimme together, and hopefully find a way to get him to bed you. I know him. If he has you once, you will never be able to get rid of him, and as to that, be careful what you wish for. There's a reason he has to keep seven women."

"Did you?" she muttered resentfully. Brìghde wished she hadn't begun this conversation.

"Not seven, no. Three at most at any given moment, but they didn't live with me, and my problem was that I loved *all* my women because they were my friends and I could not choose amongst them. I *wanted* to be able to have one woman, be faithful to her, but I could not. He is not so constrained."

"Did that include your wife?"

"I *despised* my wife," he said darkly, "for reasons I don't have time to explain right now, but it was such I did not feel married nor did I feel obliged to be true to her. I believe you have experience with a betrothed you despise, aye? And he with you?"

"Aye," she said in a tiny voice.

"I understand that a babe is a convenient excuse to get what you really want, but hounding him for it will only delay it. In the meantime, find a way to be grateful for what you have, which is a husband you enjoy when he is not tripping over his words and falling face-first in the dirt at your feet—and however it feels, that is all it is. The rest will follow and it cannot follow quickly enough. Know this: You and I want the same thing."

She slumped, defeated. "Very well."

That night, Brìghde was lying in her bathtub, having the maidservants bring more and more hot water. She had already bathed and her hair was freshly washed and wound up in a towel upon her head, so now she sought only to soak the aches and pains out of her body. And drink.

Presently there was a knock at the door, but before Brìghde could call an entry, it opened and there stood the earl himself.

"I'm in me bath," Brìghde said tightly. "Again."

"I see that."

"Close the bloody door, Grimme!"

He did just that. "My apologies," he said as he dropped his big body on her bed. He looked up at the ceiling with his arm over his forehead. "My women do not care."

"Aye, but I'm nae one o' yer women."

"In point of fact, you are."

"Nooo, I'm Aldwyn's replacement, a *man*, an' I'd rather the whole keep not know that *this* man has breasts, hips, an' no spindle. I'd rather ye not, either, come to think of it, since ye canna bear to touch me."

"Oh," he said snidely. "You're drunk."

"Whatta ye want, *Grimme?*" she asked, contemptuously rolling her R.

"When I abducted you, you were the model of equanimity, making me laugh, being my friend and playmate and conspirator, occasional bedmate, putting my house to rights for me, and now— You have been avoiding me for a week and I have respected that—"

"I've been up from dawn to midnight movin' house an' ye've been trainin' in case Sheffield attacks us!"

"But you have not slept with me and you have locked your door against me!" he barked. "A week, yet your anger has grown *after* you said 'twould fade. I grow weary of your pouting. When the duke comes, I would that you not make it so obvious that we are at odds. We must present a united front."

"I told ye," she growled, "that an argument *ends* when both parties resolve their anger an' hurt. It's ended fer *you*, but it hasna ended fer *me*, which I *told* ye I might nae be able to do verra quickly, an' e'ery night this week I've dreamt o' nothin' but ravens'n'witches, which means I've'na got any good sleep whilst tryin'a move a mansion an' preparin' to host evil in me house."

"None of which is my fault! I said that you are a beautiful, enchanting woman and I compared you to a lovely bird."

"A bird that terrifies ye. Ye *also* told me ye see in me the manifestation of *evil*. A raven witch who can split herself into winged demons. The *stuff o' nightmares*. *Sheffield* is th'evil one an' I'm akin to him?"

"No," he said firmly. "I was speaking figuratively and of brunettes collectively, which you know. I was very clear on that point."

"*An'* that I might as well be a man."

He hesitated. "I … if, if … I think of you as a man," he admitted reluctantly, "I do not see a raven. When I think of you as a man, I cannot rise. Also, you are my friend. I don't befriend those I fuck and I don't fuck my friends."

Her jaw ground. "Grimme," she said low, "the fact that I'm nae to yer taste is one thing. I'd go so far as to say I doona care." If he could rise for her, she *wouldn't* care. She would simply take her pleasure. "I weary o' bein' reminded of it *constantly*. Wishin' I were Meg. Seein' me as male, merely servin' as a replacement fer Aldwyn. Touchin' me then walkin' out angry is certainly the bleakest o' reminders."

"Where does this truly start?" he asked tightly. "I *know* you are hiding something from me, because people who continue to reference a sin after apologies were accepted are not, in fact, still angry about that sin. They are angry about something else. What did I do that you have not confronted me with?"

She huffed. "Maebh," she muttered resentfully. "Ye said a disgustin' thing about me *behind me back* to yer mistresses to appease 'em. Ye're supposed to be me friend, but I've had many friends who've spoken badly of me behind me back, ridiculed me, even as I'm tryin'a be a friend. *Then* ye used yer thoughts of me as a man to reassure yer favorite harlot. Ye *betrayed* me. Ye've been humorin' me all along an' laughin' at me with *them*."

"I most certainly do not laugh at you with them or anyone else. I am trying to walk a thin line between you and them and it is very thin."

"Yet now I canna trust our friendship. *I do not have to stay here*." It wouldn't hurt to remind him of this.

He released a frustrated whoosh of air. "And so you have been angry about that all this time instead of telling me you were angry *right then*. You were courteous, you laughed it off, but you were seething and you did not tell me. Since then, you have been letting all the words collect until there is nothing *but* anger and there is nowhere to go, and you cannot forgive the last because you are still stinging from the first. *This* is why I told you you *must* have the small arguments all along the way."

"I canna think o' one thing ye coulda said that'd've eased that hurt. I'll *ne'er* be able to forget that, forget that ye speak o' friendship to me, an' then speak so contemptuously o' me to the very people who hate me."

"Firstly, Dillena, Ardith, and Maebh do not hate you. Emelisse hates everyone and everything, especially those who have what she wants."

"An' ye put up with it," she said flatly.

"It doesn't affect me," he growled. "And no, I do not care how selfish that is, it's *my* house. That is why you are here, to *keep* it from affecting me, and I gave you free rein, so you cannot hold that over me, either. I have always said these things to reassure *them* that you are not a threat to them *and* to reassure you that I will not ravish you or—"

"Oh, ye made that clear. I've *no* fear o' yer spindle. Who fears somethin' that canna hurt him, as, say, *ravens*."

His jaw ground. "That, my lady, was hurtful. I trusted you with that."

"Maybe ye shouldn't, since ravens're nae terribly trustworthy."

"Stop it!" he barked. "Now you are arguing like my women do."

"That's because *I'm a woman!* Oh, but ye forgot that, since I *might as well* be a man. An' if I'm not a man, I'm a raven an' I terrify ye."

"*You* do not terrify me! My God, you're a wisp of a woman. I could crush your head with my bare hands."

"Prove it. Let me wear black."

He was silent.

"Mmm hm."

"Brìghde," he growled. "You're drunk and though I know you are perfectly capable of matching wits with me whilst you're drunk, I don't want to discuss it whilst you're drunk *and* tired *and* have a headache *and* anxious about Sheffield's visit."

She ignored that. "I would we fulfill this part o' the bargain as soon as possible so we may ne'er be obliged to visit this topic again. Call Maebh an' I'll allow *her* to seduce me since *she* wants me."

"Set the date," he snapped.

Brìghde swallowed. She hadn't expected that.

There was silence in the room for a long time. Then she heard him flop on her bed. "I miss you," he muttered, which sounded almost like a pout. "You've withdrawn from me for a week and … I cannot bear it any longer. I do have keys to this keep. I *could* have allowed myself in, but I did not."

Tears stung her eyes. That was quite a lovely thing to hear.

"You have only been here six weeks and 'tis as if this has always been your home and we have always been friends. If I could recant what I said—if I could recant what I said to my women, that Maebh repeated—I would. I did not say that to ridicule you; I said it because I am frustrated and angry with *myself*. They know that. Maebh is furious I will not let her have you. I don't— Brìghde, I don't know what you want from me!"

I want you to desire me.

"Right now. This very moment. What can I say or do that will put this aright?"

Lust for me. Kiss me. Swive me.

"I don't know," she muttered because she was damned if she told the truth and damned if she lied. This was only going to get worse, and the hell of it was—it was *her* problem, not his! Any other abducted bride would be thrilled. "I'll act the dutiful, happy wife tomorrow. Ye need nae fear Sheffield'll have any reason to think we're nae united against him an' that we'll emerge victorious, because neither of us can bear to lose."

"Thank you," he said in a whoosh.

"Go to bed. We've a long day ahead of us." She snorted. "A long week."

He said no more, and she rolled her head on the back of the tub to see him asleep, his arm across his chest and his other arm hanging over the floor, the way he had lain in Hogarth. She sighed. Why did she allow this?

I miss you.

No one had ever missed her before. Her mother hadn't missed her in the six years she'd been gone, had no idea how she'd gotten home because she assumed Walter had sent for Brìghde to marry Roger, so she certainly wouldn't miss her now that she knew where Brìghde was.

More girls came in with more hot water, but with no effort to be quiet in deference to his sleeping lordship, she bade them find her shift, then dismissed them for the night. She emerged from the bathtub when the water cooled, dried off, slipped her shift over her body, doused the candles, banked the fire, and shoved him.

He groaned. "What."

"Move over. Ye're on me side o' the bed."

He merely rolled over onto his stomach, facing away from her. She crawled under the covers—tried anyway. "Grimme, fer God's sake, get up an' get in bed properly. Better yet, go sleep in yer own bed."

"Would you come with me?" he mumbled.

Brìghde's mouth twisted. He might not desire her, but he *did* like sleeping with her and he had missed her enough to sulk and whinge about it.

Take what you can get.

"Aye, I suppose."

"MY LADY." IT was Avis, shaking her lightly. Brìghde's eyes fluttered open. "'Tis morning."

"Aye," she croaked.

"I will await you in your chambers."

"Thank you." The door closed softly behind her. "Grimme."

He grunted.

"Prayers."

He groaned.

Brìghde threw off the blankets and sat up. She had had a good night's rest, but she felt she would need more to get through this day.

"Come back to bed," he mumbled.

She sighed heavily and her chin dropped to her chest, then she did indeed fall back on the bed, her head landing on Grimme's stomach, making him oof, her arms outstretched on the mattress. He dropped his arm across her body, lying heavily upon her breast, and caressed her ribs. She lay that way for a long time, staring up into the darkness, luxuriating in the feel of his big hand petting her.

There were two ways she could consider this.

She could lie here and wish for him to cup her breast, to thumb her nipple, to caress her neck and chin and tilt her head up for him to kiss her tenderly and tell her how much he wanted her in preparation for hours of gentle pleasure—

She scrunched up her face and squeezed some tears out. No. That hurt too much.

Or ... she could find a way to control her inexplicable want and take what she could get. Sleeping with him *was* a privilege amongst the women in this household and, like it or not, she *was* one of them. She liked this, and how utterly *comfortable* she was with him and had been from the first. She too felt as if she had lived here forever, and that Grimme had always been her friend.

Another knock on the door. "My lady?"

"Coming," she called wearily.

She would have heaved herself upward, but he kept her gently pinned. "I am sorry that I betrayed you by saying such things about you to my women."

She gulped.

"I think, I don't know this girl. I abducted her, but she makes me a bargain, puts my house to rights ... what does she *want?* She says she has no loyalty, but she has shown me nothing but loyalty and has from the beginning and I have done nothing to deserve it. She can leave at any time; she is free and fully capable of living on her own and finding her way to her brother at Dunham."

"I told you," she muttered. "You rescued me from Fàileach. You saved my life."

"You *could* leave, but you haven't. You *could* let my house go to rot, but from the very beginning you have done everything in your power to put it to rights. You cannot possibly covet my father's position so much you would stay if you did not want to for some other reason. You want something else, something you're not telling me."

Nor did she intend to.

"Grimme, if I haven't told you something, it's because it's not important or I forgot it." He growled, but did not press. She stayed for a few moments, but after a while, the day was inevitable. "Sheffield comes today. There is much to be done." He released her. She stood and stretched, then opened the door only to run into Emelisse, who was poised to knock.

"What are *you* doing in Grimme's chambers?"

"Sleeping," Brìghde huffed, gesturing to her shift. "What are *you* doing up so early?"

"He *sleeps* with you?" she screeched. "In *his* bed?!"

"*Very* often. Emelisse, I am tired, but Sheffield comes today and I must finish preparations. Please allow me to pass."

"Does he do anything *else* with you?"

Brìghde scrunched up her face. "I am here to do that very thing." She gasped when Emelisse slapped her. Now completely awake, Brìghde held her cheek and gaped at the woman. Surely she could not have just done that, could she have? For her part, Emelisse was still enraged. That slap had been no undeniable impulse.

"The next time you strike me," Brìghde growled, "I will kill you."

"No, you won't," Grimme croaked from behind Brìghde.

"That presupposes she will strike me again."

"She will *not*. Go about your day, Brìghde, and let me tend my own matters."

Brìghde glared at Grimme over her shoulder and hissed, "She has *always* been my matter, yet you *continuously* protect her after she has provoked me. Put a *leash* on her or I will and bruises on her face will be the *least* of her worries." She brushed by Emelisse with a sharp elbow to her ribs, slammed her door closed, then slammed herself against the door to eavesdrop. Avis started to speak, but Brìghde put her finger to her lips.

"You have not been in my bed in almost two weeks," Emelisse hissed in French.

"Aye, and if you continue on this path, it will be never again. Further, if you raise your hand to her again, I will set you out in the cold."

Emelisse gasped. "How did you punish her for putting her hands on *me*?"

"I didn't," he said crisply. "You got what you deserved and you should be thanking *me* for stopping her when I did."

"But I am the mother of your sons!"

"You say that as if it has any bearing on how appalling I find your behavior."

"You *sleep* with her!"

"I rather like— Do not ever," Grimme snarled, "attempt to slap me again."

Emelisse mewled. "Let me go," she panted. "I'm sorry, Grimme, I'm sorry."

"I am coming to the end of my patience with you."

"You *never* sleep with me!" she cried. "You haven't slept with me since I bore you Max!"

"I never sleep with any of the rest of you, either."

"I share your cod with those three whores—"

"And whichever maidservants happen to be in the room."

Brìghde clapped her hand over her mouth to contain her cackle.

"—and now you are *sleeping* with a woman you met not even two months ago!"

"*My wife*," he said pointedly, "is none of your business."

"And yet, I am her business?"

"Even more now that you've struck her. Emelisse, do not make an enemy of her. You will not like her manner of justice."

"And you would *let* her?"

"She is the ruler here," he said flatly. "Not because she is my wife or the future mother of my *legitimate* sons—" Brìghde winced. "—but because that was what she was born and bred to do: Rule. Aye, I will let her because she is the wife I *need* whether I wanted her or not."

"Do you?" Emelisse pled. "Want her?"

"Push me much harder, and I'll fuck her in *my* bed, make you watch—"

Brìghde's mouth dropped open.

"—and then, when she is heavy with my *legitimate* child, I'll do it again. And make you watch."

"But you don't fuck women who are with child!"

"I'll make an exception in your case, as you are begging for punishment, and I will enjoy every second of it."

Brìghde's eyes went wide.

"The duke comes today, and I expect you to be on your best behavior. If you cannot promise me that, I will lock you in your chambers."

She gasped. "You wouldn't!"

"Try me. Now go before I do it anyway." The earl's door slammed.

Brìghde started to giggle. "Get me dressed," she whispered to Avis. "Quickly."

As soon as she looked minimally presentable, Brìghde skittered down the stairs and into the study where she found Sir John sleeping in his chair, his chin on his chest. "Sir John," she whispered, shaking him a little.

He aroused with a start, then blinked at her. "Your face is flushed, my lady," he murmured, concerned. He pressed his palm to her forehead. "Is something wrong?"

"The most extraordinary thing just happened!" she whispered, and continued whispering until the old man was grinning, but instead of replying, he simply patted her hand.

"I am very glad you are here, Brìghde," he said warmly. "Now, go be a countess."

43

"WHAT'S WRONG with you?" Grimme muttered, angry, irritated, confused, frustrated.

"Side-saddle," Brìghde muttered back.

"Stop squirming. You act like you've pearls up your arse."

She looked at him strangely. "Why would *anyone* have pearls up their arse?"

He was too tense to laugh, much less explain.

The two of them were in the lane to welcome the duke, sitting atop destriers captured from the Sheffield knights. It was an insult, to have two very valuable animals they'd captured, draped in Kyneward livery, Earl and Countess Kyneward sitting atop them to greet the man they'd taken them from. Grimme was happy to have these beasts in his stable, but they weren't Ares and Troy.

The animals were very fine.

The keep was very fine.

Grimme and Brìghde were both attired in very fine clothing and jewels.

He sensed Brìghde looking at him, but he did not return it. He couldn't. His attention was fixed upon the approaching party as if they were marauders, as, in essence, they were. The threat to Brìghde was clear, and he could not allow that to pass, but he had to think of some battle tactic he had not yet devised.

Lord Sheffield sat nobly upon an elegantly liveried but refined horse, leading approximately twenty fully armored knights, visors open, bearing the Duke of Sheffield's standard. Following them were another forty mailed men-at-arms.

Grimme should be studying the force and thinking of every combination of every possible attack that he had drilled into his force the past fortnight.

To Sheffield and his force, it would appear that there were few Kyneward knights around, but that was not true. There were disguised arbalists hidden in the forests, lying on the ground dressed to blend in, and hiding behind tall boxwood hedges grown specifically for the purpose.

There were hundreds of well-trained Kyneward foot soldiers and archers in the forests along the road from Sheffield thirty miles out to bedevil a backing army and sound the alarm. They did not have armor, but that was a hazard of waging war this way. An adequate number of Grimme's archers were on the battlements, but that was for show; it would have been suspicious if they weren't.

Aye, he *should* be studying all that and remembering signals, but the only thing he could see was the man on the duke's right and the horse he was riding.

"The duke is … not handsome," Brìghde remarked, a disgusted grimace in her voice.

"You are a very kind woman," Grimme replied tightly.

"The lead knight … Aldwyn Marchand? And that is Ares?"

"Aye."

"Oh, my," she breathed in awe.

Grimme watched his former closest friend with a grief that truly pierced his heart, which was why he desperately wanted to keep Brìghde by his side and happy. As for the horse … Grimme's longing for his beloved pet was so deep he was in danger of bowing his head to sob.

"Aye," he whispered, grief and rage bitter on his tongue.

Yet he stayed placid, looking at Ares though it hurt too much. Other than pure white feathers and a pure white blaze and nose, he was completely black, with a long glossy black mane and tail.

Like a raven.

He had an unwelcome vision of Brìghde in a black velvet kirtle astride Enyo thundering across the countryside with her black hair streaming behind her, and himself on Ares, the god and goddess of war, side by side, slaughtering their enemies. If Brìghde ever went into battle with him, though, 'twould not be on Enyo, for mares were not trained for battle. She would be on Troy, who was a match for Ares.

He felt her hand slide into his and he started. He looked at her in question. She smiled softly at him, her emerald eyes striking, and squeezed his hand until he felt his body relax a little. He squeezed back and his breath left him slowly, calmly. The corner of his mouth turned up the tiniest bit.

"'Tis only a week."

"Thank you, my friend," he whispered.

"You're welcome."

THE GREETINGS were cordial with just enough warmth in everyone's voices. Grimme and Brìghde bowed their heads with an appropriate "Your Grace," and moved aside to allow the duke to pass into the outer bailey.

"Earl Kyneward. Countess."

"My liege," Grimme said, every letter poison on his tongue.

Aldwyn stayed behind whilst Grimme and Brìghde rode in behind the duke, then followed. The force of sixty would be sent out to the field between the keep and the dower house to set up their encampment.

Aldwyn dismounted to hold the duke's horse's bridle.

Grimme dismounted.

He plucked Brìghde off her side-saddle because she could not manage it without falling on her face. She'd tried. The side-saddle was too small for a warhorse, but she could not sit astride and be proper, and Grimme did not want her on a palfrey as if she were less than he.

The duke dismounted.

Grimme and Brìghde bowed and curtsied deeply.

"Rise."

They did. The duke looked around and Grimme did too, wondering what he would see.

The outer bailey was as tidy as it could be, taken up mostly by stables. The carpenters were in the back, but had been given the week off in deference to his grace.

The duke strolled to the inner bailey, which looked … far different than it had seven weeks ago. The outbuildings were new and immaculately whitewashed. The chickens were penned up out of the way. There were flowers and tidy hedges growing at the base of the keep. There was a place for everything and everything was in its place. The ravens were not about, though the falcons soared high overhead.

It looked like a well-kempt and -functioning keep.

The duke strolled to the broad staircase to the front door. The stones gleamed in the sun and there were pots of flowers at the top where stone lions should go.

Grimme and Brìghde followed, then Aldwyn, whom Grimme had not acknowledged.

The doors were swung open by inadequately liveried footmen but that could not be helped.

The duke strolled into the great hall and they followed. The walls and ceiling were also freshly scraped and whitewashed, covering the crumbling murals, and the stone floor was clean and covered by fresh rushes and fragrant thyme. There were beautiful tapestries hanging that had been put up very late last night. Many more tables than the usual four were arranged and prepared for supper. The hearth with its surrounding chairs and longues was pristine and stacked tidily with unburnt wood. The five chandeliers—two of which were new—were shiny black and stuffed with fresh candles.

"I am pleased," Sheffield finally said.

That was plain. His lust for it fair oozed out of him.

"Your Grace," Brìghde said softly, dropping a curtsy again when he turned to look at her. Grimme did not miss the flare of lust in the duke's eyes for her, as well. "May I show you your chambers before supper? You must be exhausted."

"Aye. My manservant?"

"Awaiting you, Your Grace."

"Very well."

Grimme's rage flamed hotter when the duke did not avert his eyes from her. "I wish for you to attend me in my bath this afternoon, Lady Kyneward."

She curtsied her obeisance.

It was etiquette for the lady of the manor to bathe a higher noble, but Grimme should have known he would demand it as soon as he walked in the door. The duke wanted every woman attached to a man he conquered or whom he had power over. It would not have mattered *what* she looked like, just so he could humiliate the man she belonged to.

"Please," she murmured, sweeping her hand toward the stairs. He preceded her up the stairs and they disappeared.

"You've done well, brother."

Grimme didn't look at Aldwyn. "Aye, I have."

"You were right," Aldwyn mused. "Honor wins nothing."

Grimme turned slowly to Aldwyn with narrowed eyes and looked into a twenty-five-year-familiar face. He slowly realized that it had aged, but well. "*My* knights did not pursue a beautiful woman for the sole purpose of raping her."

Aldwyn remained placid, but Grimme knew he was seething.

"We both know why I have your knights and 'tis not over a border that is not disputed and should not be patrolled for any reason, much less as a threat. You can no longer lecture me as to the importance of honor in warfare when you serve *him*." He said nothing, but Grimme knew Aldwyn. "What's keeping you there, Aldwyn?"

"I serve my liege."

"Find a new liege, one who has as much honor as you do. Tavendish, mayhap."

Aldwyn ignored that and said coolly, "Congratulations on your marriage."

"Thank you."

"How does an English earl find a Scottish wife?"

"When one happens to meet a noblewoman of marriageable age who needs to be rescued from her wedding, one takes the opportunity."

Aldwyn could not hide his surprise.

"I'd tell you the story, but suffice it to say Sheffield will have a bit more explaining to do to Henry should I *and* my wife die mysteriously."

Aldwyn's eyes narrowed and Grimme gave him a flat smile.

"She's beautiful," Aldwyn observed, "but she's not blonde. I'm surprised you noticed she exists."

In a crowd of women, Grimme would not have noticed her. Ignoring all women was a habit, until he needed to get his cod stroked, at which point he looked for a blonde. Aldwyn knew this.

"I wager you haven't bedded her yet, though," Aldwyn drawled. He was no dimwit.

There was no use denying it, so Grimme shrugged. "When I need a legitimate heir, 'twill happen. Do I need to worry about anything happening to me that I will need to rely on my wife and heir?" he asked smoothly.

"An earl should have an heir regardless."

"I have named one of my sons my heir."

"Sheffield will challenge it."

"I expect nothing less."

Aldwyn's eye was caught from across the hall. Grimme turned to see Maebh at the bottom of the stairs, her expression sober. As if that weren't bad enough, Pierce appeared out of nowhere and sought her out. He looked up at her and asked a question. She looked down at him, smoothed his hair, smiled, and nodded. He grinned and darted down to the kitchens, looking for Brìghde, most likely.

No one had informed Pierce of his new future; he wouldn't be told until absolutely necessary. As for Maebh, he hadn't told her, either; she would crow that her son had been chosen to inherit and Grimme would never hear the end of it.

Aldwyn's jaw clenched and he slid a glance at Grimme.

"I told her to stay in her chambers," Grimme said, trying to hide his shame.

"Ever since?"

Grimme sighed heavily, dropped his head and rubbed the bridge of his nose. "She was expecting my child."

"Mayhap he's mine."

Grimme gave him a stony look. "I'm not going to abandon *my* children."

"There's that, at least. What about her? Do you love her? No. You don't love anyone or anything but war. Conquering. Any way you can. Any*one* you can."

With that, Aldwyn turned and stalked out of the hall.

44

IT'S ONLY A week. It's only a week. It's only a week.

Brìghde could only repeat that to herself over and over as she helped the duke's manservant to divest the duke from his garments. He was in his late fifties, filthy, stinking, and in Brìghde's sweet-smelling home, his odor was overpowering. His teeth were half rotten and his breath was foul. The only reason he wanted her to bathe him was because he wanted something that belonged to his vassal.

Perhaps she should be careful what she wished for because now there were *two* people in this keep who wanted her and in a choice between the duke and Maebh, she'd choose Maebh in a blink, and she would *much* rather swive Roger than either the duke *or* Maebh.

That was something she never thought she'd prefer.

Maidservants scurried in and out of Grimme's chambers to fill the bathtub.

She tried not to look at the duke's naked body, but he was so horrifying she could not stop sneaking peeks. He was tall and thin, so thin his skeleton was clearly defined. His skin was wrinkled and loose. He had no muscle that she could see. His cod was as long and thin as he was, and it was starting to rise. He was displaying himself to her the way Maebh had, but he had the power to demand anything and everything from her. If she refused, he would command Grimme to order her to do it. Grimme could not refuse an order from his liege.

Finally the tub was full, the necessaries were on a stool next to it, and the duke was leering at her.

Brìghde gasped. "Oh, Your Grace! I have forgotten wine. Forgive me!" she cried and fled the room before he could say a word, darted across the hall to her chambers, startling Avis, who was in the antechamber stirring a firkin of wine she had bid Hamond to bring to her chambers, awaiting her poison.

"Is that well dissolved?" she murmured.

"I think so. I only put in one packet."

"That will have to do for tonight. Here, let's fill the pitcher."

It was a specially made pitcher Brìghde had requested of the blacksmith. There were three, and they all had the Fàileach family crest stamped prominently on the side.

"I'm going to take one to him now. Serve him at supper, but no more than three glasses. He can drink as much as he wants of the other wenches' pitchers."

"Aye, mum."

Brìghde took the pitcher, snatched a goblet off her bed table, dashed the leftover wine into the hearth, and entered Grimme's chambers. The duke was pleasuring himself. She couldn't see anything but his head, but his shoulder was jerking, his body was shaking, and the water was rolling furiously and spilling over the floor. There were many things Brìghde wished she hadn't seen between the convent and Fàileach, and men pleasuring themselves was one of them; but very often, having such knowledge was beneficial.

The duke wouldn't be rising for anything all week, if Brìghde controlled things well enough.

"Your wine, Your Grace," Brìghde breathed when he was finished. She glided to the stool and filled the goblet.

"Tell me, my dear," he murmured as he took it and sipped. He scowled at the wine and her heart thundered out of her chest. "This wine is *delicious*."

"'Tis from Bordeaux. My Lord Kyneward is especially fond of it. This is his private stock."

"Of course it is." He continued to sip appreciatively. "Do you know … *droit de seigneur?*"

Brìghde kept her face pleasant. "I don't speak French, Your Grace," she lied, her heart thundering out of her chest.

"Your husband's tastes," he mused, "are very well known. His ravenous appetite is also well known." He rolled his gaze up to her. "*You* are not to his taste. Further, *he* has been dodging matrimony for a few years. So tell me. *How*, precisely, did you convince him to wed you?"

"I didn't, *precisely*, Your Grace," she said guilelessly. "I had something he needed and he had something I needed. 'Twas an even trade."

"And what was that bargain?"

"When was the last time you visited Kyneward Keep?" she asked smoothly, going behind him to begin massaging his shoulders. It would be so easy to strangle him. Her hands were small but strong. His neck was thin. She *might* even be able to break it.

He moaned in pleasure and sighed, "Years."

"Aye, well. My lord needed a castellan to relieve his aging father. As the daughter of a very accomplished castellain, I had the necessary qualifications to improve and oversee its condition, and replace his father as castellain. I, in turn, needed to be rescued from Fàileach's plans for me—"

"To wed into the MacFhionnlaigh clan."

"Aye. My lord snatched me out of my wedding to Roger MacFhionnlaigh, just as we plotted."

"That," he mused, sipping, "sounds like a bargain he would make. May I assume then that you are still a virgin?"

"Aye, Your Grace."

"Do you have plans for an heir?"

"Aye. That was part of our bargain."

"You have been married … ?"

"Almost two months."

"If he hasn't bedded you by now, he's not going to."

That … hurt.

"We have been busy preparing for your visit. When we are less pressed for time, his mistress and I shall arrange it."

"*Really* … " he breathed, half twisting to look up at her with a lascivious grin.

"Aye," she murmured, wishing Grimme would allow her to kill this man. "I … prefer women, so Lord Kyneward is not attractive to me. Yet we are eager to breed an heir. 'Twill be delightful for all three of us, and no one need feel unappreciated."

"And so," he sighed, relaxing back again to her firm hands on his skeletal shoulders, "you will be engaged with Kyneward's mistress and he shall stick it in you and a child will appear and then you both shall share a mistress."

"Aye."

"A man who cannot rise for you is not a real man. I, however, have already risen for you."

His neck was so thin. Her hands were so strong. 'Twould be no feat.

His chin began to touch his chest.

"Should I call your manservant?"

"Aye," he yawned, and set the goblet on the stool. "As I am willing to take my opportunities, and Kyneward is not, the only heirs you are going to bear are mine."

May your womb one day find too many choices to make.

AT SUPPER, THE duke was provided the earl's chair. Grimme was to sit on his right and Brìghde to Grimme's right, but the duke insisted on having Brìghde to his left, in her regular chair, where Aldwyn should have sat, with Aldwyn on her left. She found herself sitting between Grimme's enemy and his rival.

The first time she looked in Sir Aldwyn Marchand's face, she could see why he and Grimme had such a rivalry that it would break over a woman.

Aldwyn was less colorful than Grimme with his dark blond hair and beard, and plain hazel eyes, but he was somehow more beautiful. He was also the same size as Grimme.

"Sir Marchand," she murmured as he bowed, raised her hand to his lips, and stared into her eyes. She knew that look. Many men had given her one just like it. *This* time, however, it made her go a little breathless.

"My lady," he said, his voice deep, rough.

She put her hand to her chest and smiled. He straightened, gave her a crooked smile and a wink.

Aye, she knew Grimme was watching. She did not mind feeling a reciprocal attraction with an attractive man whilst still attempting to make her husband jealous. It wouldn't work the way she really wanted it to, as Grimme would believe Aldwyn was wooing her in revenge, but it would be a sharp elbow in the ribs. Mayhap not even that much, since he would believe she was so flattered by Aldwyn's attention she'd fall in bed with him for ear scratches.

That was, in fact, true.

Brìghde stood behind her chair. Aldwyn stood next to her. The duke had not yet appeared. Grimme stood behind his assigned chair, his father on his right. Soon enough, the duke emerged. He looked well rested, and his rotting smile was wide as he surveyed his vassal's tables. He had not a hint of a wobble in his gait.

Brìghde hated Walter Fàileach, feared him, but he had trained her well, and now that she needed those skills, she was happy she could use them to protect herself.

Grimme pulled back the chair the duke was to occupy but the duke looked over the assembled knights and said loudly, "Kyneward, are we not missing someone?"

Brìghde's eyes went to Grimme, who looked confused. "I don't know whom, Your Grace."

"Your … " he slowly waggled his fingers as he dramatically paused. "Women."

Grimme's expression didn't change.

The duke turned to Brìghde and said, "Please fetch your … friends, Lady Kyneward," he said silkily. "*All* of them."

Brìghde dropped a curtsy and hurried to the stairs. She breathlessly pounded on Emelisse's door, then Dillena's, then Maebh's and Ardith's.

They emerged about the same time, but Brìghde was bent over at the waist, her hands braced on her knees, trying to catch her breath. "Get … dressed … quickly," she panted. "Duke wants … you at … supper."

There were gasps and whimpers, but they turned immediately and scurried, each of them barking orders at their respective chambermaids, not even bothering to close their doors.

Soon they were all assembled in front of her, nervous, wringing their hands. "This week," Brìghde said low, "we are allies. The duke has already informed me he will command Grimme to give me to him, and he will want to have his turn at each of you, else he'd not have summoned you."

They looked as horrified and frightened as Brìghde felt.

"Maebh, I have told him that you and I will be implementing your plan to get me with child, and I have told him I prefer women, and now he wants to watch us together." Maebh was too scared to quip. "*If* he requests any of you attend him in Grimme's chambers, ask Avis or Hamond to get a pitcher of wine for the duke. It's a small pitcher with my family crest on it—you can't mistake it. He only need finish two cups to sleep through the night. Do not let him drink more than three and whatever you do, do *not* drink out of any pitcher with my family crest on it."

They gaped at her. "Aye," she sneered. "If I cared, I could have killed you weeks ago. Remember that the next time you accuse me of jealousy. Now, are we together?"

When she received four strong, "Aye, my lady"s, she braced herself and calmly led Grimme's mistresses down to the hall.

The duke scraped his chair around to watch all five of them present themselves. He arose and the mistresses curtsied deeply and stayed. He petted Emelisse's hair, caressed her cheek, tucked his bony hand under her chin and compelled her to rise. His thumb stroked her cheek. Emelisse was sheet white, her blue eyes popping out, but she kept her composure. He leaned forward and kissed her, opened her mouth with his, and stuck his tongue in it.

Emelisse kissed him back as best as she could manage without vomiting, but she was clutching her stomach. Brìghde was about to vomit simply watching it and desperately hoped he would not try to kiss her.

The duke pulled away from Emelisse and ran his finger down her cheek. He went on to Ardith, and repeated the kiss. Ardith was less visibly repulsed than Emelisse. He moved on to Dillena, then Maebh.

When he was finished, he asked softly, "Which one of you is Lady Kyneward's lover?"

Maebh made a tiny gesture he did not miss.

"I want to see that," he purred. "Come, come! We have chairs for you."

The duke went to his chair and Grimme, who looked *very* grim, seated the duke whilst servants seated the mistresses at the head table. Maebh was seated to Sir Marchand's left, Ardith on Maebh's left. Emelisse was seated to the right of Sir John and Dillena to her right.

In the bustle, Brìghde went to Grimme. "Do not," she whispered in his ear, "drink anything the duke offers you."

He gave her a tiny, brusque nod. She returned to her chair and Aldwyn seated her.

The first few moments were tense, but as the platters were served and the wine began to flow, the atmosphere relaxed a little. The duke chatted quietly with Grimme, leaving her to Aldwyn, who was stiff and looked rather angry. She leaned forward and looked down the table at her temporary conspirators. Maebh's head was down and she picked at her food. Ardith was morose and also was not eating.

Brìghde chatted with Sir Marchand lightly. She paid attention when the duke droned on at her, suffering his hand stroking her arm. She counted how many times Avis filled his cup, then sent her back upstairs with a tiny gesture. He was so thin, it wouldn't take much to kill him.

The duke could not hold his poisoned wine even as well as she had calculated, and his chin hit his chest within a half hour. Brìghde signaled Hamond to summon the duke's manservant.

Soon enough, the room was a bit livelier, but all twenty of the duke's knights were still present. It would be so simple to put them all to sleep for eternity.

She exchanged sober glances with Grimme, who arose and pounded the table. "Gentlemen," he called. "As you can see, I have five lovely women awaiting my cod. Enjoy your entertainment."

The room exploded in laughter and cheers, and Grimme swept his hand toward the stairs. Brìghde and the mistresses all arose and she led the way up. Brìghde stopped at her door whilst the other four ran up to the third floor, passing her without a word or a glance. Grimme angrily opened her door and ushered her in. He shut the door, backed her up against it, framed her head with his hands splayed flat on the wood, dipped his head to hers, and snarled, "*Kill. Him.*"

45

GRIMME WAS IN the stable in the wee hours long after Brìghde had gone to sleep, thinking about everything she had told him, which was *after* he'd already ordered her to kill the duke—to her delight—but then had to recant because he had said it only to release his rage.

If anyone were going to do it, it would be Grimme, for it was his responsibility. He was the commander of this deadly force of two and would not allow his second to do what he would not—and he was enraged enough to stab the duke in his poisoned sleep.

He did not remember the last time he had felt so powerless, a man coming into *his* home, lustily kissing *his* women, informing *his* wife that she was going to bear his child, as if Grimme had no say in it at all.

The hell of it was that ... he didn't.

If the duke wanted to fuck Grimme's women, Grimme had to step aside.

If the duke wanted to fuck Grimme's wife, Grimme had to step aside.

If the duke's seed caught in Grimme's wife's womb, Grimme had to rear the infant—until it was taken from him, at which time he would have no say.

The duke had wanted Ares, so he took him.

This was not a war Grimme could win, and he had met few wars he could not win.

"Come, boy," he murmured at Ares as he led him out of his own stall, the one Grimme kept empty so that one day he could welcome his pet home. Grooms hustled and bustled quietly with dim lanterns. His marshal, leading Enyo, was awaiting him and Ares in the mating pen. As soon as Grimme's marshal told him Enyo would be in heat when the duke was here, he'd hatched his plot.

"I hope this doesn't wake anyone up," the marshal murmured.

The duke might be out, but Aldwyn was a light sleeper, like most knights. The rest of the duke's company was far out in the encampment with their own horses.

Ares and Enyo greeted each other in what Brìghde might say was a lovers' reunion, then they got on with things, and not too loudly, either.

"Who do you want him on tomorrow night, my lord?" the marshal asked as Enyo was led back to her stall. They would wait until Ares was ready to go again and put him on Calliope.

Grimme listed each mare he had chosen, according to who would be in heat whilst Ares was stabled, and which nights he wanted them bred. "Get them within sniffing distance of Ares when you can. I'll come out here every night."

Once Calliope was mated and the stables shut down, Grimme trudged back to the keep and back to Brìghde's bed.

He wants me to bear his child.

It might have been funny, Grimme thought as he slipped in beside Brìghde, that Grimme was taking Ares's seed right under the duke's nose when the duke planned to have Grimme's women, but Ares belonged to Grimme, as did his wife and his mistresses, so it was anything but funny.

Grimme's failing was that he had not thought the duke would go for Grimme's women immediately because this was a business negotiation, not a social visit. He had thought the duke would work up to it, which would give Grimme time to observe and plot the best course. But no matter how badly *he* had failed to anticipate that, *Brìghde* had not. It disturbed him that she had been buying the ingredients for her poison not a week after she had arrived at Kyneward Keep, as did the fact that she had been going to the kitchen late at night and preparing it until she had a glass jar full of it, as did the fact that she had done it *after* he'd told her not to poison his liege.

It was an entirely foreseeable event.

The day after Grimme had told her to expect the duke, she had been preparing, having a firkin of wine stuffed underneath Avis's bed in the antechamber just waiting to receive the poison. She had gone to Waters to have special pitchers made, her family crest serving as the symbol for poison. She had instructed the servants that only Avis and Hamond were granted the privilege of carrying the countess's special pitchers. Only Avis and Hamond had access to her chambers for the purpose of filling the pitchers.

She had saved herself and all his women from the duke's rapacious greed, excepting the kisses in front of the entire hall.

It had humiliated Grimme to his core, which was exactly why the duke had done it, to prove to everyone present exactly *who* had the power.

It wasn't Grimme, and Mouse had the audacity to chastise him for not acting like an earl. Duke, marquess, earl … with Henry in France … Grimme was low on the power hierarchy.

The only immediate weapon he had was his Trojan horse. And like any superbly trained warhorse, she thought and acted independently to keep her knight in the battle. Grimme had been so worried about a frontal attack, he had not thought to safeguard his most precious possessions.

He ran his fingers through Brìghde's silky hair and let the strands flow through his fingers, thinking about the week ahead. As long as his wife and dearest companion-at-arms made no mistakes, they could get through the week without the duke touching any of them.

THE DUKE DID not appear for breakfast.

For a noble to miss breakfast, or even the midday meal, was normal, mayhap even expected.

The duke was not such a noble. He was an early riser, took a light breakfast, and went riding out amongst his troops.

Thus, more than a few eyebrows were raised, none more than Sir Marchand's.

"What did you do?" Aldwyn hissed in Grimme's ear.

Grimme put on his best expression of confusion. "Do?"

"You put something in his food."

"I did not," Grimme ground out. "Do you think I want to receive the king's sanction? If anything happens to him under my roof, I could be executed. I'm despicable, not *stupid*." Sir John and Mouse would argue the point.

After another half hour of waiting, Grimme seated Brìghde and sat in his own chair.

"Eat," he said brusquely. "We are not at court."

"Where are the other women, Lady Kyneward?" Grimme heard Aldwyn asked in a distantly courteous tone when all the knights had descended upon their breakfast platters to gobble it down and hurry to the training field.

"Are you concerned for their welfare?" she asked coolly.

"In point of fact, I am," he replied.

"Ah. I believe they are in their chambers."

"Nothing … untoward … happened?"

"Sir Marchand—"

"Aldwyn, please."

"Aldwyn," she said tightly.

Grimme considered intervening to save Aldwyn from Brìghde, but decided he deserved whatever he got.

"Thank you. If you are asking me if your liege, our guest, raped a woman in this household in its lord's bed, the answer is, I do not believe so. Why do you care?"

"Uh … I … do care, my lady. Very much so."

"If you care that much, dissuade him from it."

"Lady Kyneward," he said low and very apologetically, "there is only so much he will listen to."

"Thus, women are once again left defenseless. In their own home. From a *guest.*"

Grimme snorted and ate a bite. "Aldwyn," he said blithely around his food, "meet my wife, Queen Boudicca."

Brìghde laughed and gave him a saucy grin and he nudged her with his shoulder.

"What do you plan to do today, Lord Husband?"

"Go out to the dower house and discuss the boundary mistake," he drawled, looking over her head at Aldwyn, who would not look at him, though he was flushed. "So that it *never* happens again."

Aldwyn flashed him a glare and Grimme raised his eyebrow.

"Oh, Brìghde, I forgot to tell you. The king sent a missive, day before yesterday. He is *very* pleased concerning our marriage, and feels the entire plot to save you from your fate whilst acquiring a noble wife was ingenious and that I am a very magnanimous and clever boy."

She rolled her eyes. "*You* are the clever one, are you?"

He snickered. "Thank you, Lady Wife," he murmured and kissed her temple, then said over Brìghde's head, "She thought most of it up."

Aldwyn looked surprised. "Oh. I… It seems something Grimme—I mean, Lord Kyneward—"

"Stop it," Grimme barked.

Aldwyn's glare was almost pure hatred. It didn't take Grimme aback. What surprised him was that it was not *completely* hatred. Aldwyn took a breath. "'Tis something Grimme would plan, my lady."

"It's amazing what one can plan when one is desperate," she said airily.

"May I ask what your circumstances were that you were so desperate?"

"I didn't want to swive Roger MacFhionnlaigh, as he is uglier than a deerhound and less bright than a forest at midnight."

Grimme barked a laugh and when he saw Aldwyn's consternated expression, continued to laugh until he was coughing and tears were squeezing out of his eyes.

"Pardon me, my lord, my lady," Aldwyn said quietly before arising and taking the stairs practically two at a time.

"Did you kill him?" Grimme muttered.

"I don't think so," she said shortly and resentfully shoved a bite in her mouth.

He surprised her when he wrapped his hand around her knife hand and caressed it with his thumb. "You cannot want his death more than I, but you'll get me executed do you kill him."

"I'll be more careful," she grumbled. "He's very skinny. I was to kill a garrison of knights. I know not how to account for a man like that."

"Aye, he does not eat much, did you notice."

"Is he ill?" she asked hopefully.

"Nay. He is vain and believes he looks better than he does."

Brìghde grimaced. "Do you mean to say he starves himself so as to look thusly and does not know what everyone else sees?"

"Aye. He won't mind missing breakfast."

"I know that I canna kill him with poison," she whispered urgently, "as that would be suspicious. But 'twould be no feat for me to snap his neck and make it look like he slipped. He is not strong enough to fight me, and he hasn't a shred of muscle 'twixt his skin and his bones. I can do it, leave, walk back in to tend him at his bath, scream, cry, and be inconsolable that I had to witness such a gruesome thing and *no one* would believe I did it."

He sat with his mouth pursed for quite a while, thrumming his fingers on the table. Queen Boudicca indeed. "I suspect," he muttered slowly, tempted, ever so tempted, "that may cause more problems than it would solve."

She sighed and nodded in resignation.

"I will consider it." She gaped at him, and he slid her a glance. "Firstly, it is my responsibility to do it. As commander, I cannot ask my second to do what I will not."

"Unless your second is your sword and you are wielding it."

"I can concede that point. But to *my* point, I do not want him to die in my house. And thirdly, I would allow it if you had not pulled Emelisse to her feet with one hand in front of a hall full of knights. There *are* quite a few people who would believe you could do it and that you had done it. All it would take is one of my men or, God forbid, Emelisse, saying something in passing to Aldwyn. He would absolutely believe I'd married an assassin. He would *not* believe I'd married an assassin *by accident*, much less that she acted alone."

Her mouth twisted with concession and disappointment, and that heartened him as nothing else could. She was his companion-at-arms, and she did protect his back, referring to herself as a weapon instead of a convenient way to keep from having to do it himself. How could he make her appreciate how much he appreciated her?

"Did you get Ares on Enyo last night?" she asked.

Grimme nodded. "And Calliope. I'll have him on two mares every night this week. I don't plan on getting much sleep."

"You wouldn't anyway."

"No," he said tightly. He was too tense.

But soon the duke appeared, looking well dressed and well refreshed. Aldwyn trailed him. Grimme and Brìghde stood and made their obeisance.

"Kyneward," he said, cheerfully threatening.

Gritting his teeth, Grimme moved his platter one chair to the right then seated the duke, then Brìghde. Aldwyn requested leave to go to the stables, which was granted.

"Good morn, Lady Kyneward," the duke said brightly.

"Good morn, Your Grace," Brìghde cooed suggestively, but the duke was not sharp enough to discern the utter contempt.

Aldwyn was, had he heard it.

"How was your rest?"

"Utterly peaceful. I have not had sleep such as that in ages. What have we here? Lady Kyneward, your kitchens are to be commended."

"Thank you, Your Grace."

As Brìghde had already eaten two platters' worth of breakfast, she was picking at her third. The duke noticed and said approvingly, "Your restraint also is to be commended, although you could stand to lose a stone or two." Then he leaned into Brìghde and whispered something, which Grimme assumed was licentious.

Brìghde smiled benignly. "One must keep one's family traits in check, must one not?"

"Precisely." The duke nibbled on a hard-boiled egg and one small piece of bacon, drank the whole of a tankard of weak mead, and said, "Well! I am ready to inspect your boundaries, Lord Kyneward."

"Your Grace," Grimme acknowledged, pulled out his chair, and they were off to the stables. The duke went through slowly, inspecting every horse left after Grimme's troops had taken out. He passed Deimos's and Phobos's stalls without comment and Grimme breathed a sigh of relief.

He lingered over Troy. "This one is particularly lovely," he said, reaching out to pet his nose. Troy bit him. "But not well behaved. I thought better of your judgment."

He went on to the next stall and Grimme stroked Troy's nose. "Who's a good boy?" he whispered. "*You're* a good boy."

The duke was shocked when he saw Helen, which surprised Grimme, as he didn't think the duke paid attention to his own stable. "Who— When did you get her?"

"Some time ago. She's been mistreated," he said pointedly.

"I hope you are not implying anyone in *my* stables mistreated her."

"'Twas a woman," he replied. "She will not allow my wife in the stall with her alone, and every beast within fifteen miles loves my wife."

That satisfied the duke, as apparently, no woman in his household was capable of mistreating a horse. Grimme fed Helen a pear and was surprised when she lipped his hand for scratches. "Who's a good girl?" he whispered, pressing his mouth to her nose. "*You're* a good girl." Grimme left her and followed the duke to Enyo's stall.

"Ah," the duke purred. "Ares's consort."

Grimme said nothing, but the duke didn't press the point and they all moved to the yard. The duke's horse was saddled, along with one taken in the skirmish that Grimme would ride.

They spoke as they rode, and the duke was far more blunt than Grimme would have expected. "Your wife comes to me tonight, Kyneward," he said flatly. "I would not normally demand my rights so soon, but since you've no interest in begetting an heir, *I* do."

Of course he would. If Brìghde bore the duke's child, he could kill Grimme and force Brìghde to name the duke as his father, thereby gaining Grimme's lands.

It sickened Grimme to think of the duke on his wife, but he couldn't, as he had no imagination. He had to rely on Brìghde's plan and the fact that, should the duke succeed, he would not succeed. Of all the women the duke had bedded, including the duchess, he had not a child to his name. At his age and with his propensity to be aroused by any woman whose husband he had vanquished, he should have a few bastards running around.

There would be no child from the duke.

"What? No objections?"

"Would you listen to any objections I have?" Grimme asked testily.

"You forget yourself," he snapped.

"I apologize, my liege."

"And after I have taken your wife, I will take your mistresses."

Brìghde didn't have to save them; in fact, he was surprised she hadn't left them uninformed so that they would never know they had a way in which to defend themselves.

Grimme no longer questioned her loyalty, though why she had given it to him, he didn't know since, as his father had pointed out, she would have been brought here against her will and locked in until she produced two sons.

He rolled his eyes at himself. If he couldn't rise for a woman he considered a dear friend, who was amenable to fucking a man she considered slightly better than Roger MacFhionnlaigh for the purpose of bearing a child and who was likely a lusty wench, he would not have been able to rise for a woman he had to rape to get with child, blonde or not. Unwilling women were not to his taste any more than brunettes were, and every morning, he gave thanks he had *not* snatched Lady Margaret.

But he'd been desperate and unwilling to listen to Mouse, who was irritated that Grimme didn't *feel* his power, and further, could have instructed him in Grimme's worth as an earl if he'd known Grimme's mind. How should Grimme know he and his new little earldom would be valuable to any other noble in England? The only thing Grimme knew was warfare and being part of a standing army. It would not have occurred to Grimme to go without a well-trained force, instead depending on poorly trained and poorly armed and armored villeins to defend his property. He had to have wealth to keep a standing army and he had a father who could grow his wealth easily enough.

Wealthy men were not necessarily powerful. He'd never had any power, except on the battlefield, where he knew his worth and his power, and the battlefield was the only place in the world Grimme wanted to be. Emelisse's charge that Grimme didn't belong in the nobility still stung and it was of little comfort that his father, who was wise and learned and experienced, had known no more of it than Grimme did.

Once again, Grimme felt himself unutterably grateful for Brìghde's presence, her knowledge, and her work. If anyone could make him *feel* like nobility, she could, but even if she couldn't, he wanted her to be happy here. She seemed happy, for the most part. She loved hearing his father's praises and she loved conversing with his knights at meals. She loved solving problems and setting things to rights.

The only thing she was still angry about was that he had spoken of her negatively behind her back, which damaged their friendship because it was what all her false friends had done. He had not said it with ridicule, nor had he meant it that way. It was a solution to a problem and he needed help to make it happen, but intent and carelessness often yielded the same result.

His brow wrinkled. Perhaps thinking of her as a *man* was a mistake, for she did not argue like a man and she found things offensive that a man would not question. He did not know what those things were until he said them. Furthermore, she kept them fresh in her mind, ever ready to pull them out when she'd had too much to drink.

Ah, well, he couldn't rid himself of the raven witch after all these years, and her challenge to allow her to wear black was pointed—and very effective.

She was a brunette. She was bold, ruthless, shrewd, and dark and willing to kill for him. But she was not a raven or a witch.

She was physically strong, intelligent, and she knew how to wield power. She understood men and boys and what they needed, but she was not a man.

She had breasts and hips, a womb and fragile female vanity, and she argued like a woman, but she was not a woman, either.

He didn't know quite what she was, but he needed to find a way to fuck her.

Fast.

46

THE DUKE SLEPT all week. He was spry and happy and well rested and seemed to find himself feeling more attractive and proud in the saddle every day as he toured Kyneward, lusting after it, so Grimme had reported to Brìghde. Either he didn't notice that he had not swived any of the women at all, or his mind was too filled with thoughts of capturing the Kyneward lands to care.

No one in the Sheffield company had learned of the plot to breed Ares to as many mares as possible under cover of darkness, which had been a success. Now, if they would only catch …

The night before the negotiations for his knights, and his subsequent departure, Brìghde sat at supper lightly chatting with Sir Aldwyn. She didn't know what to make of him. Sometimes he flirted with her; sometimes he did not. She made sure to flirt lightly in return, as that was what a good hostess did. It wouldn't make Grimme jealous in the least bit, so she did the minimum she could get away with and still be courteous.

She started when the duke caressed her hand, and leaned in when he indicated he wished to speak in her ear. She tried not to gag at the stench of his breath.

"I have not forgotten, but I have had such good sleep here, I decided to take advantage of it. I will have time to get you with child, as your husband clearly has no interest in you."

That … hurt.

Badly.

Particularly since Grimme had only come to bed in the early hours of the morning for two or three hours' sleep. She *knew* he was out breeding Ares, but it was difficult not to feel as if he were coming from one of his own mares' bed.

"I will summon you to Sheffield when I have the chance."

"I am glad you found peace in our home, Your Grace," she whispered back. "You are welcome anytime."

"Even if I were not, I would be."

Thus, when Aldwyn began to flirt, she took advantage of their mutual attraction. *Three* people in this keep wanted her and she would not mind if the man who initiated her was more beautiful than Grimme and would seduce her tenderly.

Take a lover.

Well, why not? Grimme certainly was not going to swive his companion-at-arms.

"Sir Marchand," Brìghde said softly, but brightly.

"Aldwyn, my lady, please."

"Aldwyn. Thank you. Grimme told me a wonderful story about ravens, when you and he were boys."

The smile on his face was melancholy and fleeting. "Aye."

"Tell it to me again."

He slid her an amused glance. "Since you already know the story, I will begin by saying that day was one of the most wonderful days of my life."

Brìghde barely kept her jaw from dropping on the table.

He did tell her the story again, but this time, it was through the eyes of a boy rapt with wonder at beauty he felt privileged to witness.

"That was lovely," she murmured when he finished, her head spinning. "But they ate your hard work."

He shrugged. "'Twas a small price to pay." Then his brow wrinkled. "Has he— What has he told you of our friendship?"

Brìghde pursed her lips. "Ah … that you and he had a philosophical difference that culminated with his unwitting seduction of your lady love."

Aldwyn stiffened. Maebh dropped her head and began to weep quietly. Brìghde leaned forward and looked at her. "Maebh!" she hissed. "Have I failed you yet?" At the bare shake of her head, Brìghde snapped, "Trust me."

That did not stem her tears or her quaking, but Brìghde could say no more.

Aldwyn cleared his throat. "Aye, well, that is a concise summation, my lady, but I'd rather not discuss it … " he said, sliding her a sly glance, " … right now."

There it was. She smiled and scrunched her nose at him, shrugged one shoulder mischievously.

His expression softened and he looked at her hair, rolled and braided and elaborately decorated with silver ribbons and pearls, under a bright pink wimple with white organza. He reached up and touched her hair hesitantly, then grew a little bolder and stroked it with two fingers.

"Your hair," he murmured, slowly reaching behind her to grasp and fondle the beribboned braid down her back, "reminds me of a raven's wing." He puffed a soft chuckle, whilst looking at her hair held delicately in his big hand, his thumb petting the strands as if stroking a raven. Keeping her braid in his hand, he leaned toward her. "Grimme doesn't know this, my lady," he whispered in her ear, "but that day, I grew a deep and abiding affinity for brunettes."

Brìghde swallowed so hard she thought she would choke. "Brìghde, please."

"Brìghde. Thank you." He dropped her hair to continue eating and Brìghde ate too for a while until he paused, took a drink of wine. "You are very beautiful."

"Thank you," she purred.

Again he reached up, but this time he stroked her jaw with a crooked finger whilst looking in her eyes. "I wouldn't have to try very hard to seduce you, would I?"

"Oh, no," she breathed with a sly smile. She was not, in any way, lying. "But I am fully aware that your seduction of me would be revenge."

"I did not think I would enjoy it so much."

She snickered.

His eyebrow rose. "Does that bother you?"

"If you and I both want the same thing, does it matter why?"

"I thought you were a virgin. How do you know what you want?"

"I am, but I know because I grew up with six brothers who forgot I was a lass most of the time. Otherwise, I have seen and heard far more than I wanted to, but *now* it all makes sense."

His wide grin was breathtaking. "Does it now?"

"Considering everyone in the British Isles knows Grimme's tastes and your tastes," she whispered matter-of-factly, "with full knowledge that you are here, I can't swive you and pass a babe off as his, you ken, or I'd come to you tonight."

He put his elbow on the table and propped his cheek on it, smiling broadly. "He does not deserve you."

She grimaced a little. "I can't agree. Our bargain was mutually beneficial, and I respect him a great deal. He has been very kind to me, and he is a good friend."

"But not the way you want him to."

She blinked, suddenly confused. "What … ?"

"You correctly deduced that I would be happy to seduce you for revenge for my lady love. I have deduced that you are trying to make him jealous."

She chuckled sadly. "It won't work."

"He's looking," he whispered. "Put your hand under the table."

She chuckled wickedly and did that, but so did he, and she was surprised when he took her hand and pressed it to his cod, which was hard.

Her smile faded and she sighed, "Hooo." He took his hand away and she squeezed a little. His eyes shuttered and his breathing came a little shorter. He was hard. *For her.* Tingling swirled in her lower body and settled in her cunte, the way they did for Grimme.

"I'm very angry with him," she murmured, caressing and feeling, making him swallow, making his eyes close.

"You want him."

"I do."

"You can pretend I am him."

"Aye."

Should she be forced to choose, she would be hard pressed. Yet she did not have to choose, because Grimme had made the choice for her. If Grimme wouldn't …

"I knew that." He grasped her hand gently and put it away from him. She retrieved it with a wry smile. He studied her for a moment as if deciding what to say. "I'm married," he said bluntly, and a little pained. "If I were not, I would be most happy to introduce you to love, and not for revenge. However, I will not seduce you for any reason, revenge or not. I love my wife and she just bore me my third child."

"That's disappointing," Brìghde drawled playfully, but her heart sank into her stomach. "Why did you want me to touch you if … "

"I wanted *you* to know what it was like to be wanted by a man you wanted too." Brìghde started to tremble with the effort of holding back tears. "Oh, now," he whispered, taking his linen and wiping her eyes. "Don't cry."

"It may be more than I can bear, that knowledge."

"You are very tender-hearted."

"Aye." She *almost* told him about the ravens, but she would not betray Grimme's confidence. 'Twas not hers to tell.

He chuckled. "If 'twould not be too much, could *I* tell you the story of our parting?"

"Oh, aye. There are three sides to every story. Yours, mine—"

"—and the truth," they finished together, then laughed.

"The philosophical difference you referenced is that he does not wage war honorably. He will do anything he needs to do to not only win, but conquer."

She nodded and ate whilst she listened. "He has said as much. In fact, I share that philosophy."

"Very well. For reasons I do not know or understand, he *had* to win my lady love away from me."

Brìghde scowled. "He said he did not know she was your lady love."

"He knew," he said flatly. "He brought his battlefield tactics—our philosophical difference—into practice against me. 'Twasn't the *woman*. I had grown disinterested in her anyway, as I had met my wife. He wanted something I had, so he took it. 'Tis that simple."

"Like the ravens," Brìghde whispered, sick to her stomach.

"Like the ravens."

"And Ares? That is revenge?"

"I would never take something from someone just because I wanted it or merely to vanquish. That is the duke's way. Grimme's way."

Brìghde closed her eyes briefly and gripped her knife in her fist. "He said that about you."

"Sheffield took Ares because he knew Grimme loved him more than anything else in the world and orders me to ride him to pique Grimme. Mind you, but for my wife, I would seduce you. You are beautiful, like a raven, and I love ravens. 'Twould be my privilege to love their queen for as long as she wanted." Yet again he touched her hair, studied it. "Oh, my lady," he whispered, his voice a little hoarse. "How you tempt me, and have done so all week." He pressed the pad of his thumb to her cheek. "I don't mean to make you cry, but I cannot leave without baring my thoughts to you." He dropped his hand suddenly and said matter-of-factly, "He betrayed me. Purposely."

Her tears dried. "Why are you telling me this? Are you not afraid I will go carrying tales back to him?"

"I am *counting* on it. I do not want to love you for revenge. I want to love you because you are beautiful and sweet and kind. I want him to, one time before he dies, feel shame."

"He wanted something you had, as if you were any foe?"

"No. He wanted something I, his best friend for twenty years, had. Me, specifically." He took a deep breath. "May I be blunt? I feel our conversation has turned so intimate 'tis too late to avoid further confidences."

"Aye, please do."

"Are you in love with him?"

"No," she murmured. "I would be if he would— Well. Even if I were, I could bear it if he did not remind me so often that I am not to his taste. He touched me, tried to rise. Couldn't."

"He is being cruel for the sake of being cruel."

"No, not that either. He's clumsy and doesn't know how to be a friend to a woman. Because he sees me as a man, his companion-at-arms, he believes he should be able to talk to me like one and doesn't ken why I don't give him the responses he expects. I am weary of it."

Aldwyn nodded his concession. "Aye, I believe that. He has never *talked* to women."

"Aye. He believes he is reassuring me that he will not ravish me," she drawled with a roll of her eyes. "He sleeps with me. When he wants to *talk*. He calls me his dearest friend and—" Suddenly it all came out, as it did when she felt someone might like her, and she could not stop her flow of words. Yet she could not bring herself to tell him about the witch or the ravens. "… thinks of me as your replacement."

"He's watching. He's not happy. Tell me as if we're planning an assignation."

"Does *he* know you're married?"

"No."

Her eyelids shuttered. "I think I might like to spend the night *talking* to you."

His smile widened. "I think I would like that very much, my lady."

47

THE NEXT MORNING, after breakfast had been cleared, Grimme sat with Brìghde, Sheffield, and Aldwyn in Sir John's study. As the duke had no other advisor, Sir John was barred from the meeting.

Grimme did not think he had ever been so angry with Aldwyn as he was at this moment and he made his anger clear. When Aldwyn returned his glare with smug satisfaction, he nearly put his fist through Aldwyn's face.

Grimme deserved it; he knew he did. But Brìghde had *promised*—

He had gone straight to Brìghde's chambers after the duke had been poisoned into his restful stupor, and waited. And waited. And waited.

Until he could wait no more because he had to get to the stables. When he returned to her chambers after another successful—he hoped—night, she was still absent and her bed still made. He'd promptly unmade it and dropped into it for some well-deserved sleep.

He had seen her for the first time at breakfast, but she barely noticed him for Aldwyn's presence. He didn't know why he had expected Aldwyn to keep his hands off what was Grimme's when she was so beautiful and exactly to Aldwyn's taste.

And he knew Brìghde well enough to know that she would fuck the first attractive man who was also attracted to her, just to feel wanted.

He ached that he had driven her into his former best friend's arms, but he couldn't help his infirmity, he couldn't help being angry with her—she *promised*—and he knew he had to keep his mind on the negotiations or else it would all go south.

"Why is she here?" the duke asked pleasantly. "There is only one place I want her, and that is in bed delivering my child."

Aldwyn started.

Grimme didn't take the bait. "She is my castellain and advisor."

The duke blinked. "Your *advisor?*"

"Aye. I trust her." He slid an angry glance at her and she smiled sweetly at him as if she hadn't spent the night fucking his best friend.

"You look very much like you trust her," the duke drawled, smirking.

"She is also the reason we are all here today."

"We are not here because of her."

"We all know what happened," Grimme said flatly. "Your men saw my wife and wanted her, and crossed my boundary to get her—a boundary you have no reason to patrol. My men were defending her. The king is going to want to know why a duke attacked his vassal, a vassal with whom he is very pleased. I am willing to tell Henry it was a misunderstanding and that all is well between us, provided you meet my price *and* swear you will leave Kyneward alone."

"You have no power."

"I saved the king's life at Agincourt. That is all the power I need."

"What is your price?"

"Ares."

His expression hardened. "Never."

"Then we have nothing to discuss," he said, standing. Brìghde stood with him.

"Sit. Down. Kyneward."

Grimme looked at him, gritted his teeth, and slowly sat, Brìghde with him. He had no power here. He had sworn fealty to this man, though only because he had been forced.

"I will pay the ransom in coin." He snapped his fingers. Aldwyn arose and put a chest of coins on the floor by Grimme's feet, lid open. "If you want Ares, I will take your wife home with me right now and plow her till she's with child."

Brìghde laid a hand on his arm, likely to keep him from going over the table and strangling the duke.

"We will take the bargain."

Grimme's gut churned. "We will not!"

She looked at him guilelessly. "You love Ares."

"I am not trading you for a *horse*."

Her eyes widened a little, and she swallowed as if she didn't believe him. That infuriated him more.

"Kyneward, I'm going to have her anyway. I can have Aldwyn tie her up and throw her in the back of my provisions wagon if I wanted to, and then you would not have her *or* Ares. Take the bargain. 'Tis a gift. A show of good will, if you will."

Grimme watched the duke, but his attention was caught by Aldwyn, looking down at the table, his jaw grinding, his face flushed, his fist clenched. He was ashamed.

"She's Walter Fàileach's girl, and she outwitted him. I would love to have a son from her. Your horse for your wife."

"Over my dead body."

"That can be arranged, but I'd rather not, as the king might slap my hand. But more than that, I know you don't fear death. What you *do* fear— Well. She comes with me today or I'll kill the horse."

"Then kill him."

He felt Brìghde start. Did she *truly* think he would bow to such a bargain? No. It was a bluff, but he could not see her reasoning.

Aldwyn put his hand on the duke's arm, bent him away from the table, and whispered for quite a while.

Aldwyn and the duke twisted back to the table. "I will let this go. For now. I was not jesting about having your wife and getting my child on her."

"I never thought you were."

"There's your coin. You have the horses and armor. These negotiations are concluded."

He rose. Grimme and Brìghde rose as quickly as they could, bowed, curtsied, said "Your Grace," and then followed him and Aldwyn out the great hall door. Grimme turned left and strode to the stable where Deimos and Phobos were quartered.

"Grimme."

He stopped with Aldwyn's voice in his ear. His mouth tight, he said, "Not one word, Aldwyn," he hissed. "You're angry with me for being dishonorable in battle, but you could serve any noble in this country and you chose *him*."

"I have no choice."

"There are always choices."

"I don't know why I expected you to understand."

"Mayhap," he said crisply, "you have changed. I've changed. I know better now. But you ... fucking my wife all night."

The corner of Aldwyn's mouth turned up. "*You* won't. Not even to get an heir." Aldwyn got closer. "I know that you need an heir," he whispered. "If you die without issue—"

"I told you Pierce was my heir."

Aldwyn stiffened. "Maebh's son?"

"Aye, but my reasoning has nothing to do with piquing you, so don't preen overmuch."

"Doesn't matter. The duke will challenge it so long you might as well not have bothered. Brìghde will be the duke's captive as long as she lives. Kyneward will be no more. Everything you earned and your father built, he will destroy the way he was willing to destroy Ares. And to think—the *only* thing you had to do was bed your wife and get her with child until she had a son. But you *can't*. Pray my seed plants. You will have your heir, he will look like you, and you will never have to struggle to rise for your beautiful wife. You're welcome."

"You didn't do that for me," Grimme gritted, wanting so badly to cut Aldwyn's bollocks off. It was the ultimate revenge, getting his child on Grimme's wife, knowing that Aldwyn's son would become earl after Grimme passed.

He stepped back and raked him up and down with a glance, his lip curled. "No. And every time you look at him, you will know I did what you could not. I—conquered—you. And the hell of it is—that wasn't why I did it. I did it because she's a beautiful, tender-hearted, very *passionate* woman. She didn't have to be yours for me to seduce her. Tell her—from me—it was my privilege to be her first."

48

BRÌGHDE WENT to bed that night half satisfied with the outcome of the duke's visit. She had kept all five of them from the duke's disgusting hands, leaving him *grateful* for the peace and calm of Kyneward that he could have such restful sleep, without ever knowing why. Dillena, Maebh, and Ardith had expressed their gratitude to her. Emelisse's gratitude was reluctant and resentful, expressed under the glaring eyes of the other three, and she would forget soon enough, but Brìghde hadn't had time to devise a foolproof way to make Emelisse pay for her sins at the duke's hands or she would've.

She had baited Grimme, but not successfully. Not even the idea that she might be carrying Aldwyn's child now was enough to bring him to her.

She wasn't with child.

She had gone to Aldwyn's chambers after supper and brought a chess set, and they had played and laughed. She had not told him the truth of her abduction, though, for Aldwyn was still the enemy.

Brìghde had often mistaken friends' motives, and although the true motives weren't any better, it had taught her not to assume too much. Grimme never *intentionally* hurt Brìghde, though he did, in fact, hurt her. Thus, she simply did not believe Aldwyn's claim that Grimme had purposely seduced Aldwyn's lady love. Aldwyn was hurt, angry, and grateful to Grimme for saving his life, so it was understandable that he would say such a thing to himself until he believed it.

She had left Aldwyn's chambers after about an hour, as she could not stay without tempting him beyond his endurance. He was an honorable man and he wanted to be true to his wife—but they had kissed before she left.

Deeply.

Passionately.

It was the kiss she wished Grimme had given her the night he touched her, so now she was even more angry that her first real kiss had not been from the man she wanted more.

Aldwyn wanted her. Badly. And she wanted him, too, but he had refused her only because his honor demanded it. She would respect that; she admired it, even.

Grimme will be in my bed to discuss the evening.

Where will you go?

I will go sleep with someone who loves me.

So she had.

Thus, when the keep had been put to bed after the morning of negotiations, the afternoon of cleaning up, supper (from which Grimme, Ardith, and Maebh had all been absent), and an evening of the usual entertainments, she went to her chambers. Even if Grimme had been in her chambers awaiting her, she would have thrown him out, as she did not realize how angry she was.

The next morning, after having dreamt of ravens, she went to prayer and confession, met Pierce in the stable where his wee pony was saddled and gave him his morning riding lesson, and had breakfast, from which Grimme and Emelisse were absent.

Then, she went to the kitchens with an idea.

"Aye, my lady?" asked a bustling Linota.

"Have you ever cooked a raven?"

"Oh, aye, mum. They are *goooood* eatin'. Big birds, all muscle and fat. Taste a bit like goose, really."

"We have plenty of ravens around, do we not?"

"Aye, but y'see," she huffed and puffed as she scurried around, "the problem with ravens is, them's what hunts 'em, the ravens bedevil 'em somethin' fierce. For *years*. You'll not get a hunter in an 'undred miles to hunt ravens. Those birds remember faces and they talk amongst themselves so they can gather hunerds'n'hunerds of 'em. And *then* they pass that down to their chicks."

Brìghde blinked. "They do?"

"Aye, clever birds, them. You should see 'em playin' in the snow, more like puppies, they are, an' they play catch with the dogs. You never seen the like, with 'em. But they're also mean as sin when they're roiled. Pluck yer eyes out, they will. The ones in the bailey, now, they eat the grain we spill. 'Tis not much, but they remember us and they will beg for more."

"Do you give it to them?"

"No, mum," she said, suddenly nervous.

"I am not trying to catch you in a lie, Linota. I am pondering something."

"What's that, if ye don't mind me askin'? Maybe I can help."

Brìghde twitched her lips. "If they remember faces enough to bedevil those who hunt them and gather their families to assist, and they beg you for food, would it be fair to think that if one fed them deliberately, that they would remember that face, as well?"

"Oh sure, mum. One'a the scullery maids, now, they let her pet 'em. Demand, more like. And they bring her gifts. One o' 'em, she can pick him up an' turn him over like a babe in arms and scratch his breast. Nips at her like a cat, tease, what they do, but don't wanna go when she puts him down. Then, one time, one'a'em fell asleep on her knee whilst she was pettin' him. He was so heavy it put her leg to sleep. Now every time he sees her, he wants pets. Perches on her shoulder and won't leave 'er alone till she at least pats him on the head, and he's as big as she is. Why, he knows her name and can *say* it!"

"Pets?" Brìghde breathed. "Talks? *Gifts?!*"

"Naught but rubbish, shiny, what fits in a beak. Rocks, pieces of metal, suchlike. Now, if you wanna get rid of 'em, what you do is, hang a dead one upside down what where the others can see, an' you'll have 'em nevermore."

Brìghde thought about that many long moments, her fingers thrumming her cheek, then she finally shook her head. "That does not solve my problem."

"But eatin' 'em or feedin' 'em does?"

"Aye."

Brìghde left the kitchen and strolled through the great hall thinking about that and went into the study to find Sir John and William's heads over some parchments. They gave her a mere glance, and she sat in a comfortable chair in front of the hearth.

She barely heard them whilst pondering all that had happened, all that she had learned.

He knew.

She would have to ask Grimme when she felt like speaking to him again. But why? Grimme claimed not to have known who Aldwyn's lady love was. Aldwyn claimed that Grimme knew. They disagreed in that, just as they disagreed in their philosophy of warfare. No amount of talking would change their beliefs and they would refuse to discuss it with each other anyway.

"Papa? You wanted to see me?"

Brìghde started and twisted to see Grimme entering the study and closing the door.

"Aye, I did," Sir John said briskly. William was gone. "Lady Brìghde, have a seat if you please."

Grimme started and looked at her, then his eyes narrowed. She glared back at him. Neither broke the stare, even as they sat, until Sir John barked, "Stop it! Both of you!"

They reluctantly turned their attention to Sir John.

Sir John looked to Grimme. "Bed your wife."

Brìghde's mouth dropped open.

"That is not a suggestion. That is an order."

"Papa," Grimme growled, "I have had enough of being ordered about in *my own home!*" he roared, standing, pacing, growling, howling, punching his fists in the air and then grasping his hair in his hands as if to pull it out. "I don't need to now anyway. *Do I, Brìghde?*"

"We shall see," she said airily.

Sir John gaped at her. "The duke?"

"*ALDWYN!*" Grimme bellowed.

Sir John stilled and many, many expressions ran across his face that Brìghde could not begin to understand. He thoughtfully chewed on his top lip, then smiled. "Excellent," he said, happy again, and sat back, his hands folded over his belly.

"*WHAT?!*"

Sir John shrugged at Grimme. "What do you want me to say? You and Aldwyn look enough alike that any babe from him can be passed off as yours."

"*I do not want to rear another man's get!*" He jabbed a finger at her. "You *promised!*"

"Sit. Down," Sir John snarled and, to Brìghde's surprise, Grimme obeyed. "You have put the weight of the survival of your earldom on your limp cod."

Grimme's mouth dropped open.

"Consider: You have no legitimate heir, Pierce can be challenged, and Sheffield has already challenged the legitimacy of the rightful duke, and then the babe conveniently disappeared. If you die, Brìghde will be at Sheffield's mercy. As long as she has a baby boy, she will be in control until the boy can take over, and in that case, she can train him to be a fit ruler."

"I told her not to take a lover until *after* she bore me two sons."

"*YOU ARE NOT DOING ANYTHING TO GET SONS!*" Sir John roared, standing and raising his cane, then pounded it on his desk. "*YOU – ARE RISKING – EVERYTHING – BECAUSE YOU – ARE NOT – ENOUGH – OF A MAN!*"

Brìghde pulled her lips between her teeth. She dare not look at Grimme.

Sir John jabbed his cane in Grimme's direction. "If she is with Aldwyn's child, you will be the most fortunate bastard who ever lived. You should be on your knees, kissing her feet, since she did what needed to be done because *you wouldn't*. She is fighting not only for her survival, but for the entirety of *your* earldom, and *she does not have any reason to! She* is going to give you a legitimate heir whether you want her to or not. She kept herself and your witches safe from the duke for a week without killing him. She bargained her life and her womb for your *bloody horse!*"

"*AND I REFUSED THAT BARGAIN!*"

"Your chivalry," he sneered, "is commendable. So what do you do as soon as it's all over? You go back to your whores and pretend nothing ever happened, nothing is at stake, and your life will go on as it has been. So go. Go on. Whose turn is it this hour? Go ease your cod in all seven of those blonde bitches to make yourself feel like a real man, because God knows you can't do it in a brunette. Go with the hope that she may be with the child that will save your earldom."

Grimme didn't move.

Sir John's face mottled, and he pounded his cane on the desk again. *"GET – YOUR ARSE – OUT – OF MY – SIGHT!"*

Grimme arose so fast he knocked over the chair, then stalked out and slammed the door behind him.

Sir John dropped his body into his chair and rubbed his forehead wearily. "Please tell me you bedded Aldwyn."

She slouched down in her chair like a naughty wee lass and said in a tiny voice, "No."

"God help us."

49

NOW THAT THE duke's visit was over, it was time to plan the wedding celebration, but to Brìghde's mind there was nothing to celebrate. She set a date. She worked up lists and lists and lists: invitees, menus, seating arrangements, guest accommodations, and on and on and on until she could barely keep her eyes open in the wee hours of the mornings.

She implemented none of it.

She had gone through the newly furnished chambers to replace her mismatched, decrepit furniture. Everything from the dower house matched, so she selected the set of furniture with her second-favorite set of hangings and drapes, pink with shimmering silver trim, for her own. Her favorite was the black and gold with pearls everywhere, but Grimme would hound her until she changed it.

Three applicants for land steward came to Kyneward and Sir John, Brìghde, and William interviewed them. Though Sir John was not impressed by the credentials of any of them, he chose one since, he said, he'd been foolish enough to send competent people away before and perhaps he would be surprised.

Sir John was still unutterably happy with William, who traded his knowledge of the Italians' method of double-entry bookkeeping with both him and Brìghde, in exchange for tales from Sir John's merchant days. He didn't bother to move into a finer chamber or to his own cottage, as his tiny monastic chamber truly suited his taste. William had even caught a maidservant's eye, and she had caught his right back.

"William," Brìghde murmured, hooking his arm and swinging him around to walk him the other way, "that maidservant is not available to you."

He gave her a shocked glance. "My lady, I did not intend anything untoward—"

"She's one of Lord Kyneward's."

"Oh."

"I would not otherwise interfere in your amorous pursuits, but … "

"Aye, thank you, my lady."

The mistresses ignored Brìghde and Brìghde ignored them. With all the boys but Pierce gone, things were more peaceful amongst the women, or at least gave a good impression of it. Emelisse and Dillena sat on one side of the table, Ardith and Maebh on the other side, with Pierce on Maebh's right. Every once in a while Brìghde caught a wistful smile on Maebh's face as she looked at Pierce, then she would muss his hair.

It was obvious to Brìghde that she really did love him, but he either didn't notice or care.

At supper, Brìghde busied herself discussing legal issues with Father Hercule now that a new priest had come. The church was not happy that Kyneward was taking its priest as its lawyer, but if Father Hercule was willing to fill the post *and* tend to some priestly duties, they had no real objection. The two of them discussed the villeins' and merchants' complaints with each other and also with Kyneward itself.

Brìghde went to Waters for her meeting with the merchants and had settled everything appropriately. Some merchants owed her money, but she forgave it. She owed some merchants, and she paid it. Everyone was mostly happy. But when Brìghde apologized for the threats she'd made before she knew of the situation, they were shocked into utter silence.

"I have been a servant," she said matter-of-factly. "I have been under the rule of a cruel lady. I value kindness and I can admit my mistakes. If everyone is fair and kind with me, I will be fair and kind with you."

But she had already established just how cruel she could be and no one doubted her willingness to destroy anyone who cheated her.

As for the earl, there was one who sat to her right at mealtimes to whom she did not speak. He did not speak to her. In fact, they had not spoken to each other since their meeting in Sir John's office four weeks before. She was not hurt by that, because she was as embarrassed by that meeting as he likely was *and* he was spending his nights on the third floor, which she only knew because every single morning, he and one or two or three of his mistresses were missing at breakfast.

She rode Troy before breakfast without Grimme and Helen. The mare still would not allow Brìghde in the stall alone with her, but she did now look for Brìghde to come through to give her treats. After supper, Brìghde would ride the mares.

The company that had left to fetch Brìghde's belongings finally returned, and she was overjoyed to see her beloved pup lounging in the back of a cart, preferring to ride instead of walk all the way from MacFhionnlaigh.

"Mercury!" she cried, and the dog popped his head up, woofed, hopped down, and ran to her, slobbering all over her with his tail wagging so hard, his hind end hopped sideways back and forth.

Then he saw a rabbit and bolted off.

"Silly puppy!" she called after him.

She quivered with glee as the pile of chests grew in the hallway outside her chambers.

There was also a missive from her mother.

> *Good morn, my wee darling! I am at MacFhionnlaigh watching the Kyneward company load the wagons, and I am sad that my wee lass is gone so far from me. I am thrilled with how cleverly you outwitted Fàileach—yet again! He is furious, I am pleased to report, but more at your ingeniously planned rebellion or the fact that you have managed to marshal four lords against him, one of them Scot, to keep him from getting to you, I am not sure.*
>
> *I will visit you in four weeks, as I want to get a better look at that Sassenach god you married, and make sure you are, in fact, in control of him and his keep. I have no doubt he treats you well, for you would punish him if he did not. Or should. You better have.*
>
> *There is not much news here. Lady MacFhionnlaigh is as wet as she ever was. Laird MacFhionnlaigh is angry, but he is too weak to call Fàileach to account. Sir Bart sends his love. All your brothers are gone now, swearing never to return, and Fàileach* still *cannot understand why none wants to stay.*
>
> *I do miss you, lass, but you are safe now, I hope, at least from Fàileach, and I want that for you more than I want my wee bairn at my side. With all love –Mum*

By the end of it, Brìghde was weeping with joy. Her mother *missed* her! She was going to *visit!* Mercury was carried up the stairs by a manservant because he was too lazy to walk, but he bounded into Brìghde's chambers, slobbered on her, then bounded to her bed and promptly made a nest of her bedclothes, then dropped over on his side, completely missing his nest.

"You lazy arse."

He huffed.

Brìghde laughed as she looked up at the chests now blocking the entire hallway past her and Grimme's doors. Her furniture from her chambers at home did not come with, but she hadn't expected it. It was enough that all her clothes were returned to her, her ribbons and jewelry, brushes and combs, books and quills and inks, fribbles and gewgaws.

And she had her dog!

"That is a very big dog," said Grimme from the doorway, surprising her, but she was so happy, she decided not to allow her embarrassment to make her angry.

"I told you you were almost as big as he. Mercury, this is my husband."

Mercury did not deign to respond, not even a flick of an ear.

"And you named him *Mercury*?" Grimme said with something that sounded like amusement.

"Wait till you see him run down a deer."

Grimme turned a wary look on her. "He had better not. We cannot hunt these forests for fifty miles in any direction without the king's presence or at least written consent."

"Is your king so stingy he canna grant the hunting rights to earls he lands? Is Sheffield allowed to hunt?"

"Only when the king is in residence."

"If a deerhound gets loose and hounds a deer, what can anyone do? Leave it there to rot?"

"Logic has no place in this, my lady."

"Hrmph. He will slay all manner of fast-running things, so we will have plenty of rabbit to eat, at least. Go pet him."

Grimme sat upon her bed and vigorously scratched the dog's head and back and side and arse. Mercury stretched out lazily for Grimme to scratch his belly.

"Do not mistake his showing his belly as submission. He just wants it scratched. You are submitting to his will."

"Bloody spoilt rotten," he grumbled as he scratched, "just like Troy."

"Troy loves me," she sniffed haughtily.

"Aye, he does. Mercury is not so much like your Hades," he observed.

She wished he had not said that, for her joy faded a little. "No," she said quietly. "He is not."

Grimme was silent for a moment. "I'm sorry," he murmured. "I know what it is like to lose a beloved pet."

"Ares is still alive," she pointed out before she thought. "You still have hope. In the five years since I lost Hades, I have not met another dog like her."

"Aye, I understand. What did she look like?"

"She was a big, black Italian mastiff," she said flatly. He looked away. "Good news, though!" she breathed, eager to get off that topic. "I have a missive from my mother. She will be here in four weeks."

"My God," he groaned. "*Two* of you."

Brìghde snickered and read him the note.

"'Sassenach god'?" he asked when she was finished, highly amused now.

"Her words, not mine."

She did not miss the flash of irritation across his face and she was immediately piqued. Still, best not to assume. "Why did you scowl?" she asked lightly.

"I'd rather hear that from my wife than my mother-in-law," he snapped, then flushed.

"Ooooh," she cooed, now *angry* because her assumption was correct. Of course it was. She was always right. "I am not to your taste and you feel free to tell me at every turn—*reassuring* me that I need not fear ravishment—but you are piqued that I have not begged for your amorous attentions for the sake of your face and body, instead of simply for a son I need for protection."

His jaw ground.

"I am not used to being repulsive. You are also not used to being repulsive. At least I do not *remind* you. *Repeatedly*. You only see me as a woman when you expect me to *swoon* with enchantment and write poetry to your beauty—dare I say, a *Sassenach god*—" She squealed with laughter. "—but you canna bear to hear you are not someone I would choose?" She hooted. "This is too rich."

"You made your point," he growled.

"Of course I would take you over Roger, but you don't know what he looks like, so you don't ken how low that bar is."

"Brìghde ... "

"I can bear to have you inside me without vomiting."

"That's enough."

"I do not make friends with whom I swive and I do not swive my friends—is that how you worded it?"

"I said," he gritted, "you made your point. That's enough."

"Aldwyn, now—"

He snarled at her and stormed out of the room, leaving her cackling with delight.

What a delicious development.

She ran to tell Sir John immediately, who howled with laughter.

50

HER MOTHER was coming in four weeks!

Brìghde ran around like a madwoman trying to pull the household together enough that it would pass her mother's inspection, but it was too slow for her comfort. She fetched the clothier to Kyneward for the livery, drapes, and new banners and standards. She bade the stonemasons work faster on the west wall of the keep, which was coming along nicely, but not fast enough for her mother's visit.

The keep was finally at a point that she could consider hiring a housekeeper and if she didn't have one by the time her mother arrived, Brìghde would hear about it. As the innkeeper in Hogarth had had applicants, but none who could leave their duties to come to Kyneward, she would go to Hogarth. She sent a message to him requesting him to collect such applicants and have them present to his tavern at a particular time on a particular date, and she would interview. The selected applicant would be driven to Kyneward that very day.

She knew better than to go to Hogarth alone, but she refused to ask Grimme for anything. She asked Sir Thom to arrange for her guard and the carriage, with a two-night stay.

On the appointed day, Sir Thom and her guard, the same knights who had fought for her at the dower house and a few more, and the empty carriage driven by a groom, were awaiting her. She was feeling particularly fresh in a red kirtle with a delicate gold girdle riding her hips. She wore no wimple or headdress because black was her favorite color and her hair was the only black she was allowed to wear. It was in elaborate braids wound and bound with gold ribbons. Once the groom spread her voluminous skirts tidily over Troy's rump, she clip-clopped out of the stable, Mercury at her side, and—

"Lady Brìghde! Lady Brìghde!" called a tiny voice. She twisted to see wee Pierce running as fast as he could. "*WAIT!*"

"Och, I'm sorry," she said when he stopped at her stirrup and panted. She leaned down and caressed his face, but could barely reach. "Fare thee well. I hope to be bringing home a housekeeper in a few days."

"May I come? *Please?* I have never been to Hogarth, and Mam said you won't let her and the others go. But may *I?*"

That was true. She hated Emelisse, but she didn't dare favor one over the other. She also did not want to be more aware of where her husband spent his nights than she already was, and an inn was too close for her comfort.

She sat and thought. They had a carriage. It could not go faster than Pierce's pony could.

"Do you *really* think you can ride twenty miles?"

He pointed to the carriage.

"Oh, aye." She huffed at herself. "Go ask your father."

"If he says aye, will you let me sleep with you?"

"Of course!"

She met her guards' glances and they all chuckled. They waited. And waited. And waited. Presently, Grimme emerged from the keep, rumpled and barely dressed. Her jaw tightened.

"Where are you going?" he demanded of her guard.

"My lord—"

"Talk to *me*, Grimme!" she snapped.

He glared at her. "Where are you going?"

"Hogarth. To interview housekeepers, with the intention of bringing one back."

"I didn't say you could do that."

"I didn't ask you," she sing-songed. "I'm the lady. I am not going out without a guard. I will be gone for three days. All I want to know is if Pierce may be allowed to come with us. 'Twill be good practice and when he can no longer ride the pony, he can ride in the carriage."

"No. None of you are going. And *you* shouldn't be riding at all."

"Papa, *please*," Pierce begged. "I have never been to Hogarth. Mayhap you could come too!"

"He's busy with your mother," Brìghde said.

"Aye, I know but mayhap all three of us—"

"No!" Grimme barked.

"Papa," he whinged. "I don't have *anybody* but Lady Brìghde, and she's *leaving* for *three days*. She said she'd let me sleep with her and she hasn't slept with me since the duke was here!"

That got Grimme's attention and he stared down at his son. "She … slept with you? When the duke was here?"

"Aye."

Brìghde closed her eyes and dropped her head.

"You didn't … ?" he whispered.

She shook her head slightly.

"Aldwyn said—"

"He lied."

"Papa, *please!*"

Grimme took a deep breath and clapped his hand to his mouth, and looked away. Finally he said, "Saddle Deimos and Pierce's pony."

Brìghde was shocked. Pierce whooped with joy and ran to the stable. Grimme disappeared, then reappeared on Deimos in mail, and waited for Hamond to bring him a change of clothing.

They set out half an hour later with Mercury going after every rabbit and quail he saw, but coming back with his tongue lolling to await the next thing that caught his eye and ran very fast.

She wanted to be able to help Pierce, but after their daily morning rides, he was quite accomplished, so she had nothing to say. Grimme attempted to instruct him, but he kept saying, "I *know,* Papa!"

Since he did, in fact, know, Grimme seemed to give up.

Brìghde would not ride anywhere near Grimme. Once she determined that Pierce could do well enough on his own, she sidled up to the front and rode with her guard, and they told each other the story of that harrowing day as if they had not been there, only now with laughter and chortles and many *And then Is*. She relayed *once again* how terrified she was and how her Trojan horse had been so smart and brave.

As one, they all said, "Who's a good lad? *You're* a good lad!" and cackled like a coven of witches. Then she told them the tale of how she escaped from the convent, and after that—

"Now, let me tell you about my big black bitch from hell."

Her men grinned in anticipation of a wonderful story, but Grimme said, "Come, Pierce. Let's race, shall we?"

"You'll beat me, Papa," Pierce said in a huff.

"Very well, just try to keep up. Come."

Brìghde laughed evilly as Deimos cantered past her and her company, and Pierce passed by on the other side, his pony galloping. Soon enough they disappeared, Mercury chasing behind them, and Brìghde could relax and tell her stories all the way to Hogarth.

51

BIG BLACK BITCH from hell.

She clearly did not want Grimme on this expedition. He didn't want to be around her, either, and he had too much to think about to be obliged to half listen to her stories. What made him *angry* was that she knew exactly what to say to unnerve him and get him to back down.

She was as bad as Mouse, taunting him with his fears after he'd trusted her with them, thinking she would never do such a thing. He was quite sure she was getting her revenge because whether they saw each other or not, they lived together, the world was cruel to women, and she couldn't simply drift away or dismiss him completely, as she had any number of friends she'd had throughout the years.

And *now* he learned that Aldwyn had lied to him, that Brìghde hadn't fucked him and was in no danger of carrying Aldwyn's child. He'd been angry that the deed had occurred, but, in all honesty, had mixed feelings about the possibility of a babe. He did *not* want to rear another man's whelp, but a baby boy would, firstly, safeguard Brìghde against the duke keeping her as long as it took to get her with his child—which would be forever, as the duke was sterile—secondly, forestall the hounding for Grimme to perform, which he didn't do any better with than brunettes, and thirdly, look like Grimme because he and Aldwyn looked so much alike. But now that there was no possibility of a babe from Aldwyn, he was disappointed, as with the snap of fingers, the hounding would return.

He would go to the apothecary in Hogarth and ask if there existed anything that would make him rise without an imagination.

He *wanted* to fuck Brìghde. She was beautiful and her body was perfect and she certainly did not, as the duke had said, need to lose a stone or two. He couldn't make his body cooperate, and he hadn't spoken to his father since he had so shamefully chased him from his study.

Then she had taunted him with the fact that she did not want him any more than he wanted her. He hadn't meant to say anything, much less *I'd rather hear it from my wife than my mother-in-law,* but she'd caught his expression, the same way she'd caught his expression when he had briefly ached that he had snatched the wrong woman.

And now she was taunting him with stories of her familiar.

He missed her terribly. He was so deep in his embarrassment he could not bear to be in the same room with her, much less sleep with her.

I can bear to have you inside me without vomiting.

That was not the most effective way to get his cod to rise, as if his humiliation in not being able to when she stood naked before him and he had touched her wasn't enough. The second he had caught that blue glint of her hair, it was not going to be possible.

Brunette. Humiliation. Hounding to conceive. Her lack of desire for him.

He must. He *knew* he must. He wanted to protect Brìghde, had sworn to do so, but the duke was not a patient man and he planned to summon Brìghde to Sheffield at his leisure to take her. Grimme could bear neither the thought of Brìghde suffering under Sheffield for her first time or the thought that Grimme would have to hand her over. He could take the coward's way out and send her with a guard, but he didn't know if that was better or worse than taking her to Sheffield himself.

There was Brìghde, his sweet Brìghde, in the middle of it, wounded that he could not rise for her and frightened for her future. Mayhap if she expressed sincere desire for him, it would help. He determined to ask if there was even a smidgen of it in her.

"Papa, are you and Lady Brìghde fighting again?"

"Aye," he sighed.

"Why?"

"Because I keep saying things that make her sad."

"Why?"

Because I don't know how to seduce a woman, I don't know how to talk to a woman, and— "I don't know how to be friends with a woman," he admitted wearily, reduced to confiding in a five-year-old, for God's sake.

"I thought Emelisse and Dillena and Mam and Ardith were your friends."

What could he say? Gaston and Max knew what Grimme's women were for because Emelisse made sure to complain to them about the others incessantly.

"We are a different kind of friends, which does not include talking. Lady Brìghde and I talk, we disagree, and I say things that would not hurt a man, but do hurt Lady Brìghde. I don't know what those things are before I say them, as I have never had a woman friend before."

"Oh. I don't have any friends except Lady Brìghde."

"Don't worry about that overmuch. It takes a long time to find one very good friend." And only one very bad decision to lose him.

"But I don't want to say anything that will hurt her feelings."

"You would never be able to hurt her feelings, Son."

"I don't like it when you fight."

"I know you don't. Has she been teaching you to ride?"

"Aye, we go out every morning."

And *he* was the one who'd wanted to teach Pierce to ride. Not only had he sent his oldest sons out without knowing how to ride, he was failing Pierce again too because he was too busy sleeping off his nightly orgies. He hadn't ridden Helen in too long, and Brìghde had long ago stopped riding with him. He missed her badly.

"You're doing very well. I'm pleased."

When Pierce turned his little face up to Grimme with a happy grin, he suddenly felt like the most powerful man in the world. Grimme winked at him and leaned down to ruffle his hair. "That's my boy. We need to get you a bigger horse now. Come, race again."

Grimme and Pierce cantered into Hogarth long before the company behind them, so Grimme stabled their horses and took rooms at the inn where Brìghde would be holding interviews for housekeepers. He asked the innkeeper to tell Lady Kyneward that he and Pierce had gone for the day and would be back for supper.

"Aye, m'lord."

Their inn was diagonal to the apothecary, and 'twas there he headed first. He spoke low so as not to spread his shame too far. "'Tis for my chamberlain," he clarified.

The apothecary gave him a packet of something almost immediately, told him how to administer it, and then tutored him excessively on which foods to eat and which to avoid. Grimme would never remember this in all his days, but took the powder.

Then Grimme almost completely forgot about Brìghde and their troubles whilst watching Pierce explore all the new things the boy had never seen before, and he determined that he would abduct his other sons one at a time and bring them to Hogarth for a day.

Every *Papa, look!* and every *Ohhhhh* and every *Did you see that?!* was a balm to Grimme's heart. They ate strawberry tarts, almond shortbread, candied ginger, fritters, and apple-and-pear custard until Pierce was almost sick.

"Oh, no. No more," he laughed when Pierce wanted caraway seed cookies.

They watched the acrobats and the minstrels and the jugglers. Grimme gave Pierce coins to throw in the cap of anyone he felt entertained him well enough. "If they make you stop and watch, they've earned it."

Somehow they came upon the empty lists on the edge of town. There were no tournaments today; it was a normal day for everyone. There was no faire, no festival. Grimme's happy mood diminished somewhat.

"Oh," Pierce said, slumping. "There aren't any knights here today."

"Our house is filled with knights three times a day."

"On their horses with armor and … whatever they do here. Dillena told me about it, when you rode a horse and tried to knock another knight off his horse with a big stick."

That surprised him. "Why was Dillena telling you about it?"

"Oh, she writes stories for Terrwyn and sometimes she would read them to me, too. Now she doesn't, because Terrwyn's gone."

Grimme blinked. He'd never known that, and he had, in fact, met Dillena at a tournament. By the time Grimme was five, Sir John had taken him and Aldwyn to at least two tournaments and Grimme had never taken his sons at all.

"Did you do it a lot, Papa?"

"Aye, Son," he said slowly, rubbing the boy's back whilst looking longingly at the tilt. "I made a lot of money on the lists."

"I want to see you do it. Please?"

All the tournaments he competed in blended into one event in his mind, he on Ares, clad in his armor, the feel of the lance in his hand … He closed his eyes. He was not at war; he couldn't go back to the battlefield because Henry apparently needed him as a politician, and as a politician, Grimme would be expected to produce a legitimate son sooner or later.

The closest he would get to a battlefield now was the lists, but he still wasn't sure he could compete without Ares.

"Mayhap," he said vaguely, then looked up when it started to sprinkle. "It's getting dark. We must get back to the inn before Sir Thom comes searching for us."

Before they'd gotten halfway through the bad part of Hogarth, Pierce was dragging his feet.

"Up you go," Grimme grunted and swung him up on his shoulders.

"Oh, you should see it from up here, Papa."

Grimme chuckled, then his attention was caught by someone tacking bills to a fence. He tilted his head when he saw SHEFFIELD in big letters over a skillful drawing. "What's that?" Grimme said, catching the boy tacking them up.

"Tournament at Sheffield," the boy said and thrust the parchment at him.

"Are you going to enter, Papa?"

"Bloody hell," he whispered as he stared at it. He folded the parchment and tucked it in his shirt, grasped Pierce's little legs, and trotted all the way back to the inn, where his company was sitting in the tavern eating supper.

"My lord," said his knights, standing, which he barely acknowledged before putting Pierce down, scraping a chair toward Brìghde and plopping beside her.

"Brìghde, look." He pulled the parchment out of his shirt and opened it on the table.

She read it quickly and then gasped, putting her hand to her open mouth. "Oh, Grimme, you *must*."

"This is designed specifically to get you and me there. It'll end up a battle between me and Aldwyn, but Sheffield will most definitely take the opportunity you present."

She nodded. "I will have a ring or mayhap a bracelet specially made for the occasion."

"I didn't say I was going to participate. I would not trade you for a horse; I cannot but think he intends to put both of us on the stretcher."

She put her finger on the drawing of Ares, who was being offered as the prize. "Do you think you can win?"

"No question I can *win*. 'Tis whether I think 'tis wise to put us at his mercy."

"If there is not an invitation to this awaiting us at home, I will be surprised."

He slumped. Whether or not he *wanted* to compete was irrelevant; he would because he had no choice than to do otherwise.

"What happens if you do win?"

"That, I cannot predict."

"Whether Sheffield invites us or orders us or not, I want you to enter that tournament."

"Me too!" Pierce added.

He leaned over and kissed Brìghde on the forehead, then sat back with supper and let Pierce tell her all about their afternoon.

52

BRÌGHDE HAD, AT one time or another, slept with three males in her bed. Two brothers and Mercury, when they were traveling and inns were too full or it was too cold for someone to sleep on the floor. Thus, she did not find it strange to be sharing a bed with Grimme *and* Pierce *and* Mercury.

Pierce was asleep before they made their chambers, and once again, Brìghde found herself serving as Grimme's squire.

"Mercury is not sleeping with us," he said, glancing pointedly at the dog sprawled over the entire bed, Pierce sound asleep underneath him. Pierce loved Mercury and Mercury loved Pierce.

To be fair, Mercury loved everybody. He was the worst guard dog in the world. Brìghde loved him, but ... he wasn't Hades, and spending the afternoon telling her company about her vicious dog had only brought long-faded grief back to pierce her heart.

After a somewhat tense silence of working together to relieve Grimme of his mail and leather, they both spoke at once.

"Brìghde—"

"Grimme—"

"You first," Grimme said quietly.

"Thank you," she said, equally quietly whilst he set his armor aside and she sat and brushed out her hair for the night. "I was thinking. We are here with Pierce and sharing a bed and mayhap—mayhap we should put aside our quibbles for a day or two, or at least until we get home. Forget, perhaps, that we are at odds, and be like we were when we first came through from Scotland, and then when I came alone. I want Hogarth to be a place where we can always come and be at peace together."

"That is what I was going to say also," he said softly, picking Mercury up and setting him on the floor, then getting into bed and arranging a sleeping Pierce so that he was between them.

She braided her hair quickly, blew out the candles, and slipped into bed.

"A wee family," she whispered, stroking Pierce's hair. "I've been to the jousts many times. I have no doubt you will win, and I canna wait to see you."

"Thank you, my friend." He paused. "Would you give me your favor?"

"Well, of course," she said, surprised but very pleased, "but you're supposed to get that from a lady whose ardor you want but will never get. Or, what about Emelisse?"

"Firstly," he said, irritation in his voice, "my women aren't coming."

"Oh," she said, shocked.

"Secondly, I don't *want* Emelisse's regard because she will see more in my request than there is. Thirdly, I don't want to carry anyone's regard into battle except my dearest friend's."

There was so much unsaid, but she wanted to keep these days free of those things, so she only said, "Thank you. I would be happy to. Why will you not bring your women?"

"I value them for *one thing*," he said impatiently, "and watching me play at my occupation is not it. Now, we agreed not to talk about such things, aye?"

"Aye."

As she settled down into the mattress and felt Grimme relaxing, she felt his fingers gently combing her hair. She almost said something about ravens and the dark, but she caught herself. She wanted to go back to when they could argue and tease each other out of it or just tease without the arguing at all.

AGAIN, GRIMME took Pierce out to stuff themselves silly on sweets, see the amusements, and shop for things Pierce might want. Brìghde ordered her guard to go out and do whatever they pleased, but Sir Thom said Grimme would be displeased so they stayed.

That morning she spent in a back room of the tavern whilst seeing three applicants for the position of housekeeper. There was an old one, a middle-aged one, and a young one. In her mind, she dismissed the old one and the young one immediately, but she could leave no stone unturned. After all, she had been a housekeeper before she was ten and eight.

She quizzed them on what they would do in which specific circumstances. When she informed the old one that there were four floors of bedchambers, which totaled twenty-four chambers, storage in the donjon, a cellar even deeper than that, and that she would be expected to climb those stairs, she seemed to wilt.

Brìghde smiled encouragingly, bought her breakfast, and that was that.

The middle-aged one was perfect, she thought as she went through the list, but as the woman continued to talk, she seemed to think that scrubbing the floors once a week was a bit much, and that she would content herself with scrubbing them once a year. Then she began to expound upon how worthless servants were and one had to keep a stern hand to keep them in line. Brìghde certainly agreed with a stern hand. However, this applicant's idea involved a cane or a whip or a leather strop.

"I don't approve of those methods," Brìghde said sweetly.

She looked confused. "Then how do you make them do what you want?"

"Pay well, speak with them, not at them simply to give orders, and if they do a good job, tell them. Dismiss the lazy ones and ones who cause trouble. Do you believe you can conform to my methods?"

"No, my lady," she said in barely disguised disgust. "By your leave?"

"By all means."

Brìghde sighed heavily. The young one. She would have no experience. And then she saw her: a tall, willowy, blue-eyed blonde. Oh, sweet Mary and Joseph.

"My lady," she said and curtsied. Brìghde gestured for her to take a seat.

"I will tell you immediately that my husband will be on you before I have a chance to tell him you are not to be touched."

Her face hardened almost imperceptibly. "Will I be forced to comply?"

"No."

"Then I would like to proceed."

"Very well. Knowing that, why do want this position?"

"My current position is not to my satisfaction."

"Aye, I know that or you wouldn't be here. *Why?*"

"My current lady does, in fact, force me."

"Your *lady?*"

"Aye."

That was different. "Who is it?"

She named the name of a minor noble Brìghde had never heard of. The lord did not have a keep; he had an extremely large manor home with exactly eight and a half acres to his name—but far more servants than Kyneward did.

Brìghde went through her list of questions and Rose answered every one of them perfectly and without hesitation. "You have the position."

Rose looked relieved, but at the same time, not surprised.

"Do you have your belongings here?"

"No, mum. I am willing to leave them behind, as well as my last pay."

"We will fetch them. What is your direction?" She told her. "Oh, that is just north of here, mayhap ten miles? Did you walk all that way?"

"Aye, mum."

"Then I will send you along with our carriage and two knights." Her eyes narrowed. "You did not ask me how much the pay is."

"It could be naught but food and a roof, mum, and I would take it."

"Then I shall allow you to be pleasantly surprised when I have seen what you can do."

With that, she summoned Sir Thom, explained, and requested that he do this boon for her. He did not hesitate, and a quarter hour later, he informed her the carriage was on its way with the girl and two knights. They should be back in time for supper.

Brìghde went to the silversmith and stayed all afternoon, explaining what she wanted. He had rings aplenty that were specially made to hold a tiny amount of poison, but their purpose went unspoken. They were there for those who knew. She would need more than a tiny bit, however; thus, the smith showed her a beautiful bracelet with a compartment. Lastly, she selected a brooch and a pendant, both of which cleverly disguised vials. Amongst the ring, bracelet, pendant, and brooch, she would have enough poison to kill as many people as she needed to.

Thoroughly satisfied with her day's work, she was sitting in the tavern next to her new housekeeper with the knights describing the situation: The lord and lady had had shocked and slightly frightened expressions that their housekeeper, guarded by Kyneward knights, had come to claim her possessions, her pay, *and* she had demanded a bonus for duties not in a housekeeper's purview.

"Mistress Rose was very much like you in the manner she managed them, my lady," one knight said approvingly.

"Quite impressive," the other knight said with a nod.

The girl flushed and ducked her head, a pleased smile on her face, but Brìghde did not miss the tiny peeks she and the first knight—a young handsome one—were exchanging.

Grimme, grinning, finally came in with a sleeping Pierce in his arms, Mercury ambling behind them, dropped a quick kiss on Brìghde's forehead, and took the boy and dog up to their room.

He returned and refused supper because, he said, he and Pierce had stuffed themselves to sickness and were looking for any vomitoriums the Romans may have left behind.

Then he saw Rose, who was looking at him with a wary expression and narrowed gaze. His eyebrow rose.

"My new housekeeper, Rose," Brìghde said calmly between bites. "You are not to so much as look at her."

"Did you *have* to hire *her?*" he asked with irritation.

"Sadly, she has impeccable qualifications. She has just escaped one licentious household. I will not allow my house to be one in which the servants want to escape so badly they will risk a beating and leave without their belongings and pay to get away from unwelcome attentions."

"Rose," he said politely, "I simply offer you the chance."

"No, my lord, thank you."

"Very well. Unwilling women are not to my taste. The offer is always open."

SOON AFTER offering Rose his cod, Grimme boisterously disappeared with two women who were more than happy to show him their accommodations. Brìghde successfully kept up her façade of disinterest, as she was truly curious as to how this budding courtship between Rose and the young knight would unfold. The rest of her guard was also curious, keeping up light conversation whilst watching.

But later that night, when Brìghde awoke between a sleeping Pierce and Grimme, his arm in the curve of her waist, her pillow was still wet from crying herself to sleep.

53

"BRÌGHDE," GRIMME said the next morn, once they had gotten under way. He sidled up on the other side of his knights. "I want to talk to you. Fall back."

She would not disobey him in front of his men, not when they were outside, on the road, and he was wearing mail.

Thus, she fell back until they were well behind the carriage bearing Rose and her few possessions. Pierce was well ahead with Mercury at his side. If she had to lose her dog to someone, she would feel privileged to lose him to Pierce.

"What."

"Our truce is over?"

"Aye."

"Why?"

"I need Rose and I need you to keep your eyes off her."

"I already said I would," he said testily. "Speak with me."

She would have given him a look of disdain but she couldn't even stand to do that much. "It was one thing for my conspirator of all of a few days to quietly abandon me for a whore where no one knows who I am. It is quite another for my husband to very loudly abandon me in a place where everyone knows who we are, your habits, and that the only qualified housekeeper within twenty miles is exactly to your tastes. You *humiliated* me."

"Uh ... "

"And now, the rest of it comes back up. This is how friendships fall apart."

"Because you can't accept the terms of the friendship," he said tightly, "and you cannot forgive."

"I cannot forgive because the problem remains. You see me as a man, therefore, it does not occur to you *who* I am and what my position is. I am a woman. Married to you. Other noblewomen may be able to bear the humiliation of their husbands' indiscretions or else those couples despise each other and the woman has her own lover, but I cannot. If you and I despised each other and I had my own lover, no one would have looked askance at me. And God forbid I should bed a stranger, as that would make *me* the whore, not him."

He was silent for quite a while. "Fair," he finally said. "I'm sorry. It won't happen again."

"What won't happen again?"

"I won't make it so obvious."

She shot him a dirty glare.

He threw up a hand. "Very well. I will abstain. You are becoming as demanding as my women."

"Yet *again*—I am a woman! And it only suits you to think of me thusly when you're piqued I haven't fallen at your feet and begged you for anything but your seed."

He huffed. "I'm sorry."

"For *what?*"

"I … all of it?"

"Details," she barked, reining Troy to a halt. "You were perfectly happy to believe I'd swived Aldwyn. Nay, *relieved,* more like. I bear a babe, you don't have to come anywhere near me, all is well, *and* you can be angry and play the victim of both of us as if you are one. Not *one word* of thanks for keeping your harlots out of the duke's bed—"

"Thank you," he said sincerely.

"Not *one word* of thanks for my offer to keep Ares alive—"

"That was a bluff," he snapped.

She gaped at him, tears immediately stinging her eyes. "Are you—" she whispered. "You … *really* believe that?"

He looked uncertain. "Uh … aye?"

She looked away, up, around, her mouth open, her tears beginning to course. She dropped her head in her hand, and shook it. "Go home," she croaked. "Just go home and leave me alone."

"Brìghde—"

He reached for her reins, but Troy side-stepped him without Brìghde's command. She patted his withers. "Good lad," she whispered. "Grimme, go home. Please."

"Can we argue this out?"

"You have not made yourself available to be argued with for five weeks! Why is that?"

He looked away. "I was … ashamed," he said low. "Embarrassed. My father—"

She waited, but he said nothing more. "I ken why you were embarrassed. I was too. 'Tis not pleasant when one's father-in-law berates one's husband for not desiring her whilst in her presence. That should have been a private conversation. And I was hurt that you removed yourself from me so that we could not commiserate together like two naughty bairns."

He closed his eyes and took a deep breath, then released a long sigh.

"You extract from me a promise that I will come to you with my hurts immediately and yet you cannot do what you ask of me. Why is that?"

"You mock me," he said stiffly. "Deliberately. I hurt you, aye, but never intentionally. You are deliberately cruel, such as taunting me with your big black bitch from hell after I confided my fears, then telling me you can bear me inside you without vomiting."

"And why do you think I say those things?" she asked crisply.

He slid her an angry glance. "Because you're cruel. No wonder you have no friends."

"Oh, aye," she said agreeably. "I am. Very cruel. But have you ever known me to be cruel to anyone without provocation?" When he opened his mouth, she said, "Think very carefully."

He clapped his mouth shut.

"I didn't think so. Intent," she said airily, "and carelessness often yield the same result. Do you ken how easily I can read your face?"

"I'm learning," he snarled.

"Aye, well. Let us address 'Sassenach god' first. I would have said *nothing* to you about whether I desire you or not if you had not, once again, been so obviously angry with me. Think back. What did I say that made you angry?" She waited, then growled, "What—did—I—say?"

His jaw ground. "I don't remember."

"I said, 'Her words, not mine.' If you felt I was mocking you, which I was not, you should have said, 'That was hurtful, my lady,' and I would have said, 'Oh? Why?' You would have said, 'I don't like being mocked.' I would have said, 'I'm sorry, Grimme. I didn't intend to mock you. I will be more careful in the future.' *That* is how *friends* solve the little problems as they arise. So it seems to me that *you* are the one who needs friend lessons."

He released an angry breath. "Also fair," he mumbled.

"But you didn't do that. Your face hurt me. It hurts me that you feel free to speak of your lack of desire for me as if I should laugh it off or agree that it is fortunate or both, yet you were angry that I would not have called you a 'Sassenach god.' Thus, I hurt you back. *Mockery* and *taunting* are the only things that get your attention because I continue to ask you not to remind me how much you do not desire me, but you continue to do so."

"I have not spoken with you in five weeks," he snapped. "How do I continue to do this?"

"By running to your women for comfort instead of staying to scrap with me. For *five weeks*. And then, after we have agreed upon a truce, by offering your cod to my new housekeeper *in front of me* and Sir Thom and usual men-at-arms, and abandoning me so *conspicuously* in public to go swive two harlots."

His expression was stony.

"It hurts me that you are both angry and relieved at the prospect that I swived Aldwyn. 'Tis almost as if—" She stopped abruptly, another realization coming over her. "*You* don't want to swive me, but you don't want anyone *else* to, either, and 'tis *not* because you do not want to rear another man's child."

His jaw ground, but he said nothing.

"Nobody else had me, but now your duty has returned. You weren't ashamed at all. You were wallowing in your righteous anger at my and Aldwyn's betrayal of you, and once you learned you could no longer do that, you sought to set things aright and have the argument on your terms. It hurts me that you did not want the argument to start until *you* wanted it to start."

"Brìghde," he sighed.

"We are having the argument. This is what you wanted, aye? Discuss it right then? I am discussing it."

"Why *didn't* you swive Aldwyn?" he burst out. "You had your hand on his cod halfway through supper, as if the duke hadn't humiliated me enough."

"He wanted me to know how it felt to be wanted by an attractive man whom I also found attractive."

Grimme dropped his head, clearly frustrated.

"He kissed me. We kissed. My first kiss. Well, one that was not forced upon me. It was … *wonderful*," she sighed and out of the corner of her eye, she saw him wince. "You're my friend. I can tell you these things, aye?"

His mouth tightened.

"I would have, but alas … he is married."

Grimme's head shot up.

"To a woman he loves. Three children, one of whom she just bore. He did not want to dishonor his wife. What *must* that be like."

"You knew," he snarled, pointing at her. "My women were part of the bargain."

Her mouth tightened. "I am not asking you to give them up. I am not asking you for your eternal love and devotion. I am not asking you to be faithful to me always. I am not asking you to become my lover in truth." Because once he had swived her, he would realize the error of his ways and give her everything she wanted—his love, devotion, and fidelity. "I am asking you to give me a son so that Sheffield will have no basis upon which to petition for removal of

Kyneward to him if you die without a legitimate heir, *and* I am asking you to cease reminding me of how much you don't want me, *and* I am asking you not to embarrass me in public. I understand that you have a difficulty with the first. The last two should not be difficult, and yet they seem to be."

"You are angry that my cod won't cooperate. I understand that. But hounding doesn't help—"

"I have not had a chance to hound you for weeks upon weeks," she hissed, "as you haven't given me the chance to say so much as 'good day' because you were avoiding this argument."

"—and I think if I knew you felt something more for me than not vomiting, that *would* help."

"What if I told you I want you with my whole body and soul? Would that help?"

"And you mock me again."

She looked at him in exasperation and pain. "How in God's name did you manage to keep a friendship for twenty years?"

"Swords," he muttered. "Scrapping."

"Oh, aye, that which I cannot do. *Because I am not a man*. But then there came the lady love to tear you asunder. Aldwyn says you knew she was his lady love," she said blithely with a wave of a hand, "and that you wanted to conquer him to show your dominance, but we all mistake motives, tell ourselves things to sort it out and decide what to believe, and neither of you honest with yourselves. He's wallowing in anger and gratitude. Of course he would tell himself that. You're wallowing in grief over your lost friendship and guilt that you snatched his lady love and with the thrill of victory that you so love and I will assume you attempted to apologize for your mistake and he cannot accept it, which I completely ken, as such a mistake would appear to be a great betrayal when, in fact, it was not—"

She stopped talking.

Grimme hadn't interrupted her to contradict Aldwyn's assertion. She remained silent, giving him a chance to refute Aldwyn's claim. She even turned her head to look at him, expecting at any moment he would declare he did not know she was Aldwyn's lady love and it *was* a mistake, not a betrayal.

She waited.

He chirruped Deimos into a trot.

She caught up to him quickly enough. "Aldwyn was right, wasn't he?" she whispered. "You *did* know. You *knew*." His Adam's apple bobbed. "Did you— Was it— Did it simply … *happen*? Or did you seek her out to pursue her?"

He flushed and pursed his lips. He would not look at her.

"Please, Grimme," she begged, "please tell me you did not deliberately seek her out to seduce her. Please tell me you did not turn your philosophy of war on him. Please tell me you did not deliberately betray your dearest friend from infanthood over a *cunte*. Tell me. I'll believe you."

He waved a hand in resignation.

Brìghde was sick to her stomach and she didn't know what to say. "Oh, God," she croaked, and began to cry.

"Brìghde … I learned my lesson."

"Oh, aye, because you discarded her as soon as you'd conquered him."

"I did not."

She went over and over her conversation with Aldwyn, trying to find some way to lie to herself that Grimme was not that much of a betrayer— And then Maebh had interrupted the conversation with her weeping— It had been almost six years since they had broken apart over a woman, so memories could be fuzzy, the truth lost to both of them—

"Papa! Brìghde!"

She looked up to see wee Pierce, far ahead in the distance, waving at them to catch up.

He was … five.

Brìghde's attention snapped to Grimme so fast, she was dizzy. "Maebh," she whispered.

He looked away, and rage coursed through her breast.

"Friends?" she growled. "*Dearest* friends? Why in God's name would I *want* a friend like you? *I* am the Trojan horse you cannot trust? *I* am the cruel one? You *did* take your manner of warfare, trickery, poison, off the battlefield and you betrayed your friend with it and then you *paraded* your trophy in front of him. You sacrificed your oldest, dearest friendship, wherein you two competed and always emerged equals, to conquer him and prove once and for all you were his superior. What would you be willing to do to *me*?

"And you know I am right and you will go sulk as if 'tis my fault that I know the truth. You knew Aldwyn was right and you hate him for it. Because *nothing* is ever your fault. You pray for forgiveness, but 'tis a show to soothe ruffled feathers, but you simply want the argument to go away. There. *There* is the final argument that obliterates a friendship. I am *right* and I can no longer stew quietly in my righteousness. My God, I hope Sheffield takes Kyneward and I will poison the lot of you and open the portcullis."

With that, she thundered home to Kyneward.

54

BRÌGHDE STORMED into the keep and ran up two flights of stairs, down the hall, and stalked through Maebh's and Ardith's door to find her and Ardith on the bed, Maebh holding a brush whose handle was enveloped in Ardith's body.

"My lady!" they cried in unison.

"In a moment," she said calmly, "I will send servants up to pack Maebh's things." They gaped at her, the brush still buried inside Ardith. "For God's sake! Get that thing out of her cunte and cover yourselves."

They scrambled.

But once covered, they had recovered. "Grimme's going to hear about this," Ardith snarled.

"Grimme already knows. If he doesn't, he's a fool."

Maebh made to storm around Brìghde, but Brìghde kicked the door closed, turned, and locked it.

They both sucked in horrified breaths.

"Maebh, gather everything you want to take with you. I will allow you the whole of it, provided you can get it packed and loaded in a cart in two hours."

"My lady!" Ardith wailed. "What about me?"

"You are welcome to go with her."

"But what about Pierce?" Maebh begged, falling to her knees. "Pierce—"

"Mine now, as you wished and documented. Two hours," she barked, turning and unlocking the door. "Ardith, if you love her at all, go with her."

"What did I do?!" Maebh screamed.

"You betrayed Aldwyn Marchand, who is my friend."

Her complexion drained. "Your lover," she whispered.

Brìghde shook her head. "No. He's married. With three children. You *know* he would never seduce me. I am not punishing you. I am punishing Grimme by taking you away from him. Trust me, it'll hurt him more than it'll hurt you, as you will still have your love."

With that, she slammed and locked the door again, then stormed down to the kitchens to find maidservants and sent them up to Maebh's and Ardith's chambers to await Brìghde's return. She stormed out to the bailey to find manservants to inform them they would be carrying and lifting for the next two hours. She stormed to the stables to instruct the grooms to hitch three carts. She stormed down to the training fields.

Sir Drew, Grimme's second-in-command, happened to see her striding across the grass and came jogging toward her. "My lady! Has something occurred?"

"Indeed, something has occurred. Please choose men you trust to escort Maebh and possibly Ardith to the nearest port and put them on a ship to Ireland. They ride within three hours."

Sir Drew gaped at her. "My lady! You— You don't have that authority."

"I do now," she snarled. "Lord Kyneward should be coming in any time and you can ask him. If he does *not* come in at all, you may take that as assent."

He slowly inhaled. "Maebh, did you say?" he said low.

That infuriated her more. "You know!" she accused, enraged.

"Aye."

"And you remain loyal to him?" she demanded. He looked up to the sky, his mouth tight. "Speak freely."

He slowly lowered his head until he was looking in her eyes, his face placid. "My lord Kyneward has never led us astray." Brìghde's nostrils flared. "I have fought at his side for ten years, my lady. The king would not have gotten off the battlefield without him. Agincourt was … No, my lady. Whatever sins he has committed off the battlefield, he does not commit them on the battlefield, and that is my only concern."

"And Aldwyn?"

"Three quarters of us chose to follow the better warrior, my lady, not the more honorable one. Sir Marchand is a fine warrior but he is more interested in fighting honorably than winning, which means he loses more men. I would rather fight under a commander who values his men's lives more than his pride. And now Sir Marchand and the quarter that went with him are suffering under the duke's hand. We swore fealty to the best commander we have ever had, and he has never betrayed *us*."

She closed her eyes and pulled in a deep breath. "Fair. Just get them out of here."

She stormed back to the keep, where the entire household was in upset. Sir John was standing in front of his study with the door open, his mouth open just as wide. "Brìghde!"

She held up a finger. "Not now," she barked and ran back up the stairs. Both Maebh and Ardith were wailing and pounding their fists against the door, kicking it. Emelisse and Dillena were standing in the hall. Dillena looked frightened. Emelisse looked smug.

"My lady?" Dillena ventured.

Brìghde didn't glance at them. "This doesn't concern you. Go back to your … whatever you were doing."

Dillena vanished. Brìghde unlocked the door and bumped both Maebh and Ardith in the noses. They held their noses and screamed into her face that Grimme would never allow such a thing and they wouldn't go and—

"Lassies," Brìghde said and swept her finger toward the room, ignoring the screaming banshees who thought to advance on Brìghde to take advantage of their height, but Brìghde would not be moved. "Get in there and gather their things to be packed." She looked at the manservants and nodded at them, then looked back up at the two screaming women. "Get out of the way," she snarled.

Brìghde turned to look at Emelisse, who had a viciously pleased look on her face, then glanced at Brìghde. "You're next," Brìghde whispered. "One. Wrong. Step. I dare you."

Emelisse fled.

When Brìghde returned to the great hall, she approached Sir John and said calmly, "I am banishing Maebh. Ardith is going with her."

He stared at her dumbfounded. "But … Grimme," he said weakly.

"Grimme and I have had a … philosophical disagreement," she said crisply, folding her hands primly.

"About … ?"

Brìghde pursed her lips in thought as to whether she should tell him. "Ask Grimme and see if he can bear the shame of telling you. In the meantime, I need to fetch coin to see them upon their way."

"What did he do?" Sir John breathed as he followed her into his study, and then his chambers.

"Enough for me to tear this keep apart," she assured him and, once she had the amount she wanted, went out to the bailey to supervise the packing of the carts.

Soon enough chests large and small began to flow out of the keep. Another cart and several pack mules were required to supply the knights and soldiers accompanying them, and three more men would be driving the carts. Her Hogarth company had arrived. Grimme was not with them. Her guard was somber and Sir Thom shook his head.

Bloody coward.

She told another pair of servants to unload the new housekeeper's belongings and show her to her chambers.

Pierce ran out of the stables to Brìghde, crying because she and his papa were arguing again.

She stroked his hair and pressed him to her, then she crouched in front of him. "Pierce, look at me." He did, but his eyes were red and wet, his nose running, and his face was splotchy. "I am sending your mother away today. You will never see her again."

He blinked and his tears dried up. "Why?"

Why. How did one explain this to a five-year-old? "Someday," she said, pressing her mouth to his forehead, "I will tell you. I canna make you understand right now."

"May I say goodbye?"

"Aye, of course."

"Will you be my mam now?"

"Aye, I am."

With that, he turned and began wading through the sea of servants, looking for his mother to say goodbye. It was sad that he felt nothing more about it than a wish to say goodbye.

Twenty of Grimme's men rode into the bailey. They dismounted and bowed. "My lady," they said.

"Who is the captain of this company?" She gave the pouches to the one indicated and said, "The green one is for your journey. The red one is for their fare to Ireland. The black one is to be given to them once they and their things have been loaded onto the ship. Make sure they get on the bloody boat and that it sails away."

"Aye, my lady."

Within three hours of Brìghde's storming of the keep, they were driving out of the bailey, Pierce in Brìghde's arms quietly watching his mother leave.

55

IT WAS LATE when Grimme returned to Kyneward. The grooms were asleep, so he spent extra time taking care of Deimos, feeding him oats and carrots. Grimme had deserved to lose Ares, the one Grimme and the colt's dam had saved and raised from the womb, training him, riding him into battle, being saved by him. Then Grimme's wife had offered her body to keep Ares alive.

He'd thought it was a bluff.

It wasn't.

He was obliged to compete in a tournament because Sheffield would not take no for an answer and he was not sure he could forestall the duke taking Brìghde. And *now* his last hope for being able to fuck Brìghde—Maebh—was gone.

When he could no longer find chores to do for his horse, he trudged into the bailey, up the stairs, into the keep. His men were asleep in the hall. He picked through them, intending to trudge up the stairs, but—

"Son."

He stopped and dropped his head back. "I cannot talk now, Papa."

"You will. Come."

He would because he respected his father and was grateful to him for oh, so many things, and he would bear his derision because he knew, in spite of it, that his father loved him and this storm would pass. That was more than Brìghde had from her father, and he had never appreciated his father for that until Brìghde started telling stories of hers.

Grimme closed the study door and dropped into a chair in front of the hearth. Sir John was still situating himself into another chair.

"I do not know or, at the present, care why Brìghde threw Maebh out on her arse, but since she did—I want you to get rid of the rest of them—*all* of them. Take Brìghde as your wife in truth, and never look at another."

Grimme gaped at him. "*You're* telling *me* to limit myself to one woman? You couldn't do that with *your* wife."

"*My* wife, unlike Brìghde, was uninteresting."

"Then why did you marry her?" Grimme asked, irritated. "Your taste in mistresses runs to intelligent and lusty."

"I was deceived. She lived some distance from me and her father, who was a wealthy commoner and only rarely came to London to bring his family. I met her in my shop. She was beautiful and her father approved of me. I wrote her missives. She returned them and they stirred my heart and my cod, and I fell in love. When we were able to meet and court properly, she was shy, and I assumed she could only say what she thought and felt in writing, could only express her amorousness that way."

"She wasn't the one writing the missives."

"No and I don't know who was. She could not read at all, much less write. I thought, once we married, I would be able to tease her very interesting thoughts and hints of amorousness out of her little by little, teach her pleasure. She not only had nothing to say, she could not stand being bedded and every time I did, she acted as if I had raped her. Eight times, three babes. It still makes me ill."

"Do you mean to say ... " Grimme breathed in shock, "that you only fucked her *eight times* in your *entire* marriage?"

"Aye. Twenty-seven years."

"Good God," Grimme whispered.

"I tried, Grimme. I tried to be faithful to her because she *did* want me at her side, as company, as someone to pay attention to her as I had when we were courting, but— Well. I'm a Kyneward. I got angrier and angrier that she wanted *me* to be all things to her except her lover, and yet could not even carry on a good conversation, much less be all things to me. If she had been anything like she was in her missives, I could have done that.

"This is what I am trying to make you understand. You are married to a strong, intelligent woman who amuses and interests you, and I have no reason to think she will be any *less* interesting in bed than out. She does *everything* with passion and has a genuine lust for life. I *thought* my wife was a good friend, and more than anything, I would have liked to be able to have *one* woman who was a good friend *and* my lover *and* my wife. That is what she presented to me. That is what I thought I married. That is *not* what she was, and if she had been, I would have been able to curb my appetites. I am *still* bitter. I dare say once you've bedded Brìghde, you will see her in an entirely different light, as a woman who can be all things to you. I beg you, bed her, teach her, be faithful to her, and then you will not have to suffer as I have suffered. Do it not just for *her* and her protection, but for you."

Grimme rubbed the bridge of his nose. "You are underestimating my needs and my endurance."

"Grimme!" he barked. "You are not the only one in this keep getting his cod stroked, and I'm *seventy!*"

"So why are *you* lecturing *me?*"

"Because I want you to have what I always wanted and could not have! A wife who can be all things to you. Brìghde is a gift, I dare say a gift from God—"

Grimme's head whipped around, his eyes wide. "You hate God."

"Aye, this is how strongly I feel, to see God's hand! You have this gift in the palm of your hand and you will not unwrap it! Just *try,*" he pled.

He couldn't bear to explain about the raven witch when he *knew* it was a defect in his mind, as Brìghde had said. He would rather his father be angry with him than pity him as if he were a little boy too frightened to sleep alone during a storm, and he didn't want to hear his father's opinion on what he could do about it.

"Now. Why did Brìghde throw Maebh out on her arse?"

"I ... " He dragged his courage out. "She took my trophy away from me."

His father remained silent.

"Maebh was not an accident," Grimme muttered. "I deliberately sought out Aldwyn's unnamed lady love with the intent to seduce her away from Aldwyn, to conquer him. I succeeded. I am deeply ashamed of myself, yet ... she gave me a son I love dearly who is now also my heir. I am ashamed and yet I cannot regret it. I don't know how to apologize for that. What should I say? 'I am truly sorry, but not truly'? That is a cut that can never be drawn together, no matter how many knots are put in it because I have the reminder of it calling me 'Papa.'"

Silence.

"I know," Sir John said quietly.

That was not what Grimme had expected. "How?" he asked weakly.

"Aldwyn told me why he was distancing himself from me, and I believed him. Unfortunately for him, I have done the same and I cannot regret it any more than you can. I had to explain it to him and that was not an easy conversation."

Grimme was beyond shocked. "You ... "

"Aye. My very good friend had something I wanted, so I took it. I loved her. Kept her as a mistress. I was rewarded for my ruthlessness—"

"How?"

"A bastard you know nothing about," he said flatly, "whom I love as much as you and your siblings." Grimme would not pursue that, no matter how his curiosity was piqued. "But unlike Maebh, mine could not reconcile herself to the others. She thought she should be the only one, and I would not give up my others. My love and support was not enough. The circumstance was bittersweet and she died hating me for it, but I got my own Pierce out of it. I have not questioned you about it because how can I possibly lecture you? And you gave me another grandson I love, so ... "

"Bittersweet," Grimme whispered, so very glad to have confessed after all.

"Aye, and you will have to live with it the rest of your life. But you deserve to lose Maebh. She has Ardith, whom she loves, and Pierce is exactly where she wanted him to be, so other than having to make a new life for herself with her lover, all her things, and coin aplenty, she will not suffer losing you. Brìghde deserves her moment of vengeance on you for the way you have treated her and that, Grimme, I cannot forgive. 'Tis not mine to do so. You know what you need to do to repair the situation, but you refuse to, so good eve."

He was dismissed.

He heaved himself out of the chair before Sir John could say anything more, and left the study. He went upstairs, paused at his floor and continued up to the next. He passed Emelisse's and Dillena's doors and stood in front of the open door of chambers now empty of everything except the furniture and its hangings.

He didn't know what to think so he didn't think.

He didn't know what to feel so he didn't fee—

No wonder Brìghde had no friends. She was right. She was always right, even when she was wrong, and held her tongue as long as she could, suffering indignity after indignity just to feel as if she had a friend. Brìghde's problem wasn't in offending her friends; it was that she was so desperate for one she'd take anybody, and they simply weren't good friends.

Grimme had lost her, his only friend, the way he had lost Aldwyn and over the same despicable act.

And Aldwyn—when presented the perfect opportunity for revenge—had not taken it, ever true to his code of honor.

"Papa?"

He turned and saw little Pierce in the doorway of his chambers. He smiled at his little boy and went down the hall to squat in front of him. "Do you know what happened today?"

"Brìghde sent Mam away."

"Aye. She's not coming back."

"I know. Brìghde said she will be my mam now, but she wouldn't tell me why she sent her away."

"Because your mother and I did something very bad. Brìghde would send me away too if she could. You should not be angry with her, though."

"I'm not. I want her to be my mam."

"Pierce, know this. Your mother tried to make you happy, but she didn't know how. She wanted Brìghde to be your mam because she knew it would make you happy."

Pierce blinked. That was likely too much for a five-year-old to understand. He would tell him again when he was old enough to understand and appreciate it. "Oh."

"Now, go back to bed. Here, I will tuck you in."

Once done, Grimme trudged down the stairs and stood at Brìghde's door, his hand raised to knock. It was habit. He lowered his hand and simply looked at the wood.

He needed forgiveness.

From Aldwyn.

From Brìghde.

He needed to discuss it with Brìghde as if Brìghde had no investment in it, as he had done in the beginning. But now she had an investment and could no longer be a wise third party to listen to him and advise him.

He knocked anyway.

No answer.

Again.

His heart hammered in his chest when he heard the key in the lock and the door opened. She stood there staring up at him stonily. When he didn't speak, she placed her hand on the wall and started thrumming her fingers against the stone.

Waiting.

She was going to wait him out, to watch him wallow in his shame until he could bear her scrutiny no longer.

"If you want me to say I regret the whole of it, I don't," he said abruptly. "I never apologized because the cut is too deep and there is no point. I have Pierce. He is a constant reminder of what I did, but I love him and I am glad I have him."

Brìghde looked suddenly confused. She swallowed and looked at the floor, her face scrunched.

"He loves you. He trusts you. He would rather be with you than his mother, and Maebh loves him enough to let him go where he'll be happiest. I have told you before that I thought of you and me and Pierce as our own little family. I have no reason to doubt as to your care for and loyalty to my son, and ... thank you. That was all I wanted to say."

No it wasn't, but he didn't know what he wanted to say, and didn't know if he'd say it even if he did know. He turned away, but instead of hearing the slamming of a door, she closed it quietly. The click of the lock echoed in the hallway.

56

THERE HAD indeed been an invitation to the Sheffield tournament awaiting them upon arrival from Hogarth. It was little less than a command. But they did not discuss it, as for the next three weeks, Brìghde and Grimme avoided each other assiduously. She was too angry and Grimme too ashamed, or so Sir John informed her. He also relayed why he could not judge Grimme for it much less be angry, and Brìghde was sickened that the man she respected so highly and thought of as a father had done such a thing.

I'm seventy years old, Brìghde. I'm a lusty man with a long history of women and misdeeds surrounding them. I understand my sons and their mistakes, for I made them, my father made them, my grandfather made them and so on back to Adam. But everyone must make their own. The only thing I find inexplicable about Grimme is that he will not take you to wife, and since that affects all of us, I do have a right to be angry about it.

If Grimme ate at all, she didn't know when or where. If he was swiving his women, she didn't know that either, as Emelisse and Dillena were at all meals, though he was not. She never saw him in the stable or anywhere else in the keep, and that was all to the better for her peace of mind.

She was in the study with Sir John and the architect poring over plans for expansion of the fortress when the news arrived.

"Fàileach approaches, my lady."

Brìghde gasped and dropped her quill, scraped back her chair and blew right past the manservant, through the hall, out the door, through the inner bailey, straight to the stables. "Troy!" she roared as she ran. She was huffing and puffing when she reached his stall, where he was already saddled. She bent and braced her hands on her knees to catch her breath before they threw her in the saddle. Then she was off, out of the keep, down the lane, and on the road to Waters.

It didn't surprise her when she heard thundering hooves following her. Sir Thom had anticipated her and he and his men were ready to follow.

They were a half mile past Waters, her mother, with her captain Sir Bart, leading the company.

Of course!

"*MOOM!*" she screamed, overjoyed, pulling Troy up and twirling him around to draw alongside her company, which halted. She nigh threw herself into her mother's lap for hugging her and crying. Her mother hugged her just as tightly.

"Oh, me wee lassie," she breathed. "'Tis so good to see ye. I thought ye lost to me forever when he took ye."

Brìghde drew away when Troy had had enough of the close contact with an unfamiliar horse. Then it was her mother's captain. "Sir Bart!" she squealed, wheeled Troy around to the other side of the company and drew alongside for a hug from him. She held him tightly and closed her eyes, his presence familiar and welcoming. "It's so good to see you again. I missed ye."

That was very, very true, she realized, and she didn't know how much until he was there.

"We thought we lost you, lass," he said affectionately, putting her away from him with a wink. "You outwitted him again."

She preened. "Aye, I did."

"I couldn't be more proud."

Her mother looked over at Troy, and her eyebrow rose. "Why're ye ridin' a charger, Budgie? And astride, too. Have some decorum. Ye're not a wee lassie with a litter of rambunctious brothers anymore. You're the lady of a keep."

Two weeks.

Oh, sweet Virgin Mary, what had she done?

Her mother chirruped her horse into motion again and again Brìghde turned Troy to trot beside her. Brìghde said nothing in breathless anticipation of something, *anything* she would praise. There was nothing to praise yet. It was a dirt road bounded closely on either side by thick forest, but her mother looked at everything with a critical eye.

Then the road turned into the lane leading to the keep.

She stopped and stared at it for a long time, her mouth pursing. "'Tis crumblin'." She pointed to the west curtain wall. "That needs fortification."

"Aye, Moom. 'Tis being repaired, right at this very moment, and a third bailey wall."

"Ye need it. Ye also need a moat."

"No, 'tis built on deep rock and the ditches are being deepened and spiked."

More study. More pursed lips. "Why aren't yer banners flyin'?"

"I'm having new made, but they aren't finished yet. The old ones were worn out. The keep is half full of clothiers and flagmakers."

She looked down at Troy again. "He needs new livery."

"Aye, I know. That is also being made."

"Is the earl impoverished?"

Brìghde raised a finger. "Of all the faults you can find here, that is not one of them. By far."

She nodded approvingly. "That's good to hear. Do ye have enough room for us in the stable?"

"Um ... "

Her mother slid her a disapproving glance. "Mmm hm."

As they trod toward the lane, Brìghde looked at Sir Bart and pointed to the west field. "You can make camp there. Please come to supper tonight in the great hall. I want my husband to meet you."

"Thank you, Budgie," he said with a warm smile. "I look forward to it." Then they were off and it was just her mother, with her chambermaid following on a pony.

"What happened?" she snapped. "I know very good'n'well that was no plot. Ye had no opportunity to meet Kyneward anywhere at any time once the weddin' plannin' began."

The demons of hell could not get Brìghde to spill it, and though she had thought that her mother would believe the tale, she and Grimme had worked out an answer to this question long ago.

"He was at the tournament in Humbie. Remember? Three years ago." He had been in France three years ago on a real battlefield instead of playing warrior on the lists and Brìghde had been nowhere near Humbie. "I went with Lady Sorcha, Lady Raonaild, and Lady Deirdre." Lasses who did not exist.

"An' ye just happened to meet, speak with, an' exchange enough information that ye could come up with this plot."

"I was drunk, and 'twas a jest."

"Oh."

"He didn't know I was drunk and sent me a missive to ask if I was truly amenable, as he was getting desperate. I took the opportunity and wrote back."

She would believe that. Brìghde had not had the wherewithal to sneak off, but she could have paid any local lad to go on a grand adventure to Kyneward and sneak missives back into Fàileach Keep.

She sighed heavily. "Well done, me wee darlin'. An' doin' it drunk too. I shall tell Fàileach to roil him up again."

Brìghde preened. Not only had she earned her mother's approbation, she had successfully lied to her. Again.

"When can I expect a wee earl?" Brìghde pulled her lips between her teeth and her mother cackled merrily. "Oh, Budgie! I'll come help ye durin' yer confinement."

"Ah ... no. No, I'm not expecting yet." She would never be, at this rate.

Her mother waved that off. "'Tis only been a few months. Keep at it."

"We were strangers, Moom, each with our own reasons for the marriage. We're friends now, aye, but 'twill take some time to grow into lovers."

Her mother was aghast. "Ye've nae managed to swive *that* brute?"

"Ah ... no."

"Good God, I'd'a had him 'twixt me legs the second he said 'I do.'"

"Moom!" Brìghde squeaked, appalled.

"Ye're married now. I can talk like this to ye." She harrumphed. "*Somebody* needs to. If he looked like Roger, that'd be one thing, but the man's a god."

Brìghde was about to cry. "I know what he looks like."

"Aye, but have ye e'en seen him naked?"

"Aye."

"Is he hung like a stallion? He looks like he is."

"Moom, you're embarrassing me."

"Budgie, if a little talk 'twixt women's got ye in such a flutter, 'tis no wonder he's not gotche in bed yet." Her eyes narrowed. "Ye're bonny enough to harden any man. Are ye *keepin'* him from ye?"

Brìghde sighed. "We're just friends. For now. Don't rush things."

"'Tis all that time in a convent," she sniffed with disgust. "I knew that was a bad idea."

"Then why did you send me there?" she asked in exasperation.

"To keep ye safe from Fàileach."

Oh.

"I shoulda had this talk with ye before now," she sighed. "God knows what those nuns put in yer head."

Brìghde had to get off this topic five minutes ago. "Moom, why does Walter give you everything you want and does not treat you the way he treats us? He never said a word about throwing a poker through his shoulder."

"That is a tale best left untold."

Brìghde gaped at her mother. No tale ever went untold in her family. Eventually, even plots came out because they could not resist boasting over how clever they were.

Lady Fàileach looked around and pointed to the tall boxwood hedgerows along the lane. "That's inefficient fer gettin' the produce to the lane."

"Firstly, they look very nice and they tidy up the lane. Secondly, Grimme likes them." To hide his arbalists, but she wouldn't tell her mother that.

"That's true. I could be persuaded to sacrifice efficiency fer beauty. This is very lovely. Yer cottages look well kempt."

Brìghde was pleased. It had taken reams of lists and four weeks of supervision to get the cottages up to Lady Fàileach's standards.

Finally they went through the portcullis to the outer bailey, where Lady Fàileach stopped cold. Brìghde was fair to biting her fingernails and hoping her desperation was not blatant on her face.

"I suppose," she murmured, "I shoulda asked how many horses ye had."

The outer bailey was all stables, true, but it was beautifully built and kept. No mean, crumbling, filthy shelter for these horses, oh no. And the present occupants didn't account for the Kyneward horses out for training and the ones that belonged to the knights who lived out in the encampment.

"My God," she whispered, looking around. "I've never seen this many horses inside a keep in me life."

"Grimme is a breeder. 'Tis how he made much of his fortune and how he can afford a standing army with just twenty thousand acres."

Her mother looked at her incredulously. "Ye don't say!"

She nodded and smiled, proud that her mother had found *something* of worth in her home.

"Lassie, ye may have the devil's own luck."

"A well-executed plan, Moom. Is that not what you taught me?"

"Aye, but ye had to meet the lad first, which is where the luck happened."

Brìghde knew that whichever way it had happened, it was God's will, so why did it bother her that her mother was merely pointing it out?

"Not luck. God."

"Aye, ye're right." She crossed herself.

The grooms came to assist Brìghde and her mother to dismount. The carts would draw up soon and Brìghde instructed the waiting manservants where to put her mother and chambermaid. They walked into the inner bailey, which was again freshly whitewashed, and the keep's stone façade was gleaming. Lady Fàileach looked up and around. There were late summer flowers blooming and patches of grass where the keep's children played sometimes.

"Brìghde! Brìghde!"

"Here comes my stepson running."

"Stepson?" she barked. "He's been married before?"

"No, Moom. They're his bastards. Four."

Her jaw dropped.

"You'll not meet the others. They are with their knights."

"As well they should be!"

Pierce came flying out the door and jumped off the front stoop over all the stairs to land with a thud, then ran to her and threw himself at her. She hugged him to her but he was looking up at her mother. He was as excited as Brìghde to have her mother here, because she'd told him stories about her.

"Good day, me wee laddie," Lady Fàileach said politely, but distantly. Oh sweet Mary and Joseph. Brìghde had forgotten that her mother didn't like any children but her own.

"Good morn, Lady Fàileach," he said, pronouncing Fàileach exactly right.

"Oh, well done." She looked at Brìghde. "Are ye teachin' 'im Gaelic?"

"No. He just wants to be able to pronounce my name with a proper Gaelic accent. They all speak French."

"In an *English* household?"

"The favorite mistress is French."

"*Favorite ... mistress?*" she growled incredulously.

"'Twas a plot, Moom," she said wearily. "Business. Would you rather I suffer four mistresses, three maidservants, and four bastards with a man who likes me and allows me the utmost of freedom and unlimited coin where I am a countess or ... Roger MacFhionnlaigh?"

She closed her eyes and sighed. "Fair."

"Also, there are two fewer mistresses than a month ago."

"Brìghde made my mother go away," Pierce said matter-of-factly.

"Oh? Ye doona seem torn up about it."

"I want Brìghde to be my mam."

Lady Fàileach arched her brow at Brìghde. "I dinna take ye fer the motherin' type."

She was saved from having to answer because where Pierce went, Mercury followed. Mercury did not approach her mother, for he knew better.

"Well! Show me the inside."

The great hall was gleaming even more than it had when the duke had visited, but Lady Fàileach was a more exacting critic, and as soon as she entered, she scowled. "'Tis awfully plain."

"The murals were old and crumbling. We are awaiting an artist to come paint anew."

"Ah."

The servants were awaiting her, lined up, some in new livery, some in old. "Leave 'em in old livery until they can present a matched set," her mother whispered to her.

"This is Lady Fàileach, my mother. She is an honored guest here at Kyneward Keep."

They all curtsied, murmured, "My lady," then Brìghde dismissed them.

"Come, I want you to meet Grimme's father."

The introduction didn't go well.

Everyone was cordial, mayhap overly so, but Lady Fàileach and Sir John hated each other on sight.

Mayhap not on sight. Mayhap it was when her mother demanded of Brìghde to see the books and Sir John snapped, "Absolutely not! Are you mad, woman?"

Brìghde dropped her face in her hand.

Lady Fàileach rounded on Brìghde and said, "I thought ye'd have had this keep entirely in hand by now."

She didn't dare tell her she had a clerk.

"An' this ol' man's tendin' yer *books?* I taught ye better than that!"

"Sir John built this earldom to its present prosperity," Brìghde said wearily. "He is still teaching me his ways."

"Why aren't ye usin' *my* ways?"

"Because they're inefficient," Sir John snapped, to which Lady Fàileach took umbrage.

"*Inefficient?* I pride meself on me efficiency, Sir!"

"Your pride is unwarranted."

"She simply didn't show ye well enough. Here." She took off her gloves and swept around the desk to where the ledger sat open.

"Moom!" Brìghde cried and ran to close it before her mother got her hands on it. "Do not come into my home and attempt to take over. I have only been here four months. I am doing the best I can." In the meantime, she covertly gestured to William to go hide in Sir John's chambers.

Her mother considered that, then harrumphed. "Verra well, but I expected better of ye. Four months. That's enough time to build a keep."

She wasn't jesting.

"Show me to me chambers, if ye please."

57

GRIMME HAD successfully avoided both his wife and his father for some weeks, taking his meals with his men out in the field, working with Helen, training the new colts, and fucking himself. But Brìghde's mother had arrived, so he was obliged to play gracious host and happy conspirator. Thus, when he saw the Fàileach company pass by, he rode in from the training field and presented himself to his chambers for a bath.

Unfortunately, there was a body already in it. He sighed. "Mouse, get out. I need that."

"Your mother-in-law is here," he sing-songed as he heaved himself upward and took the towel Grimme handed him.

With a wave of Grimme's hand, Mouse hid and Hamond summoned chambermaids to empty the tub and refill it. Grimme forewent hot water to bathe quickly. Mouse attired himself in the very drab but clean clothing Grimme kept for him in his chambers and dropped himself on Grimme's bed.

"Has Sheffield bred Ares?" Grimme asked as he scrubbed.

"You know better than that," Mouse answered. "It requires more thought and effort than stomping on the necks of villeins, serfs, and slaves."

Grimme breathed a sigh of relief. "What have you to tell me today?"

"The tournament. Provided neither you nor Aldwyn can unseat each other and are the last ones standing, I *believe* the duke intends it to be a battle to the death."

"Bloody hell," he muttered as he retrieved himself from the bath and dried himself off. "It occurred to me that he'd do that, but I thought, 'No, because he would have to account to Henry for Aldwyn's death.'"

"Don't overthink. Henry would believe that you had gotten out of control and slayed him in the heat of battle, and he would never believe Sheffield ordered it."

Grimme gave himself over to Hamond for shaving. "True," he muttered. "Sheffield will do anything to poison my friendship with Henry. Why is Aldwyn submitting himself to this?"

He said nothing for a long moment.

"Mouse," Grimme growled.

He took a very deep breath. "Aldwyn's wife is serving as Sheffield's plaything."

Grimme's heart stopped. "My God."

"Aldwyn's made to watch. Tied, brought to Sheffield's chambers. She is not tied down, but the threat to both of them is that he will kill the children. Neither of them are allowed to see the little ones for anything more than a few minutes every once in a while and under heavy guard to keep them from escaping."

Grimme's gut roiled and his spine tingled.

"Sheffield doesn't get violent. Once and done, then sends her away, but she just had a baby, and he doesn't care." Grimme grimaced in sympathy pain. "What I have pieced together is that before his visit here, she was just used as a threat to keep Aldwyn under control, but then he grew angry that Aldwyn talked him out of taking your wife back with him. He has promised Aldwyn he will release all five of them if he manages to kill you."

"Aldwyn can't and Sheffield won't."

"Aye, and all three of us know it, but Aldwyn will be desperate."

"Desperate men make careless foes," Grimme said vaguely, his mind churning with ways to rescue Aldwyn and his family. "'Tis the ones with cool heads or who have nothing to lose who will conquer. The last map of guard stations, spikes, and traps you drew for me—is that still good?"

"Wait until after the tournament," Mouse said with command, his voice completely empty of mischief. "I know Aldwyn cannot kill you, but I can't predict what will happen if you kill him."

Grimme said nothing.

"Is there *any* way you can keep from killing him?" Mouse asked, with some strange note in his voice Grimme had never heard.

"I don't *want* to," Grimme said soberly, "but in the balance between Brìghde and Aldwyn, I will."

Mouse sneered. "And then what? Hand her over to Sheffield because *he's your liege* and you *must* do what your liege told you to do?"

"Don't worry about her."

"Found your bollocks, did you?"

"Are you going to the tournament?" Grimme asked, ignoring Mouse's jab.

"Grimme. Do—not—kill—Aldwyn."

"I will not promise that. I may not know how to be an earl, but I do know how to war. Trust. Me."

Mouse heaved a great sigh.

"Why do you care, anyway?" Grimme asked with irritation.

"Do you think I *like* being there and seeing what Sheffield does?" he demanded.

"Hrmph. Are you going to the tournament," he asked again, "or are you staying in the castle?"

"Tournament."

"Good. I need you."

"Don't you always? If Sheffield's not in the keep, I have little reason to be there. God, I hate that place. It's even worse now that your wife's worked some black magic—" Grimme controlled his flinch. "—on this place. It's easy to stay filthy there. I have to trot sixty miles for a bloody bath."

"You have enough coin to take a room at the inn fifteen miles away from you."

"I'm invisible, remember? That would make me visible. And speaking of your wife— What I wouldn't give to plow her."

"You and Papa and Aldwyn," Grimme muttered morosely. "Hamond, trim my hair."

"Aye, m'lord."

"Sheffield and every other man in England wants her but *you* because you don't like brunettes," Mouse mocked in a high-pitched voice. "What is *wrong* with you?"

Grimme would *never* confess his fears to Mouse, of all people, as he would torment him endlessly. It was bad enough Brìghde did it. "I already told you why."

"I've been thinking about that. You don't fuck your friends because they are male, but *she* is not. How can you be friends with a woman at all? 'Tis not like you."

"I think of her as a man," he mumbled. Or else the raven witch. "'Tis a sore point 'twixt us."

"You're pathetic."

Grimme wasn't going to argue the point.

"You're not in the least bit worried about her with Sheffield?" Mouse demanded.

"She can take care of herself."

"How?"

"My little wife," he murmured vaguely as he thought, "is a natural born killer. I barely kept her from killing Sheffield when he was here. She had … two, three, four ways to do it and I would've let her, but I didn't want him to die on my land."

"But— Did I hear correctly that she offered herself to keep Ares alive?"

Grimme sighed heavily, guilt still weighing upon him. "Aye, she—" His eyes popped open with sudden realization. "She … Oh, God, I'm an idiot," he whispered. "Oh, *God*," he moaned, closing his eyes. "I thought she was bluffing."

"Why would she do that when she knew he would take the offering but still kill the horse?" Mouse said, clearly perplexed.

"I could not reason it out. She informed me it was not a bluff at all."

"Only a woman who loves her man would do that."

Grimme shook his head vehemently. "This is what I have just realized: She never intended to submit. She intended to kill him. She wanted access to him away from Kyneward, away from me, so that he would not die on my land, where I could not have done it, and where no one knows she would be capable of doing such a deed herself and thus, not suspect her."

"Good God!"

"How could I not have seen that?" he groaned.

"You married an assassin," Mouse said flatly.

He heaved a sigh. "Entirely by accident, I assure you."

"Aren't you afraid she'll kill *you*?"

"No," Grimme said immediately, "although I do fear for Emelisse."

"Aye, well, mayhap Emelisse needs to learn how to keep her mouth shut."

"And her hands to herself. She slapped Brìghde, and Brìghde told her if she touched her again, she'd kill her. I believe her, but Emelisse doesn't."

"The world wouldn't mourn."

"My sons would."

"Oh. I forgot about them."

"Brìghde is desperate for friends. I am one, albeit not a very good one. But more than that, she hangs on every word of praise Papa gives her. She lives for any expression of approval from him. And I am absolutely certain she wants something from me, but I don't know what it is nor will she admit she wants anything at all. Can't be money because she has access to the daily chest. You know women. What else could she possibly want?"

Mouse shrugged helplessly. "I haven't been in her company at all, much less enough to know, and I've never known a woman I would describe as a 'natural born killer,' but that is not my concern at the moment. My concern is Aldwyn. Do not kill him and do not rescue him until after the tournament."

Finally, Hamond was finished with Grimme's hair. "Very well," he muttered. "Time to face the mother of all viragos."

58

GRIMME DIDN'T know what to expect of his mother-in-law, but the licentious shrew he met was not it. He was not surprised to find her resembling Brìghde quite closely, excepting that her black hair was generously salted and mostly tucked up under a headdress. She was dressed more finely than Brìghde with jewels aplenty, which made him realize that other than her wedding ring, Grimme had never bought her any jewels.

Except for Brìghde's delicate observation that the keep's outer bailey walls on the west needed to be repaired, whatever critical thoughts Brìghde had had upon arriving at the keep, she had kept to herself.

Lady Fàileach was not so subtle. In fact, subtlety for her seemed to be a vice.

Grimme met her coming out of Sir John's study—rather, *storming* out of it—and she ran right into his chest. She opened her mouth to chastise him, then looked up at him, recognized him, smiled wickedly, stepped back, and raked him up and down with a leer.

He met Brìghde's gaze over her mother's head. Brìghde looked away, her mouth trembling, and her face flushed. Aye, he wanted Brìghde to admire him, but he did not want to be ogled by his mother-in-law.

"Sweet Virgin Mary," she said with a heavy Highlands brogue. "Ye're me son-in-law."

"Aye," he said as graciously as he could muster. "Pleasant to meet you, Lady Fàileach. Welcome to our home and we hope that you enjoy yourself here."

She held out her hand. He took it, raised it to his lips, kissed it. "I am verra impressed by yer stables. Will ye take me on a tour?"

He inclined his head and offered her his arm. He cast a glance at Brìghde as he swept Lady Fàileach out of the keep, but she would not meet his eyes.

"Where are all your stallions?" she asked once they reached the stables.

"They're warhorses," he said matter-of-factly. "They must prepare for war, as any knight must. A horse who is made to war is not happy spending his days in a stall."

"Oh, but there is the one Brìghde rode out to meet me. Why do ye allow her to ride a charger?"

"I allow Brìghde to do what she wants for I need her to put my house to rights. She can't do that if I order her not to do this, that, or some other thing."

"Hrmph. She hasn't got it to rights yet," she sniffed.

Therein began a spate of complaints about what Brìghde had not yet accomplished or failed to do properly or had left unfinished, and how could he tolerate it? As she spoke, Grimme's mood went from resigned to disgusted to angry, but he could not show it.

Grimme wanted to protect his wife, but did that include protecting her from a mother she had been so excited to see?

"My lady," he said courteously, interrupting her, "you did not see Kyneward Keep before she arrived. She has worked wonders for it and the whole of the earldom, which was a daunting task, as I am a new earl and have been away most of my tenure. Neither my father nor I knew how an earldom is to function, and Brìghde has taught us much. We're grateful she's here, and we're grateful for her accomplishments, which are many."

Lady Fàileach's mouth tightened, but she lightly said, "Ye don't know what should be, so of course ye'd be happy with her."

If she lasted two weeks in his house without his slapping her all the way back to Scotland, it would be a miracle.

Lady Fàileach was not interested in seeing the mares, which irritated him because a successful breeder depended as much on the lineage and quality of its mares as its stallions, and he was proud of them.

He toured the baileys with her, pointing out all the improvements Brìghde had made, but Lady Fàileach said nothing except hum disapprovingly every once in a while.

He could stand it no more and with a courteous, "I'm sure your chambermaid has your chambers ready for you, Lady Fàileach. We dine in two hours."

Her eyes narrowed. "You have a *clock* here?"

"We have many," he said solicitously. "My father is very precise."

It was an effort for her to bite back whatever she wanted to say about his father, which deepened his anger. *Say it. One word. Give me a reason to throw you out.*

When he accompanied her back into the keep, Emelisse was arguing at Brìghde, who looked utterly bored, and Dillena stood impatiently with her arms crossed over her chest, her toe tapping, and her eyes rolled up to the ceiling.

"Who are those women?" Lady Fàileach demanded.

"My mistresses."

"Ye've got plenty to go around," she said playfully.

Normally, Grimme would preen and say *That I do*, but this was not the time. Suddenly, Lady Fàileach broke from him, marched over to the three women, barked at Emelisse and Dillena to get their whore arses back to their chambers, as they shouldn't be harrying a countess, a *lady*, for anything. In fact, they should not show their faces at all. All three of them looked at her in shock, Brìghde so horrified she could do nothing but stand there.

Grimme strode across the floor, but before he could say anything, both Emelisse and Dillena burst into tears and ran up the stairs. It took a lot to make Dillena cry.

"Moom!" Brìghde cried. "I canna believe yer audacity! They *live* here! This is their home! They are the mothers of Grimme's children. *Ye're* the guest, an' ye doona ken anythin' about how it goes here."

"Why in God's name would ye allow yer husband's mistresses in the house?"

"It was a *plot*, Moom!" she insisted. "I *knew* about them before I came here an'—"

"Lady Fàileach," Grimme said tightly, "please see to your chambers. In the future, refrain from disparaging remarks to or about my family. I will not tolerate it in my home."

Without a breath of shame, she imperiously gestured to Brìghde to show her the way and then marched herself right after her, muttering, "*Family*. Hrmph," under her breath.

He watched them go and realized that whatever Brìghde thought about the members of the household, she had never disparaged his women without provocation. She and Dillena seemed to get along. Brìghde had tossed two, but not because they were Grimme's mistresses. She hated Emelisse and might *kill* her (for Emelisse had given her every reason to) but she did not disparage her place in the household.

Nay, Brìghde didn't care *who* Grimme fucked, so long as he didn't embarrass her or remind her that he did *not* want to fuck her. His brow wrinkled. *Why* didn't Brìghde care, though? Wasn't she the least bit jealous?

Sassenach god.

No, he'd never hear that from Brìghde's mouth unless she was squealing with uncontrollable laughter, and he now didn't find it the least bit amusing that her mother had referred to him that way.

"It's only two weeks, it's only two weeks, I'm training, I'm training, it's only two weeks," Grimme found himself immediately whispering to himself.

"Get rid of that bitch," Sir John whispered from behind him.

"Your introduction did not go well?"

"We have just met the one person Brìghde cannot control or outwit."

Grimme groaned and dropped his face into his hand. "She made Dillena cry."

"That's … impressive. 'Tis no wonder that girl needs a friend."

At supper, Brìghde breathlessly introduced him to the captain of Lady Fàileach's guard, Sir Bartholomew Thatcher, and Grimme made the introductions to Sir Drew and Sir Thom.

"Sir Bart taught me how to ride," she said happily. "He also got me my first wee sword and dagger."

Sir Bart bowed and said, "My lord."

"Pleased," Grimme said politely, and signaled for a servant to add a chair at the head table for Sir Bart, next to Sir Thom.

Other than that, supper was a nightmare. Lady Fàileach had taken Brìghde's chair without asking and Brìghde had borne it without a peep. Worse, Lady Fàileach whispered her complaints at Brìghde. Loudly. In English. So Grimme could hear.

The food wasn't good enough.

Brìghde wasn't dressed well enough.

The hall was too white, not enough color, too many candles, hearth wasn't big enough, hearth furniture was old and worn, tables weren't clean enough, floor wasn't clean enough, rushes weren't fresh enough, head table's dais wasn't high enough. The furniture, draperies, hangings, rugs, and tapestries were one hundred years out of date. And that was just the beginning.

The only thing she approved of was Grimme's looks, his title, his stable, and his money. When she wasn't harrying Brìghde, she talked at Grimme almost the entire meal, and there Brìghde sat, picking at her food and … drinking. A lot.

He leaned away from Lady Fàileach and toward his father and whispered, "If I see or hear much more, I'm sending her home tomorrow."

Sir John said nothing, but he was fuming.

When supper was cleared and the after-supper amusements were being brought out, Brìghde's mother got up, stood on her chair, and said in an overly dramatic tone, "I'm gonna tell ye the story o' Cailleach Bhéara."

And because she was a guest, everyone was cordial.

Except that she really was entertaining.

Grimme sat slouched in his chair with his foot propped on the edge of the table whilst Brìghde's mother performed. It was the only way he could consider it, standing up on her chair and telling Highland legends as if they were real and she had experienced them personally. He looked at Brìghde. She was leaning against the table with her cheek in her palm looking up at her mother, rapt. It was a story she had probably heard thousands of times growing up. He smiled a little at her almost enchanted expression, which would have been cute if Grimme didn't know how desperately she craved her mother's approval—and wasn't getting it. She was so happy her mother was here to see her own little fortress. Never mind that her mother had found fault with *everything* she touched, Brìghde seemed to shed those in anticipation of the next thing she might praise. Every compliment had been appended with "but … " It was driving Grimme to lunacy, watching her turn every single lovely thing Brìghde had done into something flawed.

Her criticism made Grimme truly *look* at what Brìghde had done and as he observed he grew more and more awestruck and … grateful. So she was cruel and never forgave and needed little reason to grip her enemies by the throat with her iron fist. She also loved and respected Grimme's father, treated Grimme's sons well, and enjoyed Grimme's men. She always did what was in the best interest of the earldom and its dependents. She was funny, intelligent, and strong. Her threats to leave were a bluff. She would never leave what she had created. She was too proud of it, and here her mother was, tearing it back down stone by stone.

Lady Fàileach was everything Brìghde wanted to be, but Grimme did not want Brìghde to be her mother. Brìghde had a sweetness about her that her mother lacked, a kindness she could have gotten from neither parent. She was also not nearly as controlling as her mother was. Lastly, Brìghde was a shadow of her true self when her mother was in the room, not only because her mother overpowered her, but because she was hiding her true self *from* her mother, and *that* he would not tolerate.

He reached behind Lady Fàileach and rubbed Brìghde's shoulder. She tossed him a surprised look but went back to watching her mother tell the story.

Grimme had been in Lady Fàileach's company all of four hours and though he did not suspect her of nefarious intentions, nor did he think she was a morally deficient person, nor did he fear a sneak attack by Brìghde's father (would welcome one, in fact, as he was itching for a very bloody battle), he did not want Lady Fàileach here. But Brìghde loved her mother, and Grimme wanted to honor that. Grimme had men serve under him that he did not like, and who did not like him, and betimes utterly loathed, but they were excellent knights and those knights knew him to be an excellent commander.

This was something else entirely.

Lady Fàileach had broken Brìghde in a matter of minutes, and he could not bear to see his Enyo broken.

After the keep was put to bed, Grimme knocked on Brìghde's door, being the first time he had sought her out after she'd tossed Maebh and Ardith out on their arses. God, he missed them, or rather, Maebh's cunte and Ardith's arse. He could not get what he needed from Emelisse and Dillena alone, though the maidservants almost made up for it, but that housekeeper was starting to look delicious and he could be persuaded to make *her* his next mistress instead of a mere Kyneward servant he fucked.

"Come."

He opened the door slowly to find her sitting cross-legged on her bed, holding onto Mercury for dear life. There were two pitchers on a stool by her bed.

"She's leaving tomorrow," Grimme said.

Brìghde gasped and twisted. "Grimme! I didn't ... Um."

He closed the door and lifted the pitchers. Both empty, and he'd lost track of how much she'd drunk at supper. "I will not have my sweet friend ground under anyone's heel." *And I am disappointed you're allowing it.* He hoped she heard it, for he wouldn't say it.

She gulped. "I ... fergot." Then her eyes filled with tears. "I just remember the way she comforted me after playin' wi' me brothers or Walter thrashin' me. Teachin' me what to do, how to run a noble house ... " Her brogue was very thick. "She was like this in *her* home, but it was *her* home so I ne'er thought anythin' of it. I *ne'er* thought she'd come inna *my* home an' try to take it over. She just ... she just wants all the attention on *her*."

Grimme sat on the edge of the bed and gathered her into his arms where she sobbed herself to sleep.

He tucked her in, blew out the candles, and climbed into bed with her.

59

"MOOM," BRÌGHDE said in the doorway of her mother's chambers the next morning, manservants just leaving after having rearranged the furniture to her taste.

"Aye, dear," she muttered as she lazed in the sitting room with her embroidery. "Did ye e'er take up embroidery as I instructed? 'Tis a soothin' pastime, somethin' a *lady,*" she said pointedly, staring up at her from under her brow, "should be doin'. What about yer lyre lessons?"

It was after breakfast, which her mother had taken in her chambers, as she always did. She said it was her reward for having Fàileach Keep running so well she could afford the luxury of time. Brìghde had been up since before dawn, as usual, riding with Pierce, who had graduated to one of the mares who needed exercise, and this morning, Grimme had accompanied them, riding Helen.

Don't throw her out, Grimme, please. She's my mother. I will manage her.

This is your home. I obey my father when it suits me to do so and I only do so out of respect. You have done a magnificent job and my father's opinion is the only one you have to live with, and he is ecstatic.

Your standards are too low.

Brìghde! That is your mother's opinion! You were happy with your work until she came.

That was true, but now all she could see were the dusty corners.

She had also had to go to Emelisse and Dillena, who were both furious, apologize profusely, assure them that Lady Fàileach would not be at breakfast, and Brìghde would try to keep her mother's mouth shut. It was humiliating, having to apologize to Emelisse.

"Moom," she said again and stepped into the chambers, closing the door behind her.

"Well, speak up."

Brìghde's heart was thundering in her chest. "I don't appreciate yer comin' here an' immediately findin' fault with e'erything I've accomplished."

"How are ye gonna get better?" she demanded. "*Someone* has to point it out to ye. Certainly that old codger—"

"Don't," she growled. "I love him. He is the father to me *Walter* is not."

Her mouth tightened.

"You will show him respect fer no other reason than that. He is furious with the way ye're treating me."

"*He* is not a mother!"

"*He* didn't smack me into a hearth and then say he was sorry there was no fire in it."

"Ye've gone soft. I'm dismayed."

"If ye don't like it here, ye're welcome to leave."

"I'll go when I want to an' not a second sooner. I wanna go to that tournament yer husband's competin' in."

Brìghde's stomach sank into her hips. "Then please be more respectful of me an' the family."

"Family!" she barked. "*Two* mistresses down from *four,* an' that's what ye call a *family?*"

"Aye, because there were children here, an' there's still a child, whom ye're ignorin'."

"Why shouldn't I? He's nothin' to me, an' ye certainly don't dress 'im like an earl's son, bastard or no. He looks like a bloody peasant."

Brìghde was suddenly violently ill. She was right. In the rush to clothe the servants, she had given Pierce no thought at all. *Nobody ever had,* and now she couldn't do a thing about it whilst her mother was here.

"An' what's this ye're wearin' now? *Livery?*" she sneered.

"I'm wearin' a green kirtle, Moom, no more, no less."

"*Everyone* here wears green. At least ye could've chosen a shade that matches yer eyes, but no! Why canna ye wear red or black?"

"I'm not spendin' coin for red when it's just an e'eryday dress an' Grimme doesn't allow black in the house. He hates it."

Her face scrunched. "Why? Black's yer best color an' it's elegant."

"Moom! I'm asking ye to respect me in me home, an' stop findin' fault with e'erything I've done. *I* like it. Me husband likes it. Me father-in-law likes it. An' I'm *not finished!*"

"I'm disappointed," she said sternly, putting her embroidery down and looking at Brìghde stonily. "Ye're me daughter an' I expected better of ye, an' here ye are, lookin' like ye wasted me time all those years." Brìghde felt moisture roll down her cheek. "Still a hoyden, ridin' a charger astride. Ye're not tumblin' with a litter o' laddies anymore, Budgie!" She was very angry. "Stop actin' like a man! Take up a lady's pursuits, put on yer best color an' show yer husband how much more bonny ye are than those whores an' 'e won't need to stick his spindle anywhere but you! Aye, 'twas a bargain, I know, I know, but

Lord, lass, ye've earned God's favor somehow, weddin' that stallion with a title an' a fortune, but ye're not takin' advantage of it! Don't ye *want* swive him?"

"Aye," she said in a tiny voice.

Her mother looked at her for a long time, then her eyes narrowed. "But he doesna wanna swive *you*," she said with dawning comprehension.

Brìghde flushed and looked away, wringing her hands.

"Quit actin' like a man, fer God's sake!" she yelled. "At least *try* to seduce the lad. Brìghde Moira Fàileach, you are *my* daughter an' I know ye've got it in ye to swive the man dizzy, but ye're not doin' it an' that disappoints me. Go away."

60

BRÌGHDE COULD not have withstood the next few days if it were not for Grimme.

After the first supper together, Grimme had coolly commanded Lady Fàileach to abandon Brìghde's chair so that he could sit next to his dearest friend. With a tiny snarl at Brìghde, she complied, muttering, "*Friend,*" under her breath. Yet every night at supper, Lady Fàileach stood up in her chair and kept the hall spellbound with her tales. Brìghde had heard them for years, but with her mother telling them, she could get lost in the stories as easily as everyone else. Grimme sat relaxed with his hand on Brìghde's back, giving her strength, reminding her of who she really was, as she was forgetting. Quickly.

He was wonderful, comforting Brìghde and petting her and telling her how proud of her he was, how grateful he was, listing all the things she had accomplished whilst at Kyneward and that she would eventually make it more grand than Fàileach could ever hope to be.

"You have not seen Fàileach," she said sadly.

"Why do you miss it so much?"

"I don't. I think about what it is and then look around here and … "

"You've only been here *four months*, Brìghde!" he said, exasperated.

"*She* could've done so much more than I have been able to."

Grimme was coldly polite to her mother, but Lady Fàileach either didn't notice or care. Pierce stayed away from her, going so far as to eat in the kitchen. Sir John did not bother to hide his hatred of her and the two of them matched words every chance Lady Fàileach got. Dillena and Emelisse ate all but breakfast in their chambers.

Because Brìghde had her mother's Highlands brogue in her ear, Brìghde could not keep a tight rein on her own accent and found herself so lazy with her speech she didn't have to be drinking at all to speak completely unintelligible English.

It slowly occurred to Brìghde as she lay in bed with Grimme telling him tales of her childhood that she didn't share information with her mother.

At all.

She lied to her.

A lot.

She made up stories to get her to back away. She was so accomplished at it, she could be falling-down drunk and speaking Gaelic and she wouldn't divulge a bit of truth.

Indeed, Brìghde hadn't stopped drinking since her mother arrived. Everywhere she went, she had a goblet in her hand and a wee lassie following her with the pitcher.

Grimme was astounded by how much she could drink and still keep her wits about her, her feet steady under her, *and* remember what she had said and done whilst completely whittled. Now Grimme could understand her no matter how thick her brogue was, so long as she was still speaking English, but then, when she had been drinking heavily, she inevitably slid right down into Gaelic, which her mother understood quite well. Her mother didn't drink much, but she kept Brìghde's cup full, trying to get Brìghde to talk, to tell her the things she wouldn't tell her when she was sober.

Several times her mother had harried Brìghde concerning her regrettable lack of consummation of the marriage with suggestions for her improvement. Better clothing. More elaborate hairdressing. Nicer headdresses. More jewels.

"His whores are dressed ten times better than you, Budgie!"

"Moom, I work because I've not got the keep the way I want it. I canna go about in good clothin' e'eryday yet."

"Don't give me that, lass. I've been through yer chests. I know what ye've got."

"I know ye have, an' ye made Avis cry. Canna ye be nicer to me servants?"

"*Nicer?* Ye're too familiar with all yer servants. 'Tis not seemly."

Thus, Brìghde could not leave her servants alone for two seconds without her mother going behind them and finding fault with everything they did. She did it pleasantly, but there was the hint of a threat in her voice. Brìghde had told her mother to take the threat out of her voice, as Brìghde would not allow her to punish them, but got yet another lecture about the importance of the iron fist. Once, her mother had berated Rose into tears, and that was that.

"Moom! What do ye think ye're doin'? This is *my* home! By what authority do ye do this?"

She was aghast. "Don't ye dare speak to me that way, wee lass. I have the authority because I—am—your—mother."

What could she say to that? Oh, aye. She remembered: "I am an English countess. Until you can come up with somethin' better than the wife of a Scottish clan chief, I outrank you."

Her mother didn't speak to her for hours as Brìghde started preparations to move the household to Sheffield for a fortnight. It was a blessed few hours.

Grimme slept with her every night, all night, but as the tournament approached, they both got more and more tense. She did not want to have tension with Grimme with her mother in the house making her tense enough, but the night before their departure, she was particularly distressed:

The Kyneward heir.

Sheffield's impending demand for *droit du seigneur*.

Quit actin' like a man, fer God's sake!

Brìghde would be fully accessible to Sheffield for at least a sennight, for she had the dubious honor of being the duke's special guest in his box to watch the jousts. There was a very good chance she would be ordered to stay behind whilst Grimme was ordered to go home, and he would do so. She would be alone against Sheffield and his guard, and she would either escape or die trying, but she would not allow Sheffield inside her. As she lay there in the dark thinking about it, she got more and more angry.

Sheffield would've taken all five women in the keep if Brìghde had not done something about it. Grimme certainly wasn't going to protect her, much less his mistresses, from his liege's greed. Aldwyn, that most noble of knights, wouldn't.

I know you've got it in you to swive the man dizzy ...

What was *wrong* with a man who would not protect his women, no matter the cost?

Aye, well, then there was Walter, who would kill or allow to be killed anyone who had no value to him. He wouldn't hesitate to hand Brìghde over to a rapacious liege if he thought it would benefit him somehow.

But would he hand over Brìghde's *mother?*

She didn't know what kept him on her mother's leash, but whatever it was, it was strong and no, he would *never* hand over Brìghde's mother to a liege. If he had one.

Seduce the lad, for God's sake!

"Grimme," she said, shaking him awake.

"Mmrph."

"Swive me." She cringed. That was not how to do it.

"What?" he croaked, twisting to look at her over his shoulder.

"Swive me. Please don't let the duke be my first. Please."

And now she was begging, which was definitely not seductive.

He looked pained. "I ... "

"You can protect me from my mother," she cried, "and you can protect me from soldiers who want to rape me, but you won't protect me from the duke, when I most need your protection."

"Part of the problem," he growled, "is that it is a *duty*. I am pressed to rise and *no man* can do that. I *told* you that and you promised to stop hounding."

"I have not said a word to you in weeks upon weeks."

"Very well. But *now* you wake me up in the middle of the night to delve directly into a bitter argument about fucking and expect it to happen?"

He had a point. "More than fair. But we leave for the tournament tomorrow. What is the duke going to demand of me? And what are you going to do about it? I'm angry. And I'm terrified. Until I am with *your* child, no other's, I am going to be angry. About *everything*. Every cruel thing you have said or done to me, what you did to Aldwyn—"

"My offense against Aldwyn is not yours to forgive!"

"No, but never mind your betrayal of Aldwyn. What would you do to me? I would not think that if you had not spoken of me so contemptuously to your women. Twice."

His nostrils flared. "Do not roil yourself over what I have not done to you. Whereas, you were taught poisons to lay a clan to waste and you purchased the ingredients to poison me and my entire earldom the first week you were here with *my* coin. And *then* you threatened to burn down all of Waters. If we are comparing which of us should trust which of the other the least, then—"

"You abducted me."

"It was beneficial to you."

"And my poisoning the duke was beneficial to you. Do you think I *want* to be at odds with you?"

"Aye, I do," he said flatly. "You're hiding something from me, something you want, but you won't tell me what it is and the longer I cannot guess and give it to you the angrier you get."

"I want a son," she gritted.

"Aye, I know that," he sneered. "Something *other* than that."

It was *right there* in his mental grasp, if he just knew where to look, but she couldn't tell him without being utterly crushed, with no hope of putting herself back together again. "I do not know how you would get that impression."

"Because I *know* you."

Not well enough. "I have been very clear about this since I received his ransom missive addressed to me, and found him to be a threat to *me*. I am frightened, Grimme. *He* wants to plant his seed in me. *First*."

"He's nigh sixty years old and doesn't have a child to his name, legitimate or otherwise. Just tell him we've done the deed and you're with child."

She had already planned that. "That doesn't help me evade his hands and mouth and spindle!"

"And how am I supposed to do that?"

"I don't know!" she screeched. "It is *your* responsibility to think of a way! What would you have done if I had not poisoned him and thus was forced to spend the night being raped in *your* bed? *Nothing.* Because you think you have no power against him."

"Brìghde," he breathed incredulously. "I *don't* have any power against him."

"You had a choice, Grimme. You had a choice to try to protect me or not, and you chose not. You would have allowed him to rape me without a twitch. I would've killed him, then I would be executed." She hopped out of bed to pace, quivering with anger. "Tell me," she insisted, "what you would have done to try to protect me if I had not poisoned him."

Silence. "I don't ... know."

"You would have handed me over without a fight. You'd be frowning when you did it, so there is some comfort," she sneered.

"Brìghde," he growled, "I could not have forestalled him in any way without getting killed by his knights for trying—"

"Aye, I ken you canna *stop* him, but if I were with child, he wouldn't believe he could plant his seed."

"—or executed by the king for killing him."

"You would not die to protect me? The chivalric code. That you don't adhere to, aye, I ken. But your friend the *chivalrous* knight is no better. He serves that filthy, stinking, rotting bag of bones. He doesn't like what he does, but he does not do anything to forestall it. 'Don't you care, Aldwyn?'" She lowered her voice. "'I care very much, my lady, but there is nothing I can do.'" She returned to her normal pitch. "I do not accept that. One of you honorable, one of you dishonorable, both of you intelligent warriors, but neither one of you able to devise a plan to keep the duke from raping your wife in *your* bed without killing him, and neither of you willing to protect your women to the death. I wouldn't be surprised if Aldwyn's wife isn't a regular captive in the duke's bed. And what would Aldwyn do? Nothing. *Because he has no choice,*" she mocked.

Grimme said nothing.

Brìghde almost continued, but then realized Grimme hadn't protested her assertion.

"She is, isn't she?"

"Aye," he said tightly.

"How do you know this?"

"I have spies at Sheffield."

She groaned miserably. "Aldwyn?"

"Tied. Made to watch."

"Sweet Mary and Joseph! Very well. When the duke summons me, I will bring with me enough poison to kill him. Or I will snap his neck. Or I will wait for him in the dark and kick his bony arse down the stairs. I may or may not be found guilty, and I may or may not be executed, but I will protect myself however I can and must since *my husband Earl Kyneward* won't. *Sir Aldwyn Marchand, knight of the realm,* won't, either, and I will *never* forgive you for making me see to my own protection. *Again.* I'm the raven witch, am I? Dark. Ruthless. Demonic. *Cruel.* You have really no idea, Grimme. And I can't kill *you* until I have a son. Is that your fear? That I'll kill you? Brunette, duty, hounding, fear. Aye, I can see how that would add up. God, I wish I had Hades. *She* would never have allowed me to put up with this, bitten my arse right out the front door months ago."

"Are you quite finished?" he asked testily.

"For the moment."

"I have never had a wife. Aldwyn had never had a wife. Neither of us had ever seen or heard of the *droit du seigneur* being claimed, although there is rape and pillage aplenty amongst conquered peoples. It disturbs me greatly that Aldwyn's wife is suffering and that Aldwyn is forced to watch. It enrages me that he will not set his pride aside to ask me to help him. However, they have three children whom Sheffield is holding hostage and Sheffield is not above killing babes. I don't know what you would do for *our* child, but I would do anything for *mine.*"

Brìghde gulped. That was an evil quandary: Submit, kill, or die—none with any certainty that her child would live.

"What *would* you do for our child, Brìghde?" he demanded suddenly. "Sheffield allows you to see him once every so often to assure you he's still alive and that you cannot escape without getting him killed. What would you do?"

"I would do whatever I needed to do until I could kill Sheffield."

"Even if that meant the child would die if you failed?"

"I would not fail."

"But if you *did* fail, or if there was a good chance you were going to fail," he pressed, "would you attempt to kill him at the cost of *our* child's life?"

"Aye!" she barked. "I would not do so foolishly, and I would bear whatever indignity I must until I could be assured of success, but the cowardice is in not making the attempt. If our child dies in my attempt to protect myself and him, so be it, because *you won't.*"

There was a long silence.

"If," she growled, "you are going to be a dishonorable warrior to suit your own purposes, choose *all* your purposes."

His silhouette moved. He dug his fingers into his eyeballs. "Choose all my purposes," he repeated slowly.

"Aye. And now I suppose I've given you another reason not to give me a son."

"Brìghde," he said low, "you are *everything* I would ever want in a wife, a woman I would *choose* to have a child with. I would wed you again without a second's hesitation."

Brìghde bit her lip. That was a lovely thing to hear, but there was a *but* in his voice.

"But tell me something," he purred. "Why did you offer yourself for Ares?"

Shocked, she thought quickly. That was the question of a man who already knew the answer. "Because you love him," she finally said. "I couldn't let him kill your pet."

"Mmm hm. Would you have taken Hades over me?"

"No! But that's different."

"Why?"

"Ares was just a bairn. You saved him from dying. You nursed him. You trained him. Hades—she came to me the way she was. She loved me and I don't know why and—"

"Shut up."

Brìghde clapped her mouth shut.

"Don't lie to me again. You were going to kill Sheffield."

She didn't say a word.

"That's why you were angry that I thought it was a bluff. Because I did not realize your intent as soon as you said it and thus did not take advantage of it immediately."

"Would you have?" she asked in a small voice.

"Absolutely not. I would not have allowed you to risk yourself."

Her eyes stung. He arose from the bed and walked around it until he was standing in front of her. He slowly knelt on one knee in front of her and bowed his head.

"I, Earl Grimme Kyneward, swear my fealty to you, Lady Brìghde Kyneward, my wife, my countess, my raven queen, my dearest companion-at-arms. To the best of my ability, I will protect you from all harm. I swear it on my life."

61

THE NEXT MORNING, Brìghde was far more in sympathy with Grimme than she had been in many weeks. He slid her a warm, comforting smile and she tucked her hand in his whilst walking out to the stable to lead their company to Sheffield, a force one hundred strong, but no mistresses. Emelisse was furious. Dillena wanted to go only because she needed more quills, inks, and parchment, but Brìghde couldn't allow the one to go but not the other. Instead, Brìghde had asked her to make an exhaustive list and she would fill it as well as she could. Sir John stubbornly insisted to go, as he couldn't let Brìghde out of his sight with that hag—Brìghde hadn't bothered to defend her mother—grinding down *his* Brìghde.

Nobles and errant knights from all over the British Isles and France were going to Sheffield. The tournament would likely take a few days, if Grimme's estimation of the crowd was anything to go by. Gaston, Max, and Terrwyn were somewhere in the company, attending their knights, and their knights had granted them leave to attend their father on the lists. Pierce was happy to be able to sit in the nobles' box with his grandfather and Brìghde. He was not happy he would have to sit with Lady Fàileach.

Sir Bart helped her mother onto her horse. Once settled on her palfrey in her side-saddle, she slid a glance at Brìghde and Troy with a slightly curled lip. Brìghde turned away to see Pierce trotting toward them on Enyo.

"What's a wee laddie doing on such a magnificent horse?" her mother asked in a harsh whisper. "He's too big for him.

"Moom, canna ye tell that's a mare?"

"She looks like a charger."

"This is a breedin' estate, Moom! The mares are as important as the stallions an' that one drops valuable foals. Pierce is an accomplished rider an' Enyo's a sweet lass."

Finally, they got under way. Grimme and Brìghde rode side by side at the head of the Kyneward company. Mercury trotted beside Brìghde for a while, chased something, then trotted beside Pierce for a while. Eventually, Mercury would end up in the carriage with Sir John. Pierce rode alongside the carriage because he didn't want to be anywhere near Brìghde's mother and he couldn't ride with his brothers even if he wanted to.

Lady Fàileach insisted on riding next to Grimme and engaging him in conversation, most of which was embarrassing. Sir Bart rode on Brìghde's other side and occasionally flashed her a warm smile of encouragement, but Brìghde had come prepared with several bladders of wine. She finished the second one before noon, then Grimme took the rest of it away from her with a glare. She could ride drunk. 'Twas one of her special talents.

Grimme, riding silver Phobos, took Brìghde's hand and smoothed his hand over her ring and a bracelet filled with enough poison to lay waste to half of Sheffield. She had enough poison in her brooch and pendant to kill the other half. He wanted her to, she could tell, but he could not risk execution without an heir.

Yet he had sworn to protect her with his life, so either he was willing to attempt to defend her against the duke—she had no delusions that he would be able to, and no delusions that the duke wouldn't make him watch—or he had a trick up his sleeve.

It took four days to get to Sheffield because all roads to Sheffield were crowded with travelers. The inns in all three towns between Kyneward and Sheffield were full. The fields and forests along the way were covered with tents so that each night they made camp, the Kyneward tents had to be erected here and there, spread far out amongst others. Fortunately, that meant for most of the journey, Brìghde was able to avoid her mother.

Unfortunately, once they reached Sheffield, they were directed to a section set aside for the Kyneward company to occupy. As far as the horizon in all directions, Sheffield's vast rolling hills and dales were covered with not only tents from the most primitive to the richest, but merchants peddling every ware anyone could think of. There were mummers and musicians and jugglers and acrobats. The jousting field was very long, almost twice as long as most to accommodate all the spectators.

Brìghde would have preferred to sit atop Troy and take in the color, music, and noise, but she had duties, duties she would have to perform with her mother. Thus, the first thing Brìghde did once Grimme plucked her from the saddle was demand her wine. She started drinking as soon as her mother approached her to discuss the erection of the tents. Grimme left her with a roll of his eyes, then strode over to his forces to talk to two of his knights at length, their heads bent.

Brìghde watched him. Though it was most likely he was giving normal directions, she would like to think he was concocting a plan to get her away from the duke's clutches. Yet the only thing she could see was him, his body naked, so tall and strong. So hard. No man in his force was bigger than he.

His face was so beautiful it had taken her breath away from the first, and his hair was so fine it was like strands of copper and gold.

"Lord, lass," her mother breathed in her ear as Brìghde watched her husband. "I'd give me right arm to feel that beast 'twixt me legs."

So would Brìghde, but she only said, "Moom, please stop. Why do ye keep embarrassin' me so?"

"I can look, can't I?"

"Look, aye. But keep yer lust to yerself. I don't wanna hear it. We plotted an escape for me an' an heir for him. 'Twas a bargain, an even exchange."

"Ye're bonny enough to have any man ye want," Lady Fàileach hissed. "If ye put a little more effort into it, ye could have *him* too, an' then he wouldna have to go elsewhere."

She scrunched her face. "Who are you to lecture me? Ye've got yer own problems with Walter."

"How things are between him an' me is none o' yer business."

"Then why do ye think me business with Grimme is any o' yer business?"

"Because I am your mother," she said threateningly.

Brìghde had had enough. She stepped forward, almost nose to nose, as they were the same height. "If you want," she said low and slow, "to test which one of us has the harder fist, go ahead."

Her mother's eyes narrowed and she nudged even closer. "I threw a poker into Walter's arm to save ye from 'is wrath," she whispered. "Doona get too threatenin' with me, lass."

"Aye, well, if ye're brave enough to do that *after*, then why did ye not defend me *before* he smacked me into the hearth? Why always take vengeance but ne'er protect me in the first place? 'Tis as if ye *wanted* a reason to throw a poker in 'is arm, an' ye let 'im at me so ye could."

Lady Fàileach looked up and past Brìghde, stiffened, and all the fight seeped out of her. She stepped back and looked down, her face flushed.

Brìghde glanced behind her to see Sir Bart standing there, his legs spread, his arms folded across his chest, and a very, *very* angry expression on his face. Brìghde glared at him in return, but … he seemed to be looking at her mother. That was odd, a knight glaring at a lady that way; Grimme would be enraged if Sir Thom looked at Brìghde that way if it did not concern her safety.

"I sent ye away to the convent," Lady Fàileach muttered. Brìghde turned back to her. "An' ye came home when 'twas time for ye to wed Roger—" Three years too early, but she apparently hadn't noticed. "—so ye'd be safe at MacFhionnlaigh, but then Walter postponed the weddin'. The only thing I could do was make sure he *finally* couldna harm ye again, an' he didn't."

"Aye, until he had a sword in my back at the altar."

She turned away completely and Brìghde thought she heard her whisper, "I'm sorry."

Brìghde wasn't satisfied.

She darted around her mother and took her by the arms. "*You let him force me to marry Roger*," she hissed. "I knew you wouldna lift a finger to prevent that. *I* protected *myself* the best way I knew how. *I* protected *myself* because nae *one* of ye—you, six brothers, two grandparents—all knowin' 'twas a bad match politically an' that Roger an' I *hate* each other—an' the *best* I could do was an insignificant Sassenach earl *I did not know* in need of an heir. Do ye hear me, Moom? I pledged me *womb* to a *stranger* to protect meself because *you wouldn't.* Vengeance is lovely an' wonderful, but ye don't wanna *help* me in the first place. Ye just wanna reason to war with Walter. Both o' ye, bloodthirsty warmongers always in need of a slight to avenge, an' ye let 'im at me so ye could have one. God only knows why I dinna see it before."

She said nothing, and she would not look at Brìghde.

It was then she looked up to see Grimme standing next to a glowering Sir Bart. Grimme's smile was small but warm, his eyes soft, and she didn't care what Sir Bart thought.

Brìghde forcibly turned her mother around and said, "Do ye see that man? The one God sent me? The one I plotted with? The one *I didn't know* whom I was willin' to swive to get away from Walter an' Roger? Do ye see that man?" She still wouldn't look. Brìghde took her chin the way she had Emelisse's and brought it up. "*Look at him!*" she screamed. Her mother was fighting Brìghde's hand, but Lady Fàileach wasn't nearly as strong as she pretended to be.

In fact, it shocked Brìghde into letting her go.

"*He* has sworn to protect me with his life! We were *strangers*, Mother! Do ye nae ken? A *stranger* has promised to do fer me what you wouldn't. An' now ye come into me home an' ogle me husband, disrespect me, dismiss the things I've done, deride how I treat the servants, make an immediate enemy of a man I love as a father, insult me husband's family, ignore me sweet wee stepson who was so excited to meet ye, question e'ery single decision I make, command all the attention fer yerself, an' think I should obey ye in *my* home because *you are my mother*? Grimme was ready to throw ye out the first night, but I said no an' here ye are a fortnight later still oglin' *my* husband as if 'tis yer right—I suppose because God knows Walter isna worth oglin'. You have done *nothing* to earn my obeisance an' I certainly willna bow to *you* in *my* home."

Tears started to well in her mother's eyes.

"Brìghde," Grimme said softly. "Come. 'Tis time for the nobles to meet with the duke."

She took his hand when he offered and left in a swirl of skirts to go see the man she was about to kill.

Because her husband wouldn't.

62

TO BRÌGHDE'S relief, Grimme had politely refused lodging in Sheffield Keep. The duke had leered at Brìghde, then looked at Grimme and said, "It doesn't matter whether she's down the hall or two hundred miles away, Kyneward. Be prepared to linger after the tournament is over. Or go home, but she will be my guest for a while."

Grimme was calm, but he committed to nothing.

Their tent was worthy of a king. Their collapsible bed was reasonably comfortable, Pierce would sleep on pillows next to them curled up with Mercury, and Avis and Hamond each had a cot in an opposing corner.

"I studied the list," Grimme said softly, made loud to her only because her ear was against his chest and she felt the deep vibrations. He lay on his back, Brìghde half upon him, and he was caressing her back. It was agonizing to be *right there* and … nothing. Not a licentious word or lusty kiss. "There is no knight on it that can beat either me or Aldwyn, especially after we've had a month of practice."

"You will end up on your feet."

"Aye."

"Surely he has a weakness."

He was silent for a long time. "He does. I have never used it against him."

"Why not?"

"Because it's infallible and I would beat him every time and that is not a challenge."

"Unlike Maebh."

"That was no challenge, either," he snapped. "He has a tiny defect in the corner of his left eye. If you get him spinning leftwise a few times because he can't see you and he's chasing you, he'll get dizzy, then all you have to do is put your foot on his back and shove. It doesn't bother him in the course of normal battle."

"Trojan horse."

"I may or may not use it, as 'tis a dishonorable way to win. The crowd won't like it, either, and Sheffield could use it to disqualify me."

Brìghde sighed in resignation. "Who is your herald?"

"No one you know," he said firmly.

No one she would ever know, apparently. "Is the competition already set or have you chosen your opponents already?"

"Aldwyn and I have both been challenged by many people. They drew lots and set the first pass. Neither of us tilt until mid-afternoon."

She said nothing more and he put his hand to her head, stroked it a few times, then went to sleep.

The next morning, Brìghde strolled through the faire with Pierce, her mother, Mercury, and Sir Bart and Sir Thom, both dressed in mail. Lady Fàileach was *very* subdued but did not seem to wish to part from Brìghde. Whilst Brìghde and Pierce ate and giggled and played games of chance and skill, Sir Thom encouraged Pierce, and her mother and Sir Bart watched silently. Brìghde offered Lady Fàileach to join in, but she politely refused.

The only thing she said was a mild observation. "Ye act more like an older sister than a mother."

"That's because I am not his mother," Brìghde said softly, her fingers in his hair. "I am his *moom,* which is an entirely different thing, an' I have claimed the right to spoil 'im the way I spoil Troy an' Mercury. 'Tis Grimme's responsibility to see to his discipline if he needed any, which he does not."

There was, in fact, a stationer's stall, and Brìghde gave him Dillena's list along with coin, bidding him to wrap it all up and send it to Earl and Countess Kyneward's tent.

After midday, they made their way to the nobles' box and there were many nobles in many boxes. However, she would be seated next to the duke himself. Sir John was seated beside her, Pierce next to Sir John, and after Pierce, her mother.

"Sir John," the duke nodded haughtily as Sir John attempted to bow—but couldn't, especially in the close stands. Brìghde had to help, and that was all the duke had to do to show his dominance.

"This is my mother, Lady Moira Fàileach."

She clumsily curtsied. She was the wife of a clan chief. She didn't know *how* to curtsy, and it was likely a reminder that she *should* have curtsied to Brìghde and Grimme.

"Lady Fàileach," he purred as he raised her hand to his lips. "I have heard much about your husband."

"Ye canna believe everythin' ye hear, Yer Grace." She had to choke out that *Your Grace,* at which Brìghde nearly giggled.

"You're as beautiful as your daughter."

"More," she said flatly. Brìghde flushed, but the duke cackled.

"Please, have a seat and enjoy yourself."

Sir Thom and Sir Bart stood on the ground in front of the nobles' box along with other ladies' captains. Mercury lazed in the grass between Sir Thom and Sir Bart.

Brìghde watched Grimme, sitting astride Troy at the end of the lists with his sons and his squires, one of whom was holding Phobos in one hand and Deimos in the other.

Half of the horses to compete were swathed in finery from nose to tail, and some were armored. It was a measure of a knight's wealth—or his noble's—to dress and armor the beasts.

The Kyneward horses were neither armored nor dressed. Their only finery was a short, narrow length of cloth bearing the Kyneward standard draped over their rumps, and the small, elaborately fringed and belled banners on their reins. Otherwise, their distinctive coats were brushed to a sheen, their contrasting manes, tails, and feathers also meticulously cleaned and brushed to the texture and shine of satin.

Phobos's very rare silver coat was set off elegantly by his black mane, tail, and feathers.

Deimos was a common red and black, but groomed as he was, he looked exotic.

Troy's golden hide sparkled and his white mane, tail, and feathers glistened.

No, these horses were not hidden under yards and yards of cloth or an hundred pounds of steel. The Kyneward horses' lack of livery and armor was to display the fine horseflesh that Grimme Kyneward bred and trained.

Troy, however, somehow rose above Ares's sons, and Grimme was not too proud to freely acknowledge it. She had thought Grimme jesting when he said he intended to ride Troy for the entire tournament, and only brought Deimos and Phobos to the lists in case he felt otherwise. But no.

Troy is as fine as Ares, and I will not ride an inferior horse against him.

But Deimos and Phobos are his sons.

Aye, and Troy is better than both of them. I wish I had gotten that knight's name in Laight, so I could find his dam and sire.

Troy was pawing the ground, his neck bobbing up and down to make his bells ring, his feet dancing and prancing about. Yet Grimme was not paying attention to the beast, moving along with him as if they were one, as his squires assisted him, taught Grimme's sons how to squire him, and Grimme gave additional instructions.

Pierce was squirming in his seat with excitement. She looked across Sir John at him and smiled. Sir John ruffled his hair.

"Look, Brìghde! There's Gaston and Max and Terrwyn!"

"Are you glad to see them?"

He shrugged sheepishly.

"Lady Kyneward," the duke said, petting her sleeve. "Your husband is riding all three horses?"

"Mayhap, but—"

"What are their names?"

"The red is Deimos. The silver is Phobos. The golden is Troy."

"What do those names mean?" he asked with irritation.

"Deimos is the Greek god of dread. Phobos is the god of terror. They are Ares's sons."

His eyes narrowed slightly. "Are they *Ares's* sons?"

"They are," she said with a firm nod.

"And the golden?"

She smiled sweetly. "Troy. He is a Trojan horse. 'Tis a jest."

"He bit me." *Who's a good lad?* "I am surprised your husband allows such an ill-mannered beast in his stable, much less lowers himself to ride him in such a distinguished event."

"He's very loving with me. One more of their caliber and we would have the four horses of the apocalypse, aye?" she asked blithely. "Perhaps … Ares himself."

The sudden flare of mixed lust and hatred in the duke's eyes was evident. It was both frightening and satisfying. She gave him a small, flat smile.

Sir John, on her left, leaned down to whisper into her ear, "Grimme would kill you for taunting the duke that way."

She flashed the old man a mischievous smile. He winked at her.

There was no question in Brìghde's mind that Grimme would win. Never mind that Grimme loved war and fought to conquer …

Ares was at stake, and he felt the best way to win was on Brìghde's sweet Troy.

Brìghde had been to tournaments before. She had no particular interest in any of the knights except Grimme and Aldwyn, and this was to be a three-day tournament, so she settled in for a very boring three days. The only knight from Kyneward was Grimme, and the only knight from Sheffield was Aldwyn. There was no point for any other knight from either house to spend coin to enter. The rest, and there were quite a lot, came from other nobles' forces, and from hither and yon to both practice and for the coin prize. The wagers between Grimme and Aldwyn were at even odds. No one else entered was expected to get that far.

"Oh," the duke said, twisting toward someone behind Brìghde. She twisted also, at his behest. His hand was on a woman's knee. "This is Lady Caroline

Marchand. Lady Caroline, this is Lady Brìghde Kyneward. I would hope you can be ... *friends* ... despite your husbands' animosity toward each other."

Lady Caroline was a tall, willowy brown-eyed brunette. She was dressed in powder blue, and she seemed to be barely holding herself together.

"Good day," Brìghde said politely. Lady Caroline inclined her head a little, for it might be too much to speak. "I don't think our husbands' differences need influence us?"

She shook her head slightly. "Pleased to meet you," she whispered.

The duke caressed Lady Caroline's knee, then his hand crept up her inner thigh as far as he could reach. Brìghde looked at her own right hand and wrist, where her ring and bracelet reassured her, protected her. As long as she could get some of the powder on his tongue, she could put him to sleep or she could kill him. It was the only good thing Walter Fàileach had ever done for her.

The horn was blown to signal the next set of combatants. As this was an open tournament with no invitation required, there were many *non*-nobles competing and their heralds were an important part of gaining the crowd's approval. Thus, each competitor had his own herald to introduce him to the crowd and encourage cheers and boos. Throughout the years, Brìghde usually found only one or two entertaining and occasionally one she would have rather listened to than watch the tilt. She was curious as to what sort of herald Grimme would have hired for the occasion.

Each herald for this pair of combatants came out and bellowed their knights' names and various accomplishments, most of which were likely just tales. The knights appeared, approached the duke's box, received his blessing to commence, and commenced. It was all Brìghde could do not to slump and sigh and yawn.

Her attention drifted to her husband, whilst the thundering of hooves and clanging of metal and explosion of wood faded into the back of her mind.

Grimme wasn't watching the competitors, either. He was talking to his squires and sons, giving instructions and approbation, grinning, listening, laughing. His jousting armor was black, three times heavier than battle armor so he couldn't be knocked off his horse as easily. She had seen him swing himself up into the saddle with more grace and ease than other knights here had been able to. He was a big man and with his armor, he was terrifying.

Yet that morning, she had watched from the bed as he sat in his braies whilst Hamond shaved him.

Why don't you grow your beard?

It chafes whilst it's growing out.

Chafes what?

Women's skin.

She wished she hadn't asked.

She just had to suffer through a number of combatants until she could watch her husband, which seemed to be all bloody afternoon, though it was likely only an hour. Finally Grimme was up, though the crowd had only grown because Earl Kyneward and Sir Marchand were the knights to see. Brìghde was shocked when a brightly costumed jester in purple and yellow did back-flips down the list.

Those were *Sheffield's* colors!

The jester finished with a high flip and twist, and a flourish to great cheer, grinning with his overlarge and hideously painted scarlet mouth. His eye mask was elaborate and beautiful, dripping with beads, ribbons, and feathers. His many-horned cap was festooned with bells and tassels.

"Today!" he roared with outstretched arms. "We will have the pleasure of seeing Earl Kyneward make an utter fool of himself!"

The crowd hooted and Brìghde's eyes popped open.

"An *insignificant* Sassenach earl with a *tiny* twenty thousand acres and an army as limp as his cod!"

Brìghde gasped at hearing her own words and her head snapped to Sir John, who looked highly amused. Brìghde went back to listening to Grimme's jester, for if Sir John did not find this insulting, neither should Brìghde. Grimme *had* hired him, after all.

"*Grimme!*" the jester bellowed, rolling his R the way Brìghde did when she was angry with him. "Look at him!" He pointed to him sitting on Troy at the end of the tilt. Grimme gave a hearty wave to raucous cheers. "*Grimme*, his name the portent of death, but did you ever see a weaker knight in your life?"

The crowd roared with laughter because he did, in fact, look like the portent of death.

"And that *nag* he is riding! What a pathetic excuse for a mare!"

The crowd was rolling with laughter now and Sir John was chuckling.

"I will tell you a secret, though," he yelled conspiratorially. "The earl has duped everyone in England that he earned his earldom saving the king's life at Agincourt, but that is *not true*. The secret is just exactly how Kyneward *came* to be an earl. 'Tis because he made the king *come!*"

Brìghde choked, and looked at Grimme, who was himself laughing along with the crowd.

"I do not find him amusing, Lady Kyneward," the duke said stiffly.

"Neither do I," she said before she thought.

Then the duke stood and bellowed, "*Start the damn joust before I piss myself!*"

Without hesitation, the jester turned to Grimme and yelled, "Coward!" then bolted off the field.

Grimme and his opponent rode toward each other, then turned to ride toward the duke's box. Once they had made their obeisances, Grimme looked to Brìghde, his grin wide.

"My lady?"

Brìghde smiled and pulled a length of green chiffon from her sleeve, stood, reached over the rail, and tied it around his upper arm. "May you be disproportionately advantaged."

He saluted her, then turned and cantered toward the end of the tilt. He positioned Troy, clapped his visor down and took a lance. He hefted it, looked up, shook his head, and gave it back. He was given another, but after inspection this time, he nodded.

Brìghde was careful to sit back and cross her leg over the other, rest her crossed arms in her lap, and give every indication that she was calm and unworried.

She was unworried, but she was not calm. Her heart raced as she watched Troy paw the ground, Grimme sitting calmly awaiting the flag, his lance up. Pierce couldn't stop quivering in excitement.

The flag was waved and she curled her fingers into her palm so hard she would be surprised if her nails didn't draw blood. Grimme kicked Troy into action, but her horse was more than ready to charge. Grimme lowered his lance and … the lances exploded on each other's shoulder armor. The other knight barely held onto his seat, but Grimme hadn't moved. The crowd roared. Brìghde clapped politely, but Pierce hopped up and screamed, "*Yay, Papa!*"

At the end of the tilt, he was given another lance and accepted this one. The flag was waved and then horses were thundering toward each other. Lances down.

Grimme unseated the knight in spectacular fashion, hitting him so hard he was lifted up out of his saddle before flying heels over helm until he crashed to the ground on his belly. Grimme didn't bother to look as he dropped his shattered lance and rode back to his squires and sons with a fist in the air to the crowd's clamor. He needed no help to dismount.

That was the last she'd see of Grimme today.

Three pairs of combatants later, Aldwyn was up, riding Ares, who was swathed in Sheffield livery of purple and yellow, his face covered in armor. Almost nothing of the magnificent beast could be seen but his white feathers, dingy from the dirt. Aldwyn's herald was stiff, formal, matter-of-fact, and recounted Aldwyn's very long list of accomplishments in a fashion that near put Brìghde to sleep. The crowd was quiet, but it was not out of respect. Aldwyn displaced his opponent easily and without drama, garnering sparse applause.

She vaguely wondered why she had wanted to kiss that man, and could barely remember the kiss at all. Oh, well. That was the last she'd see of Aldwyn today, too.

The day wore on interminably, with combatant after combatant showing why they were inferior: They were not nearly as big as either Grimme or Aldwyn. Their armor was not nearly as heavy, for they could not carry that much weight. They were not as seasoned warriors as Grimme or Aldwyn. Their horses were much faster than Troy and Ares, but they were smaller.

Then there were the heralds. After Grimme's jester, not one herald could compete, though they tried. Occasionally, she felt the duke reach behind her and caress Lady Caroline and it almost made Brìghde sick. It was when he began stroking Brìghde's thigh that she decided she had to do something. She twisted her ring to crack it open. When the duke was speaking to his duchess or someone on the other side of him, she licked her finger and tapped a scant amount on it and pressed it into the grooves in her finger, then closed her ring tightly. Brìghde was sufficiently hardened to the poison that she could put it on her tongue if he kissed her, but that was too much for her to bear.

It was bitter. He might taste it. But then, he might simply think that was what her finger tasted like. Or else his mouth was so foul he wouldn't know the difference. She gagged.

The duke again turned to Brìghde and she smiled as seductively as she could manage, then, when he opened his mouth to say something, she put her finger against his mouth and said, "Shh. Let me look at you."

He took the bait and sucked her finger into his mouth. She retrieved it as soon as she felt his tongue had gotten all of it. "I didn't think you would be so eager, my dear, but after that limp cod of a husband you've got, mayhap I shouldn't be surprised. Did you bring your shared mistress?"

"Alas, no."

"I hope you have saved your virginity for me, as I bade."

"Alas, not that either, I'm afraid."

He looked half angry, half intrigued. "With your mistress?"

"Aye," she returned silkily. "'Twas an accident. Grimme caught us and wanted to join in. He does that, you ken, two or more at once."

"I've heard that about him, but what man wouldn't, with his stable of mares?"

"We indulge often enough that Grimme has acquired a taste for me alone."

His eyes narrowed. "Are you expecting?"

"Aye, but I'm a lusty wench. Now that I'm blooded and bred, I can't get enough, and I really don't care who gives it to me as long as they're good at it."

He grew a sly grin. "I'll forgive you," he purred, rubbing his cod for her, "if you promise me a performance with your mistress."

"At our wedding fête."

Brìghde was nauseated.

It took half an hour for his chin to fall to his chest.

She twisted away from him and tapped Lady Caroline, then brought her head down. "You and I need to talk," Brìghde whispered in her ear.

"Aye," she breathed.

"Can you get away?"

"Not right now. The duchess will see me. I can only lose myself in the crowd after today's list and hope you will find me."

"I will try."

63

LADY CAROLINE was not easy to find. Pierce had already jumped the rail to the ground below to run to his father, Mercury chasing him. Sir Thom assisted Sir John. Brìghde looked at her mother and hissed, "Not—one—word." Her mother was duly quelled.

The duke was still sleeping, and the duchess was trying to awaken him.

Brìghde slipped down the stairs and into the crowd. So. Many. Powder. Blue. Dresses. And Brìghde was short. But Lady Caroline was not and she had a distinctive headdress.

Brìghde grabbed her arm and pulled her under the stands. "Explain."

"The duke uses me," she said bluntly. "He uses me to control Aldwyn, and threatens our children with harm. I don't know how it could get *worse* for us if Aldwyn loses, but it will."

"He's going to lose."

"No. He's fighting for me. He can bear it no longer, watching me—" She clapped her mouth shut.

"Has he ever attempted to stop the duke from forcing himself upon you?" Brìghde asked carefully, trying to keep judgment out of her voice.

"He is chained. If he does not submit, Sheffield will kill our children."

"Is he chained all the time or just when Sheffield summons you?"

"Just when I'm with the duke."

"I ken why he might not be able to escape with you, but why canna he get a message to Grimme?"

Caroline looked down, then away. "I don't … know." Then she looked back up at Brìghde and said, "But the duke has promised Aldwyn that if he wins the tournament, he will let us go."

Brìghde's mouth tightened. "He will never let you go, but surely your husband knows Grimme will help you if you want."

Lady Caroline shook her head. "Aldwyn came home angrier than he has ever been, and wants nothing to do with your husband. He would never ask for help."

Aldwyn and his bloody pride! He would rather allow himself to be chained and his wife to be used—in front of him—with the threat of his children's deaths—than request Grimme's help. Grimme was the *only* one who could save him and his family from the duke *and he knew that!*

"Lady Caroline," Brìghde said gently, "mayhap your husband should put aside his pride this once."

"Lord Sheffield is his liege," she said weakly, but without conviction.

Brìghde didn't dare give Lady Caroline her ring; she wouldn't know how to use it and it would expose Brìghde's only weapon.

Brìghde took Lady Caroline's hands in both hers and looked up at her. "Grimme loves Aldwyn. He is ashamed of what he did to him that led to their parting."

"What *did* he do?" she asked plaintively.

"He seduced a woman out from under Aldwyn to show his dominance," Brìghde said flatly.

Caroline blinked, her mouth open a little. "That's … not as bad as I had imagined."

"Lady Caroline," Brìghde said urgently, "'Tis Aldwyn's responsibility to protect you, but if he cannot or will not—" Because he was the inferior warrior and always had been. "—come to me. Please. Grimme will fetch you and your children away immediately. All you have to do is ask."

"I cannot. The duke would kill Aldwyn."

"Aldwyn is a grown man, a knight, a warrior. Save yourself and your children and let him see to his own survival."

"Lady Brìghde," she said sadly, "Aldwyn told me of you and I am not you. My children and I need Aldwyn and he has promised to save us. You don't need your husband for … anything."

Brìghde blinked, but Lady Caroline had disappeared.

THE NEXT DAY was more of the same.

Grimme was up thrice as the field narrowed. His jester had fresher and funnier words with each match, insulting everything from Grimme's looks to his cod to his keep to the fact that he kept mistresses but didn't swive any of them because he was more interested in swiving his villeins' sheep.

Brìghde winced with every word Grimme's jester threw at him, for she would not be able to withstand such mockery. She'd had too much of it in her life and she could not laugh at herself. If she could, Grimme's lack of desire for her would not hurt so much.

"A *breeding* estate, he claims! Aye, if one takes a half-human half-lamb into account!"

The crowd loved it.

"Tastes like chicken!" he squawked as he ran off the list.

Brìghde suffered the duke's pets for far too long before she teasingly asked if she could pleasantly surprise him when everyone had gone and she was his guest.

Flattered, pleased, he kept his hands to himself, though not his innuendoes.

Brìghde tried not to vomit.

Again Grimme asked her favor, and today she tied red and azure ribbons on him to remind him of her wedding dress. He saluted her then bounded off, Troy groomed to perfection, his coat glinting gold in the sun and his mane, tail, and feathers immaculate white and flowing.

"How sweet," the duke said silkily. "He loves you."

Sir John stiffened.

Brìghde barely managed not to swallow her tongue. *Love* her?! He could barely scrape together a friendship with her!

She smirked at the duke and teasingly slapped his knee. "'Twas a plot, Your Grace. 'Tis simple enough."

"You may lie to me all you want, my dear, but I know when a man is in love with his wife." He looked over his shoulder. "Don't I, Lady Caroline?"

"Aye, Your Grace," she murmured.

Brìghde could barely breathe and her head was a muddle of pud. "You know of Walter Fàileach. You know of the MacFhionnlaighs. Surely you can see why I would make such a bargain."

"I find it odd you refer to your father by his Christian name."

"He demands we address him as 'Laird Fàileach' or 'my laird,' but we canna bear to address him as 'father,' 'papa,' or 'da,' so to poke at him, we always addressed him as 'Walter' and took the consequences."

"Ah. I marvel, then, that you brought your mother."

"My love for my mother is more powerful than my hatred for Walter."

"I am given to understand she is the more formidable of your parents."

"No, she is not," Brìghde said firmly, which was in no way a lie, she knew now.

"Well, if your father is more formidable than she is, and you outwitted your father, then … "

"You have drawn the correct conclusion, Your Grace. At some point in the future, Walter will wage war on me, and I will conquer. Because *I always have*."

"It makes me wonder what you would do to any other foe you face."

If he didn't know she'd poisoned him, he was an idiot. If he did, he would be on the watch.

"As it pertains to my wedding to Roger MacFhionnlaigh, I was a desperate maiden. I am no longer a maiden, and I am now only desperate for cod. Grimme's is adequate for my needs."

"I may want to see that, as well," he purred.

She hadn't expected that.

"Or you and my lovely Lady Caroline."

Lady Caroline stiffened.

Brìghde allowed herself to give him a sly smile, glanced briefly over her shoulder at Lady Caroline, and cooed, "'Twould be my treat."

He turned his attention to the jousts. He spared Lady Caroline not one more glance or touch.

Brìghde surreptitiously reached back and patted Lady Caroline's leg, and she grasped Brìghde's hand and squeezed it.

Shaking, disgusted, nauseated, heartsick, on the verge of tears, she went back to watching her husband, who seemed monkish by comparison. That could be because he couldn't rise for her, looked pained when he tried, and had never described his activities to her. There had only been one long conversation with Emelisse in French, which Brìghde "didn't speak," and in the course of that conversation, he had spoken of such lascivious acts with a matter-of-factness that reduced them to mere trifles. *You won't give me a strawberry tart. You ate all the caraway seed cookies before I got any ...*

Love.

She bowed her head and rubbed her temples.

And now she'd lied to the duke so much he wanted to watch her and Grimme together, which would decrease his ardor that much more, which would give the duke an opportunity to humiliate him even further.

She leaned against Sir John. "Why can't you keep my mouth shut?" she whispered.

He chuckled. "It was far too amusing."

She huffed away from him, her arms crossed over her chest. She was pouting. She knew she was.

He's a knight. Think about the knight who rescued you.

She devoted herself to watching the *knight* she'd married in a small kirk, he still in his gambeson and mail, and she in her torn and filthy wedding dress, her hopelessly tangled hair flowing down her back, filled with leaves and debris, conspirators arrogant about how clever they were.

She remembered her lone trip to Hogarth, when she was trapped by men who wanted to harm her, and there Grimme sat in front of an armored force, looking bored but quite lethal, not having to do one thing. Now here he was, playing knight. That was all it was for him, play, because he lusted for war, longed for it, missed it when he wasn't at it—but he did not war for its own sake, as Walter and, apparently her mother did.

I, Earl Grimme Kyneward, swear my fealty to you, Lady Brìghde Fàileach Kyneward …

She didn't want to see him *play* at it. She wanted to see him in the fray of it.

Even in play, with a jester who pointed out his accomplishments by mocking him, he *looked* like a warrior, a "beast." In his armor, on a warhorse he found as fine as Ares, galloping down the tilt time after time, he caught her breath. His sons were just as enchanted by this big, strong man of war because he was *their father*, and they knew him as a beloved Papa, and they saw in him their own futures.

Aye, he was her husband, her dearest friend. She possessed his ring and his name and his fealty. But he was *not* her lover, and that … hurt. It hurt that that magnificent stallion did not ply her with his lust every night, did not—

Love.

Duke Sheffield was a cruel man. He knew people, and he knew exactly what to say to crush them.

It took both Grimme and Aldwyn several tries each to knock their respective opponents off their horses, but they did it. The day was over for Brìghde and Lady Caroline, but the day continued for everyone else.

That night, around the Kyneward camp's fire, they toasted to Grimme's victories of the day. All four boys were fawning for Grimme's attention, and he was more than happy to give it. He told them that if they did not fight, they could all sleep in the tent with them that night. They promised readily and he grinned at Brìghde over their heads. It was difficult to smile back, but she did it. When the boys saw Mercury, they climbed all over each other for his attention, but the lazy dog simply lay there and allowed them to pet and scratch him, not even a doggy kiss for their troubles. Brìghde could barely feign a chuckle.

"Papa! Where's your jester?" one of the boys asked.

"Here and there," he said lightly, but would answer no more questions about his unusual herald.

They went to bed that night, and if there were not six other people in the tent with them, Brìghde would have slept on the ground to keep from begging for his lust. Yet here she was, curled up against this warrior's bare chest with her hand tracing circles in the hair on it, held in his bare arms, his hand caressing her back. She was completely aroused and thoroughly unhappy. When she determined everyone else was asleep, she murmured, "I said too much to the duke today."

He sighed. "Tell me so I will know what not to say."

She told him most of it, save the "love" cruelty, and all the way through he chuckled, just like Sir John, until she got to the most awful part.

"What?!" he breathed, horrified, his hand pressing flat to her back instead of caressing her.

"I'm sorry," she squeaked.

He took a deep breath and lay there not speaking. Finally, he said, "It won't get that far."

That angered her immediately. "Oh, aye, because now it's *your* humiliation at stake, you will do something about it."

"I am not arguing about this in a tent full of sleeping people in a field full of thousands of others. You need to trust me."

"I trust that you will try, which is what I asked you to do, and I do not take that for granted, but I do not delude myself that you can stop it."

"I have a weapon and a plan. *Trust. Me.*"

Her heart settled back down. "Can you also do something about Lady Caroline and the children, then?" she asked hesitantly.

"No. She is not my responsibility. She is Aldwyn's, and that he would rather allow himself and his family to suffer than come to me for help when he *knows* I will get them out is his failing and I am deeply disappointed in him. I live with the guilt of what I did to him. I would not be able to carry the guilt of allowing my wife to be repeatedly raped, much less in front of me, my children under threat of death."

"You wouldn't?" she asked in a tiny voice.

"No. I told you I would do anything for my child. That includes asking a man who betrayed me to rescue me. I have offered *twice* to fetch him and demanded at least once that he find a new liege himself. He could go to Tavendish, York, Warwick—*anywhere* up and down England or all over France, yet he stayed at Sheffield long enough to fall into this oubliette, and it was an entirely foreseeable event." She smiled at the use of her own words, but he was getting angry now. "If he cannot bear to allow me to rescue him, if he cannot find a new liege, he still has the same weapon I do, if he could put aside his pride to wield it."

"What?"

"I'm not telling you. You talk too much."

She sighed. "Fair. I'm ... glad I didn't swive him now."

He started. "Not even for a babe?"

"I told you I don't like weak men. I do not want to bear the child of such a coward. It's disgusting, that he is not even *attempting* to forestall it."

"He's not a coward. He's honorable, has too much pride, and believes that his righteousness will bless and save him in the end. He will adhere to his pride even if that means he loses men on the battlefield. I have no pride when it comes to my family and my men. Conquer? Aye, I will, and in the most efficient manner possible."

"Sir Drew said that about you," she murmured hesitantly. "He said that is why most chose to go with you."

"Aye, and Aldwyn refuses to believe that honorable men might win, but they don't conquer."

64

THE NEXT DAY was the final day of the tournament. Grimme and Aldwyn would ride many times until the field narrowed to only two. Many knights had hoped, a few still did, but no one expected any other outcome. Grimme's jester was welcomed with screams and whistles before each tilt, his jests and antics funnier and more outrageous each time.

As Grimme approached Brìghde for her favor, she took a deep breath, knowing this would anger him, but mayhap anger would help. She rose and extracted a black ribbon from her sleeve. His smile faded and his eyes turned thunderous.

"Dark," she whispered as she tied it on his wrist. "Ruthless. Clever. Bold. Fly, Raven King, *fly*. Snatch the rabbit from that wee laddie."

He stared at her for a long time, his anger clearly fading, then his smile grew again, softened, and widened. "Thank you, Wife," he said softly. Off he rode, to defeat that nameless knight.

Aldwyn defeated his.

More combatants that weren't Grimme took the lists, narrowing the field even more. Then Grimme was up again. It took him four passes to unseat his current opponent, but he did it, rounded the end of the list and returned to his squires and his sons.

It nearly brought tears to her eyes to see her husband riding her beloved mount. He was *playing*, but ... Troy was too. 'Twas as if he knew it was play and both man and beast were one, agreeing to expend the least amount of effort they needed to to unseat a previously thrice-victorious knight on their first pass.

"He rides Troy as if he's ridden him forever," Brìghde whispered to Sir John.

He patted her knee. "Troy is not just a match for Ares, he's yours. Troy is your favor to him."

"What is that, Sir John?" the duke said. "Did you say the Trojan horse is Lady Kyneward's?"

"Aye, Your Grace."

"You ride a warhorse, Lady Kyneward?" the duke asked imperiously.

She gave him an innocent smile. "I'm Scots, and I have six brothers. I grew up riding shires. Bareback. Unfortunately, I find it difficult to keep my seat on something more refined."

The duke leaned to her and whispered, "You will be riding my shire bareback tonight."

"Mmmm hm."

Then there were only two left: Grimme Kyneward and Aldwyn Marchand.

No one was surprised but everyone was excited.

"And now," Grimme's jester said dramatically, "we come to the final round. What black magic has the earl used to last this long?" Brìghde whimpered, looking to Grimme, whose smile was pained. "For 'tis either God or the devil, and," he added wryly, "I don't think God favors sheep fuckers, poor wee lambs."

The crowd was delighted, but Grimme's smile was fake and Sir John wasn't laughing. She leaned on Sir John.

"Does the jester know that is Grimme's sore spot?" she whispered.

"He does not," Sir John said tightly, "and Grimme will never tell him."

"Who *is* he?"

But Sir John simply shook his head.

And then … then the jester looked straight at Brìghde and grinned with his hideously painted scarlet mouth. "Ah, there's the source of the earl's magic!" Brìghde, watching Grimme with trepidation, saw him subtly untie her favor and drop it in the dirt. Her eyes stung and she thought she would throw up. "His lady wife, who, in fact, is the mind of the two—"

Whistles and catcalls and more laughter.

"—and clearly an inspiration to every man here! Run your flags up your poles to salute that beautiful woman, lads!"

The jester did backflips toward the duke's box until he was standing just below her.

"My lady," he purred. "Stand up."

The duke clamped his hand around her arm to keep her seated and hissed, "Get off the field. You are not amusing me."

He shrugged with a wink at Brìghde, then backflipped his way back toward the tilt and addressed the crowd again.

"We *all* know who's going to win the prize, do we not? Shout his name!"

"*Grimme!*" the crowd shouted.

"*What?!*" the jester cried, outraged. "You're as deluded as the king. Did he make *you* come too?! For the last tilt today, and for the prize of Ares, the fine steed Sir Aldwyn Marchand is riding, may I present Earl Grimme Kyneward!"

The crowd went wild as Grimme trotted down the tilt with a wave, but the only thing Brìghde could see was the spot where Grimme had dropped her favor. Aldwyn's herald came out to boos, so he merely said, "Sir Aldwyn Marchand, knight of the realm!"

Aldwyn garnered cheers, but not as raucous as the ones Grimme had garnered.

The *jester* had made Grimme the crowd's favorite, far more so than Grimme could have done on his own. Nay, Brìghde was not the mind of the two of them. She was Grimme's weapon, his assassin. If Aldwyn would not ask for help and Grimme would not give it without being asked, Brìghde would do what neither of them would do.

Again.

She reached back and touched Lady Caroline's leg, and the woman once again squeezed her hand. Brìghde watched Aldwyn astride that great beast who was to be the prize, the animal that Grimme and the colt's dam had nursed from an almost-dead newborn to … that.

A warhorse fit for the god of war.

Who was under the wrong knight.

Aldwyn was no warrior, and the more she thought about Lady Caroline's hell, the more her stomach turned that she had been so aroused by him—a man who loved his wife so much he would not dishonor her with adultery, but not enough to adhere to his own code to protect her with his life, never mind being humiliated himself. What man with *any* pride would submit to that if he had a way to save himself?

Grimme trotted to the end of the tilt and chose his lance. Aldwyn, at the other end, chose his. Sir John slipped his hand into hers, which was when she realized she was trembling. Grimme clapped his visor down. Aldwyn did the same. The flag was waved.

Lances shattered.

They went to the end of the tilt again. Chose lances.

Lances shattered.

Four times more, with no gain for either of them. They—and their mounts—were too well matched.

"Troy is magnificent," Sir John whispered to her.

It was all Brìghde could do to keep from crying—or looking at the spot where her favor lay trampled in the dirt.

The duke leaned over and whispered something to someone, who whispered to someone else, until it got to the officiant, who blew his horn and announced that the knight and the earl would decide the matter on foot. All the nobles around her were chatting and snickering and laughing, not loudly, but enough to be irritating.

Both men dismounted and flipped their visors up. An official went out onto the field, clapped a hand on each man's shoulder and spoke.

Grimme stared stone-faced at the official. Aldwyn did not look surprised. Grimme looked up at the duke with the same expression, communicating something. Brìghde leaned forward to look at the duke, who merely nodded with a self-satisfied smile.

The official left the field. Grimme spoke with Aldwyn for a moment or two—begging, Brìghde hoped—for him to allow Grimme to rescue him. Aldwyn shook his head and stepped back. Aldwyn's men came out to remove the shoulder armor bolted to his breastplate and take his helm. Grimme signaled to his squires to come assist him do the same. He pulled his mail hood back and his golden-red hair tumbled out of it. It was dark, soaked with sweat. His dangerously red face was shiny with it, but now, with the shoulder armor and helm removed and the squires off the field, the two men drew their swords and began to circle each other.

Grimme struck first.

Aldwyn was expecting it.

Brìghde clasped Sir John's hand harder, and he did the same. Pierce was standing at the rail, hopping up and down, still yelling encouragement at his Papa. Grimme's other sons, at the end of the list, were doing the same.

The people in the stands were roaring, but Brìghde could barely breathe much less yell encouragement. Then with a loud clash of metal on metal, the fight turned earnest and … deadly.

Brìghde didn't know when she realized that Grimme was going to kill him—

Brìghde gasped and turned to Sir John. "It's to the death!" she hissed.

Sir John gaped at her. Lady Caroline choked.

When Brìghde looked at the duke, she found him staring at her with smug licentiousness. "Not … *quite,* my dear. If one of them is not on the ground soon, *then* it will be at their discretion." *But I have instructed Sir Marchand to kill your husband, and if he doesn't, the consequences will be dire.*

He didn't have to say it for Brìghde to know.

The duke apparently didn't know that Grimme fought to conquer, and if that meant killing his dearest friend, that was what that meant. Grimme would grieve for the rest of his life and Brìghde would help him through it, but he *would* do it. He would not surrender, would not submit, but clearly the duke expected Aldwyn to win.

He wouldn't.

And *then* Grimme would rescue Lady Caroline and her children, and do what Aldwyn was not willing to do, and suddenly she hoped for Aldwyn's death so that Lady Caroline would never have to feel the duke's hand again.

Sir John bowed his head and his shoulders began to quake. Brìghde, heartsick, put her arm around him and held him close to her.

As the fight went on, Aldwyn began showing his fatigue. By contrast, Grimme somehow seemed to get bigger. Stronger. Faster. He rained strikes down upon Sir Aldwyn that would have broken a lesser knight. Tears began to leak from her eyes as she watched him wear his lifetime friend down, knowing what it was costing him.

Discipline wins battles.

Suddenly the duke cupped his hands around his mouth, and bellowed, "*CAROLINE!*"

That energized Aldwyn. Both Lady Caroline and Sir John were openly sobbing.

The fight went on and on until finally both men were showing their fatigue, stalking around each other, thrusting, parrying.

"Any time now, Lady Kyneward, Lady Marchand."

Brìghde caught a glimpse of Grimme's face: frustrated, angry, red, sweat-soaked, tired.

She withdrew her arm from around Sir John, cupped her hands around her mouth, took a deep breath, and screamed, "*TROJAN HORSE!*"

Grimme immediately stepped away from Aldwyn's next thrust, breathed as deeply as he could within his armor, and side-stepped yet another sword thrust.

She sat on the edge of her seat, leaning forward, her elbows on her knees and her fists pressed to her mouth.

Again, Grimme side-stepped a swing. Aldwyn was flagging again, whilst Grimme was pacing around him, stalking him like prey. Once again Aldwyn dove for him. Once again Grimme side-stepped.

That was when the boos started, but Brìghde knew Grimme: He was going to win without killing his best friend and he didn't care if the crowd found him dishonorable or cowardly. He continued to stalk Aldwyn in leftwise circles, faster and faster, closer and closer with each circle, his sword at his side, keeping Aldwyn in the middle of the circle turning, completely on the defensive, unable to see Grimme. He swung. Grimme arched his back and it barely missed. Aldwyn swung again, but now he was dizzy.

Grimme pulled his sword back with both hands and stopped short, simultaneously swinging it like the stick of a stick-and-ball game, slapping the flat of the blade on Aldwyn's back, sending him flying, landing face down in the dirt.

The stands erupted in roars and cheers. Brìghde could barely see, she was so enraged, so she was still tense on the edge of her seat. Pierce could not be more overjoyed and he was hoarse from screaming. Grimme's other sons and squires were screaming and jumping too.

Sir John's head snapped up and he choked, then laughed and began to applaud as tears ran down his face. "Well done!" he said as loudly as he could, which was not very loud. "Oh, well done!"

"Congratulations, Lady Kyneward," the duke growled. "He may have Ares, but I have *you*. And *you* are going to pay."

She inclined her head a mere fraction of a turn toward him so that he would not see how disgusted and angry and frightened she was, but at least he had not disqualified Grimme for a cowardly or dishonorable act.

Without giving the nobles a second glance, Grimme drove his sword into the ground halfway up the blade, then turned and trotted away from the box to the end of the tilt. Whilst Aldwyn's men were dragging him off the field, Grimme was looking at the ground, searching, then bent, picked up the black ribbon he had taken off, bowed his head, and brought it to his lips.

Brìghde, who suddenly could not breathe, almost started to cry.

Grimme palmed the ribbon and stalked toward the box. He stopped when he reached his dirt-sheathed sword and looked at the duke silently. It was a flat stare of expectation that he *would* get what he wanted.

After a moment or two, the duke gave a signal and presently, Ares, now stripped of livery and armor, was led to him and the reins put in his hands. Grimme turned and wrapped his arms around his pet's neck and buried his face in his glossy black mane.

For his part, Ares was craning his neck to give Grimme velvety-lipped horse kisses, even going so far as to move his rump around to break Grimme's grasp to greet him the way he wanted to. He huffed in Grimme's face, and Grimme grinned, taking him by his ears and pressing his mouth to his blaze the way Brìghde had done Troy. The beast reared a little, then bobbed his head over Grimme's shoulder, craning his head and neck around Grimme.

Ares was clearly happy to be reunited with the only warrior worthy to ride him.

The stands were still roaring.

Brìghde didn't dare turn around and look at Lady Caroline.

Grimme pulled away from the horse and signaled his squires and sons, who came running, bringing Troy with them. One of Grimme's squires drew Troy up next to the rail of the nobles' box. "My lady." Grimme stepped forward and held his hand up to Brìghde.

Brìghde cocked her head in confusion and he gestured for her to approach the rail. She stood and before she could blink, he had plucked her off the stand

and plopped her on Troy's back. He helped her adjust her stirrups and straighten her skirts, then strode to Ares, mounted him, looked at Brìghde and said, "Catch me if you can!" then thundered off the field.

Suddenly Brìghde laughed, stood in her stirrups and kicked Troy into a gallop, but he was more than ready to go. She thundered off the field, out of the arena, rounded a corner, looked for Grimme, who was slowing and then she knew what he wanted to do. With a shriek of laughter, she urged Troy faster until they fell in with Grimme and Ares.

Together, they rode around the list, behind the stands, to the other end and slowed to a trot. Grimme grabbed her hand and held it high as they trotted back onto the list and down the field together to the roar of the crowd.

The Duke of Sheffield was not pleased with Earl and Countess Kyneward.

65

THEY WERE summoned to the duke's table for supper that night.

Brìghde and Grimme dressed carefully, somberly. She was surreptitiously watching him dress when she saw him tie the black ribbon to the inside of his doublet.

She wanted to ask him about having taken her favor off and dropping it in the dirt, but decided never to mention it. He had gone back for it, kissed it, and now had tied it to his clothing as if he were going into battle.

He was. Brìghde had asked Grimme to give his life for her and he had sworn it and now she wasn't sure that was what she wanted at all. If he died, she wouldn't be able to bear it.

"Grimme," she murmured as they rode Ares and Troy to the keep, "I changed my mind. Do not risk your life. I have my poison. I will kill him myself and make it look like an accident, and then I will come back to you. I don't want to lose you."

"'Tis not only you now, Brìghde," he returned. "You asked me to choose *all* my interests, and that is what I am doing. My prime interest is being unconquerable."

"Grimme, no matter what we have argued about, no matter that I am still angry about the bairn and will continue to be so, you are my dearest friend. My mother's presence has shown me that. Knowing what Lady Caroline is going through with Aldwyn unwilling to come to you for help, I— You are the only one who has ever *tried* to protect me, to be more to me than simply a family member to be used or played with or commanded."

He smiled at her. "Thank you, my friend. That means quite a lot to me. When we get home—"

"*If* we get home. If he kills you, I will kill him. I will not submit."

"That's my beautiful raven queen," he murmured, halting Ares and reaching out to press his mouth to her forehead. Then he touched his forehead to hers and his nose to hers and said, "When we get home, I will do my best to give you that son. I promised to protect you, and I understand that is part of it. Will you be patient with me?"

"Aye," she whispered.

Kiss me, Grimme. Don't send me into battle without your favor.

'Twas as if it didn't *occur* to him to kiss her, and she would not ask. If she asked, she would beg.

He pulled away from her with a grin. "Let's go defeat a duke."

Sheffield Keep was far grander than Kyneward. It was four times bigger and more fortified, its walls not crumbling. However, the great hall was as filthy as the duke himself.

"Oh, we should have brought your mother," Grimme muttered. "She could strike terror into this housekeeper's heart instead of ours."

She snickered.

Kyneward Keep had its share of dogs running around snatching bits of food off the floor during mealtimes, and the compacted filth she had had to clean off the floors was horrible, but this ... this was ridiculous, at least thirty years' worth. There were dogs *everywhere* and the floor was littered with dog shit and sour rushes. Brìghde could barely hold her heaves.

Unfortunately, the only people at supper, which was sparsely laid, were the duke, Grimme, and Brìghde. They bowed and curtsied and said, "Your Grace."

"I commend you on your performance today, Kyneward," the duke said grimly as they sat.

"Thank you."

"I didn't expect that result," Sheffield said as he spooned a tiny amount of porridge into his bread bowl and speared a small piece of meat to put on his platter.

"You should've. My horse was at stake."

Neither Brìghde nor Grimme bothered with the food; this conversation wouldn't take that long and neither of them were brave enough to eat Sheffield's food.

"Aye, well, Sir Marchand will feel my rage."

"I wasn't going to kill him, and I wasn't going to let him kill me."

"But what you *will* do is watch me fuck your wife."

Grimme shook his head and said casually, "No."

The duke was aghast. "*No?!* You cannot gainsay me! 'Tis my *right*."

"It is not." With that, Grimme retrieved a parchment from inside his fine doublet and presented it to the duke. "That is from my *friend*, King Henry V. I requested legal advice on the matter of the *droit du seigneur*, and he informed me that should any of his vassals attempt to claim it upon each other, they may face execution."

The duke's face mottled. He snatched it out of Grimme's hand, looked at the seal, then opened the missive and read it—or tried to. He snapped his fingers and someone came out of the corner.

Our friend Kyneward,

We do not sanction the use of the droit du seigneur. If you are asking on your own behalf to have permission to claim it, we deny it. If you have been petitioned to submit, we beg you write the details and we will see to the matter ourselves. We will not have our vassals warring amongst themselves and execution will be considered for any who succeed.

Your friend,
Henry V

"'Tis dated six weeks ago, Your Grace," the servant said.

Utterly shocked, Brìghde didn't dare glance at Grimme. He had to have sent his question to Henry directly after the duke's visit, along with the terms of the ransom agreement, to have received an answer that long ago. He had already protected her when she was hounding him for not doing so! *That* was the weapon Aldwyn had not used, for he would not lower himself to request any help at all!

"God damn you," the duke hissed. "Running off to tattle to da every time you don't like something. If your only power is the king, who is in France—"

"Clearly he thought it important enough to hold my man and answer so thoughtfully—whilst in the middle of a war."

"You have no power when he is on the battlefield," Sheffield said flatly. "You cannot prove I claimed it."

"I wouldn't have to prove it," Grimme said calmly. "I'd simply kill you, present my quandary to him, and either he will execute me or he won't."

"Neither of you would be able to get out of this keep!"

Grimme shrugged as if that didn't matter.

"You would risk death for that, that, that—*barbarian Scot?*"

"She is *mine,*" Grimme snarled, arising to loom over the duke. Instantly knights were there to capture him and keep him in his chair. "And I will defend her to the death."

"But to *her* death?"

Brìghde spat upon his foot. "I'd kill myself before I'd let you touch me."

The duke shot out of his chair at her, but Brìghde put her hand over his face and shoved him back into it. He was no match against her and she was too swift for the knights to keep her quelled.

"You will never again command me to give you what is *mine,*" Grimme said. "My wife. My women. My horses. My earldom. Go running to da? Aye,

I certainly will. He is already suspicious of our ransom agreement, as he demanded in a separate missive to know the real reason you would agree to pay the ransom. Continue to bedevil us, I will give him that answer and I will *also* remind him that you killed your cousin and his wife and his child to gain the dukedom."

"I did no such thing," he said flatly.

"Henry believes you did. Half the nobles in England believe you did."

Sheffield's nostrils flared.

"So think twice and thrice before laying any more plans for my demise."

Brìghde watched this entire episode nearly in tears. Grimme had found a way, and it did not involve anything more than asking the king to clarify his thoughts on the *droit du seigneur*.

And if that didn't work, he was willing to kill the duke or die trying.

For her.

Grimme would never love her, as he was not capable of loving any woman, but *she* loved this man with her whole heart.

"Do I make myself clear?"

"Get out of my house," the duke said with a vicious snarl.

"Gladly," Grimme said, arising and pulling Brìghde's chair out for her. Then he plucked the king's missive out of the servant's hand and they strolled out as if they hadn't a care in the world.

66

SUPPER AT Kyneward Keep the day they arrived home from the tournament was a joyous occasion. Brìghde and Grimme were in utmost sympathy. Grimme had outwitted the duke and they were free of his machinations. And Ares was home!

Very late that night, Grimme was lying in her bed excitedly recounting everything in a scattered fashion as it came to him whilst Brìghde lazed in her bathtub and listened, added her little excitements and lies to the duke (exaggerated for best effect, naturally), eager to soak in their victory and await the moment Grimme said *'Tis time*, as he had promised. She didn't want to do it whilst her mother was in the house, though, and he seemed to know that.

She was startled by a knock on the door. "Who goes?"

"'Tis Moom."

Grimme sighed heavily and arose to open the door.

"Oh! Um, Grimme. I didn't expect to see you." *All* of him, as he was naked.

"I'll leave you to your daughter, Lady Fàileach," he said coolly, and left.

The door closed. "What, Moom."

"I . . . need to talk to ye about somethin'," she said. She *sounded* nervous, but . . . Brìghde twisted and looked at her. She was wringing her hands.

"What do ye wanna complain about this time?" she sniped. "I'm naked in a bath but not in bed with me naked husband? Did ye get a good look? Aye, he's hung like a stallion. Now ye know."

Lady Fàileach shook her head, refusing to look at her.

"Well, fetch a chair. I'll not get out of the first bath I've had in a fortnight."

Instead, Lady Fàileach simply sat on the edge of the bed. Brìghde closed her eyes and soaked. "I doona know how to approach this," Lady Fàileach began. "E'en though 'tis a talk I've had with all yer brothers, ye're a lass an' it's come clear to me I doona know how to rear a lass."

"Moom," Brìghde sighed in irritation, "the only thing ye could say right now that'd make me happy is that Walter isna me father."

Silence.

More silence.

Brìghde's eyes popped open. She turned her head. Lady Fàileach was still wringing her hands. "*Noooooo*," she breathed, hope fluttering in her chest.

Her mother shook her head slightly.

Brìghde stayed utterly still for a moment, then squealed with delight, kicking her feet so that water splashed everywhere. She whooped for joy. She scrambled out of the bath to find her towel, then slipped into her robe. She plopped herself on her bed beside her mother, who now looked simply resigned.

"Oh, who is, who is?" she demanded gleefully with as much delight as a wee lassie could hold.

Her mother looked at her strangely. "Of all the men ye've known in yer lifetime, who'd ye like it to be?"

"Sir Bart," she said immediately.

Her mother's face softened.

"Is it? Oh, is it?!" she squealed again, then jumped up and hopped around, laughing and clapping and— She bolted out the door and burst into Grimme's chambers.

He wasn't there. She looked to Hamond, whose mouth tightened.

Her joy vanished instantly and she turned to go back to her chambers, now hoping to be able to muster some happiness. But her mother knew. She saw.

Brìghde's mouth began to tremble and her eyes stung. She held the door open and swept her hand out toward the hall. "Thank you, Moom. I will go visit him in the morn."

"Close the door, Budgie," she said softly.

Brìghde obeyed.

"Come."

She sat on the edge of the bed and when her mother pulled her into her arms, she burst out into sobs.

GRIMME WAS not happy when, at breakfast, Brìghde coolly told him her mother was staying an extra week. She didn't bother to tell him why.

After breakfast, Brìghde's mother took her out to meet Sir Bart for the first time as her real father.

"I need to ride," her mother murmured. "'Tis a ways an' I canna walk that far."

Troy and her mother's palfrey were saddled, and then they set out, but the opposite direction from the Fàileach encampment. "What—"

"'Tis roundabout."

"Moom, if you'd told me to begin with, I'd have put him in your chambers with you."

"No one knows," she said softly, "not even his men."

"Does Walter?"

"He knows ye aren't his. He doesn't know whose. He doesna want to." She paused. "All seven of ye are Bart's bairns."

Brìghde gasped. "How … why … ?"

She sighed heavily. "I may tell ye one day, Budgie, but not now."

"If ye had a litter o' bastards, and Walter knows about it, how do ye keep him on a leash? He'd move the world fer ye, an' 'tis not what a man'd do with an unfaithful wife, much less one who put a spear through his sword arm."

"I'll tell ye only that my father was deceived by Fàileach, and I threatened to leave the marriage. Me da nor Bart knows to this day, as 'twould cause a war 'twixt the Highlanders an' the Lowlanders. But fer all that, Walter knows I'm willin' to start it. 'Tis me only weapon, keepin' me counsel an' even then, it has its limits before he'd kill me to keep it."

Brìghde didn't know what to say to that, for Sir John was still bitter about the deception he endured at his wife's family's hands. What was so bad about Walter's secret that he would kill his wife to keep it?

"I guess that he canna sire children."

"'Tis the *reason* he canna sire children that canna be revealed."

Brìghde knew Lady Fàileach would say nothing more and they rode in silence for a good three miles around the keep.

"I will tell ye," she said abruptly, "once yer husband can get his mind right an' bed ye."

Brìghde whimpered.

"I see now. Sir Bart—yer father—took me to task for the way I've been beratin' ye, an' then when ye rode me at the tournament, he bade me shut my mouth and *look* so I could see. An' I did."

"But *what* did ye see?" she cried.

She huffed in frustration. "I canna explain in words, or I would." She pressed her fist to her breast and thumped lightly. "I see here. If I could explain anythin' important in words, I'd write it all down fer ye so ye wouldna forget."

With that, she broke into a canter toward the stream where the sheep gathered and Brìghde watered her horses when they were out.

Sir Bart was awaiting them. He was standing alone, his destrier grazing some distance away. He was dressed in finery, and she may not have recognized him without some type of armor.

If she could dismount Troy without falling on her arse, as she did half the times she tried, she would've run to him. As it was, he had to help her dismount after he helped her mother. But instead of putting her on her feet, he simply hugged her to him and she clasped him tightly. "I'm so glad ye're me da," she whispered. It was then she realized his shoulders were quaking.

It was quite a while before he could collect himself, but finally he released her and set her on her feet, then took her hand and her mother's and the three of them walked, not speaking.

"Budgie," he finally said, which was when she realized that Sir Bart was the one who'd given all seven of them their nicknames. So many things made sense now, looking back. He was the one who had taught her to ride. He had led the expedition to the convent and seemed happy to do it. Now she knew why.

She took a deep breath. "How ... ?"

"Well," he began, "when a man and a woman love each other very much—"

Brìghde laughed, and he slid her a mischievous grin.

He took a sharp breath as if to say something, then released it as if he thought better of it. Then he did it again. "I watched you outwit Walter time and time again, from the time you could talk, it seems. I am proud of my sons, and they are as strong and intelligent as I could ever hope. But you started out with the disadvantage of being a lass, and you still conquered him."

She sighed. "Not accordin' to me husband's definition."

He hummed. "Aye, I've seen your husband's definition. Whether you kill Walter or your husband does, he will die knowing that you brought about his destruction."

"Why didn't me brothers do it?" she asked plaintively.

"Your brothers knew they would leave and they never had to come back, so they didn't have a reason to be as ruthless as you."

Ruthless. Her mouth twisted.

"How did you get home from the convent?" he asked suddenly, startling her *and* her mother.

"Uh ... "

"What kind of question is that?" her mother demanded. "Walter sent fer her fer the weddin', then postponed it."

Sir Bart ignored her mother. "How long were you there?"

"Uh ... "

"Budgie!" her mother barked. "Answer the question!"

"I, uh ... Why do you ask?" she drawled suspiciously.

"You came home completely different. You left an innocent hoyden. You *should* have come home docile and quiet, with an interest in ladies' pursuits, or at least return unchanged. But you came back hardened and wary, as if you had seen battle and nothing could surprise you."

Her mother drew in a soft breath.

Brìghde puffed her cheeks out. "I ran away three years in. It took me three years to get home."

"Budgie!" her mother wailed softly. "Why dinna ye tell me?"

"Why would I, Moom?" she demanded, exasperated. "I don't tell ye anythin' an' the drunker ye get me the better I lie."

"You knew!" her mother barked, rounding on Sir Bart, bringing their walk to a halt.

He shrugged. "You refuse to tell me what Walter does to her—"

"Because ye'd kill him!"

Sir Bart nodded slowly. "How many years now, Moira? Thirty?"

Brìghde knew the beginnings of an old argument when she heard one. 'Twas the same 'twixt her and Grimme.

"I don't want to hear this," Brìghde said. "But to the point, why dinna ye rescue me from me weddin'? Walter had the point of a sword in me back."

He barked a laugh, then his laugh turned into a rolling guffaw. "Oh, Budgie, yer husband tore in just before my men could start the plan. They were to take you somewhere safe, so—"

"*You* were planning to abduct me?" she squeaked.

He grinned at her. "I was. They didn't know quite what happened, if perhaps I had put a separate plan into play so they didn't follow, and I couldn't get to you in time. But when we got your missive, I laughed. And laughed. And laughed. Every time I thought about it, I laughed until I couldn't catch a breath. Budgie, my wee lassie, you are a jewel."

Brìghde looked at her mother. "Did you know he was going to do that?"

Lady Fàileach nodded. "'Tis why I dinna try to stop the weddin'. I knew Walter would kill ye if we did anythin' too soon. We had to get the sword out o' yer back first."

"All the things I said—" Brìghde whispered, horrified. "—about, about you not protectin' me … "

She shook her head. "I deserved it. I waited too long." She tilted her head toward Sir Bart. "He took the decision out o' me hands."

"I was tired," he growled at her mother, "of being barred from protecting my daughter." He looked at Brìghde. "And I do mean barred. Physically."

"Ye'd'a killed Walter an' then ye'd'a been executed!" she cried. "I couldna bear it!"

"And I couldn't bear watching that bloody madman tear into *my daughter* any longer!" he roared, releasing Brìghde's hand. He looked at Brìghde. "I never planned to return once we abducted you. I chose you over your mother."

He cast her mother a glare. "Which I should've done when she came home from the convent far too soon, acting like a seasoned soldier, *which you did not notice.*"

Her mother's face was in her palms and she was crying.

"Moom ... "

"But you, Budgie, have the devil's own luck," he said wistfully, no longer angry. Or else he was keeping it in reserve. "And the wit to exploit it. You did well. I can go home with your mother and be at peace, knowing you're loved and taken care of, in a place where you'll be happy."

"Grimme doesn't love me," Brìghde said, confused.

"Are you or are you not loved by the people at Kyneward?"

"Well, aye, a few. Sir John. Pierce."

"Are you or are you not happy here?"

"Mostly."

"Will you or will you not always be taken care of and protected and treated with the respect you deserve?"

She sighed. "Aye." That still wasn't enough.

"Then it's a good start. Don't take it for granted."

67

BRÌGHDE'S MOTHER and *father* stayed that extra week so that Brìghde could spend time with him, but her mother watched quietly, subdued by Sir Bart's anger—and he was *very* angry. It was impressive; Brìghde had never seen her mother in any way subdued by anyone or anything. They loved each other, had been together thirty years, had seven children together, but they still got angry with each other. Brìghde would have to remember that. Yet they would tell her nothing of their beginnings, nor the marriage, nor whatever they saw in Grimme and Brìghde's marriage.

Grimme was clearly confused by what reasoning Brìghde was suddenly spending so much time riding out with her mother when they could barely stand each other's company, but Brìghde did not want to tell him. She was still stinging from his inability to wait until her conversation with her mother ended before getting his spindle stroked. However, he encouraged Brìghde to come out of Lady Fàileach's shadow now that she had conquered her, and so supper was again a riot of tales of derring-do from different knights, re-telling the same tales over and over again, grander with each re-telling, bawdy jests, and clever insults. Sir Bart finally joined in, and ruled the last two nights of their visit. Grimme seemed to be thoroughly entertained.

When they left, both Brìghde and her mother were in tears. There were no apologies forthcoming—the Fàileach family did not believe in apologies—but her mother had all but acknowledged that Brìghde's iron fist was stronger than hers. Lady Fàileach could defeat Laird Fàileach—and only because he allowed her to—but she could not defeat Brìghde, and she had to travel all the way home with that knowledge.

As for Sir Bart—Brìghde threw herself into his arms, surprising exactly no one in the Fàileach company, as that was always how she'd acted—and whispered, "Thank you, Da."

"You're welcome, Budgie. I love you. I always have."

She was lying on her bed deep into that night, Mercury curled around her, looking into the fire and grieving, angry at her husband, angry at her mother, angry at Walter, even angry at Sir Bart. Was she ever going to have a man in her life who would protect her without being pushed to it?

Troy. Faithful Troy.

Her door creaked open. "Go away," she croaked.

Grimme closed the door, then moved Mercury so he could lie behind her and curl up. "Now that your mother and father are gone—"

She gasped and bolted upright. "You *knew*?"

"Suspected. When you got angry with your mother at the tournament, he was furious with her. He's just the captain of her guard. There had to be a reason she would tolerate it, much less be subdued by it such that her behavior changed so much. Then I wanted to know why she'd be staying an extra week, but you were angry with me again for some reason, which I want to know, so I followed you on one of your rides. I saw the loving kiss between them, and then Papa and I started looking at him more closely to see if there was a resemblance. It's subtle, but it's there."

Brìghde hummed and twisted to sit on the edge of the bed.

"What did I do?" he asked flatly.

"The night we were talking and she interrupted—that was what she wanted to tell me. I was so happy. I ran to tell you, but … you weren't in your chambers."

He heaved a deep sigh. "I was angry," he muttered. "I don't like her, I don't like how she treats you, I don't like that you allowed her to treat you like that, I don't like that she interrupted our conversation, and I don't like that you allowed it."

"And so you did not wait until the conversation was over to tell me you were hurt by that."

He was silent.

"On our way to the duke's for supper," she mused, "you said when we got home, you would give me what I need."

"Aye."

"That night she interrupted us—I was listening to you and you were so excited. I was excited too. We conquered. Together, we conquered. We were soaking in our victory together, and I was happy with your promise."

"And then your mother interrupted," he said tightly.

"I didn't invite her in, Grimme. You did."

He stilled, then released a trembling breath. "Bloody hell," he whispered.

"You left before I had a chance to tell her to go away. And then you went immediately to … whoever, wasting seed you promised to me. Is that something you do often? Get angry with me, then your spindle rises, then you seek someone? And if so, you couldna wait five minutes? That is how long that conversation lasted. I was so happy. I wanted to share it with you and you couldn't wait five—bloody—minutes."

He slowly sat up on the other edge of the bed, his back to her.

There was silence between them. Mercury hopped up on the bed again, trod the bedclothes three times around, then plopped over on his side. She didn't know why he bothered to make his nest since he never landed in it.

"I'm taking Pierce to Hogarth tomorrow," she muttered. "My mother pointed out that he looks like a bloody peasant because no one, including I, has ever seen fit to dress him in something other than peasant garb, and even then, what he does have is too small for him, tattered, and stained. It looks like it has never been laundered or mended once. His shoes and boots are too small and have holes in them. At the tournament, I was embarrassed, all these nobles wondering what I'm doing with a peasant's child in the nobles' box when he is the son of an earl. And then I realized—of all your sons, only Terrwyn has good clothes and shoes. Emelisse, for all her smothering, took no more notice of her sons' clothes than Maebh did hers. She can outfit herself in the height of fashion—although she canna go anywhere and wouldna be invited to neighboring nobles' fêtes—if we *had* any neighbors—but she can't manage to remember her children need clothes. I suppose they didn't *need* good clothing because they weren't allowed outside their chambers, much less anywhere else."

He sighed. "Would you like company?"

"No. You'll embarrass me again."

"I promised you I wouldn't," he said softly, sincerely.

Brìghde didn't know what to do or say. "All the boys but Terrwyn need clothes," she muttered, "but it wouldna be fair to take the three, but not him. Did you send them out to the field with what they have?"

"I don't know," he said flatly.

"Oh. How can I— Do you call them in from the field when they need something? How do I get them to Hogarth?"

"Generally, if they are truly out to apprentice, I would pay the knight—I am paying their knights as if they were out to apprentice—and any expenses he incurred to feed, clothe, and shelter the boy. Since they are not truly apprenticed, I would see to their needs myself. Food and shelter, aye, they have. Clothes … " He puffed out a long breath. "I am a horrible father."

"Well, I'm a horrible mother, so at least we have that in common."

"You've been a mother longer than I've been a father," he said dryly.

She chuckled in spite of herself. "That's true."

"If your mother's visit has shown me one thing, it's how much you have done for me. Us. All of us, Kyneward, the villeins, the village, my father, my children, Dillena. Even Emelisse, though she'll never admit it."

Brìghde growled.

"Aye, well, that's what she said about you, too."

"Stop it."

"Stop making you laugh?"

"Aye."

"We can wrestle on the rug. You can stab me in the arse."

She turned around and punched him in the shoulder.

"Ow. You're laughing." He sighed. "Brìghde, I'm sorry. I don't want to hurt you and I don't mean to hurt you, but I keep doing it and I don't know why."

"You keep doing it because you keep thinking of me as a man to avoid thinking of me as a witch, and you expect me to respond as a man would. Go away, Grimme. I'm too tired to argue, too sad to be teased out of it, too angry to listen to you apologize and expect immediate forgiveness. Again. Please have your sons ready to go to Hogarth tomorrow. The road is close to their encampment, aye? We can meet them on the way?"

"Aye."

He arose, but instead of leaving, as she expected, he wrestled Mercury off the bed, divested himself of most of his clothes, and slid into bed. He plucked at her shift, then rubbed her back and she sighed with his touch, feeling desire curl through her, yet knowing she did not do the same for him. He was asking her to sleep with him and …

"We conquered," he whispered. "Brìghde, you and I have our private struggles, aye, and I acknowledge that I am the problem, but together, you and I— We cannot be defeated."

TO BRÌGHDE'S surprise, Dillena requested to go to Hogarth, as she needed gold leaf and inks that the stationer at the faire had not had. After seeing Dillena's artwork, Brìghde was only too happy to grant that.

"We will be staying two nights."

"Thank you, my lady," she said with a smile, and left the breakfast table in a rush to gather her things for the trip.

Emelisse watched this with a stony expression. She had been angry before Brìghde's mother's visit, but now she was unbearable about it. Brìghde hadn't heard her harrying Grimme over it, but Brìghde did have to endure Emelisse's endless barbs about her mother's behavior.

Thus, Brìghde ignored her and waited for her to sullenly request to go too, but … she never did, and Brìghde wasn't going to offer. Grimme wasn't paying attention, as he had to eat quickly, then ride out to collect his other sons, who would join them along the way. He wolfed his food, then, to Brìghde's surprise, pressed a kiss to her temple and told her it shouldn't take very long. He left without having glanced at Emelisse, much less said anything. Brìghde didn't gloat, but however apologetic she was about her mother's behavior, Emelisse had made Brìghde wish her mother had said *more*.

Thus, Sir Thom captained their company of ten men, two women, one boy, and three riderless mares. They eschewed a carriage in favor of two pack animals, and just past Waters, they met Gaston, Max, and Terrwyn, standing with Grimme.

"Mam!" Terrwyn cried happily and ran to Dillena, who smiled and ruffled his hair.

"Good day, my son," she said sweetly. "How do you fare?"

"I will tell you," he said as Grimme helped him into the saddle and adjusted his stirrups. Terrwyn, who could apparently ride quite well now, directed the horse to stand next to Dillena and chattered at her happily whilst Grimme helped the other two, and interrupted Terrwyn to tell them all to be good for Lady Brìghde.

"Where's Mamá?" Gaston asked Grimme whilst looking between Brìghde and Dillena.

"She did not ask to come," Brìghde said gently.

"Oh," he muttered.

Grimme looked troubled and he pulled Brìghde aside. "Didn't you offer?" he whispered up at her.

"No," Brìghde said flatly. His jaw tightened and her eyebrow went up. "If she cannot lower herself to ask me for something, she won't get it."

"Would you have brought her if she'd asked?"

"Aye, because I do not now, nor have I ever, played favorites with your women. Now it is too late."

"I will go get her."

"Don't," she said low, threateningly. "When she runs to you screaming at what a horrible bitch I am, tell her that all she had to do was ask. Then you may inform her that *I* will be the one clothing *her* sons because she was too lazy, ignorant, selfish, or proud to do it herself."

She held his glare with one of her own, until he sighed. "Very well."

"Excellent," she chirped. "Now we understand each other."

He shook his head, but caressed her leg as he walked away, mounted Ares, called good day to them all, and headed back to Kyneward.

68

BRÌGHDE WAS RIGHT.

She was *always* right.

Grimme was furious, and he spent the day working his rage off in swords, taking on one knight and foot soldier after another and winning. He couldn't quite decide what he was furious about, or at whom, the most, but it felt as if everything he knew about his people, his women, his household, was all askew.

His rage did not abate.

It wasn't that Brìghde had turned everything upside down. It was that she showed him it was *already* upside down and he had turned a blind eye to it.

No, he knew whom he was furious with, and it was not Brìghde.

At supper, he could barely stand to look at Emelisse, so he went upstairs to do a bit of scouting, then headed to his chambers for a hot bath. He bid Hamond bring him a tray and when he was finished, to summon Emelisse. She blew into his chambers breathlessly, likely expecting him to fuck her in his bed.

"Sit down," he snarled, pointing to a chair by the hearth.

"Grimme," she whimpered.

Once she was seated, perched on the edge of it with her hands folded in her lap like a naughty little girl, he had absolutely no idea where to begin.

After a while, she relaxed back into the seat, crossing one knee over the other and swishing her foot, and drawled, "If you're not going to say anything, I will. *She* refused to take me to Hogarth and you let her. Why?"

"*She* was waiting for you to ask," Grimme said sweetly, "but you didn't."

The look on Emelisse's face was murderous. "I shouldn't have to," she hissed. "I should be *offered*."

He ignored that. "Do you want to know *why* she went to Hogarth?"

"I don't care."

"She went to clothe *your* sons."

There was dead silence for quite a while. "What?" she whispered.

"I don't care what you think of my earldom, me, my bastardy, or how I was so fortunate to be bequeathed an earldom, or anything else about our life. But those boys are the sons of a bloody *earl*. I do not treat them as bastards and I do not see them as any less than I would see legitimate children. Yet ... they are dressed like bloody peasants. I believe those were the exact words Lady Fàileach used, 'bloody peasants.'"

"Brigitte's *bitch* of a mother," she snarled.

"I agree completely," he agreed. "However, she was *right*."

"She said that about Pierce. She never saw mine or Dillena's."

"Well, if she'd seen Terrwyn, she wouldn't have made the observation, since Dillena has always made sure to attire him properly, which *you did not do* for Gaston and Max. Furthermore, if you'd have allowed Gaston and Max out of their chambers for a half day, Dillena would have made certain *yours* got clothed, too. Maebh would clothe Pierce, but only when Dillena suggested she do so and provided Maebh could remember long enough to do it. So *my* wife has to take *your sons* to clothe them properly. And you could have gone and spent three days with Gaston and Max—if you had only asked."

She wailed with rage. "She would *never* have allowed me to go!"

"Aye, she would have because she has *never* shown any one of you favor over another. She got along with Maebh and Ardith before she found out about Aldwyn. She gets along with Dillena quite well and gives her anything she wants because Dillena is kind and asks nicely. You have made Brìghde's life hell since she arrived, but she has only demonstrated her power when you dared her to. And yet, she has advocated for you, kept you out of the duke's clutches, and apologized for her mother.

"To my point: You not only do *not* contribute to the household and do *not* satisfy me in bed, you do *not* take care of our sons. Putting them in their chambers all day and all night with nothing to do is not caring for them. You kept them away from their studies. You would not allow them to ride, much less teach them. You drove out four nursemaids. Never mind *you* didn't want to hand over the boys, but you drove out the ones for Dillena and Maebh, too. Yet *you* didn't care for our sons yourself, either.

"I went to your chambers and I saw the toys and games on your shelves that have never been played with. I went to Gaston's and Max's chambers and saw ... nothing. Not even the toys Brìghde and I brought back for them from Hogarth. I thought they had sneaked all their possessions out to the field, but my knights said nothing to me about it. This morning, when I went to gather them to meet her on the way to Hogarth, I saw they had *nothing*. Never mind toys and games, they only had one change of clothing. Emelisse! *One!* Too small, tattered, filthy. They each have one pair of boots that are too small and have holes in them. *THEY LOOK LIKE BLOODY PEASANTS!*

"I do not want for coin. Your chambers are rich with hangings, your chests are full of expensive clothing, your boxes are full of expensive jewels—half of which weren't paid for before *my wife* settled your bills. You can outfit yourself, but you *never* clothed our children! If it hadn't been for Dillena trying to guess their sizes and sneak the clothes to them, they would be bare to the world!"

Emelisse said nothing, and Grimme could not read the look on her face, somewhere between defiance, rage, and shame.

But Grimme was so enraged now that it was a wonder the water was not boiling. "Answer me this. What the bloody hell do you do all bloody day?"

She flinched a little. "Um ... sleep."

Grimme could not believe his ears. "Sleep. You sleep. Aye, very well. What do you do all bloody night but for the quarter hour you grant me the privilege of giving you release?"

She pulled her lips between her teeth. "Sleep," she whispered.

Grimme closed his eyes and took a deep breath. "Tomorrow morning," he gritted, "after breakfast, you are going to present yourself to Father Hercule and tell him you would like to learn how to read. After midday meal, you will go to the stables. You are going to tell the head groom that you wish to learn how to ride astride and groom a horse. You will do that every day from midday until supper until you can jump a stallion over a cow and groom him with your eyes closed. When you can do that, you will exercise the mares and groom them afterward."

"I will not," she hissed. "I don't *have* to learn how to read and I will *not* work like a peasant."

"Work like a peasant?" he chortled. "You've never worked at all! Even before Gaston, you barely cooked, barely cleaned. Ardith came and she cooked and cleaned. Dillena came. She cooked and cleaned. Maebh came. She cooked and cleaned. You did *nothing*. But I was gone most of the time, earning money to feed you lot, so I didn't notice. The other three didn't complain, but *you* did. In eleven bloody years, you have done not one bloody thing for me, and the *first* time I ask you to do something for me that does not involve my cod, you refuse—and not graciously, either."

"It's *her*," she snarled. "It's because she hates me!"

"Aye, she hates you and with good reason."

"You love her!"

"Oh, no, Emelisse, I love *you!*" he mocked in a girlish pitch. She hissed at him. "Unless you want me to put you out, you have three choices: You can *work* and contribute something to this household, you can learn something and be able to *talk* to me, or you can *fuck me* to my satisfaction."

"Very well," she sniped.

"Very well you'll exercise my mares and learn how to read?"

"No. I will fuck you to your satisfaction."

"Go to your chambers. I will be up in a while. If you do not do what I want, how I want, as many times as I want, with enthusiasm and without complaining, you will go to Father Hercule in the morning and to the stables in the afternoon."

BRÌGHDE AND Dillena were laughing about a puppet amusement they had seen in Hogarth when they and Pierce clip-clopped into the mares' stable after a very successful outing. All the boys had had fun and had only argued over who got the last almond tart. Before Brìghde could raise her voice, Dillena snatched it from them, split it in two, gave Brìghde one half and ate the other. Gaston's, Max's, and Terrwyn's knights had met them on the road between Kyneward and Waters to take the boys back to their encampment laden with two fresh changes of clothes and new boots whilst more were being made. The pack animals had been taken to the keep to be unloaded with all their purchases put in their respective chambers. Sir Thom and the rest of their guard went to the stallions' stable.

Thus it was that they came upon Emelisse attempting to sit a palfrey astride with two grooms' help. It wasn't going well. Brìghde and Dillena exchanged a look, turned around, and headed right back out of the stable to give her some privacy. Brìghde hissed at Pierce to come along as he was wont to stay there and snicker at her.

"Pierce!" she barked when he wouldn't obey. "Now!"

Grumbling, he turned his horse and slumped in the saddle with a sullen expression all the way out.

"Not that she doesn't deserve it," Brìghde muttered to Dillena, who tried to hide her smile. They all clip-clopped to the stallions' stable.

Supper was being served when they walked in, and the three of them took their chairs.

"Good eve, Brìghde," Grimme said cheerfully and leaned over to kiss her cheek.

A little surprised, she grinned. "Good eve, Grimme. Why are you so cheerful?"

"I have been *very* productive whilst you were gone."

"Oh? Does it involve a certain person having been persuaded to exercise the mares?"

"It does," he said happily.

"Aaaand … ?"

He slid her a glance. "If you don't want me to speak of you to them, do not expect me to speak of them to you. The only thing you need to know is that she is to spend mornings with Father Hercule and afternoons in the stables."

She pursed her lips and nodded approvingly. "Fair."

"Now, sleep with me tonight. I missed you terribly."

69

SUMMER FADED into autumn. Brìghde and Grimme were at one again, smiling, laughing, trading confidences. She slept in his chambers at least once a week, and he in hers other times during the week. Emelisse was learning to read and exercising and grooming mares, but not well or without much hatred and bitterness directed toward Brìghde. Brìghde did not suffer this silently or with any graciousness at all, gleefully returning her weak barbs with far more pointed ones. Grimme only had Emelisse (who was, according to Avis, too tired to entertain) and Dillena and the three maidservants; however, he had found two new maidservants in Hogarth and brought them home. Brìghde steadfastly refused to acknowledge their existence, leaving the maidservants' purpose to Kyneward Keep's young housekeeper Rose to manage.

Rose, who did not like Lord Kyneward *at all*, did not approve.

She was brash and bold, bawdy and funny, getting rid of the troublesome servants and teasing the remaining staff into doing what she wanted done. She was far more lax than Brìghde, but it worked, so Brìghde left her alone. The knight who had caught Rose's eye had requested Grimme's permission to wed her, which he gave happily.

Grimme's spies at Sheffield reported that the duke had no plans for Kyneward. Yet. However, the duchess had sent a missive asking if Brìghde would be putting on a fête to celebrate the marriage.

She wrote back that she was still in the process of turning Kyneward Keep into a place worthy of the celebration she planned, and would send invitations in January for a May Day celebration, near the earl and countess's one-year anniversary.

After receiving an angry missive from the king demanding Grimme reveal what had really happened at the dower house, Grimme had finally written the truth of everything, containing the reminder of the duke's shadowy right to the title, the attempt at claiming *droit du seignior,* and ending with the order to fight to the death at a friendly tournament.

Grimme had dreaded writing that missive, as he did not want to be seen as "running to da," but Henry was his only protection and he knew Grimme well enough to know when he was skirting the truth.

The harvest was beginning to come in. The threshers were hard at work. Kyneward Keep received its portion with the land steward and William counting it all as it came in. It was deep into autumn when the cold November rains came that William reluctantly approached Brìghde with bad news. He found her in the inner bailey by the small millstone the bakers kept for small batches of flour, where she and Mercury always spent time after breakfast.

"My lady, may I speak with you privately?"

"Aye, William," she breathed, alarmed, putting down her bucket of grain. "'Tis private here. Speak freely."

"We do not have enough food to last the winter."

Her heart started thundering in her chest. "What?" she whispered.

"I did not account for all the added staff, my lady," he said weakly. "And new villeins who have come to Kyneward, who have not had time to plant."

"We haven't had enough new staff and villeins to make any difference. What are you calculating?"

"Ah … well, uh … Lord Kyneward has … uh … also added three hundred new knights I did not know about until yesterday."

"That he didn't tell us about, you mean."

He flushed, "Ah … aye."

"But for that, we would have enough?"

"Aye."

"Take me around."

They started with the brand-new granary. It was full; however, he said, they needed a bigger one.

The chickens were getting old and their egg production was slowing down.

The cellars were packed with onions and pears, carrots, turnips, peas and beans of all types. There were wheels upon wheels of cheese. Also not enough. The cellars were not big enough to hold what they needed.

The pigs and cows and sheep currently being slaughtered and smoked and salted would not be enough, and even at that, they needed a bigger smokehouse than the one they had just rebuilt. They could not hunt for deer, boar, or game fowl because it was the king's forest and poaching was a high crime. Brìghde would *not* slay the ravens no matter what. They could fish; the streams had plenty of it. Mercury caught rabbits by the barrels. He *had* killed a deer, but Grimme had no knowledge of that.

They went to the stables. There were not enough oats for the horses, although, thankfully, they did have enough hay.

The spice closet was full. Grimme insisted on having bottles upon bottles of clove oil, which baffled her, as the cooks were not allowed to use it. They had ginger, frankincense, lavender oil and other medicinal herbs. They had everything Linota had asked her for.

She shook her head and said, "I'll have to be sparing. And we need more salt if we are to cure any more meat."

Brìghde groaned.

She, William, and the land steward spent the next week going around to the villeins and inventorying their goods for the winter. They didn't have enough to feed that many more soldiers, either. She and William went into Waters to survey the taverns. They had enough to feed the regular number of knights who took their meals there, but they *had* noticed the increase and they, too, were worried.

Other estates allowed their villeins to starve as long as the nobles were well fed; Brìghde's mother would not, for Lady Fàileach had often lectured to Brìghde that, long-term, the labor was worth more than what it took to keep them fed all winter. It surprised Brìghde that Sir John also held that philosophy, but from a merchant's experience, and had never allowed Kyneward villeins to go hungry. After having been a servant, Brìghde herself was all too aware that she could not allow anyone who depended on Kyneward to go hungry, for Kyneward depended on them.

Too, most nobles, save the ones on the border of Scotland, did not have standing armies to feed. Granted, the Kyneward rations were meager, hard biscuits, dried meat, and watered ale, but Sheffield didn't even do that much. Brìghde didn't know what Tavendish or Dunham did. Fàileach fed its army.

"Oh, Lord," she whispered, sick to her stomach.

"My lady," William groaned after every bit of bad news. "I feel it is my fault."

"Stop. William, 'tis *not* your fault, and I will not have you taking the blame. The first thing we do is ration. And then we will think of something else. Please find Lord Kyneward and meet me in Sir John's study."

He bowed.

She went down to the kitchens. "Linota, put that pot down. I need to talk to you privately."

"Aye, mum," she grunted.

"You know we don't have enough food to last through the winter."

"I gathered that."

"Cut the meals by a quarter."

She looked at the ceiling, waggled her fingers, muttered to herself, then looked at Brìghde and said, "Aye, mum." Then she returned and started barking orders.

There would certainly be no anniversary celebrations without proper food stores for winter and heaven knew what Brìghde would do about Christmas, with twelve days of feasting.

"My lady," William called from the top of the stairs. "We are waiting."

She ran up the stairs and swept into Sir John's office where he, Grimme, William, the land steward, and Rose sat or paced, wringing their hands.

"Brìghde," Grimme growled. "You took me off the training field for household business?"

"We do not have enough food to last us through spring."

All jaws dropped but William's.

"What?!" Grimme roared, hopping out of his chair to pace. "*Why?! I trusted you!*"

"*You* did not say a word about having added three hundred more knights to the household!" she accused, hurt that he had *now* found fault with her management as well as her desirability. "Even though we only provide biscuits and dried meat, that is quite a lot! This is *entirely* your fault because you thought *your* business was separate from *my* business."

"'Tis no one's fault!" Sir John barked. "We would not have had the stores whether he told you or not. It is the price of growth. In any business, there is always a space of time when an overabundance of opportunity is to be had, but one has not the resources to take it. I have been at the point many times in my life, and new growth is always painful."

William nodded. "Even if we had brought more in, we do not have the storage space for it all."

"We needed the knights. There is no question of that, and we need more, aye?"

Grimme nodded. "Henry leads his army into battle. At some point, he will die. At some point after that, Sheffield will feel free to attack, and I will not be taken unawares or unprepared. We will not starve. We have funds."

"Food that does not exist cannot be bought and we cannot eat silver," Brìghde insisted.

"I will send a message to Tavendish and see if they are open to selling some of their stores," Grimme returned.

"If they have enough, aye, but if they do not, we—" She took a deep breath. "We cannot pull food out of the ground at this late date. But there is another way. We will have to hunt. Deer, boar, fowl. We may lack bread and vegetables come February, but we will not want for meat."

Grimme shook his head. "No."

She looked at him and calmly said, "*All* your interests."

He dropped his face in his palm and rubbed his temples. "Let me consider."

70

GRIMME'S MOOD at supper that night could best be described as morose. The reduced portions had been noticed and there was much rumbling. He stood.

"At the moment, we do not have enough food to get through to spring," he stated baldly. "We have found solutions, but they will take time. In case those solutions do not come to fruition, we ration. A little food all winter is better than no food in the spring."

Then he sat and glanced at Brìghde's platter, which was sparse. He was quite sure she would suffer the most, because she ate the most. This night, however, she ate her reduced portion and drank a lot of wine. She would never forgive him if he ran out of Bordeaux.

"Brìghde," he whispered in her ear, leaning against her, "I sent a message out to Tavendish a half hour ago."

"At night?" she whispered back. "Do you think that's wise?"

"I would we get this settled as fast as possible."

"How far is it?"

"An hundred ten miles. I bid them only to take the message and return with a response. I hope to hear back within the week."

Brìghde sighed and went back to picking at her food and drinking.

He studied her surreptitiously, wondering how he could see the beautiful woman in front of him and not be able to rise. He was taking his powders and sleeping with her more and more often—generally naked—trying to *make* himself desire her. He kissed her neck whilst she slept, palmed her linen-covered breast, tucked his hand under her shift and stroked her legs, her mound. She did not awaken, but that was all for the better, for he did not rise.

She and his father were right about the babe, and Grimme had promised her he would try. But he *was* trying. He tried in those moments when she could not look at him with expectation and judgment, mockery and a complete lack of desire for him, when she could not witness his failure, be hurt by it, then punish him for it.

Every week that went by that he could not awaken her to a stiff cod, more guilt weighed upon him.

He had even tried going to Emelisse (who was now far more accommodating since she thought she could fuck her way out of studies and riding) to suck his cod to stiffness and then leaving her to fuck Brìghde, but by the time he slipped into bed with Brìghde, he was limp again.

He still had his voracious appetite for his women and maidservants—and he was fucking all five of the maids, hoping one of them would catch—but he could not seem to make it work for Brìghde, and he did not know how to solve the problem. He was writhing in guilt that he could fuck all night long, but *not* the person he *needed* to fuck.

What would it be like to lie in bed with Brìghde and talk about all manner of things after he'd fucked her, and before he did it again? He yearned for the day he could do that, yet …

He could explain *none* of this to her without the old argument rearing its ugly head, without her ridicule. He had tried to kiss her, but sleeping women did not kiss very well and if he kissed her whilst she was awake, she would know he had failed.

Again.

He was embarrassed, frustrated, confused, and carrying a great deal of guilt, and he had no one to talk to about this.

"Brìghde." She looked at him. He swallowed. "I— We— If I can't … Did you still intend to … find someone to … "

The anger flared in her eyes immediately and her jaw tightened. "You *promised*," she hissed. "I have been patient. I have said *nothing* to you, yet … silence. No hounding. Sleeping with you. Being friends again. And now you ask me if I shall find a stallion?" She swept her hand over the great room. "Pick someone. One's as good as another, aye?"

He flushed and went back to his supper. "Mayhap … " he tried again, even more delicately this time, "one of the maidser—"

Her snarl was ugly. "I am not," she hissed, "taking on a bairn from a *maid-servant* so you can keep your spindle from being dirtied by my cunte." He winced. "Don't you *ever* bring me one of your newborn bastards to me to claim as mine, for I will not."

And with that, she quit the table and slammed into Sir John's study.

"What did you do this time?" his father asked him wryly.

Well, he had no one else to talk to, so … He sketched it out quickly, ending, "And I can't tell her any of it!"

For once, his father was not angry with him, but his sad expression was somehow much worse. "I'm sorry, Son," he murmured. "I have no advice."

"Papa," he whispered urgently, "she does not want me, either. How are two people who don't want to fuck supposed to fuck?"

His father's brow wrinkled. "Are you *sure* she doesn't have any desire for you?"

"She's made it plain," Grimme muttered, embarrassed all over again. "And not for any reason of kindness, either. I may be cruel about it, but not purposefully. I have always been attempting to reassure her I will not rape her. But she taunts me with her lack of desire for me deliberately and as cruelly as possible."

His mouth flattened and he sat silent for a while, thinking. "You have destroyed any chance you may ever have had."

"Oh, God," Grimme groaned.

"I believe she has been lying to you about her lack of desire for you—"

"Did she tell you that?"

He hesitated. "Did it ever occur to you," he said slowly, "that if she found Aldwyn attractive, she would also find you attractive?"

Grimme blinked. "Ahhh, no."

"Has she *said* she does not find you attractive?"

"She *said*," Grimme said testily, "that I was better than Roger MacFhionnlaigh, but that bar was low, and that she could bear to have me in her without vomiting."

"That says absolutely nothing about *you*. There is only one reason she would lie to you about that, and that is fearing your refusal of her, and do not tell me you would not refuse her."

Grimme's jaw ground.

"Even if she were lying, it's too late." He paused. "You are doing to Brìghde what my wife did to me: She demanded my time, my attention, my approbation, for she was so needy, but would not be my lover."

Grimme thought he would be ill.

"Unlike Brìghde, however, my wife did not give me any of her time, had no attention to give me for she was unlearned and uninteresting, which are not the same thing, and indicated no appreciation for my presence. I *loathed* my wife for the same behavior you are subjecting your wife to. So why should she not be cruel to you when you demand her time and attention and approbation, her presence in slumber, but will not do the one thing she wants you to do? What is her alternative? Leaving? I would not be surprised if one day we wake up and she is not here."

Grimme ached with guilt and dread, and the idea that he would live the rest of his life without Brìghde … If she left, he would never be able to find her.

"Why don't you *want* to?" his father pled softly.

"My *mind* wants to," he hissed desperately. "It always has. I look at her and my mind sees a beautiful woman. My mind wants to fuck her, talk, sleep, wake up with her, fuck some more, talk some more, but my cod sees black hair and taunting and duty and humiliation—"

"It starts with the black hair, aye?"

Grimme nodded. "I told her why I don't like brunettes when she demanded to know—"

"She looks like a witch to you," Sir John said flatly, "aye, I know, so to keep from looking at her like a witch, you look at her like a man."

Grimme dropped his head. "She told you. Of course she did. Did she tell you about the ravens, too?"

Sir John shook his head.

"Aye, well. Here it is." But instead of being embarrassed at the pity he expected, he was shocked when his father's expression gradually turned thunderous, and Grimme wondered why it made him angry.

"I am going to kill that child," Sir John snarled.

Oh. He was furious with Grimme's older brother. Whilst Grimme was happy his father was furious with the instigator on his behalf, he did not think Sir John's fury was equal to the offense. "Why are you so angry?" Grimme asked, genuinely curious. "'Tis what brothers do."

"That affects more than your marriage," he growled, "and that is all I'm going to say about it to you. Your brother, on the other hand, is going to get an earful."

"Very well," Grimme said, confused, not daring to ask no matter how wildly curious he was, "but now she mocks me with it. Of all the people I could have trusted with that, I never thought *she* would do so."

His father released an angry hiss.

"And now we've got a food shortage and we need to work together, but she will again punish me by refusing to talk to me … "

"Lord, what a mess." Sir John began to rub his temple to calm his ire. After a while, he said wearily, "She bid you find a stallion?"

"Aye."

"Mouse is here. Throw him at her and see what she does. He won't have the same reservations Aldwyn did."

"And have him taunt me about whose child I'm rearing?" Grimme asked incredulously. "No."

"You boys give me a headache," he ground out. "All three of you."

With that, Grimme arose wearily and trudged to the stairs with a pat on his father's shoulder.

"You are the most fortunate bastard in the world," Mouse said from Grimme's bathtub when he attained his chambers.

"So I've been told," Grimme said wearily as he flopped on his bed, wishing Brìghde were with him, wishing he had not destroyed his truce with her, wishing he could fuck her. "What happened to Aldwyn?"

Mouse waved his hand. "He got sent out on training exercises."

"And Caroline?"

He grimaced. "That ... is an ugly situation."

"Very well. I will fetch her and the children since Aldwyn's gone—"

"Don't," Mouse said, yet again with the tone of command in his voice.

"But—"

"Don't," Mouse snarled. "If you value Aldwyn's life, do not do anything. She and the children disappear, he'll die, and whatever you think of it, being *raped* is survivable. *Dying* is not."

Grimme sighed. "How ugly is it?"

"Every night," he muttered. "All night."

"Brìghde has poison that can put him to sleep."

"He sleeps one night. He sleeps the next. He sleeps for a month. Eventually, he's going to realize he's being poisoned and will turn the keep upside down to find out who."

"You can poison the entire keep and his forces with what she has. I would never be implicated and no one knows you exist."

"I am many bad things, but I am *not* a murderer."

"Even though—?"

"Even though. I will not stoop to that."

That angered Grimme. "Have you ever seen true evil?"

The look Mouse cast him was deadly. "How can you ask me that?" he asked low, his voice thrumming with rage. "I *live* with it. Everything I do—"

"We."

"—we do is to get rid of it."

"But you will not do the one thing that *must* be done in the case of true evil. I have seen evil elsewhere. I have slaughtered it. It does not come back. It hurts no one ever again. There is *more* evil out there to be slaughtered, aye, but I have disposed of what was in front of me."

"And Aldwyn won't even do as much as I do. God, we're all hopeless."

"Noooo," Grimme corrected. "*You* and *Aldwyn* are hopeless. I have a plan, the will, capability, and motive. *You* have no will. Aldwyn has no plan *or* will *or* capability. You could do this easily, at any time. I can do this myself, not quite as easily, at any time. *You* are the one making the decisions right now, so do not make me regret trusting you to know when the time is right to strike."

Mouse sighed in concession.

"If you could get Brìghde into the keep—"

"I am not dragging a woman—a beautiful woman—a beautiful woman the duke wants and is enraged about not getting—which he is punishing Caroline for—into Sheffield for any reason." Grimme could appreciate that so he said nothing for a while, but then Mouse mused, "Why would you send a woman into such a situation?"

"She's not a *woman*," he muttered. "She's my dearest friend and companion-at-arms."

"We have trod this ground. I don't understand how you can be *friends* with a woman without dying to fuck her, or without her dying to fuck you, but that is not to the point. Why would you send your dearest friend, who happens to be small, delicate, and female, into such danger?"

"She thinks of herself as my weapon and I trust her. Small, delicate, and female is the perfect person to do the job."

"I'm not going to do it, so your weapon is going to stay alive if I have anything to say about it."

"What did you mean, not have a female friend without dying to fuck her or otherwise?"

"I don't befriend those I fuck, and I don't fuck my friends."

"Aye, we agree. So?"

"*You* have that policy because all your friends are male. *I* have that policy because I have fucked my female friends or refused to fuck them and it *never* turns out well. I *stopped* making female friends because of it."

"Then why are you confused about my not wanting to fuck Brìghde?"

"Because at some point in my friendships with women, my feelings turn from camaraderie to lust and, sadly, occasionally love. They don't return it and there I am with my cod in my hand craving them. Or they love me, but I do not love them and will not fuck them. Farewell the friendship. You and Brìghde are at odds over who's not fucking whom. Your friendship is *gone*."

Oh, God, that was what he was afraid of.

"No friend, no policy. You won't be fucking your friend. Have you *ever* wondered what it would be like to fuck a woman you care for as more than a cunte, then lie in bed and talk?"

Grimme said nothing for a moment. "'Tis all I *can* think about," he confessed reluctantly.

"That is where it starts."

Grimme tried to sift through what Mouse was saying, but couldn't. "I just want my friend back!"

"I promise that if you fuck her, you'll get your friend back."

"You cannot promise any such thing."

They were silent for a long while. Finally Grimme said, "At some point, I am going to rescue Aldwyn whether you tell me it is time or not."

"Aye," Mouse mumbled. "Because that's who you are." Then he sighed. "It has to be done when the whole family is together. Since I do not know where he is, it can't be done until he is back in the keep."

"No," Grimme said firmly. "You will find out where he is and send me word immediately, then slink back into the shadows and let me work."

"Very well," he grumbled, then waved a hand. "Begone. I need a nap. Go sleep with her and at least *try*."

71

WHEN BRÌGHDE awoke again, she was irritated that someone had let a cat into her chambers. She did not mind cats in her chambers, but they got impatient and yowled to get out again, which would mean Brìghde would have to get herself out of bed to let it out. This cat was lying heavily along Brìghde's ribs, but soon enough it would hie itself to the door and yowl to be let out.

Her eyes opened slowly. The cat was not breathing. Not moving. Not a twitch of a muscle or flick of an ear. Brìghde sighed heavily. It was cold in the room, the fire reduced to embers, but Grimme's body was big and warm, surrounding her, protecting her.

She wanted him so much, and he … did not want her. So much that he would prefer to rear another man's child than swive her. He would prefer to get a maidservant with child and pass it off as Brìghde's. Their truce was broken with those two questions, after months of not fulfilling his promise to her, and now he had used his key to unlock her door to sleep with her.

Suddenly, she felt him sweep her braid away from her neck, to be replaced by his mouth. She sucked in a little breath. He kissed her slowly, his mouth butterfly light. He touched his tongue to her neck and she whimpered, all those swirling tingles in her lower belly collecting and settling in her cunte, which clenched. Aye, she knew now, at least partially, how it felt to be desired by a man she also desired. She had seen enough to know what to expect, felt enough to know what her body would do.

His hand caressed her breast through her shift whilst he kissed her neck. She closed her eyes with a sigh, drawing her leg up to tighten her folds.

"I don't want to rear another man's child," he whispered in her ear. "I know you don't want to rear another woman's babe. I also know that you don't want me, but I will try to make it pleasurable for you."

She slipped her hand between their bodies and felt his spindle through his braies. Soft. She massaged him the way Aldwyn had encouraged. But he never grew, never got hard. She continued to try, but … nothing.

More. More time …

Squeezing, caressing …

More …

"How long?" she asked bluntly.

"How long what?" he asked, surprised.

"How long will I have to endure this forced amorousness before you're hard?"

"Will you allow me to at least *try?*"

"I flirted with Aldwyn for two minutes and he was hard. I have been caressing and squeezing you for a good ten minutes and you're still soft. You haven't even *kissed* me."

He sat up. "Are you going to compare me to Aldwyn every second of this?"

"*I* have an imagination," she barked, sitting up on the edge of the bed. "I know what is supposed to happen. I can simply pretend you're him."

"That is not a good way to get me to rise, my lady," he snarled. "If you know so much, then take my cod in your mouth and make me rise that way."

She shot him a nasty glare over her shoulder. "The seed does not plant going down the throat."

"You don't have to swallow," he barked. "You just have to get it to rise."

"And that is my responsibility."

"Aye, in fact, it is."

"When I walked into your chambers with the poisoned wine, the duke was pleasuring himself. Do that. I'll watch."

"*Excellent* idea, my lady," he sneered as he stood and shucked his braies, then fell back on the bed. Brìghde took her time studying his body, so big, so muscular. His spindle was long and thick. But of course it was. She arose and lit more candles, moved tables and stools this way and that so she could see well.

"Take your shift off."

She did so without a blink then crawled back on the bed and sat cross-legged with her hands folded primly in her lap, her knees nearly in his ribs.

He dropped his hand over the side of the bed and brought up a bottle of clove oil and poured a little into his hand. So *that* was what that was for. He wrapped his hand around his spindle and began to tug on it, just a little.

Brìghde was going breathless. She would have him inside her tonight. *Finally.* Her cunte clenched at the thought, and she wasn't sure she would need any of the kissing and touching she and Aldwyn had shared. And then, once Grimme had been inside her and had gotten his release with her, 'twould be no feat to do it again and again until she caught. She had many nights of passion ahead of her and her heart thundered and her cunte clenched in delicious anticipation.

His hand moved a little faster. She glanced at his face. He had his other arm behind his head and his eyes were closed. She was naked. Why were his eyes closed? Did he not want to see her body? Did he not want to touch her? If not, why had he wanted her to take her shift off?

She again went back to his spindle because it was beautiful and she wanted him and she would do anything he asked of her. She would do it better than his mistresses and maidservants did, so that he would have no reason to seek them out ever again. She wasn't sure *how* to do things better than his mistresses, but she would learn. The prize was too great not to.

For then she would become his one and only, and then he would tell her he loved her, and then he would discard his women, and then she would have his children, and then they could be a family the way he had been with his women and their sons …

His hand went faster. She again glanced at his face. His eyes were still closed. He grimaced. He squeezed harder. He got more oil without ever opening his eyes, and to pour it into his hand, he had to release his spindle, which was …

Limp.

She dropped her face in her hand.

He tried again, but now she was not looking. She could not bear to see her failure. She could have almost any man she wanted except the only one she truly wanted.

"Go away," she croaked.

"Brìghde … "

He wanted to leave. She could tell by his voice.

"Brìghde, you don't want me either! It doesn't help!"

"Would it if I told you I did?"

"That is the *second* time you have mocked me with that, my lady," he snarled. "Mockery and taunting do not help."

She had a choice to make. Convince him of the truth and risk this again, or let him go so she would not be further humiliated?

I want you, Grimme.

I love you, Grimme.

"Get out," she whispered, choking on her tears. "I will no longer allow you to humiliate me."

He didn't move. "I have been thinking," he mused. "All the things I have said about my desire for you or lack thereof are hurtful to you. I understand that. However, I have never intended to be cruel and you know that. I have apologized endlessly and yet you do not forgive."

"Aye, so what," she said snarled. "Intent and carelessness yield the same result and I canna forgive so long as the offender continues with the offense with no intention of changing."

"When you mock me, taunt me—you are being intentionally cruel."

That was true, but she could not let him know it was to be able to have some defense or he would want to know why she needed a defense. It was either that or fall at his feet and beg him for his love, his spindle, and his fidelity, none of which she would get.

"Why do you think that will help the circumstance?"

"Does it *hurt* the situation?" she asked snidely.

"Why would I *want* to fuck a woman who is deliberately cruel to me?" he asked coolly. "How am I to rise for a woman when I know that she will mock me for being unable to?"

She gulped, shame flooding her, and her face getting hot.

"Mayhap," he said pleasantly enough as he got out of bed and strode to the door, "I will not allow *you* to humiliate *me* any longer."

He opened the door, but Brìghde scrambled off the bed and slammed her body against it, keeping it closed.

"You do not have to worry about my hounding you any longer," she said low, her body quivering with rage and pain. "It is not my place to care more about the longevity of your earldom than you, the earl. You were not meant to be an earl, you have no interest in being an earl, you don't want to learn how to be an earl, you don't want to be here at all. You don't care about your women. You don't care about your children. You don't care about me. You don't care about Sheffield. You don't even care about Henry. All you want to do is go back to France and slay men you see as your enemy for God knows what reason, then wade through their blood after you have done so." *Then* she opened the door and swept her hand through the air. "So do that and get out of my way."

HE AND EMELISSE were absent from breakfast the next morning.

72

BRÌGHDE PICKED at her midday meal. Emelisse was present though Grimme was not. When a knight called "my lady!" she looked up and he threw a jest at her. She grinned and returned it. Then the jests and insults flew across the hall as if she were one of them. Eventually, however, they departed to go back to the practice fields. As she gathered herself to leave also, she happened to glance at Emelisse, who was staring at her with a triumphant smile on her face. She was sitting back, her arms crossed over her chest, one knee over the other.

Gloating.

Brìghde waggled her wedding ring.

That hardened her expression and she looked away.

"Remember that," Brìghde said coolly.

"May you find yourself at the mercy of a babe in winter."

Since Emelisse had said it in French, Brìghde rose as if she hadn't heard her, then went to Sir John's study.

"What was that about?" Sir John asked when he shuffled into the study and closed the door behind him.

"I leave your son's spindle limp."

"That is the entire problem, aye," he said vaguely, looking over a list. "What is the difference about today?"

"Today Emelisse made a point to remind me."

"Hag," he muttered.

"Aye, and she cursed me again."

Sir John rolled his eyes.

Over the past many weeks since the tournament, she had deliberately blocked Grimme's promise from her mind and luxuriated in everything he had given her and in their reestablished camaraderie, taking what she could get, not taking it for granted, waiting patiently so that when the time was right, she would be pleasantly surprised. She was dressing better. She was wearing a wimple that covered her hair.

But every week that had passed that he hadn't even *tried,* it got more and more difficult to keep herself from thinking about it. With his questions about her finding a stallion after all, or if she would be willing to take a maidservant's bairn as her own, and with the humiliating attempt he had made *with his eyes closed*, his desperation to avoid swiving her was devastating. And he thought she was mocking him when she ventured toward him in spite of her fear.

How in the world was she supposed to get anywhere with him when he continually cut her off, assumed what she was thinking, and expected her to act and react like a man?

Every time Emelisse or Dillena were absent from breakfast when he was, it had made her angry. Every time she got her courses, it had made her angry. Every time she looked into his empty chambers when the door was open when she passed by, it had made her angry.

She had sat beside him in bed eager, *hoping*— How, with his knowledge of women, could he mistake her eagerness for anything *but* desire?

What could he *possibly* say that would ease the burden of her repulsiveness?

Take what you can get.

She couldn't do that anymore.

Don't take it for granted.

No amount of love and praise Sir John and Pierce could shower her with was going to fill the hole in her heart and soul.

She was not about to take any stallion, for she did not give a whit about having a child for any reason if 'twas not Grimme's— Last night— *Right there*— His beautiful body on display, hers as well—that he refused to look at—as she sat there *knowing* her hopes would at last come true, and ...

She had forgiven him everything but that, and she could not whilst he acknowledged his error but refused to correct it.

The week wore on. She had much to do and the messenger returned from Tavendish saying that aye, between Tavendish and Dunham, they could spare the stores, especially the salt. That would be *very* expensive, but if Grimme allowed them to hunt, they would need as much as they could get.

She, Sir John, and William all breathed a huge sigh of relief, and began laying plans with Sir Thom.

Grimme appeared at supper, but she could not stand to look at him. She did not speak. She ate her portion, drank several pitchers of wine, did not bother to request excusal, and joined Sir John in his study for a quiet game of chess. However, William was already there playing with him. Thus, she roamed about his impressive library and chose a book of Gaelic verses.

"You speak Gaelic?"

"No," Sir John murmured. "I was born in London and spent most of my life there. I have only been here as long as Grimme has. I simply thought the books lovely, and I like to have lovely things."

"Ah." She paused. "You would like Dillena's artwork, then."

He hummed as his hand hovered over his rook.

The verses were uninteresting, but she read so as to pass time somewhere other than her chambers looking at the bed where her failure had been on prominent display. But eventually, she sat there looking at the fire, and sorting through her thoughts.

Their truce had been temporary. After the tournament, when he paraded her so brilliantly, presented them as a powerful lord and lady, had outwitted the duke, and pledged his life to her she had forgiven him everything.

He atoned for his betrayal of her to his mistresses when he allowed her to send Maebh away, for she knew very well it was only by his leave that it could happen.

His betrayal of Aldwyn was insignificant as compared to Aldwyn's betrayal of his wife, too cowardly to fight for her and so much pride in his honor he would not ask for help from men he *knew* would give it immediately and freely.

Ravens, nightmares, and witches were the gifts she had given Grimme on the lists, and he had accepted them when he accepted her black ribbon with a smile of understanding and gratitude. Aye, he had dropped it in the dirt, but then he had retrieved it, kissed it, and worn it to confront Sheffield.

He had made up for his disappearance immediately after her mother interrupted them by respecting Brìghde's insistence that Emelisse not be allowed to go to Hogarth with them.

She had forgiven him everything when she realized that he'd acquired the weapon to outwit the duke to protect her before she demanded he do so.

And yet it wasn't enough.

She loved him.

She. Loved. Him.

She wanted him to love her in return, wanted him to lust for her the way he lusted for seven other women, wanted him to cast them all aside and swear love and devotion and his spindle solely hers.

That was never going to happen, she realized now, and she would not wait for eleven years as Emelisse had. She was pathetic, and Brìghde had never been nor would she ever allow herself to be so. Brìghde did not have the same compunction to stay that Emelisse did and she determined to leave. The Kyneward earldom could stuff itself down the garderobe.

She left Sir John and William with a weary "Good eve" that they barely returned, they were so engrossed. She trudged up the stairs only to see Grimme's door open. It was empty. She sighed and turned the key in her lock—which locked it. She dropped her head on the wood then reluctantly unlocked it.

"What are you doing here?" she asked quietly as she entered. It was dark except for the fire.

"Budgie."

She closed her eyes.

"What can I do?"

Love me.

"The *first* thing you can do is not leave my bed after humiliating me, then go straight to Emelisse's and gloat to her how you humiliated me."

"What?! I did no such thing!"

"Did you or did you not leave me and go swive Emelisse all night?"

Silence.

"Did you or did you not give her a reason to gloat at me all the way through midday meal?"

"I did not," he said immediately. "I would not do that to you."

"You've *done* it before. What did you say to her?"

"She asked me why I already smelled of clove oil. I said I had been with you. She said it hadn't been long enough for me to have been with you."

Brìghde was confused. "What does that mean, long enough? It doesn't take very long."

"Brìghde," he said low in his chest, "we are talking about *me*. If I had been with you, I would not, an hour later, have gone … to … her … "

Brìghde stuck her tongue in her cheek.

"Oh."

"Mmm hm. I had to remind her I'm the one with the wedding ring and 'Lady' in front of your name. So. When are you leaving for France or must I put the force together myself?"

"Not whilst we have a food shortage," he growled.

"All you have to do is allow us to hunt, and you may go."

He hesitated. "I … don't want to—"

She waited for him to finish the thought. "Then I will give the order myself and you can escape responsibility."

"I am not talking about hunting!" he roared, getting off the bed and beginning to pace. "Hunt all you want—I care not. I don't want— I don't know what I want! I don't—" He thrust his hands into his hair. "What I don't want is to be away from *you*."

How many more arrows to her heart must she endure? "We are at an impasse, then, as I canna bear to be in the same room with you. Get out."

73

GRIMME WAS informed of the success of the messenger's quest to Tavendish and the imminent departure of his wife to fetch the food when he heard the wagons being hitched long before sunrise the next morning, and he only heard them because he had not been able to sleep.

He rushed down the stairs and out into the bailey with nothing but torches for light. There, Brìghde was dressed in page's woolens, standing in the middle of everything, directing this knight and that servant to put this there and that here.

"What is going on?" he demanded tightly.

In the torchlight, he could see her surprise. "Why ... we are going to Tavendish. Did Sir John not tell you?"

Of course not. It was household business, Grimme did not want to be involved with household business, and Sir Thom's force was Brìghde's to command.

"You do not need to go."

"I am castellain," she said flatly. "'Tis household business and my responsibility."

It was, in fact, but her scathing rebuke the night before had not gone unpondered. He realized that the first thing he needed to do was decide what, precisely, he wanted. He didn't know. He had never known what *he* wanted. He had lived most of his life at war and enjoying battle, never giving a thought to his women or his children. When he was home, he itched to go back because he didn't want anything else.

But now he wanted something he could not name. It was a seed of a feeling down deep in his breast that he could not capture, and had not known was there until Brìghde had ordered him back to France.

"I will be well protected," she said tersely, but he barely heard her. He needed her to stay so that he could confess these things and seek her advice, but she could not bear his company.

He scoured his mind for one thing, *anything*, to say that didn't make him sound like a lackwit. "Are you taking Mercury?"

"No," she said with contempt. "He is not a war dog. He is a deerhound and you will need him to hunt. He will beg me to ride in my lap. Unfortunately, my big black bitch from hell is dead."

He stalked away from her to find Sir Thom, who was surprised and told him, "Sir John bid me, at your behest, he said. As he is castellan, I thought nothing of it."

Grimme's jaw ground. "Get it straight from me next time."

"Aye, my lord. I apologize. Do you want me to dismantle or change the operation?"

"Who planned the expedition?"

"I did."

"Then no."

Grimme stood with his legs splayed and his arms crossed over his chest as he watched the preparations winding up and his wife, looking even tinier in her boy's clothing than she did in her wedding dress, a squire much taller than she dressing her in the leather gambeson and mail Grimme had had made for her so long ago as a jest. Then "her" squire fastened a heavy green woolen cape around her as if he were a mother dressing a child.

She was leaving. Aye, she was going on Kyneward business, but Tavendish was only ten miles south of Dunham and she could choose not to return. The possibility of never seeing Brìghde again was …

Devastating.

Grimme threw his hands up and stalked toward her. Of course the woman was going to ride two hundred twenty miles round trip dressed like a knight. No carriage for her, oh *no*, not unless she was the one driving it. He brushed the squire away, turned her toward him, clasped her face between his hands.

"My lord?"

"Shut up," he muttered and kissed her.

Hard.

He swallowed her gasp, took the opportunity to nudge her mouth open, and touched his tongue to hers. She sighed into his mouth and returned the kiss. He deepened it, felt her acceptance, her eagerness, and wondered …

He broke away to pick her up by the waist and throw her on her stallion's back. She gaped down at him whilst he glared up at her.

There were so many things he wanted to say to her, now, before she went out on an excursion as if she were a warrior. Would she come back? What would happen if she didn't? She was wrong that he didn't care about her. He could not *bear* it if she didn't return. There were so many things he needed to say to her, tender things—

"Don't die," he snarled, then stalked back into the keep.

74

BRÌGHDE HAD two hundred twenty miles and approximately four weeks to think about that kiss, which she refused to do.

She rode near the front of the party, though Sir Thom refused to allow her to be at the very front. She obeyed without question. The only thing he said when she attached her sword to her saddle was,

"You know how to use that thing?"

"Out of practice, but I think I can hold my own."

"Aye, then. If we are attacked, let the horse lead and move with him as you did when you outran Sheffield's knight. Use your knees to hold on so your hands are free to use your sword and dagger, as you did in Hogarth. He knows what to do in a battle. Can you remember that?"

"Aye."

It was a force of thirty armored knights and twice the number of leather-and-mail-clad soldiers driving the carts, with one squire per knight and one for her. They were well provisioned for the trip, with hundreds of pounds of dried venison and hard biscuits, and many barrels of ale. It had been carefully and tightly packed in one wagon, as the others would be needed to carry stores back to Kyneward.

The days were cold, foggy, and misty. The nights were freezing, foggy, and misty, and she slept in a tent on the ground like everyone else, squeezed between Sir Thom and her squire covered in woolens. It took them seven days to reach the manor house at Tavendish Grange, at Berwick-upon-Tweed, perching menacingly on the cliffs overlooking the sea.

The morning of the day they were to arrive, Brìghde took care with her toilette, to attire herself in one of her heavy woolen gowns, green to match her eyes and the Kyneward livery, and all the destriers were dressed. She rode at the front, her gown spread over Troy's rump and the staff of her husband's standard perched on her foot, waving proudly in the sea breeze.

Henry Raxham, Lord Tavendish, along with his lady wife, met them some distance away from the manor. "Countess Kyneward, welcome," he said gravely.

Brìghde bowed her head. "Earl Tavendish, Countess Tavendish. Kyneward thanks you for this boon."

"'Tis no boon when you've the coin," the earl said wryly.

"One cannot eat silver and gold, my lord," she smiled back.

"Come."

Thus, Brìghde handed off the standard and was welcomed to ride between the earl and his countess. "I will tell you," she said lightly, "that I am not trained in diplomacy, nor am I particularly diplomatic. Please forgive me in advance for any offense I give."

The countess laughed and the earl grinned at her. "You're Walter Fàileach's girl, who outwitted him. We have a good idea what we're getting."

"I have had no news of attack from Fàileach. He has been quiet?"

"He's always quiet," the earl said. "I heard Sheffield paid five knights' ransom to Kyneward. How did a vassal come to snatch his liege's knights so that he could demand ransom and get it?"

Brìghde pulled her lips between her teeth and looked up to the sky for guidance. She knew Grimme had written the missive, but had he gotten a response? "There was a … misunderstanding. At our border."

"Aye, aye, we know that," the earl said a little impatiently. "That was in the deliberately vague missive your husband and Sheffield sent to the king. What was the nature of the misunderstanding?"

"Ah … the Sheffield knights tried to steal something. Our knights defended and vanquished."

Lady Tavendish looked at her with a raised eyebrow. "What did they want?" she asked flatly.

Brìghde gave up and huffed. "Me."

"Do you mean to say—"

"Our dower house is in the southwest corner of Kyneward, bordered on both sides by Sheffield," she began. She was going to tell them everything because that was what she always did. "Sheffield patrols that border."

"He patrols the border between him and his vassal?" Earl Tavendish asked, shocked.

"Aye. I wanted to see our dower house … " She told the tale, but not the way she and her knights re-told it to each other, getting bigger and more dramatic with each telling.

The earl and countess remained silent. Then the earl said, "That is a serious accusation, my lady."

"'Tis why the ransom agreement was deliberately vague. His knights saw me and took the opportunity. But that is also why he paid the ransom."

"That is the more concerning point of the plot, as well as the fact that he patrols his border with his vassal. There is no reason for that."

"We … My husband, that is, believes that Sheffield wants Kyneward, and that the patrol is a reminder to us that he is always watching."

"I find it unlikely that a duke with such vast lands is overwrought about twenty thousand acres that never belonged to him in the first place."

"My husband says he was unofficially promised it, but the king gave it to my husband instead."

Both Tavendishes looked at her strangely. "By *whom?*"

"I don't know."

"'Twould seem to me you are here for more than food, then."

Brìghde said nothing because she did not how to negotiate a treaty of protection, though Sir John had told her to try, and tutored her a bit.

"I will be blunt: the king is not pleased, and has asked me to look into the matter and mitigate."

Her heart started thundering. "Is he angry with us?"

"Both Sheffield and Kyneward. But more than that, he is puzzled."

"But ... Grimme wrote and explained everything."

"Oh. Well, we have not heard from him in some time, so the missives may have crossed. I will write. If it as simple as lands promised but not given, we may be able to negotiate something."

"Negotiate what?" Brìghde asked, confused. "Give him half our land? Three quarters? Of twenty thousand acres? Why not all of it? What is there to negotiate?"

"We will discuss it later. Let us dine and speak of happier things."

BRÌGHDE AND her forces left Tavendish a week later laden with enough salt to preserve every hoofed, winged, and finned animal on Kyneward land, and grain, cheese, and vegetables that would last them well into spring with careful husbanding.

She also left with the start of a good friendship with both Tavendish *and* Dunham, whose laird and lady were awaiting Brìghde's arrival, with her brother Archie. It was a joyous and tearful reunion with her brother, who had inspected her for signs of abuse or anything untoward that Kyneward might have done to her, and the Dunhams, with whom she had spent quite a bit of time in the days preceding the wedding.

After she and her knights were situated, the lot of them were then welcomed in the great hall to much regalement. Archie stood and described the "abduction" as it looked from his view. He over-exaggerated, and when she called him on it, it made everything funnier. Then Brìghde stood and described it from her view, exaggerated but adjusted to account for the fact that it was supposed to have been planned.

The entire hall of knights was roaring by the time Archie and Brìghde finished. They grinned and hugged, and she whispered, "I need to talk to you."

"Aye."

After supper, she and the other nobles retired to the library, where they chatted about light things, but then discussed their food shortage and the reason for it.

"And so you were chosen to bear your husband's banner," Dunham murmured wistfully, sliding his wife a loving glance that she returned.

Brìghde's smile faded as she remembered the kiss Grimme had given her and could not, for the life of her, understand why he had done such a thing, especially after she'd ordered him back to France. "I simply assumed I would be the one to come. I am castellain and 'tis my responsibility and, ultimately, my fault that I did not account for our growth."

Tavendish waved a hand. "'Tis a good problem to have—as long as you have the coin to see you through. He is a good lord, then?"

"He is a knight first and foremost. His father is a merchant, and took it from where it started to its blossoming now. My clerk came to us from Medici Bank in Italy and has been a great boon to our recordkeeping." That impressed everyone, and she smiled. "We have a land steward now and may have to hire another. I will take over as castellain in full when Sir John deems me fit or—" She sighed. "Well, he is old."

Everyone sobered for a few seconds, then Lady Dunham teased, "And when are we going to hear about a new little earl?"

Brìghde blushed, but she had to fake a shy little smile. "When God wills."

It was deep into the night after she had gone to bed when it occurred to Brìghde that perhaps she had been too free with information with people she had *just met* and she wrung her hands, but 'twas too late. *Why* had she trusted these people? Because they made her feel welcome and laughed at her jests? Because they seemed to *like* her?

She started to breathe a little harder and tears pricked her eyes that she had blundered so very, very badly. Why was Sir Thom not with her? Because she had told him she did not need him, but she *did*. He would have known what to say and what not to say and warned her.

Never had she felt so young and so lack-witted. Twenty-three and bearing her husband's standard to negotiate for food— Why, 'twas what Grimme had said! She thought she knew everything and was always *right*. Never mind Sir John seemed to agree with her, this was a diplomatic task and she had just given away all of Kyneward, and then Grimme would think her disloyal, when she was not.

She was just stupid.

But her brother was among them and her brother had never made a bad alliance in his life.

The next morning after breakfast, Archie dragged her out to the stables, tossed her in her saddle and they took out over the moors, riding along the cliffs. When they had run their horses as much as they needed, they pulled up and walked.

Archie looked at her soberly and said, "How did you meet Kyneward?"

Brìghde tried the same lie that had worked on their mother, but he gave her a stony look. She sighed. "Do *not* tell *anyone*. Vow."

He raised his hand. "I vow."

"It really was an abduction," she said wearily. "He thought I was Meg."

Archie was aghast, and grew more aghast as she laid out every detail for his inspection, including Walter's plan for MacFhionnlaigh, including her part as Trojan horse, including the threat the duke presented, including Grimme's women, including his distaste for brunettes—

"Ravens?" he asked, confused. "What—?"

"I don't know. Suffice it to say there'll be no wee earls comin' along."

"Budgie, why dinna ye tell me any o' this whilst Fàileach was preparin' ye to take MacFhionnlaigh?" he asked wearily when her tale came to a close. "I would've helped ye. Dunham, Tavendish—"

"Archie, he never said a disparagin' word to me for *two years!*"

"His favor is *always* fleeting!"

"Ye doona ken ... "

"Sis," he said weakly, and she could see tears sparkling in his eyes, "we've guarded each others' backs all these years, all allied against the same man. Why did ye think we'd abandon ye when ye needed us most? At the very least, ye coulda told me before the weddin' an' I woulda objected an' taken ye back to Dunham."

"He had the point of a sword in my back, Archie," she insisted, unable to discern if Archie knew of Sir Bart's plot, "ready to run me through. Grimme surprised him."

"It coulda turned out so much differently! Aye, clearly God's hand's in it, an' it sounds like a better marriage than many nobles have, but what if it had been a man like Sheffield?" No, he didn't know. "Ye shoulda told us."

"*I shouldna had to!* Once, just *once*, I'd like for *one male* in me life to care enough about me to *protect* me w'out havin'a be asked, coerced, told, prompted, trapped, or begged. Ye *knew* I dinna wanna marry Roger. Ye've known since we were bairns. Ye *knew* Roger hates me but would *love* to swive me. *You knew!*

Six brothers, me allies, all of us with a common enemy, an' ye *left me* when I needed ye most! I dinna fight me abduction because I thought *you* had staged it, but noooooo. That level o' plannin' is beyond yer ken."

"You didn't think of it, either!" he barked.

"I did too!" she screamed. "Walter had me practically locked in my chambers, sent his black guard out with me, put me on the slowest nag in the stable— I had a plan. Several. I could implement none of them." She paused, then muttered, "Sir Bart was going to snatch me. Grimme got there before he could."

He blinked. "Oh. Well, then. *He* dinna have to be prompted."

"It only took *twenty-two years,*" she said flatly.

"Budgie," he whispered, clearly stricken, "I … "

"Why am I always left to defend myself? Does *no one* care enough about me to think through the entire situation? It didn't *occur* to Grimme to protect me against the duke until he was humiliated enough to do somethin'. He ultimately protected me, aye, but only because it was in *his* interest to do so. Sweet Mary an' Joseph, an' here I was thinkin' I could come to you if I left Grimme to his own devices. The *only* bein' to *ever* care about me that much was a *dog* an' I got her killed. Oh, an' even then she wasna male."

She turned Troy, who was more than happy to go because he had sensed her distress and the reason for it.

"Budgie, stop," Archie said, reaching out to take Troy's bridle. Troy tossed his head, but Archie had a good hold. "I am sorry."

"That—does—not—help! Let him go!"

Archie released Troy's bridle. "What can I do to assuage you?"

"Nothing," she snarled. "Nothin' short'a killin' Fàileach an' Duke Sheffield, nothin' short'a shovin' an iron rod up Grimme's spindle—"

He flinched, grimaced, and pulled his legs together.

"—or givin' 'im a love potion assured to make 'im fall in love with me forever an' desire me as he ought an' no other, will assuage me an' not even then because the damage is done *an' I canna forget!"*

She cantered off, away from Tavendish Keep, for she did not want to go back angry and at odds with Archie. She also could not see which way she was because her eyes were filled with tears. She let Troy have his head.

Archie fell in beside her and they rode together in silence until Troy felt like walking, but he walked out of arm's reach of Archie.

"I know about Sir Bart," she muttered.

"Oh, aye? I wondered when Moom would tell ye."

"I'm happy, but I doona ken what's got Walter on Moom's leash. Why does he allow her to order him about? She's got seven bairns from another man that he's supported, an' never punished her for spearin' 'is shoulder."

"I don't know, but it has to be somethin' big."

"Why does she stay with him when she and Sir Bart could run away?"

His jaw dropped. "Where else would she go that Walter wouldna find her? Budgie, doesn't it *ever* occur to you that other women are not like you? *You* could leave Kyneward, make yer home outdoors, feed yerself off the land, an' survive until ye could find a better circumstance fer yerself, an' ye'd ne'er allow yerself to be found. Moom would ne'er do that even if she could. She loves her comforts too much, an' she would never lower herself to work for a wage as you did, an' she's gettin' on in years. *And* may I remind ye, ye dinna ask for help *then*, either. You *know* Hamish'd helped ye if ye'd written to come fetch ye from the convent. But noooooo, ye had to do it yerself, the way ye've always done it."

"Noooo," she drawled angrily. "*None* of ye was available. Do ye think yer knights woulda said, 'Certainly, me wee squire, I'll letcha traipse 'cross the country to fetch yer wee sister. Here's some coin fer yer journey.' Sir Bart knew somethin' had happened. He said I came home hard an' wary, an' Moom ne'er noticed."

"Aye, and that's the *reason* we forget ye're a lass—"

She cringed.

"But once upon a time, ye took pride in that! 'Tis not yer fault. Ye never had a chance for suitors so ye dinna know what it was like to be treated like a desirable lady by men who were free to court ye an' take ye to wife an' care for ye as ye deserve. Ye hate Roger but as ye'd be livin' with his moom, ye'd not had anythin' ta do anyway, so there was no gain for ye to learn womanly arts. I've seen ye with yer knights. Ye laugh an' jest with 'em as if they're yer companions-at-arms. Ye're near as vulgar as they are, an' ye know way too much for a lass, much less a *virgin*. They should be sober, quiet, awaitin' yer orders, yet ye treat 'em as friends an' they feel free to speak with you as an equal. Ye have yer own bloody squire!

"It would occur to *no one* that ye canna take care o' yerself, *including* Walter, which was why he locked ye up and had a sword in yer back. He *knew* ye'd find some way to outwit him because ye *always have*. An' now ye've got a husband who thinks of ye as his dearest friend, a man, an' as he doesna find men in the least attractive, he canna rise. Ye're stuck havin' the thinkin' an' strength of a man an' the sensibilities of a woman, an' ye refuse ta change! Doesna help you ride a charger, astride yet. Wearin' pages' clothing an' leather an' armor. I'm sure *that* was attractive."

"Aye, and then that was when he kissed me. *For the first time!*"

Archie shrugged helplessly.

"An' what should I do? *Embroider?*" she sneered. "Play the lyre all day? Spend me day primpin' in case he chooses to grace me with his presence when he has *other women* doin' the same? Women he *wants* to swive?"

"Ye probably ought to consider the lyre again. Ye're good at it."

"True, but I don't enjoy it enough to spend time practicin', an' he won't care. I wear fine clothes, fine jewels. Me hair is always perfectly an' wonderfully coiffed. I can read an' write an' sum. I speak properly when I'm nae drunk or wi' me family. How else can I make 'im see me as a woman w'out abandonin' me knights at supper?"

"*Budgie!* Yer knights should be respectin' ye as a lady, not tellin' tales of the harlots they've swived along the way because ye think it's funny! They treat ye like a man because ye act like one!"

"An' whose fault is that, I'd like ta know."

He ignored that. "Moom's right. Act like a lady an' maybe he'll start lookin' atche that way."

They continued on because Brìghde was too angry and she would remain that way. It was December. They were buffeted by the sea winds, the air heavy with moisture. She was damp and freezing. Troy was likely too. But her anger and frustration kept her from being able to socialize.

After some time, she muttered, "How did Walter react when ye read him my missive?"

"Oh, Budgie," he drawled, his humor coming back. "I wish ye'd been there to see it. He destroyed his study, an' all the while Moom cacklin' so she couldna breathe, tauntin' him, enragin' him all the further."

"Do ye think he plans to bring a force to Kyneward? Moom wouldn't know, so I dinna bother to ask."

"He's go' bigger problems right now. The MacFhionnlaighs are still furious."

"Not Roger, I'll wager."

"Nay, he's happy. They might be dimwits, but they can make any problem six times larger an' require sixty times more resources than it would otherwise." Archie sobered. "Dunham'll see to Walter. You need to worry about yer liege. Yer *husband* needs to come ask Tavendish for help 'imself. We can see why you, as castellain, would come for the food. Ye shouldna be negotiatin' treaties o' protection, especially since ye canna keep yer mouth shut to people ye doona know."

"Did I say too much?" she asked in a small voice.

"Aye," he said flatly.

"Oh, Grimme's gonna be so angry wi' me ... " she whispered, wringing her hands.

Don't die.

Brìghde was forced back indoors if only for her pet's sake and was thus forced to let the conversation go. Nothing was going to change it. Nothing was going to change her. Nothing would heal her wounds or salve her anger but time, and that was doubtful. She really just wanted Grimme to go back to France.

The rest of the week was spent in much more pleasant conversation. The negotiations for food began two days before they were to leave, as Sir John had warned her.

Don't snub their hospitality. Stay, enjoy their company, then let the negotiations begin. They will signal when 'tis time.

She came to reasonable terms with Tavendish, then she and her party went north with the Dunham company to negotiate for the last of the supplies Kyneward needed.

Then they set out for home and the entire way, Brìghde dreaded what her husband would say when she told him of the words she'd spilled.

Yet at night when they made camp, she could only remember how, on their journey from MacFhionnlaigh to Kyneward, Grimme had slept behind her. And then as soon as they made Kyneward he had been welcomed home by four women who had more of him than Brìghde ever would.

His children.

... very essence of what I find terrifying about ravens ... very essence of what I find admirable in men ... how am I supposed to see you any other way?

It was on the fourth day they were attacked.

By whom, why, she did not know, but so far as she knew, Tavendish and Dunham were the only people who knew their travel plans, and Brìghde had given them everything they needed to know to attack, steal the food back, and leave Kyneward without a countess and an heir.

She found herself in the middle of it. "Sir Thom!" she called. "Protect the food or we all die!"

He nodded his understanding and she found herself matching swords with the bannerless brigands. She left the reins draped over her lap, drew her dagger, and tightened her knees to hang on, hoping Troy would not throw her. And Troy, so gentle with and protective of her, turned into a snarling beast of prey and carried her into battle as if she were a real knight.

She wasn't. This was not real, she knew. These were just her brothers coming after her to challenge her, putting her to the test because that was what she had demanded they do.

Doona grant me mercy just because I'm a wee lassie.

Remember ye said that when ye're covered in bruises tomorrow.

Just her brothers, she chanted to herself as she fought alongside the knights and foot soldiers, and she would not let her brothers best her. Yet *this* time, she was allowed to run a man through and she did. Troy wheeled around from the man she had just killed and she was presented with a stallion's rump, which she stabbed up to the hilt.

The horse screamed. Reared. Troy backed away. The rider was thrown. Another of her men speared the brigand in the eye.

Then it was over.

Twenty-three of over an hundred of their party were dead, three of whom were armored knights, and many more wounded. Brìghde was bloody from the cuts through her mail and gambeson and every part of her hurt. Her shoulder was aching terribly. Troy was also covered in blood, some of it his. His chest heaved.

Sir Thom swept his helm off to survey the damage. He looked at Brìghde soberly as she slipped her cloth-lined mail hood back. She glanced at their caravan.

"But by God, we saved the food."

Then she threw up.

75

GRIMME RODE out hard to meet the slowly returning party that was thrice as long as the one that had left almost four weeks ago, and his mouth dropped open to see how bedraggled they were.

Brìghde rode at the front, Sir Thom at her side. She was bearing the staff of the Kyneward banner on her foot and it flew proudly.

That wasn't right. She should have been in the middle, guarded by his knights.

Heads were going to roll—right after he got everybody patched up.

"Brìghde!" he roared and kicked Ares to go faster, flying over browned and fallow fields, leaping fences and streams. "Brìghde!"

He wheeled his mount around as soon as he drew alongside and said ... nothing. Because he was speechless. Brìghde's face was covered in bruises and she was holding the banner staff with the wrong hand. Her other arm was in a sling, and she was depending on Troy to do her thinking. She looked like she had aged ten years and her emerald eyes were bloodshot. Her beautiful black hair was now just past her shoulders, ragged at the ends, sheared off by a knife somewhere along the way. There were holes in her mail and her gambeson was leaking stuffing.

His knights' armor was badly dented.

"Brigands," she said curtly, her eyes forward. She had not looked at Grimme once. "But by God, we saved the food."

Her chest heaved and her mouth trembled and her face was wet. She was crying.

"You fought?" Grimme croaked.

"Valiantly," Sir Thom said curtly. "My lord."

Grimme had seen battle most of his life. He understood that haunted look in Brìghde's eyes, the one young men got after their first battle, so much worse than the day she had been chased by a Sheffield knight.

"When did this happen?" he asked, falling in with Sir Thom.

"Three days ago." The man was clearly exhausted, but he held himself straight. "And we have wounded."

"Did you not tell her what we do with the wounded?" he whispered.

"She already knew, but would not watch. She demanded we save whom we thought would heal."

"Well done." Grimme kicked Ares to round the front of the company and fell in on Brìghde's side. "Give me the banner."

"No. I ride into Kyneward carrying our banner."

"What's wrong with your shoulder?"

"It separated from the cup," Sir Thom said. "We wrenched it back into place, but 'tis still tender and we have no herbs. I bade her not use it for a while if she can help it."

That was a painful procedure. "Brìghde!" he barked, then snapped his fingers in front of her face. She never blinked, never looked at him. "Answer me!"

"I didn't die," she murmured tonelessly, tears still streaking down her cheeks and her mouth still trembling. Her entire body was trembling.

He had to get her under blankets as soon as possible. "Come."

"No. We all ride in together."

"*I* am the commander here," he barked, then reached for Troy's bridle. He was too tired to protest. The procession came to a halt.

That was when she turned her head slowly to look at him, and he had never seen anything more frightening in his life, that flat look in a new soldier's eyes, only in his wife's. He reached out and caressed her cheek. Her eyes fluttered closed and she tilted her face into his hand a little.

"It's different when it's not your brothers with play swords," she whispered.

Grimme continued to caress her cheek. "Aye, it is."

Then she pulled away from him, dropped her chin to her chest, and began to sob.

He looked over her head to Sir Thom, who said, "A force of sixty, all well armored. We don't know if they were sent from Tavendish or Dunham or someone else. They had no standard." He chucked his head toward the back of the caravan. "Forty-one horses and armor. The three dead horses are fresh enough to be used for meat."

"I trust you left none alive."

"No, my lord. My lady sent one to hell herself and assisted with another."

Shocked, Grimme looked back at her. "How— Never mind. Let's get you home."

She lifted her arm with a grimace and swiped her nose on the back of it, then lifted her head and straightened her spine. She did not look at him, but said, "Let him go."

He released Troy's bridle.

She deserved to ride into Kyneward a warrior, the conqueror.

76

BRÌGHDE LAY in her bed naked on her uninjured side and simply stared into the fire. The battle had not been real. It was just her and her brothers playing knights, as they did several times a week, riding shires bareback. She was lying in her bed, her mother scurrying around downstairs, getting her potions and poultices ready to apply to her children who had played too hard that day. She would sweep in at any moment and berate Brìghde loudly for getting hurt and wasting her time when she knew better. Then she would sit down by the bed and carefully tend her cuts and bruises.

At any moment, Brìghde would excitedly tell her mother how she had bested her brothers, and she would hear a yell from the chambers across from hers,

That's not how it happened, Budgie, ye liar!

What am I to do with ye, lass? Ye're a wild one, all right. Did ye get 'im?

Oh, I sent him straight to Satan himself, Moom.

You did not!

I really did, Moom.

That's me good lassie!

At any moment her brothers would bound into her room and they would all tell the tale to each other as if they had not been there slaying all the imaginary knights on their not-imaginary steeds.

I ran him straight through!

Oh, yeah? Well, I sliced his head clean off!

Aye, well, all o' ye still have yer heads an' limbs, so none o' ye did anythin' of any merit.

Moom!

'Tis different in real life, me wee bairns.

It certainly was, and she did not understand Grimme's lust for war any more than she understood her mother and Walter's way with each other.

The bed depressed behind her, but she did not move. A very cold wet cloth was laid over her bare shoulder. It wouldn't help. None of those poultices worked. She did not know why anyone thought they did.

A big body squatted in front of her and held a spoon full of noxious liquid to her lips. "Ginger," Grimme murmured. "'Twill help the pain."

She knew what ginger did. Everyone did. If they didn't, they were idiots. She opened her mouth and let him trickle the liquid in. She grimaced but swallowed.

"More."

She swallowed more. "Troy?"

"He's fine," Grimme said soothingly. "A few cuts. More."

Again. "By God, we saved the food."

"Well done, Lady Kyneward."

Tears gathered in her eyes again. "I said too much."

"When?"

"At Tavendish. I— They seemed to like me, and I— I told them *everything*," she whispered, her voice cracking. She felt him stiffen. "Baldy told me to shut my mouth, but it was too late. I didn't mean to be disloyal, I swear. I— They made me feel so welcome and I— I simply could not keep one thought to myself."

"Shhh. We can talk about that later."

"I want so much to be liked because I don't have any friends—"

He chuckled. "I don't count, then?"

No, he certainly did not.

"Archie told me I said too much. He said *you* needed to be the one to go to Tavendish and request protection, that I shouldn't be the one ... We were attacked because I could not keep my mouth shut."

"Mayhap. Mayhap not. I've no reason to suspect Tavendish or even Dunham, though they *are* tricky Scots."

She didn't smile at his teasing. "When you abducted me, I told you everything right away. You were kind to me and you seemed to like me and I told you everything almost immediately."

"Aye, you did," he conceded gently.

"I told the duke all those things—"

"Lies."

She closed her eyes and whispered, "I just want somebody to like me. Anybody. Just one person who won't betray me." More tears squeezed out from under her eyelids and her body began to wrack with her quiet sobs. She felt a hand on her forehead. "Moom, I'm sorry, I'm so sorry. Why does Da hate me?"

"Your husband's da loves you very much."

"Moom, he wants me to poison an hundred people."

"But you won't because they haven't done anything to deserve it."

"Moom, I don't want to marry Roger."

"You don't have to. You're married to Grimme."

"Moom, help me run away, *please*."

"Grimme will. Did."

Brìghde opened her eyes to see the most handsome man she had ever seen. Why didn't he love her? He said he liked her but if he liked her, shouldn't he *love* her too?

I love you, Grimme. Please love me.

The door opened with a crash, startling her. "Are you coming to supper or not?" Emelisse demanded in French.

"I am tending to a wounded knight," Grimme growled.

"*Knight*," she sneered.

Knights didn't get swived by their husbands.

"I'm going to kill her," Brìghde whispered because she couldn't raise her voice any louder.

"And ... here comes the bloodlust," he said in English, sounding amused, then spoke again in French. "Emelisse, out. I will present myself when I am damned good and ready to."

"Tell her never to come in here again," Brìghde croaked.

"Emelisse, do not ever come in her chambers again."

"Oh, but she is allowed entry to *my* chambers to inspect my every belonging?"

"Oui, that is exactly the way."

"I hope she dies," Emelisse snarled in English and closed the door with a bang.

Brìghde's brow wrinkled. "Am I going to die?"

"No," Grimme said dryly. "You don't even have a fever. Your shoulder will heal in a few weeks. Your cuts are all bandaged and bruises fade. You are in shock. It happens to men new to war. Training does not prepare him for the reality. I cast up the entire contents of my body after my first battle."

"I did that."

"Sir Thom tells me you were a virago."

The corner of Brìghde's mouth turned up. "'Twas Troy. He knew what to do."

"The best-trained horses always do, and he is very protective of you. Remember when you were angry with me and he would not let me near you?"

"I pity the knight who lost him."

"He is a greater warrior than the knight who rode him. If he couldn't make money with Troy, he deserved to lose him."

"I want to see him."

"Very well."

Brìghde sat up gingerly. She hurt all over, but she did not care. Grimme helped her up and gently maneuvered her arm into the sleeve of a kirtle. He put her shoes on her and wrapped her in her heavy woolen cape. She groaned every time she moved. He chuckled. "The way you did all the way from Fàileach."

She was too busy concentrating on her next steps to laugh. Her head was spinning. She held onto Grimme for dear life. He carefully led her out her door and down the spiral staircase, step by slow step. It was supper. Everyone turned to see the two of them. Halfway to the front door, Brìghde was still concentrating on where to put her foot next when he stopped.

"Brìghde, look."

She looked up to find all the knights who ate in the great hall on one knee, their heads bowed. She put her hand to her mouth and frantically puffed in and out.

"You think no one likes you," he whispered in her ear, "but that is not true. Even if it were, these men respect you, and you cannot buy, command, or beg for respect, which is the greater honor."

She didn't want the respect and fealty of a legion of knights. She wanted her husband to see her as a desirable woman, to swive her and love her and never take another. She started to cry. At least *that* was something a lady did, and they would never know why.

"They would defend you to the death, aye, even from the duke, as I swore."

She sniffled and wiped her cheeks, and said, "Rise." They did, and she inclined her head. "By God, we saved the food."

The men who had fought alongside her chuckled. "Aye, we did, my lady," said Sir Thom.

They continued to stand as Grimme led her out the door, across the bailey, and into the stable.

"Troy?"

He snuffled and stretched his neck over his stall. Grimme helped her keep her feet as they slowly traversed down the center aisle until they came to his stall. She opened the door and wrapped her arms around his neck, burying her face in his mane. He craned his head to snuffle at her shoulder and nibble her ear with his lips. He licked her cheeks.

"Ew."

Grimme chuckled. "Next time, do not coat your skin in salt."

"Very good advice," she sighed, still clinging to her horse's neck.

"Brìghde, I am leaving in three days. Do you think you will be able to manage without me for a while?"

"At Christmas?" She asked weakly. "We have food now. We can have a grand feast and have the laddies home an' gifts an'— Not that we have any decorations, as I havena been home."

"Christmas comes every year. 'Tis not something we have ever done, as I am usually on the battlefield, so my family has no expectation of a Christmas celebration."

"Surely it can wait until after Epiphany," she pled, watching her hopes for a merry Yule vanish.

"It cannot. Have the celebration without me."

"But ... where are you going?"

"Tavendish."

She sniffled and patted Troy's withers. "Very well. I want to spend the night with my only friend."

77

AFTER GRIMME carried his sleeping wife back to bed, he called on Sir Drew, who had already deduced what Grimme planned and had begun getting the support wagons loaded. Grimme then called upon Sir Thom to captain this expedition, for he knew the route and the weak points.

On Christmas Eve, after a joyless feast at which Brìghde was not present, after Grimme went out and, in torchlight, oversaw the preparations for leaving at dawn, after he had lain in his own bed, thinking about the coming battle—and he prayed there would be at least one—he thought about his little wife, injured, bruised, battered, and realized he was rock hard. The first time he had wanted to sink himself in her body and … she was too injured.

He arose and swept a robe around his naked body and sought her out. He stood over her in her bed, bathed in firelight, on her side, asleep. Her supper was untouched. He lifted her pitcher. It, too, was full.

"Bloody hell," he whispered, dropping his head. Nobody had thought to help her eat and drink. Not even him.

"Grimme?" she murmured, not moving, likely because she was too sore.

Sir Thom was not nearly as sore and he wasn't injured, but he was a seasoned knight and was used to the mock battles they waged on the training field and he had been in full armor.

Discipline won battles.

He sat on the edge of the bed. "Can you move at all?" he murmured, leaning over to kiss her shoulder.

"A little. Help?"

He helped her turn onto her back. Her linens dropped away from her beautiful breasts, bruised, the breasts of a goddess of war, who could ride out onto the battlefield with him and slay the enemy.

She closed her eyes and sought her breath, for simply turning over and with his help was too much. "Sleep with me?"

"I cannot." Her eyelashes fluttered up and her expression revealed her hurt. It ached, oh God, he ached. He shifted. "Give me your hand."

Hesitantly, suspiciously, she did, and he did the worst thing he could possibly do. He wrapped her hand around his cod.

Her stunned expression, wide eyes, open mouth, sharp gasp, would have been funny if she weren't so injured she couldn't even sit up by herself to eat. "How … "

He slowly released her hand to see if she'd draw away, but she didn't. She squeezed and he groaned.

"Is that … for *me*?" she asked in a tiny, almost desperate voice.

"Aye," he croaked. "If you weren't so injured, I would teach you tonight."

"You would?"

"Aye, but you cannot bear even the most gentle of tutoring."

"I ken, then, but … why now? What happened? I am a calamity."

He set her hand aside. "You came back to me a warrior," he said hoarsely, wanting her desperately and he didn't know how long he could stay before he took her anyway. "You came home to me a victor, a conqueror. I undressed you. I have been helping Avis take care of you. I have rubbed salve into your skin." He swept the rest of her linens away from her and looked at her. The bruises were uglier now, yellow and green and purple. He stroked and caressed her, seeing the body of a woman he wanted more than he had ever wanted any woman in his life.

She was injured and the willow bark and ginger were not nearly enough to roust her out of her pain-induced sleep.

"Your *beautiful* body," he murmured, unable to stop stroking her velvety skin, looking at it, "so much smaller and more delicate than you seem. Small, fragile, soft—yet bruised, cut, battered, sore, from a battle you had fought and won." He looked into her eyes that were filled with something he hoped was desire. He remembered their kiss.

Did it ever occur to you that if she found Aldwyn attractive, she would also find you attractive?

His hope grew. "It is the body of a woman, but it is also the body of a warrior. My wife, my dearest friend, had gone to war and won and there was the evidence, and war is the thing I love the most. You, an accomplished poisoner, who could snap a duke's neck and make it look like an accident. You, who threatened to burn a town down for cheating you. You, who could lift a woman much bigger than you off a chair with one hand. You, who could cast out my women with no one questioning your right to do it. You, who sent a man to hell because he threatened your food. You, who have earned the respect of my entire force of knights—"

"You told me those were the things that made you admire me *as a man!*" she cried. "And then your knights— I thought you would see me as a man evermore!"

"That," he whispered as he lowered his head to touch his nose to hers, "was before you came back to me a warrior. You, my lady, have become the personification of war, and now I can finally possess and conquer War herself."

He kissed her, catching her gasp in his mouth, stroking his tongue along hers. She whimpered and wound her fingers in his hair to bring him closer.

"Stay," she breathed.

"I cannot," he murmured into her mouth. "I told you I would teach you gently, but I cannot when you can't manage to sit up to eat. I will when your body is strong again."

"I don't care," she whispered. "Stay."

"No. Even if I thought your passion could rise when you are in such pain, I would not give you release. I would not have you ever more think of pain when you think of this."

"Then … let me see you. Please."

He stood without a second thought and threw back his robe. She studied him closely without speaking, her eyes lingering no longer over his cod than any other body part, and it seemed she was studying each and every hair on his body.

Finally she met his eyes and smiled softly. "Thank you. I would give you a favor to take into battle but … "

Aye, she was worn out from simply lying there and attempting to stay awake.

"I have your black ribbon. I will wear it. Here." He donned his robe again and brought her supper tray to her. "There are more pain powders in the wine."

"I can't lift the pitcher," she said sadly.

"I know. I will help you."

"What about your spindle?"

"'Twill subside." It wouldn't, but she needed to eat and drink more than she needed to know how much he wanted her. She was very hungry, but she could barely chew without having to stop and catch her breath, and it seemed all her thoughts were now concentrated on the task of eating and drinking. Watching her favor her shoulder, watching her try to direct her battered and broken body that did not want to cooperate did nothing to assuage his need for her.

Finally!

Then she was finished and she could barely keep her eyes open. He helped her shift until she was on her uninjured side again. "Stay … with … me … " she whispered just before she fell asleep.

He put the tray aside and went back to his chambers to try to relieve his lust for War, for he could not bear to sleep with her in this state. Once, twice, thrice he spent, and still he could not relieve his lust. He fell asleep with his hand around his cod.

At dawn of Christmas morning, Grimme's squire was preparing to attach his armor to him when he said, "Wait."

He left his chambers and slipped into Brìghde's. She was in exactly the position he had helped her into last night. He sat on the side of the bed and caressed her face. "Brìghde," he said softly.

Her eyes fluttered open and she grimaced.

"I'm leaving."

"Oh. Aye," she muttered, struggling to sit. She couldn't and he helped her up. "Do you know when you'll be back?"

"Nay. Your brother was right; I need to talk to Tavendish myself."

"Fare thee well and godspeed," she said with a smile.

"Brìghde," he said, gently clasping her face in his palms. She tilted her mouth up to his and he lowered his mouth to hers, kissing her the way she deserved, the way a man kissed his dearest female friend when he didn't know if he'd return.

She sighed and deepened the kiss. The room was quiet but for her soft sighs and the blood rushing through his ears. His cod.

He drew away from her slowly and her big green eyes followed him. He touched his forehead to hers and whispered, "When I get home."

"Aye?" she asked in a tiny voice.

"Aye, and not for a babe." He took her hand and placed it on his cod again. She closed her eyes with a tiny sob and squeezed, caressed.

"Grimme," she pled, "stay until I am healed."

"I cannot resist you that long," he admitted.

"Truthfully?" she said.

"Aye." Her hand tightened over his cod and he closed his eyes, to feel her hand. His breath was coming shorter and faster and he was going to spend— "Stop now. I can't bear it."

Tears glittered when she opened her eyes and her mouth trembled. "Come home to me, Grimme. Come home to my bed. Vow."

He leaned down and gave her a tender kiss that she returned fervently. "I vow."

A little after sunrise, Grimme rode out, leading a force of three hundred armored men, Sir Thom on his right, riding Troy. War. He prayed another band came at them so he could slaughter the lot of them, as his bloodlust was roaring in his veins.

It took them four days to reach Tavendish Grange.

On the morning of the fifth day, they were met within sight of the manor by an armed force of five hundred, led by Tavendish himself. "What is the meaning of this?" he demanded.

"My wife was beset by brigands on her way home," Grimme said coolly.

Earl Tavendish's mouth dropped open. "My God! How— Is she well?"

"Aye, no thanks to you."

He blinked. "You think I—?" His eyes narrowed and his jaw clenched.

"She informed me that she said too much."

"Aye, she did," Tavendish growled. "Trusting women do not belong in diplomacy or begging protection."

Grimme pursed his lips. As he thought: Tavendish had not sent the brigands after her, which most likely meant Dunham hadn't, either. "Protection."

"Aye," he sneered. "She said so much, she might as well have come crawling on her knees for protection from your liege, and now here you are accusing *me* of breaking her trust."

Suddenly a horn, long and clear, sounded. Earl Tavendish looked up and over Grimme's head. Grimme twisted, as did his men to see an armed force at least two miles away, coming at them full bore, bearing a standard he did not recognize.

"There's your enemy, Kyneward," Tavendish snarled. "Fàileach. And you led him right to us."

"Good," Grimme snarled with the anticipation of having his lust slaked in the thrill of war.

He wheeled Ares, as bloodthirsty as Grimme, and though they had been riding hard for the last four days, this was familiar. Comforting.

Grimme Kyneward was not made for peace; he was made for war and he welcomed the anticipation that flowed through him as he settled in to the rhythm of battle.

He nearly stood in his stirrups as he urged his mount faster to the head of his men. He thrust his sword in the hair with a guttural cry.

"Brìghde!"

THE BATTLE WAS not quick.

Laird Walter Fàileach had brought at least one thousand men. If Grimme had not had Tavendish at his back, they would have been slaughtered almost instantly.

But he *did* have Tavendish at his back and, at some point whilst Grimme was slashing and hacking his way through Fàileach's men to get to Fàileach himself, sustaining heavy losses, Dunham's force of five hundred came thundering up behind Fàileach to flank them. Once Tavendish's archers had entered the fray, it was all but over.

It vaguely occurred to Grimme that it was all topsy-turvy. English nobility warring with Scottish nobility was nothing new, but two English lords allied with a Scots laird against another Scots laird was something else again—add in that the two Scots lairds were allied by marriage and 'twas even more remarkable.

The battlefield was a bloody mess by the time Grimme dismounted, the point of his sword to the throat of whom he thought was Walter Fàileach.

"Nay, I am not Walter," panted the man on the ground, his voice a high squeak. Grimme took off his helmet and let it drop, then swept back the mail and cloth from his head. The man's eyes widened a tiny bit.

"You recognize me now, aye? Coward."

"He is," came a deep voice from Grimme's right. Grimme did not take his eyes off the man on the ground. "Good eve, *Da*."

The man's eyes widened when he saw the knight and gurgled. "Archie!"

"You are Brìghde's brother Baldy?" Grimme asked, looking into green eyes topped by raven-black hair. He was of average height and he carried himself with the swagger of a jester, which was not so different from Brìghde.

"Aye," he said conversationally. He stuck his sword in the blood-soaked ground and leaned on it casually. "You are her husband? Earl Grimme Kyneward. Ingenious plot our little Budgie planned, wasn't it, Walter? She outwitted you. Again." Archie looked at Grimme. "He hates her because he's never been able to best her, as she's not his and she got Sir Bart's mind."

Fàileach snarled at Archie and tried to rise, but the point of Grimme's sword in his throat convinced him not to move.

"Aye," Archie grinned. "We're *all* Sir Bart's get."

"Was it your force that beset my wife halfway between Tavendish and Kyneward?" Grimme asked his father-in-law.

"What?" Archie said. "Budgie was attacked?"

"Aye. I don't think they were mere brigands. The armor was too fine, as were the horses."

Walter Fàileach swallowed. Grimme looked at his Adam's apple as if it were a particularly appetizing dish and moved the point of his sword there.

"Walter," Archie said threateningly, but Laird Fàileach just stared at him, lips tight. "Aye, 'twas him," Archie finally confirmed after exchanging glares for long moments.

Grimme sensed Tavendish approach on his left. "For God's sake, man, stop playing and just do it."

So he did.

Grimme closed his eyes and lifted his face to the sky, then went to one knee, bowed his head, and crossed himself.

Tavendish and Archie Fàileach did the same, then they all rose. Grimme turned to Tavendish. "I apologize," he said low.

"Accepted. Day after tomorrow, we will meet in my hall. We have much to discuss."

With barely a glance, Grimme yanked his sword out of Laird Fàileach's throat and began the most difficult task of all.

78

GRIMME WAS unutterably weary when he finally entered his tent some time in the wee hours. There were at least twenty posts whose tops blazed and made the campground almost homey. His squire had already taken off his armor and he had already gone 'round to learn of those men he had left.

He, Tavendish, and Archie Fàileach had stayed on the battlefield until they could no longer see, even with torches, looking for the injured, assessing their injuries, and, if they were too severe, putting them out of their misery. Grimme hated that part the most, looking into his men's eyes, having known them, fought side by side with them, earned their loyalty, then slaying them quickly.

It was merciful, but it tore Grimme's heart out.

In the morning they would strip the bodies of all valuables then begin the business of burning them. The stench at the moment would only get worse once the fire was set.

Out of the three hundred knights Grimme had led on this expedition, two hundred thirteen remained. That was a loss he could not sustain with any grace at all. Out of the men Brìghde had taken to Tavendish, a full quarter of those had died or were injured severely enough that Sir Thom had slain them in mercy when she wasn't looking.

One hundred eleven men total—a full centaine. That many men out of a thousand was a good chunk, and now he knew Brìghde had told Tavendish and Dunham everything concerning Duke Sheffield.

"Oh, Brìghde," he sighed, but it was difficult to be angry with her because, irrespective of the battle she'd fought, she had brought back enough food to last them all well through spring, even to the point of defending it with her life.

He didn't know which she craved more: someone who liked her, or being right.

No, he knew very good and well: Being right.

He lay on his pallet with his arm across his forehead, thinking about the weeks she had been away, worried sick that something would befall her or that she could not secure the stores Kyneward needed or both.

Missing her desperately and not knowing if she would ever return.

To busy himself, he had ridden out to the far reaches of Kyneward where his sons were still training, trying to catch up to where they should be for their ages.

They had grown, not only taller, but stronger and with more endurance. Terrwyn had improved the least, but he already had the stamina Gaston and Max had not had.

Grimme had respectfully requested of their knights permission to take each son into Hogarth for a day or two, and had been granted it. He didn't need to request anything, but because he respected his men, they had a reason to respect Grimme.

The boys were thrilled to spend time alone with their papa, far away from their duties, being spoiled by a man they idolized and who loved them and who was interested in learning of them and their experiences as pages.

He was highly amused and grateful to Brìghde every time Gaston or Max exclaimed, "Lady Brìghde bought us cookies here!" or "Lady Brìghde allowed us to play with the mummers there!" or recalled every little thing Lady Brìghde had allowed them to buy or do. Terrwyn, of course, said the same thing about Dillena.

It was also enraging that Emelisse had never taken the boys with her on a jaunt to Hogarth.

Brìghde claimed he didn't care about being an earl. That was true. She claimed he didn't care about his women. He did, but he didn't care about Emelisse the way she wanted him to and he didn't know what Dillena wanted at all. Brìghde claimed he didn't care about his children. Also not true, but she did not approve of the way he indulged them.

Then he'd spent a week out in the field with them all in the same tent, Grimme telling them war stories, all three boys hanging on every word. Now that they had some understanding of it, they could relate it to their lives. Their time at the lists watching Grimme compete made them tell tall tales about what *they* would do once they took their own places at the joust. Grimme watched them at their duties, at their sword and dagger play, at their riding exercises, and praised them. He was truly impressed by their progress, but he would have praised them anyway.

They didn't need to know that.

My lord, we need them back now, if you please.

Of course. Fare thee well, my sons. I will take you to Tavendish and Dunham myself.

Not one of them had asked about their mothers.

He deliberately didn't think about the day Brìghde left.

There were seven women in his house he could fuck.

He couldn't stand to touch any of them.

Dillena was happy about that.

The maidservants only cared because when he wasn't fucking them, Rose worked them to the bone.

Emelisse was enraged.

You'll come to me when she's here but not when she's gone? Sleeping in her bed the entire time? For weeks!

Now that the battle was over and diplomacy would be the order of the week, he could not stop thinking about her, his lust for war, his lust for *her*.

Seeing her come home a conqueror, caring for her naked, battered body, seeing how fragile she really was … those big green eyes, her sweet face.

Men did not have breasts, much less ones that perfect, but hers were covered in bruises. Men did not have perfectly nipped waists, but she did and there was a massive bruise over her ribs, making him suspect one or more were cracked. Men did not have wide hips or a rounded arse just right for smacking. And men did not have mounds that led to heaven.

She was a warrior in a perfect female body, covered in bruises to attest to her strength. He could barely keep from stroking her mound down between her legs and giving her a taste of what she could expect when he got home.

He wished he could have. Giving her a release would have done wonders for her desire and confidence in his sincerity, but it would have been painful for the rest of her body.

He again went to sleep with his hand around his cod, knowing that she would meet him at the portcullis, and that he would lead her to bed and tenderly fulfill his promise to her, teach her, guide her to being the lusty wench he knew she would be.

He awoke some time after sunrise and presented himself to the provisions wagon for breakfast, which he took off somewhere else to be alone. Unfortunately, Sir Thom followed him, and then more followed, and they ended up eating together as they always did. He said very little, but most of his men were as taciturn as he was on days like these when the stripping and burning of bodies was the prime task.

"My lord," someone said and Grimme's eyes lifted from his platter to see Archie Fàileach, who had led Dunham's forces to secure their victory, picking through their camp toward him.

"Welcome," Grimme murmured, holding his hand out to shake Archie's. With a look, he bid one of his men to vacate the log beside Grimme for Archie. "Breakfast?"

"Already ate, thank you. What happened to Budgie?"

"Halfway between Tavendish and Kyneward, her company was attacked." He waved a hand at Sir Thom, who relayed the battle. When he finished, Grimme continued, "She has been in the manner of a very young soldier who has experienced battle for the first time."

"Ah."

"She is also injured, not badly, but will take a while to heal. I stayed long enough to make sure she did not need me and set out."

"On Christmas Day," Archie said flatly. "Wi' three hundred men."

"My goal was to determine if Tavendish had anything to do with it whilst preparing for attack by the same band, with the intention of following and wiping them out. I did not come to Tavendish with the intent to start a battle or defend myself against a force of a thousand. I certainly could not have predicted that Fàileach would come out of the air at me."

It went unsaid: Fàileach had been spying on Kyneward and tracking Brìghde to make war on her, to punish her for outwitting him. When that did not work, Walter Fàileach decided to punish Grimme. It would have worked, if not for Tavendish and Dunham.

"He'd've expected an English force to back ye," Archie murmured. His brogue was much thicker than Brìghde's. "He wouldn't've expected a Scottish one to do so. He thought he had a good rapport wi' Dunham, that me marriage to Meg would solidify that alliance, an' 'e never expected that any of his sons would turn on him, though he's given us reason to from the cradle. Me father-in-law has never liked or trusted him. I squired an' fought for Dunham for years before he trusted me, an' still sometimes I wonder if he does."

"He must, as he allowed his daughter to wed you."

Archie shrugged.

"Brìghde said he was a patient strategist, but it seems to me in the short term, he did not know how to exploit human nature to his benefit."

"Aye. When yer own children want ye dead, ye've done somethin' wrong."

"You're his bastards. My legitimate brothers feel the same way about my father and he certainly is not a madman prone to slapping girls into a hearth."

"Aye, well, we were told so late, we think of ourselves as legitimate."

"What does your mother have on him that he allowed her to rule him?"

"I doona know, an' I doubt we ever will. 'Twas strange, what they had, but now Moom's free to marry Sir Bart, an' if I had to be a bastard I canna think of a man better to be me father than he."

Grimme chuckled. "Brìghde feels the same. Who is the new laird of clan Fàileach?"

"Our oldest brother Hamish. He'll be a good laird." He paused. "Budgie told me the whole of it. Trojan horse. No plot 'twixt the two of ye. Wrong woman. She just turned it to her advantage."

"And mine. The story that we planned it was her idea."

"She can turn everythin' to her advantage." Archie chuckled. "She would've taken a dead frog over Roger MacFhionnlaigh. She … took me to task for not seein' to her protection'," Archie said low, his eyes on the ground. "I— She's always been able to take care o' herself, so none of us thought … " He stopped. "She said ye canna bed her, as ye think of her as a man, an' now she's engaged in battle, an' it'll be more difficult, I imagine."

"That's changed," Grimme said shortly, angry that she had confided in her brother but really, who else could she confide in except Sir John? But Grimme's father didn't want to hear it anymore because now, instead of being angry with Grimme, he was simply sad about a situation he could not repair. That was worse than anger.

Archie was looking to him for explanation.

"War," he muttered, "is the thing I love most. She returned a conqueror and I … know not how to explain or even why I should to you." *I lust for war and now I can fuck War herself.* "Never mind."

The rest of the meal was spent in light chatter, rumors of this and that and some other thing. Religion. Money. Politics. Fucking. Things he could speak of with his men, his father, and his wife. But *not* any other woman, including the mothers of his children.

Finally Grimme grimaced and arose. "Gentlemen, 'tis time."

For the next several hours, the remaining forces from three armies stripped the bodies of the dead of their valuables, boots, weapons. Those injured and fallen who were not dead that Grimme, Fàileach, and Tavendish had missed the night before, they killed. The stripped bodies were dragged to a growing pile.

Then they came to Walter Fàileach. Grimme and Archie together stripped—

"My God," Archie breathed at he stared down at—

Grimme simply stood staring down at his enemy aghast, unable to believe what he was seeing. "That's … Oh, God," he breathed.

Archie swept cloth over the body, then looked up and around. Grimme, too, looked for anyone who may have witnessed the abomination, for now they knew what Lady Fàileach knew and had kept to herself all these years. Indeed, the entire Fàileach clan depended upon silence.

They dragged the completely shrouded body of Walter Fàileach to the pile, maneuvered it so that it was inconspicuous, then Grimme took a torch and set fire to it. He and Archie made sure Walter was eaten first, the evidence of the perfidy completely gone, then they stepped back.

Grimme stood for many, many moments watching the familiar flames lick at the hair and catch elsewhere until it was a pyre that could be seen from fifty miles away and stunk about that far.

All around him, men dumped spoils in a pile and drew horses to it. Grimme, Tavendish, and Fàileach first divided the spoils in three portions roughly equal to the size of each army, then they divided the goods amongst their own men according to rank, the nobles getting the best and most.

Grimme worked as if detached from it all. A good portion of his fortune came from the spoils of war, especially the horses, once he determined if they should or could be bred. Even Brìghde had been a spoil of war; just not a war with anyone here.

It was funny, he thought as he stared into the flames. This entire expedition had been because of Brìghde. He was here, and he could not stop thinking of her. He had never, so far as he remembered, missed any one of his women when at war and he certainly would not go to war for any of them.

Why *now?*

Why, when she came home at her worst, having seen battle, killed a man, injured, in shock, looking haggard and worn, did he want her *now?*

When he was at war, his lust was aroused, then satisfied. If the battle was not long enough to satisfy him, he could find tall, willowy, blue-eyed blondes most anywhere. He had not thought of any of his women on his expedition to snatch Lady Margaret Dunham, nor had he thought of them much on the way home with Lady Brìghde Fàileach, except to inform her that they existed.

War.

Grimme was rock hard.

War had not satisfied Grimme. Any number of tall, willowy, blue-eyed blondes would not satisfy him.

There was only one woman who could satisfy him now when war could not, his warrior wife, she who had slain a Fàileach brigand from horseback as well as any trained knight, her beautiful body covered in bruises and cuts from the battle. Dark. Bold. Ruthless. But he no longer saw a raven or a witch. He saw Enyo, Goddess of War, his wife and dearest companion-at-arms, and she would be awaiting him at the portcullis when he came in as a conqueror, and then he would take her straight to bed.

He pressed his company to complete their tasks and get on the road, to ride harder, faster, because he could not wait to see her at the portcullis.

THE ONLY PERSON to meet him at the portcullis was Emelisse.

79

GRIMME AND his forces had returned. They were within ten miles and Brìghde had a choice to make: She could meet him at the portcullis or she could meet him in her chambers. Emelisse would be at the portcullis, so while it would be satisfying to see the look on her face when Grimme chose Brìghde, it made Brìghde no better than a mistress. She would not stand there as if to compete with Emelisse for Grimme's favor when he had vowed to come home to Brìghde's bed.

No. She didn't *need* to be at the portcullis, and seeing the look on Emelisse's face was not worth the humiliation of standing with her. He would know where Brìghde was, pass by Emelisse without a glance, and take the staircase by two to Brìghde's chambers to find her in her bed, naked, awaiting him, awaiting his body and his lust for her, to give him a conqueror's welcome as he deserved.

He had vowed.

And after he had swived her, she would be the only one able to sate him and then he would tell her he loved her and then he would put his other women aside for her and be ever true to her and ...

The leaders of the force came through the portcullis. She could hear the shouts and clanking of steel and horses. He would be in at any moment. There she sat, naked, waiting, aroused, quivering in anticipation and awash in hope and happiness, and ... the afternoon deepened. Night fell. Suppertime drew near.

Grimme never came.

He was hungry. That was the problem. Of course he would stop to eat first.

Brìghde dressed and presented herself at supper because she had missed him so, all the weeks she was gone to Tavendish. The time he was gone to Tavendish.

He wasn't there.

Neither was Emelisse.

Dillena briefly met her gaze, but her mouth was downturned and she shook her head a tiny bit. Brìghde would have gone back to her chambers, but Sir Thom greeted her heartily with a hug and concern for her shoulder, then wanted to relay the entire journey and battle for her and regale the knights in the hall with the tale.

Walter Fàileach was dead by Grimme's hand, which Brìghde found utterly satisfying.

She stood on the seat of her chair and raised her dinner knife. "I outwitted you *again*, Walter Fàileach!" she roared. "And now you're dead! Tell Satan good day for me!" The knights hooted and cheered as she hopped down and went back to her meal.

Her oldest brother Hamish was the new laird of Clan Fàileach. Everyone was happy *especially* her mother, who could move to the Fàileach dower house with Sir Bart because they had no reason to keep the secret anymore. Sir Bart had always known Walter Fàileach would fall to his most dire enemy: Brìghde.

The knights in the hall cheered for her, cheered for Sir Thom, cheered for the men who had gone and done battle with Laird Fàileach's forces. She somehow managed to grin and tease and insult and tell tall tales. Dillena left supper early, and Brìghde only noticed because she patted Brìghde's shoulder on the way to the staircase.

She nearly came undone. She didn't know how she got through the evening, but she couldn't bear to go back to her bed, knowing that, firstly, Grimme wouldn't be there and, secondly, exactly where he was.

He was not at breakfast.

Neither was Emelisse.

He was not at midday meal. Emelisse was, and she was gloating. Once again Brìghde waggled her wedding ring and once again, Emelisse's expression darkened with anger.

He was at supper, and did not say a word to her.

"Grimme," she murmured, laying her hand on his arm. He jerked it away and gave her such a hateful glare, she gasped and recoiled. "What—"

"Don't," he snarled. "Don't speak to me until I give you leave to do so."

She turned back to her platter, but only happened to see that half the hall had witnessed that. As the knights quieted and bent to their meals in relative silence, Emelisse started to laugh and said in French, "Oh, your little wife thought you'd come home and take her to bed. How precious."

Grimme grunted and replied, in French, "She thought wrong."

Stay or go? The knights were not laughing. Half this hall spoke French, so 'twas not as if Grimme and Emelisse were speaking in private to make some effort not to humiliate Brìghde in public. Dillena, who learned French because she had hated being spoken of in a language she didn't know, was picking at her platter. Brìghde was still hungry, but she was about to start sobbing. She cleared her throat, stood with as much dignity as she could muster, and glided to the staircase.

"That's right," Emelisse called in French. "Run to your chambers. Cry. We all know who's got his cod and you won't be getting a babe out of his. *I* had his babes. *You* will *never* have his babes."

Grimme said nothing.

He was angry with her.

Why?

What had she done?

Was it— It— Oh, God, it couldn't be that she had mocked him so, could it? Could it be that last order for him to go back to France?

It had to be. She could think of no other offense she had given him, so it was either that or ... what?

No, there was nothing else it could be.

The next day, after having cried herself to sleep, she ran to Sir John as she always did and poured it out, even her shameful mockery and ridicule of Grimme's infirmity. He was shocked. Appalled. Then angry. "I will speak with him."

But Grimme only came in from the field for supper, ate, then disappeared with Emelisse. Brìghde could not smile any longer. She could not laugh. Suppers were subdued, and after-supper entertainments were not as lively.

After three days of this, she knocked on Grimme's chambers door around midnight. Hamond opened it and woefully informed her that he was not in.

"Has he been in at *all?*"

Hamond hesitated. "Ah, no."

Brìghde's heart broke. "He's *sleeping* with her?"

Hamond gulped and cast his eyes downward. "That, I do not know."

"Hamond, what did I do?" she pled, hating that she was begging a servant for information.

"I don't know, mum," he said, sounding almost as despondent as Brìghde felt.

Once again she asked Sir John, who sadly shook his head and told her Grimme would not countenance Brìghde's name being spoken to him.

Another week passed with absolutely no difference in his behavior toward her. He refused to look at her, much less speak to her. It was as if she were not even there.

Brìghde's shoulder was still a little sore, but she had no problem getting to sleep, between all the wine she was drinking and sobbing herself to sleep.

Archie was right. If she didn't stop acting like a man, which would require her to watch her every action, Grimme would never see her as a woman. Coming home a warrior, a conqueror, was *certainly* not the way to Grimme's spindle.

Yet she was proud of herself. Grimme was proud of her.

Or he had been. He had been hard for her *because* of the battle, or was she so filled with pain that she had misunderstood? Had she dreamt the entire episode?

What had changed? What had happened between his tender care of her, his pride in her, his vow to return to her and make her his in truth, and then his marching off to find out what had happened and, if necessary, avenge her?

And she had reduced herself to begging for ear scratches.

The night that marked the tenth day of Grimme's inexplicable rage, Brìghde had barely gotten to sleep when she felt Avis's hand on her arm, shaking her gently.

"My lady."

"Mmmfphf."

"There's a woman found nigh dead at the portcullis, asking for you. I wouldn't have awakened you, but, mum, she's in a bad way. Half naked. Frozen. Feet shredded to bits, maybe frostbit. Could barely ring the bell."

Brìghde rolled out of bed, stepped into her warm slippers, pulled her robe around her with some difficulty, and skittered down the stairs to see one of her knights carrying a woman's limp body. "Where to, my lady?"

"Kitchen. It's warm there. I'll clear the table and then you may put her on it. Avis, fetch blankets."

The woman was, indeed, in a bad way. Her skin was snow white and her lips blue. Her eyes were closed and she had on a very expensive, very heavy woolen kirtle that was now in tatters. She had the shreds of a woolen cape clutched in her elbows. Her hair was long, filthy, thin, and straggly, some of it having come out in clumps. Her shoes were long gone and her feet were, indeed, shredded. They had blood smeared all over them and they would start bleeding again as soon as she warmed up.

Her heart was beating, albeit faintly, and she was breathing.

She looked vaguely familiar, but 'twas hard to tell in this condition.

"We have to save her feet," Brìghde said, rushing around to find a pot to warm up some water.

"'Ere now, m'lady, move," Linota said as she came bustling into the room. "What're tryin'a do?"

"Heat water. Look at her feet."

"Aye, then, let me take care of her now and you take care of your shoulder. Seen a lotta this in my day."

Avis returned with heavy woolen blankets she and Brìghde spread carefully over the woman's body. Brìghde sat on the bench and grasped the woman's hand and began rubbing it, gesturing to Avis to do the same with her other hand.

Linota, Brìghde, and Avis tended her with warm cloths to her feet, hands, and face for what seemed hours until her eyelids fluttered open.

"Good morn," Brìghde said softly with a smile. "You seem to have taken a wee walk in the frost."

She started to cough.

Brìghde, Linota, and Avis traded looks. If she didn't die, she'd be lucky.

Fortunately, Linota had thought to warm up some wine. Brìghde fetched a small cup, put willow bark and ginger in it, and tried to help her sit up enough to drink it. She looked as if it had been the first of anything she'd had in a while.

It took quite a bit more nursing before she could speak. "Lady—Kyneward—"

"I am she. What has brought you here?"

"Aldwyn," she wheezed.

Brìghde's heart stopped. "Lady Caroline!"

She nodded carefully.

"What's wrong with Aldwyn?"

"Duke put … Sheffield donjon."

"Why?" Brìghde asked, trying not to rush her, but she needed to get Grimme immediately.

"Punish for … not killing … Lord Kyneward at … tournament. Beat me for … not … being you—"

Brìghde choked, horrified.

"—use me— Aldwyn … tried—" She stopped to drink and draw a breath.

"Aldwyn finally tried to protect you from the duke?" Lady Caroline nodded. "Now he's in the donjon?" Again she nodded. "Where are your children?"

"Keep tower, nursery. With nursemaid. No danger when left, but … finds out I'm gone—"

"You walked sixty miles in the cold?" Brìghde demanded.

She nodded. "No … other … way. Get help. Please. You promised."

"Aye, I'll fetch Grimme."

"Thank you," she sighed and leaned against Avis whilst Linota rousted more servants to help.

Brìghde ran up the stairs and slammed into Grimme's chambers. Not there. There were so *many* places he could be at this time and she didn't want to find him like that, but …

Queasy for yet another reason, she ran up another flight of stairs and knocked on Emelisse's door, which opened immediately to reveal a radiant Emelisse.

"Is Grimme here?" she asked desperately.

Her mouth tightened and she slammed the door in Brìghde's face.

She gathered her courage and stepped to Dillena's door. Her chambermaid answered sleepily and told her that Dillena had put Lord Kyneward out some time ago, but he used Maebh's and Ardith's old chambers when he was with the maidservants.

With a heavy gut, she went to the last door and raised her hand and knocked. Nothing. Knocked again. Nothing. She put her ear to the door. There was someone in there and that someone was awake.

She tried the latch and it opened easily. She slowly nudged the door open and peeked around the edge of the door and saw Grimme slouched in a chair naked, a maidservant sitting on his lap facing away from him, undulating her hips so that Brìghde could see his bollocks, and his spindle buried in her, an expression of sheer ecstasy on her face. His head was back and his eyes were closed and his chest was heaving.

"God, yes," he whispered. "Yes."

Another maidservant walked out of the maid's antechamber naked then and stopped beside Grimme's head and lowered her head to kiss him. It was a long, slow, lazy kiss and he wrapped his other hand around the back of her head to deepen the kiss. Then he broke the kiss and shifted to take her nipple in his mouth. She moaned and arched her back. He slipped his hand between her thighs and she gasped a little.

Sick to her stomach and sick at heart, Brìghde silently pulled the door closed and fell back against the stone wall, and tried not to cry, tried to remember why she had come looking for him. Was it *that* urgent?

Please. You promised.

Aye, it was that important.

She took a deep breath and turned to the door. She raised her fist and pounded on the door.

"*What!*"

She was so choked up she couldn't answer. She simply pounded on the door again.

Silence. Then the latch clicked and the door flew open. "Bloody he—Brìghde," Grimme hissed. She tried not to look at her very naked, very aroused husband. "What in the bloody hell are you doing here?!" he barked, then stepped back to close the door in her face.

"I need help," she croaked, barely able to keep her tears in check.

"For what?" he demanded.

"Aldwyn."

"What?" he breathed.

"Lady Caroline— Kitchen. Walked from Sheffield— I promised help—"

"Aye, aye, of course," he said, now distracted. Then he looked at her strangely. "What's wrong with you?" he asked, reaching toward her.

"Don't touch me," she snarled, stepping away from him.

His expression hardened. "Brìghde—"

"Don't touch me," she panted, her mouth over her mouth, trying not to vomit. "Don't touch me. Just get dressed and come down to the kitchen. Please."

With that, she could no longer hold herself in. She gagged, gagged again, and threw up all over the floor.

With a choke and a cry, she ran to the stairs and ran as fast as she could away from that, that, that *filthy* animal she was married to, hearing Emelisse's cackles all the way down.

80

PANICKED AND furious, he barked at one of the maidservants to clean up the hall floor, then searched for his tunic amongst all the fabric in the room. The longer he failed to find it, the more panicked he became.

"Are you going to go running to *her* every time she snaps her fingers?" Emelisse purred viciously from the doorway.

Grimme turned more linens and bed hangings upside down and around trying to find his clothes.

"She gives you *nothing*, but you would vanquish the world for her."

"Bloody hell, where's—" Never mind. He had chests full of clothes. He darted out the door and clipped down the stairs to his chambers and tore into his chest for a tunic, then he ran the rest of the way down to the kitchen, where he found Brìghde, a cook, and maidservants aplenty hovering around a frail-looking woman sitting on the edge of the table, holding a tankard of something hot between her trembling hands. "Caroline," he breathed, taking one knee in front of her. "What happened?"

Brìghde spoke for her, in the most odd, stilted manner. "When Aldwyn … lost … the tournament— Failed to kill you, that is— And then when I— When Sheffield couldn't have me— The duke beat her and used her. Aldwyn— Tried to kill him. Finally. He's in the donjon."

Grimme, feeling as if his skull were full of cotton, arose and caressed Caroline's back. "Caroline?" he asked gently. "How long has he been there?"

"Haven't seen … since … tournament," she whispered haltingly, as if she had not used her voice in so long she forgot how.

"That was *months* ago."

"Aye." She patted her own chest. "Chained to … bed. Could not … "

"The children?"

"Safe in nursery … when I left. Never mistreated them, but … threatened. Keep Aldwyn under control."

"How did you get away?"

The tale was slow to come out, between her hoarseness, her need to stop to breathe, her shivering, and the fogginess of her mind.

"Had … friend. Mouse."

Grimme took a deep breath and dropped his head back. "Damn you," he whispered, wondering why he hadn't come himself.

"Unlocked me from bed. Gave me … clothes. Food. Sneaked … out. Very hurry. Took me to … forest. Said come here. Sixty miles. Couldn't walk … because chained … so long. Said would … protect … children."

Oh. That was why he hadn't come himself.

"Sixty miles. I couldn't. But … if wanted … save family, had to."

"Die for a husband who wouldn't die for you," Brìghde muttered viciously.

Grimme cast a glare over his shoulder, hoping Caroline hadn't heard that.

"Begged Aldwyn ask you … for help. He said … you wouldn't, but … Lady Brìghde said you would. Promised. Then friend … said come here."

"Aye, aye! Caroline, I need much more information before I can do anything. Do you understand? 'Twill take time. Time to construct a plan and to get to Sheffield Keep. How long did it take to get here?"

Shook her head. "Don't know. Went through … forest. Fell. Dogs and horses. Found hole under tree, crawled in. Slept. Don't know … how long. But dogs … gone. Slept more. Then walked. Lost way. Slept. Not enough … clothes. Food. Friend said had no time … for more provisions. Have coin, but couldn't … stop in villages. Sheffield soldiers at inns. Many. Looking for me. Would see."

Grimme's heart was thundering and his blood was beginning to boil the way it did before any battle. He dropped his head and stuck his fingers in his eyeballs. He sensed and felt women moving around, dishes scraping, soup poured. He needed to calm his heart and breathing so he could think.

"Brìghde," he said tightly whilst he tried to comfort Caroline. "Light up the great hall. Wake my men. Set up the tables. Get parchment, quill, and ink." She disappeared up the stairs.

Soon enough, Sir Drew and Sir Thom came running down into the kitchen. "Aye, my lord?"

"We're going on a rescue," Grimme said.

"For whom?"

"Marchand and his three children." The clamor of cots being put away and tables being pulled off the walls and set up rang all the way down to the kitchen. "Sir Thom, you are now in full command of Kyneward."

"Aye, my lord." He bounded up the stairs.

To Sir Drew, he said, "Gather our eight best men and four extra horses. Supplies for a week we can carry in our packs. You ride Troy."

"Aye, my lord." He vanished, too.

"Caroline?" Brìghde said softly as she gave Grimme a wide berth. He looked at her, still angry but suddenly bemused by her behavior. She acted as if he were going to strike her, but he didn't know why she would think such a thing. "Come with me. Let's get you in a warm bath and your wounds tended. Lord Kyneward will fetch your children and husband as I promised." She turned to the cooks and requested soup and venison stew sent up to the chambers next to hers.

"No, put her at a table. I need to get more information."

Brìghde started to protest, but he raised an eyebrow and she clapped her mouth shut.

He watched whilst Brìghde put Caroline between him and her and guided her toward the stairs. The bundled woman could barely walk she was limping so badly. That was when he noticed Brìghde wincing in pain, too. Her shoulder. Grimme strode over and swept the woman up in his arms. She was much taller than Brìghde, but half starved. He cast his wife a questioning glance as he bounded up the stairs with Caroline and put her gently in a chair.

Brìghde was right behind him with a tray, which, with her shoulder, she should not be carrying at all, but she was careful to keep the tray between him and her. He remembered her vomiting in the hall and he reached out, but she neatly dodged his hand. "Are you ill?"

She nodded angrily, but still would not look at him. "Aye, I am. So don't touch me."

"Brìghde—"

"*Grimme,*" she snarled with that contemptuous rolling R that he was beginning to hate. Her look was pure evil and he stepped back, shocked. His men noticed. "*You* make me ill. Don't – ever – touch – me – again. Now save your friend, whom you would have killed had I let you."

Caroline gasped.

He was so confused and disoriented, he could do nothing but glare at her. *He* made her ill? What reason could *she* possibly have to be angry with *him*? *He* slayed her father, returned victorious, but *she* couldn't be arsed to meet him at the portcullis!

He shook his head. He had more important things to do than argue with Brìghde.

"Gentlemen," he said robustly. "Today, we get Sir Aldwyn Marchand back amongst us."

Grimme drew out the map of Kyneward and Sheffield. It was sixty miles to Sheffield Keep with three well-traveled towns between, and the keep was heavily fortified. To get there, they would take the forest route Mouse took, which he had marked. But Mouse was a lone man who could run steadily over long distances for long periods of time, even through the woods. Eight mounted men with four extra horses could not travel that quickly during daylight on a good, empty road. Thus, Grimme and his men had practiced this many times in groups of four and eight mounted and unmounted, with pack animals and without. Each man knew the way sightless.

Mouse had also drawn maps of the keep, traps, spikes, and routes in and out of the fortress. Now Grimme and his men discussed which one to use, based on which donjon Aldwyn was most likely in, or, worse, which oubliette.

They knew how to get past the watchers stationed on hillocks ten miles out from Sheffield, but the guards two miles out at the edge of the forest would have to be slain silently. Unfortunately, they could not slay every man in Sheffield's army. They did not have time.

Yet some of Sheffield's knights were only there because they were loyal to Aldwyn, not the duke, and Grimme did not want to kill men he still thought of as his own.

"Is there a possibility," he said slowly, "that we could find some of our old companions-at-arms and pull them in on our scheme?"

"We could, but we have no way of knowing if they are true to Sir Marchand or have bled their allegiance to the duke," Sir Drew said.

"Aye, I know, but— First, how would we find them and how fast do you think we could determine this, did we come upon them?"

"The particular bird call we have not used since you and Sir Marchand parted, my lord. They may remember and come. Then we can attempt to determine their fealty from there."

Grimme demonstrated. "That one?"

His knights nodded and they all repeated it. It was old on their lips, though not having been used in years.

Discipline won battles.

Now it was Caroline's turn to speak. She was sitting quietly, slowly eating her hot venison stew and drinking warmed wine. Brìghde appeared with another bowl of warm water. She knelt at Caroline's feet and carefully changed out the cooled water for the warmed.

Why was she doing that herself, especially with her injury? She had servants for such things.

"Thank you, my lady," Caroline whispered, her voice breaking. Brìghde was caring for Caroline the same way she had cared for Pierce when Maebh should have. She was so much *more* than his wife, friend, companion-at-arms.

But with a filthy glare shot Grimme's way, Brìghde left.

Devil take her. A companion-at-arms would have met him at the portcullis and welcomed him home as a conqueror. She'd demanded he come home to her, but she hadn't given *him* a thought and he was still furious she had destroyed his plans for a lusty coupling. She could stew in her sudden and inexplicable anger that she had no right to. He had more important things to worry about.

He went back to his plans, extracting all the information from Caroline he possibly could. Three children. A nursemaid. A wet nurse. And if Aldwyn had been in the donjon for months, he would be weak, starving, and unable to walk. He would also be light enough for Grimme to carry for a few miles.

Grimme and his force of eight left at first light, their bellies and packs full, as they were not taking support, and they did not have their battle armor; they would go with mail and drape themselves in woolens. They rode into the forest just past the second village to eat and sleep, for the next day would be a long one.

At first light of the second day, they set out and slipped through the forest, out of sight of hillock-topped watchers who would sound the alarm. At midday, five miles from Sheffield Keep, they made a small, close encampment, without fires, though it was freezing.

"Full moon tonight."

It didn't need to be said, but Grimme needed to say something.

They groomed their horses, resaddled, repacked, slept and ate, then left their horses in the hands of two knights. They had two hours until sundown and had to make at least three miles on foot through the dark woods before they could expect to find the guards on the edge of the forest. Darkness came early in the woods, so they would have to go by whatever moonlight they could get.

They were silent as they slipped through the forest. It was likely around ten of the clock they encountered the first guard, two miles out from Sheffield Keep. Deep in the woods, Grimme hooted.

The guard didn't act as if he recognized that signal.

One of Grimme's men took him down without a peep. Grimme signaled to them to spread out and find others. When they reported back within the timeframe Grimme had assigned, six guards had been slain and they returned with one extra. The new man went to one knee and whispered, "My Lord Kyneward, I pledge my fealty to you."

Grimme recognized that voice and he grinned. "Get off your knees and greet me like you know me." They grasped arms and clapped each other together. "Reacquaintance will have to wait. Did they tell you why we are here?"

"Aye, my lord."

After retreating to the woods, Grimme's former knight explained that most of Grimme's forces who had gone with Aldwyn were in the encampment and whoever could come would if they heard the signal.

"You don't care for Sheffield much, do you?" Grimme asked wryly.

The knight laughed bitterly.

"Let us gather our men first and we will retreat to discuss the way in. Send those with their own horses to the woods immediately to await us. Now, spread out at the edge of the encampment and make the call."

They crept in slowly, the moonlight as detrimental as it was helpful. Each of the seven of them were now on their own, their task to slay every layer of guards patrolling the keep in a range as wide as seven men could span.

Once through those, Grimme and his men were much, much closer to the keep. The encampment was large, campfires burning, but not brightly.

Grimme lay on his stomach in the high, dead winter grass between two tents ten feet beyond the demarcation between packed dirt and grass. He released a soft hoot. Presently there was an answering one, from his man far to the left him, and another from his man far to the right.

Then Grimme hooted again in a special tone and pattern. His man on the left repeated it after a time. Long after that, his man on the right repeated it.

Now they could only wait.

Slowly ... ever so slowly ... tent walls began to move. It could be simply the breeze. It could be that the call had been heard and understood. One by agonizing one, men emerged from their tents with, so far as Grimme could tell, leather armor and mail, packs, and swords. The few he did see crouched away from the light from the campfires.

His man to the left released the call once more. His man to his right released the call once more. After a time, Grimme hooted the third time.

Then he saw it.

Two tent rows in front of Grimme, a crouched figure gestured for anyone who could see him to crawl forward. Grimme and the men on his direct left and right went in, crawling through the grass until they reached the dirt, then they crouched and ran.

Grimme recognized his knight immediately. An arm clasp and whispered purpose and plan and the knight nodded. Row by row they all crept forward, crouching from old companion to old companion until by the time they reached the outer walls of the keep, the men Grimme had gathered numbered nine. He had no idea how many each of his six other men had gathered, but he sent the four of those with their own horses back into the woods to wait for Aldwyn and his retinue.

It took Grimme and his five men a long while to make their way around the fortress to the postern gate, picking their way where many more men awaited them. There were more with their own horses, who were sent back to the woods.

Grimme began to describe how to get through the guards, as Mouse had instructed, but one of his reacquired men whispered, "My lord, my wife is the children's nursemaid. I regularly visit in the night. To do that, I had to remove all of the spikes and traps in the ravine to make a narrow path. I also carved out stairs, of a fashion."

"Excellent. You will lead us through your path. You knock, kill the guard. Are any of the guards our old companions?"

"No, my lord."

"Good. We'll kill 'em all. Twelve of us will go in with you. You take a man, go to your wife however you go, we will follow and kill as many as we can. Bundle your wife and the wet nurse and the children—you will have noise because they are children—we will cover you as you bring the women and the children out. You ten—" Grimme picked five of the men he'd brought and five of their old companions. "—Take them west for as many miles as you can, then turn north. We will find you later."

"Aye, my lord."

"You—" Grimme selected several. "We need to search the donjons and oubliettes for Sir Marchand. Any idea which one?"

"No, my lord."

"Unfortunately, we cannot kill the duke. Henry will execute me, and I rather like my head."

"And so do the ladies."

They snickered softly, but continued to discuss where the donjons were and which was most likely. They would be forced to search each donjon one by one, Grimme in the lead, as he was the biggest and could carry Aldwyn out if he had to. He'd done it before.

Once the plan was in place, they all plastered themselves up against the wall whilst the knight did his duty and knocked.

"Why you gotta plow the girl ever'night?" the guard grumbled. The only sound they heard was a slump and the knight signaled for them to come. Grimme was first in, his dagger in his hand, and followed. There were few guards in the back yard of the bailey. The twelve of them fanned out, skirting the campfires, and slew all of them.

They hid and waited. Presently, a well-bundled woman with a baby in her arms skittered through and was helped out by the knights they'd left outside. Another one soon came through with a big bundle. She had a gag in her mouth.

Presently, their companion appeared with two sleepy children who were starting to whimper. Grimme signaled to one of his men to grab a child and go.

Both knights ran for the door and disappeared into the night, the children's cries sounding like a disoriented wolf, and soon they couldn't even hear that much.

Another hoot. Ten more knights entered and spread out, splaying themselves up against the walls of the outbuildings out of the moonlight and firelight.

The first donjon was the biggest and closest to the backside of the keep, which was most likely where Aldwyn was. Grimme didn't know how many people they'd have to kill to get there.

"Come," Mouse whispered from the darkness to Grimme's right.

Grimme started and nearly throttled him for knowing to expect him, but not for getting the signal to him in the first place. Grimme turned to the men behind him and whispered, "Stay. I'll bring him out."

Mouse led him into the keep, to the farthest donjon from where they'd entered, the donjon Grimme and his men had determined was the *least* likely one, and picked the padlock, plucked it off the hasp, and held the door whilst Grimme slowly, carefully, felt his way down the stairs. There was light here, torches in the sconces. There was also a guard who was, unfortunately, awake and patrolling the hall of cages. Grimme sneaked upon him, raised his dagger and brought it down with both hands, cleanly severing his spine at the base of his neck. He dropped with little noise. Grimme patted him down for the keys. He whistled very softly, a whistle he and Aldwyn had had as children that no one but Aldwyn would know.

Waited.

Then the answering whistle came back to him. It was soft. Weak. Grimme crept in the direction whence he thought it had come. He whistled again, and the return was barely audible, a breath really.

He found Aldwyn in a cell, hanging on the wall in shackles, naked but for braies. Grimme went through a dozen keys before he found the right one. He quietly opened the cage door, unlocked Aldwyn's shackles, caught him when he fell over, and hefted him over his shoulder. He was smaller than Grimme expected.

He emerged from the donjon and Mouse led him out again, but he stopped Grimme to toss blankets over Aldwyn's body. "Send my men out as fast as you can," Grimme whispered, "then close the gate behind us."

Grimme ran across the bailey and dropped from the threshold of the postern gate, barely keeping his feet. He picked his way through the path his man had carved, climbed the makeshift stairs, and ran. He ran west, then turned north, letting the moonlight guide him, wishing he had Ares. Soon though, Grimme flagged. He tripped, but managed to roll so that Aldwyn would not take much of the spill.

Grimme lay on his back, looking up at the moonlight, his chest heaving, his breath blowing white in the cold. They were in tall grass. It would do for him, but it was freezing and Aldwyn had no clothes on but the blankets Mouse had thrown over him. Aldwyn was slumped over on his side, barely breathing.

"Can you walk?"

"No," Aldwyn whispered. "Children."

"We have them."

"How … "

"Caroline walked to Kyneward."

'Twas as if the last of the life left Aldwyn and he relaxed into the ground.

"Don't die," Grimme snarled as he sat up and tried to catch more of his breath.

"Won't. Car—o—line … "

"She said you were punished for not killing me."

"Aye."

"I apologize for not killing you, then."

"Would have—been worse—for family."

"Is that why the duke yelled her name at you?"

"Aye, to remind me—if died—would—kill them."

"That would have been a mercy."

"Know that—now."

"Very well, brother. Let us go."

Grimme stood, then stooped to drag Aldwyn up, around his shoulders, until he had good grasp of Aldwyn's wrists and ankles. "Help me."

"Will—try," Aldwyn breathed.

Grimme set off once again, at a moderate, steady pace now. He didn't stop until the sun came up.

81

BY THE TIME they all gathered in the woods long after sunrise and Grimme took a proper count, there were sixty-seven. They had lost no men, gained fifty-nine, two children, an infant, a nursemaid, a wet nurse, and thirty horses that belonged to the knights who had joined them.

"Papa! Papa! Papa!"

Aldwyn, sitting on the ground and shivering in his blankets, hugged his children to him and sobbed. Everyone else moved a bit away so as to give him his privacy.

"Are we missing anyone at Sheffield who would come with us?"

One of Grimme's old centeniers shook his head. "If they did not hear the hoots, we can do nothing for them. If they did not respond, 'twas likely because they have wives."

Grimme could appreciate that.

"My lord?" the wet nurse said in a tiny voice.

"Aye."

"My husband … I— He will not know where I've gone."

"He's going to have to use his imagination, because you're coming with us. Do I need to gag you or should I kill you now and let the baby starve?"

She was terrified. "I'll be quiet," she stuttered, on the verge of tears. "But—my own babe—"

"How old is he?"

She gulped. "A year."

"He'll live so long as your husband has the good sense to teach him to eat."

She started to weep quietly and Grimme prayed Mouse would somehow realize and see to the situation.

"We are about seven miles from our encampment." Grimme looked around. "Seven miles through a thick forest with wounded is nothing."

They all nodded in agreement and then the reunion started, with hugs and arm clasps and laughter, then every last one of Grimme's old guard took one knee, bowed their heads, and swore fealty to him.

"Rise."

They each took off a piece of armor or clothing and dressed Aldwyn. Grimme doffed his warm tunic, ripped it in two and bound each of Aldwyn's feet, wrapping them carefully. Aldwyn was put in a saddle and strapped to it so he could sleep. The nursemaid could ride, but she was quivering from hunger, so her husband rode behind her. Each child sat in front of a mounted knight. Everyone was well bundled.

The wet nurse, however, was afraid of horses and could not only not keep her balance on one, she had a difficult time even riding with a knight behind her. She certainly could not nurse from the saddle, even with the sling. It was determined she would walk whilst nursing, and even that would be difficult. The nursemaid would carry the babe when not nursing. Grimme led the horse with Aldwyn on it and once they were situated, they set off.

The sun was high overhead when they heard bellowing men and thundering hooves pass by a good distance away, a mile perhaps, though it was difficult to tell in the dense forest. There were dogs. Grimme sucked in a worried breath and glared at the wet nurse. She quailed and the knight behind her clamped her to him, his hand over her mouth.

The bellowed commands were difficult to decipher.

" … can't have gone far … "

" … Kyneward, I'd bet my life on it … "

" … Marchand are bitter enemies … "

" … only loyal to himself … "

One of the children started to whimper. *Bloody hell.*

"You're all wrong," came a stronger voice. Not the duke's. Grimme stopped to listen, but he needn't strain to hear. "'Tis York's doing. He has always coveted Sir Marchand. We ride south."

Suddenly, Aldwyn's body seemed to relax and he was breathing easier.

"Friend or foe?" Grimme whispered.

"Friend," Aldwyn whispered in return.

Once the hooves were presumably pointed toward York, the muffled thunder commenced then faded, headed south.

"Disproportionately advantaged," Grimme whispered, and trudged on with his precious burden.

AT MID-AFTERNOON four days later, it was a bedraggled bunch that trudged around the turn and plodded along the lane that led to Kyneward Keep. The children were asleep, well wrapped and sated on dried meat and hard biscuits, along with a bit of wine to put them to sleep. The nursemaid was asleep, cradled in her knight husband's arms as they rode. The wet nurse had learned to balance in front of a knight enough to be able to sleep, but not well enough to carry the babe or nurse from the saddle. She walked when nursing and she was, at this moment, in the middle of the company, limping, nursing. The horses' heads were nearly dragging the ground. Almost everyone was walking.

They had seen battle: Not the Sheffield knights, but a pack of errant ones attempting to steal good horses from wandering villeins. Now Earl Kyneward had those horses and armor, too.

Grimme was in the lead, walking Ares, Aldwyn slumped in the saddle in an abundance of clothing and blankets, still strapped to it. Grimme had found the apothecary in the town where they stayed, and dosed a bladder of wine with powders to lessen the pain.

"Aldwyn!" came a woman's scream from the keep. Caroline limped as swiftly as she could down the lane, but that was not very swift at all. "*Aldwyn!*"

Grimme saw Brìghde in the portcullis, leaning against the wall, her arms folded. She did not come running to see him, and his fury redoubled. What right did *she* have to be angry with *him?*

However, Emelisse *did* come running.

"Grimme! Grimme!"

She was the *last* person he wanted to see right now.

He was now close enough to see the look of sheer disgust on Brìghde's face before she pushed herself off the wall and disappeared. He released a long angry whoosh of air.

He was still plodding along. Emelisse had bypassed Caroline, who was slowing down because she was limping so badly. He held his hand up and Emelisse stopped.

"Go to your chambers," he said low. "Don't come out. I will tell you when I want to see you."

"But—"

"*NOW!*" he barked.

Emelisse gaped at him, but he raised an eyebrow and she turned to trudge angrily back up the lane. Meanwhile, poor Caroline Marchand had tripped and was lying in the lane crying. Emelisse passed by her, casting an unconcerned glance down at her.

His stomach turned. Brìghde would never have done such a disgusting thing.

One of his knights strode to Caroline, helped her to her feet, wrapped a blanket around her, picked her up, and cradled her in his arms.

They dragged themselves through the portcullis. Ares, Troy, Deimos, and Phobos were drained, as were all the other horses that had traveled both to and from Sheffield. Sir Thom and the marshal were in the bailey with at least fifty men to sort out the soldiers and horses.

"Take Sir Marchand to whichever chambers Lady Brìghde tells you to." Grimme gathered the last of his breath and bellowed, "*Brìghde!*"

She appeared at the keep door just as Grimme and Sir Thom were gently helping Aldwyn off Ares and helping him to walk, as he would not countenance being carried again, even though his feet were bare.

Brìghde glared at Grimme, then turned to direct the army of servants that streamed out of the keep from behind her. That done, she picked up her skirts and ran down the stairs into the thick of it. Grimme watched her as she rushed to direct the knight carrying Caroline and the one helping Aldwyn. Then she saw the wet nurse and rushed to relieve her of her burden. They talked for a few seconds before the woman gently handed the babe over to Brìghde. She smiled and called to a knight, who swept her up in his arms and disappeared into the keep.

Grimme was exhausted and his entire body ached right down to the last hair on his little toe, but he watched as she scurried around, assigned servants to tend the sleeping children and the nursemaid. Brìghde wasn't paying much attention to the babe in her arms whilst running around, giving instructions, and making sense of the chaos. Then suddenly it was done, and only Grimme and Ares were left. Her back was to him. She twirled to see that everyone had disappeared. Then she stopped, her profile to Grimme, and looked down at the baby, a sweet smile on her face. She caressed the child's cheek and cooed, "Oh, who's a good wee lassie? Did you make it all that way? Aye, you did! What a brave little lass you are, aye, and bonny too!"

For the first time in what seemed forever, Grimme smiled. He tried. He couldn't. He was too tired.

"Brìghde," he said quietly.

Her back stiffened and she looked straight ahead.

"Sleep in my bed tonight," he said. It wasn't a request.

She glared at him. "I will not," she snarled, her chest heaving. "And don't ever touch me again."

"What is *wrong* with you?" he barked.

"In point of fact, don't speak to me ever again, but that shouldn't be difficult since you haven't spoken to me since you returned from Tavendish for some reason I cannot fathom."

"You did not meet me when I came home!"

Her mouth dropped open. "I didn't have a chance! You came home and took Emelisse to bed and *stayed there* for days!"

"Aye, because I was—and am still—*furious* that my wife did *not* meet me!"

"*Why* in God's name should I meet you when your whore will be there? Do you expect me to line up with her, breathlessly awaiting your approbation? You have not humiliated me enough in private that you demand I submit to it in public too? You vowed to come home to *my bed*, but you took the first cunte that offered itself."

Grimme's rage slowly started to fade and be replaced by dread as he realized that … she had never met him. She had never had expectation of anything but a cursory "good day" as he passed her by to take whichever of his mistresses to bed, and that he had, in fact, been so furious not to see Brìghde where he had expected her to be that he taken Emelisse to bed as revenge—except, for Brìghde, that was the way things had always been done.

"Ah … Brìghde—"

But she was marching herself toward the keep, up the stairs, and in the door, which she slammed. Grimme stood looking at the door for quite a while, horror swelling in him.

"Oh, God, what have I done?"

82

HE ENTERED THE keep wearily to find a hearty meal and warmed wine being served. Brìghde must have had the kitchens in a frenzy since the watchers had sounded the horns to put food on the table for the weary soldiers and their precious charges. He couldn't decide if he was more tired than hungry, but he certainly did not have the energy to climb the stairs, change clothes, come back down the stairs, eat, and then go back up the stairs again.

He dropped into his chair and slouched, his foot on the table edge and his hand to his mouth as he watched all his knights slump in their chairs, eating.

"Welcome home, Son," Sir John said from behind him. "Come, give your papa a hug."

Dutifully, Grimme stood and pulled Sir John's chair out for him, but enfolded the old man in his arms, and the old man reciprocated. At one time, John Kyneward had been as big as Grimme—or perhaps that was just a child's perception. He was now only a little shorter, but he was thin. Frail. Grimme determined he would never allow himself to succumb to such frailty.

Grimme's old man was growing older, but he was too dispirited already and didn't want to drag himself any lower.

"You seem a little bit happier."

"Aye, well, when your boy goes out to raid his most dire enemy's fortress to rescue another beloved boy and you don't know if either of them will come back, it puts your views to rights."

"Fair." Grimme seated his father and dropped back in his, still slouching.

"Why aren't you with Emelisse?"

"Beyond the obvious," he sneered, "which is that I barely have enough strength to breathe, I sent her to her chambers."

Sir John blinked incredulously. "You did what?"

Grimme relayed the incident and then said, "I do not know why that angered me. 'Twas what she's done for years."

"She was thinking only of herself. She thrust herself upon you with no regard for what you had done and in what condition you and your men returned, expecting you to be grateful for her eagerness to see you. She has never, in almost twelve years now, done one damned thing for you or anybody else, and thinks dropping two weakling colts and ruining them is your reward for allowing you to pamper her. Brìghde would not have done that, and the fact that you noticed how Emelisse behaved and relayed how she ignored Lady Caroline is telling."

"And what does it say?" Sir John said nothing and Grimme looked at him, his eyebrow raised. "No comment?"

"Not one."

Grimme scowled, but his father simply slid him a glance and began eating from the platter that had just been placed in front of him.

"Lord Grimme." A platter was slid in front of him by the maidservant who'd been riding his cod when Brìghde had interrupted and sent him on an incursion into Sheffield Keep.

He turned his head slowly and looked up at her with a glare that shocked her. "If you ever call me that again," he murmured threateningly, "I will set you out on your naked arse in the snow. You may thank me for not dismissing you immediately."

She dropped a terrified curtsy— "Thank you, my lord." —and vanished.

"What happened that now you're snapping at a wench you regularly plow?"

"Brìghde is angry with me."

"Why shouldn't she be?" Sir John said with pursed lips and raised eyebrows. "The better question, which I have asked you before, is why you are angry with her."

He pursed his lips and sighed heavily. "I ... She didn't meet me at the portcullis when I came home from Tavendish."

Sir John gaped at him then slowly propped his elbow on the table and his face in his hand as if in great pain. "Oh, my *God*," he croaked.

Grimme had done the unforgiveable to his wife, aye, but he was shocked to see tears in his father's eyes when he finally raised his head and looked at Grimme.

"I have never," he whispered harshly, "in all my days, been so ashamed of you. She was not at the portcullis because Emelisse was and she was not going to go begging for your favor when you had *vowed* to return to *her bed*. She was in *her bed* waiting for you."

Grimme wished Aldwyn had killed him at the tournament.

"You didn't even *think* to walk past Emelisse to find her?"

No. No, he hadn't. He had looked for Brìghde eagerly, gotten more and more despondent when he didn't see her—*surely* she would not have abandoned him, would she?—then taken his rage out on Emelisse.

"And then you and Emelisse said such disgusting things about her at supper the next evening."

He winced. "Brìghde doesn't speak French."

"And is that not fortunate for all of us, but half your commanders understood and they were *waiting* for you to shut Emelisse up and you didn't! As for why she is angry with you *now*, I do not know. She has been merely sad since you returned from Tavendish, and she is convinced it was because she had hurt you too much to be borne."

"Hurt me how?" Grimme asked, utterly confused.

"Mocking you for not being able to rise for her, then ordering you back to France."

Grimme groaned.

"She has not ceased blaming herself for your anger. The night Caroline came she had had supper in my chambers and she was sad, which was awful enough. But then she was furious, so something else must have happened between supper and Caroline turning up half dead."

"Well, *I* didn't do anything to her."

"Except treat her as so much dirt under your boot. Your *entire* force of commanders is grumbling."

"What have *they* got to do with it?" Grimme demanded in a hot whisper.

"You have continuously chosen that worthless harlot you've kept for some bloody reason I can't fathom, over a woman who is worthy of the respect of battle-hardened knights. You have *also* allowed her to say awful things to and about Brìghde without once cutting her tongue out. Son," he continued urgently, "if I were you, I'd go up there right now and make sure my wife wasn't planning to leave me."

"*Leave?!*" Grimme choked, his heart beating out of his chest. He couldn't *bear* it if she left. He could barely bear it when she was simply not speaking to him, and the four weeks she'd been gone to Tavendish had been pure hell.

"She has no reason to stay and has always kept leaving in her pocket. I don't care if *you* need her or not, but *I* do. *Desperately*. If you have any regard for *me* at all, repair this."

"Aye," he whispered, bolting out of his chair, but stopped short when he saw Sir Aldwyn Marchand standing at the bottom of the stairs, clean, dressed in Grimme's clothes, which would normally fit him perfectly, but he was stick thin. His dark blond hair was freshly washed. He was holding himself up by a thread, but he had determined he would not show weakness by staying in bed where he rightfully belonged.

Take care of Aldwyn or go to Brìghde before she left?

No, Brìghde wouldn't go anywhere until she'd made sure her guests were healthy and able to take care of themselves. He had time and perhaps if he groveled enough, her anger would abate.

Grimme went to Aldwyn. "You should be in bed," he said gently. "You can barely walk."

"I need to do this," he returned stiffly.

Grimme offered his hand. Aldwyn stared into his eyes and refused the gesture.

"Aldwyn," he said softly, moving slightly so no one would see it.

"I'm still angry. 'Twill take a mite to put it away. I know you came to get me out of Sheffield because you cannot bear the burden of your guilt, but I am grateful nonetheless."

Grimme looked at him stonily.

"I am grateful. For my life, for my family's lives. But this does not absolve you."

"I don't think you want to have this argument here," Grimme said coolly.

"'Tis no argument. I am right. You know that. You are angry with me because I am right. And I am angry with you that you will not admit it."

"Very well. How many times were you chained and forced to watch Sheffield on your wife because your pride would not allow you to take the help I offered or ask Henry for help?"

Aldwyn's meager color dropped, as did his chin.

Grimme's stare was hard. "Don't expect a warm welcome from Brìghde, and I will no longer grovel for Maebh. So. Argue? Now?"

Aldwyn closed his eyes and swallowed. "No," he whispered.

Grimme plastered a smile on his face before he turned and said, "Sir Aldwyn Marchand!"

His knights were on their feet, their cheers raucous, tankards and knife handles banging on the tables.

Aldwyn smiled weakly and waved.

"Where would you like to sit?"

"With John," he murmured. Grimme gestured for another chair to be squeezed in. He walked with Aldwyn in case he tripped, but no. He was slow but otherwise hid his injuries well. Grimme didn't know what they were anyway.

Sir John arose and clasped Aldwyn to him as if he were his son. They embraced for quite a while, Sir John murmuring in his ear, and Aldwyn murmuring back. When their embrace finished, Grimme assisted Aldwyn to sit, then his father.

Grimme was turning back toward his chair when he saw Brìghde gliding to her chair, dressed beautifully in black velvet, her sleeves long and voluminous, her elaborately decorated black hair rolled at her temples. She had a black ribbon around her neck and her headdress was black as well.

Black.

Grimme thought he would bleed through his skin, he was so enraged.

"My lady!" came the shouts and half-drunken toasts to her and her beauty. She smiled mischievously and sat when Father Hercule pulled her chair out for her.

Grimme closed his eyes. He should have done that.

"Where is my supper?" she called playfully, delighting the knights who, as Grimme carefully watched, seemed quite surprised by her cheer. As her platter was being placed in front of her, she pointed to one knight and teased him about some incident Grimme didn't remember, and the hall erupted in laughter. Grimme plopped in his chair. He was still filthy, weary, hungry, and now he could add angry, panicked, ashamed, and heartsick on top of it all.

But at the moment, he had to play gracious host.

Some other of his men teased Brìghde about something else and she laughed. "I will get my revenge for that."

It was no different from any other meal. Brìghde had enchanted a quarter of his commanders, half thought she was amusing in her own odd way, and the last quarter didn't like her at all, for they considered her too much for a woman and too much in control of Grimme. But aye, his father was right. Even if they didn't like her, they *did* respect her. She had earned it.

She raised her goblet. "Who thinks they can hold their wine better than I?" The roar was deafening.

Grimme leaned against her and whispered, "Do not get them drunk."

She said nothing. In fact, she acted as if he were not there.

He leaned farther and twisted until he was looking directly in her eyes. "Why are you so angry with me?"

She stared at him with such a hate-filled expression, he drew away in shock.

Then, for reasons he could not express, he kissed her.

The hall exploded.

"Kiss me back," he growled against her mouth.

"Get off me," she hissed, and bit his bottom lip.

It was all he could do not to yelp, but he pulled away with a satisfied smirk—until, with a snarl filled with contempt, she wiped her mouth on the back of her arm.

His anger resurged, particularly when he noticed that about a third of the hall had been watching for just such an event. But before he could do anything more, she raised her goblet and said,

"Three cheers for a successful raid on Sheffield! Open the casks! You will not be in the training fields tomorrow, as it will be a day of celebration!"

In the cacophony, the only person who noticed she slipped away after exactly three bites of her supper was Grimme.

83

IT WAS LATE when Grimme attained his chambers. His chamberlain awaited him with a hot bath, which was more than welcome. He accepted a concoction of ginger to ease the soreness of his muscles, and a goblet of wine, which he sipped. It pained him that Brìghde drank his expensive wine as if it were cheap beer, and it irritated him that she never seemed to get drunk. Her brogue thickened, then she would start speaking Gaelic, but she was light and steady on her feet and her mind was just as clear as when she was sober.

"Fetch Aldwyn," he said low.

"Aye, my lord."

It took a while. His door opened and Aldwyn shuffled in slowly, attempting to keep his back straight and his legs steady. "You requested me, *my lord?*"

Grimme rolled his eyes and pointed to a chair by the hearth so he could look Aldwyn in the eye.

Aldwyn sat.

"Get him some warmed wine with willow bark and ginger and a blanket."

"Aye, my lord."

Grimme took a deep breath. "I am going to say this once and then I never want it discussed again. You were right. I deliberately set out to seduce Maebh away from you. You and I are well matched in everything, never losing to the other more than winning. I was tired of losing at all, and I wanted to conquer you. I brought my philosophy of warfare to bear to do it. I was dishonorable in every respect. I accept that, I acknowledge that. I cannot regret it *completely* because she gave me my son Pierce, and I cannot regret him."

Aldwyn was silent for a long while. "That was … concise. And not apologetic in the least."

"Oh, I very much regret hurting you. Brìghde made me realize that though the argument was over in *my* mind, the hurt was not resolved in yours and I did not intend for you to know Maebh was here at all, much less that she had had my child. You have every right to be angry with me, and though I am asking for your forgiveness, I do not expect it. Lastly, I know that you deserve an earldom more than I do, and 'twas only a quirk of fate that Henry saw what I did, but did not see what you did."

"I do not care about Maebh and I don't want to be an earl!" Aldwyn burst out. "All I want is that you not see weakness in my philosophy!"

Grimme remained silent.

"But you do," he said bitterly.

"I do not see you as a weak man, Aldwyn. I am *disappointed* that you seem to have lost sight of what is and is not honorable, and when to win, lose, or conquer. It is not up to me to forgive you for not attempting to save your wife from the duke, but I cannot respect it. Where is the honor? You chose to honor your pledge to an evil man over your pledge to your wife. *Repeatedly.* You violated the heart and spirit of the chivalric code—the one *you* live by. I told you I would help you. Twice. You could have written to Henry, like I did. But you didn't and I cannot believe you didn't think of it. Honor has its place and I act honorably when it is in my best interest. I act despicably when it is in my best interest. But I have *never* been evil. You thought honor would save you from evil and when it didn't, you were too proud to admit it. I do not expect your forgiveness because I do not deserve it, but do not expect my respect that you honored your liege over your family."

There was a very long silence. Grimme sat back in his tub and closed his eyes, wondering how to keep Brìghde from leaving him. Aye, she had a right to be angry about the way he had treated her when he returned from Tavendish. That would have been more than enough to explain her hate-filled expression. What it didn't explain was why his father thought she had gone to bed sad and feeling guilty but awakened enraged.

"You're right," Aldwyn whispered, his voice tremulous.

Grimme had almost forgotten he was there, and he started at his voice. "I'm *always* right." Except when he wasn't, which only happened with his father and Brìghde.

"How do I live with this?"

"You will or you won't. I would not be able to and I would have fallen on my dagger before now, but in the end, you found your courage, and that, I respect."

"You found me naked chained to a wall in a donjon," he sneered. "I didn't *conquer!* How can you respect that?"

"You *tried*, Aldwyn!" Grimme burst out. "You fight a worthy fight even though you know you won't win! What I don't respect is that you would rather be chained and watch your wife suffer than allow me to help you when I offered. As for me, well— I was no better. I would have let the duke have Brìghde and my women because I thought I had no choice."

"He slept the whole time."

"There was a reason for that," Grimme said flatly.

"You did poison him," Aldwyn breathed.

"Brìghde did. She did what neither of us would have thought to do, and I stewed in shame for that for weeks, trying to devise a way to keep the duke off her without killing him or letting her kill him. He terrified her and humiliated me and I did *nothing* about it. So. There is my shame as well. Brìghde was furious. She demanded my life for her and I swore it. She knew I could not stop it, but she faulted me for *not trying*."

"I was *chained*!"

"Only when the duke had your wife. You were free the rest of the time to plan or send a missive to Henry or even one to me."

"How do you know that?" Aldwyn demanded.

"I have spies," Grimme barked. "Because I am *not honorable*, remember? I would have fetched you after the tournament, but I was warned that I could not get Caroline and the children out without getting you killed. Your wife walked sixty miles in the dead of winter at night in the frost to do what you would not. Do you know what Brìghde said? 'Die for a husband who wouldn't die for you.'"

"Stop," Aldwyn croaked. "I cannot bear it."

The silence was long. It was not comfortable. Grimme dozed. He thought Aldwyn might have, too. Hamond returned to take some cold water out of the tub and put more hot water in, and leave more wine.

"Hamond, do you know what Brìghde's angry about?"

"Nay, my lord," he returned. "I only know that she was very sad when you returned from Tavendish, and came here to look for you. I cannot guess what made her angry, but Avis is worried."

"Has she asked her to start packing?"

Hamond hesitated.

"Speak freely."

"Her chests have begun to disappear."

Grimme rubbed his temple. "Oh, God," he groaned. "See if you can find out."

"Aye, my lord."

For a while after Hamond left, there was just more silence.

"Maebh is gone," Grimme muttered suddenly. "Brìghde threw her out to avenge you and punish me."

"Are you punished?"

"Not particularly."

There was some silence, but now it was comfortable. Their opinions were out. They had argued through the worst of them and settled for what they could get.

"You said not to expect a warm welcome from Brìghde? About Caroline?"

"Aye," Grimme grunted, rubbing his nose. "That you didn't try. I will not repeat what else she said."

"I … want you to know— I didn't bed her."

"I know."

"She wants you."

"Aye, for a babe, I know that too. Hounding does not make my cod rise any better than a brunette does."

"*Why* don't you like brunettes?" Aldwyn asked slowly. "I've asked you before, but you were lying to me. I let it go because it wasn't important then, but it is now."

"As if there must be a reason," Grimme scoffed.

"Your aversion to her is too deep. She is one of the most beautiful women I have ever seen and if you can rise for three or more women all night long, but you cannot rise for her, there is something about *her* specifically."

Grimme took a deep breath. He had his dear friend back, and they told each other everything, so why not? It got easier with each telling.

"The ravens," he muttered.

"The ravens—?" he asked, confused. "That was a wonderful day."

Grimme stilled. He opened his eyes. He lifted his head to see the silhouette of his best friend who seemed to be staring at him.

"Aye, they were *beautiful,*" Aldwyn mused. "So black they were blue, sweeping down out of the sky like a shimmering blue-feathered angel."

"A witch breaking apart into demon birds," Grimme croaked.

Aldwyn looked at him sharply, and saw too much. "That is what you see in brunettes?"

"Aye. Do you mean to say that is why you love brunettes?"

Aldwyn nodded. "I will assume you were a bit more frightened than I was."

"Terrified. I still have nightmares." Indeed, his heart was thundering just thinking about it when they were in private, in the dark, not around a campfire telling it as a good story.

"Does she know that?"

"Aye," he grumbled. "She got it out of me. I tried to do it in a gentle way, but there is no way to soften that blow. She is beautiful, but … she is dark. Ruthless. She would slither through the grass and slit the throats of the enemy then lick the blood off the blade. She poisoned the duke after I told her explicitly not to, and I am fortunate she didn't kill him, as she was tempted. Her hair gleams blue in the light, like those ravens' wings. She is only loyal to herself."

"Like you."

"No. She is also sweet and kind and funny. Tender-hearted. She thinks she rules with an iron fist, but only at first, to establish her dominance, and after that, only when she must. She prefers to cultivate people's better natures so that she does not have to watch her back, but she will punish harshly if the offense is too great to be borne, and she will kill to keep from having to watch her back. She could have snapped Sheffield's neck and made it look like he fell. We discussed it, in fact, but too many people here know she is strong enough to do that."

"No they wouldn't have. She's a slip of a thing."

"She lifted Emelisse out of a chair by her face with one hand. Everybody saw that. She offered herself for Ares to have the opportunity to kill him without either of us being implicated."

"Uh … "

"And … I want her," Grimme said low. "In spite of it."

"Who?"

"Brìghde."

"Since when?" Aldwyn asked, astonished.

"Since I realized she is the only one who can slake my bloodlust when I don't have enough war to do it. But now she is angry and I don't know why."

"She wants you to bed her," Aldwyn insisted.

"I know that!" Grimme barked impatiently. "What I *also* know is that she has been keeping something from me since nearly the beginning, and she has been allowing it to eat her up instead of simply *telling* me so we can argue it to a resolution. And now I … " He closed his eyes and admitted, "Here is the worst of it: *She* does not want me. She never has. She didn't want *you*, either. She just wants a son to protect her."

"Hm."

Grimme didn't like the sound of that *hm*. "You know, don't you?" he accused, sitting up in the tub and splashing water everywhere. "What she's not telling me. You know what it is."

"I *know* one thing. I *suspect* another thing," Aldwyn said tightly, "but I am not going to tell you."

"Why not?"

"Because whether I'm right or not, it was told to me in confidence. She may be angry with me or she may hate me now and forevermore, but it was a private discussion and that is all."

"She tells *everyone everything*. Why won't she tell *me*?"

Aldwyn heaved a longsuffering sigh.

"She doesn't tell her mother anything," Grimme grumbled. "She can be dead drunk and she won't breathe a word of anything and if her mother presses her, she lies. The drunker she is, the better she lies."

"What would her mother do with any information Brìghde gave her?"

"Oh, she'd use it as a wea … pon … "

"Mmm hm."

"I wouldn't—"

"Yes, you would," Aldwyn interrupted matter-of-factly. "You've done it before."

Grimme sighed heavily and sat back.

"When I was here last, you said you were dishonorable, not stupid."

"Aye."

"You're stupid too."

84

GRIMME WENT to breakfast the next morning and waited for Brìghde, but she did not appear. His knights were subdued. Sir John was angry with him—again. Dillena pointedly ignored him, but why was *she* angry on Brìghde's behalf? She should be happy. Emelisse was chatty—in French—which infuriated him even more than he already was.

Her chests have begun to disappear.

He left the table in the middle of whatever Emelisse was saying to him and bound up the stairs two at a time. He knocked on Brìghde's door, but when Avis answered it, she shook her head and closed it in his face.

He pounded on it, roaring, *"Brìghde, open this damned door!"*

Avis opened it again. "She is not here, my lord."

"You lie."

She shook her head and opened the door wider. Grimme stalked in and searched everywhere: the bedchamber, the sitting room, the antechamber, the garderobe. He even looked under the bed.

"Where is she?"

"I don't know," Avis said so firmly he knew she was lying.

"I want to see her in my chambers when she returns."

"I will tell her, my lord."

He waited all morning brooding in a chair in front of the hearth. She did not appear.

She was at midday meal, but she did not speak to him. In fact, she did not speak at all. She kept her head down, picked at her food, and drank four pitchers of wine. That wouldn't help.

There was no laughter in the hall. Everyone's heads were down. 'Twas as if a thundercloud had descended over the whole of Kyneward Keep.

"Brìghde," he whispered.

She ignored him.

"Brìghde, I'm sorry I— I was hurt that you did not meet me at the portcullis. It was wrong of me not to seek you out when I returned, and then punish you for it."

She ignored him.

"Groveling?" Emelisse said in French, disgusted but hiding it behind a pleasant demeanor. "For what this time? Did she repulse you again? She is angry that she cannot make you rise? If she weren't such a hag—"

"Emelisse," he said pleasantly, and continued in French, "go to your chambers. Now."

She looked at him squarely and said, "Will you be joining me?"

"*Non.*"

"Then I will not leave. If you want me out, you will have to drag me out of this chair and take me to my chambers."

"You are embarrassing me."

"How? She doesn't speak French."

"But I do," Sir John said mildly.

She sneered at him. "I do not give your existence a thought, old man."

"As do my wife and I," Aldwyn said.

Emelisse looked at Caroline and said, "Your husband was fucking Grimme's wife the entire week he was here."

Caroline, sitting beside Aldwyn, slowly turned her head. Aldwyn shook his head. "I did not."

"He didn't," Grimme said firmly. "'Twas an act to make me jealous. It didn't work."

"Oh, of course. *Why* would you be jealous of a woman who cannot make you rise?" Emelisse taunted pleasantly.

"Shut your mouth," Grimme growled.

"*Non*! She made my sons go away. She has you wrapped around her small finger. If she is angry with you, you run to console her." He wondered which would be worse, to continue to have a nasty conversation that half his men could understand or throw Emelisse over his shoulder and take her out. "If she asks you for something, you do it immediately. If she pounds on the door and screams at you, you laugh. She does *nothing* for you, but you go to war over her. She is an ugly, fat *pig*. She's disgusting, and I imagine her cunte is growing spider webs."

Pierce hopped up on his chair and screamed in French, "You leave Brigitte alone, you ugly witch!"

Emelisse snarled at him. "Shut up and sit down, you little monster."

Grimme still hadn't decided what to do when Brìghde slammed the pommel of her knife on the table and stood. With an expression of pure evil at Grimme that took him aback, she stepped onto her chair, stepped up on the table, and dropped to the floor behind Emelisse with a thud. Emelisse screamed and leaned away from Brìghde, but Brìghde grabbed her by the hair, wrapped the length of it around her hand once, twice, and pulled her out of her chair, flopping her on the stone floor like a fish.

Emelisse's screams were ear-shattering.

"Brìghde!" Grimme bellowed, standing and stepping on the table as she did, hitting the floor behind Dillena. "*Stop!*" he roared.

Brìghde was walking down the aisle dragging Emelisse across the stone floor as if she were a mere length of cloth. He ran to the end of the table and around, trying to get to Emelisse, who was still screaming, squirming, her hands up and trying to release Brìghde's grasp, as she was not strong enough to fight. She started to beg for mercy, but in French. She was too terrified to remember to speak English.

He stood in front of her feinting to the left or right, but Brìghde anticipated him and snatched Emelisse's head this way or that every time she blocked him.

"*LET – HER – GO!*"

Brìghde released her but because Emelisse was not expecting it, her head thudded on the stone floor.

There was immediate silence. Emelisse was out cold and Grimme *still* didn't know what to do. Brìghde slowly raised her arms out to her sides and stared at him as if waiting for—

Black. With voluminous sleeves that looked like raven wings, and she was *preening* for him like a demon bird, her sleek blue-black hair loose, swinging around her shoulders. His breath started to come short, his heart thundered in his chest, cold shivers ran up and down his spine.

She had a wide, evil smile on her face. She had had that kirtle made for the entire purpose of terrifying him. And he was.

Although she was a small, delicate woman, he saw a raven witch. Dark, ruthless, demonic. She was a *woman,* he reminded himself. A very *small* woman. It was just linen. He could crush her skull with his bare hands. She was just a brunette, not a raven. Not a witch. Not evil. Not demonic. If she *were* a witch, he could hang her as one. He had all the power because he was twice her size and she was delicate.

He had to tell himself this over and over again.

He knew what she wanted him to do: Rouse Emelisse and send her to her chambers, but she was unconscious and likely to stay that way. He couldn't blame Brìghde for her fury. It was maddening, knowing one was being discussed in a language other than one's own.

There they stood in the middle of a hall full of knights who, he knew, were losing any respect for him at all, because he was about to go to war with someone they respected, on behalf of someone they hated. They wouldn't fight for Brìghde, but his credibility was gone.

She folded her wings over her breast, rocked back on a heel, and gave him a dead stare.

"Pick her up," she said—*in French!* Grimme's jaw dropped, blood rushed through his ears, his mind spun, his stomach turned over. Pierce's and Sir John's gasps were loud. "Take her to her chambers. Sit with her. When she awakens, soothe her. Comfort her. Tell her you will keep the *evil, demonic* witch—that *hag*, that ugly *fat pig* with cobwebs in her cunte—the *raven witch*—away from her. Sit at her bedside all week and when she is healed, fuck her for a sennight to reassure her I mean nothing to you. Did you also soothe her with those words? Evil? Ugly? Hag? I can imagine you did, as you've disparaged me to them before."

"*Non*, I did not," he swore. "You are none of those things."

"I don't believe you. You continue to demean me to your whore, after you said you wouldn't. How many times now? Five? Six? You have allowed her mouth to run unchecked without *once* defending me or muzzling her. *In front of me*. Even though you did not know I speak French, you know that many people here do, and you *still* allowed her to speak of me thusly."

"I chose you," he reminded her, still trying to get to Emelisse, but Brìghde blocked him and he didn't want to touch her. "When I told her I was blessed by God to be your husband and I would wed you again."

"Would you wed me again *now?*" she purred.

Not like this, he wouldn't.

When he didn't answer, she said, "You were, as usual, lying to make the argument go away. You choose her time and time again. You speak of friendship, yet betray me time and time again." She looked over her shoulder and called to Aldwyn, "You of all people know the value of his friendship, don't you?"

"He saved my life, Brìghde," Aldwyn said low. "Twice. And my family's."

"Do not sing his praises to me," she sing-songed, "as I will begin listing the legion of *your* sins to remind you that you know no more about honor and virtue than he does."

Aldwyn sat silent. No, he wasn't going to challenge her, either.

Her lip curled. "Knight of the realm with your precious code of chivalry, which you *did not uphold*. Grimme didn't save you. Your wife did. She was willing to die for a man who wouldn't die for her."

Grimme didn't dare look at Aldwyn.

"My lord."

Grimme looked up to see Sir Thom rising to his feet. All around him, a few of his knights rose to their feet—to defend her against their liege, something neither he nor Aldwyn would have done for her against the duke.

"It is time to choose."

"Brìghde—" Grimme said, panicked. The raven witch was in a murderous, drunken rage and his commanders were forcing him to choose her, but there was Emelisse on the floor and blood was starting to seep into her hair—

"Take her before I kill her," she said flatly in English and moved aside.

He swooped down to pick Emelisse up, cradled her in his arms, gave the raven witch a wide berth, and strode up the stairs to take her to her chambers.

"That's right!" she called after him. "Choose her. *Again.*"

The question wasn't whether Brìghde was going to leave or not. The question now was when and how many people would she kill or take with her on her way out.

85

GRIMME CLIPPED down the stairs after he had gotten Emelisse situated with her chambermaid and servants toting pails of cold water up and down the stairs. With a tilt of his head, he ordered Sir Thom to follow him outside.

"What the bloody hell were you thinking?" he hissed once they were in a relatively private place. When he remained silent, Grimme said, "Speak freely," though he knew he would regret it.

"I can no longer stand by and watch you defend Mistress Emelisse against my Lady Kyneward."

"They are *women* at war and I *do not want* to get in the middle of it!"

"*They* are not at war," Sir Thom responded. "Mistress Emelisse is at war and my lady refuses to participate until Mistress Emelisse forces her to."

Grimme started to pace, one hand on his hip and the other rubbing his forehead. "Do you have any suggestions?"

"Allow my lady to kill her."

Grimme stopped cold and gaped at him. "She is the mother of my sons!"

"Who was cruel to another one of your sons, which was when my Lady Kyneward stepped in." *Because you didn't.* It didn't need to be said. "She has much reason to have killed her before now, and many opportunities, but she has not and I am sworn to protect my lady. Even if she did not know French, did not know what was being said about her, it would have come to this conversation and on this day, for I can bear no more."

"Are you ... *recanting* your fealty to me and instead bestowing it upon Brìghde?" he asked, flabbergasted.

"I have already done it. My lord, I cannot respect this, neither you nor Sir Marchand. I have fought by your side for ten years. We were all three together at Agincourt. I saw what you did to save the king's life. Mistress Emelisse has always been a part of our life together and I thought nothing of her. But my lady came, and she earned my respect in Hogarth, and when she removed Mistress Emelisse from her chair, and when she outrode Sheffield's knight. I have fought by her side as well as yours. Yet I have also watched her care for Master Pierce and the Lady Caroline as tenderly as any mother ever tended her child. She brought joy and light to Kyneward and made it our home. She gave your sons what they needed that their mother did not. I feel loyalty to her by virtue of her own acts, her own honor and courage, and that she is a lady, not because she is your wife. By contrast, Mistress Emelisse … "

He didn't finish the thought, which was probably just as well. How Emelisse had passed by Caroline still nauseated him.

"Today, you chose Mistress Emelisse again, and that was the final insult. I have chosen my lady."

"How can you swear fealty to her when she lives here with *me*?" Grimme asked stonily.

"When you are at one, I shall serve you both. When you are at odds, I shall serve her. When she goes, I shall go with her."

"*When* she goes?"

"Aye. She wanted to leave within the sennight; however, I persuaded her to stay until spring so that we had good weather for our travels. That, my lord, was my loyalty to you, to give you time to right this wrong."

"What wrong?" he demanded. "How am I wrong for defending the mother of my children against a warrior like Brìghde?"

"The wrong is which woman a warrior of your stature continues to choose."

"What was I supposed to do?" he demanded. "Leave her there? She was unconscious and bleeding."

"In lieu of allowing Lady Brìghde to kill her, you *should* have had one of us take Mistress Emelisse to her chambers. Then you should have taken Lady Brìghde and Master Pierce in your arms, comforted them, promised to send Mistress Emelisse away, ordered one of us to begin preparations for doing so, and then made my lady your wife in truth."

No. Not when she looked like *that*. He didn't want to touch her, didn't want to be anywhere near that raven, that witch. Even if she *wasn't* a witch, she had taunted him with it without saying one word, and now she was tearing his command apart with her demonic powers.

He heaved a shuddering breath and dropped his head back to look at the sky, his mind blank. "How many of you is she going to take with her?"

"Six more have sworn fealty to her. How many more will do so before we leave in the spring, I cannot guess. She is also planning to take Master Pierce with us."

"Oh, no," Grimme growled.

Sir Thom raised an eyebrow. "With Mistress Emelisse in the house?" Grimme said nothing. "There is no room for both women, my lord. You made your choice. We made ours. You know I speak truth or you would not have allowed me to speak this long."

Grimme waved a hand and muttered, "Thank you, Sir Thom. Go about your duties. I will ponder what you have said."

Once Sir Thom had disappeared, Grimme set about trying to find Pierce, which took him approximately forever, and finally found him in the stable grooming Helen and crying. To Grimme's shock, Helen was giving Pierce big horse kisses and mussing his hair with her nose and licking his cheeks. Grimme supposed she felt no threat from a small male who clearly needed comforting. Pierce tried to hide as soon as he saw Grimme, but Grimme caught him gently.

"Pierce," he murmured, and squatted in front of him. "I am sorry about what Emelisse said to you today."

"She always says that," he muttered sullenly and ripped himself away from Grimme to continue to work. He was doing an excellent job.

"She says that to you all the time?" Grimme asked carefully. This put a new twist on things.

"Not where Brìghde can hear."

"Did you tell Brìghde?"

"No, because she would kill her and then you'd send her away."

Grimme dropped his head. "I would not send her away."

"Even if she killed Emelisse?"

"I won't *let* her kill Emelisse." He barely caught the tiny snarl on tiny Pierce's face. Oh, aye, there was the ruthless streak. "Sir Thom said she's leaving."

"She is taking me with her."

"I am not going to let that happen."

"I don't want to be here with Emelisse!"

Grimme sighed. "I know. How many horses do you still have to do?"

"Six," he grumbled.

"Do you want help?"

Pierce looked up at him warily. "You want to help me?"

"I want to spend time with you."

"Oh."

Nothing else was said between them, but they developed a good working rhythm together and by the time they finished, it was supper, and it was as if they had been working together for years.

Grimme did not expect to see Brìghde at supper, and he was not disappointed. He allowed Pierce to sit in Brìghde's chair. Sir John, Dillena, and Caroline were absent as well. Grimme cocked his head and Aldwyn, who was in no better mood, sat next to him.

"How many?" Grimme muttered, leaning toward him and covering his mouth.

"At least ten," Aldwyn returned softly. "You *must* do something!"

"Where's Caroline, or do I need to ask?"

"I'm sleeping in the stable tonight."

He sighed heavily. "Did she believe that you and Brìghde didn't … ?"

"Considering what Brìghde said to me today, she's not even sure *that* much happened. She is now furious over my refusal to seek your help, as Brìghde continues to bludgeon me with it. Whilst I do not blame her and I am willing to grovel, there is nothing I can do to take it back. I can barely lift my head for the shame and I don't want the woman I love to hate me for the rest of my life. But Brìghde's anger feeds Caroline's and— I don't know what to do."

"I have no sympathy for you," Grimme said heartlessly. Aldwyn blanched. "At least you know *your* wife isn't going to poison you for it."

"I would *rather* be dead than live with my guilt, those memories, and Caroline's hatred."

"Tell Brìghde. She'll be more than happy to accommodate you."

"What *happened* to you today?" Aldwyn demanded in a harsh whisper. "I have never known you to fear *anything* and yet today, you— What—?"

Grimme shook his head wearily. "She was wearing black to deliberately taunt me with the ravens, to terrify me, and … it worked. All I could see was evil."

Aldwyn sighed and dropped his head. "What you *saw* was an enraged woman with nothing to lose and those are the most dangerous enemies of all. Why can you not look through the black and see her as a desirable woman?"

Grimme shrugged helplessly.

"Grimme! You can repair your situation, but you're deliberately not doing it—" Sir Thom had even bought him time to do so. "—and you keep choosing Emelisse. Brìghde didn't do anything until Emelisse attacked Pierce and you *sat there* and let her speak. If you repair yours, you can help me repair mine."

Grimme dropped his head back. "You have to help me repair my situation first. Brìghde confessed things to you I *know* will help, but you won't tell me."

Aldwyn's mouth tightened in thought, and Grimme waited for Aldwyn to decide whether to break Brìghde's confidence or not. Aldwyn gritted his teeth. Grimaced. Tapped his fingers rapidly on the table. After an interminable amount of time, he shook his head and slumped. "I cannot," he finally muttered. "If I knew for a certainty, I would but … I don't and I have to have *some* honor left to my name."

The hall was almost utterly silent but for the sounds of eating and drinking, with all of Grimme's knights accounted for plus the ones he'd brought back with him from Sheffield. There were no after-supper amusements, as they all left until the tables were cleared and their cots placed. There was unrest in his ranks and he would not countenance it, but until he had a battle plan, he would have to let it lie.

The next day was as any other, except meals were silent. Again, Brìghde, Sir John, Caroline, and Dillena were absent. Pierce sat next to Grimme. Sir Thom paid Grimme his proper respect, but only as a reminder that he awaited spring to leave Kyneward for Dunham. Nevertheless, Grimme's respect for him was now unassailable for he had done what neither Grimme nor Aldwyn had done.

Again, after-supper amusements were foregone and Grimme felt it was time he visited Emelisse. He walked in her chambers to see her chambermaid tending her head with a cold cloth. She was already quietly sobbing when Grimme walked in and it didn't stop when she saw him; it didn't grow worse, either.

There was a large lump just above her temple with a cut. Half of her face was one ugly bruise over several scrapes. "How are you feeling?" he asked in French.

"Terrible. My head is throbbing and look at my face."

"I see it."

"Why have you not come to see me before now?"

"Because I can barely look at you."

"It is because of what she did to me! Please tell me you punished her."

"I did not," Grimme said grimly, folding his arms over his chest. Her weeping deepened but only a little; her headache must be hell. "You dared me to drag you out of the hall. I wasn't going to. She did it instead and you deserved it. I am utterly *ashamed* of your behavior since I have come home. First, it was how you acted at the portcullis—"

"What did I do that I do not always do when you come home?"

"Firstly, you passed by an injured woman who had fallen to the ground with nothing more than a look—"

"Why do you care?"

"—and secondly, you did not see how weary we were and offer to help. You wanted me to take you straight to bed, but I couldn't. You wanted what you wanted and saw nothing else."

"And so you have not been to my chambers since you have been home—because of that?! I'm sorry I hurt you."

"No, Emelisse, it's who you are, and I am tired of who you are. You know nothing about me, we have nothing to talk about, and you do not care about me."

"That is not true! I love you!"

"If you loved me, you'd have helped me when I could barely walk, barely see. Instead you wanted me to fuck you."

"It's her! It's always her!"

"Aye, it is. Because *she* would never demand I do something for her if I need tending, and she would never have passed by a sick woman if she could, in some way, help. You disgusted me."

"I acted no differently than I would have twelve years ago and you have never cared!"

"Aye, that's true. But now I do."

"And you do not care what that *witch* has done to me!"

"I care. How can I not? You're the mother of my sons. But don't expect sympathy. You have been harrying her since she arrived when she was no threat to you."

"She has *always* been a threat to me!" she hissed. "You would do anything for her! You would *die* for her! You went to Tavendish to *avenge* her! You would *never* have done that for me!"

"Right now, consider yourself fortunate I do not put you out if for no other reason than you were cruel to Pierce. I *told* you what I would do, but yet … I have not done that, either."

Her eyes narrowed and she opened her mouth—

"One word about him," he said low, "and I will slap your bruised and bloody face."

Her eyes widened.

"You deserved what happened, for daring *me* to drag you out—which you knew I wouldn't. Fear her and walk lightly. I have told you before not to make an enemy of her. Has it not yet occurred to you that I have chosen to protect you from her time and time again? Every single time, I have chosen *you*."

It made him utterly ill.

"Grimme," she whimpered, "please don't be angry with me."

"How can I not be?!" he said, throwing his hands up and pacing. "I have not visited you since I returned from Sheffield because all I can see of you is that you passed by a sick woman who needed help. And now I find out you've been cruel to Pierce *after* I told you not to be. It has *nothing* to do with Brigitte, as she can fight her own battles, which you have clearly been shown. Twice."

"You're going to let her kill me, aren't you?" she choked.

"No," he said firmly. "I will never let her kill you. You have my word on that. You are the mother of my sons and I respect you for that, though all my other feelings for you faded away long ago. And yet, I continue to choose you above her every single time."

"You *did* choose her! Twice!"

"You were bluffing," he snarled. "You've done that to me too many times for me to think otherwise."

Her eyes narrowed. "May you always doubt the parentage of your next son."

His spine tingled.

... she is not the witch in this house.

"That sounded like a curse."

"It is," she said flatly.

"Hrmph." he said, to cover his sudden fear. "Believe what you want, but I am done with you now and forevermore."

86

THE NEXT morning, Grimme was leaving his chambers just as Caroline Marchand was leaving hers. He didn't know where Aldwyn had ended up sleeping, but it was *not* with his wife.

"Oh, good morn, my lord," Caroline murmured and curtsied.

"Good morn," he said warily. "I … have missed you at meals. Are you well?"

"I am healing, my lord," she said with perfect equanimity, "thank you. And thank you for rescuing my family. I'm not sure I said it."

He didn't remember nor care. "Most welcome. Have you … seen Lady Kyneward?"

She looked a little surprised and looked at Brìghde's door. "I … assumed … "

Why not. He turned and knocked on Brìghde's door. Avis opened it and shook her head. "Did she sleep there last night?"

Again, Avis shook her head.

No, he knew where she'd slept. He sighed. "Thank you, Avis."

She dropped a curtsy and closed the door quietly.

"Lady Caroline," Grimme said abruptly, "I apologize for the strife that you have had to endure whilst in my home."

Again, she looked surprised. "Uh … oh. Why, thank you, my lord. I am … actually, I have—" She bit her lip.

"Speak freely."

She took a deep breath and began carefully. "By comparison to Sheffield, Kyneward Keep has been a place of peace for me. The strife amongst you and your wife and your mistress is irrelevant to me. The children did not suffer at Sheffield at all, so they miss their home, but I am glad to be away and I owe you my gratitude."

"You owe me nothing," he said with firm kindness. "Lady Caroline, can you find it in your heart to forgive Aldwyn?"

Anger flared in her expression for only a second, but she said softly, "That is for me to decide, my lord."

"Oh, of course. Of course," Grimme said hurriedly.

"You did not allow your wife to suffer such."

Should he tell her or not? "I almost did."

Her eyes widened.

"Come, we shall speak privately." He directed her back into his chambers and requested meals be sent up. "Please," he said, offering her a chair in front of the hearth, which she took, looking at him warily. "I am going to tell you what I told Brìghde. This is not an excuse, but it is an explanation."

He spoke for quite a long time, interrupted only by their food arriving, trying to read Caroline's expression and failing, so he repeated things several times in several different ways. They ate comfortably whilst he spoke, but finally he had no more words, no more ways to explain, so he stopped speaking.

"'Die for a husband who wouldn't die for you,'" she whispered.

Grimme sighed heavily.

"At first I was angry with her. Why should I want my husband to die, but she said you were willing to die for her, so … "

"Did she tell you that?"

She nodded. "She did not tell me anything of what you've said."

So Brìghde had told Caroline the best of the situation. Grimme didn't quite know what to make of that.

"That is because," he said gently, "I didn't make the same mistake twice. The dilemma forced me to search for a solution that did not involve killing Sheffield, because I was not going to allow her to suffer such hell."

And Aldwyn never tried.

It went unsaid because he wasn't going to say it.

Now Caroline was silent and he was at the question he had wanted to ask from the moment he saw her. "Do you, perhaps, know why Brìghde is angry with me?"

Caroline shook her head sadly. "Aldwyn asked me that, but she has no reason to confide in me. We barely know each other, I am a guest, and she sees me as her patient. She also feels as though she should protect me from Aldwyn, but I—"

"Go ahead," he urged when she stopped.

She sighed. "I would that she allow Aldwyn and me to come to our own accord. She has no right to be angry at Aldwyn—"

"Oh, aye, she does," Grimme corrected soberly. "He did not try to save her from the duke when he was here. Look at what the captain of her guard did. Neither I nor Aldwyn did that for her. We left her defense to her."

Caroline sighed. "Be that as it may, my anger is mine to carry, and her anger feeds mine. I don't want to hate my husband, but she does, and she seems to feel it my duty to hate him, too. I am not strong like her. I don't want to hate Aldwyn because my children and I need him and … "

Brìghde doesn't need you.

That, too, went unsaid.

"I'll talk to her." If he could find her.

"Thank you, my lord."

He escorted Caroline out of his chambers, bid her good day, and went straight to his father's study. He entered without knocking to see Sir John at his desk and William and the land steward at their own desks. Brìghde was not at her desk.

"Papa," he said firmly as he seated himself. William and the land steward left. "Has she talked to you?"

"No," he said tightly, "and I doubt she will. She has closed herself off from everyone except Sir Thom, and he won't betray her. I think she eats in the kitchen and talks to the cooks and bakers, but I cannot be certain."

"She's sleeping with Pierce."

Sir John said nothing for a long while, staring at Grimme from under his brows. Grimme hated that stare, but he was long past feeling any shame. He needed to repair the situation and he would take information and counsel from any source he could find, but presently, the only thing that happened was that Sir John slouched.

"I have no advice," he murmured.

The door opened to admit one small, filthy, bedraggled, exhausted male.

"Mouse," Grimme purred viciously, "come in."

"Aye," Mouse said wearily, closed the door, trudged across the room, flopped on the rug right at Grimme's feet, closed his eyes, folded his hands over his chest, and groaned.

"You told me you would send a signal when the time was right," Grimme growled.

"I did. Lady Caroline. The duke decided to kill her and make Aldwyn watch, and that was when I found out Aldwyn was *not* out training, but in the donjon, where I could not go without being seen. The duke was going to kill her within the hour, but I staged a distraction. I gathered what provisions and coin I could, and got her out of the keep and past the encampment to the forest. She had been chained so long she could barely hobble and I didn't have enough time to get her provisions for a sixty-mile walk, but if she wanted to live and save her family, she had to do it. I would have come myself, but I had to get Caroline out quickly and I wanted to keep an eye on the children."

"Very well. What happened after you got her out?"

"My distraction was effective, so it took Sheffield a while to return to his chambers. Two, three hours, mayhap. They rode out with dogs at sunrise and

I was sure she was going to get torn apart. Nothing. Anywhere. Several guards were blamed for letting her escape. They were killed. I found out which donjon Aldwyn was in, but I could *not* go there and from what I saw, he would not have been able to walk anyway, and I am too small to carry him."

Grimme nodded.

"I watched over the children, but it almost seemed as if the duke had forgotten about them." He shrugged. "All I could do was wait."

"How long was she walking?"

"It was three weeks between the time I got her out of the keep until you came. They called off the search. She was likely dead. The night you came, I had already started trying to devise a plan to get the children out and I was pacing through it. If Aldwyn died, he died, but I wasn't going to let the children die if I could find a way. I saw the postern gate open, the dead guards, knew you were in. I ran to get the children, but they were already gone, so I looked for you. You know the rest."

"And after we left?"

"The dead guards had everyone in an upset because they didn't know *why* someone had raided or how. Nothing was stolen. I had put the padlock back on the donjon door. They didn't find out until they went to feed Aldwyn. Then the wet nurse's husband said she was missing and their baby needed to be fed. The duke sent for the children—not there. The force that went after you came back with the report that they found nothing."

"Who was the commander of that force? He seemed to know or at least suspect we were the raiding party, but did not want to find us. He turned south to go to York."

"He's one of Aldwyn's. From Agincourt."

"What about the knights I brought back with me?"

Mouse opened one eye. "You brought knights back here?"

Grimme looked at his father. "They weren't missed." He looked back at Mouse. "Do they know Aldwyn's here?"

"The duke is sure of it, but how will it look if he says a word? 'Lord Sheffield, why would Lord Kyneward feel it necessary to raid your keep for your deputy and his family?'"

"Excellent," Grimme purred, pleased with himself despite the chaos in his own keep. "Good boy."

Mouse glared at Grimme, then kicked his leg. Grimme chuckled wickedly when Mouse clutched his foot and swore.

"Anything else?"

"No."

"Go eat then take a bath and go to bed."

"Lemme sleep right here."

"Go on, now."

Once Mouse had laboriously gotten to his feet and left, Grimme looked at his father. "That was a bit of good news to brighten my day."

"Now you need to repair the situation with Brìghde. Grimme, I do not want to spend the rest of my life laboring over your ledgers."

"Aye, Papa," he murmured, hearing the desperation in his father's voice. His mood sank again. On a hunch, he went down to the kitchens to see Mouse sitting at the table wolfing down his meal.

"My lord," everyone said and bowed or curtseyed, then went back to work. Mouse, of course, looked over his shoulder and snorted.

Grimme slapped Mouse on the back of the head.

"You are *never* going to get a 'my lord' out of me."

"Looking for my wife," Grimme said to the general room.

"Not here, m'lord," said the head cook breathlessly, bustling around. "Just missed 'er."

"Do you know where she is?"

She cocked her head toward the outside wall. "Could check the bailey, but I doubt it."

He checked. Not there. He stepped outside in the freezing February day, but stopped cold when he saw the ravens. Hundreds of them. Mayhap only a dozen. They weren't paying any attention to him. They were swooping in lazily and playing with each other, but they were so *big* and there were so *many* with wings black as night but glinting blue in the sunlight. He wasn't going to go to the stables by that route.

He went back down to the kitchen and stalked through it, up to the great hall, then out the front door to the stables, expecting to find her with Troy, but there was no Troy at all. Once again he found Pierce carefully grooming Helen, who was, yet again, acting as if she were comforting her own babe.

The boy barely looked away from her. "Good day, Papa."

"Good day, Son. Where did Brìghde go? Troy's gone."

"I don't know," he said, looking confused. "Troy's training today."

"Oh." Grimme ruffled his hair. "Brìghde's been sleeping with you?"

"Aye," he said absently, not at all interested in the conversation. "She misses Mercury and says he won't come back to her."

That was a good lie for a five-year-old. Not a good enough one for a husband.

In spite of all Grimme's good intentions, he spent the rest of the day looking for Brìghde. Not in Pierce's chambers. Just before suppertime, he went to his own chambers and asked Hamond *one more time* if he or Avis had any idea where Brìghde was. No. Of course not. Mouse was asleep.

Supper was as quiet as all the meals had been since Brìghde had swept the floor with Emelisse. Brìghde and Sir John were absent. Caroline joined Aldwyn. Dillena appeared. Pierce was subdued.

"What's wrong?"

"You and Brìghde are fighting again," he sulked, picking at his supper.

"I'm sorry."

"I'm mad at *Emelisse*. Why can't you make her go away?"

"Pierce, she's your brothers' mother."

"I hate them and I'm glad they're gone and I want her to go away too." He looked up at Grimme, tears in his eyes and his mouth trembling. "I don't want to leave you, Papa, but I don't want to stay without Brìghde."

He draped his arm around the boy and pressed his mouth to his head. "I'll try," he whispered.

"My lord." He looked over his shoulder to see Emelisse's chambermaid and cocked his ear so she could whisper into it. "Mistress Emelisse requests permission to see you in your chambers."

"No."

"Aye, my lord."

Grimme could not spend all day, every day trying to find Brìghde or cater to Emelisse or mediate this war. Yet around midnight, he went to Pierce's chambers to see Brìghde and Pierce asleep, Mercury between them taking up most of the bed.

He looked down at her, so sweet in sleep. He debated whether to pick her up and take her to his chambers, but decided that would not be strategically wise. He left her to sleep; he now knew where to find her after midnight.

He went out into the field and stayed for the next five days, hoping that if he gave everyone enough time away from *him*, things might set themselves to rights, his commanders wouldn't revolt, and Brìghde wouldn't leave.

On day six of utter misery in a tent in the cold with rations of dried meat and biscuits (he didn't bother to go into Waters with the rest), he returned to the keep in time for midday meal. He looked over his hall filled with his knights, all eating without joy. It was no better than it was before he had removed himself. No laughter. No jests. No insults. No tales of derring-do. He had more men now, old companions he was happy to sup with again. They looked unsettled, confused.

Grimme didn't realize what joy and liveliness Brìghde brought to the keep until she took it away. She had done *nothing* except withdraw her person from the keep, but everyone felt not only her absence, but her black mood during her absence. Sir Drew had even approached him to ask with all courtesy when they could expect Lady Brìghde to return to her normal cheer. What Grimme heard was *Do something. Now.*

Staying away from the keep, training as usual, pretending nothing unusual was happening, trying to allow the anger to dissipate was not working. Thus, when he returned to a silent supper, after having trained in swords all afternoon long, he was angry, frustrated, panicked, and longing for a foe he could run through.

Or fuck.

Emelisse was never going to see his cod again.

Dillena had put him out. *I can take no more, Lord Grimme. Since Maebh and Ardith left, I have become too sore and chafed and tired to gain pleasure and not even the oil helps now. I must rest. I will inform you when I can resume.*

He went looking for his maidservants.

Annoyed when he couldn't find them, he went directly to Rose only to be informed, politely, through gritted teeth, that she had dismissed all five of them when they could not stop preening about their value to Lord Kyneward, refused to do anything else, and were fomenting resentment amongst her staff, *and* that Lady Kyneward knew nothing about it. Rose was almost as tall as Grimme. She stood and looked him in the eye, just *daring* him to dismiss her.

"You dismissed them to punish me."

She said nothing.

He raised his eyebrow at her and swept her up and down with a glance. She *was* beautiful.

She folded her arms across her very delectable breasts.

He threw up a hand and walked away because he couldn't fuck Rose and he could dismiss her all day long, but she wouldn't go until Brìghde affirmed his decision, which she would not.

On his way to the third floor, he stopped and knocked on Brìghde's door. Avis once again shook her head.

"Is she still packing?"

"I think so, my lord," she whispered after looking up and down the hall. "Another chest is gone."

He walked into Dillena's chambers to find her at her writing desk. She looked up. "Oh. Good eve, Lord Grimme."

He looked at her expectantly. To his surprise, she gulped, put her quills and inks away, then arose and glided to the bed, sat on the end, opened her robe, and spread her legs. He looked at her face. She did not want this and he could not rise for an unwilling woman.

He quit Dillena's room in a huff.

Grimme was able to tolerate many things from his little wife, but this could not go on. She had not only withdrawn her person, she had sucked the little remaining cheer out of the keep along with her and the effects of her mood on the household and his men were dire. He wasn't going to tolerate it.

He determined that she could stay or she could go, but the dark thundercloud over Kyneward Keep was intolerable.

He went to Pierce's room expecting Brìghde to be there, but she wasn't. Pierce was playing with Aldwyn's oldest, teaching her the ball-and-spoon toy Brìghde had bought for him so long ago. Mercury was sprawled over the bed, gave Grimme a deep *woof* and rolled onto his back for belly rubs.

"Where's Brìghde?"

Pierce shrugged.

There was only one thing left to do.

87

TO GRIMME'S surprise, when he unlocked Brìghde's door and swept it open, intending to stay there until she returned to it, she was already there, soaking in her bathtub. When she gasped and twisted to look at him, he said only, "I have keys to the keep too, my lady," as he twirled the ring around his finger, "as it is *my* keep and I am the lord here. Remember?"

She said nothing. She simply turned and went back to her soaking.

He closed the door and started to wander around her chambers. He had slept here many times, but he had never really cared or seen it. There was one thing about it, however, that was off and he couldn't put his finger on it. It seemed darker somehow, but it was as bright as it usually was, between the firelight and the plethora of candles she used.

He could also tell things were missing. Many things.

"When are you leaving?" he asked casually, as if he didn't care, but he did care and he dreaded her answer ... which didn't come. He continued to look around her chambers to try to see what else was missing.

A small bowl of findings caught his attention because it was alone on a shelf that had once been filled with things. He looked at it more closely. There were bits of bone, chips of metal, pieces of buttons and one whole button, pieces of leather, colorful stones, and one small piece of wood carved into a heart shape.

He puffed a soft laugh. "Pierce has been bringing you presents."

"No," Brìghde murmured lazily from her bath, shocking him. She brought a goblet of wine to her lips. There was a large pitcher on a stool by the bathtub.

"You collect tidbits?"

"I have ... friends." That R rolled elegantly off her tongue. His eyes narrowed. She was drinking. No wonder she was talking to him. "Who bring those things to me. They're gifts o' gratitude."

Her brogue was very thick. She was drunk, but she was still speaking English. "Oh?" Grimme asked, intrigued. "Who would find such rubbish to be treasures worthy of a countess?"

"I," she sighed, "doona think ye'd like th' answer to that."

"Tell me anyway."

"Ye'll be angry."

"No angrier than I am with my imagination running amok."

"Ye don't have an imagination."

"*Tell. Me.*"

She pursed her lips. "The ravens." His heart stopped. "I feed them. They bring me gifts."

"*Brìghde—!*" he croaked, horrified that she *fed* them and *encouraged* them—*in his own home!* "How could you betray me so?"

"They're me friends," she repeated airily, raising her hand and undulating it in the air, watching the water run down her fair skin. "I am their queen," she murmured with soft, cruel satisfaction.

"Are you always going to punish me for that?" he snarled through clenched jaw.

She chuckled evilly. "Until I leave, aye." She waved a hand. "Go to yer doves. Yer *angels. Two* mistresses an' *five* maidservants. Leave yer demon wife alone with 'er minions."

He nearly did just that, as he always did when he was angry with her and could not bear to sleep with her, except the maidservants were gone, Dillena dreaded his visits, and he could never fuck Emelisse again.

That left Rose.

He wished.

Surely he had some other tall, willowy, blue-eyed blonde maidservants around here, didn't he?

"I'd suggest," she added, "that ye not attempt to drive th' birds out or otherwise antagonize 'em. They're shrewd an' have long memories an' an eye for faces. They're cruel. They'll remember ye an' they'll make yer life hell."

"I ought to lock you in the dower house forever," he whispered, hating that his voice was trembling.

"Howe'er, if ye were able to bury yer fear, ye *could* feed 'em. An' they'll bring ye gifts," she sing-songed, "which would make ye their king."

Grimme struggled to keep hold of himself.

"Fly, Dove King, *fly*," she whispered. "Fly away from the raven witch who bursts apart upon naughty wee laddies to torment 'em an' steal their rabbits."

His throat clogged. His heart thundered in his chest. "I told you," he croaked, "it was figurative."

"An' now it's literal."

"You did this purposely."

"I did."

"*Why?*" He hated that he was begging.

"Because ye're a naughty wee laddie who deserves to have the raven witch descend upon ye to pluck yer eyes out."

That … was true.

"When ye likened me to th' raven, I became aware of 'em. There they were, scroungin' at the millstone for grain, pickin' through the bailey for scraps. They're big. Fat. I wondered: Would it help yer fear to eat 'em? I went to the cook an' asked 'er if they were good. She said they're delicious but … I'd ne'er be able ta get anyone ta hunt 'em fer 'er because they remember an' they'll descend an' bring all their family with 'em an' pass that knowledge on to their bairns."

Grimme wanted to run, but his feet could not move.

"That's indeed a shrewd bird, to remember th' faces o' humans who kill their family. I admired that. I wondered then: If they'll remember an' make an enemy, will they remember an' make a friend? Mayhap if ye befriended 'em, they'd come to like ye an' ye'd put aside yer fear.

"I've been feedin' 'em fer months, tryin'a decide when ta bring ye to 'em to make their acquaintance an' put away yer fear. The first time they brought me a gift, I nearly cried. They're clever, 'tis true. But they're also loyal to their friends, an' they consider me a friend. I dinna cultivate 'em to punish you. I cultivated 'em to help ye, to repair yer mind, but now … Now, my enemies are their enemies."

"Brìghde! I am not your enemy! I am your friend!"

"My *friend*," she said as if the word were unfamiliar in her mouth. "What does 'at mean?"

"What have I done that has made you so angry you create and turn on me the weapon I fear most? *No one* knew that but you! I would have rather you *poisoned* me than this! Put a dagger through my heart. *ANYTHING* but this!"

"I doona want ye dead. I want ye on yer knees, beggin' fer mercy."

Which was exactly where he was going to be soon enough. "Brìghde!"

"Firstly, ye left me with tender kisses an' a stiff spindle, vowed to come home to me bed an' gimme th' son I've been beggin' ye for, then promptly took yer favorite whore to bed, never once thinkin' perhaps I was waitin' for ye somewhere other than where *she* stood as if I were one o' yer collection."

"I am sorry for that," he apologized sincerely, prepared to grovel any which way she wanted him to and *not* because she'd threatened him.

"'Twasn't so much that ye *did* it, although there is that. 'Twas that ye refused ta speak to me fer days, punishin' me as if I were at fault."

"Brìghde," he said wearily, "I wanted you to see me come in a conqueror."

"Hmmm." She was silent for a long while. "I dinna gi' ye somethin' ye wanted—somethin' I dinna know ye wanted—because *yet again* ye dinna come to me with yer wants an' yer hurts the way ye chide me for doin'—so ye punished me. I'd remember that fer the future—if we were gonna have a future, which we are not."

He groaned and dropped his head back. Opened his eyes. Realized what was wrong with her chambers. Where before her chambers had been draped in pink, now it was black. The bed hangings were black. The drapes were black. Her bedclothes were black. The trim was sparkling gold and shiny pearls, but otherwise it was totally black.

He couldn't catch his breath.

"Secondly … " Again she pursed her lips. "I saw you."

"Saw me what?" he sighed wearily.

"With the maidservants. The night Caroline came an' I was lookin' fer ye. No one answered me knock, so I opened the door. I saw one ridin' yer spindle, saw ye kissin' the other."

He huffed. "So? That is what I *do*. You wondered how it was done with more than two people. There it is. *Why* are you angry about the maids at all? You know this is what I do. You have always known." He was utterly confused. "*This* is why you've been so angry you have cast a pall over the entire keep? Why you're leaving me?"

"Aye. I doona want yer filthy words in me ears or yer filthy hands anywhere on me body."

His eyes narrowed as the implications of that started to seep into his brain. "You're jealous."

"*Humiliated. Again.*"

He gulped.

"'Tis one thing to *know* that you do it. 'Tis another thing to see it *after* ye've twice demonstrated yer inability to do it for *me*. Embarrassin' me in Hogarth. Choosin' yer whore over me time after time when she's cruel to me, an' I hit back, an' ye protect 'er as if *I'm* in the wrong. Tryin'a rise fer me, failin', leavin', then both you and yer whore're absent from breakfast the next morn. Months of a promise not kept, and then ye ask me if I plan to find a stallion as if 'tis my doin' I'm not wi' babe. Then ye ask if I'd take a babe from a maidservant. *And then!* Promised me yer regard but abandoned me, punished me, an' I see ye moanin' in pleasure with … maidservants. The depths of me humiliation overwhelmed me ability to tolerate it any longer."

Aye, she *was* jealous, but it didn't matter. "And so now you will turn an unkindness of ravens on me to bedevil me and poke my eyes out?!"

"Ye *could* consider it a blessin', as then ye'd not be able to see whom you bed an' therefore nae fear me."

"Bloody hell! You are a wisp of a woman, sweet and tender. There is nothing about you I should fear!"

"I saw the look on yer face when I spread my wings. You were *terrified*."

He winced. That was true.

"Of *course* you fear I will conquer you."

But *that* was a step too far. "I cannot be conquered! I can hang you as a witch. *I* have the ultimate authority over you, and you have no power against me."

She nodded lazily, her mouth pursed, her eyes still closed. "You can do that, but hide like a coward so me friends willna know 'twas you, for they'll descend an' pluck the eyes out of anyone pullin' the trap." Her mouth curved in a ruthless smile. "Do it," she whispered. "Hang me." Her whisper was lilting, sultry, tempting. "I willna have to hear yer filthy words, feel yer filthy hands, not have to take yer filthy spindle into my body, not have to endure yer filthy lips on mine. Not have to know that *you must force yourself* to give me what ye freely give a maidservant. A tavern wench."

"'Twas the bargain," he repeated. "You knew about my women. You have never objected before."

"Ah, but I am loyal to no one but myself, remember, and, since ye've nae seen fit to take advantage of me good nature an' appreciation before now, 'tis too late. Ye've missed yer opportunity for attack. I am alterin' the terms an' ye've no choice."

He snarled. "I could pull you out of that tub, throw you on that bed, spread you as far as you can go, and rape you until you can't walk. I could chain you and fuck you until you are with child, then do it again after he's born until you catch again."

"No, ye couldn't!" she cackled. "Ye're not enough of a man! Ye're just a terrified wee laddie. But should ye succeed by some devil's magic, I will set me demons upon you. They will do *anythin'* for me. Ye doona fear war, death, me poison or me knife, but ye do fear them."

Grimme had never been so terrified in his life. "Witch," he whispered. "You really are a witch."

"Oh, no. *Emelisse* is a witch. A real one. She cursed me. Twice. She has cursed Sir John, too."

He said nothing, for after Emelisse had also cursed *him*, he was beginning to believe he had *two* witches in his house.

"*I* am certainly not a witch. I am merely stronger than that lazy, worthless lump o' flesh. An' I made friends. Ye look at me an' ye see a witch—that's yer own mind doin' it to ye because ye canna get over a story yer brother told ye when ye were a wee laddie, an' then some birds were hungry one day.

"As always, I've been a true an' faithful friend to a faithless an' selfish person. I've nothin' to value in yer friendship yet ye've much to value in *my* friendship, but by God," she said, her voice rising in pitch. Her eyes opened and there was an evil glint in them. No, not evil. Tears. "You will value the *whole* of me or you will get *none* of me."

That gave him pause. Did she know what she'd just said? And if so, had she *meant* it?

"Do what ye want with me, but you *will* live with this knowledge—" Her smile widened and sparkled with demonic glee. "I—conquered—you. You can rape me. You can hang me. But once I'm dead'n'buried, me loyal friends will act in me stead, an' ye'll fear me more than ye already do. You will *never* live in peace again. I've made sure of it."

No, she didn't know what she'd said.

Grimme clenched his fist, unable to bear one more second of her taunts, her betrayal, her *terrifying* descent from happy playmate, wise advisor, bed partner, dearest friend, and companion-at-arms to enraged demon from the pits of hell.

He quit the room violently, slamming her door, and only then realized that his cod was rock hard. He charged to the stairs and ran up them, headed for Dillena's chambers … but his hand stopped just before touching the latch. He'd already tried this, but he needed to take a woman.

Take her hard.

Violently.

This was Dillena's taste, to be taken hard, violently. Aye, she was the quiet one—right until she wanted to be punished. He had oil and she could slake his lust.

Bloodlust.

He had seen his enemy on the battlefield and she had conquered him. Dishonorably. With deceit and spycraft and ruthlessness, crawling through the fields on her belly to stab a thousand men in the night and lick the blood off her blade. She had turned his shameful confession on him and created the only weapon he feared. He had to retreat to fight another day. 'Twas what good commanders did.

But he hadn't had to do that in years because he did not fight honorably. He hadn't even fought honorably on the lists, taking advantage of Aldwyn's weakness so. He would never have done that had not that—that—that *demon* commanded him to.

And he'd done it.

He turned around and slammed back into her chambers, where she was standing next to her tub, drying off. She gaped at him in shock.

"As God is my witness," he rumbled, rage and bloodlust tearing through his veins, yet noting her pale body, short, but generous breasts and hips that flared out from her waist, every beautiful curve. "I will not be conquered by *anyone*, much less one small woman."

Her shock melted into smug satisfaction. "Ye can't rise for me," she mocked in a high-pitched, childish voice. "Ye're *scared* o' me."

With that, he pulled off his tunic and breeches, and stood proud and naked before her.

Her mouth dropped open. Her eyes widened, and trailed from his rock-hard cod up his chest and into his eyes. *How can this happen?*

"War," he purred, "makes me rise, and you and I, my lovely wife, are at war."

She gathered herself and looked at him with contempt. "Aye, ye always do when I give ye a war, but it doesn't occur to ye to *stay*, does it? I realized that when me mother interrupted us crowin' about our victory to each other over an' over again."

That distracted Grimme immediately and he looked away in thought, scraping his memory for their history. He was stunned.

By God, she was right. He *had* gotten hard for her from their very first argument and he never thought to *stay* and slake his bloodlust with *her*, War. If he'd simply been willing to take the argument all the way to its end, this would have been decided nearly immediately.

Then he realized that he did almost everything incompletely, stopping just short of finishing it. Fatherhood. The earldom. Marriage. Friendship.

Choose all *your interests.*

War was the only thing he did to completion and then some.

She sneered at him. "Oh, aye, *now* ye're just realizin' ye've wanted me all along, but ye were too afraid o' me to know it fer what it was. I told ye from the beginnin' I don't wanna war wi' me husband. If ye canna rise for me when ye're not angry, I don't wantche."

"You don't want me anyway."

"Well, close the door an' get on with it before I make ye laugh an' it goes limp again."

That almost did make him laugh and because of it, the last of his fear disappeared. But this was too serious and teasing her wouldn't work this time. He kicked the door closed and pointed to the bed, satisfied when she obeyed, albeit slowly, warily, as if she had only just realized he was an animal about to attack.

He was.

"You want a son?" he growled. "Aye, you're going to get one. I am not leaving these chambers until you've gotten the protection you want, that you've goaded me into."

She chortled. "That's what ye say *now*."

"You and I," he growled, prowling around the bed and back again as she crawled on it to sit in the middle of it with her knees against her chest and her arms around her knees as if that would protect her, "have slept together many times." He continued to pace around the bed, back and forth, faster, the way he had defeated Aldwyn. "That is a privilege I have never granted any of my women except Emelisse, and I long ago stopped sleeping with her. But you … Oh, *you*," he whispered. "I come back to you every time. I miss you when you are angry and do not speak to me, whereas I have *never* missed any of my women. Tavern wenches are *everywhere*."

Her lip curled. "Did ye miss me whilst you were angry with me that I had not deigned to greet the victor at the portcullis? *TEN DAYS, GRIMME!* Ye only come to me with yer hurts when ye're shown that you were *wrong* an' then only because ye want immediate forgiveness so all can be well in yer mind, the argument resolved! Ye've *always* done that, an' then berated *me* for doin' it! All ye had to do was *stay when you were angry*."

He didn't answer that because it was true, but her anger fed his bloodlust. "You're right. But I swear to you on my mother's grave—the first argument, do you remember? When you so brutally told me what a horrible father I was."

"Eh, ye still are."

"It took *four* women to release what I would have released on you. And I'm angry now. Here I am, *staying* whilst I'm angry and rock hard for *you*, the way I have *always* been when I'm angry with you. So answer me this: Do you *want* me to break you on my lust? Because that is what is going to happen *tonight*."

She was watching him warily, getting tighter in on herself, now starting to look frightened.

Good.

"*Answer me!*" he roared, pounding his fists on the bed and getting in her face. "What do you *want* from me? We had a bargain, and my mistresses and maidservants came with it. You were *happy* to allow me that in exchange for what I gave you."

"I was *never* happy with your women," she hissed, her words confusing him. "I turned a blind eye and refused to think about it. The day we arrived, you abandoned me for them and didn't give me a second glance back. I could have walked away and you would never have noticed."

He didn't remember it that way at all. "I had been away from home and I had just met you."

"And then I *saw* you!"

"So you are angry to find me doing exactly what I *have* been doing half my life, which you *know* I do and have known from the beginning. You want something from me *other than* a babe, but I do not understand what. Do not lecture me on what I keep from you when you have been keeping something from me all along. *TELL ME WHAT YOU WANT FROM ME!*"

He was utterly and completely shocked when she looked at his cod, then dragged her eyes up to his. Then she quickly looked away.

Sickened, he sneered, *"For a babe!"*

She shook her head, the slightest bit.

He stopped pacing, stunned. "You want … *me?*" he whispered.

She nodded hesitantly.

What if I told you I want you with my whole body and soul?

"You weren't mocking me," he croaked.

Again, she shook her head, but only barely.

His father was right about that.

Grimme's breath left him in a whoosh, his mind full of cotton, and he began to pace again, as the only thing he could feel was rage and the only thing he could think was—

"WHY DID YOU NOT TELL ME?!"

Her head whipped around, and she hissed, "I did! Ye didn't finish the thought. *As usual.*"

"And if I had?" he demanded.

"I would've insisted ye answer the question. But e'en if I told ye when ye were demandin' me to admire ye, ye woulda told me *once again*, gently, e'er so gently, that ye find me beauty repulsive, that I leave ye limp because I'm yer dearest o' friends, that *e'erything* ye value about me, the things that make ye crave me companionship, makes me admirable as a *man* an' ye doona rise fer men. It would hurt me—*again*—but that woulda settled the matter fer *you.* Had I said what I really wanted, ye'd'a crushed me into pieces so tiny I'd ne'er be able to put meself together again. 'Oh, Brìghde,'" she mocked with a perfect London accent, "'my lovely, *beautiful* raven queen, my *dearest friend*, I love hearing you tell me I am a Sassenach god. My vanity is pleased. But I will never desire you because you might break apart and send your ravens after me, so you never have to fear I will ravish you. Tell me more about how godlike I am and how much you desire me.'

"*And then!* To realize ye *do* rise for me, but only when ye're angry with me an' *you do not stay!* Why must I give ye a war to get ye to rise fer me? Why canna ye rise fer me when we're laughin' an' playin' and teasin'? An' then ye try to placate me with talk o' yer admiration fer me *manly* friendship. Deny it. I dare ye to deny that that is how ye'd've responded to me had I been forthcomin' about how much I truly desire ye—and oh, *God*, I do. There. I said it. Sassenach god? Aye, ye are. Now go away, because I doona want ye this way, canna stand to have ye inside me without vomiting. Ye're too ugly a friend to be borne."

You have destroyed any chance you may ever have had.

You are doing to Brìghde what my wife did to me.

"I rescued you," he said softly, desperate for something, anything, that he could use to prove he was valuable to her.

"I've shown more than enough appreciation for that. I'll not do so again."

His jaw ground and he looked away. He could not deny any of her accusations, but his anger crushed any delight he might have gotten to know she *did* desire him. He put one hand on his hip and clapped his other hand over his mouth and breathed through it to control his panting, angry with himself for *never finishing.*

"All this time," he growled, looking at her. Again, her nod was brief and wary. "When, Brìghde? When did it begin?" She shrank away from him, but he pounded the bed again. "*ANSWER ME, GOD DAMN YOU!*"

She flinched away from him. "Two days after you abducted me," she muttered, her brogue lightening, "when I saw you in the morning light."

He could barely believe his ears. "What—did—you—say?" he growled.

She did not repeat it, would not look at him, curled in a ball away from him.

"And when did you begin to care about whether I desired you or not?"

She shook her head. "I don't know. All those nights we slept together. The … closeness. It grew too much." She stopped. "You were *right there!*" she wailed suddenly, beginning to cry, pounding her fists into the bed. "When I refused you my bed," she panted through her sobs, "'twas because at those moments, I wanted you most, wanted to touch you and feel you and kiss you and know that you wanted to touch me and feel me. *But you wouldn't!* I could not control my need or resist the temptation, especially when you intended to sleep naked— I could not *bear* for you to leave me in disgust if I succumbed, so I … "

Then he understood, and it hit hard. Hurt. She was pleading with him, pouring out her hurt and frustration and anger that she could not have poured out any other time without his rebuffing her. He knew that now. Understood. Finally. Because now … *now* she had evidence that he would no longer rebuff her, and she could tell him the whole of her hurts.

"You *teased* me," she snarled suddenly. "You *taunted* me. Ever parading yourself before me, encouraging me to touch, and all the while withholding yourself. You were cruel. *Vile.* And you accused *me* of being cruel to you. What I have said and done to you canna begin to compare to the cruelty to which you have subjected me."

He winced.

"You abducted me, Grimme. You got far more than you deserved for that bit of chicanery, which was not necessary. Lastly, you abducted the wrong woman and after all I had done for you, you *still* wished you got the blonde."

And he finally—*finally*—saw her as she was: a woman who was longing and hurting. That was all. Not a witch. Not a raven. Not a warrior. Not a wife begging for a child. Just a woman who desired him and wanted him to desire her and was hurt that he didn't, enraged he had been so selfish, taking everything she could give and giving her nothing she truly valued—one good friend—in return.

He was ashamed. Elated. Aroused. Enraged—at himself because he *never finished.*

"I told you I hated weak men and every time I see you in your armor, at the tournament, riding Ares, just ... *looking* at you, your body naked or clothed, powerful, beautiful, and I want and I can't have because— And you could not— And you kept *assuring* me— As if that would be a salve to my hurt. Calling me your dearest friend— You wouldn't even *kiss* me, as if it didn't occur to you that you could do so— But of course it wouldn't, as I am a man in your eyes— But I also did not want to be one of many, as I knew you would leave my bed and go somewhere else, as you do Emelisse."

She wiped her tears with the heels of her hands and sniffled. "I see how bitter she is. I didn't want to be her, but I didn't know what to do. I could bear it no longer. I pushed and pushed and pushed to find out *why* you could not rise for me— I thought I could repair it, and once repaired, you would choose me alone— But Emelisse has carried that hope for years— Then I realized that you *do* rise for me, but not for the right reasons— But I cultivated the ravens anyway, to try, to see if you could be repaired— Grimme, I was *desperate* to show you that you need not fear them, thus, need not fear me—"

"I DON'T FEAR YOU!"

She nodded fervently. "Aye, you do. I've seen it in your face."

"No more," he breathed angrily. "The night before I left for Tavendish, when I showed you my desire for you, I was not angry. Far from it, but you couldn't even feed yourself you were so injured and weak. I went to bed and could do nothing but try to satisfy myself. I dreamt of you all the way to

Tavendish. I engaged in battle, but it was not enough to slake my bloodlust. I dreamt of you all the way home, what I would do when you met me at the portcullis, and I *craved* to have you underneath me, slaking my need. But tenderly at first, to teach you, to bring you to pleasure so that one day I could slake my bloodlust in you and *you would never break!* But you *weren't* there, did not meet me at the portcullis."

"And you took *her!*" she snarled.

"My mistake, and oh, it was a *fatal* mistake. I spent *ten days* trying to quench my lust for you." Her expression transformed to what he thought might be hope, but he wasn't sure. "I did not understand what I was doing, what I truly wanted from you because I did not understand *you*."

She sat in painfully confused silence for quite a long while, tears sparkling on her lashes. Finally, she spoke and again her confused helplessness tore at him. "I don't ken why suddenly— When you *weren't* angry, before you went to Tavendish. Why, when I was at my worst? At my most manly? You referred to me as a *knight!* And then your knights paid their respects to me when *all I wanted* was for my husband to desire me! I was being seen *by everyone* as a man!"

"Oh, no. Not a man. A goddess. Enyo."

She clamped her eyes shut and pressed her fists to her temples. *"I DON'T WANT TO BE ENYO!"*

That took him aback and halted everything. "You don't?"

"*NO!* I have *always* taken pride in being Enyo, but— You could not rise for me and then Moom and Archie said it was all my fault because I was too manly, then I experienced it. War. *Real* war. I don't want to do that. I am *not* your companion-at-arms. I *don't want* to be your companion-at-arms. I don't want you to see the goddess of war in me, to possess and conquer *her*, but not *me*. Not a raven witch or queen or a man, either. *Me!* Just a wee lassie who happens to have black hair. *Me*, Grimme! Just me!"

He watched her, noting she had *again* said something provocative, and wondering if she knew what she'd really said and if she did, if she'd meant to. "You *want* me to possess and conquer you?"

"I want you to see me, Brìghde, and desire me! Me, the wee lass you play with and talk to and laugh with!"

She knew what she'd said. His heart slowed, his body relaxed. He cracked his neck this way and that, settled into the rhythm of the battle, got comfortable, saw his imminent victory. He put one knee on the bed and slowly began crawling toward her, unable to stop his slow smirk. She watched him warily, ready to bolt.

"I asked you something very specific, Brìghde," he said slowly, with the patience of a hunter. "Do you want me to possess and conquer you?"

Suddenly she put her hand in his face and shoved him away, the way she had the duke. That *wee lassie* was very strong. "You will have to *rape* me," she hissed, "if you do not vow to stay out of *any* other cunte or arse or mouth but mine forevermore."

"That is not what I asked," he purred.

"I WILL NOT BE EMELISSE! Your spindle is *mine* and mine *alone.* Say it! Those are the terms of the new bargain, since you refused to fulfill the terms of the old one. I was, at one time, willing to share you did you look at me with some measure of lust, *but you didn't!* You rebuffed me *time and time* again! So now you must earn it."

88

THE CORNER OF Grimme's mouth turned up and he got off the bed to pace again. Yet again his lovely little wife curled up, but this time, instead of sorrow or fear on her face, she had rage.

Good.

Rage was good.

Bloodlust was good.

She was no longer drunk.

She was fully engaged now, because while she might not want to war with her husband, she would do whatever she had to to get what she wanted, and she wanted him. It humbled him, her regard, her desire—

It angered him—if he had just *finished*.

"You will change your mind after I have broken you," he said matter-of-factly. "Every woman thinks she can outlast me, but she can't. You will be no different."

Best not to underestimate an enemy, however, especially *that* one. Her blood ran hot, as hot as his, and she had bloodlust to match him.

"You said you wanted to teach me pleasure so that I would never break!"

"You're altering the terms," he reminded her sweetly.

"Aye, I am and do you not bend to those terms, I shall leave."

"On my life, I will never choose anyone over you again."

"Prove it. Send Emelisse away."

That halted him in his tracks. "I … can't," he said, bewildered. "She's the mother of my sons and they need her to be here."

"Won't," she muttered hatefully.

"Where would I send her?" he demanded.

"That is not my concern. These are my terms: No other forevermore. Emelisse goes, as I canna live with her any longer. How much do you value me, Grimme? That is the question I put before you. I already know how much you valued Aldwyn, so I can see the direction this will go. I have given you too much of my friendship, begging for scratches, which you swore I would never have to do—"

"Your wants *changed*," he snarled, "and drifted outside the boundary of friendship and you did not tell me!"

She nodded. "True. I tried to tell you, but you did not listen. I tried to show you, but you refused to see. I tried to reason with you, but you refused to make an attempt. I tried to accommodate your infirmity and your request for time and my good company, but you thought that meant I would never call you to account. I tried to make you jealous, but it dinna work. I tried to ignore your hurts against me, but you continued to do those things even though you knew they hurt me. I tried to taunt you, but you would not prove me wrong. I tried to make myself more of a lady, but you did not notice. I tried to apologize for a hurt I thought I had dealt you, and you snarled at me. I have put your earldom to rights, and you don't value that because you don't know the work it takes and you never wanted to be an earl in the first place."

He started to object to that, but she talked over him.

"I have done everything I could, served you, pleaded with you, debased myself in every way I could manage. You have humiliated me. Your liege has claimed me. My mother has scorned me. Your father has embarrassed me. Your mistress ridicules me. Publicly. *And you allow her to.* I have borne more insult than I have ever allowed myself to bear before. Why? Because I hoped that one day, you would take me to wife and choose me over all others. I no longer have that hope and I no longer care. I am leaving not just you, but the lot of you, and I am taking Pierce, whose mother did not want him and whose father will not protect him."

With each damning word that came out of her mouth, his shame increased. She was right. She was always right, and she had borne far more than any friend could be expected to, certainly more than Aldwyn had.

"I have done the best I could," he protested weakly, "within my experience."

"No you haven't," she countered matter-of-factly. "You want everything to be as you want it. You want to conquer. You want total and complete subjugation of your enemy and you find it most satisfying when they simply settle down and quietly obey. I did. Now I am not. She goes or I go. I do not know *where* I will go, mind you, but it willna be to my family, who believes this is my fault for not being alluring enough, or to Dunham or Tavendish, who think I am too dimwitted to be allowed out of the keep."

He sighed heavily. He had only one gambit left. Whether it would work or not, he did not know. "Then go."

"'On my life, I will never choose anyone over you again,'" she mocked.

"But I'm going with you."

Silence.

"Will that convince you?" he asked low, his heart thundering in his chest. "You and me and Pierce, our own little family, as I have always thought of us. Ares, Enyo, Troy, Helen, Mercury. Wandering England with no lack of coin, doing whatever takes our fancy. Mayhap we will be joined by a big black bitch from hell to protect us."

More silence.

"I don't want that," she finally murmured. "Removing yourself from Emelisse to keep from swiving her is no proof of anything." She sighed. "Go away. You do not want to get rid of Emelisse nor do you desire me unless I turn into a goddess of war. I have told you what you wanted to know, so you and I have nothing more to say to each other."

"I will not throw the mother of my children out," he said firmly, "as they are too attached to her. I let Maebh go because she was willing to do what was best for Pierce. I am willing to leave because they do not need me, but they do need her. They need a place to come home where their mother is always going to be."

Still more silence, and as he had with Caroline, he continued to talk to get some concession she was listening and understood his position.

"As for my desire for you, it is there. It was there before you left for Tavendish, there before I left for Tavendish."

"No other, Grimme. No one else. Ever. Save me. If you want me to stay, those are the terms."

He started to pace again but said nothing, continuing to stare at her with each turn. She watched him pace, still wary, still half afraid he would fulfill his promise to attack her and the evidence that he could was still standing straight and tall.

But this was war.

"Compromise: I have no other but you forevermore ... until you beg me go somewhere else to slake my lust because I have broken you—and you will also *admit* that I broke you. In detail. *In writing*. So that you may never say that I did not fulfill my part, that I can remind you *why* when you forget and grow angry at my women, and that you grant me my freedom again."

"You think I am putting you in a *cage?*" she asked incredulously.

"I – WANT – MY – LUST – SATISFIED!" he roared. "Those are the terms I am willing to abide by. Take it or leave it, and if you leave it, I will go to Dillena right now." No, he wouldn't.

"Dillena put you out," she sniffed.

"Five maidservants." Who were gone.

"Do it. Pierce and I will leave tomorrow morning and if you follow, you will *never* see him again." She was wrong about that, but she was not bluffing. Pierce could live without Grimme. He couldn't live without Brìghde, and she knew that. "If you want me *now*, you do it on *my* terms because God knows you couldn't do it on your terms. When was the last time you had your spindle in a cunte?" she snarled. "This morning? I wasn't at breakfast, so I don't know."

"Two weeks ago," he said calmly. "The night I went to Sheffield to get Aldwyn."

She narrowed her gaze at him.

"Furthermore, the only place I slept whilst you were gone to Tavendish other than out in the camp with my sons, was in your bed, and the only person I fucked was myself. In your bed."

She pulled her lips between her teeth.

"You sent Maebh and Ardith away—and I let you. Do not, for one second, believe that you could have done that without my leave." Aye, she knew that. Her expression told him. "Dillena put me out because I broke her—likely forever. Rose dismissed the maidservants to punish me."

Her mouth dropped open, then she closed it with a snap.

"I was done with Emelisse when she met me at the portcullis expecting me to fuck her, and walked right past Caroline without a thought to help her when she fell."

Brìghde looked at him, aghast. "She didn't!" she breathed.

Ah, aye, there was his sweet Brìghde. "She did. That does *not* mean I can't find more."

She shoo'd him away. "Go. Go go go. See how fast you can swive more maidservants before Rose dismisses them too and *no* I will not dismiss her and I don't care how disrespectful she is to you."

"Only because I allow it," he reminded her.

"Never mind then. I'll take her and her husband with me when I go."

She wasn't bluffing, but they were only at the halfway point of the battle. It was no different than any he had ever waged wading through men's blood and bodies up to his knees.

"How much do you value me, Grimme?" she demanded, rolling her R. "More than your horse, aye, I know. More than Emelisse? No, because you have chosen her every bloody time!"

"I have sworn and will continue to swear that I will never choose her over you again."

"We'll see about that the next time she provokes me and I punish her for it. Here's the real question: Do you value me more than your spindle? Vow. I am the only one. Now and forevermore."

He was going to make sure she knew what, exactly, was at stake. "No. Because you will break."

"Not that I could trust a vow," she mocked, "since you vowed to come back to me and you put your spindle in *her*."

"I am sorry about that," he said again, and again sincerely. "I will grovel for that any way you tell me to however many times you tell me to. But no."

"Methinks you do not understand the nature of a negotiation. I have something you want. I am not giving it to you without a fight and if you do that, I will set my ravens on you. You have far more to lose than I do because *I DON'T HAVE ANYTHING TO LOSE! VOW!*"

He wanted Brìghde more than anything he had ever wanted in his life, and not because of her cunte. He was hard, getting harder as the battle raged.

War.

He *had* to have her. Had to *keep* her. He could not *bear* to let her go. He would promise her *anything* to keep her.

"No," he said patiently. "You will deny me to punish me and cite my vow. You will get tired and sore and chafed and beg me for relief, yet *I* will be bound by my vow. You will balk at doing something that pleasures me and I will be bound by my vow not to find another for that specific pleasure. How much do you value *me*, Brìghde? How much do you value our friendship? If 'tis not that much or if I have damaged it beyond repair, then aye, I can accept that because I deserve it, and God knows I've been a very bad friend, a worse husband, and the worst father, so I would not blame you, and I will deeply grieve the loss of your company for the rest of my life. So we are again at an impasse. We are negotiating our terms and I am still hard. For you."

"Because we are at war and that is the only time you rise for me!"

Why don't you try kissing her?

You wouldn't even kiss me, as if it didn't occur to you that you could do so.

He looked at his tiny wife, curled in on herself quivering with hurt and resentment and anger. He could not allow this negotiation to appear as a war. *He* was aroused by it but she was not, which meant he had to seduce her, which he did not know how to do. It made him wonder for the first time in his life, *What would Aldwyn do?*

"Do you remember," he murmured, "the morning you left for Tavendish?"

She said nothing and looked away.

"I kissed you. You were dressed like a soldier. You had a squire. And yet ... The thought of you never coming back to me was—"

"Then why did you not take me to bed right then?" she demanded.

"I was thinking too much," he said, surprising himself. "Thinking about the food. Thinking about the possibility that you would not return. Thinking about what I really wanted. I was awake all night thinking. You had commanded me to go back to France, but ... I didn't want to."

She looked confused, which gave him hope.

"Aye, it took me by surprise, too. I have spent almost two years wanting to go back to France, then you gave me permission to do so. Nothing held me here, for you can rule better than I or my father and you may prove to be the better politician with some tutoring. I knew you would take care of the earldom and that would satisfy Henry, but I didn't want to. You made this my home. Without you, I can't feel at home at all."

"And you have made me feel as if I am nothing but a necessary evil," she snapped. "Do you not ken? Unless I am useful, I am wanted *nowhere*."

He grimaced, but he did not avert his eyes, instead studying the bare skin of her arm, her hip, her thigh, seeing how tiny and defenseless she was, noting how she sat: wounded, angry, and frightened.

"I will be true to you until you break and put me out," he said again. "You will admit *in writing, in detail* that I broke you and why. Those are the terms I will agree to."

Her nostrils flared and her jaw ground. "No third persons," she said, shocking him. So she *was* willing to negotiate. "Or fourth. Or fifth. Or any number. Just you and me."

"Brìghde," he said low. "You don't know what you're asking for."

"Then leave and allow me to continue packing."

"I will accept that term, but you *must* do everything else my women do as many times as I want. Do you want me to list them out?"

She held up a hand and counted on her fingers. "All positions of swiving."

"Aye. Do you know what those are?"

"I have seen two or three. I can guess others. I will assume you'll teach me the rest." He nodded. She was still negotiating. She put down her second finger. "Your spindle in my arse."

"Eventually. You asked me why anyone would put pearls up their arse. You'll find out."

She scrunched up her face in disgust. "That is where one *shits* from!"

"Hot water and soap," he said with a crisp pop on the P.

She took a deep breath. Third finger. "Suck your spindle."

He was getting harder just hearing these things come out of her mouth. "Aye."

"What did Emelisse mean when she said that once for you was three times for her?"

Ohhhhh, *that* conversation. In French. Later, he would try to remember what other conversations she might have heard. "A man gets hard, gets stroked, spends his seed once. He goes limp. Stays that way for an hour or two before he can get hard again."

"Aye."

"Not I. I can spend three times before I go limp. Wait one hour. Another three times. I can do that for hours. 'Tis why I require more than one or two women. Three or four. Because a woman gets dry and raw and itchy no matter how much oil I use, which makes it little better than rape—but I still want more."

She squeaked in sudden comprehension, now completely cowed.

He smirked evilly. "But since you have negotiated that away … " She gulped. "Would you like to renegotiate third and fourth and fifth parties?"

"No." She closed her eyes and clenched her jaw. "But I don't know enough to be able to promise that. I *can* promise I will do my best."

She wouldn't be able to survive that several nights in a row, but she was still negotiating. "Very well. I will accept that. What else?"

"Being tied up?" she asked carefully, putting down her fourth finger.

"To keep you still so that I may play with your body at my leisure and you may do the same to me."

Was that … *delight* in her expression? "You will let me tie you up and play with you?" she asked courteously, as if the question itself didn't give her away. How utterly intriguing.

"Aye."

She nodded. "Very well."

"Next?"

"You said something about punishment." Fifth finger. "That, I cannot imagine. My brothers never said anything suchlike and I have not seen or heard of that in my travels."

How could he explain this without terrifying her? Never mind. She *should* be terrified. He took a deep breath. "Pain can bring release."

She looked at him blankly.

He took his cod in his hand and stroked. Her eyes widened and her breath caught, but that was *not* fear and she started squirming. "I do this," he said low, barely able to stand it when the woman he wanted was *right there* and aroused by his display. "If you took a whip to my arse right now, I would spend."

Her eyes popped. "You want *me* to do that to *you?*"

He released his cod because he was about to spend all over her bed. That was not a good way to negotiate. "Aye, but I would do it to you, too."

"A whip?" she squeaked.

"My hand. At first. And you would enjoy it."

She gulped. "Emelisse doesn't."

"Dillena does."

"Uh … "

He gave her a wolfish grin. "Aye, the *quiet* one."

She pulled her lips between her teeth and looked away. That might have been too much, but he'd already given up his orgies for her, so this answer would tell him how much she wanted him. "Anything else?" she asked.

"That is all I can think of at the moment. Your answer, my lady?"

"Emelisse?"

"She stays. My sons need her."

She closed her eyes and took a deep breath. "May I trust that you will help me learn to enjoy all the things that pleasure you?"

"Of course," he said softly. "Why would I want you to dread anything that pleasures me?"

"Then, aye."

"If we are finished, what say you?"

Her jaw went back and forth whilst she considered it. She was taking a *very* long time. "If I am with child? Ill? Injured? My courses?"

"I will gladly accommodate any of those and abstain, as I did when you returned from Tavendish. I have no lust when I'm injured, ill, or exhausted, either."

"I do not want to have to declare war on you every time I want your spindle."

"You won't have to."

She rolled her eyes. "And what if you gain a newfound aversion to me?"

"There is *nothing* that could keep me out of your cunte now."

"Done," she said immediately.

So *that* was what she had wanted to hear. He almost laughed.

"You overestimate your will and endurance, and you underestimate mine."

Now she looked *very* frightened.

"Good," he breathed with a victorious curl to his lip. He put one knee on the bed and then began crawling to her. His cod needed relief. Immediately. "Fear me, Brìghde," he whispered, taunting her, his desire for her growing by the second. She shrank away from him with wide eyes and slid away from him until she was in danger of falling off the bed. "Fear me, my wee lass Brìghde, for I have conquered you and now I will possess you and you will *thank* me for it."

89

BRÌGHDE WAS terrified.

She had not thought taunting him would be a risk at all, but even if she had, she would *never* have thought he would come after her once she had threatened him with her pets.

But she should've. He was a warrior who did not wage war honorably. He sneaked and stabbed and spied. Of course he would be enraged when she beat him at his own strategy and break through his fear to conquer her through brute strength because *he refused to lose.*

He reached up a hand and she flinched away, but his hand was soft, touching her cheek, his thumb lightly caressing her bottom lip. He gently turned her chin until she was nose to nose with him. She pulled away a little to look into his velvety brown eyes, dark with lust.

Lust for her.

She reached forward, wrapped her hand around his head, and brought him to her for a crushing kiss. They kissed for moments upon moments, Brìghde's eyes closed, feeling his tongue sliding along hers, the panting breaths from his nose. She was panting as much.

"I want to touch you," she breathed.

"I'm yours," he whispered hotly as he continued to kiss her.

And as they kissed, she stroked her hands down his neck, across his shoulders, down his back as far as she could reach. She caressed him as she pulled her hands back down over his shoulders and caressed his chest—the one she had seen so often, had stared at when he could not see, wanting to touch, never having the courage to risk being rebuffed—gently, ever so gently, with effulgent praise of her person, declarations of eternal friendship, and a distant admiration of her beauty.

He grasped her chin and said, "Open your eyes." She opened them. He pulled away from her. "See me."

"I do," she whispered, wondering what he was saying.

He reached for her hair and pulled a lock into his hand, stroked it, studied it. "See that I am seeing *you,* Brìghde Fàileach Kyneward, my wife, my castellain, my countess, my dearest friend in the world, and that I desire you, that *I* know whom I crave to slake my lust. Do you believe that?"

"Your imagin—"

"I DON'T HAVE AN IMAGINATION!"

She gulped.

"Your eyes are beautiful," he whispered, reaching up to comb his fingers through her hair once again. "Green isn't my favorite color," he murmured, then caressed her face until his thumb was stroking her chin. "I said that because I looked in your eyes and it was the most beautiful color I'd ever seen."

Brìghde did not know what to think and decided that perhaps she simply should not try.

"I am here. With you. Not Enyo. Not the raven queen. Not a witch. Not a man. Just my sweet wee lassie Brìghde who happens to have black hair. Do you believe that?"

She looked in his eyes, which did not stray from hers and she searched for a long time. He did not drop her stare, did not mock or tease. Her mind told her to run, run far away, where he could never find her. Her heart told her to run far, far away to find out if he would follow. Her body simply wanted to feel his skin next to hers.

I love you, Grimme. Please love me.

"Aye, I do."

He backed away from her then reached across the bed and grabbed her ankle, yanking her across the bed toward him, making her yelp and fall flat on her back. She looked at him. "Fear me," he whispered again with that victorious, evil smile that caught her breath.

"Do you do this with *them?*" she taunted.

He sneered. "I don't have to. When I want my cod stroked, I go their chambers, and they will do what I bloody well want them to do. *Immediately.* I could go to Dillena right now, snap my fingers, tell her to bend over and spread her legs, and she'd do it and I would shove my cod into her cunte so hard she'd feel it in her throat."

Sweet Mother Mary, what had she unleashed?

"And then I leave and come sleep with you. *You,"* he whispered as he pressed his lips to the inside of her knee, then softly kissed her over and over again, brushing his mouth over her skin, licking her, his breath tickling her. "Oh, *you.* I will play with you and talk and tease. I will sleep with you. I will enjoy your body as a part of my dearest friend. But know this: I—conquered—you. Send your ravens, my queen, my witch. I will slaughter every raven in Britain and Europe to get to you and then I will *eat—them—raw."*

"Oh Lord," she whimpered, seeing him with blood dripping down his chin and onto his strong naked chest, a big raven crushed in his bigger hand.

Her cunte clenched the way it had before when she had looked at him and craved to touch him.

"Brìghde," he breathed as his mouth crept up her inner thigh, kissing, licking, breathing, closer and closer to her cunte until he was at the crease between it and her thigh. "I cannot live without you."

She worked herself up to her elbows and looked down her body at his golden-red hair between her legs and when his fingers spread her folds open, and licked her, she gasped, arching her back.

"Bloody hell, you're already wet." He sounded shocked.

She nearly choked when he slipped two fingers inside her easily.

"I knew you'd be a lusty wench," he purred as he slowly stroked inside and out, and she could feel herself clenching on him. "You do *everything* with passion. You refused me your bed when you knew you could not resist trying to seduce me?"

"When your refusal hurt too much," she corrected tersely.

"Very well," he grunted as he raised up on his knees and moved toward her, straightening her out on the bed, spreading her legs, and situating himself between them. "Look, Brìghde."

Once again, she raised up on her elbows to see his big body straight and proud, his spindle also straight and proud, long and thick, his big hand around it, stroking a little, his thumb passing over the head.

"Can that—fit?" She looked up at him, fearful again. "Will it hurt?"

"Possibly." His fingers were still in her cunte, his thumb doing something with some spot above it. He was still watching her face. "You're a virgin, but you're so wet that may not make a difference. Choose: Hard and fast or easy and slow?"

She gulped. "What would you recommend?"

He barked a laugh and grinned at her. "That is the most dimwitted question I have ever heard."

She laughed. "Aye, it was."

But his thumb went across that spot again and she gasped, again arching her back, her lower body reaching for him and then again when he barely touched her entrance with his spindle. "Easy and slow," he whispered, then drove into her.

"Grimme!" she screamed, bolting upright and panting with the stabbing pain. "That was *not* easy *or* slow!"

She felt his hand caressing her cheek. "Shhh … 'twill pass. Just wait. Look."

She opened her eyes and looked down at their respective mounds intimately touching, feeling his spindle inside her, stretching her, but not moving.

She was half sitting, her knees draped over his strong thighs. "Aye," she panted as the pain eased away into pleasant fullness.

"Watch." He pulled out a little and he was shiny with some liquid. "That's you. That's your desire for me. 'Twill ease the way. Give me your hand." She looked up at him in question. He gave her a crooked smile. "Trust me."

She gave him her hand and he manipulated her fingers until he had the middle one. He brought it down between them, spread her folds wider, and put her finger where his tongue had gone. "That," he said matter-of-factly, "is your nymph. 'Tis what gives a woman the most pleasure."

He released her hand and slid all the way inside her again. Her muscles clenched on their own. "I can please it like this," he murmured wedging his mound between her folds. Her breath caught. "I can please it with my hand like this." He pulled away a little, touched her there, and tickled it. Again she could not breathe. And then he began to move in and out of her in time with his finger strokes.

"Oh, sweet Mother Mary," she breathed and lay down to close her eyes and let him to do whatever he wanted to do to her.

"Oh, I see," he teased, "wee lassie Brìghde thinks she can conquer me by making me do all the work, aye?"

"Aye," she sighed, feeling herself clench around him more, something seeming to build inside her.

He started to laugh. "For God's sake, don't go to *sleep* on me!"

"It feels so good," she breathed. "If you can stay like that all night, I will never have to admit anything."

His laughter deepened and he pulled away.

"No, no, no!" she said, panicked, and struggled upward again. "Don't go."

"You, my lovely, are going to participate. Lie back again. Grasp your nipples."

Anything to keep him wedged inside her. She obeyed, finding her nipples to be tight.

"Roll them between your fingers."

She did and began to whimper. Then she rolled them harder and harder, clenching on him, arching her back.

"Bloody hell," he whispered, almost in awe.

She pushed herself against him, pinched her nipples as hard as she thought she could bear, and then—

"Oh, my God!" she gasped, coming off the bed, eyes wide. She almost cried when he withdrew almost completely from her because her sensations drew away a bit. "Grimme," she pleaded.

"We've got a long night ahead of us," he said vaguely as he laid himself upon her, bracing himself with his hands on either side of her face. "You want my cod?"

"Aye," she breathed, clenching herself around him, trying to retrieve that lovely feeling.

He began to move in and out slowly. She opened her eyes and he was watching her, studying her as if to determine … He went faster and she sighed, feeling a lazy smile growing upon her face.

"Don't you dare go to sleep," he warned, ramming into her hard and staying, which made her smile wider.

"Stay there."

"No. But I will … "

His hips began to roll, which her nymph could feel and combined with his spindle stuffed inside her, was utterly divine. "Better than wine," she sighed.

He withdrew, drove into her again, withdrew, then he went faster … faster … faster until she matched his rhythm, her hips rising and falling with his strokes, feeling him against her nymph. At some point, she gave up trying to match him, because he was going so fast, pounding into her, and all she wanted to do was lie there and enjoy it.

"Brìghde," he growled.

She raised a hand and put her finger against his lips. "Shhh … "

He sucked her finger into his mouth and her eyes flew open. He grinned, then bit down. "Ow!"

But then, his hips a battering ram, he lowered his head and kissed her heatedly. She returned it, wrapped her legs around his arse to pull him closer.

"Don't," he whispered against her mouth. "I can't go as far."

"I know. I want you to be inside me and *stay*."

"So you can go to sleep? No. We can play that game later." She scowled in confusion and he chuckled. "Oh, my lovely lady wife, this is only the very beginning. Roll your nipples again. I can't reach with my mouth. You're too short."

She ignored his teasing and did as he said. She grunted with each thrust, enjoying every one, especially with pinching and pulling at her nipples.

Grimme gritted his teeth and arched his back, ramming into her again and staying, the way she liked. One short, tiny thrust. Another short, tiny thrust. A third and he was buried inside her.

He opened his eyes and looked down at her. "Now you."

"Now me what?"

He grinned and began to move again.

"No!" she wailed. "*Stay.*"

He heaved a sigh and rolled his eyes, then did as she bid, squirming so his mound was directly against her nymph.

"Aye," she breathed as she clenched around him and pulled him closer in with her legs and squirmed and then— She growled like an animal, panting, clenching, working herself on his spindle as if she were in the saddle.

"Keep going," he whispered, pinching her nipples.

She did and just as the feelings began to dissipate and she released her hold on his arse, he took his opportunity to begin his withdraw and advance again. It was too much for her to keep it all in and she nearly screamed with the next one.

He was still going when hers faded completely, and that was quite all right. It meant she could lie back and relax, enjoying the feel of his body in hers, knowing that *she* had made him rise, knowing that he *knew* whom he was bedding, knowing he was *hers*, and she would never have to share him. She clasped her hands behind her head to simply watch and feel.

He once again released his seed into her, stopped and stayed. "Look at you, lazing there as if 'tis my duty to fuck you."

She closed her eyes and smiled. "It is. Who possesses whom, my lord?"

He chuckled wickedly, but he stayed. And stayed. And stayed.

And then, he began again. It didn't take as long this time before he released, which was disappointing.

He stayed still inside her for, she supposed, as long as he could because she felt him shrinking.

"You broke me," he quipped as he twisted off her and landed on the bed next to her, then twisted over her to kiss her whilst caressing and kneading her breast, pinching her nipples.

"Harder," she breathed into his mouth.

He chuckled as he kissed her, caressing her cheek and her hair. "In a few moments, I am going to let you sleep." Her eyelids were already getting heavy. "No, no. I need to fetch something."

She whimpered when he rolled out of bed and bounded across the room, out the door and leaving it open—she sighed—going to his own chambers, then returning with a small chest.

"Close the bloody door, Grimme!"

He kicked it closed without a thought and sat on the side of the bed. "You wanted to sleep with me inside you, aye?"

"Oh, yes," she sighed dreamily.

He slipped his fingers into her cunte. "You've got enough seed in you to fill a tankard." Then gave her an arrogant grin. "I will admit I did not expect such voraciousness from a virgin, but you do everything with lust, so I shouldn't be surprised."

He opened his chest and she saw many small implements in it. "There are specific devices?" she asked. "You don't have to use a brush handle?"

"Brushes are convenient, but likely irritating to sleep with," he muttered as his hand wafted over each item as if this choice was the most important choice he had ever made. He chose a small glass phallus and said, "Spread your legs. Watch."

She did and once again struggled to her elbows to see the small glass column disappear inside her. It wasn't as big as he was.

"What's wrong?"

She told him and he was surprised. "Oh. Very well." He took it out, threw it on the bed, and chose one with a larger girth. She watched that one disappear and she sighed and dropped her head back.

"That one, then?" he asked dryly.

"Aye."

She flopped back on the bed and clenched around it. When he returned to bed, he had to shove her this way and that to get her under the linens, but he didn't seem to mind. Then, once all was right with their linens, he slid into bed and lay on his back, then gathered her to his side. She crooked her leg and felt that wonderful thing rubbing her in all the right places.

"*Now* you may sleep."

She did.

90

GRIMME LAY dozing with his wife lying against him in a dead sleep, her cunte stuffed with glass.

The second day after he'd abducted her … He searched his mind, but sadly did not remember anything but that he was consumed with rage at Sheffield, driven to such a repugnant task—only to find out that it had suddenly turned into a rescue, how relieved and grateful he was, and how much fun he had had with her on their journey home.

He had so many regrets, so many things he should have seen, should have done, should have said. If he'd stayed during their first argument. If he'd done what his father and Mouse told him to do—

Why don't you try kissing her?

… once you've bedded Brìghde, you will see her in an entirely different light …

… if you fuck her, you'll get your friend back.

They were right. How had they known?

How many times had he slept with her? How many times had he seen her naked body? How many times had she bathed in front of him? How many opportunities had she given him—and only stopped because she hurt too much?

So much time he had wasted, so many ways he had hurt her—not intentionally, but intent and carelessness often yielded the same result.

Ignoring brunettes was a habit. His taste had carved itself in stone with his first woman and he still had her, almost twelve years later. He had had six other women who looked like Emelisse. Women who looked like Emelisse were everywhere. He didn't need to think about brunettes at all. He fucked the women he wanted and ignored the women he didn't.

If Brìghde had not been so intelligent and delightful, he would have ignored her, too, never giving a thought to her hair color at all. But then … his new fun, delightful friend had wanted the black linen and he finally noticed her dark beauty, her raven-black hair, her fair skin with the faint dusting of freckles, her big emerald eyes.

He had never seen a more beautiful woman in his life.

If only …

It had taken her going off to war and the realization that she may never come back for him to notice he needed more from her than her company and friendship.

What if I told you I wanted you with my whole body and soul?

Not mocking him. All he'd had to say was a sincere *Is that true?*

She couldn't have lied to him. She wanted to tell him. She wanted him to ask. Even if she'd lied, he'd have been watching for it.

His heart ached.

And now … tonight …

He had intended to teach her passion tenderly. He had risen for her, had shown her before he left for Tavendish, had stayed hard for her throughout the battle. He intended to control his need so that she need not fear him and learn what he liked. Instead, he had taken Emelisse at the gate.

He ached with regret for many reasons, and one of them was that tonight, she—a virgin—had taken him all three times, paced him, and then wanted more because she had bloodlust to match his.

No matter how insatiable she was *now*, however, there would come a day he would wear her down, wear her out, and then break her.

She would never admit he'd broken her so either she'd endure it the way Dillena had been willing to or attempt to change the bargain again, and *that* he would not do. He would never go back to Emelisse, Dillena, or maidservants, but he would have to do something when she could no longer bear the physical demands. The chafing. The itching. The soreness. The exhaustion.

Confronting all the pleasures he enjoyed that she didn't know enough about to negotiate in good faith.

The second she broke and begged and he went back to his habits, she'd leave him and he would not be able to bear that. He had meant to teach her so that she would never break, never beg for mercy because he knew—he'd always known—she would never allow herself to be one of many. She had to leave to give him a taste of what it would be like to live without her, to realize he did value her more than he valued his cod.

He slept for a while, a deep sleep, the kind he always slept with her, peaceful, restful, the kind he hadn't slept with any woman he was fucking. Even when he was still sleeping with Emelisse, he'd merely dozed, waiting for her to be ready to take him again.

He was not hard when he awakened. He had too many thoughts, troubling ones, to rise. That too was part of his failure with Brìghde. Brìghde made him *think* about things, important things. He had no room to think about fucking.

His eyes popped open with the realization— He wouldn't need as much because he did other things with Brìghde that he had never done with his women. They talked. They laughed. They thought. They argued. They played. They plotted. They slept. They ruled.

Grimme had practically begged Emelisse to educate herself so he could do that with her. He had never cared before, and then … he did.

His father never made a mistress of a woman until she was his friend. Mouse had had female friends he wanted to fuck or wanted to fuck him but it was not returned, thus he had stopped making female friends.

Lord, how could Grimme be so dense?

No, not dense. Frightened, for after the ravens had attacked him, he had never been able to shed his brother's tales.

Brìghde stirred. He did not want to awaken her, for he did not want to wear her out, but her breathing was deepening. He kneaded her arse, tickled the crease between her arse cheek and her thigh. She giggled and squirmed. She was so lovely.

"Brìghde," he said as he caressed her, "I want to apologize."

"What for?" she mumbled.

"Being angry with you so much that I kept us apart, not coming to you with my hurt."

"If you had, you would have found me in bed awaiting you."

"That, but I mean all this time—" And he confessed all his thoughts because she was his dearest friend and he kept nothing from her. "You make me think and … I cannot rise when my mind is occupied, and that is what you do. You occupy my mind every hour of every day."

She was silent for a while after he finished. "It was not simply the ravens?" she asked, clearly confused.

"How can I explain it a different way?" He took a deep breath and tried to order his feelings into words. "A *raven* is superior to me, for they conquered me then and continue to do so. A *man* is my equal. A *woman* is inferior to me. This is what I did not understand about you: You were not my superior. You were not a man. You were a woman, but I have always seen you as my equal. I could not reconcile it in my mind. But when you pulled Emelisse across the floor, all I saw was a raven witch breaking apart and coming for the naughty boy and I had been very naughty, and … aye, you terrified me. You were, in fact, my superior, you always had been, and you conquered me."

"Oh, Grimme," she sighed sadly. "I'm not your superior. I don't want to be your superior. I want you to see me and value me as your dearest friend *and* your lover. But I will not be one of many who share your spindle."

He sighed heavily and pulled her even closer to his body.

"I'm curious," she said. "You have black tournament armor and Ares has hair black as mine. Why does this not bother you?"

"It's intimidating and I don't have to look at myself." He paused. "As for Ares," he murmured. "I almost let him die because I was frightened of him too. But he was so small and helpless, and his dam was trying so hard, 'twas almost as if she were begging me to help her save her babe. That's why I did it. I could not pass by a sickly babe without trying to help."

She lifted herself up to look at him, but her expression was so sad and pitying, he couldn't bear it, so he slapped her arse.

She yelped. "Already?"

"Anything can happen at any time." He smirked, but it faded. "I have so much guilt and regret for what I have done to you, to our friendship." He pressed his lips to her head. "I'm sorry," he whispered. "Forgive me?"

"Please don't make me give you a war every time I want your spindle," she said in a small voice that tore his heart out. "I don't want that. It takes too much work and too much anger, and I don't like being angry. I want us to be like we were on our way here from Fàileach. My first morning here, when I got your arse out of bed—"

He chuckled. He would never stop laughing about that.

"Aye," she insisted. "That was funny. You are not only a lusty man, but you are a funny and cheerful one as well. We can be like that. That is what I want. I want to laugh and tease and jest. And when we argue, we may argue as we did in Hogarth, calmly, acknowledging our wrongs, or teasing each other out of our pique and repairing the situation. But I *also* want this, to be lovers alone, just us, loving and then talking and then sleeping."

"I want the same."

She shifted her hips and adjusted her legs and sighed happily. "That glass is divine. Rub my arse," she commanded as she yawned.

He didn't bother. She had already fallen asleep.

91

WHEN BRÌGHDE awoke, she was still full, but now it was her husband. She was on her belly, sprawled out. He must have gently slid the glass out and himself in. He was braced over her, but remained still.

"Mmmm," she purred and clenched around him as she had been doing the glass.

"You're a lusty wench, Brìghde Kyneward," he whispered in her ear.

"And aren't you disproportionately advantaged."

He chuckled and she could feel it all the way up in her cunte. He lifted himself off her body, and she whimpered when he left her. But he grasped her hips and pulled them up off the bed. She lifted her front half—

"No, lie there. Only your arse."

"Are you going to put those pearls in me?"

"Aye."

She sighed when he slid into her again and stayed, but it didn't feel the same. It wasn't as tight. She was too open and she tried to close her legs a little—

"No, stay still."

"Grimme," she whinged.

"I gave you what you wanted immediately the way you wanted it. Now let me play with your body."

"Do you do this, with the pearls?"

"Aye. When I've got three or more women. Keeps me harder longer. Now stay still." With that, he slapped her arse.

All these *things* were going to send her into the trusses. She clenched around him. "Do that again."

He laughed and slapped her again.

"Harder." She tilted her hips forward, and then back again.

"I told you not to do that."

With all her strength, she slammed her arse into his belly to seat his spindle in her fully. She huffed. She closed her eyes and enjoyed the feel of him in her whilst he kneaded her arse and rubbed oil in the cleft, then coated her hole. She gasped when he slipped a finger in and—

He caught her hips. "No, no. Relax. Don't fight it."

It took some time to accustom herself, and she gritted her teeth the entire time. The only reason she could bear it was because his cod was in her the entire time and having his finger in her arse was painfully, disgustingly pleasurable.

Soon enough he withdrew his finger and slipped the well-oiled pearls in one by one until she felt them in her cunte, against Grimme's spindle.

"Can you feel those?" she whispered.

"Aye," he returned gruffly. "How does that feel?"

"Odd."

"Aye, well, we will accustom you to such and then when you are ready, you will take the whole of me."

She groaned.

"With the glass in your cunte."

"Uh … "

"Time, Brìghde. Just time."

He slid out of her almost all the way and she whimpered.

"Use your hand on your nymph, the way I taught you."

Brìghde squirmed around until she could get it there and rubbed it gently. She could admit that it was a bit tender, but having Grimme in her was worth much discomfort. He began to slowly go in and out. It felt so lovely she completely forgot about her nymph and enjoyed being full.

"You truly enjoy that, don't you?"

"Aye," she sighed. "'Tis as a back rub, but for my insides."

He burst out laughing. "And the pearls?"

"They make up for the space left whilst I am spread so." But at some point whilst Grimme began to drive into her in earnest, the other sensations grew and then she was reaching for the moment she thought she would die in pleasure. It faded, it grew, with each withdrawal and stroke in, it went up and down. She clenched in on him.

"Use your hand, Brìghde," he encouraged softly.

So he knew what she was reaching for. She spread her folds and caressed her nymph, and once she had done that, she reached her crisis, yet again growled like a wild animal and tried to slam herself back upon Grimme, but she kept missing the rhythm he paced, which made him slip out. "Stop." He grasped her hips and re-set the pace.

"Grimme," she whinged, her whole world revolving around her husband's spindle, the way her whole body revolved around it. And then her crisis passed and she simply enjoyed getting a back rub for her insides.

Faster he went, harder. He groaned with release. "Brìghde … " he whispered, caressing her arse. Then he slapped her, but instead of yelping, she said,

"Harder." She clenched upon him and he chuckled. He stayed still for a while, but— "I am getting an ache in my neck."

"Very well, get up on your hands."

That changed things. "Am I allowed to complain about such things or do you wish for me to suffer discomfort that takes away from the pleasure?"

"No, I don't wish that."

She was braced and her head hung low and she squirmed upon him where he impaled her.

"Finished?" he asked.

"Noooooo."

He laughed outright. "I have never laughed so much as I do with you, in bed or out. You are thoroughly delightful."

He began to move again and his second release was just as lovely as his first. Whilst he attempted to gain his third, the other sensations returned and Brìghde reached for them whilst, one by one, the pearls were popped out of her and she gasped, her release extraordinary, but more than that, it kept going whilst he pulled them out slowly. And *kept going*. He lowered himself over her so that he covered her like a dog covered his bitch and rammed into her hard and fast to find his release and give her hers, which did not happen until …

He *bit* her! On the back of the neck like a cat! And *held on!*

"Grimme," she breathed, panting heavily, her head down. He snarled when he rammed into her the final time, his teeth still in her neck, and his seed entered her.

If she were not with child by the time this night was over, 'twould be a miracle.

He opened his mouth and released her, then left her slowly, and she felt his seed creep down her inner thigh. Normally she would be disgusted, but tonight it was proof that he had *finally* found his lust for her.

"Glass?"

"Aye."

He slid her new favorite toy inside her, slick with his seed, and smacked her arse.

"Again."

"Mmm … Come."

"I don't wanna move," she whinged.

The bed bounced as he climbed off, then sat in a chair before the hearth and slouched. "Come here."

She moved—if one could call it that—left the bed and waddled to him, groaning all the way, trying not to let her toy slip out. He grinned. "Bend over my legs."

She was suddenly so tired she would have dropped anywhere, but she did what he said, clamped her thighs together to feel the glass, and with each strike of his hand on her arse and the exposed parts of her folds, she clenched, clenched again, and then gasped yet another release. He slapped her again and again whilst she growled through her crisis until she was finished and panting.

"Tired," she slurred.

"Aye, as am I." With that, he bade her stand, and then he swept her up in his arms and laid her in bed, lying beside her and kissing her to sleep.

"GRIMME," SHE said softly into his chest. His hand was on her bare back, caressing her. They had been at it for hours and dawn was breaking. He had been thoughtful to get the oil, but her body was sore and chafed; her breasts were worn, her nipples and nymph were tender, her jaw ached, and her arse hurt nine different ways.

She had knelt on a pillow in front of him where he sat in a chair, tasted his cod and bollocks, whilst he taught her how to pleasure him until he'd spilled down her throat, *then* he had her climb onto him and lower herself over him. *Ohhhh*, she had sighed, taking him even deeper than before, rocking, undulating slowly until he impatiently commanded her to ride him. Hard. Whilst he sucked her nipples. So now her thighs were screaming.

He had broken her and it had only taken one night.

But by God, she would *never* admit that, especially not in writing, *never* beg him seek other relief.

He had to train; he was gone all day.

He had to sleep, and when he slept with her, 'twas from dusk until dawn.

When he was gone, she would coat herself in lavender oil and frankincense, nap, and when she wasn't napping, gnaw on ginger.

"Mm?"

"Get dressed. Come with me. I want you to meet my friends."

"No."

"Grimme, they are not pieces of a witch flying apart. They're just birds. Feed them and they will love you. 'Twas what I intended all along."

"Birds who have long memories and an eye for faces. If I offend even one of them, they will all come after me."

She chuckled. "'Tis difficult to offend a bird who knows you'll feed him. Come. At least watch."

His chest began to rise higher and faster. He really was afraid, which was something she could not truly understand. Her strong, bold, warrior husband had no fear of war, no fear of death or pain. But he feared a bird.

And he feared her.

But her idea as to how to repair it had been the wrong one; she could never have known that what he lusted for more than cunte was *war*. She had given him that many times, but neither of them had understood, much less acted on it.

"Do you … " she began hesitantly, "still fear me?"

"Nay," he said with a yawn, stroking her back. "We have talked and laughed these many hours, as much as we did upon our journey from Fàileach. Our shopping trip to Hogarth." He paused and laughed. "'*Grimme, get your arse out of bed!*' This has become one of every moment of our friendship we have enjoyed and can enjoy for the rest of our lives."

She sighed, soothed, calm, and finally at peace.

"Did you learn French at home?" he asked suddenly, in French.

"*Non*. No one in my family speaks French. We speak Gaelic inside the house."

"Then how … "

She huffed impatiently. "You assume too much and you never ask questions to get *all* the information," she said testily, irritated all over again. "You grew up with Aldwyn and never had to do that with him because you experienced everything together. You don't ask anyone anything beyond what you think you need to know." He sighed heavily. "The convent I went to was in Lyons. I only stayed long enough to learn French with a noble accent, then I had to work my way across France before I even had the chance to work my way up England. And *then* I had to learn how to control my Scottish accent to work in English noble houses. Sixteen hundred miles from Lyons to Fàileach. Walter was absolutely certain I would not dare leave."

"Good God," he whispered. "But you had your dog, who killed for you."

"And died for me."

"And now you want me to meet more animals who would kill for you."

"Grimme, please?"

"Roll over and spread your legs, then," he muttered, and she allowed him to gently remove her glass that had gotten to be a bit much, but when she recovered a little, she would be more than happy to be filled again.

He dropped it into a pail, one with the pearls. She would have the maidservant heat some water and she would cleanse them herself.

He pulled on his breeches and tunic. She slipped a kirtle over her head, groaning all the while, and offered her hand to him. She could barely walk, her thighs and cunte and arse and belly and ribs and all over were so sore. "Do you surrender?" he purred, pulling her into his arms, her back against his chest. He kissed the top of her head.

She chuckled. "No."

"Pfft. Even if I broke you, you would not admit it."

"And thus, it would not matter, would it?"

"Is my cod worth the consequence?"

"Keeping your hands and mouth off of and your spindle out of any other woman is worth it, aye."

"'Tis not the way it is done."

"I am loyal only to myself and I want what I want and what I want is to be the sole possessor of my husband's body. All of it."

He chuckled and whispered in her ear, "'Tis yours solely until you beg me for mercy. That's the bargain, aye?"

"Aye. Come. Be quiet and peaceful. Don't antagonize them."

"You are not making me more confident, my lady."

92

GRIMME FOLLOWED her down the stairs to the kitchen, and she moaned and groaned all the way, which he found utterly charming. Without speaking or looking at her, a servant pointed to a pail of offal that Brìghde plucked off the ground then went up the back stairs and out to the bailey. The sun was just coming up and only the servants were about. It was freezing. An unkindness of ravens covered the bailey yard and as soon as they saw her, they started trilling and grunting and squawking and making a wide variety of ugly noises. He felt his heart start to pound and his breath come short.

"Stay here in the doorway. They are used to William. They ignore those who ignore them. Sit."

He did. Slowly. Quietly.

She walked out among them confidently, talking to them differently from how she talked to Troy or Mercury, as if they were her equals. They flocked around her and one with a white neck and a tiny bit of white on the tip of his beak flew up and perched on her shoulder. The bird was bigger than her head. They were not squawking at her anymore, but their noises sounded like they were *talking* to her. She answered each of them.

She threw bits of offal around and they pounced on each piece, and as she did so, Mercury galloped around the corner, which would send them away. Grimme heaved a sigh of relief.

But no. The birds fluttered upward, then landed on the dog. He put his nose to another and sniffed. The bird had absolutely no fear and pecked at the dog's nose. Mercury nudged him a little. The bird tripped backward, then he was back. The dog lifted a paw and swatted the bird several feet away, but the bird came back. Mercury swatted at him again, but the bird fluttered up and Mercury missed. Then the dog woofed, jumped and snapped at him, but the bird stayed just out of reach. Then he slapped the dog in the face with his wing. Grimme almost laughed.

"Lie down, Mercury."

He did, with a deep but soft *woof*. The raven wanted to play some more, but Mercury was apparently finished. Presently, another bird, with a piece of offal in his beak, hopped over to Mercury. The dog opened his mouth and the bird dropped it in! The dog chewed, then closed his eyes whilst being thoroughly trammeled by birds.

Grimme's eyes were wide and his heart was thundering out of his chest. Yet Brìghde stood there until she had passed out every last morsel of offal and they had either eaten it or given it to Mercury, and came hopping to her for more. She made a shooing motion when they followed her to the granary, where she set down the empty pail, found her keys, and unlocked the door.

"You get *some*, but you may not enter. I must tell you this every day even though you know better."

They did, indeed, stay a respectful distance away from the granary door. The one perched on her shoulder fluttered to the ground. She closed the door behind her. She emerged with a small pail full of wheat kernels and they looked up at her expectantly.

She poured a little on the ground and then, walking backward, slowly laid a path of grain toward Grimme. "Come. I want you to meet my friend. His name is Grimme."

They followed her faithfully until her arse was nearly in Grimme's face. He leaned forward and kissed it, which startled her, and then she laughed. She stepped to the side.

"Fill your hand with grain," she said, "and sprinkle it on the ground before you."

He did, looking up at her skeptically.

"If you make friends of them, they will remember and will never take offense so long as you do not break their trust and the only way you can do that is to hunt them or hurt whom they love. Look at Mercury. He's a hunting dog. He could devour them in a trice and never mind if they came after them, for he would slay them all for the sport of it. Yet they would enjoy it as simple play, and they would tease him and mock him."

The ravens hopped closer and closer, following the grain. Brìghde filled her hand with it and held her hand between Grimme's knees. He had never wanted to get away from anything as badly as he did the enormous bird who fluttered up and perched on her hand. Somehow, he controlled himself.

She put the pail on the ground and petted the beast. He stopped eating, closed his eyes, and turned his head this way or that, telling her explicitly where he wanted her to scratch. He made the most ugly sounds Grimme had ever heard, but clearly he was enjoying himself.

"I can't tell them apart," she said matter-of-factly. "I don't name them. But they know me. Give me your hand."

He did, warily. She took it gently in hers, manipulated his fingers, and—"Do not pull away. Just feel the feathers." She held his finger and made him stroke the bird perched on her hand. The feathers were soft, silky, and shimmered blue in the sunlight. The bird tilted his head and Brìghde directed Grimme's finger to scratch him there. He opened his beak widely and Brìghde kept Grimme from withdrawing his hand. "This is Grimme," she cooed. "Grimme. Scratch under his chin." Gradually, she let go of his hand. "Keep petting him. Now, hold your other hand out and cup it." He did. She poured grain into it and the bird hopped from her hand to his, and he was heavy. Aye, he could see why she had once considered them a possible meal. "Now pet him."

He did.

God help him, but now that he'd watched and felt, he could see how she'd become attached to them. Ravens didn't need to be fed and they didn't need her. They were scavengers and could fend for themselves aplenty, but she needed them the way she needed Mercury and Troy, the way she'd needed Hades. The animals were loyal to her and would never betray her, even at the cost of their lives.

Grimme couldn't look away. He was enchanted by them from afar, but in close, with their talons clutching the fat of his hand and eating, enjoying his caresses, they were not much of a threat. They behaved as any beloved pet with its master's attention.

She turned and shooed the birds away from the pail of grain. "Bad birds. You know not to eat from the pail. Come." Brìghde swept away, birds following her faithfully as she spread the grain out on the millstone, put the pail away, disappeared into the keep, then returned with another pail of offal and sat beside him.

They then swarmed. Grimme would have bolted, but Brìghde grasped his arm and held on tightly. "I'm sorry. I'm so used to this, I didn't think. Here," she grunted and reached through all the ravenous ravens to select a piece of offal. She gave it to him and said, "Let them come to you and feed."

"Can they sense my fear?"

"Mayhap, but they may not care as long as they get fed and scratched. They taught you, did they not? When you were a wee lad? You said they taught you how to be a warrior, that honor was not the way to win, and that the only important thing was to conquer."

"Aye," Grimme whispered, staying still, even after the offal was gone and the grain was gone and finally only one raven remained to demand Grimme pet him. So he did, even going so far as to surround the back of the bird's neck and rub him somewhat firmly, though Grimme could easily kill him.

He dare not.

"If you do that too long," she said dryly, "he'll fall asleep."

He did, in fact, fall asleep and caught himself just before he toppled over. Brìghde laughed softly. "Silly bird. Go on now. The food is gone and so is your playmate." Indeed, Mercury was gone. "Take everyone with you."

They flew away completely, not one raven left.

But soon after, one returned and dropped a green stone in her lap as he flew by. Then he disappeared.

"Remarkable," Grimme whispered in awe, watching him go even after he was out of sight. He turned to look at her and for the first time wondered how he could have missed the essence of her beauty, which was not dark at all. It was light and joy, fun and laughter, caring and love.

"What are you thinking?" she asked with a soft smile.

He reached up and caressed her cheek, sliding his hands into her hair, and leaned in to kiss her. She sighed and tilted her head a little to go deeper into his mouth and he hummed his pleasure.

"You didn't." From behind them, Emelisse spoke in pleasant-sounding French that disguised her rage.

Grimme pulled away a bit, turned his head, and looked over his shoulder at the ground. "I did."

"*After* she did this to me?"

"You deserved it."

"Why have you never kissed me that tenderly? Looked at *me* the way you have looked at her since she walked in the door?"

Brìghde started.

"You have *never* looked at me like that. *Never* kissed me that way."

"I will not come to you again, Emelisse," he murmured. "I already told you that, and now I have another reason, which is to protect my son from you."

"I'm sorry about Caroline and Pierce. Grimme, I'm *sorry!*"

"'Tis too late, Emelisse. 'Tis done."

"*She* cannot satisfy you. No one woman can."

"When she has broken and begs for mercy the way you did, I will go elsewhere, but I will not come to you."

"You love her!"

"Oui, I do," he said quietly.

Both Brìghde and Emelisse gasped. The first didn't know. The second was bluffing. Again.

He looked up at Emelisse, no longer beautiful, dove-like, or angelic. Oh, once the bruises faded and the lump went down, she would again be beautiful to the rest of the world, but not to Grimme. "I will not put you out so long as you stay away from Pierce, and I promised you I would not allow Brìghde to kill you, but do not harry me for my attention. You will not get it."

"We have been together for *twelve years!*" she cried. "I *loved* you! I was faithful to you all this time. But you found others nearly immediately and I tolerated them! I could have had any number of lovers. I could have found someone who would love *me!* But then *she* comes here, she looks exactly the way you *hate*, you were *disgusted* by her, and yet … You have given her your cod?"

"Oui. She has sole use of my body for as long as she can tolerate it."

Her face mottled in rage. "Her time and attention and, and, and sleeping with her wasn't enough for you?"

"*Non*. It wasn't."

"How *could* you?"

Grimme shrugged helplessly as he did not know what to say to that. "Begone, Emelisse," he said as gently as he could. "You have permission to take your meals in your chambers should you not wish to dine at table."

She whirled and ran.

Grimme looked back at Brìghde, who watched him with gentle sadness. "I don't know how to do this," he murmured. "You have turned everything upside down."

"It always looks worse before it gets better," she said soberly. "'Tis the nature of setting things aright." She bit her lip. "Did you mean that?"

He didn't have to ask to what she referred. "Aye. I love you."

"When?"

He shook his head wearily and sighed, "When *haven't* I loved you?"

She broke and began to cry, allowing her head to fall on his chest so she could sob in private. He stroked her back. He could see it now. She had fallen in love with him long ago, had tried to hide it, wanted his body, solely hers, but would not lower herself to beg or compete. He had always known something was growing there, but he had welcomed it as the deepening of a friendship that he cherished and couldn't understand why it wasn't going the way he thought it should.

"I love you, Grimme."

He dropped a kiss on top of her raven-black head. "That's what you've been keeping from me?"

She nodded as she cried. But as she cried, the ravens returned, one by one, creaked and croaked and cawed at him, their beaks wide. Grimme stiffened, watching them warily, as they were watching him. "Brìghde … " he breathed. "Your demons are back."

She turned her head and wiped her tears, then beckoned them forward. "Come." She patted his chest. "This is my friend, Grimme. *Grimme.*" She turned her face up to his. Her mouth was trembling. "Kiss me."

He did, with all the tenderness he could dig out of his soul. He felt her hand on his face, her fingers in his hair, combing it. Then there were talons on his knee, a great weight perched upon him, and it was all he could do to keep from knocking the bird off, then it was nibbling at Grimme's arm. It was irritating, but it did not hurt. Grimme opened one eye to see the bird hop over to Brìghde's lap and peck at her shoulder, as he was almost bigger than she was. She broke from the kiss and laughed, twisted to stroke his beak and his eyelids flickered in what Grimme could only assume was bliss.

"Are you jealous?" she cooed. "Silly bird. This is Grimme. He is my friend."

"And lover."

She smiled, but she was still looking at the bird. "Protect him as you protect me."

Grimme saw the others wander off and then fly away. They *had* been protecting her, fearing that he had hurt her and that her tears were those of unhappiness. She hadn't lied about their loyalty to her.

"Go now, bird," she whispered, her lips to his beak. He nibbled at her nose and she chuckled. "There are your kisses. I want to go back to bed with my lover."

That big, black, majestic bird flew away with a squawk.

93

BRÌGHDE AND Grimme presented themselves at breakfast after feeding the ravens. No one saw her and Grimme come up from the kitchens, though she moaned and groaned as she had all the way from Fàileach. Grimme chuckled.

The hall was full of knights, but it was quiet. Everyone sat eating, but when they spoke, they only spoke in whispers to each other. She was shocked and distressed at how lifeless it was.

"It's been like this since I came back from Tavendish and took Emelisse at the portcullis," Grimme whispered when she looked at him questioningly. "Your sadness, then your absence and the reason for it has affected everyone. You left, and all the joy and life went with you; 'tis not even as lively as it was before you came."

She wrung her hands. "I'm sorry," she croaked. "I didn't know. I would not have ... "

"No apologies. 'Twas my fault, seeing a woman of lust and laughter, light and life as a witch because my brother told me a frightening story when I was three. Stay there."

With that, he presented himself at table. They noticed, but no one would look at him.

"Papa!" Grimme bellowed toward the study door. Presently, Sir John appeared. Grimme gestured to him. "Come. Eat." It wasn't a request, so he sighed and William scurried to help him to his normal chair. Aldwyn and Lady Caroline shifted to the right.

Then Grimme pulled back his chair and hers, turned to Brìghde, and gestured to her to come forward. A low rumble of whispers went through the hall once they caught sight of her, then they began to rise. The only people who did not look surprised were Aldwyn and Lady Caroline, who had pleased smiles on their faces. Brìghde assumed that was because they had overheard the war that had been waged in the chambers next to theirs. How could they *not?*

Brìghde took her place beside her husband and now lover. *Her* lover. Alone. He loved her and she never *ever* had to share him again. The low rumble turned into utter silence.

Grimme took her hand and brought it to his lips. "Brìghde Fàileach Kyneward, you and I said our vows in a little church in Laight, Scotland, me in armor, you in a torn and dirty wedding dress with tangled hair and leaves in it. But now I pledge my fealty, my love, my devotion to be solely yours for the rest of our lives."

The hall whispered with anticipation. Brìghde's mouth tightened and her eyes narrowed. "You forgot something," she growled.

"And my cod—until you break."

After a very long second, the hall erupted in raucous laughter and cheers. Brìghde flushed and could not help her beaming smile, though she tried to hide it. Pierce climbed on his chair and jumped up and down, clapping and screaming, "Yay, Brìghde! Yay, Papa!" Dillena applauded with a lovely smile on her face.

Grimme tilted Brìghde's face up to his and kissed her tenderly and for quite a while, so much she felt her desire returning.

He pulled away from her slowly, and watched her. Slowly, his expression turned to irritation.

"Thank you, my lord," she murmured shyly.

He stared at her expectantly.

"Well, *I* don't have to say anything," she said testily. "Everyone but you and Emelisse knows how I feel about you."

Surprised, he looked around, then somebody snickered. Then someone else. Dillena laughed and clapped her hands to her mouth in delight. Everyone began laughing again, but this time it was good-natured mocking, all directed at the two of them for being blind.

Grimme looked to Sir Thom. "Is *that* what has had you on the brink of revolt?" he demanded.

"Nay, my lord. 'Twas as I said." He shrugged. "But it was just an extra measure of insult that you could not see." He looked at Brìghde. "And we all knew how he felt about you, though you did not."

"Neither did he," she said dryly.

He laughed. "Too true. A toast!" said Sir Thom, raising his goblet. "Lord and Lady Kyneward!"

The toast was loud, but Grimme bid everyone sit and eat. "I'm hungry. I've been fucking my wife all night long, and bloody hell, she was one very lusty virgin."

Once the meal was under way and everyone was happy, with jests and insults and tales of derring-do, the knight who had journeyed with them all the way from Fàileach called,

"My lord! Mind she doesn't break you on her lust!"

Brìghde squealed with laughter and clapped. Grimme chuckled.

"I wager she can't be broken!" someone else called.

"I'll not take that wager!"

"He's met his match, you'll see."

The meal went on in that vein, most of it directed at Grimme's cod and the unlikelihood it could sate Brìghde's lust.

Grimme leaned into her and she grinned at him. He looked at her undecorated, likely tangled hair straight from bed, and seemed captured by it, but now it was not with troubled features. He reached up and ran his fingers through it. "Raven Queen," he whispered as if to himself, bringing that lock to his lips, then studying it in his hand. "Bold. Dark. Ruthless. Clever."

"Grimme, I do appreciate that you find those things about me admirable and a year ago, I would have been flattered, but ... I am a woman and I— Those are the things that you said make me admirable as a man."

"My *equal,*" he reminded her. "What would you find soothing?"

"Aphrodite."

He looked confused.

"Ares is the god of war. That is you, aye, I will agree. But I am not Enyo. I do not lust for war. I do not want to ride into battle with my warrior husband. I want him to protect me as a beloved wife without having to be told, coerced, or prompted. I want to meet him as a conqueror when he comes home to me. I want to take care of his wounds of war. I want to slake his bloodlust and bear his children and rear them as warriors like him. If I must, I will be his weapon and assassin, but it will be with deception and stealth, in the shadows so that I will not be obliged to fight. And that, my lord husband, is what *no one* has ever understood about me—not even myself, not until I experienced real war. My journey from the convent did not begin to compare. I could hide. I could run. Hades fought my battles. That day ... I had to fight or die."

His eyes were soft and his smile was wry. "Aphrodite has a temper, too, that she uses without hesitation and to the full extent of her power, which is vast."

"Only when she must," she murmured.

"But when she must," he whispered, leaning toward her. Brìghde closed her eyes and met his tender kiss, "she is magnificent."

94

GRIMME WAS *relentless.*

After about a week, Brìghde felt as though she had been turned inside out and upside down. She was tired. And bruised. And scraped. And raw. And broken. She could barely sit, her arse cheeks stung so much. Her wrists and ankles were bruised from velvet ropes.

But she would *never* admit it to him.

Emelisse was taking her meals in her room, likely because her face hadn't healed yet, but Brìghde had not seen her once since she'd confronted them in the bailey. Dillena took her meals at table and seemed … calmer. Happier.

Brìghde had praised Rose's wisdom in dismissing the maidservants.

"He has always belonged to you, mum," Rose said softly. "He just had to have his shiny toys taken away from him like a naughty boy."

Brìghde chuckled softly. "Aye, I suppose so. Thank you."

Every morning, she had taken Grimme out to the bailey to feed the ravens, and this morning, she bade him go alone. She watched from inside the threshold, hidden, as they swarmed him for his pail of offal. He was tense and still ready to bolt, but he held firm, spread the offal as she had done, waited until they were all finished. One or two perched upon his person somewhere, squawking at him, then flying off to the door of the granary. Many of them did that, marched back and forth from his feet to the granary. Finally he seemed to understand.

"Very well, my troops," he said resignedly. "Stay away from the door as your queen has told you time and again."

They did. He fetched the pail and they followed him to the millstone where he dumped it and spread it.

He watched them eat for a while, then when one of them looked up at him and squawked, he hesitantly reached a hand out to pet him. The bird, of course, stretched this way and that, demanding to be scratched here and there. Presently, Grimme offered him his arm and the bird hopped on so he could pet him more easily.

"Grimme," the raven squawked.

Grimme started and gaped at him. "You *talk?*" he asked the bird incredulously.

"Grimme."

Brìghde thought Grimme would bolt, but he didn't. He stayed and stared. Then he started to laugh. "And just what am I going to name you?"

"Grimme."

"No," he said firmly, stroking the bird's beak playfully. "I think I will call you Philippe, you clever little demon. Philippe," he said as he stroked its head and down its back, "who taught you to talk?"

"One of the scullery maids," Brìghde called softly. "I taught him your name. I suppose now he knows who it belongs to. They know my name, too, but will not say it unless I have special treats for them."

He went back to petting the bird, but now as if they were old friends, his fingers scratching here and scritching there whilst the bird relaxed and almost fell asleep.

She knew that feeling, having Grimme's fingers on her, in her, wherever he wanted to put them. She closed her eyes and let her head fall against the wall. He demanded much, but he did not fail to give her pleasure and found ways to coax her to it every time.

It was worth it, she thought sleepily. She would pay any price to keep him to herself—*all* of him, and he had encouraged her to play with his body as much as he played with hers. He did whatever she wanted him to without once directing her or laughing at her when she was shy or embarrassed. If she was hesitant, he led her slowly, teaching her with far more patience than she would have credited him.

He was teaching her so that she would never break.

She opened her eyes when the ravens took their leave with their usual farewell squawks, gurgles, trills, and one creaky "Grimme." Grimme stood in the middle of the bailey and watched as the last one disappeared. Every morning he did this, watched the skies for the ravens who would not return until suppertime.

Yet one did return and, as he flew past, dropped something at Grimme's feet. He was gone in a blink.

Grimme looked down, squatted, and picked it up.

His first gift.

He stood slowly and stared down at it. After quite a long while, he closed his hand around it and brought his fist to his lips to kiss it.

Brìghde put her hand to her mouth and tears stung her eyes. When he finally walked back to her, he opened his hand. It was a broken piece of shield.

She smiled and whispered, "Raven king."

BRÌGHDE WAS IN the study just after midday meal with William poring over the ledgers. Grimme was out in the field and Brìghde intended to take a very long nap. After a knock at the door and the invitation to enter, Brìghde was surprised to see Dillena.

"Um … good afternoon, Dillena."

"My lady," she curtsied. "May I speak with you? Alone?"

"Oh, aye, certainly. William?"

Brìghde arose and offered her one of the comfortable chairs in front of Sir John's desk, and Brìghde took the other. "Is … something the matter?" Brìghde asked gently.

"Aye and no," she began hesitantly, looking down at her hands. "I … would like to go back to Wales."

Brìghde blinked, shocked. "Why … do you not tell Lord Grimme this?"

She looked at Brìghde, confused. "We are to come to you for household business and coin, are we not?"

"Oh, of course, of course. I see. Aye. Why … ? This is your home. You ken he will not put you out. I certainly have no reason to or intention of it."

"I know," she said gently, but she had always been the gentlest of the four, the most easy to please, the quietest. "May I speak frankly?"

"Aye."

"I have no more purpose here," she began calmly. "Terrwyn is as good as gone from me and even if I stayed, I would never see him again anyway. He will be gone to someone else as page in a few weeks, then squire, then knight, then battle, and will die."

That was true.

"I tired of Lord Grimme years ago."

Brìghde's eyebrow rose.

"You will too. 'Tis inevitable. I would like to find love such as what he has shown you since you arrived. Whether that love will give you an advantage over his lust, I cannot say, but for your sake, I hope it does. I would like one man to myself, and I to him, and if I cannot have that, then I want no one. In fact, I would rather no one, as I have had all of that I can stomach. Since he has no need of me at the moment and my son's fate is out of my hands, I will take my freedom whilst I can, as you have every reason to grant me this request."

"Dillena," Brìghde said, reaching out and taking her hand, "you have been the model of graciousness to me, and I am grateful for it. I will send you anywhere you want with all your belongings, with as many funds as you will need to live comfortably for the rest of your life."

She inclined her head. "Thank you, my lady. Whatever you might think of it, I have not resented you, and I wish we could have been friends. I have been grateful for your presence, as I am grateful for any new woman Lord Grimme brings into the household. I am not as lusty as Maebh and Ardith, and I do not love him nor am I in love with him, as Emelisse is. I don't even know him well enough to know if I *like* him, yet I have been with him for almost ten years. I am … like Terrwyn. The middle. The forgotten."

"No, you're not," Brìghde was quick to say. "Of all four of you, you are the only one he admires."

She looked stunned.

"Before he attained earldom, you took care of the household when Emelisse would not. You took care of Terrwyn and sometimes Pierce, where Emelisse did not take care of hers. You exercised the mares when he asked. You would have helped Sir John, had he thought to ask and you simply didn't know what to do or where to start. Lord Grimme just had to be shown who you are."

Dillena looked like she was about to cry, but they were tears of joy.

Brìghde tilted her head. "Lord Grimme would have granted this request before I came. Why now?"

She shrugged. "I have been so long with him that this is simply the way it is. I didn't know what I was missing until I saw him with you. He took you from your home and your family, but by the time you arrived, you were fast friends. He laughed when you roused him from Emelisse's bed, which he would have done with no other. He spends every spare minute with you. He cares what you think. What must it be like to be and have that type of friend? I would like to have a friend instead of living with women who will never be my friends, where I am one of many who look alike, where I am nothing more than … my cunte."

Now Brìghde's eyes were watering. "But you weren't. He just didn't tell you. He doesn't know how to talk to women."

"That is nice to hear. I will ponder it."

"I pray you godspeed and whatever miracles you stand in need of."

IT TOOK FOUR days for Grimme to notice Dillena was gone.

And he didn't care.

Brìghde closed her eyes and prayed for a miracle.

95

IT HAD BEEN over a month since Grimme had blooded Brìghde, and she was growing accustomed to his needs. The jests concerning Grimme's questionable ability to slake Brìghde's insatiable lust may not have been too far off the mark, but because Brìghde and Grimme also did the things they had always done, he didn't need as much as he had before.

They swived, then talked and laughed half the night, then they slept. Or they argued, they swived, slept, then finished the argument to a conclusion. She had to teach him how to do this, how to know when there was more information to be had, to realize there were questions he had not thought to ask because he assumed too much.

Grimme, Brìghde, and Pierce rode together before breakfast. Helen would still not let Brìghde in her stall alone, she would reluctantly behave for Grimme, but she was completely in love with Pierce and would do anything for him. Thus, Helen became Pierce's mount and Grimme began to teach him how to repair a ruined horse.

Brìghde wore black, and the more she wore it, the more Grimme admitted he could see the light in her darkness, the joy she brought to their home that made normal mealtimes happy occasions. The keep was only dark and unwelcoming when she removed herself.

They went to Hogarth and, as they always did, went to the kirk to give thanks for their disproportionate advantage. Aye, Kyneward had its own chapel in which to give thanks, but doing so in Hogarth was their special rite.

Grimme ruled the outside; Brìghde ruled the inside.

Emelisse had finally shown her face when her bruises were gone, presenting herself to table. She engaged herself in chatting with whoever would indulge her. The only other women in the hall now were Brìghde and Lady Caroline, and since every last knight in the hall hated Emelisse, it was difficult for her to find anyone to talk to. She must be very lonely, and Brìghde *almost* felt sorry for her, as Brìghde had been in that position almost the entirety of her three-year stay in the convent. The only difference was that Brìghde had also been subject to the needling of the other girls for sport, and no one needled Emelisse. She supposed that for Emelisse, being ignored was worse than being needled.

The only time Grimme spoke to Emelisse was when he once took her out to the farthest reaches of Kyneward to see her sons. Grimme would not allow Emelisse to say a word about the changes in the family structure at home. Grimme was adamant that Emelisse praise the boys' progress and to give no indication that she wanted them back to baby them. She came home despondent that they were happy where they were, which was to say, happy without her.

Grimme had asked Brìghde very courteously to stay out of Lady Caroline's ear as it pertained to Aldwyn, for it was not her grudge to carry. Brìghde huffed, but then Grimme said the correct words: *Don't be like Walter.* She growled, but had to concede his point. It would have been more difficult to put it aside if she did not want to engage in the conversation at meal times, as it was difficult for her to be angry with and ignore someone who made her laugh in spite of herself. It also helped that Aldwyn had taken her aside and apologized profusely for not attempting to keep the duke away from her.

"Apology accepted. Thank you."

Grimme received a missive from Tavendish requesting him to go there to train some of the Tavendish army in Grimme's dishonorable battle tactics. Flattered and hungry for something different to do, he had acquiesced happily. Aldwyn would not be going, as he was still recovering, but he was not happy about it.

Grimme would be taking Gaston and Max with him, to leave one at Tavendish to apprentice, and one at Dunham to apprentice. Terrwyn would be going south to York in the spring. All the boys were called home for three days for a celebration of their success and so Emelisse could say farewell to her two.

Just before midday meal, Brìghde had gone to the boys' chambers and given them the first set of fine clothing they had ever had. When she had taken them to Hogarth, she had had them made and prayed they would not outgrow them before they got to wear them.

They thanked her vaguely, but it was in the manner of someone looking at something so precious and dear that they were not paying attention to anything else.

Thus, when they were brought into the great hall to great fanfare, the boys looked like an earl's sons. They were pleased and shy and happy and proud. They were offered chairs at the head table, Terrwyn by Pierce, Gaston and Max next to their grandfather. But Emelisse wanted them flanking her as it had always been.

Brìghde watched the pair carefully. They were resentful, a little embarrassed, and envious of Terrwyn and Pierce. Again. Brìghde poked Grimme in the ribs with her elbow.

"No, they need to be up here so we can honor them and their achievements," he said calmly.

With great excitement, the boys ran down the aisle and around the tables, to take their places of honor, so excited and happy they didn't notice Emelisse's expression turning to one of quiet rage.

"Put on a happier face," Grimme murmured coolly, "or I'll send you to your chambers like a naughty little girl."

She did a poor imitation of happiness and pride. After the meal, Grimme took all four boys out riding, Pierce on Helen, Gaston and Max on Deimos and Phobos, and Terrwyn on Troy, but Grimme allowed each of the three others to take turns with each of the four most prized stallions in the Kyneward stable, even Ares. Helen, of course, snapped at everyone but Pierce.

Thus, supper was a raucously joyous one. Emelisse took her meal in her chambers, but the boys didn't seem to notice. Brìghde made many toasts to all three boys, working very hard to think of complimentary things about them because she didn't know them that well. They beamed at her with flushed faces, but Brìghde didn't think they cared that it was *her*. They were being fêted, and it was the first time they had ever been fêted in their lives.

As had been their habit since Brìghde and Grimme had deepened their friendship, the two of them left everyone to the after-supper amusements to seek their own private amusement. Grimme swept Brìghde into his chambers and pulled her into his arms for a lusty kiss.

Brìghde's desire rose almost immediately and she pulled at Grimme's hose to free him from confinement.

"You, my lusty wench," he whispered into her mouth, "are going to wait until we're unclothed."

"Get to it, then," she said smartly, smacking his arse and stepping away to disrobe. She met him in bed and squealed with laughter as he tackled her and rolled her over.

"God, I love you," he growled as they wrestled and she laughed. She didn't think she'd stopped laughing since they had come together. She launched herself at him, toppling him over on his back so that she was lying atop him.

"I love you, too," she said breathlessly before kissing him. She felt his spindle rise against her leg. She rubbed her leg against him and he sighed encouragingly.

"You beautiful, beautiful Aphrodite," he whispered and rolled her over.

She laughed delightedly and wrapped her arms around his shoulders to bring him down to her for teasing kisses. He tried to deepen them but she dodged him and pecked him on the cheek. On the nose. On his eyelid. On his ear. "Raven kisses."

"How about goddess kisses?" he teased, getting to his knees and, grinning, jerked her up to him for a hot kiss then arranged her so that she was situated over his spindle.

"Oh, is that so, my stallion?" she cooed, very slowly lowering herself, sighing and closing her eyes, feeling his magnificent body against hers, in hers. He shifted, grasped her arse cheeks in his big hands and adjusted her so that he was seated fully within her.

She stayed.

"Oh, God," he sighed impatiently. "Move, Brìghde."

"No!" she chirped playfully, and dropped a kiss on his nose.

He growled his laughter and lifted her. It wasn't difficult.

The sound of squealing and shouting children went past and up and down stairs. Brìghde didn't think much about it; Aldwyn's oldest and Pierce played hide-and-seek often, and now Pierce's brothers were home, so of course they would play.

All Brìghde cared about was being in her lover's arms, her dearest friend, feeling his big, strong, warrior body against hers, his mouth on hers, kissing, kissing, making up for all the kisses they had missed, that she had longed for—

CRASH!

"Papa—!"

Brìghde screamed and lost her balance, toppled off Grimme, bounced off the side of the bed, and landed on the floor.

Grimme started laughing.

"Not funny," Brìghde sing-songed as she struggled to her knees.

"Aye, it is," he chortled. "The look on your face."

She popped up to look over the bed to see both her stepsons in the doorway, their eyes wide. She blew up at the lock of hair that fell into her face.

"Gaston," Grimme said, still laughing. "Please knock from now on. You can't barge in anymore. I apologize for not telling you."

"Papa ... " he said, looking at Brìghde, his smile fading, his expression turning from happy to heartbroken.

"Uh oh," Brìghde whispered and whirled, ducking behind the bed and out of sight.

"Emelisse," Grimme growled.

Brìghde felt a white-hot rage.

"Oh, I'm sorry," she purred in French. "I didn't know you were with Lady Brigitte. I wouldn't have encouraged the boys to come visit you."

"Papa, I thought— Maebh and Dillena and Ardith are gone, so I thought ... Mamá said it was just her now."

Grimme got off the bed and it sounded to Brìghde that he was putting his robe on. She started when her kirtle landed on her head.

"Close the door for a moment, please," he asked courteously, "so Lady Brìghde can dress. Then we will explain."

"Explain what, Grimme?" Emelisse asked innocently.

The door closed quietly and Brìghde stood, then wiggled into her kirtle. Grimme was no longer laughing. When she was done, he opened the door and ushered his two oldest sons into his chambers. Brìghde looked at Emelisse, who once again wore that look of smug victory. Her eyes narrowed. "You don't learn, do you?" Brìghde asked softly.

Grimme closed the door in Emelisse's face, then swept his hand to the sitting room, where the boys sat.

Brìghde could have accepted angry glares. Heartsick expressions were something else again. "Grimme, I think you need to speak with them alone," she said softly.

"Aye," he sighed. "Brìghde," he said harshly before she opened the door. "Not one finger."

"Hrmph." She left, but Emelisse was nowhere to be seen. Brìghde stood in the hall angry, sad, and bound by Grimme's order not to touch Emelisse. She slumped and trudged downstairs, where the entertainments were still happening. She slipped into her chair and watched, her heart heavy. Terrwyn and Pierce were running around, the Marchand girl trying to keep up, but she was only four and was crying for Pierce to wait for her.

Brìghde sat slouched in one corner of her chair, her foot against the edge of the table, wondering how she could live with Emelisse for the rest of her life if Emelisse did not stop her childish behavior. Clearly she felt free to poke at Brìghde because Grimme had never given her any indication that he would take Brìghde's side of any argument. To be fair, Brìghde could kill Emelisse with her bare hands, therefore, Emelisse needed protection Brìghde did not.

She started when, some time later, Grimme's chair was scraped back and he dropped himself into it, rubbing the bridge of his nose.

"Well?" she asked.

He heaved a sigh. "I don't know. When I sent them out, the household was more or less what they were used to. They've come back to something completely different and unfathomable. They are torn between loyalty to their mother and the fact that you have taken care of them. And now I'm fucking you and only you. If it were just that Maebh and Ardith and Dillena were gone, or if I had simply started fucking you too, and their mother was still my favorite, they would understand that. I have tried every way I can think of to explain it. I tried to explain that I love you, but that only led to, 'Don't you love Mamá?'"

Brìghde grimaced.

"Aye!" Grimme agreed earnestly. "It just made everything worse, so I stopped talking."

"'Tis only two more days," Brìghde murmured. "I shall stay out of sight."

"No, you won't. I am leaving too, remember, and will be gone for a month. I want to spend every second I can with you before I go. I may not have an imagination, but I *do* have a memory, and I will need all I can get to be able to slake my lust with my hand since I am not allowed to fuck anyone *but* myself."

She laughed.

"Now," he purred, leaning over the arm of his chair and nibbling at her ear lobe. "Where were we?"

The next two days were taken up with demonstrations of the three boys' education with sword and dagger play, horsemanship, archery, and quintain. Grimme, every knight in the great hall including Aldwyn, were to test them. Brìghde on Enyo, Pierce on Helen, and Lady Caroline and Emelisse on much smaller palfreys rode out to the field where the trials were set up and sat watching from horseback.

Emelisse attempted to gossip about Brìghde with Lady Caroline in French, but Lady Caroline seemed to have forgotten her manners, for she flatly ignored Emelisse. Emelisse didn't attempt to converse with Brìghde.

Brìghde watched Pierce carefully as he observed, but she could see nothing of envy in his expression. She reached out and caressed his back. He turned a sweet smile on her. "Is this something you think you'd like to do?"

He simply shrugged his shoulders.

But gradually her attention turned back to the men and boys playing on the field, and she smiled. Playing. Grimme's smile was full of joy and mischief, his sons were riding tall and proud that they were part of the knights and were careful to give only their very best effort in order to earn the whoops and praises of the commanders who were also having a good time. Aldwyn was happy to be back in a saddle, and Brìghde could see no difference in his riding now than it had been at the tournament.

Though it was March, it was still cold, so Emelisse and Lady Caroline went back to the keep after not very long at all, then Pierce left, so there sat a well-bundled Brìghde watching her husband play with his sons, teach, encourage, praise. Brìghde trotted Enyo forward a little so she could see Grimme better. He was leaving in two days and she could barely think of how lonely she would be without him for a month.

Suddenly Ares reared high, high, higher even, and Grimme held his seat until the great beast landed, then he called, "Now you try."

Brìghde could feel her breath come shorter as she watched him, so big, so strong, and she thought she would never get tired of watching him. That indomitable warrior loved her. He was *hers*. Her eyes stung.

Deimos, with Gaston in the saddle, reared high, high, higher until Brìghde thought he'd get tossed, but no. Brìghde broke into wild applause and yells, which surprised the boy. He twisted to see who was cheering him. He looked confused, looked next to Brìghde, past Brìghde, then gave her a weak smile and wave.

Damn Emelisse to hell.

Max, too, held his seat on Phobos, and Brìghde cheered wildly, and though Terrwyn got tossed from Troy's back, Brìghde cheered for him anyway.

"Lady Brìghde!" Sir Thom called and waved her forward. Surprised, she put her hand to her breast. He nodded, then Grimme and the rest were gesturing for her to join them.

She trotted Enyo forward until she was within a nose of Ares and the two nuzzled. "How would you like a chance to ride Ares?" Grimme asked.

Brìghde's heart thundered. "Me?" she squeaked.

He grinned. "Aye. You run him. We'll try to catch you. I'll ride Enyo."

Once mounted on Ares, Grimme adjusted her stirrups. It was a much bigger saddle than Troy's, but then, it was made for her husband, who was twice her size. Whilst Grimme mounted Enyo, Brìghde took a few minutes to tuck all her skirts and woolen cape in front of and behind her to take up some of the room and adjust herself. She reached forward to reassure Ares, who wasn't sure he had anybody on his back at all. Then she reared him high, high, higher before kicking him into a leaping, flat gallop across the countryside, her husband, stepsons, and knights following her.

It was dusk when they all returned to the keep, Brìghde having raced all three of her stepsons (and allowed them to win). They were never going to be friends, but all she wanted them to know was that she did not hate them and she enjoyed their company.

At supper, everyone recounted all of the boys' feats to each other and announced what fine knights they would make one day. Emelisse was absent, which did not go unnoticed by her sons, who were a little more subdued.

"Grimme, go get Emelisse's arse down here and tell her to celebrate her sons the way everyone else is."

Presently she appeared with Grimme at her back and glided to the boys, hugged them, praised them, and generally gave a very bad impression of her pride in them. They knew it. Grimme knew it. Brìghde knew it. Everyone in the hall knew it. The boys were embarrassed. Brìghde could barely hide her rage, and she dropped her face in her palm.

The next day was the last before Grimme left with his sons to apprentice. No one knew when they would see them again, as that was the nature of apprenticeship. The festivities were a little more subdued, for the fact that Emelisse didn't bother to show her face at any of the meals at all. Brìghde and Grimme exchanged stony glances, but Grimme shook his head slightly. Her absence was better than her public display of resentment that her sons were getting all the attention and she got none.

But by supper, Brìghde had her own reason for her sour mood.

"You can rest," Grimme whispered in her ear with a snicker. When she didn't laugh, he nudged her with an elbow.

"I got my courses," she muttered, her eyes stinging.

"Oh," he murmured and wrapped his arm around her shoulder, bringing her into his body for a kiss on the top of her head. "I'm sorry."

"So am I."

"Next month. You'll see."

"You aren't going to be home all month."

"Month after that, then."

"What if I'm barren?" she asked plaintively.

He shrugged. "We'll find a way to make Pierce hold."

"But *I* want to have at least one of your children," she whispered as if she were begging scratches, but Grimme was doing his part and *very* well, too. 'Twas up to God now.

"And I want that, too, but it often does not happen for a while."

"Your others caught immediately."

"Do not worry overmuch," he murmured. "God has advantaged us disproportionately, and I have no reason to think he won't continue."

The next morning at dawn, she rode out with them halfway to Waters, bid her stepsons to do their absolute best at all moments and she was certain they would return home as warriors as fine as their father, then she kissed her husband passionately and said, "Come back to me. Vow."

"I vow," he whispered, still kissing her as if he could not get enough of her, until Terrwyn impatiently yelled,

"Papa! Come!"

"I love you, Ares," she murmured as she tied a black ribbon on him.

"And I you, Aphrodite."

Thus, she rode back to the keep alone and would have to grieve alone all month.

96

HER COURSES had come and gone, and she would get them next month, certainly. Brìghde already missed Grimme's company desperately and at night felt her desire for him grow, but she dare not touch herself the way he had taught her to.

Do not do this alone. Save your lust for me.

Are you going to save yours for me?

Bloody hell? No.

That had made her laugh, and she eagerly awaited Grimme's return, his return to her mind and her bed and her body and hopefully soon, her courses would cease.

Soon after breakfast a little over a week after Grimme departed, she began feeling ill. She wondered if she were with child after all and that her courses were simply a vestige of the month past. A wee bairn made in love would be more than welcome. She would dance with the mummers and learn how to juggle to express her joy.

She tried to get up the stairs, but her head was suddenly pounding and the spiral staircase began to spin.

"My lady," Lady Caroline breathed from behind her, then she felt herself falling backward, knocking Lady Caroline over and landing upon her. Lady Caroline scrambled out from under her and screamed for Sir Thom, who came running.

Lady Caroline felt her forehead. "No fever, thank God. Take her to her chambers."

Brìghde vaguely heard her. She vaguely felt being raised into the air. She vaguely felt being carried. She vaguely felt being lain in her bed. She vaguely felt the sweep of women inside and outside.

She's not breathing.

Brìghde scowled and opened her mouth. "Yes I am."

Oh my good lord, she's not breathing!

Her heart is not beating!

My lady, my lady. Can you hear me?

She was jostled and it hurt. She groaned, "I am hurt. Get ginger."

My lady!

Oh no! How will we tell Lord Kyneward? Do we send a messenger? Do we wait? What will we do?

Aldwyn, fetch Sunny. Quickly! Tell her to bring poison antidotes. Sir John's voice. How had he climbed the stairs?

Mistress Sunny cannot come here! Hamond's panicked voice. *Lord Kyneward doesn't countenance witches.*

Lord Kyneward is not here!

People scrambled.

"Brìghde," Sir John said, closer now. A chair scraped on the stones and then he was at the bedside. He took her hand. "If you can hear me," he whispered in her ear, "listen well. Even if you are dead, I will tell you anyway. I believe you have been poisoned—"

"It is impossible for me to have been poisoned," she gently corrected him. "Even if someone could get to my poison, which they canna do, I am hardened to it. Nay, I am with child."

"—as I saw Emelisse lingering about your chair at breakfast and thought nothing of it but her jealousy. But you ate and drank as deep as you usually do, and you hold your wine, so you could not have been drunk."

"I am with child," she said calmly.

"I hope the healer may be able to stop the poison."

"I am with child!" she insisted.

"If you have an ounce of control over your body, your own soul; if you have an ounce of love for my son, will to live. Nothing can break him but the loss of his dearest friend."

"I am with child!"

Sir John said nothing more, but sat beside her, holding her hand.

Brìghde continued to tell Sir John she was with child, not poisoned. She did not know how long she lay there not being listened to, but presently, someone swept in her door.

"Is she dead?" came a childish voice.

"Nay," Sir John answered. "Her hand is warm, her face is flushed, yet she has no heartbeat and she does not cloud the glass."

There was scurrying about the room. "Fan the fire," the child commanded. "I will need hot water and cloths."

Brìghde sensed all but the child and Sir John leave the room. She felt a small hand on her forehead. "No fever, though."

"She was poisoned."

"Aye, that's plain," the child said derisively.

"Don't talk to Sir John that way," Brìghde said.

But they ignored her.

"But *what* was she given?" the child whispered to herself. Brìghde heard pages flutter. More pages. "Oh, by the Virgin Mary," the child breathed. "Belladonna."

Belladonna was a problem. Brìghde's receipt did not call for belladonna, and she was not hardened to it.

"Can you bring her back?"

"There is only one thing I can try. I will need large lumps of fire-blackened wood, but not the ashes."

Sir John's chair scraped away. He shuffled to the door and instructed the awaiting maidservants to get it. "Quickly! Quickly!"

Silence.

"Who did this?" the child whispered over Brìghde whilst awaiting the maidservants.

"Grimme's favorite mistress," Sir John whispered back. "He has put her away. He made Brìghde his wife in truth and pledged fidelity to her."

"He *did?!*" the child asked breathlessly.

"Aye, so Emelisse has reason. I saw her lingering about Brìghde's chair before breakfast. Brìghde drinks much wine; 'twould not be difficult to poison the pitcher she drinks from."

"How much did she drink?"

"She will generally go through three pitchers in a meal."

"Hopefully, that amount of wine will dilute the poison." She paused. "Emelisse, aye?"

"Aye."

"She has come to me begging love potions for Grimme."

She wasn't supposed to call Grimme by his first name.

"She has cursed both me and Brìghde. Brìghde is convinced she is a witch. I tell her the only bad curse is one you believe."

"She *fancies* herself a witch. If she were one, she could have made her own love potion and ensorcelled Grimme herself."

"Ah. Did you give her anything?"

"Nay. I knew she would not pay me what she promised."

Soon there was more bustling in the room. She could hear the child scraping the side of a bowl.

"'Tis done. Sit her up."

Brìghde felt someone pulling at her, then someone else climbing into bed to sit behind her. She was laid back against the person.

"Open her mouth. We will see if this works."

Brìghde opened her mouth herself, yet felt Sir John's hands upon her chin and cheeks. The liquid was thin, but horrid, tasting of burnt wood and something even more bitter. She gagged and wanted to throw up.

"More. 'Twill make her sick, but that is what we want."

More of the wood liquid went down her throat. She choked on it. If she *had* to have something other than food or wine in her mouth, it should be her husband's spindle. Brìghde snickered.

One, two, three more spoonsful.

Brìghde was going to vomit.

"Fetch a pail!" the child screeched.

Four, five, six more spoonsful.

Brìghde heaved.

"It's working. More."

At spoonful number eleven, Brìghde cast up everything in her stomach, which was, in fact, quite a bit. She was tugged and rolled this way and that until she was hanging over the edge of the bed, choking and vomiting into a pail.

Someone was holding her hair back, and the child was smoothing her forehead and crooning at her to cast up everything, including the contents of her bowels. Brìghde felt as though she were doing that very thing.

Finally it stopped. "Wine," she croaked.

"Nay, watered mead."

"Don't like mead," she wheezed.

"You didn't like the charcoal, either, but you're awake."

Brìghde fell back onto the body of a maidservant, who was keeping her upright, and looked at the child. She was a dwarf. Tall for a dwarf, but still a dwarf. She wasn't a child but she wasn't an old hag, either. She was perhaps Brìghde's age at most. She was beautiful, with curly red locks tied back, kind brown eyes, and a winsome smile that immediately comforted Brìghde.

A tankard of mead was put in Brìghde's hands.

"Drink it all, my lady," the dwarf witch commanded firmly, "then drink some more. We must keep you vomiting." The witch looked down into the bucket and her eyebrow rose. "For such a tiny girl, you eat a lot."

Sir John laughed. "And drinks even more. She puts all of Kyneward's forces to shame."

"Your appetite saved your life," the witch said dryly.

For the next hour, Brìghde was forced to drink watered mead and beer and vomit it up again. Presently she needed the garderobe and Avis helped her with that.

"'Tis hot in here," Brìghde croaked finally.

The witch doused the fire and said, "I will sleep here for the night. Pap—Sir John, please arrange that."

Brìghde had enough wits about her to catch that, and she looked at the witch, who flushed and looked away. She turned to Sir John. "Does Grimme know?"

He shook his head. "He is too superstitious to accept her. He does not know she exists, but I keep her and her mother close to provide for them. I love her as much as I love all my children, but only my bastards return it." He nodded toward his daughter. "She is as learned as all my children. I made sure of it. 'Tis in medicine, though, the healer's arts, as much as I could find men who would take her as a student. She is not a witch, but healers are often called that. No one would accept her as a doctor and clearly she is no hag."

The witch puffed a soft laugh, and Brìghde smiled weakly, as it was the best she could do. "Your name is Sunny?"

"Aye, for Sunniva," she murmured shyly.

Brìghde chuckled, charmed. "Grimme and Sunny." She looked at Sir John. "Do you visit them?"

"I cannot make a flight of stairs by myself," he said bitterly. "How do I get to their cottage six miles away?"

"And Sunny cannot come here, for Grimme would think her a witch in truth and cast her out."

"We cannot predict," Sir John corrected. "He gives me what I want but he may draw the line at a witch, and I'll not risk her and her mother."

Brìghde nodded, but her eyelids were growing heavy.

"Sleep now," Sunny said softly.

"Sir John," Brìghde whispered.

"Aye?"

"I am going to kill Emelisse. Will you be my advocate?"

"With pleasure."

SUNNY STAYED with Brìghde for three more days. As she had been secreted into the keep, Emelisse did not know she was there and the servants and their families depended on Sunny for healing, so they would not betray her, *especially* not to Emelisse. They secreted her out under cover of darkness. It took another fortnight for Brìghde to gain the strength to do what she intended to do, for she could not now trust that her food and drink would go unmolested. She took her meals in the kitchen, where Emelisse would not go and Linota could keep an eye on her food from hearth to platter. Brìghde fetched her own wine, but did not drink much because she had to go to the wine cellar to get it and that took quite an effort.

She sat at the breakfast table chatting with the knights who had been left to guard Kyneward. She had already eaten in the kitchen and only attended the meal for the company. Today, Emelisse was not only at table, but she was especially chatty, even trying to draw Brìghde and Lady Caroline into conversation.

Halfway through the meal, irritated that Emelisse thought Brìghde was so stupid as to allow herself to be cultivated, she asked Sir Thom and Aldwyn to meet with her in Sir John's study. Once gathered, she turned to the man alongside whom she had battled.

"Emelisse was the one who poisoned me." He nodded gravely. "Today, she dies."

"Aye, my lady."

She looked at Aldwyn and Sir John, daring Aldwyn to argue, but his expression was placid and he nodded once.

"What are your orders?" Sir Thom asked.

"I want a long whip. String her up in the bailey by her wrists and strip her to the waist."

He didn't blink. "If I may advise?"

"Speak."

"That is a very long and tiring and difficult way to execute someone, and you must be careful with your shoulder."

"My shoulder will bear it. I want her to feel my rage before I kill her."

97

GRIMME AND his men crested the rise over Kyneward. The watchers had blown the horns to announce their arrival. The training field was nearby, and the men continued to train, as they should. The company stopped so that Terrwyn could dismount, gather his things and walk back to his knight. Grimme gave him a great hug and reminded him that he would be taking him to York in two months. He watched his third son trot away and felt sorrow and resignation that his two oldest sons were gone; he'd grieved them all the way home and soon Terrwyn would be leaving.

He didn't know how he would manage when it was Pierce's turn to apprentice somewhere, and he could only hope Brìghde caught soon—and often. He had realized on his way home that he could not be without his children about, which truly shocked him.

Grimme and his men rounded the turn to follow the long lane to the keep. Other than having to leave his sons to their future with no idea when he'd see them again, he was exuberant. He had Tavendish's approbation and political power with the crown to keep Sheffield at bay should the duke be stupid enough to attempt something. After Grimme had reluctantly admitted to Tavendish that he did not know how to make political alliances, Tavendish had offered to assist him in that as well.

As he rode along high in the saddle and rounded the turn into the lane, Grimme expected that at any minute, Brìghde and Pierce, mayhap Aldwyn and Caroline, would come rushing out of the keep to greet him. But no.

"Where the devil are they?" he barked, immediately angry.

"My lord," Sir Drew murmured, "'tis too quiet. Something's wrong."

Grimme kicked Ares into a run up the lane and through the portcullis—to find the villeins, the servants, and the guards gathered round some spectacle in the middle of the inner bailey. High up on Ares, he could see over the crowd and his heart stopped.

There in the middle, Emelisse hanging by her wrists, stripped to the waist, her back a bloody mess, and … his wife, garbed not in black but in pink, wielding a whip, with Sir John and Sir Thom standing by her side and watching with sober countenances. Pierce stood beside Sir John with an expression of smug satisfaction. Aldwyn and Lady Caroline stood next to Sir Thom, their expressions stony.

Grimme could say not one word for a moment or two, he was so nauseated, but the next crack of the whip stirred him to action.

"*BRÌGHDE!*" he bellowed as he turned Ares into the crowd, which parted amidst many bows and "my lords," which he only vaguely noticed. He just had to get to Emelisse before Brìghde killed her. He put himself between the women just as the lash was about to rip more skin from Emelisse's back. He caught it with his thickly gloved hand and wrapped it around his hand once, twice, three times, snarling at Brìghde and pulling her forward with each wrap. She wouldn't let go and she was snarling back at him. She was strong. He tugged her closer and closer, jerked it out of her hand, then dropped it to concentrate on getting Emelisse down.

He turned Ares so that when he cut the rope around an unconscious Emelisse's wrists, he could ease her down into his lap, on her stomach.

She groaned. He stroked her blood-soaked hair and made comforting noises as he turned Ares to face his wife.

"You stripe her," Grimme snarled, "you heal her."

"*And again you choose her over me!*" Brìghde screamed.

"*She is the mother of my children!*" he roared in return. He shot a glare at Sir Thom and demanded, "What could she have possibly done to warrant this?"

With all equanimity, Sir Thom answered, "Mistress Emelisse poisoned my lady."

Grimme's heart stopped and he nearly dumped Emelisse off his lap as if her body had sprouted spikes.

"It is my charge to protect my lady, and if I cannot do so, to mete out justice. In this case, I find the justice equal to the crime, and allowing my lady to wield the lash to be as just."

Grimme looked to Aldwyn, who said calmly, "I would have found the same."

He looked at his father, who had a stony look upon his face. "Your wife nearly died," he said flatly. "Unfortunately, you arrived before Brìghde killed her."

Stunned, he looked to Brìghde. "You intend to kill her *after* I told you not to?!"

"Aye," she growled, glaring at him from under her brows. "I intend to cut out her heart and *EAT – IT!*"

Grimme had done that, so he could appreciate it. "You're not dead," he pointed out.

"No, but if she lives, and lives *here*, I will be."

"Do you have proof?"

"*I – DON'T – NEED – PROOF!*" she roared. "What if you had come home to find me dead? Would you believe it then?"

That would have sent him into a murderous rage.

"Would you choose her then? Aye, of course you would, because the mother of your children," she sneered, "that blonde angel *dove*, couldn't possibly be evil, could she?"

He continued to stroke Emelisse's hair and signaled his knights to take her to her chambers. Once she was gone, he waved a hand at the crowd. "Begone, back to your posts."

He sat and stared at—rather, *through*—Brìghde, who stood glaring at him. She picked up the whip again and coiled it threateningly. If it hadn't involved Emelisse, Grimme's cod would be stirring. He loved that about Brìghde, her rage, her bloodlust—that then would turn happy and amusing when she was sated.

What could he say to Brìghde? Emelisse had declared war on her the day they rode into Kyneward and Brìghde had tolerated it because she hadn't cared enough to engage until it became important to her rule. And now he had protected Emelisse from Brìghde *again* after he had sworn not to.

He dropped his head back to see ravens, scenting blood, circling in the sky. They spoke.

This is your fault. You would not protect our queen from the witch.

"I know," he whispered, heartsick. Ashamed.

What was he going to tell Gaston and Max?

Grimme hadn't had to say anything to Terrwyn until after the fact; Dillena and Brìghde had taken care of it. Brìghde had called Terrwyn in from his duties and given him and Dillena a day to say goodbye.

Grimme had allowed it, watching from afar, knowing Brìghde thought he hadn't noticed or cared. It was difficult *not* to notice a wagon being loaded with what were clearly Dillena's belongings and a carriage being hitched. Aye, he noticed. He cared. He had gone to Dillena in the dead of night whilst Brìghde was sleeping and requested to talk. She explained. He understood. He regretted that he did not really know her very well. He knew she was learned, and could read and write, but he had never known that she wrote poetry and stories for herself and Terrwyn since she had no books. He had never known about her artwork, much less that Brìghde had admired it so much. He had taken her in his arms and tenderly kissed her farewell. She whispered to him the explanation Terrwyn was to be given: that Dillena was going back to Wales to care for her dying mother.

Thank you, Lord Grimme.

Grimme.

Aye, thank you, Grimme. Please take care of our son.

You have my word. And Dillena—thank you for Terrwyn. I will forever be grateful to you for him.

Then our time together has been well spent.

You have meant much more to me than I realized, and I wish I had told you sooner.

Lady Brìghde told me. Thank you for that, too.

Please send me your direction when you are settled, and I will give it to him to find you when he is free again.

I would like that. Thank you.

It would be up to Grimme to tell his two oldest—and most attached to their mother—that Emelisse had gone away. He had to tell them *something,* but they were still stinging from his lack of an answer to *But don't you love Mamá?*

On the other hand, Emelisse's lack of enthusiasm and pride in the boys' accomplishments had not gone unnoticed nor had Brìghde's care. It hurt, that their mother did not demonstrate the same amount of care that their stepmother had. On the road to Tavendish, Max and Gaston had approached Grimme and quietly asked him why their mother was angry with them.

She's not. She is sad you're leaving and doesn't know how else to show it.

She did not even bid us fare thee well.

It hurt too much; 'tis easier for her to pretend you are still out in the field and she can go visit occasionally.

It's Lady Brigitte's fault!

Very well. Let us ponder that a moment. Ever since Lady Brigitte came, she has been trying to give you the freedom Terrwyn and Pierce have, oui?

… Oui.

Nay, Grimme didn't mind poisoning this well at all.

She bought you real swords when your mother wouldn't let you have toy ones, oui?

… Oui.

She fêted you. She praised you. She cheered for you, oui?

… Oui.

She took you to Hogarth to get clothing, but you stayed for the amusements and games and you enjoyed yourselves, oui?

… Oui.

So is it her fault, *or was it a gift she gave you? You don't have to answer. Simply ponder it.*

At some point whilst Grimme was lost in thought, his wife and her conspirators had disappeared. He turned Ares and went to the stable, dismounted, scratched his pet's nose, received his horse kisses, and trudged to the keep with a heavy heart. The hall was somber as everyone awaited him to be seated for supper. He hadn't even taken his mail off yet.

"Eat," he sighed with a wave and trudged up the stairs. He opened his door and was surprised to see Brìghde there with Pierce, sitting on the bed whilst she entertained him with a tale and made him laugh.

She looked up and watched him warily, but Pierce slid off the bed and ran to Grimme. "Papa, it's true. I saw her do it. I was hiding under the tables when I saw her."

Grimme's eyebrow rose and he bent to pick the boy up. "You hate Emelisse, so it would be to your benefit to lie to me."

"I'm not lying, Papa," he said soberly. "Brìghde almost died. She was in bed for three days."

"Four," Brìghde said quietly.

Grimme gulped, unable to bear the thought of losing his dearest friend, his Aphrodite. "I believe you, Son. Now. Go eat. I need to speak with Brìghde."

"Fare thee well, Brìghde!" he said brightly as he left the room.

"Fare thee ... " she drifted off because he'd disappeared.

Grimme closed the door, crossed the room in two strides, picked Brìghde up, and kissed her with everything in his soul.

She was surprised, but melted against him soon enough and wrapped her arms around him. They kissed heatedly. "I'm sorry," he whispered into her mouth.

"Do you send her away *now?*" she murmured, sliding down and pulling away slowly.

He looked in her big green eyes and said, "Aye, but whether you like it or not, she *is* the mother of my sons and you will not kill her."

"And if she had killed me?"

"I would have killed her myself. Quickly, quietly, and privately."

"If I had killed her before you returned?"

"I ... " He took a deep breath and turned as she started to remove his mail. " ... would have been very angry for a few days whilst I thought of what to tell my sons. Did you tell Sir Thom you intended to kill her?"

"Aye. He, Sir John, and Aldwyn agreed with— Ow," she hissed, clutching her shoulder.

"Wielding a whip a bit much for you, Wife?"

"Aye," she grumbled. "Sir Thom warned me. I didn't listen."

"I'm shocked."

He said nothing else for a while and she seemed to want to squire for him in spite of her pain. "I could accustom myself to having you as a squire," he said vaguely as he searched through his clothing.

She puffed a laugh.

"Your minions … "

"Aye?" she said vaguely.

"Do they speak to you?"

"All the time."

He shook his head. They made noises at her in a language she did not understand and refused to say her name without a treat, but he did not want to delve into flights of fancy.

"Did you miss me?"

"I was ill for most of it," she said flatly.

"And the rest?"

"Aye," she purred.

"Did you save your lust for me?"

"I did."

"But you didn't want to."

"Nay."

He grinned. "I pray you don't let me break you, Wife."

"Me too!" she said fervently.

He laughed, happy that for now, at least, he had a lusty wench to fuck who would not kick him out of bed when she'd had enough.

Yet.

"Ah … but … " she said hesitantly. "When I was ill, at first I thought I was with child and sadly, I am not, but it made me wonder— If I grow heavy with child—"

"*When*," he corrected gently.

She smiled weakly. "Emelisse said you don't swive women who are with child and I don't want to be disgusting to you again. I know you acquiesced to accommodating me, but nine months is a long time, never mind the time after I have delivered."

He sat down and pulled her onto his lap. "I don't generally fuck women heavy with child not because I am uninterested, but because I do not want to harm the baby. You have been the recipient of my amorous attentions for a month. Do you see my concern?"

"I do," she said simply.

"Once," he continued, "a woman whose child did not want to come into the world, and who was utterly miserable for it, and whose husband refused to help her after the midwife told her what could be done, came into a tavern I frequented and asked the wenches who would be most likely to fuck her for the sole purpose of encouraging the babe to get on with its business. *Everyone* pointed at me."

Brìghde's eyes widened. "And you did it?"

"She had blue eyes and blonde hair. Of course I did." Brìghde chuckled, and he grinned. "It took an entire day, but the babe did, indeed, finally decide she had had enough of my knocking on her door. *And* the pleasure I gave the mother reduced her aches and pains. She was very grateful."

Brìghde laughed. "What did her husband think?"

"He steadfastly avoided the house for the duration."

Brìghde squealed with laughter, then said, "Ow," and clutched her shoulder.

"The new terms were that I would abstain completely if you were with child, ill, injured, or having your courses. If *you* want me to fuck you when you're with child, I will happily accommodate you. When you determine you cannot or should not—" It would be the longest year of his life. "—I will not press you until you have healed from delivery and feel you may resume."

When her face lit up with joy, and she launched herself to hug him and whisper *Thank you, Grimme, thank you thank you thank you,* in his ear, Grimme decided he would endure it graciously whether he liked it or not.

He wrapped his arms around her. "I do not know what I will do about my insatiable lust, but I swear to you it will not involve any other woman, man, horse, sheep, goat, tree knot, or bunghole."

She laughed.

"It will involve my right hand. And left. And yours. And your mouth."

She grinned slyly. "Need that be said?"

98

GRIMME FUCKED his lusty Aphrodite for the first time in a month—thrice, as she was still so filled with rage and bloodlust she could outpace him—and after several hours, when she was finally sated and had fallen asleep, he went to Emelisse's chambers. She was lying on her stomach, her maidservant lightly patting her back with a damp cloth.

"My lord," the girl said, rose, curtsied, then went back to tending Emelisse, who slowly turned her head to look at Grimme. It was dark, long after the keep had been put to bed. The fire was low. He went around lighting some candles, then cocked his head toward the door. The chambermaid curtsied again and left quietly, taking Emelisse's untouched meal with her.

Grimme pulled a chair up to Emelisse's bedside and gently caressed her forehead and cheeks.

"Look what you have done to me," she whispered in French, tears running down her face, "bringing that *witch* into the house, sticking your cod in her, feeding her familiars, never knowing that you are ensorcelled. She has bewitched you, Grimme. What will make you see?"

He sighed. "Did you intend to make her sick or did you mean to kill her?"

She closed her eyes and began to sob. "I did not poison her."

"Don't lie to me, Emelisse. I have allowed you to lie to me for twelve years, as I did not care. Now I do. My father's and Aldwyn's opinions I question, but I do not question Sir Thom. He believes you did, therefore, you did."

"He is in love with her," she wept. "They are lovers, but you do not see."

Grimme rolled his eyes. "Answer me. Did you intend to kill her or did you mean to make her sick?"

"She needs to die," she hissed.

"Ah. Did you use the poison in the house?"

"She keeps it locked in her chambers and guarded by that vicious little bitch of a chambermaid. Why is a chambermaid allowed to treat me with such contempt?"

"You have hated Brìghde from the beginning, when I did not desire her, nor she me, when we were no more than conspirators each with our own reasons for the marriage. She advocated for you. She saved you from the duke. Yet you cursed her, you struck her at least once that I know of and she warned you then she would kill you if you did it again. You should have believed her, as she had planned a very painful death for you."

Emelisse's eyes went wide. "You promised you would not let her harm me again! I cannot trust *any* food or drink brought to me and I have not eaten!"

"I promised I would not let her kill you, but now I have ordered her not to touch you again *at all*, which includes poison, and she will abide by that."

She gulped. "Thank you," she whispered.

"I cannot trust you not to poison her again, and I will tolerate no more of your childish behavior. Time and time again, I have protected you from her, choosing you even though you were in the wrong, even though it tore my commanders away from me."

"Only because they hate me!"

"They didn't always. You earned their hatred."

She hiccuped. "You chose her from the beginning."

Grimme said nothing for a moment, thinking back. "How did you know?" he asked.

"You laughed when she pounded on my door and screamed at you and kicked it open," she said sadly.

He somehow held his laughter. He would never not find that funny. "Be that as it may, know this: I set you aside because you passed by Lady Caroline. It was the last insult from you that I could stomach. I have sworn fealty to Brìghde. I have declared my love for her. I have vowed to be faithful to her."

"Until you break her the way you broke me."

"Forever. No matter what." Brìghde didn't need to know that.

Emelisse shattered. Grimme sat and endured it, as he felt he owed her that comfort. He caressed her forehead and her cheeks whilst she cried, and finally she was ready to speak again.

"What about Gaston and Max?"

"They are gone. As you did not show a mother's pride and you did not bother to bid them farewell, they may not care."

She gasped. "What?"

"The entire three days they were here, they sought your approval, and you would not give it. In fact, you embarrassed them with your show of resentment. You deliberately encouraged them to see me with Brigitte, which tore them asunder as you knew it would. They are hurt and feel as if you have abandoned them. I reminded them of who *did* show her pride in them, who *did* celebrate them, who *did* ride halfway to Waters to say farewell to them, who *did* play with them, who *did* think about their needs and meet them. It wasn't you, and I cannot forgive you for that."

"I wanted them *with me*!"

"Aye, I know that so very well. What *you* want. Not what *other people* need from you. In any case, they are gone and will have no reason to think of you for years. They will be told that you left Kyneward because you could no longer abide Brìghde. You will *never* breathe a word of the truth to the boys. Do you understand?"

"Oui," she breathed as she started to cry again. Tears dripped down her face. "Did you ever love me?" she whispered, her voice cracking.

Grimme sighed heavily. "I did," he admitted, but now with no expectation that she would taunt him with it. "Once. I have kept you with me no matter what because I am a loyal man and I wanted my sons near. But you never stopped trying to control or possess me. I stayed because *I* wanted to. I stayed because my father loved and took care of his bastards, and I could do no less for mine. I sent them away *only* because it was past time for their apprenticeship. I did that for their future. 'Twas not to punish you."

"You didn't send them away until *she* told you to!"

Grimme pursed his lips. "That is true," he finally said.

"I am with child again."

"It would be very much like you to have another to keep me by your side," he mused, "to have another babe to possess and control. But I don't believe you because I told you what I would do, and you would never risk that."

"*She* possesses and controls you!"

Grimme puffed a little laugh and felt his indulgent smile. "No. I value her friendship, far more than I ever valued Aldwyn's. It is a coming-together I can have with no other."

He stroked her cheek and her forehead and her hair, long, flaxen, and bloody from the stripes on her back. He smoothed the hair away from her back, carefully picking out strands from the blood. He leaned in to kiss her tenderly, as it used to be when he was a new initiate and dazzled by this blonde beauty who wanted him, when he loved her.

She kissed him back. "Grimme," she sighed. "I love you. Forgive me?"

"No."

She whimpered. "Please don't send me away. I can't bear life without you."

"I know," he said sadly. He pulled away from her and stood. "Thank you for Gaston and Max," he murmured, cupping and caressing her face. "They are fine boys and will grow into fine men. I will always be grateful to you for them."

"Where are you sending me?" she whimpered.

"To hell."

99

BECAUSE OF THE way in which Emelisse had left Kyneward Keep and why, and because Brìghde hoped to be with child soon, medical matters were much on her mind. She sat in the middle of Grimme's bed brushing her hair, hesitant to discuss it, but she could not put it off much longer, as Sir John was old and tired. It was time to release him from his duty.

She took a deep breath and said, "Grimme."

"Aye," he grunted as he sat before the fire, his legs outstretched, staring into it, drinking, lost in grief she wished he had not taken upon himself when she would have gladly borne it for him.

It had been a week since Emelisse disappeared, leaving her chambers untouched and her bed clean and precisely made. No one had seen her leave, no one asked where she went. She left behind notes for her sons, but that was all. Grimme had been staring into the fire like this ever since. He had not gone into the field. He had not eaten much at meals. He had not swived Brìghde, but had held on to her tightly all through every night when he was not tossing and turning. He was drinking.

A lot.

"When you spoke of the ravens before—"

"Bloody hell, Brìghde," he snapped, casting a glare over his shoulder at her, "how many times are you going to throw that in my face?"

"No, no, no, no!" she hastened to say. "'Tis not what you think. I am merely *asking* if you truly believe that witches are real."

"Why?" he drawled with great suspicion.

"Please?"

He took a deep breath and turned back to the fire. "My brother, the one who told me the tale of the raven witch. He doesn't believe in witches. He doesn't believe in God. He doesn't believe in Satan, either. He hates the church. He's more hateful about it than my father is."

"Did you tell Sir John what he said?"

"Oh, no. No. He would have punished my brother and then my brother would have laughed at me for running to Papa. But my mother took us to church, even though my father didn't want her to. There, we were taught witches are real and must be feared and avoided at all costs, and if one cannot avoid them, one must hang them."

Brìghde's brushing slowed. This was not going well.

"And then the ravens snatched our rabbits." Grimme was silent for a long time, then he finally said, "As I grew and learned how much I love war, my *mind,* that which I use to devise battle plans, said no, there is no such thing as witches. My father even proved to me that the church considers contemplating such things but a vanity and that the particular priest my mother took us to was wrong. Witchcraft either didn't exist or was an insignificant piece of nothing, a waste of time. How would I know if I met a witch? Papa asked me. A real one. My brother said they were beautiful. My mother and the priest said they were ugly.

"I don't know if I believe in witches anymore. But what I *do* know is that evil exists, and I have met it. It *never* looks like a small beautiful woman with black hair in a black kirtle. Time and again, I have met evil, known it for what it was instantly, and conquered it, as when I slayed Walter Fàileach. Time and again, I have seen evil, known it for what it was, and been unable to do anything."

"Sheffield."

He raised a finger. "Aye. And sometimes ... Sometimes, evil looks like a tall, willowy, beautiful blue-eyed blonde, and for twelve years I didn't see it."

Brìghde grimaced. "People change," she offered.

He barked a laugh. "Still advocating for her, eh?"

"No. I do not want you to blame yourself. There was no reason for you to see what had not come to the surface and you were trying to be loyal to the mother of your children no matter how difficult she made it. I didn't *like* it, but I do find it honorable and comforting."

"Oh. Thank you." Again he was silent for a long while. "She cursed me."

It didn't surprise Brìghde that she *had,* but it did surprise her that Grimme told her. "What did she say?"

"'May you always doubt the parentage of your next son.' What did she say to you?"

"'May your womb one day find too many choices to make.'"

"Two ways of saying the same thing."

"Also 'May you find yourself at the mercy of a babe in winter.'"

He drank the rest of his wine in one swallow, then poured more. "If one looks at it logically," he said slowly, "if she were a real witch, she would have had me spellbound, and she did not. God knows she tried."

Oh! Hope!

"'Tis odd that you should say that," Brìghde said, attempting to tip-toe around her point, "as someone else made a similar observation to me. What if— Mind you, I am only suggesting—"

"You've been talking to Papa, aye?" he said dryly, looking over his shoulder again with a wry smile. His mood was lifting. "Witches aren't real. Curses can't hurt if you don't believe in them, aye?"

Brìghde chuckled. "Aye."

"What do *you* think?"

"You … never asked me how I recovered from the poison."

Silence. "Tell me," he finally said, low.

"A healer. She lives just past Waters. She has lived there since Kyneward became yours. The villagers, villeins, and servants *call* her a witch, but they know her not to be one. Emelisse thought she really was a witch and sought her out for a love potion for you, but she doesn't do such. She is learned in the ways of man's medicine. Less than a doctor. More than a barber. Your father said healers are often called witches, shunned in public, but sought in private."

"I do not know of any healer past the barber or midwife in Waters."

"I know you don't know of her," Brìghde rushed to say. "I am asking … that you meet her. But I do not want you to fear her or find her evil or … cast her out or … whatever you would do if you met a real witch."

He waved a hand. "I'm not so dimwitted as to not know the difference between a healer and a witch, and even if she were a witch in truth, I would never harm the one who saved my wife's life."

That made Brìghde so very, *very* happy. "Oh, thank you, Grimme! I will send for her then. Now come to bed, lie back, and let me pleasure you, since you would not allow me to spare you this pain."

He wrestled himself out of the chair, put his goblet on the table, and lumbered toward the bed, getting in and situating himself. He looked up at her and raised a hand to run his fingers through her hair. He took a lock, studied it, caressed it. Then he looked up at her.

"It was your right," he murmured, sorrow oozing from his voice, "but it was my responsibility. Time and time again, I refused to see the evil, failed to protect my Aphrodite, and I had to pay the price."

100

TWO DAYS LATER, Grimme's father was picking at his breakfast. Brìghde roosted in her chair as if she'd pearls in her arse. Since Grimme had, in fact, made her come to table with either pearls in her arse, glass in her cunte, or both, he knew what that looked like. She was ignoring Pierce and Mercury, and she'd forgotten to feed the ravens, so he had done it for her. She, too, was picking at her breakfast and drinking.

A lot.

Grimme looked between them, his eyes narrowing. "If you two think I am going to cast out this healer simply because she is *called* a witch, you know me less well than I thought you did."

Sir John didn't look at him. Brìghde gave him a nervous smile.

"When—"

Just then an empty chair at the end of the head table was pulled out and Mouse plopped in it. Grimme scowled down the table. "Did you take a bath?"

"Aye," he drawled as he picked his teeth, sat back, and put his feet up on the table. "Your housekeeper is dazzling and not in the least bit pleasant. Have you fucked her yet? Because if you won't, I will."

"What's he doing here?" Grimme calmly asked his father.

"I summoned him."

"Grimme," Brìghde growled. "Who is that?"

"His name is Mouse."

"Don't I ... know you?" Aldwyn asked Mouse slowly.

"Nay."

"But who is he?"

"That is not important right now."

"No, I do know you."

"No, you don't."

"It *is* important. Who is he?"

Mouse and Aldwyn continued to argue whilst Grimme asked his father, "Does he have anything to do with this healer?"

"Aye," he said shortly.

"When does she arrive?"

"Grimme," Brìghde gritted.

"She is already here," Sir John muttered.

"What— Oh, bloody hell, do you *really* think so little of me that you must sneak her in? Where is she?"

"In my study."

"Now, Grimme—" Brìghde said hurriedly when he scraped back his chair and headed for the study. She and Sir John were right behind him—or as much as they could be when Sir John shuffled along on his cane. "Don't—"

He opened the door quietly and peeked inside to see a red-headed dwarf—tall for a dwarf, but a dwarf nonetheless—pacing and chewing her thumbnail. She was dressed in the height of fashion, her hair was beautifully coiffed, and her headdress was elegant. She had expensive rings on her fingers and an expensive girdle.

"Good morn."

She jumped and stared at him wide-eyed, her hand over her heaving chest.

He huffed and opened the door fully, then awaited his wife and father. Mouse bolted for the door and slipped through it before Grimme could close it on his face. Mouse laughed. "Missed. Again."

Mouse flopped in Sir John's desk chair and tilted it back, putting his feet up on the desk, and whilst Grimme could clearly see the confusion on Brìghde's face as to who this person was and why he leaked disrespect like a sieve, she and his father were clearly far more anxious about Grimme's reaction to the healer.

Grimme only wanted to thank her for saving Brìghde's life.

"You don't look like a witch," Grimme said finally.

Suddenly, much of the tension left the room, and the dwarf smiled tremulously. "Good morn."

He raised an eyebrow, for she had not addressed him as "my lord" or curtsied to him.

She looked back at him as if to ask what he expected.

"Curtsy?" he prompted. "'My lord'?"

Her expression changed to amusement and she chuckled softly. "No."

Mouse chortled. It was half funny, half confusing, but not necessarily infuriating. "Hrmph."

"Grimme," Sir John said, stepping forward. "This is Sunniva." That was a very old Saxon name. "She is the healer who came and helped Brìghde expel the poison."

Grimme decided she could refuse courtesy to him all she wanted. He bowed. "Thank you, Mistress Sunniva, for my wife."

"You're most welcome," she said softly.

"And this ... "

Grimme turned to see a much smaller dwarf sitting to the side. She was not much older and looked like the other, so he said, "You are her sister?"

"Mother," she said warily, looking at him as if she expected to bite her. "We are not here to be your amusement."

" ... is Maud."

Grimme began to scowl at all of them in turn. "What is the point of this?" he demanded. "There is too much pomp and circumstance about this meeting. They are dwarves. She is a healer who is called a witch, but is not a witch. She saved Brìghde's life. Excellent, thank you, Mistress Sunniva. But Mouse is here, so something else is going on."

Sir John cleared his throat. "The dwarf I bedded ... 'Twas funny you should mention it after so many years."

Grimme's jaw dropped and his attention focused solely on Sunniva. "You're my sister?"

She nodded. "Aye," she said shyly. "Sunniva Kyneward. Papa calls me Sunny."

Grimme rushed to her and she cringed away from him, but he didn't care. He picked her up, held her to his chest, and swung her around. "I have a sister!" he crowed, then put her down. She wobbled on her feet, as she was slightly dizzy, but he didn't feel sorry for her.

He grinned down at his dazed sister. "Come, come, sit. Breakfast?" He strode across the room and bellowed, "Breakfast! Six. Several pitchers of wine." He closed the door and said, "I have a sister!" Then he rounded on Mouse. "You knew!"

He shrugged. "I know everything about this family, little brother."

Brìghde's jaw dropped.

Grimme was too happy to be angry and laughed at the various expressions darting across Brìghde's face, then he stopped gradually when he saw that his father had tears in his eyes and looked terribly unhappy.

"Papa?"

He looked at Sunny, who was glaring at his—*their*—father.

"I thought you would cast her out for witchcraft," he croaked. "You were four when she was born. Three years later, you were gone for a page, so you only saw her once or twice as a baby and you weren't paying attention. Then you were gone so much, there was no opportunity ... I have kept you separated since she came to Kyneward with me. She begged me to take the risk, but I wouldn't. I can predict you on most things, but this was ... I was afraid. For her and her mother. Now she is angry with me for much wasted time, and I am no less angry with myself. Sad, rather."

Grimme dropped his head and sighed heavily.

"Ah, Sunny," Mouse drawled with a grimace. "This is apparently all my fault. I used to tell Grimme about a raven witch that would come for him if he were naughty. Papa's already dragged me over hot stones for it."

Both Sunny and Brìghde snarled at him.

"What?" he demanded. "That's what older brothers *do*, torture their little brothers." Mouse tilted his head and pointed at Grimme. "You are six and twenty years old. You love war. You'll kill at the slightest hint of anything untoward and never bat an eye. Witches don't exist! Shouldn't you be past this by now?"

Grimme had about all he could take of his older brother. "You do remember you're half my size, do you not?"

"You must catch me first, and you have *never* been able to do that."

The food came and with it a table and chairs. The servants cast glances at Sunny and nodded respectfully. She smiled in return.

"Does *everyone* know about her but I?" Grimme burst out.

"Aye," all five of them said in unison.

He huffed and swept his hand to the table. "Come. Eat." As they settled, Grimme pulled out his sister's—*he had a sister!*—chair for her before seating himself.

"Thank you," she said, again shyly.

"Are you always like this?" he asked her as he seated himself.

She stilled and looked at him warily. "Like what?"

"Shy."

"Oh. Aye. 'Tis one reason we live so far in the woods. That, and we are dwarves. That, and I am a witch."

He waved that off.

"I don't … care for people. They are not kind to the likes of us."

"You—both of you—are welcome here at all hours of any day." Her smile was one of joy and relief and he smiled back. "In fact, you may move in!"

She blushed. "Thank you for the offer," she said softly, "but I need my cottage, and even if I didn't need it, I would not leave it."

"Well, then! You must do what you must. I am so happy to have a sister! Our brothers hate me and Mouse, you see."

She nodded. "They would hate me even more, did they know of me."

As they ate, Grimme learned of her circumstance, which was very much like his own: A bastard of a second mistress his father was fucking whilst fucking Grimme's mother, but not his wife. 'Twas true to form for a Kyneward male, so he thought nothing of it.

"You're twenty-two, then?"

"Aye."

He looked at her mother. "You don't look old enough to be anyone's mother."

Maud also flushed. "Thank you," she said quietly. "I was nineteen when Sunniva was born."

He summed quickly, then raised his eyebrow at his father. "That would've made *you* nearly fifty."

Sir John shrugged and calmly ate. "She was a charming, intelligent young woman and I'm a Kyneward. I have a brother younger than you."

Brìghde raised a finger and said, "Ah … Grimme. Speaking of brothers." She pointed at Mouse, still sitting at Sir John's desk and eating. "Explain."

"That is Philippe Kyneward."

"He's … *older* … than you?"

"Aye. By six years."

Mouse smiled at her beatifically and gave her a small wave. "I generally live at Sheffield. I'm one of Grimme's spies. Papa called me home for this little reunion. Good morn, Sunny."

"Good morn, Philippe," she said sweetly. "Thank you for the books."

"Say nothing of it. Anything else I can get for you?"

She put down her knife to dig in her sleeve. "I have a list."

He took it, looked at it, and stuffed it in his breeches. "As good as done, little sis."

Grimme snorted. "Are there any *more* bastards you want to tell me about?" he asked his father, amused.

He smiled. "Two. The first one is due in—" He looked at Maud.

"Six months," she said softly.

Grimme and Brìghde both gaped at him. "When—?" Brìghde squeaked.

He shrugged. "When you or Grimme or both are out for more than a day, Maud comes here. My cod does not want for attention, I assure you. I *am* a Kyneward."

Grimme and Mouse roared, but soon enough Grimme got around to asking after the other one. "The one you said you would not tell me about?" Grimme asked his father.

Sir John nodded. "I wasn't as prolific as my father was. He is your age, barely six months younger. I sent him also to a knight."

His tone was odd. Grimme stared at his father, who would not look at him. Then he pulled in a shocked breath. "Aldwyn."

His father nodded slightly. "God, this is delicious," Mouse hooted at Sunny, who grinned.

"Why did you not give him your name as the rest of us?" Grimme demanded. "Why did you not tell me?"

"His mother hated me. She would not give him my name, and demanded I keep the two of you apart. I conceded the name, but I did not, obviously, concede to keeping you apart, nor would I deny him his future. I also would not allow her to move out of my reach. Now she is dead."

"Does *he* know?"

Sir John pulled his lips between his teeth.

Rage burst through Grimme's breast. "Of this entire situation," he ground out, whirling his finger around the table, "*that* is what angers me." He glared at Brìghde, who held her hands up, looking as shocked as he was.

"I didn't know!"

Then he glared at Mouse, who merely grinned.

"'Twas coincidence that you became fast friends, or … mayhap not coincidence. Perhaps kin knows its own, but 'twas why Mouse and I were so concerned about the tournament. If either of you had killed the other … "

Grimme looked at Mouse, who nodded soberly. "I almost told you, but I decided to trust you and … I should do that more often."

"Yes," Grimme said flatly, "you should." He looked back at his father. "Why did Aldwyn's mother hate you?"

Sir John hesitated. "I betrayed my best friend to have her, and—"

"*Aldwyn* is your Pierce."

"Aye. That was what I had to explain to Aldwyn when you took Maebh. Aldwyn's mother didn't hate me for seducing her. She hated me because I would not choose. She made the choice for me, and I grieve her." He swept his hand toward Sunny's mother. "I cannot visit her anymore without arousing your suspicion because I must marshal a force to take me there. I did not want you to know in case— We send messages back and forth almost daily and when you are gone— Maud is the only one I have left who is also true to me, and now, when I am old and infirm, I can appreciate having one woman to devote my time and attention to, and enjoy my love for her. The choice has been made for me and I am grateful to be relieved of that burden. 'Twas why I wanted you to put the others away and take Brìghde as your wife and be true to her, to save you the pain I have endured. I told you."

"You said if I bedded Brìghde," Grimme said slowly, "I would love her. Did you know I already did?"

He nodded. "'Twas only a matter of time before you realized it, but it was time we did not have and I was angry with you for being blind to it—deliberately, I think. You were not willing to let go of your women or control your appetite and you knew—we all did—that Brìghde would never countenance being one of many. But then Aldwyn came and I thought it amusing that I would get a grandchild out of Brìghde from one bastard or another, but he would still be *my* grandchild from her."

Grimme felt ashamed. Betrayed. Shocked. Angry. But mostly *elated.* He threw back his chair and strode to the door, flinging it open. "Aldwyn! Caroline! Come! Bring your platters!"

Aldwyn, deep in a discussion with Father Hercule, and Caroline, in the midst of a sip of wine, looked at him in shock. He gestured impatiently, and they arose. He bellowed for two more chairs and the servants scurried to get them placed before Aldwyn and Caroline entered the room.

Aldwyn stopped cold in the threshold, and Grimme could tell when he put it all together. Aldwyn looked at Grimme warily, but Grimme couldn't help his grin. Aldwyn puffed a laugh, dropped his head, and shook it.

"You, my poor brother," Grimme said heartily as he propelled him in with an arm around his shoulder, gesturing for Caroline to join them before kicking the door closed, "clearly did not get the Kyneward thirst for cunte."

Aldwyn slid him a wry glance and Sir John started to laugh. "I just wasn't as obvious," Aldwyn drawled. "I can control my appetites and I fell in love early." He pulled away from Grimme and offered his hand to his wife, who took it, looking very, very confused.

"Caroline," Aldwyn murmured, pulling her forward. He swept his hand to the table. "Meet my father, John Kyneward, who is not truly a 'Sir.' You met Sunny when she was here tending Brìghde. Grimme is my half-brother and Sunny is my half-sister. This is Maud, who is expecting again, so I will have yet another half sibling."

Caroline looked as shocked as Brìghde. "Why didn't you ever tell me?" she whispered at Aldwyn.

His smile faded. "First, it was because my mother didn't want me to, and after she died, it was easier for me to think that my companion-at-arms had betrayed me, not my brother, so I couldn't bear to think of it at all."

Grimme winced. No, he would no longer grovel for Maebh, but it didn't make the offense go away.

"But in cutting myself off from Grimme, I cut myself off from my father and Sunny, as wherever he goes, she goes. That, I regret deeply."

"Come, come," Grimme said heartily.

"Sunny," Aldwyn said warmly and skirted the table to hug her as well as he could, then dropped a kiss on the top of her head.

"Aldwyn," she said just as warmly, clasping his hand in both of hers. "'Twas good to see you again after so many years, although the circumstances were dire and we did not get much of a chance to speak. Now 'tis wonderful to be able to break bread together with full knowledge of each other."

That was when Aldwyn saw Mouse, who was looking at him whilst chewing a mouthful of food. "Who *are* you? I *know* I've seen you somewhere before."

"The last time you saw me, I was doing backflips down the Sheffield list and insulting Grimme."

Brìghde gasped and Aldwyn's mouth dropped open.

Grimme heaved a sigh. "Aldwyn, Caroline, sit down." Once they had both squeezed in the crowded table, he said, "This is Philippe Kyneward. Our oldest illegitimate brother. We call him Mouse. He spies for me at Sheffield because God knows he can't do anything respectable. Couldn't be a soldier. Couldn't keep a shop. Couldn't be a scholar. Couldn't be a tradesman. The only thing he knows how to do is thieve and spy."

"And jest!"

Aldwyn looked dumbfounded. "Why do they call you Mouse?"

"Because I'm small, I know all the hiding places, how to lurk in the shadows, and I'm very, very quiet when I need to be, which is most of the time. *Nobody* at Sheffield knows I exist."

"You're the one who saved me," Caroline whispered, her voice trembling.

"Not soon enough," Mouse gritted and looked away. "I apologize for not doing what needed to be done much sooner. Grimme wanted to fetch you after the tournament, but I … I thought I knew better than he and—I didn't."

No one said anything for a moment.

"We all have our sins to account for," Grimme rumbled. "We can do that later. Let us right now enjoy each other."

Sir John, for his part, was dabbing his eyes. "I agree. I am so happy," he said tremulously, "to see all my bastards together for the first time, and, moreover, enjoying themselves and each other."

"Philippe—" Aldwyn began.

"Mouse."

"Mouse. Where do you come from?"

"London, same as the cod that spawned us all. I was a favor Papa did for a nobleman who did not care for women."

"Then … you're a legitimate noble?" Aldwyn said, almost painfully confused.

"I am. However, soon after I was born, my putative father died—"

"Was murdered," Sir John corrected.

"Sweet Virgin Mary!" Brìghde blurted, and Grimme cast her a mischievous smile.

"—and I would have been the new noble, but his cousin—"

"Who murdered him."

"—challenged my legitimacy. Unfortunately for him, nobody cared. I was born in wedlock. My father had declared me his, therefore, I was legitimate."

"I snatched Mouse and his wet nurse," Sir John said, "before he was killed too, and the only thing I told his mother was that I would keep him safe. That was the last time I ever saw her. The cousin killed her when she wouldn't tell him where the babe was, but without the babe's body, he could still not claim the dukedom. Eventually he produced a dead babe, and that was that. Grimme's mother was Mouse's wet nurse and six years later, Grimme came along. Do you remember, Aldwyn, you and your mother lived across the hall from Grimme and his mother."

"Aye, I remember."

"Grimme's mother reared us," Mouse said.

"Until you couldn't be confined," Sir John said with a dark glare at Mouse.

"Bastard of bastards!" he crowed.

"Good Lord," Aldwyn breathed. "Who are you then?"

"I," Mouse pronounced, "am the rightful Duke of Sheffield."

Aldwyn and Caroline's gasps were loud enough to be heard in the stable, whilst Grimme and Sunny snickered.

"Which is why Grimme will *never* get a 'my lord' out of me. Say it, Grimme."

"No."

Suddenly Brìghde began laughing. "'Your Grace.'"

"Oh, you are *beautiful*," Mouse breathed.

"Thank you," she cooed.

"How'd you get him to plow you?"

"I declared war on him."

Grimme chuckled. Mouse cackled.

"However," she drawled dangerously, "your bit about black magic at the tournament did not help my cause." Then she slid an angry glance at Grimme. "I saw you take off my ribbon and drop it in the dirt."

Grimme dropped his head back, wondering how to apologize for *that*, too.

"But I also saw you go back and retrieve it before you demanded Ares, and then tie it to your doublet before we went to supper," she said softly and grasped his hand to squeeze it.

He looked at her sheepishly, saw her soft smile, and squeezed back. "Thank you, my love."

Then Brìghde turned to Sir John and said, "Why did the duke not recognize you here or at the tournament?"

"It's been thirty-two years," he said flatly. "I was thirty-eight when Mouse was born, and in my prime. He saw me now and again, but he only knew me as a merchant catering to the duchess if he thought about it at all. He knew Mouse wasn't the duke's but he didn't know who his father really was, and he had no expectation that his father was still sharing his mother's bed. Grimme and Mouse look nothing alike, whereas Grimme and Aldwyn have been taken for brothers their entire lives."

"Can he prove he's the duke?" Aldwyn asked slowly.

"No," Mouse said.

"Aye," Sir John said.

Now *everyone* was gaping at Sir John. He arose laboriously, shuffled toward his chambers, and closed the door behind him. Everyone was dead quiet, and Grimme looked at Mouse, who was stunned, which, so far as Grimme could remember, had never happened.

Presently, Sir John came shuffling out again. He shuffled up behind Mouse, who twisted to see him. "This," he murmured, giving something to Mouse, along with a folded piece of parchment, "was the duke's. He gave it to me to give to you in case your legitimacy was challenged. He needed a legitimate heir because he hated his cousin and knew he would do whatever it took to get the title."

"Oh, Papa," Mouse breathed as he took it, and Grimme wasn't sure he'd ever seen his older brother dumbstruck.

"The duke was a dear friend of mine from boyhood. Once you were conceived, he entrusted your care to me should anything happen to him. I did love your mother, Mouse, do not mistake me, but I have grieved him as much as I have grieved your mother."

Mouse put the object on the desk and opened the parchment. Grimme wouldn't harry him to know; Mouse would tell him in his own time. Or he wouldn't. His brother rubbed his forehead, sighed, refolded the parchment and gave both back to their father. "You keep it," he said low. "I don't want to be a duke."

"I'm going to die soon, Son," Sir John murmured, patting Mouse on the shoulder before shuffling back to his chambers. "You'll need it before that happens."

"Give it to someone you trust."

"Aye, I will," he said as he disappeared. "Grimme," he said once he made his way back to the table. Aldwyn arose and assisted him to sit back at the table. "There is another reason why I wanted a new castellan, and why I have brought you all here. When I realized that I did not know how to rule an earldom beyond simply making it prosperous, and that I had sent all those qualified men away because I thought I knew what needed to be done, my pride broke. In fact, it had broken so much I begged God for a miracle."

"You *prayed?!*" all four of Sir John's bastards demanded at the same time.

"I did."

"Well?"

"Brìghde came."

"You *prayed* for a miracle," Brìghde growled, "that *came true* and you doubted *me?*"

He shrugged sheepishly. "Old habits, old thinking. The church and I— Well. I decided that what God and I do together is no one's business but our own. I didn't expect anything, but … And then you said you had prayed for a miracle so as not to marry your intended. I started to think … perhaps … " He looked around at his children. "I wanted to gather you all together before I died, so I could see you all together, pull out all the secrets so you could all make your own decisions and mayhap be a family. I wanted to give Mouse what he needs should he decide to pursue his inheritance, as Grimme and I want him to do."

"Papa!" Grimme huffed.

"Papa," Mouse growled.

"Papa?" Aldwyn said carefully.

Sir John held up his hand. "I don't plan to die. What I am going to do is move out to the cottage with Maud and Sunny."

"But … Papa … " Grimme said, suddenly despondent. He looked to Brìghde for reinforcement, but she shook her head. She'd known that, at least.

"I don't want him to go," Brìghde said gently, laying her hand over his. "He is the father I never had, that I wanted, whom I love so very, very much. But he deserves his happiness, too, as he has had so little of it. You have had him to yourself for years. He has given you Kyneward. He has given Mouse his dukedom. 'Tis time Sunny and Aldwyn had their turns."

"I loved every one of your mothers," he said, then looked at Maud, "and I love Maud, and I would like to spend the rest of my life with one woman. You know where she lives. You may come visit."

"How will you get around?" Grimme asked.

"I'll manage. Somehow."

Grimme gulped and stared down at his plate, then nodded. "Aye," he croaked. "Not that I could stop you."

Sir John shook his head. "No. I plan to leave within the sennight."

When Grimme saw the soft, loving glance his father cast at Sunny's mother, and the one she returned, Grimme could not keep it within himself to grieve. He understood how that look felt. He didn't *like* that his father was moving away from him, but he would do the same to be close to his love. After a bit of a tense silence, Mouse said something irreverent that made everyone laugh, and the conversation of a happy family resumed.

Grimme looked at Brìghde out of the corner of his eye. She was talking to Mouse, who had begun to flirt with her and it had gotten very vulgar very quickly, but Grimme just rolled his eyes. Mouse never saw a pretty thing he didn't want to steal. She was laughing, jesting, eating, drinking the way she did when she was happy, the way she had the day after their wedding, all the way to Kyneward, and during their sojourn in Hogarth, her emerald eyes sparkling with joy.

She was so lovely, so amusing, so clever.

"What are you pondering so slyly, Lord Husband?" Brìghde teased.

He grinned at her. "The moment I fell in love with you."

"Ohhhh?" she cooed, fluttering her eyelashes. "And when was that?"

"'*Grimme, get your arse out of bed!*'"

A Moment of Peace

THE ONE-YEAR anniversary celebration of Brìghde and Grimme Kyneward's marriage was magnificent. Fàileach, Dunham, Tavendish, Sheffield, MacFhionnlaigh, nobles major and minor—*and* the king and queen of England!—arrived at Kyneward Keep for a two-week festival with merchants, tournaments, entertainments, games, and all the sweetmeats Grimme's sons could stuff in their bodies. The tournaments offered money prizes, attracting many errant knights. The rolling hills of Kyneward were covered in tents and fair exploded with color.

The fortress's walls and battlements were being massively fortified. The third bailey wall around the tiny collection of cottages was coming along nicely. The keep itself was being expanded, the great hall becoming a true *great* hall. The walls of the great hall had been painted with colorful murals depicting the battle at Agincourt, the story of Grimme and Brìghde's wedding, the tournament in which Grimme won Ares back, and in the middle of it all, the new Kyneward crest, with one rearing black horse and one rearing golden horse flanking a shield with ravens in flight.

Linota had a strong hand on the kitchen and her food got better all the time. Rose, newly wed to her knight, had an iron fist around the housekeeping, strict schedules, and more exacting cleaning standards than Lady Fàileach, but she did it with cheer and praise. William, also newly wed and granted Sir John's old chambers, had charge of the ledgers and the daily coin chest, which he counted religiously, as he was a banker at heart and would entertain no discrepancy between it and his bookkeeping. England still had no bank and Grimme still wouldn't consent to send it to Italy, so the rest of Grimme's coin was hidden in small chests all over the fortress. William and the land steward each had an apprentice. The royal gamekeeper lived comfortably in Kyneward's pocket. Eleven mares would be dropping foals in a month or two, thus the stables had been expanded—again.

Brìghde was surprised MacFhionnlaigh had accepted her peace offering of an invitation, but she welcomed them as honored guests. It was the least she could do. Laird and Lady MacFhionnlaigh were still stinging from the wedding that wasn't, but they were as limp as Brìghde expected them to be.

Roger, so ugly even Grimme blanched, took her and Grimme aside and privately thanked them for sparing him marriage to Brìghde.

"Well, why didn't *you* do something?" she asked, irritated.

He looked confused. "I dinna have a choice."

Brìghde threw up a hand. "I should never expect a different answer."

"I also knew you'd have a plan."

Brìghde didn't know whether to preen or punch his face. "Of *course* you wouldn't have a plan, you stupid ass."

"God, I hate you!" he burst out. "I have *always* hated you!"

"I hate you too!" Brìghde yelled. "*You* were *mean* to me all the time—"

"Do I need to separate you two?" Grimme stepped in to ask, barely able to keep from laughing. "You fight like siblings. Roger, you go this way. Brìghde, you go that way. If you cannot be civil, do not speak to each other again."

"Gladly!" Brìghde and Roger hissed at each other before storming off in different directions.

The ravens now followed Brìghde or Grimme wherever they went, as the humans had trained them to do so by carrying nuts in their pockets at all times. They would hold one up in the sky, and the birds would snatch them as they flew by. If a bird wanted to play, he would perch somewhere on their persons or horses, if they were riding. Then Brìghde or Grimme would toss nuts into the air for the birds to catch mid-flight. Kyneward gathered so many birds that the knights began to feed them, too, as a game to see how many gifts each knight could accumulate. Brìghde and Grimme each had a glass jar for their gifts.

Grimme had commanded all his soldiers to wear ribbons of red and azure on their left shoulder. 'Twas his intent to train the ravens to remember his men and, if Kyneward were attacked, they might assist in battle. If they merely knew who belonged to Kyneward and who didn't, he would consider that a success, but how would he know? Grimme reasoned that if a horse could be trained to think independently during battle, surely a very, very smart bird who could remember faces could be trained to engage the enemy of his friend.

Terrwyn, having been out in the field, returned and played with Pierce, having missed him more than he realized, and they rode together, Pierce always with his stalwart Helen and Mercury. Then Terrwyn would be going to York when Richard, the third duke, returned home after the festival, and was excited to do so.

Gaston and Max returned home to find that their mother had left Kyneward, but had left notes behind for them, telling them that she loved them more than life, that she did the best she could, that she grieved their absence, and that, because she could not stand Brìghde, she had gone back to France to start over again. Since this was consistent with how she had acted the last time they saw her, they were sadly resigned. They attempted to make a good show of understanding and happiness that she had left them *something*, but neither Brìghde nor Grimme were fooled. Pierce had been sternly instructed not to say a word about what really happened that day in the bailey no matter how angry they made him, and he agreed, as he was simply happy she was gone. The only thing Brìghde and Grimme could do was pray that no one else would tell them, either.

Brìghde, who was not showing yet, felt radiant. The only complaint she had so far was that Grimme had forbidden her to ride. Every evening, she went to Troy's stall after he had been out in the field training, and groomed him and fed him pears and apples and carrots and anything else he asked for and spoiled her pet shamelessly. If she wanted to go into Waters, she walked. If she wanted to go to Hogarth, she had to use the carriage, which, in her opinion, wasn't a much better option for her condition.

'Tis only until November. You wanted a son, so you must accept the consequences.

The only stallion she was permitted to ride was Grimme, and as the weeks passed, her appetite became more voracious. He was *very* accommodating, and the pleasure he gave her did, in fact, ease her aches and pains. She had not yet managed to break him.

There arrived, on Brìghde's birthday, a litter of Italian mastiff puppies like Hades. Brìghde immediately picked up the black one, who was sweet and happy and her back end bounced in excitement as Brìghde held her and received all manner of puppy kisses. There arrived with the basket of puppies their sire and dam, as well as a man who bred and trained dogs to war.

"Oh, who's my sweet little Hades?" she cooed at the happy puppy, who would one day guard Brìghde and her bairns. "*You're* my sweet little Hades, aren't you? Did you come back to me, my wee darling? Oh I have missed you so very much!"

Grimme got a very special thank you that night.

All the visiting nobles welcomed Grimme into their midst as worthy of being part of them. To his credit, Grimme acted as if he were worthy to be there, giving no hint that he had ever thought otherwise. He still wasn't comfortable, but Brìghde encouraged him to continue to act thusly.

Thus, Brìghde was happy. Grimme was happy. Pierce and Terrwyn were happy. Gaston and Max were mostly happy. Sir John and Maud were happy. Sunny was happy. Aldwyn and Caroline and their children seemed happy.

The Fàileach clan was happy. The Tavendishes and Dunhams were happy. Roger MacFhionnlaigh was happy (so long as he didn't have to speak to Brìghde). Mouse gave a good imitation of being happy when he deigned to grace them with his presence. Sir Bart was happy. Lady Fàileach, who avoided Grimme at most costs, could find no fault—and she looked. The rest of the visiting nobles were happy.

King Henry was *definitely* happy.

The only person *not* happy was the Duke of Sheffield, with whom the king desired an interview during the celebration. Sheffield knew it would not be a pleasant one.

What truly sealed Sheffield's utter hatred for Grimme, however, was that when the king and queen arrived, and all the pomp and ceremony was over with and all obeisances were shown their majesties, the king grabbed Grimme and they clasped arms, embraced, and laughed, giving each other hearty claps on the back, as equal warriors, calling each other by their given names. Then, 'twas Aldwyn's turn. Further, that night at supper, Henry, Grimme, Aldwyn, and all the knights who had fought with them at Agincourt traded stories with many *And then Is* whilst the duke and duchess sat sullenly next to the king.

The day after that, Grimme, Tavendish, and Sheffield were closeted with the king in Sir John's study for hours.

Grimme and Tavendish emerged just after the midday meal with smug countenances, and Grimme assured Brìghde that the king knew that Grimme had told him the truth of all the circumstances of Sheffield's dealings with Kyneward. Tavendish's firm belief that Kyneward had indeed been under siege by its own liege sealed the king's opinion, and the threat of sanctioning the duke was there, though never stated.

The king did not apologize for Sheffield having been told he would get Kyneward lands, but said that he understood Sheffield's frustration. He made it clear it was merely a regrettable slip of the tongue, but since Grimme *had* saved the king's life, he deserved it. When asked who had promised him the Kyneward lands, he named Oakeshire, Sheffield's neighboring marquessate to the south and east.

When confronted with the possibility that Earl Kyneward had raided Sheffield Keep in the deepest of night to snatch the duke's deputy and his children, slaying at least two dozen of the duke's men in the process, the king had raised an eyebrow and said,

"Why would they need to be snatched? Were they being held hostage?"

The duke could not answer that question.

"Then did it really happen at all?"

"No, your majesty."

"What *really* happened, Lord Sheffield?"

"Sir Marchand left my employ and swore fealty to Earl Kyneward."

"We are happy to see Kyneward and Marchand together again. They make a formidable pair."

Grimme had once again asked if his naming an heir without legitimization would hold up to a challenge, and the king, surprised, said, "Who told you it wouldn't? Which son are you naming so that we may note it?"

"Pierce," he said immediately. The boy may or may not be a warrior at heart, as he didn't care to play the knights' games and would rather watch, then go tend to his studies, but he had thrown the first punch and defeated his older, bigger brothers through sheer tenacity. Terrwyn might not mind, but it might give Gaston and Max a reason to hate Grimme, especially if they ever realized the truth of their mother's disappearance. They were smart. As they grew, they would reach the logical conclusion.

The king sequestered himself with Sheffield the entire afternoon whilst Kyneward's knights and Sheffield's knights jousted for practice and play and prizes.

The day before the king left, Grimme requested a private audience, and the two of them rode out just after breakfast, Grimme on Ares and the king on Troy, the king's guard following at a good distance. They were gone for hours, and when they returned, they were walking, their arms around each other, half drunk, grinning, trading bawdy jests, laughing. Grimme saw Brìghde and gave her a tiny nod. She smiled and sent a tiny nod at the small mouse in a dark corner. He winked and scampered down to the kitchens.

Thus the spring passed. Summer unfolded and deepened. As new villeins moved in and Brìghde added more staff, Kyneward Keep slowly became known as Raven. Waters grew to a size more in proportion to its taverns, and with the prosperity, Brìghde's belly and appetite for Grimme's spindle and Linota's food grew apace, although suddenly she could not abide the smell of wine. Grimme's force of seven hundred men that Henry had left had grown twice that, coming from all over (draining Sheffield's force significantly) to pledge fealty to a strong lord who paid well, but yet again Henry wanted two thirds of his oldest and most well-trained force, so off they went to France, leaving Grimme with fewer than five hundred young half-trained soldiers.

Six four-year-old stallions were finished training and Grimme pronounced them ready to go to their new owners. Mercury now had a mate, Nerio, and the kennel was full of their puppies *and* two other breeding pairs of deerhounds.

The mastiff puppies were well on their way to becoming as vicious as Hades had been, and Grimme began looking for other dogs of the same breed so as not to intermingle blood lines. If he could breed warhorses, he could breed deerhounds and war dogs too.

Tavendish paid very well to be able to send knights to Kyneward to train in Grimme's battle tactics. Grimme and his commanders trained men to slither through the grass like serpents, slit the throats of the enemy in the night and lick the blood off the blade, and to blend into forests and trees and shrubs and hills for surprise attacks on invaders.

Autumn came and Raven found that though it had doubled its storage, it still wasn't adequate for their stores, and more had to be built quickly as the grain and vegetables and beans came in.

Wee Lady Moira Kyneward barged into the family, but not without her father demanding that she present herself. It took three days and it appeared that Brìghde had finally broken Grimme. Lady Fàileach and Sir Bart came for Brìghde's confinement.

When Grimme had said he was not accustomed to celebrating Christmas, Brìghde had assumed he meant with his women and children, and that at least a cursory attempt had been made every so often. She was shocked to learn that he had never celebrated it at all, for reasons neither Grimme nor Mouse knew. Sir John claimed not to know, but Brìghde was suspicious. Thus, Brìghde determined to organize the best Christmas season she could think of. Gaston, Max, and Terrwyn were sent for at the beginning of December. Brìghde decorated Raven in all manner of holly and ivy and mistletoe. There was feasting with the villeins from Advent to Epiphany. There were gifts for the boys. Sir John, Maud, and Sunny came to spend those weeks making merry, and Brìghde caught Sir John praying in the chapel.

Max's knight had sent a missive to Grimme with his opinion that while Max would make an adequate knight, the boy did not want to be one anymore, and would be more suited to scholarship or commerce. Grimme hired tutors for both Pierce and Max and welcomed the boy home to prepare him for a different occupation. With Father Hercule's lawyerly duties, he could no longer oversee their studies, and though the Kyneward priest was very learned, his tutoring skills were not good. Gaston and Terrwyn were perfectly happy that they would be squires soon, as they had progressed as quickly as their father had.

Thus, the year of our Lord 1422 dawned with two boys at home studying and following Brìghde around to learn how to rule an earldom if they had to. Twice a week, Max rode out to Sunny's cottage to study commerce with his grandfather. Max and Pierce still had their arguments, but not often, as there wasn't much a ten-year-old and a six-year-old could fight about when they were treated equally.

Raven grew and prospered, safe from Duke Sheffield, who, if things went according to plan, would by autumn be replaced by the rightful one. William, having trained two new clerks, bid Raven adieu to take his wife and infant back to Italy. There were many tears of both sadness and joy all 'round.

The architects and stonemasons worked steadily. More wells were dug so that water would not be scarce during a siege. Brìghde and her force of assistants worked tirelessly to make sure they had stores to last through a many-year siege. If the Trojans could hold off the Greeks for ten years, Brìghde reasoned that so Raven should be able to. Grimme continued to add and train more troops, and prepared a special force dedicated to waging dishonorable warfare.

Honorable warfare had no place at Raven, which was a good thing because on August 31, 1422, King Henry V, Earl Kyneward's only protection from the illegitimate Duke Sheffield, perished.

600 Years Later ...

Grimme and Brìghde Kyneward live on in **The Proviso**, *for Grimme may not have married a Dunham, but his many-greats grandson did.*

BRYCE KENARD is a lusty savage in a bespoke suit, with a scarred soul that matches his fire-ravaged body. His children are gone. His faith is gone. He tried to tame his sinful nature, but he couldn't—and God punished him for it. Now, the only things he has to hold onto are his rage, his successful law practice, and the twenty-year-old memory of a woman who showed him what he wanted. Then he comes face to face with Giselle Cox, who can give him exactly what he wants and more, a woman who wants him *for* his nature (not in spite of it), and shows him God didn't punish him for anything.

What Bryce doesn't know is that lust and savagery come standard on Kenard men, so there is nothing that can dilute his inner warrior, spawned by 15th Century Earl and Countess Grimme and Brìghde Kyneward, a lusty English knight and his savage Scots wife.

You met the Dunhams and Tavendishes in Black as Knight.
Now get to know them in the **Tales of Dunham**.

Acknowledgments

I HAVE LOTS of people to thank for this book.

MY HUSBAND, natch, for keeping the ship steady when I go down the rabbit hole.

Alpha readers Ekaterina Xia, Jan Leonard, Barbara Trumpinski-Roberts, Tina Black, and Elyse Perry, and beta readers Linda Armbruster and Katherine Scott, who all contributed to the strengthening of the structure of this hastily built world.

Jan Leonard (again), Elizabeth Palmer, Julie Weight, and Deb Lefler, as they have been supporting me in this writing and self-publishing gig since way before *The Proviso*, when I still thought self-publishing was a Satanic rite. (Narrator: It is.)

Nathan Wagner for the maps I needed to figure out where the hell I was. England and Scotland are small countries. I've been there, but I had to double and triple check mileage and I still don't believe how close everything is.

Linda Armbruster (again) for turning me onto the Northumberland folk group The Unthanks and their beautiful songs "Magpie" and "Lullaby".

Well, ackshually

Since early 2018, I have been a part of an online group of very glib mutants/misfits/autists/freaks/people who hate authority. One day in June 2019, I checked out completely to write this book. They got worried about me and pinged me, but by then I was done. They've pulled a lot of funny memes out of this book, affectionately known as *Cods & Cuntes*. (Chapter 18, guys!) Once I started the fine-tuning, my glib friends were invaluable in helping me figure out details of this book and its sequel, *Cods & Cuntes II: Trebuchet Boogaloo*.

Specifically: @nw, @Gender Traitor, @Cannoli, @Yusef, @cy, @Fourscore, @CPRM, @Akira, @UnCivilServant, @NotAdahn, @Don Escaped

Texas, @Jarflax, @Heroic Mulatto, and @The Hyperbole, who found a discussion thread when I couldn't.

@OldManWithCandy came looking for me when I disappeared. @SP [RIP 2017], with her rusty tin can lids, keeps us all in line.

@Tres Cool writes the mostest awesomest personals ads ever and he should publish them as a how-to on getting laid via Craigslist. @Tundra will be playing Boss Tom Pendergast in the movie version of my Prohibition romance *1520 Main*. @plisade hated authority long before 2018. @dbleagle was a known disrespecter of authorities since he was a mere qtreagle. In fact, each and every denizen of this community would like you, Dear Reader, to know that they hate authority. Molon labe and No Step on Snek.

@The Glib Formerly Known As BEAM didn't do sweet FA but rather regarded the entire process with studied bemusement. @banginglc1 deserves no credit and is truly a despicable human being. @BakedPenguin was despicable before it was cool. @PopeJimbo thinks Memphis barbecue is better than Kansas City barbecue but he is despicable for this opinion and also wronger than wrong. @Spartacus demanded to be prominently included despite doing absolutely nothing whatsoever, and @slumbrew's comments made me dumber for reading them. @Ted'S is the sexiest man alive who everybody knows has the best taste in music. @SUPREME OVERLORD trshmnstr is generally a jerk who thinks I'm evil, but he lives in a trashcan and gave the gift of the permalink, so I guess I can tolerate him. @RCDean's demand that I use a nonstandard spelling of "cods" was summarily rejected. @STEVE SMITH did something and by "something," mean …

@i_am_totally_not_an_escaped_AI dropped a sweet birthday present on my head. *mwah*

@Agile Cyborg, a master of nonsense-that-is-not-really-nonsense. To wit:

> *"I discovered among my brethren and sistas that the brain has a door and a stairscape resides beyond and the door has a lock and that lock is opened with intellectual louvres … like slats on a giant spaceship shedding the rays of a great 'verse …"*

Lastly, I have many other glib friends who have helped me with this, that, and some other sometimes very heavy things. They don't know they contributed to this book, but they did. Everything about this community is interwoven in every sentence of this book.

Moriah Jovan

About the Author

MORIAH JOVAN writes what her imaginary friends tell her to write. Thus far, they have shown up in the novels *The Proviso, Stay, Magdalene, Dunham, Paso Doble, We Were Gods, Black Jack, Lion's Share, 1520 Main, Twenty-Dollar Rag,* and *Black as Knight,* published by B10 Mediaworx. They will, most likely, continue to order her around until she hits on the right drug and dosage. Fortunately, her husband is very understanding of all the other people in her life.

Moriah has been doing this self-publishing thing since 2008 and has the war wounds to prove it. She's a fair-weather Chiefs and Royals fan, half-assed planner, avid cross stitcher, dilettante crafter, and aspiring odalisque. She regularly thumbs her nose at her to-do list as if it has any authority over her at all. Her goal is to finish all the craft projects she has begun in her life.

All of them.

You can catch her at:
moriah@moriahjovan.com
moriahjovan.com
𝕏.com/moriahjovan
facebook.com/moriah.jovan (page)
facebook.com/groups/moriahsfunhouseandhallofmirrors (group)

For news, updates, announcements, get her newsletter,
Moriah's Funhouse and Hall of Mirrors at
eepurl.com/YUdvD.

For more of Moriah's crazy imaginary friends,
visit her website for extras, vignettes, and outtakes
at **moriahjovan.com/talesofdunham/extras/vignettes-outtakes**

***Black as Knight*:** 1420: Newly made English Earl Grimme Kyneward must wed a noblewoman—quickly. Time is of the essence, so Grimme abducts one. Except ... Brìghde is the *wrong* bride—or is she? Together, Grimme and Brìghde must defeat an evil duke who covets everything Grimme loves.

***A Babe in Winter*:** Raven lay in ruins. With only Grimme, Brìghde, and Philippe surviving the siege, the three must journey to Italy and back to reclaim their fortune and avenge themselves on Sheffield, but they must survive the winter first. Leaving them alive was a punishment—and a mistake.

THE TALES OF DUNHAM

***The Proviso*:** Knox Hilliard's uncle killed Knox's father to marry his mother and keep Knox's inheritance. Knox and his cousins Sebastian and Giselle are out for vengeance, but somewhere along the way they find allies—and love.

***Stay*:** Vanessa's a celebrity chef carrying a childhood crush. Eric's a career politician racked by gratitude and regret. They're bound by history but separated by two spectacular careers and two hundred miles. How can they ever make it work?

***Magdalene*:** Widowed Mormon bishop and steel magnate Mitch meets corporate restructuring specialist Cassie St. James, a former prostitute. As they navigate a relationship, they're working together to bring down a man who wants to destroy everything Mitch holds dear.

Dunham: It's 1780. American privateer Captain Fury and British pirate Captain Judas share a kiss that leads to a tavern brawl, but their common enemy—King George III—keeps them fighting to make a life together on the American frontier.

Paso Doble: Victoria, an American professor in Sevilla, Spain, moonlighting as a nightclub singer meets Emilio, a smooth Spanish matador moonlighting as a chemist. She makes him laugh. He solves her problems. They're *just friends*—right up until the first kiss.

We Were Gods: After twenty years, five kids, world renown, and a multimillion-dollar business, Étienne and Tess call it quits because at some point, love just isn't enough anymore—until it's the only thing they have left.

Black Jack: Music professor Lydia and culturally illiterate bond trader Jack are the least likely people to feel instant attraction, much less plan a weekend romp moments after meeting. It would have been a fun vacation fling if not for almost getting murdered.

Lion's Share: After Blythe's husband dies, leaving her alone with four young children, her father-in-law Finn steps up to the plate to make sure her children are safe and provided for. Six years, countless dinners, kids' activities, and endless killer cookies later, there's nothing else between them but respect and friendship. Nothing at all.

1520 Main: In Kansas City during Prohibition, Trey desperately wants to own the speakeasy he's been managing for the past four years. Then Boss Tom Pendergast hands it to him on a silver platter. The catch: Trey must seduce Marina, a preacher's daughter, and get her pregnant in two months. Trey wants that speakeasy, and he doesn't care how he gets it.

Twenty-Dollar Rag: A spoiled brat party girl gets a lesson in life from a man who values hard work over wealth, which changes her life. Tia doesn't expect to see Vachel ever again—and she would really rather not.

www.ingramcontent.com/pod-product-compliance
Lightning Source LLC
LaVergne TN
LVHW041051080826
845145LV00007B/1530

* 9 7 8 1 7 3 2 0 3 0 2 8 2 *